Nancy Drew
Mystery Stories

VOLUMES

CAROLYN KEENE

1 The Secret of the Old Clock

2 The Hidden Staircase

3 The Bungalow Mystery

SMITHMARK

This edition published in 1999 by SMITHMARK Publishers,
a division of U.S. Media Holdings, Inc.,
115 West 18th Street, New York, NY 10011; 212-519-1300.

SMITHMARK books are available for bulk purchase for sales promotion
and premium use. For details write or call the manager of special sales,
SMITHMARK Publishers, 115 West 18th Street, New York, NY 10011.

ISBN: 0-7651-1728-2

Library of Congress Cataloging-in-Publication Data

Keene, Carolyn.
    The secret of the old clock ; The hidden staircase ; The bungalow
mystery / Carolyn Keene.
        p.   cm. — (Nancy Drew mystery stories)
    ISBN 0-7651-1728-2 (hardcover)
    1. Detective and mystery stories, American. 2. Children's
stories, American. [1. Mystery and detective stories.] I. Title.
II. Title: Secret of the old clock ; The hidden staircase ; The
bungalow mystery. III. Title: Hidden staircase. IV. Title:
Bungalow mystery. V. Series: Keene, Carolyn. Nancy Drew mystery
stories.
PZ7.K23Ser 1999
[Fic]—dc21   99-20940
                                          CIP

Printed in the U.S.A.

10 9 8 7 6 5 4 3 2 1

Contents

VOLUMES

The Secret of the Old Clock

"The Crowley clock at last!" Nancy exclaimed

CHAPTER I

The Rescue

NANCY DREW, an attractive girl of eighteen, was driving home along a country road in her new, dark-blue convertible. She had just delivered some legal papers for her father.

"It was sweet of Dad to give me this car for my birthday," she thought. "And it's fun to help him in his work."

Her father, Carson Drew, a well-known lawyer in their home town of River Heights, frequently discussed puzzling aspects of cases with his blond, blue-eyed daughter.

Smiling, Nancy said to herself, "Dad depends on my intuition."

An instant later she gasped in horror. From the lawn of a house just ahead of her a little girl about five years of age had darted into the roadway. A van, turning out of the driveway of the house, was barely fifty feet away from her. As the driver vigorously sounded the horn in warning, the child became confused and ran directly in front of the van. Miraculously, the little girl managed to cross the road safely and pull herself up onto a low wall, which formed one side of a bridge. But the next second, as the van sped away, the child lost her balance and toppled off the wall out of sight!

"Oh my goodness!" Nancy cried out, slamming on her brakes. She had visions of the child plunging into the water below, perhaps striking her head fatally on a rock!

Nancy leaped out of her car and dashed across the road. At the foot of the embankment, she could see the curly-haired little girl lying motionless, the right side of her body in the water.

"I hope—" Nancy dared not complete the harrowing thought as she climbed down the steep slope.

When she reached the child, she saw to her great relief that the little girl was breathing normally and no water had entered her nose or mouth. A quick examination showed that she had suffered no broken bones.

Gently Nancy lifted the little girl, and holding her firmly in both arms, struggled to the top of the embankment. Then she hurried across the road and up the driveway to the child's house.

At this moment the front door flew open and an elderly woman rushed out, crying, "Judy! Judy!"

The next second, the child lost her balance

"I'm sure she'll be all right," said Nancy quickly.

The woman, seeing Nancy's car, asked excitedly, "Did you run into her?"

"No, no. Judy fell off the bridge." Nancy quickly explained what had taken place.

By this time another woman, slightly younger, had hurried from the house. "Our baby! What has happened to her?"

As the woman reached out to take Judy, Nancy said soothingly, "Judy's going to be all right. I'll carry her into the house and lay her on a couch."

One of the women opened the screen door and the other directed, "This way."

Nancy carried her little burden through a hallway and into a small, old-fashioned living room. As soon as she laid the child on the couch, Judy began to murmur and turn her head from side to side.

"I believe she'll come to in a few minutes," said Nancy.

The two women watched Judy intently as they introduced themselves as Edna and Mary Turner, great-aunts of the little girl.

"Judy lives with us," explained Edna, the older sister. "We're bringing her up."

Nancy was somewhat surprised to hear that these elderly women were rearing such a small child. She gave her name and address, just as Judy opened her eyes and looked around. Seeing Nancy, she asked, "Who are you?"

"My name is Nancy. I'm glad to know you, Judy."

"Did you see me fall?"

Nancy nodded, as the child's Aunt Mary said, "She rescued you from the river after you fell in."

Judy began to cry. "I'll never, never run into the road again, really I won't!" she told her aunts.

Nancy said she was sure that Judy never would. She patted the child, who smiled up at her. Although Nancy felt that Judy would be all right, she decided to stay a few minutes longer to see if she could be of help. The child's wet clothes were removed and a robe put on her.

Mary Turner started for the kitchen door. "I'd better get some medication and wet compresses for Judy. She's getting a good-sized lump on her head. Nancy, will you come with me?"

She led the way to the kitchen and headed for a first-aid cabinet which hung on the wall.

"I want to apologize to you, Nancy, for thinking you hit Judy," the woman said. "I guess Edna and I lost our heads. You see, Judy is very precious to us. We brought up her mother, who had been an only child and was orphaned when she was a little girl. The same thing happened to Judy. Her parents were killed in a boat explosion three years ago. The poor little girl has no close relatives except Edna and me."

"Judy looks very healthy and happy," Nancy said quickly, "so I'm sure she must love it here."

Mary smiled. "We do the best we can on our small income. Sometimes it just doesn't suffice, though. We sold some old furniture to the two men in that van you saw. I don't know who they were, but I guess the price was all right."

Mary Turner's thoughts went back to little Judy. "She's so little now that Edna and I are able to manage with our small income. But we worry about the future. We're dressmakers but our fingers aren't so nimble with the needle as they used to be.

"To tell you the truth, Nancy, at the time Judy's parents were killed, Edna and I wondered whether we would be able to take care of Judy properly. But we decided to try it and now we wouldn't part with her for anything in the world. She's won our hearts completely."

Nancy was touched by the story. She knew what was in the minds of the Turner sisters—living costs would become higher, and with their advancing years, their own income would become lower.

"Unfortunately," Mary went on, "Judy's parents left very little money. But they were extremely bright people and Judy is going to be like them. She ought to study music and dancing, and have a college education. But I'm afraid we'll never be able to give her those things."

Nancy said reassuringly, "Judy may be able to win a scholarship, or get other financial aid."

Mary, finding Nancy a sympathetic listener, continued, "A cousin of our father's named Josiah Crowley used to help us. But he passed away a couple of months ago. For years he used to pay us long visits and was very generous with his money." Miss Turner sighed. "He always promised to remember us in his will—he loved little Judy—and I am afraid Edna and I came to depend on that in our plans for her. But he did not carry out his promise."

Nancy smiled understandingly and made. no comment. But she did wonder why Mr. Crowley had changed his mind.

"Josiah went to live with some other cousins. After that, things changed. He rarely came to see us. But he was here just last February and said the same thing—that Edna and I were to inherit money from him. He had always helped us and it seemed strange that he should stop so suddenly."

Mary Turner looked at Nancy. "Maybe you know our well-to-do cousins that he went to stay with. They live in River Heights. They're the Richard Tophams."

"Do they have two daughters named Ada and Isabel?" Nancy asked. "If so, I know them."

"That's the family all right," replied Mary.

Nancy detected a hint of coolness in the woman's voice. "Do you like those two girls?" Miss Turner asked.

Nancy did not answer at once. She had been taught never to gossip. But finally she said tactfully, "Ada and Isabel were in high school with me. They were never my close friends. We—uh —didn't see eye to eye on various things."

By this time Mary Turner had selected a few items from the first-aid chest. Now she went to the refrigerator for some ice cubes. As she arranged the various articles on a tray, she said, "Well, when Cousin Josiah passed away, to our amazement Richard Topham produced a will which made him executor of the Crowley estate and left all the money to him, his wife, and the two girls."

"Yes. I did read that in the newspaper," Nancy recalled. "Is the estate a large one?"

"I understand there's considerable money in it," Mary Turner replied. "Some of Josiah's other cousins say he told them the same thing he told us, and they are planning to go to court about the matter." The woman shrugged. "But I guess a fight to break the will would be hopeless. Nevertheless, Edna and I cannot help feeling there *must* be a later will, although as yet no one has presented it."

Nancy followed Miss Turner into the living room. The cold compresses helped to reduce the swelling where Judy had hit her head on a rock. Convinced now that the little girl was all right, Nancy said she must leave.

"Come to see me again soon," Judy spoke up. "I like you, Nancy. "You're my saving girl."

"You bet I'll come," Nancy answered. "I like you too. You're a good sport!"

The child's great-aunts profusely thanked Nancy again for rescuing Judy. The visitor had barely reached the door when Edna suddenly said, "Mary, where's our silver teapot?"

"Why, right there on the tea table— Oh, it's gone!"

Edna ran into the dining room. "The silver candlesticks! They're gone too!"

Nancy had paused in the doorway, startled. "Do you mean the pieces have been stolen?" she asked.

"They must have been," replied Mary Turner, who was white with apprehension. "By those men who bought some furniture from us!"

Instantly Nancy thought of the men in the van. "Who were the men?" she asked.

"Oh, Mary, how could we have been so careless?" Edna Turner wailed. "We don't know who the men were. They just knocked on the door and asked if we had any old furniture that we wanted to sell. We'll never get the silver back!"

"Maybe you will!" said Nancy. "I'll call the police."

"Oh dear!" Mary said woefully. "Our phone is out of order."

"Then I'll try to catch up to the van!" Nancy declared. "What did the men look like?"

"They were short and heavy-set. One had dark hair, the other light. They had kind of large noses. That's about all I noticed."

"Me too," said Edna.

With a hasty good-by Nancy dashed from the house and ran to her car.

CHAPTER II

A Missing Will

THE BLUE convertible sped along the country road. Nancy smiled grimly.

"I'm afraid I'm exceeding the speed limit," she thought. "But I almost wish a trooper would stop me. Then I could tell him what happened to the poor Turner sisters."

Nancy watched the tire marks which the van driven by the thieves had evidently made in the dirt road. But a few miles farther on a feeling of dismay came over her. She had reached a V-shaped intersection of two highways. Both roads were paved, and since no tire impressions could be seen, Nancy did not know which highway the thieves had taken.

"Oh dear!" she sighed. "Now what shall I do?"

Nancy concluded that her wisest move would be to take the road which led to River Heights. There was a State Police barracks just a few miles ahead.

"I'll stop there and report the theft."

She kept looking for the van, which she recalled as charcoal gray. "I wish I'd seen the license number or the name of the firm that owns the van," Nancy said to herself ruefully.

When she reached State Police headquarters Nancy introduced herself to Captain Runcie and told about the robbery, giving what meager information she could about the suspects. The officer promised to send out an alarm immediately for the thieves and their charcoal-gray moving van.

Nancy continued her journey home, thinking of the Turners and their problems.

"I wonder why Mr. Josiah Crowley left all his money to the Tophams and none to his other relatives. Why did he change his mind? Those Tophams are well to do and don't need money as much as the Turners."

Nancy did not know Richard Topham, but she was acquainted with his wife, as well as his daughters. They were arrogant and unreasonable, and disliked by many of the shopkeepers in town. Ada and Isabel had been unpopular in high school. They had talked incessantly of money and social position, making themselves very obnoxious to the other students.

"I wonder," Nancy thought, "if a way can't be found so the Turners could get a share of the Crowley money. I'll ask Dad."

Five minutes later Nancy pulled into the double

garage and hurried across the lawn to the kitchen
door of the Drews' large red-brick house. The
building stood well back from the street, and was
surrounded by tall, beautiful trees.

"Hello, Nancy," greeted the pleasant, slightly
plump woman who opened the door. She was
Hannah Gruen, housekeeper for the Drews, who
had helped rear Nancy since the death of the girl's
own mother many years before.

Nancy gave her a hug, then asked, "Dad home?
I see his car is in the garage."

"Your father's in the living room and dinner
will be ready in a few minutes."

Nancy went to say hello to her tall, handsome
father, then hurried to wash her hands and comb
her hair before the three who formed the Drew
household sat down to dinner. During the meal
Nancy related her adventure of the afternoon.

"What tricky thieves!" Hannah Gruen burst
out. "Oh, I hope the police capture them!"

"They certainly took advantage of those Turner
sisters," Mr. Drew commented.

"Mary and Edna are in financial difficulties,"
Nancy commented. "Isn't it a shame that Josiah
Crowley didn't bequeath some of his estate to the
Turners and other relatives who need the money?"

Carson Drew smiled affectionately at his only
child, then said, "Yes, it is, Nancy. But unless a
will written later turns up, that's the way it has
to be."

"The Turners think there is another will," Nancy told him. "Wouldn't it be wonderful if it can be found?"

"I agree," spoke up Hannah. "It's well known in town that Mrs. Topham and her daughters were unkind to Josiah Crowley for some time before he died. Their excuse was that Josiah's eccentricities were extremely trying."

"The Tophams have never been noted for any charitable inclinations," Mr. Drew observed with a smile. "However, they did give Josiah a home."

"Only because they knew he was going to leave all his money to them," said Hannah. "If I'd been Josiah I wouldn't have stayed there." The housekeeper sighed. "But when people get old, they don't like change. And probably he put up with things rather than move."

She said the treatment the Tophams had accorded old Josiah Crowley had aroused a great deal of unfavorable comment throughout River Heights. Nancy had not known him personally, but she had often seen the elderly man on the street. Secretly she had regarded him as a rather nice, kindly person.

His wife had died during an influenza epidemic and after that he had made his home with various relatives. According to rumors, all these people had admitted that he had paid his board and done many favors for them. They in turn had

been very kind to him, and though poor themselves, had tried to make Josiah Crowley comfortable and happy.

"Tell me everything you know about Mr. Crowley," Nancy urged her father.

The lawyer said that the old man had publicly
declared he intended to provide in his will for several deserving relatives and friends. Then, three
years before his death, the Topham family, who
had never shown an interest in him, had experienced a sudden change of heart. They had begged
Josiah Crowley to make his home with them, and
at last he had consented. Shortly after he moved
into the Topham house, Mr. Drew was told that
the old man had decided to leave all his money to
them.

Mr. Crowley, though failing in health, main-
tained a firm grip on life. But as time went on,
he became more and more unhappy. He continued to live with the Tophams, but it was whispered about that he frequently slipped away to
visit his other relatives and friends, and that he
intended to change his will again.

"Then there must be a later will!" Nancy said
hopefully.

Mr. Drew nodded, and went on, "One day Josiah Crowley became critically ill. Just before his
death he attempted to communicate something to
the doctor who attended him, but his words, other

than 'will,' were unintelligible. After the funeral only one will came to light, giving the entire fortune to the Tophams."

"Dad, do you suppose Mr. Crowley was trying to tell the doctor something about another will which he had put some place where the Tophams couldn't find it?" Nancy asked.

"Very likely," the lawyer replied. "Probably he intended to leave his money to relatives who had been kind to him. But fate cheated him of the opportunity."

"Do you think anybody has looked for another will?" Nancy questioned.

"I don't know. But I'm sure of this. If another will shows up, Richard Topham will fight it. The estate is a considerable one, I understand, and they aren't the kind of people to share good fortune."

"Can't the present will be contested?" Nancy asked.

"I hear that other relatives have filed a claim, declaring they were told another will had been made in their favor. But unless it is located, I doubt that the matter will ever go further."

"But the Tophams don't deserve the fortune," Hannah Gruen remarked. "And besides, they don't need the money. It doesn't seem fair."

"It may not seem fair, but it is legal," Mr. Drew told her, "and I'm afraid nothing can be done about the situation."

"Poor Judy and her aunts!" said Nancy.

"There are others affected in the same way," her father remarked. "For instance, two young women who live on the River Road. I don't know their names. I understand they were not related to Mr. Crowley, but were great favorites of his. They are having a struggle and could use some extra money."

Nancy lapsed into silence. She felt strongly that a mystery lurked behind the Crowley case.

"Dad, don't *you* believe Josiah Crowley made a second will?" Nancy questioned suddenly.

"You sound like a trial lawyer, the way you cross-examine me," Mr. Drew protested, but with evident enjoyment. "To tell the truth, Nancy, I don't know what to think, but something did happen which might indicate that Mr. Crowley at least intended to make another will."

"Please go on!" Nancy begged impatiently.

"Well, one day nearly a year ago I was in the First National Bank when Crowley came in with Henry Rolsted."

"The attorney who specializes in wills and other estate matters?" Nancy inquired.

"Yes. I had no intention of listening to their conversation, but I couldn't help overhearing a few words that made me think they were discussing a will. Crowley made an appointment to call at Rolsted's office the following day."

"Oh!" cried Nancy excitedly. "That looks as though Mr. Crowley had made a new will, doesn't it? But why didn't Mr. Rolsted say something about it at the time of Mr. Crowley's death?"

"For one of many reasons," Mr. Drew replied. "In the first place, he may never have drawn a new will for Mr. Crowley. And even if he had, the old man might have changed his mind again and torn it up."

Before Nancy spoke again, she finished the delicious apple pudding which Hannah had made. Then she looked thoughtfully at her father. "Dad, Mr. Rolsted is an old friend of yours, isn't he?"

"Yes. An old friend and college classmate."

"Then won't you please ask him if he ever drew up a will for Mr. Crowley, or knows anything that might solve this mystery?"

"That's a rather delicate question, young lady. He may tell me it's none of my business!"

"You know he won't. You're such good friends he'll understand why you're taking a special interest in this case. Will you do it? Please!"

"I know you like to help people who are in trouble," her father said. "I suppose I could invite Mr. Rolsted to have lunch with me tomorrow—"

"Wonderful!" Nancy interrupted eagerly. "That would be a splendid opportunity to find out what he knows about a later will."

"All right. I'll try to arrange a date. How about joining us?"

Nancy's face lighted up as she said, "Oh, thank you, Dad. I'd love to. I hope it can be tomorrow, so we won't have to waste any time trying to find another will."

Mr. Drew smiled. "We?" he said. "You mean you might try to find a hidden will if Mr. Crowley wrote one?"

"I might." Nancy's eyes sparkled in anticipation.

CHAPTER III

An Unpleasant Meeting

"WHAT are your plans for this morning, Nancy?" her father asked at the breakfast table.

"I thought I'd do a little shopping," she replied. Her eyes twinkled. "There's a dance coming up at the country club and I'd like to get a new dress."

"Then will you phone me about lunch? Or better still, how about eating with me, whether Mr. Rolsted comes or not?"

"I'll be there!" Nancy declared gaily.

"All right. Drop in at my office about twelve-thirty. If Mr. Rolsted does accept my invitation, we'll try to find out something about Josiah Crowley's wills." Mr. Drew pushed back his chair. "I must hurry now or I'll be late getting downtown."

After her father had left, Nancy finished her breakfast, then went to the kitchen to help Hannah Gruen, who had already left the table.

"Any errands for me?" Nancy asked.

"Yes, dear. Here's a list," the housekeeper replied. "And good luck with your detective work."

Hannah Gruen gazed at the girl affectionately and several thoughts raced through her mind. In school Nancy had been very popular and had made many friends. But through no fault of her own, she had made two enemies, Ada and Isabel Topham. This worried Hannah. The sisters, intensely jealous of Nancy, had tried to discredit her in positions she had held in school. But loyal friends had always sprung to Nancy's defense. As a result, Ada and Isabel had become more unpleasant than ever to Nancy.

"Thanks for your encouragement," she said to Hannah a little later, giving her a hug.

"Whatever you do, Nancy, beware of those Topham sisters. They'd be only too happy to make things difficult for you."

"I promise to be on my guard."

Before leaving the house, Nancy phoned the Turners. She was glad to hear that Judy had suffered no ill effects from her fall. But she was disappointed that the police had found no clue to the thieves who had stolen the silverware.

"Please let me know if you learn anything," Nancy said, and Edna promised to do so.

Becomingly dressed in a tan cotton suit, Nancy set off in her convertible for the shopping district. She drove down the boulevard, and upon reaching the more congested streets, made her way skillfully through heavy traffic, then pulled into a parking lot.

"I think I'll try Taylor's Department Store first for a dress," she decided.

Taylor's was one of River Heights' finest stores. Nancy purchased several items for Hannah on the main floor, then went directly to the misses' wearing apparel section on the second floor.

Usually Nancy had no trouble finding a sales-clerk. But this particular morning seemed to be an especially busy one in the department, and an extra rush of customers had temporarily over-whelmed the sales force.

Nancy sat down in a convenient chair to await her turn. Her thoughts wandered to the Turner sisters and little Judy. Would she be able to help them? She was suddenly brought out of her rev-erie by loud-voiced complaints.

"We've been standing here nearly ten minutes!" a shrill voice declared. "Send a saleswoman to us immediately!"

Nancy turned to see Ada and Isabel Topham speaking to the floor manager.

"I'm afraid I can't," the man replied regretfully. "There are a number of others ahead of you. All our salespeople are—"

"Perhaps you don't know who we are!" Ada in-terrupted rudely.

"Indeed I do," the floor manager told her wea-

rily. "I will have a saleswoman here in a few moments. If you will only wait—"

"We're not accustomed to waiting," Isabel Topham told him icily.

"Such service!" Ada chimed in. "Do you realize that my father owns considerable stock in Taylor's? If we report your conduct to him, he could
have you discharged."

"I'm sorry," the harassed man apologized.
"But it is a rule of the store. You must await your
turn."

Ada tossed her head and her eyes flashed angrily. This did nothing to improve her looks. In
spite of the expensive clothes she wore, Ada was
not attractive. She was very thin and sallow, with
an expression of petulance. Now that her face
was distorted with anger, she was almost ugly.

Isabel, the pride of the Topham family, was
rather pretty, but her face lacked character. She
had acquired an artificially elegant manner of
speaking which, although irritating, was sometimes amusing. It was her mother's ambition that
Isabel marry into a socially prominent family.

"I pity any future husband of hers!" Nancy
thought with a chuckle.

Suddenly Ada and Isabel saw Nancy, who
nodded a greeting. Isabel coldly returned the
nod, but Ada gave no indication that she had even
noticed Nancy.

At that moment a saleswoman hurried toward

the Topham sisters. At once they began to shower abuse upon the young woman for her failure to wait on them sooner.

"What is it you wish to look at, Miss Topham?" the clerk said, flushing.

"Evening dresses."

The saleswoman brought out several dresses. Nancy watched curiously as the Tophams, in an unpleasant frame of mind, tossed aside beautiful models with scarcely a second glance. They found fault with every garment.

"This is a very chic gown," the saleswoman told them hopefully, as she displayed a particularly attractive dress of lace and chiffon. "It arrived only this morning."

Ada picked it up, gave the dress one careless glance, then tossed it into a chair, as the distracted clerk went off to bring other frocks.

The fluffy gown slipped to the floor in a crumpled mass. To Nancy's horror Ada stepped on it as she turned to examine another dress. In disgust, Nancy went to pick it up.

"Leave that alone!" Ada cried out, her eyes blazing. "Nobody asked for your help."

"Are you buying this?" Nancy asked evenly.

"It's none of your business!"

As Nancy continued to hold the dress, Ada in a rage snatched it from her hands, causing a long tear in the chiffon skirt.

"Oh!" Isabel cried out. "Now you've done it! We'd better get out of here, Ada!"

"And why?" her haughty sister shrilled. "It was Nancy Drew's fault! She's always making trouble."

"It was *not* my fault," Nancy said.

"Come on, Ada," Isabel urged, "before that clerk gets back."

Reluctantly Ada followed Isabel out of the department. As they rushed toward a waiting elevator, Nancy gazed after them. At this moment the saleswoman reappeared with an armful of lovely frocks. She stared in bewilderment at the torn dress.

"Where did my customers go?" she asked Nancy worriedly.

Nancy pointed toward the elevator, but made no comment. Instead she said, "I'm looking for an evening dress myself. This torn one is very pretty. Do you think it could be mended?"

"Oh, I don't know," the woebegone clerk wailed. "I'll probably be held responsible and I can't afford to pay for the dress."

"I'm sure Taylor's wouldn't ask you to do that," Nancy said kindly. "If there's any trouble, I'll speak to the manager myself. What usually happens is that such a dress is greatly reduced."

"Thank you," the clerk replied. "I'll call Miss Reed, the fitter, and see what can be done."

"First, let me try on the dress," Nancy said, smiling.

They found a vacant fitting room and Nancy took off her suit and blouse. Then she slipped the lovely pale-blue dance creation over her head and the saleswoman zipped it up.

"It's darling on you," she said enthusiastically.

Nancy grinned. "I kind of like myself in it," she said. "Please call the fitter now."

Presently Miss Reed, a gray-haired woman, appeared. Within seconds she had made a change in an overlap of the chiffon skirt. The tear was no longer visible and the style of the dress was actually improved.

"I told our manager what happened," said the saleswoman. "If you want the dress, he will reduce the price fifty percent."

"How wonderful!" Nancy exclaimed. Laughing, she said, "That price will fit into my budget nicely. I'll take the dress. Please send it." She gave her name and address. To herself she added, "Ada Topham did me a favor. But if she ever finds out what happened, she'll certainly be burned up!" Nancy suppressed a giggle.

"It's been a real pleasure waiting on you, Miss Drew," the saleswoman said after Miss Reed left and Nancy was putting on her suit. "But how I dread to see those Topham sisters come in here! They're so unreasonable. And they'll be even worse when they get Josiah Crowley's money."

The woman lowered her voice. "The estate hasn't been settled, but the girls are counting on the fortune already. Last week I heard Ada say to her sister, 'Oh, I guess there's no question about our getting old Crowley's fortune. But I wish Father would stop worrying that somebody is going to show up with a later will which may do us out of it.'"

Nancy was too discreet to engage in gossip with the saleswoman. But she was interested and excited about the information. The fact that Mr. Topham was disturbed indicated to her that he too suspected Josiah Crowley had made a second will!

The conversation reminded Nancy of her date. She glanced at her wrist watch and saw that it was after twelve o'clock.

"I must hurry or I'll be late for an appointment with my dad," she told the saleswoman.

Nancy drove directly to her father's office. Although she was a few minutes ahead of the appointed time, she found that he was ready to leave.

"What luck, Dad?" Nancy asked eagerly. "Did Mr. Rolsted accept your luncheon invitation?"

"Yes. We are to meet him at the Royal Hotel in ten minutes. Do you still think I should quiz him about the Crowley will?"

"Oh, I'm more interested than ever in the case." She told her father about the saleswoman's gossipy remarks.

"Hm," said Mr. Drew. "It's not what you'd call evidence, but the old saying usually holds good, 'Where there's smoke, there's fire.' Come, let's go!"

The Royal Hotel was located less than a block away, and Nancy and her father quickly walked the distance. Mr. Rolsted was waiting in the lobby. Carson Drew introduced his daughter, then the three made their way to the dining room where a table had been reserved for them.

At first the conversation centered about a variety of subjects. As the luncheon progressed the two lawyers talked enthusiastically of their college days together and finally of their profession. Nancy began to fear that the subject of the Crowley estate might never be brought up.

Then, after the dessert course, Mr. Drew skillfully turned the conversation into a new channel and mentioned some strange cases which he had handled.

"By the way," he said, "I haven't heard the details of the Crowley case. How are the Tophams making out? I understand other relatives are trying to break the will."

For a moment Mr. Rolsted remained silent. Was he reluctant to enter into a discussion of the matter? Nancy wondered.

Finally the lawyer said quietly, "The settlement of the estate wasn't given to me, Carson. But I confess I've followed it rather closely because of something that happened a year ago. As the present will stands, I do not believe it can be broken."

"Then the Tophams fall heir to the entire estate," Mr. Drew commented.

"Yes, unless a more recent will is uncovered."

"Another will?" Carson Drew inquired innocently. "Then you believe Crowley made a second one?"

Mr. Rolsted hesitated as though uncertain whether or not he should divulge any further information. Then, with a quick glance about, he lowered his voice and said, "Of course this is strictly confidential—"

CHAPTER IV

Racing the Storm

"CONFIDENTIAL?" Mr. Drew repeated, looking at Mr. Rolsted. "You may rest assured that whatever you tell us will not be repeated to anyone."

"Well, I'll say this much," Mr. Rolsted went on, "about a year ago Josiah Crowley came to me and said he wanted to draw up a new will. He indicated that he intended to spread out his bequests among several people. He expressed a desire to write the will himself, and asked me a number of questions. I took him to my office and told him exactly how to proceed. When he left, he promised to have me look over the document after he had drawn it up."

"Then you actually saw the will?" Mr. Drew asked in surprise.

"No. Strange to say, Crowley never came back. I don't know whether he ever wrote the will or not."

"And if he did, there would be a chance that it would not be legal?" Nancy spoke up.

"Yes. He might have typed it and signed the paper without a witness. In this state at least two witnesses are required and three are advisable."

"What would happen," Nancy asked, "if a person were ill or dying and had no witness, and wanted to make a will?"

Mr. Rolsted smiled. "That sometimes happens. If the person writes the will himself by hand and signs it, so there's no doubt the same person did both, the surrogate's office will accept it for probate."

"Then if Mr. Crowley wrote out and signed a new will, it would be legal," Nancy commented.

"That's right. But there's another thing to remember. It's pretty risky for someone who is not a lawyer to draw up a will that cannot be broken."

Mr. Drew nodded. "If Josiah Crowley left any loophole in a will he wrote personally, the Tophams would drag the matter into court."

"Yes. It's a foregone conclusion that the Tophams will fight to keep the fortune whether they have a right to it or not. I believe some other relatives have filed a claim, but up to the moment they have no proof that a later will exists."

Although Nancy gave no indication of her feelings, the possibility that Mr. Crowley had made a new will thrilled her. As soon as Mr. Drew paid the luncheon check, the three arose and left the dining room. Mr. Rolsted took leave of Nancy and her father in the lobby.

"Well, Nancy, did you find out what you wanted to know?" Mr. Drew asked after the lawyer had left.

"Oh, Dad, it's just as I suspected. I'm sure Mr. Crowley did make a later will! He hid it some place! If only I could find out where!"

"It would be like looking for a needle in a haystack," Mr. Drew commented.

"I must figure out a way!" Nancy said with determination. "I want to help little Judy."

She awoke the next morning thinking about the mystery. But where should she start hunting for possible clues to a second will? She continued pondering about it while she showered and dressed.

As she entered the dining room, she was greeted with a cheery "Good morning" from her father and Hannah Gruen. During breakfast Mr. Drew said, "Nancy, would you do a little errand for me this morning?"

"Why, of course, Dad."

"I have a number of legal documents which must be delivered to Judge Hart at Masonville some time before noon. I'd take them myself, but I have several important appointments. I'd appreciate it if you would drive over there with them."

"I'll be glad to go," Nancy promised willingly.

"Besides, it's such a wonderful day. I'll enjoy the trip. Where are the papers?"

"At the office. You can drive me down and I'll get them for you."

Nancy, wearing a yellow sunback dress and jacket, hurried away to get her gloves and handbag. Before Mr. Drew had collected his own belongings, she had brought her car from the garage and was waiting for him at the front door.

"I put the top down so I can enjoy the sun," she explained as her father climbed in.

"Good idea. I haven't heard you mention the Crowley case yet today," Mr. Drew teased as they rode along. "Have you forgotten about it?"

Nancy's face clouded. "No, I haven't forgotten, but I must admit I *am* stumped as to where to search for clues."

"Maybe I can help you. I've learned that the two girls on River Road who expected to be remembered in the will are named Hoover. You might look them up on your return trip."

"That's great. I'll watch the mailboxes for their name."

When they reached the building where Mr. Drew had his office, Nancy parked the car and waited while her father went upstairs to get the legal documents to be delivered to Judge Hart. Returning a few minutes later, he placed a fat Manila envelope in his daughter's hand.

"Give this to the judge. You know where to find him?"

"Yes, Dad. In the old Merchants Trust Company Building."

"That's right."

Selecting a recently constructed highway, Nancy rode along, glancing occasionally at the neatly planted fields on either side. Beyond were rolling hills.

"Pretty," she commented to herself. "Oh, why can't all people be nice like this scenery and not make trouble?"

It was nearly eleven o'clock when she finally drove into Masonville. Nancy went at once to Judge Hart's office but was informed he had gone to the courthouse. Recalling that her father had mentioned the necessity of the papers being delivered before noon, she set off in search of the judge.

Nancy had considerable trouble trying to see him, and it was twelve o'clock when at last she delivered the Manila envelope into his hands.

"Thank you very much," he said. "I'll need these directly after lunch."

Nancy smiled. "Then I'm glad I found you."

When Judge Hart learned that Nancy was the daughter of Carson Drew, he at once insisted that she have luncheon with him and his wife at their home before returning to River Heights.

She accepted the invitation and spent a very

pleasant hour with the Harts. During the meal the judge laughingly asked if Nancy was still playing aide to her father.

"Oh, yes," she said, and at once told him about the Drews' interest in the Crowley case.

"Did you know Josiah Crowley or ever hear of him?" she asked.

Both the Harts nodded. "A maid who used to be with them, came to work for us after Mrs. Crowley's death," the judge explained. "Jane herself passed away a short time ago."

"We never met Josiah," Mrs. Hart added, "but Jane pointed him out to my husband and me one time down on Main Street."

"Did he have relatives or friends in town?" Nancy inquired.

"I think not," the judge replied.

Nancy wondered what old Josiah had been doing in Masonville if he had no relatives or friends there. The town was not known as a spot for sight-seeing. Her interest was further quickened when Mrs. Hart remarked that she had seen Mr. Crowley in town at another time also.

"How long ago was that?" the girl asked.

Mrs. Hart thought a minute, then replied, "Oh, less than a year, I'd say."

When luncheon was over, the judge said he must leave. Nancy told the Harts she too should go. She thanked them for their hospitality, then said good-by. Soon she was driving homeward.

"Why had Mr. Crowley gone to Masonville?" she asked herself. "Could it have had anything to do with a later will?"

Nancy had chosen a route which would take her to River Road. Half an hour later she turned into the beautiful country road which wound in and out along the Muskoka River, and began to look at the names on the mailboxes. "Hoover," she reminded herself.

About halfway to River Heights, while enjoying the pastoral scenes of cows standing knee-high in shallow sections of the stream, and sheep grazing on flower-dotted hillsides, Nancy suddenly realized the sun had been blotted out.

"A thunderstorm's on the way," she told herself, glancing at black clouds scudding across the sky. "Guess I'd better put the top of the car up."

She pressed the button on the dashboard to raise the top, but nothing happened. Puzzled, Nancy tried again. Still there was no response. By this time large drops of rain had started to fall.

"I'll get soaked," Nancy thought, as she looked around.

There was no shelter in sight. But ahead, past a steep rise, was a sharp bend in the road. Hopeful that there would be a house or barn beyond, Nancy started the car again.

Vivid forked lightning streaked across the sky. It was followed by an earth-shaking clap of thunder. The rain came down harder,

"Oh, why didn't I bring a raincoat?" Nancy wailed.

When Nancy swung around the bend, she was delighted to see a barn with lightning rods about a quarter mile ahead. Farther on stood a small white house.

"I wonder if that's the Hoover place," Nancy mused.

By now the storm was letting loose in all its fury. The sky was as dark as night and Nancy had to switch on her headlights to see the road. She was already thoroughly drenched and her thought of shelter at this point was one of safety rather than of keeping dry.

Nancy turned on the windshield wipers, but the rain was so blinding in its intensity, it was impossible to see more than a few feet ahead. Almost in an instant the road had dissolved into a sea of mud.

Nancy had been caught in a number of storms, but never one as violent as this. She feared a bad skid might land her in a ditch before she could reach the shelter of the barn.

"How much farther is it?" she worried. "It didn't seem this far away."

The next instant, to Nancy's right, a ball of fire rocketed down from the sky.

"Oh! That was close!" she thought fearfully. Her skin tingled from the electrical vibrations in the air.

A moment later a surge of relief swept over Nancy. "At last!" she breathed.

At the side of the road the barn loomed up. Its large double doors were wide open. Without hesitation, Nancy headed straight for the building and drove in.

The next moment she heard a piercing scream!

CHAPTER V

A Surprising Story

NANCY froze behind the wheel. Had she inadvertently hit someone? Her heart pounding in fright, she opened the car door to step out.

At the same instant a shadowy figure arose from a pile of hay near her. "I guess I must have scared you silly when I screamed," said a girl of Nancy's age, stepping forward.

"You— You're all right?" Nancy gasped.

"Yes. And I'm sorry I yelled. I came out here to check on our supply of feed for the chickens. I didn't think it was going to be a bad storm, so I didn't bother to go back to the house."

"It's pretty bad," said Nancy.

"Well, the storm terrified me," the girl continued. "I didn't hear your car coming, and when it rushed in here, I panicked."

Nancy began to breathe normally again, then

told the stranger her name and the fact that the mechanism for raising the top of the convertible was not working.

"That's a shame," said the girl. "And you must get your clothes dried. The storm is letting up. Let's dash over to the house. Grace will help you too. She's my sister. My name's Allison Hoover."

Hoover! Nancy was tempted to tell Allison that she had been planning to call, but she decided not to mention it at the moment. It might be better to do her sleuthing more subtly.

Nancy smiled at Allison. "Thanks a million. But first I'd like to wipe out the car. Are there any rags around the barn?"

Allison produced several and together the two girls mopped the water from the cushions and floor. By this time the rain had stopped. As Nancy and Allison sloshed through a series of puddles to the farmhouse, Nancy had a better chance to study her companion. She was tall, with reddish-blond hair and very fair skin. Her voice was musical and she had an attractive, lilting laugh.

The girls reached the run-down farmhouse and stamped the mud from their shoes on the back porch. Then Allison flung open the door, and they entered a cheerful kitchen.

As the door shut behind them, another girl who was just closing the oven of an old-fashioned range turned toward them in surprise.

"Grace, I've brought a visitor," Allison said

quickly. "Nancy, I want you to meet my sister. She's the mainstay of our family of two."

Grace Hoover cordially acknowledged the introduction and greeted Nancy with a warm smile. Nancy judged her to be at least four years older than Allison. Her face was rather serious, and it was evident from her manner that responsibility had fallen on her shoulders at an early age.

Nancy was attracted to both girls and responded to their friendly welcome. She put on a robe which Allison brought her and Grace hung her wet clothes near the range. Presently Grace pulled an ironing board from a closet with the intention of pressing Nancy's garments. But Nancy would not hear of this and began to iron them herself.

"This is fun," she said to the sisters. "I don't know what I would have done without you girls."

"It's great for us," Allison spoke up. "We don't have much company. To tell you the truth, we can't afford it."

Grace stepped to the stove, removed a golden-brown cake from the oven, and set it on the table to cool.

"But today we're not talking about money. It's Allison's birthday and this is a birthday cake. Nancy, if you're not in too much of a hurry, I wish you'd join us in a little celebration."

"Why, I'd love to," Nancy said.

"Grace's cakes are yummy," Allison declared.

"I'm not much of a cook myself. My department is taking care of the barn and the chickens."

Soon Nancy finished pressing her clothes and put them back on. Meanwhile, the cake had cooled and Grace started to spread the chocolate frosting.

"Suppose you two go into the living room and wait," she suggested. "I'll bring in the cake and tea."

Nancy followed Allison to the adjoining room. Although it was comfortable, the room did not contain much furniture. The floor had been painted and was scantily covered with handmade rag rugs. With the exception of an old-fashioned sofa, an inexpensive table, a few straight-backed chairs and an old oil stove which furnished heat in cold weather, there was little else in the room. However, dainty white curtains covered the windows, and Nancy realized that although the Hoovers were poor, they had tried hard to make their home attractive.

"Do you two girls live here alone all the time?" Nancy inquired.

Allison nodded. "Grace and I have been living here since Father died. That was two years ago. Mother passed away just before that," the girl added with a slight catch in her voice. "Their illnesses took every penny we had."

"I'm terribly sorry," Nancy remarked sympathetically. "It must be dreadfully hard for two girls to run the farm by themselves."

"Our farm isn't as large as it once was," Allison said quietly. "We have only a few acres left. I know you are too polite to ask how we manage, Nancy. Grace helps a dressmaker at Masonville whenever she can get work. She makes all her own clothes and mine too. And I raise chickens."

From just beyond the doorway suddenly came the strains of "Happy Birthday to you! Happy Birth—"

By this time Nancy had joined in. She and Grace finished "—day to you. Happy Birthday, dear Allison. Happy Birthday to you!"

Grace set the cake with eighteen lighted candles on the table. She and Nancy sang the second verse with the words "May you have many more!"

Tears stood in Allison's eyes. When the song ended, she grasped her sister in a tremendous hug. Then she gave Nancy one.

"This—this is the nicest birthday I've had in years," she quavered.

"And it's one of the most enjoyable I've ever attended," Nancy said sincerely.

Suddenly Allison began to sing a tuneful old English ballad about the birthday of a village lass. Nancy listened entranced to Allison's clear, bell-like tones. When she finished, Nancy applauded, then said:

"That was perfectly lovely. You have a beautiful voice, Allison!"

The singer laughed gaily. "Thank you, Nancy. I've always wanted to take lessons, but as you know, voice training is pretty expensive."

At that moment Grace brought in a tray of fragrant tea. As she poured three cups, Allison blew out the candles and served the cake.

"I've never tasted anything more delicious in all my life," Nancy said enthusiastically.

The three girls chatted like old friends. Finally the sun broke through the clouds. As Nancy rose to leave, she noticed an unusual picture on the wall opposite her and commented on its beauty.

"Uncle Josiah Crowley gave it to us," Allison told her. "If he were only alive now, things would be different."

At the mention of the name, Nancy sat down again. Was she going to pick up a clue to the possibility that Mr. Crowley had made a later will?

"He wasn't really our uncle," Grace explained. "But we loved him as much as though he were a relative." Her voice broke and for a moment she could not go on. Then, gaining control of herself, she continued, "He lived on the farm next to us— that was when Mother and Father were alive. All of Allison's and my misfortunes seemed to come at once."

"He was the dearest man you ever saw," Allison

added. "Some people thought him queer, but you never minded his peculiar ways after you knew him. Uncle Josiah was very good to us. He always told me that he'd back me in a singing career."

"Yes," Grace added. "Uncle Josiah used to say Allison sang as sweetly as a bird and he wanted to pay for lessons with a famous teacher. But after he went to live with the Tophams, he never said any more about it."

"He never liked it with the Tophams, though," Allison declared. "They weren't kind to him, and he used to slip away to visit us."

"Uncle Josiah often said that we seemed like his own children," Grace spoke up. "He brought us many nice gifts, but we loved him for himself and not his money. I remember, though, the very last day we saw him alive, he told us 'I have planned a big surprise to make you girls happy. But I can't tell you now what it is. You'll see it in my will.' Those were his very words."

"And then the Tophams got everything," Allison said. "He must have changed his mind for some reason."

"It's hard to believe he would forget his promise to us," Grace said sadly.

"Oh, wouldn't it be wonderful if a later will could be found!" Allison exclaimed.

"Yes," Nancy replied slowly. "I've heard that

Mr. Crowley told other people he was leaving money to them. The Turner sisters, for instance. Do you know them?"

"Slightly," Grace answered.

"My dad," Nancy went on, "is a lawyer and he and I are very much interested in this case. He even mentioned you girls, and to tell the truth I was on my way here to talk to you."

Allison impulsively grasped Nancy's arm. "You say your father is a lawyer? Grace and I are positive Uncle Josiah made a later will. Oh, if we could only engage your father to help us prove this!" Then a sad look came over her face. "But I'm forgetting—we wouldn't have any money to pay him if we should lose the case."

"Don't let that worry you," said Nancy kindly. "This is your birthday and you must be happy, Allison. My special wish for you is that before you're one year older, you'll inherit some of the Crowley money, so that you can take those singing lessons!"

CHAPTER VI

An Exciting Appointment

THE HOOVER girls walked out to the barn with Nancy. "Do come to see us again," Grace called, as the young detective climbed into her car.

"Yes, please do," Allison added.

Nancy promised that she would. "As soon as I have some news," she said.

Although the weather had cleared, the River Road remained muddy and slippery. Nancy found it necessary to drive with extreme care for the next two miles until she reached the main highway.

"No wonder this River Road isn't used much," she thought. "And how do Grace and Allison get to town?" Nancy wondered. She had not seen a car at the Hoover home and knew that no bus passed their door.

"I certainly wish," she thought, "that I or somebody else could locate a later will of Josiah Crowley's by which the Hoovers and the Turners would receive some much-needed money. I must tell Dad about this latest development."

She decided to see if her father was in his office and drove directly there. Nancy parked the car in a nearby lot. She surveyed the convertible ruefully as she climbed out.

"Poor thing! It certainly needs a bath!"

Nancy found Mr. Drew in. As she entered his private office, he arose from the desk chair to kiss her. "I'm glad you're here—and safe," the lawyer said. "I was worried about you when that violent storm came up. When Hannah phoned me that you weren't back, I began to regret I'd sent you on the errand."

His daughter grinned. "I'm back, all in one piece. I delivered the papers to Judge Hart and learned that he and his wife saw Mr. Crowley in Masonville a couple of times. Also, I talked to the Hoover girls."

She described her meeting with Allison and Grace Hoover and ended by asking her father if he could help them.

"From what you say, it does look as though Josiah Crowley might have made another will which included them as beneficiaries," Mr. Drew commented thoughtfully. "I'll be glad to do anything I can to help the Hoover girls."

He asked whether the sisters had given Nancy any specific information about Mr. Crowley's habits or other helpful clues. When Nancy shook her head, Mr. Drew suggested that she invite the girls to his office for a little conference. "Perhaps if I ask them some questions, it will recall helpful incidents." The lawyer studied his desk calendar for a moment, then looked up at his daughter. "How about tomorrow afternoon at two-forty-five? I can give them about half an hour."

For answer, Nancy gave her father a hug and then asked if she might use his telephone to call the Hoovers at once.

Grace and Allison eagerly accepted the Drews' invitation, and Nancy said she would drive out to bring them to the conference and take them home afterward.

"You're a doll!" cried Allison, who had answered the telephone. "Nancy, I just know you're going to solve this mystery!"

Suddenly an idea came to Nancy. She asked Allison how long the girls would be able to stay in River Heights.

"Oh, as long as you need us," Allison replied.

"Good. Then I'd like you both to stay and have supper with us," Nancy said.

"Sorry I can't join you," Mr. Drew told his daughter as she hung up. "I have a dinner engagement and conference in the evening."

Just then, the mayor of River Heights was shown into the lawyer's office, and Nancy arose to leave. She spoke to the mayor for a moment, then said, "See you later, Dad."

Before Nancy returned home, she stopped at an old-fashioned house on a side street. It was the home of Signor Mascagni, a famous voice teacher who had retired to the small city the year before, but took a few outstanding pupils. Nancy introduced herself to the white bushy-haired, florid-faced man, then said:

"Signor Mascagni, would you be willing to listen to the voice of a friend of mine and give your honest opinion as to whether or not she might become a great singer? If she might, and she can obtain the money for lessons, would you be able to take her as a pupil?"

Signor Mascagni studied Nancy for several minutes before replying. Finally he said, "You do not look like the kind of girl who would come here on a foolish errand. Ordinarily I do not accept beginners. But in this case I would be willing to hear your friend sing." He laughed. "Mind you, I will give you nothing but the truth, and if your friend does not measure up, I hope her feelings will not be hurt too deeply."

Nancy laughed too. "I like honesty," she said. "As a matter of fact, this girl knows nothing about what I am asking you. Coming here will be a complete surprise to her. I'm probably no judge of voices, but I think she's a natural. However, we will both appreciate having your opinion, and will certainly abide by it."

She arranged for a meeting the following afternoon at four o'clock and left Signor Mascagni's house in an excited mood. "Maybe I'm going way out on a limb," Nancy mused, "but this is another one of those hunches of mine that Dad talks about, and I must carry through."

When she picked up the Hoovers the following day, Nancy did not mention the appointment with the voice teacher. The three girls went directly to Mr. Drew's office and at once he began to quiz Grace and Allison about Mr. Crowley.

"I understand that he was a rather eccentric man," the lawyer began. "Suppose you tell me everything you can remember about what Josiah Crowley did and what he said which would help us figure out where he might have secreted a later will."

"Uncle Josiah was rather absent-minded," Grace spoke up. "I often saw him hunting for his spectacles, which he had pushed up on his head."

"Did he ever hide things?" Mr. Drew asked.

"Oh, yes." Allison laughed. "Uncle Josiah was always putting articles away in what he called a safe place. But the places were so safe he never could find the things again!"

"Then," Nancy spoke up excitedly, "Mr. Crowley could have hidden a will and then forgotten where?"

"I suppose so," Grace replied. "While living with the Tophams, I'm sure that's just what he would have done. One day when he was calling at our house he talked about the Tophams and the way they were trying to get all his money. 'I guess they think—just because I stay on—that they're going to get everything. But they'll be fooled when they find I've made another will,' he said with that odd little chuckle of his. 'This time I'm not going to trust it to any lawyer. I'll put it away in a place that I know will be safe.' "

Allison asked Mr. Drew, "Do you think Uncle Josiah hid another will somewhere in the Tophams' house?"

The lawyer looked down at his desk for several seconds before replying. "If he did, we would have a great fight on our hands, I'm afraid, trying to persuade the Tophams to let us make a search."

Another thought had come to Nancy and she shuddered at the idea. Perhaps the Tophams had been alerted by all the talk of a later will, had searched for it, discovered one, and by now destroyed it!

She flashed her father a questioning look and got the impression that he had the same thought. But there was no point in discouraging the Hoover girls by telling them this.

Mr. Drew continued to question the sisters until three-thirty, then said he had another appointment. He would do all he could to help the girls and would not charge them for his services.

"Unless they bring results," he added with a smile.

"You're very kind, just like your daughter," said Grace as she arose and shook hands with the lawyer. "You have no idea how much Allison and I appreciate what you're doing for us."

When the three girls reached Nancy's car, she told the sisters she wanted them to meet someone special in town, and drove directly to Signor Mascagni's home. As they went up to the front porch they could hear the sounds of a soprano voice singing an aria from *Tosca*.

"How beautiful!" Allison exclaimed softly.

The girls were admitted by a maid and asked to wait in a small room while Signor Mascagni's pupil finished her lesson. Puzzled, Allison waited for Nancy to explain.

"I have a surprise for you," Nancy said with a grin. "Signor Mascagni has promised to listen to your voice. If you pass the test, he'll consider taking you as a pupil—that is, after we find the money for voice lessons."

Allison was too dumfounded to speak, but Grace cried out, "Oh, Nancy, what are you going to do next? We've known you only twenty-four hours and you've already boosted our morale sky-high."

At this moment the door to the studio opened. The young soprano came out, followed by Signor Mascagni. He said good-by to his pupil, then invited the three callers into the studio. Nancy quickly introduced the Hoover sisters.

"And you are the singer," the man said almost

at once, addressing Allison. "I can tell from your speaking voice."

Apparently the teacher sensed that Allison had been taken by surprise and was a little nervous. Accordingly he began to talk on other subjects than music. He showed the girls several paintings in the room and pieces of statuary which had come from Italy.

"I prize them highly," he said.

"They are exquisite," Allison remarked.

Signor Mascagni walked to a rear window and pointed out a lovely garden in back of the house. Then, evidently satisfied that Allison was at ease, he led the way to the grand piano and sat down.

"Now what would you like to sing?" he asked Allison with a smile. "Please stand right here facing me."

"Something very simple," she replied. " 'America the Beautiful'?"

The teacher nodded, asked her what key she would like it played in, then began to accompany her. Allison sang as though inspired. Her voice sounded even more beautiful than it had at the farmhouse, Nancy thought. When Allison finished the song, Signor Mascagni made no comment. Instead he asked her to try a scale, then to sing single tones, jumping from octave to octave.

"You have a very fine range, Miss Hoover," was his only comment.

For half an hour he had Allison try short songs

in various keys and at one point joined with her in a duet. At last he turned around on the piano bench and faced Nancy and Grace.

"I believe," he said slowly, "I believe that some day we shall know Allison Hoover as an operatic star!"

Before the girls could say anything, he jumped up and turned to shake Allison's hand fervently. By this time the full import of his words had dawned on the young singer. Tears began to roll down her cheeks.

"Bravissimo! Bravissimo!" he exclaimed. "You sing, you cry, you smile! *Magnifico!* You will also be a dramatic actress *splendida."*

Nancy and Grace were nearly on the verge of tears also, they were so overwhelmed by the happy news. Then suddenly the three girls became serious, remembering that there was still the problem of money for lessons from this great man. They knew his fee per hour must be very high.

Allison suddenly began to talk and poured out her whole story to the white-haired teacher. "But I know," she declared with a brave smile, "that somehow I'm going to get the money for the lessons and I wouldn't want to take them from anybody but you, Signor Mascagni. I'll come back to you just as soon as I can. Thank you very, very much. Please, girls, I'd like to leave now."

As Allison rushed toward the front door, Signor Mascagni detained Nancy and Grace. "This Allison, she is wonderful!" he exclaimed. "I want to give her lessons to see that her training is correct." He threw up his hands and shook his head. "But I cannot afford to give the lessons free. Perhaps I could cut my price—"

"We'll find the money somehow, signor!" Nancy promised. Then she and Grace thanked the teacher and followed Allison outside.

At the Drew home that evening there were mixed emotions on everyone's part. Hannah Gruen had taken a great fancy to the Hoover sisters and the news of Allison's talent had thrilled her, as well as the girls. Conversation at supper was gay and animated. Nancy and Mrs. Gruen drove the sisters to their farm and on parting Nancy again promised to do all she could to help find a will from which the girls might possibly benefit.

But figuring out how to do this became a problem that seemed insurmountable to Nancy. At breakfast the following day, Mr. Drew suggested, "Nancy, perhaps if you'd give your mind a little rest from the Crowley matter, an inspiration about the case might come to you."

His daughter smiled. "Good idea, Dad. I think I'll take a walk in the fresh air and clear the cobwebs from my brain."

As soon as she finished eating, Nancy set out at a brisk pace. She headed for River Heights' attractive park to view the display of roses which was

Signor Muscugni shook Allison's hand fervently

always very beautiful. She had gone only a short distance along one of the paths when she caught sight of Isabel and Ada Topham seated on a bench not far ahead.

"They're the last people in the world I want to see right now," Nancy thought. "They'll probably say something mean to me and I'll lose my temper. When I think how Grace and Allison and the Turners could use just one-tenth of the Crowley money which the Tophams are going to inherit, I could just burst!"

Nancy had paused, wondering whether she should turn back. "No," she told herself, "I'll go on to see the roses. I'll take that path back of the Tophams and they won't notice me."

Nancy made her way along quietly, with no intention of eavesdropping on the two girls. But suddenly two words of their conversation came to her ears, bringing Nancy to an involuntary halt.

She had distinctly heard Isabel say—"the will."

In a flash Nancy's detective instincts were aroused and her heart pounded excitedly. " It must be Josiah Crowley's will they're talking about," she reasoned.

CHAPTER VII

The Angry Dog

WITH the instinct of a detective who dared not miss a clue, Nancy deliberately moved closer to the bench on which the Topham girls were seated.

"If there *should* be another will, I'm afraid we'd be out of luck." The words, in Ada's nasal voice, came clearly to Nancy.

Isabel's reply was in so low a tone that the young sleuth could just manage to catch the words, "Well, I, for one, don't believe Josiah Crowley ever made a later will." She gave a low laugh. "Mother watched him like a hawk."

"Or thought she did," Isabel retorted. "The old man got out of her clutches several times, don't forget."

"Yes, and what's worse, I'm sure Nancy Drew thinks he made a later will. That's why she's taking such an interest in those Hoover girls. I actually saw them go into Mr. Drew's office yesterday and it wasn't to deliver eggs! If Nancy gets her father interested, he might dig up another will. Oh, how I hate that interfering girl!"

At this Nancy could barely refrain from laughing. So the Tophams *were* concerned about the existence of a second will. With bated breath she listened further.

"You're such a worry wart, Ada. You can trust Dad and Mother to take care of things, no matter what happens," Isabel commented dryly. "They won't let that pile of money get away from us. It's ours by right, anyhow."

"You've got something there," Ada conceded. "We should have old Josiah's money after supporting and putting up with him for three years. That was pretty clever of Mother, never accepting any board money from Josiah Crowley!"

The conversation ended as Isabel and Ada arose from the bench and walked away. Nancy waited until they were out of sight, then emerged from her hiding place. Seating herself on the bench vacated by the Topham sisters, Nancy mulled over the remarks she had just overheard.

"There's no doubt in my mind now that if there is a later will, the Tophams haven't destroyed it. How thrilling! But where can it be?"

Nancy realized that to find it was a real challenge. "And I'd better hurry up before the Tophams stumble on it!"

For another ten minutes Nancy sat lost in

thought, sifting all the facts she had gleaned so far.

"There must be some clue I've overlooked," she told herself. Suddenly, with a cry of delight, she sprang to her feet. "Why didn't I think of that before! The Hoover girls and the Turners aren't the only ones who should have figured in this will. There are other relatives of Mr. Crowley who have filed a claim. I wonder who they are. If I could only talk with them, I might pick up a clue!"

Immediately Nancy set off for her father's office. He was engaged in an important conference when she arrived, and she had to wait ten minutes before being admitted to the inner office.

"Now what?" Mr. Drew asked, smiling, as she burst in upon him. "Have you solved the mystery or is your purse in need of a little change?"

Nancy's cheeks were flushed and her eyes danced with excitement. "Don't tease me," she protested. "I need some information!"

"At your service, Nancy."

The young sleuth poured out the story of the Topham sisters' conversation in the park, and told him of her own conclusions. Mr. Drew listened with interest until she had finished.

"Excellent deducting," he praised his daughter. "I'm afraid, though, I can't help you obtain the relatives' names. I don't know any of them."

Nancy looked disappointed. "Oh dear!" she sighed. "And I'm so anxious to find out right away. If I delay even a single day the Tophams may locate that other will—and destroy it."

The next instant her face brightened. "I know! I'll drive out and see the Turner sisters. They might be able to tell me who the other relatives are." Nancy arose and headed for the door.

"Just a minute," said the lawyer. "I wonder if you realize just what you are getting into, Nancy?"

"What do you mean?"

"Only this. Detective work isn't always the safest occupation in which to engage. I happen to know that Richard Topham is an unpleasant man when crossed. If you do find out anything which may frustrate him, the entire Topham family could make things extremely difficult for you."

"I'm not afraid of them, Dad."

"Good!" Mr. Drew exclaimed. "I was hoping you would say that. I'm glad you have the courage of your convictions, but I didn't want you to march off into battle without a knowledge of what you might be up against."

"Battle?"

"Yes. The Tophams won't give up the fortune without a bitter struggle. However, if they attempt to make serious trouble, I promise to deal with them myself."

"And if I do find the will?"

"I'll take the matter into court."

"Oh. thank you! There's no one like you in all the world."

After leaving her father's office, Nancy went directly home to get her car. When she told Hannah Gruen her plans, the housekeeper warned, "Don't become too deeply involved in this matter, dear. In your zeal to help other people, you may forget to be on your guard."

"I promise to be as careful as a pussycat walking up a slippery roof," Nancy assured the housekeeper with a grin, and left the house.

Quickly backing her car from the garage, she set off in the direction of the Turner home. The miles seemed to melt away as Nancy's thoughts raced from one idea to another. Before the young sleuth knew it she had reached the house.

"Hi, Judy!" she called to the little girl, who was playing in the yard with a midget badminton set.

The child looked very cunning in a pink play suit. The hand-embroidered Teddy bears on it were surely the work of her loving aunts.

"Hi, Nancy! I'm glad you came. Now I'll have somebody to play with," Judy said, running up to the visitor.

Obligingly Nancy took a racket and batted the feathered shuttlecock toward the child. "Hit the birdie," she called.

Judy missed but picked up the shuttlecock and whammed it nicely across the net. Nancy hit it back and this time the little girl caught the birdie on her racket and sent it over.

The game went on for several minutes, with

Judy crying out in delight. "You're the bestest batter I ever played with, Nancy," she declared.

After ten minutes of play, Nancy said, "Let's go into the house now, Judy. I want to talk to your aunties."

Judy skipped ahead and announced her new playmate's arrival.

"Hello, Nancy," the women said as she entered the living room.

"We were watching the game from the window," said Mary Turner. "This is a real thrill for Judy. Edna and I are very poor at hitting the birdie."

"It was lots of fun," Nancy replied. "I'm glad to see you all again."

She now asked whether the police had located the thieves who had taken the silver heirlooms from the house.

"Not yet," Mary answered. "And what's worse, we found that several other pieces had been taken too."

"What a shame!" Nancy exclaimed. "But I'm sure the stolen articles will be found." Then she added, "I came here on a particular mission."

"Yes?"

"Your story about Mr. Josiah Crowley intrigued me. Then, the other day, I met two girls, Grace and Allison Hoover, who told me of a similar promise from him regarding his will."

"How amazing!" Edna Turner exclaimed. "I

heard Josiah mention the Hoovers and Allison's beautiful voice."

"Dad and I have become very much interested in the case and are inclined to agree with you and the Hoovers that Mr. Crowley may have written another will shortly before his death and hidden it some place."

"Oh, wouldn't it be wonderful if such a will could be found!" Mary exclaimed. "It might mean all the difference in the world to Judy's future."

"What I want to do," Nancy went on, "is talk to as many of Mr. Crowley's relatives as I can find. Some place I may pick up a clue to where a more recent will is hidden. Tell me, do any of his other relatives live around here?"

"Yes. Three that I can think of," Edna answered.

She went on to say that two cousins, who had never married, lived on a farm just outside Titusville. "Their names are Fred and William Mathews."

Suddenly the Turner sisters blushed a deep pink. They glanced at each other, then back at Nancy. Finally Edna said:

"Many years ago Fred proposed to Mary, and William to me, and we came near accepting. But just at that time we had the great tragedy in the family and took Judy's mother to rear, so we decided not to marry."

An embarrassing pause was broken by Judy. "Some day my aunties are going to give me one of my mother's dollies, Nancy. Isn't that nice?"

"It certainly is," Nancy agreed. "And you must be sure to show it to me." Then she asked the sisters, "What relation are the Mathews to Mr. Crowley?"

"First cousins on his mother's side."

"Do you think they would mind my asking them some questions, even though I'm a stranger?"

"Not at all," Mary replied. "They're very fine gentlemen."

"And tell them Mary and I sent you," Edna added.

"How far is Titusville from here?" Nancy inquired.

"Oh, not more than five miles on Route 10A. You could drive there in a few minutes. It's on the way to Masonville. Nancy, won't you stay and have lunch with us?"

Eager to continue her work, the young sleuth was about to refuse, but Judy put in an invitation also. "Please, oh please, Nancy. And while my aunties are fixing it, you and I can play badminton."

"All right," Nancy agreed. "And thank you very much."

It was nearly two o'clock when she finally was ready to depart.

"Oh, Mary," said Edna suddenly, "we forgot to

tell Nancy about Josiah's wife's cousin, Mrs. Abby Rowen. She'd be apt to know more about the will than anyone else."

"That's right! You really should call on her, Nancy. She took care of Josiah one time when he was sick, and he thought the world of her. He often declared he intended to leave her something. She's a widow and has very little."

"Even a few thousand dollars would mean a lot to her," Edna added. "Abby must be over eighty years of age, and growing forgetful. She has no children and there's no one to look after her."

"Where shall I find Mrs. Rowen?" Nancy asked, hoping it was not far away.

"Abby lives on the West Lake Road," Edna responded. "It's a good many miles from here."

"Then I shan't have time to go there today," the young sleuth said. "But I'll surely see her as soon as I can. And now I must be going."

Nancy thanked the Turner sisters and said good-by. But before she could leave, Judy insisted upon showing how she could jump rope and do all kinds of dancing steps with a hoop on the lawn.

"Judy entertains us all the time," Mary remarked. "We believe she's very talented."

Nancy thought so too. As she drove off, she again hoped that money would become available for a very special education for Judy.

After Nancy had gone five miles along the designated route, she began to watch the mailboxes.

Soon she noticed one which bore the name *Mathews*. The farmhouse stood back a distance from the road and had a wide sweep of lawn in front of it. Near the house a man was riding a small tractor, mowing the grass.

Nancy drove down the narrow lane which led into the grounds, and stopped opposite the spot where the man was working. The man's back was toward her, and he apparently had not heard the car above the noise of the tractor, so she waited.

Looking toward the house, Nancy suddenly saw a sight that appalled her. Wedged between two stones of a broken wall was a police dog puppy whining pitifully. Nancy dashed forward and released the little animal. As it continued to whimper, she cuddled the pup in her arms and began to examine its paws.

"Why, you poor thing!" Nancy said, seeing a tear in the flesh of one hind leg. "This must be taken care of right away."

She decided to carry the puppy over to the man on the mower. As Nancy walked across the lane, she suddenly heard an angry growl near her. Looking back, she saw a huge police dog, evidently the pup's mother, bounding toward her.

"It's all right," Nancy called soothingly to the dog. "I'm not going to take your baby away."

She took two more strides, but got no farther. With a fierce snarl the dog leaped on Nancy, knocking her flat!

CHAPTER VIII

A Forgotten Secret

NANCY screamed for help, hoping to attract the farmer's attention. She expected momentarily to be bitten by the angry dog, but to her great relief the animal did not harm her.

The young sleuth's sudden fall had caused the puppy to fly from her arms. With a leap its mother was at the pup's side. She grabbed her baby by the back of its neck and trotted off toward the barn.

"O-o, that was a narrow escape." Nancy took a deep breath as she got to her feet, brushed herself off, and ruefully surveyed a tear in her sweater.

By this time the man on the tractor, having changed direction, saw the fracas and came running. He apologized for the dog's actions, but Nancy said quickly:

"It was my fault. I should have set the pup

down. Its mother probably thought I was trying to dognap her baby!"

"Possibly."

Nancy explained why she had picked up the little animal and the farmer said he would look at the cut later.

"I'm glad you weren't hurt," he added. "Thanks for being such a good scout about it. Did you come to see me or my brother?" he asked. "I'm Fred Mathews."

Nancy gave her name, and added that she was acquainted with the Turner sisters and others who had been told they would benefit under Josiah Crowley's will.

"My dad—the lawyer Carson Drew—and I are working on the case. We believe there might have been a later will than the one presented by Mr. Topham, and we'd like to find it."

"And you came to see if William and I could give you a clue?" Fred's bright blue eyes sparkled boyishly.

"That's right, Mr. Mathews. Also, did Mr. Crowley ever tell you he was going to leave you some money?"

"Indeed he did."

At this moment another man came from the house and Fred introduced him as his brother William. Both were tall, spare, and strong-muscled. Though their hair was gray, the men's faces were youthful and unwrinkled.

"Let's sit down under the tree here and discuss this," Fred suggested, leading the way to a group of rustic chairs. He told William of Nancy's request, then asked him, "Did Cousin Josiah ever give you any idea he'd made a will in which we were not beneficiaries?"

"No. I thought one would come to light when he died. To tell the truth, Miss Drew, Fred and I were thunderstruck at the will which left everything to the Tophams. That wasn't what Cousin Josiah led us to believe."

"It certainly wasn't," Fred spoke up. "But I guess William and I counted our chickens before they were hatched. We just about make ends meet here with our small fruit farm. Help and equipment cost such a lot. One thing we've always wanted to do, but couldn't afford, was to travel. We thought we'd use the money from Cousin Josiah to do that."

"But our dream bubble burst," said William. "No trips for us."

Nancy smiled. "Don't give up hope yet. Dad and I haven't."

She was disappointed that the brothers could offer her no clues about a place to look for another will. A little while later she left the farm and returned home.

"No new evidence," she told her father. "Let's hope Mrs. Abby Rowen has some!"

Early the next morning she set off for the elderly

woman's home, and reached her destination by asking directions of people living along West Lake Road.

"This must be Abby Rowen's house," Nancy told herself. "It fits the description."

She climbed out of her car and stood before the one-story frame building which was badly in need of paint and repair. The yard around it was over-grown with weeds, and the picket fence enclosing the cottage sagged dejectedly.

"The place looks deserted," Nancy mused. "But I'll see if Mrs. Rowen is at home."

Nancy made her way up the scraggly path to the house and rapped on the front door. There was no response. After a moment, she knocked again.

This time a muffled voice called, "Who's there? If you're a peddler, I don't want anything."

"I'm not selling anything," Nancy called out reassuringly. "Won't you let me in, please?"

There was a long silence, then the quavering voice replied, "I can't open the door. I've hurt myself and can't walk."

Nancy hesitated an instant before pushing open the door. As she stepped into the dreary living room, she saw a frail figure on the couch. Abby Rowen lay huddled under an old shawl, her with-ered face drawn with pain.

"I am Nancy Drew and I've come to help you, Mrs. Rowen."

The old lady turned her head and regarded Nancy with a stare of wonder.

"You've come to help me?" she repeated unbelievingly. "I didn't think anyone would ever bother about old Abby again."

"Here, let me arrange the pillows for you." Gently Nancy moved the old woman into a more comfortable position.

"Yesterday I fell down the cellar stairs," Mrs. Rowen explained. "I hurt my hip and sprained my ankle."

"Haven't you had a doctor?" Nancy asked in astonishment.

"No." Abby Rowen sighed. "Not a soul has been here and I couldn't get in touch with anybody. I have no telephone."

"Can you walk at all?" Nancy asked.

"A little."

"Then your hip isn't broken," Nancy said in relief. "Let me see your ankle. Oh my, it is swollen! I'll bandage it for you."

"There's a clean cloth in the closet in the kitchen," Abby told her. "I haven't any regular bandage."

"You really should have a doctor," Nancy remarked. "Let me drive you to one."

"I can't afford it," the old woman murmured. "My pension check hasn't come, and it's too small, anyway."

"Let me pay the doctor," Nancy offered.

Abby Rowen shook her head stubbornly. "I'll not take charity. I'd rather die first."

"Well, if you insist upon not having a doctor, I'm going to the nearest drugstore and get some bandaging and a few other things," Nancy told her. "But before I go, I'll make you a cup of tea."

"There's no tea in the house."

"Then I'll get a box. What else do you need?"

"I need 'most everything, but I can't afford anything right now. You might get me some tea and a loaf of bread. That's enough. You'll find the money in a jar in the cupboard. It's not very much, but it's all I have."

"I'll be back in a few minutes," Nancy promised.

She stopped in the kitchen long enough to examine the cupboards. With the exception of a little flour and sugar and a can of soup, there appeared to be nothing in the house to eat. Nancy found that the money jar contained less than five dollars.

"I'll not take any of it," she decided.

Quietly the young sleuth slipped out the back door. She drove quickly to the nearest store and ordered a stock of groceries. Then she stopped at a drugstore and purchased bandages and liniment.

Reaching the cottage, she carried the supplies inside and adeptly set about making Abby Rowen more comfortable. She bathed the swollen ankle and bound it neatly with the antiseptic bandage.

"It feels better already," Mrs. Rowen told her gratefully. "I don't know what would have happened to me if you hadn't come."

"Oh, someone would have dropped in," said Nancy cheerfully. She went to the kitchen and in a short while prepared tea and a light lunch for the elderly woman.

As Abby Rowen ate the nourishing meal, Nancy was gratified to observe that almost immediately her patient became more cheerful and seemed to gain strength. She sat up on the couch and appeared eager to talk with Nancy.

"There aren't many folks willing to come in and help an old lady. If Josiah Crowley had lived, things would have been different," she declared. "I could have paid someone to look after me."

"It's strange that he didn't provide for you in his will," Nancy replied quietly.

She did not wish to excite the woman by telling her real mission. Yet Nancy hoped that she might lead her tactfully into a discussion of Josiah Crowley's affairs without raising hopes which might never be realized.

"It's my opinion that Josiah did provide for me," Mrs. Rowen returned emphatically. "Many a time he said to me, 'Abby, you'll never need to worry. When I'm gone you'll be well taken care of by my will.'"

"And then everything was left to the Tophams," Nancy encouraged her to proceed.

"That was according to the first will," Abby Rowen stated.

"You mean there was another will?" Nancy inquired eagerly.

"Of course. Why, I saw that will with my own eyes!"

"You saw it!" Nancy gasped.

The old woman nodded gravely. "Mind, I didn't see what was in the will. One day Josiah came to call and give me some money. Right off I noticed he had a bunch of papers in his hand. 'Abby,' he said, 'I've made a new will. I didn't bother with a lawyer. I wrote it myself.' "

"How long ago was that?" Nancy asked quickly.

"Let me see." Abby Rowen frowned thoughtfully. "I can't remember the exact date. It was this past spring. Anyway, Josiah hinted that he'd done well by me. 'But, Josiah,' I said, 'are you sure it's legal to write it yourself?' 'Of course it is,' he said. 'A lawyer told me it was all right, just so long as I wrote it myself and signed it. But I did have it witnessed.' "

"Do you know who witnessed the will?" Nancy broke in.

"No. He didn't say."

"Haven't you any idea what became of the will?" Nancy asked hopefully.

"Well, I remember Josiah did say something about putting it where nobody could get it unless they had legal authority. But I really don't know what became of it."

"Are you certain that was all Mr. Crowley said?" Nancy inquired gently. She recalled the Turners saying that Abby had become forgetful.

The elderly woman shook her head and sighed. "Many a night I've lain awake trying to think what else he did say about where he would put the will. I just can't recollect."

"Try to think!" Nancy begged.

"I can't remember," Abby Rowen murmured hopelessly. "I've tried and tried." She leaned against the cushions and closed her eyes, as though the effort had exhausted her.

At that very moment the clock on the mantel chimed twelve. Abby's eyes fluttered open and an odd expression passed over her face.

For an instant she stared straight before her, then slowly turned her head and fastened her eyes on the clock.

CHAPTER IX

Helpful Disclosures

NANCY watched Abby Rowen intently as the mantel clock finished striking. The elderly woman's lips had begun to move.

"The clock!" she whispered. "That was it! The clock!"

Nancy gripped the arms of her chair in excitement. "Josiah Crowley hid the will in a clock?" she prompted.

"No—no, it wasn't that," Abby murmured, sighing again. "I know Josiah said something about a clock, but whatever it was has slipped my mind."

Silence descended over the room. Nancy was wondering what connection the timepiece could have with the missing will. Mrs. Rowen was staring at the clock, evidently still trying to probe her memory.

Suddenly she gave a low cry. "There! It came to me just like that!"

"What, Mrs. Rowen?" Nancy urged quietly, lest she startle the old woman into forgetfulness.

"A notebook!" Abby exclaimed triumphantly.

Nancy's heart gave a leap, but she forced herself to say calmly, "Please tell me more about this notebook."

"Well, one day not long before he passed away, Josiah said to me, 'Abby, after I'm dead, if my last will isn't found, you can learn about it in this little book of mine.' "

"Do you know what became of the notebook, Mrs. Rowen?"

"Oh dearie me! There goes my memory again. No, I don't."

Although baffled, Nancy felt a growing conviction that the whereabouts of the Crowley will was definitely tied up with a clock of some kind. But, she pondered, why did the striking of the mantel clock remind Abby Rowen of the notebook?

Impulsively Nancy got up and went over to the mantel. She looked inside the glass front and in the back. There were no papers inside.

Returning to her chair, Nancy asked the elderly woman, "What became of the furnishings of the Crowley home when he gave it up?"

"The Tophams got 'most everything."

"There must have been a family clock," Nancy mused, half to herself.

"A family clock?" Abby repeated. "Oh, yes, there was a clock."

"Can you describe it?"

"It was just an ordinary mantel type, something like mine—tall, with a square face," the woman told Nancy. "Only Josiah's was fancier. Had some kind of a moon on top."

"What became of the clock?" Nancy questioned.

"I suppose the Tophams got it, too."

At last Nancy, sure she had done all she could for Abby, and that she had learned as much as possible for the present, rose to depart. After saying good-by, she stopped at a neighboring house and asked the occupants to look in occasionally on the ailing woman.

"I think maybe one of the county's visiting nurses should see Mrs. Rowen," she suggested.

"I'll phone the agency," the neighbor offered. "Meanwhile, I'll go over myself. I'm so sorry I didn't know about Mrs. Rowen."

As Nancy drove toward River Heights, she jubilantly reviewed the new facts in the case. "Now, if I can only locate Mr. Crowley's notebook—or clock—or both!"

Nancy's brow knit in concentration. How would she go about tracking down the old timepiece?

"I guess," she concluded, "if the Tophams *do* have the clock, I'll have to pay them a visit!"

While she did not relish the idea of calling on

the unpleasant family, Nancy was determined to pursue every possible clue. "I can just see Ada's and Isabel's expressions when I appear at their front door," Nancy thought wryly. "Well, I'll think of some excuse to see them."

She was still mulling over the problem when she pulled into the driveway of her home and heard a familiar voice calling her name.

"Why, Helen Corning!" exclaimed Nancy, as a slim, attractive school friend of hers ran up. "I haven't seen you for days."

"I've been busy lately," Helen explained, "trying to sell six tickets for a charity ball. But I haven't had much luck. Would you like a couple?"

A sudden idea flashed into Nancy's mind at her friend's words. "Helen," she said excitedly, "I'll buy two of your tickets and sell the rest for you."

The other girl stared in astonishment. "Why, that's a wonderful offer, Nance. But—"

Nancy's eyes danced. "I know you think I've lost my mind. I really mean it, though. Please let me take the tickets! I can't tell you my reasons yet—except my cause is a worthy one."

Helen, looking relieved but bewildered, handed over the tickets. "This is really a break for me," she said. "Now I can leave for my aunt's Camp Avondale this evening as I'd hoped. It's at Moon Lake. I thought I'd never get off, with those tickets unsold!"

Nancy smiled "Have a grand time, Helen," she said.

"How about coming along? It's not expensive and there's room for lots more girls. We'd have loads of fun."

"I'd love to," Nancy replied, "but right now I can't get away."

"Maybe you can make it later," Helen suggested. "If so, just zip on up. I'll be there for two weeks before the regular summer camp opens."

The two friends chatted a little longer, then said good-by. Nancy put the car away, then walked slowly toward her house, looking meditatively at the charity tickets in her hand.

"These are to be my passport to the Tophams' stronghold!"

It was the following afternoon when Nancy approached the large pretentious house belonging to the Tophams.

Bracing herself for what she realized would be a trying interview, Nancy mounted the steps and rang the doorbell. "Here goes," she thought. "I must be subtle in this maneuver to keep from arousing the Tophams' suspicions!"

At that moment a maid opened the door, and with a condescending look, waited for Nancy to state her mission.

"Will you please tell Mrs. Topham that Nancy Drew is calling?" she requested. "I'm selling tickets for a charity dance. It's one of the most im-

portant functions of the year in River Heights,"
Nancy added impressively.

It seemed ages to the young sleuth before the
maid returned and said that "Madame" would see
her. Nancy was ushered into the living room,
which was so bizarre in its decor she was startled.

"Such an expensive hodge-podge!" Nancy observed to herself, sitting down. She glanced at the
pink carpet—which to her clashed with the red
window draperies—and at an indiscriminate assortment of period furniture mixed with modern.

A haughty voice interrupted her thoughts.
"Well, what do you want, Nancy?" Mrs. Topham
had sailed grandly into the room and seated herself opposite Nancy.

"I'm selling—" Nancy began pleasantly.

"Oh, if you're selling things I'm not interested,"
the woman broke in rudely. "I can't be handing
out money to every solicitor who comes along."

With difficulty Nancy suppressed an angry retort
to the cutting remark. "Mrs. Topham," she said
evenly, "perhaps your maid didn't make it clear.
I am selling tickets to a charity ball which will be
one of the loveliest affairs in River Heights this
year."

"Oh!" A slight change came over Mrs. Topham's
face. Nancy sensed that her words had struck a
responsive chord. The woman was well known
for her aspirations to be accepted by the best families in River Heights. "Well—"

To Nancy's dismay Mrs. Topham's response was cut off by the arrival of Ada and Isabel. The sisters entered the room, but did not at first notice Nancy's presence. They were intently carrying on a disgruntled conversation.

"Really!" Ada was complaining. "I'm positive that woman snubbed us deliberately."

Then she and Isabel caught sight of Nancy and stopped short. They stared coldly at the visitor.

"What are *you* doing here?" Isabel asked with a patronizing air.

Mrs. Topham answered her daughter's question. "Nancy is selling tickets to a charity dance, dear. It's to be a very important affair and I think it will be—er—beneficial—for us to be present."

Isabel tossed her head disdainfully. "Don't waste your money, Mother."

"Isabel's right," Ada chimed in. "We don't want to go to a ball just anybody can go to. We only attend the most exclusive affairs."

"Absolutely," Isabel declared in her haughtiest tone. "After all, Ada and I are very particular about the people we choose to meet."

Mrs. Topham hesitated, evidently influenced by her daughters' argument. Nancy's heart sank, and she feared her cause was lost. She fully realized that Ada and Isabel would stay away from the dance just to spite her.

As she debated what her next move should be, Richard Topham walked into the living room.

He was a thin man, with sparse graying hair. His manner was rather nervous. Mrs. Topham perfunctorily introduced Nancy to her husband.

"I gather you have some tickets to dispose of, Miss Drew," he said without ceremony. "How many?"

"Why, four," Nancy replied in some surprise.

"I'll take them all." Mr. Topham opened his wallet with a flourish and drew out a hundred-dollar bill. Here you are. Keep the change for your charity."

His daughters gasped and his wife exclaimed, "Richard! Have you lost your senses? All that money!"

"Listen," Mr. Topham retorted bluntly. "This donation will entitle us to have our names on the programs as patrons."

With this remark he slumped into a chair and buried himself in the financial section of the newspaper. His family stared at one another, but they knew that the matter was closed. They never dared disturb him when he was absorbed in the stock-market reports.

Nancy arose reluctantly. She still had not accomplished the real purpose of her visit, but she had no excuse for prolonging her stay. How could she find out about the Crowley clock? Was it the one on the mantelpiece?

"I must be going," she said. Then, looking at her wrist watch, she pretended that it had stopped and began to wind it. "What time is it, please?"

"There's a clock right in front of you—on the mantel," Ada said sharply.

Nancy looked at the timepiece. "So there is," she remarked casually. "Is it an heirloom, perhaps the old Crowley clock I've heard so much about?"

Mrs. Topham looked down her nose. "I should say not! This is a far more expensive one!"

Isabel also rose to Nancy's bait. "Cousin Josiah's old clock was a monstrosity. We wouldn't even have it cluttering up the attic!"

Nancy's hopes waned, but she asked quickly, "Oh, then you sold it?"

"No," Ada spoke up contemptuously. "Who'd give any money for that piece of junk? We sent it up to our bungalow at Moon Lake."

Moon Lake! The words hit Nancy like a thunderbolt. Not only had the Topham girl given Nancy the very information she sought, but Helen Corning's invitation to Camp Avondale provided a valid reason to visit the resort! Now if she could only figure out how to see the old clock!

As if Ada had read the visitor's thoughts, she said airily, "We have some really fine pieces up at the cottage, Nancy. If you ever get up that way, drop in to see them. The caretaker will show you around."

"Thank you. Thank you so much for everything," Nancy said, trying hard to conceal her excitement. As the door closed behind her, Nancy grinned in anticipation.

"What luck!" she told herself. "Moon Lake, here I come!"

CHAPTER X

Following a Clue

WITH soaring spirits, Nancy walked homeward. "I wonder," she thought, "how the Tophams will feel about Josiah Crowley's old clock if it costs them the inheritance they're counting on."

At dinner that night Nancy chatted with unusual animation, deciding not to tell of her exciting plans until after Hannah had served dessert.

Mr. Drew, however, sensed that big news was coming. "My dear," he said, laying a hand on his daughter's arm, "you look like the cat that swallowed the canary. What's the big scoop?"

Nancy giggled. "Oh, Dad. I can't keep any secrets from you." Then, as the table was cleared, the young sleuth told of her great stroke of luck. "And just think, Helen invited me to her aunt's camp!"

"Good," her father commented, smiling. "You

can combine business with pleasure, Nancy. Swimming and boating and fun with the girls will provide a much-needed vacation."

"May I start first thing in the morning?" his daughter asked.

"An excellent idea, Nancy. The change will do wonders for you. Go, by all means."

Hurriedly she packed a suitcase and the next morning was off to an early start.

Moon Lake was about a fifty-mile drive. One way to go was past the Hoover girls' farm and Nancy decided to stop there. As she approached the house, the young sleuth heard singing. It was coming from the barn.

"How beautiful!" Nancy thought, as the clear soprano voice went through a series of trills and flutelike scales.

In a moment the singer appeared and Nancy teasingly applauded. Allison's eyes danced. "Thanks. I was just trying to imitate some of the greats."

"You'll be great yourself one of these days," Nancy prophesied.

"Not unless I get some money to finance lessons," Allison said. "Any news, Nancy?"

"Sort of. I've had a little luck." At this moment Grace appeared and instantly invited Nancy to stay, but the young detective said she too had work to do. "I hope to have a good report for you soon," she added, and waved good-by.

Grace's face brightened and Allison declared cheerfully, "Then there's still hope? We are so lucky to have you as a friend, Nancy. Come see us again soon. Please."

Resuming her journey, Nancy soon branched off from the River Road and headed toward Moon Lake. As she drove along, her thoughts revolved constantly around the Crowley relatives and the Hoovers.

She sighed. "How different things would be for them now if Josiah Crowley hadn't been so secretive!"

Her reverie was ended by the sudden strange actions of her car. It kept veering to the left of the road in spite of her efforts to keep it in the middle. With foreboding, Nancy stopped and got out to make an inspection. As she had suspected, a rear tire was flat.

"Oh dear!" she murmured in disgust. "Such luck!"

Though Nancy was able to change a tire, she never relished the task. Quickly she took out the spare tire from the rear compartment, found the jack and lug wrench, and went to work. By the

time her job was completed, she was hot and a little breathless.

"Whew!" she exclaimed, as she started on her way again. "I'll be ready for a nice, cool swim in Moon Lake!"

It was after twelve o'clock when she came in sight of Camp Avondale, run by Helen's aunt. Through the tall trees Nancy caught a glimpse of cabins and tents. Beyond, the blue lake sparkled and glimmered in the sunlight.

As Nancy drove into the camp, a group of girls gathered about her car. Helen came running out of a cabin to greet her chum.

"Girls, it's Nancy Drew!" she exclaimed joyfully and made introductions. Nancy did not know any of the campers, but in no time they made her feel warmly welcome.

"Nancy," said Helen, "park your car back of the dining hall, then come have lunch."

"That sounds wonderful." Nancy laughed. "I'm nearly starved!"

First, she was escorted to the main building where she met Aunt Martha, the camp director, and registered.

"May she stay with me?" Helen asked.

"Certainly, dear. And I hope you have a splendid time, Nancy."

"I'm sure I shall, Aunt Martha."

As the two girls walked off Nancy told Helen

about selling the charity-dance tickets and gave her the money paid by Mr. Topham.

"He surely was generous!" Helen commented in surprise. Then she smiled wryly. "I have a feeling he did it more for social prestige than sympathy for the cause."

Nancy scarcely had time to deposit her suitcase under her cot and freshen up after the long ride when lunch was announced by the ringing of a bell. Campers hurried from all directions to the dining hall. The food was plain but appetizing and Nancy ate with zest.

The meal over, she was rushed from one activity to another. The girls insisted that she join them in a hike. Then came a cooling dip in the lake. Nancy enjoyed herself immensely, but the Crowley mystery was never far from her mind.

"I must find out where the Tophams' cottage is located," she reminded herself. "And next, manage to go there alone."

Nancy's opportunity to accomplish the first part of her quest came when Helen suggested about five o'clock, "How about going for a ride around the lake in the camp launch? There's just time before supper."

"Wonderful!" Nancy accepted readily. "By the way, can you see many of the summer cottages from the water?"

"Oh, yes. Lots of them."

Helen led her friend down to a small dock and with four other girls climbed into the launch, a medium-sized craft.

As one of the campers started the motor, Helen remarked, "It's always a relief to us when this engine starts. Once in a while it balks, but you never know when or where."

"Yes," spoke up a girl named Barby. "And when you're stuck this time of year, you're stuck. There are hardly any cottagers up here yet, so their boats are still in winter storage."

As the little launch turned out into the lake, Nancy was entranced with the beautiful sight before her. The delicate azure blue of the sky and the mellow gold of the late afternoon sun were reflected in the shimmering surface of the water.

"What a lovely scene for an oil painting!" she thought.

As they sped along, however, Nancy kept glancing at the cottages, intermingled with tall evergreen trees that bordered the shore line.

"The Tophams have a bungalow up here, haven't they?" she questioned casually.

"Yes, it's across the lake," Helen replied. "We'll come to it soon."

"Is anyone staying there now?"

"Oh, no, the cottage is closed. It's being looked after by Jeff Tucker, the caretaker. He's the tallest, skinniest man I've ever seen outside a circus."

"Is it hard to get to the place?"

"Not if you go by launch. But it's a long way if you take the road around the lake." Helen looked at her friend. "I didn't know you were particularly interested in the Tophams, Nancy."

"Oh, they're not friends of mine, as you know," Nancy returned hastily. "I was merely curious."

After a time, as the launch slowed down and chugged along close to shore, Helen pointed out a wide path through the woods. At the end of it stood a large, rambling white cottage.

"That's the Topham place," she said.

Trying not to appear too eager, Nancy looked intently at the bungalow. She made a quick mental note of its location.

"Tomorrow I'll visit that place and try to solve the mystery!" she told herself.

CHAPTER XI

An Unexpected Adventure

NANCY awoke the next morning to the fragrant odor of pines. Eager to start out for the Topham bungalow, she dressed quickly.

But in her plans she had reckoned without Helen Corning and her friends. From the moment breakfast was over, Nancy was swept into another whirlwind of activity by the campers of Avondale. The entire day passed without a chance for her to break away.

"Oh, Helen!" Nancy groaned as she tumbled into bed that night. "Tennis matches, canoe races, swimming, water skiing—it's been fun. But tomorrow I think I'll stay out of the activities."

Helen laughed gaily. "You'll change your mind after a sound sleep, Nancy. Wait and see."

For answer, Nancy murmured a sleepy good night. But even as she slipped into slumber, she vowed that in the morning she would not be deterred again from visiting the Tophams' summer place!

After breakfast the next day, Nancy stood firm in her resolve. When Helen urged her to accompany the girls on an all-day hike, Nancy shook her head.

"Thanks a lot, but please excuse me today, Helen."

Normally Nancy would have loved going on such a hike. But she had to achieve her plan of sleuthing. Helen, though disappointed, heeded her friend's plea and trudged off with the other campers into the woods.

As soon as they were out of sight, Nancy leaped into action. After obtaining Aunt Martha's permission to use the launch, she hurried down to the dock. Nancy had frequently handled motorboats and was confident she could manage this one.

"Now. Full speed ahead for the Tophams'!"

To her delight the motor started immediately, and Nancy steered out into the lake. As the launch cut through the water, a cool spray blew into her face. The young sleuth felt a thrill of excitement as she guided the craft toward her destination which might hold a solution to the mystery.

"If only the Tophams' caretaker will let me in when I get there!" she thought.

Nancy's heart beat somewhat faster as she neared her goal. But all of a sudden there was a sputter from the engine. The next instant, to Nancy's utter dismay, the motor gave one long wheeze and died.

"Oh!" she cried aloud.

Nancy knew that the tank held plenty of fuel, for she had checked this before departing. A moment later she recalled Helen's remark about the engine becoming balky at times.

With a sigh of impatience at the unexpected delay, Nancy examined the motor. For over an hour she worked on it, trying every adjustment she could think of. But her efforts were useless. There was not a sound of response from the motor.

"What miserable luck!" she said aloud. "Of all days for the motor to conk out! This means I won't get to the Topham cottage after all!"

For a moment Nancy was tempted to swim ashore. To be so close to the bungalow and not be able to reach it was tantalizing. But she resisted the impulse; she could not leave the boat stranded—it would drift off and she would be responsible.

"I'll just have to wait for a passing boat to rescue me," Nancy decided.

But fate was against her. The hours dragged by and not another craft appeared in sight. Nancy became increasingly uncomfortable as the hot sun beat down on her. Also, she was growing weak from hunger.

"And worst of all," Nancy thought gloomily,

"another whole day is being wasted. I want to get to the bottom of this mystery!"

To occupy her mind, Nancy concentrated once more on the motor. Determinedly she bent over the engine. It was not until the sun sank low in the sky that she sat up and drew a long breath.

"There!" she declared. "I've done everything. If it doesn't start now, it never will."

To her relief and astonishment, it responded with a steady roar as if nothing had ever gone wrong!

Nancy lost no time in heading back toward camp. She dared not attempt to visit the bungalow, since it would be dark very soon.

When finally she eased up to the dock, Nancy saw Helen and her friends awaiting her. They greeted her with delight.

"We were just going to send out a search party for you!" Helen exclaimed. She stopped abruptly and stared at her friend. "You're sunburned and covered with grease! What happened?"

Nancy laughed. "I had an extended sun bath." Then she gave a lighthearted account of her mishap as the campers trooped back to their cabins. When Helen learned that Nancy had had nothing to eat since breakfast, she went to the kitchen and brought back some food.

The following morning the young sleuth decided on her next move. Directly after breakfast she began packing.

When Helen entered the cabin she exclaimed in amazement, "Why, Nancy Drew! You're not leaving camp already!"

"I'm afraid I'll have to, Helen. Right after lunch. I may be back but I'm not sure, so I'd better take my bag with me."

"Don't you like it here?"

"Of course!" Nancy assured her. "I've had a wonderful time. It's just that there's something very important I must attend to at once."

Helen looked at her friend searchingly, then grinned. "Nancy Drew, you're working on some mystery with your father!"

"Well, sort of," Nancy admitted. "But I'll try to get back. Okay?"

"Oh, please do," Helen begged.

Nancy went to the office to pay Aunt Martha and explain her hasty departure. After lunch she set off in her car to a chorus of farewells from the campers, who sadly watched her depart.

She headed the car toward the end of the lake, then took the dirt road leading to the Topham cottage. Soon she came to a fork in the woods.

"Now, which way shall I turn for the bungalow?" she wondered. After a moment's hesitation, Nancy calculated that she should turn left toward the water and did so.

The going was rather rough due to ruts in the road. Two of them, deeper than the others, apparently had been made by a heavy truck.

"The tracks appear fresh," Nancy mused.

As she drove along, the young sleuth noticed a number of summer cottages. Most of them were still boarded up, since it was early in the season. As she gazed at one of them, the steering wheel was nearly wrenched from her hand by a crooked rut. As Nancy turned the steering wheel, to bring the car back to the center of the narrow road, one hand accidentally touched the horn. It blared loudly in the still woods.

"That must have scared all the birds and animals." Nancy chuckled.

Around a bend in the road, she caught sight of a white bungalow ahead on the right side of the road.

There was no sign at the entrance to the driveway to indicate who the owner was, but a wooded path leading down to the lake looked like the one she had seen from the water.

"I think I'll walk down to the shore and look at the cottage from there," Nancy determined. "Then I'll know for sure if this is the place Helen pointed out."

Nancy parked at the edge of the road and got out. To her surprise, she observed that the truck's tire marks turned into the driveway. A second set of tracks indicated that the vehicle had backed out and gone on down the road.

"Delivering supplies for the summer, no doubt," Nancy told herself.

She went down the path to the water, then turned around to look at the cottage.

"It's the Tophams' all right," Nancy decided.

Instead of coming back by way of the path, she decided to take a short cut through the woods. With mounting anticipation of solving the Crowley mystery, she reached the road and hurried up the driveway.

"I hope the caretaker is here," she thought.

Nancy suddenly stopped short with a gasp of astonishment. "Why, the Tophams must be moving out!"

The front and side doors of the cottage stood wide open. Some of the furniture on the porch was overturned and various small household items were strewn along the driveway.

Nancy bent to examine some marks in the soft earth. She noted that several were boot prints, while others were long lines probably caused by dragging cartons and furniture across the lawn.

"That must have been a moving van's tracks I saw," Nancy told herself. "But the Tophams didn't say anything about moving." She frowned in puzzlement.

Her feeling persisted and grew strong as she walked up the steps of the cottage porch. Nancy knocked loudly on the opened door. No response. Nancy rapped again. Silence.

Where was Jeff Tucker, the caretaker? Why wasn't he on hand to keep an eye on the moving activities? An air of complete desertion hung over the place.

"There's something very strange about this," she thought.

Curious and puzzled, Nancy entered the living room. Again her eyes met a scene of disorder. Except for a few small pieces, the room was bare of furniture. Even the draperies had been pulled from their rods and all floor coverings were gone.

"Hm! Most of the furnishings have been taken out," Nancy thought. "I suppose the movers will be back for the other odds and ends."

She made a careful tour of the first floor. All but one room had been virtually emptied. This was a small study. As Nancy entered it, she noticed that the rug lay rolled up and tied, and some of the furniture had evidently been shifted in readiness for moving.

"Funny I didn't hear anything about the Tophams deciding to give up their cottage," she murmured. "And I must say those moving men were awfully careless—"

A vague suspicion that had been forming in the back of Nancy's mind now came into startling focus. "Those men may not be movers!" she burst out. "They may be thieves!"

At once Nancy thought of the dark-gray van which had stopped at the Turners. "Those men may be the same ones who robbed them!"

That would explain, Nancy thought fearfully,

the evidences of the truck's hasty departure. "Probably the thieves were scared away when I sounded my horn!"

Nancy glanced about uneasily. What if the men were still nearby, watching for a chance to return and pick up the remaining valuables? The realization that she was alone, some distance from the nearest house, swept over her. A tingling sensation crept up Nancy's spine.

But resolutely she shook off her nervousness. "At least I must see if the Crowley clock is still here," Nancy reminded herself, and then went through the bungalow again.

She found no trace of the timepiece, however. "I guess the thieves took that too," Nancy concluded. "I'd better report this robbery to the police right now." She looked about for a phone but there was none. "I'll have to drive to the nearest State Police headquarters."

Nancy started toward the front door. Passing a window, she glanced out, then paused in sheer fright. A man, wearing a cap pulled low over his eyes, was stalking up the driveway toward the cottage. He was not tall and slender like the caretaker. This stranger was rather short and heavyset.

"This man fits the Turners' description! He must be one of the thieves who stole the silver heirlooms!" Nancy thought wildly.

CHAPTER XII

A Desperate Situation

FOR A moment Nancy stood frozen to the spot, positive that the man who was coming to the Topham cottage was one of the thieves.

But she hesitated only an instant. Then she turned and ran back into the study. Too late she realized that she had trapped herself, for this room had no other door.

Nancy started back toward the living room. But before she had taken half a dozen steps she knew that escape had been cut off from that direction. The man had reached the porch steps.

"It won't do a bit of good to talk to him," she reasoned. "I'll hide, and when he leaves, I'll follow him in my car and report him to the police!"

Frantically the young sleuth glanced about for a hiding place. A closet offered the only possible refuge. She scurried inside and closed the door.

Nancy was not a second too soon. She had scarcely shut the door when she heard the tread of the man's heavy shoes on the floor just outside. Peeping cautiously through a tiny crack in the door, she saw the heavy-set man come into the study. His face wore a cruel expression.

As he turned toward the closet where she huddled, Nancy hardly dared to breathe, lest her presence be detected. Apparently the man noticed nothing amiss, because his eyes rested only casually on the door.

Nancy's hiding place was anything but comfortable. It was dark and musty, and old clothing hung from nails on the walls. As dust assailed her nostrils, she held a handkerchief to her face.

"If I sneeze he'll surely find me," she told herself.

She felt around and once came close to ripping her hand on a sharp nail. Then she came upon something soft on a shelf and imagined it was a sleeping cat. She drew back, then touched it more cautiously.

"Only an old fur cap," she told herself in disgust. "O-oo, now I feel like sneezing more than ever!"

She held one hand over her mouth hard and waited in agony. But presently the desire to sneeze passed and Nancy breathed more freely.

When she dared to peep out through the crack a second time, she saw that two other rough-looking men had come into the room. One was short and stout, the other taller. Nancy was sure that

neither of these two men was the caretaker, because
Helen Corning had mentioned that the man was
skinny.

The heavy-set man who had come in first seemed
to be the leader, for he proceeded to issue orders.
"Get a move on!" he growled. "We haven't got
all day unless we want to be caught. That girl
you saw, Jake, may be back any time from the
shore. And she just might get snoopy."

The man addressed as Jake scowled. "What's
the matter with you, Sid? Going chicken? If
that girl comes around, we'll just give her a smooth
story and send her on her way."

"Cut out the yaking," said Sid. "Parky, you
and Jake take that desk out of here."

There was no doubt now in Nancy's mind. She
was trapped by a clever gang of thieves! She
could only continue to watch and listen helplessly
from her hiding place.

The two men lifted the heavy piece of furniture
and started with it to the door. But they did not
move swiftly enough to satisfy the leader, and he
berated them savagely.

Jake turned on him. "If you're in such a hurry,
why don't you bring the van back to the driveway,
instead of leaving it hidden on that road in the
woods?"

"And have someone driving past here see us!"
sneered the leader. "Now get going!"

Little by little the men stripped the room of

everything valuable. Nancy was given no opportunity to escape. Sid remained in the room while
the others made several trips to the van.

"Well, I guess we have all the stuff that's worth
anything now," Sid muttered at last.

He turned to follow his companions, who already had left the room, but in the doorway he
paused for a final careful survey of the room.

At that same moment Nancy felt an uncontrol-
lable urge to sneeze. She tried to muffle the
sound, but to no avail.

The thief wheeled about. "Hey! What—"

Walking directly to the closet, he flung open the
door. Instantly he spotted Nancy and angrily
jerked her out.

"Spying on us, eh?" he snarled.

Nancy faced the man defiantly. "I wasn't spying
on anyone."

"Then what were you doing in that closet?" the
thief demanded, his eyes narrowing to slits.

"I came to see the caretaker."

"Looking for him in a funny place, ain't you?"
the man sneered.

Nancy realized that she was in a desperate situation. But she steeled herself not to show any of
her inward fears.

"I must keep calm," she told herself firmly.
Aloud, she explained coolly, "I heard someone
coming and I just felt a bit nervous."

"Well, you're going to be a lot more nervous,"

the man said threateningly. "This will be the last time you'll ever stick your nose in business that doesn't concern you!"

A fresh wave of fright swept over Nancy, but resolutely she held on to her courage. "You have no right to be here, helping yourself to the Tophams' furniture!" she retorted. "You should be turned over to the police!"

"Well, you'll never get the chance to do it." The ringleader laughed loudly. "You'll wish you'd never come snoopin' around here. I'll give you the same treatment the caretaker got."

"The caretaker!" Nancy gasped in horror. "What have you done to him?"

"You'll find out in good time."

Nancy gave a sudden agile twist, darted past the man, and raced for the door. The thief gave a cry of rage, and in one long leap overtook her. He caught Nancy roughly by the arm.

"Think you're smart, eh?" he snarled. "Well, I'm smarter!"

Nancy struggled to get away. She twisted and squirmed, kicked and clawed. But she was helpless in the viselike grip of the powerful man.

"Let me go!" Nancy cried, struggling harder. "Let me go!"

Sid, ignoring her pleas, half dragged her across the room. Opening the closet door, he flung her inside.

Nancy heard a key turn.

"Now you can spy all you want!" Sid sneered. "But to make sure nobody'll let you out, I'll just take this key along."

When Nancy could no longer hear the tramp of his heavy boots she was sure Sid had left the house. For a moment a feeling of great relief engulfed her.

But the next instant Nancy's heart gave a leap. As she heard the muffled roar of the van starting up in the distance, a horrifying realization gripped her.

"They've left me here to—to starve!" she thought frantically.

CHAPTER XIII

The Frustrating Wait

AT FIRST Nancy was too frightened to think logically. She beat upon the door with her fists, but the heavy oak panels would not give way.

"Help! Help!" she screamed.

At last, exhausted by her efforts to force the door open, she sank down on the floor. The house was as silent as a tomb. Bad as her predicament was, Nancy felt thankful that enough air seeped into the closet to permit normal breathing.

Although she had little hope that there was anyone within miles of the cottage, Nancy got to her feet, raised her voice, and again shouted for help. Her cries echoed through the empty house and seemed to mock her.

"Oh, why didn't I have enough sense to tell Helen where I was going?" she berated herself miserably. "The girls at camp will never dream that I came here."

Then Nancy remembered mournfully that her father thought she intended to remain at Camp Avondale for a week! He would not become alarmed over her absence until it was too late.

"Someone may find my car at the side of the road," Nancy reasoned, "but it isn't very likely. Few persons pass this way so early in the season."

She wondered, with a shudder, what had become of Jeff Tucker. The thief called Sid had hinted that the caretaker had received the same treatment as Nancy. If he was locked up somewhere, she could expect no aid from him.

"Those thieves will get so far away that even if I could get out of here, I'd be too late."

As the full significance of the situation dawned upon Nancy, panic again took possession of her. In a desperate attempt to break down the door, she threw her weight against it again and again. She pounded on the panels until her fingers were bruised and bleeding. At last she sank down again on the floor to rest and tried to force herself to reason calmly.

"I'm only wasting my strength this way. I *must* try to think logically."

Nancy recalled that it was sometimes possible to pick a lock with a wire. She removed a bobby pin from her hair, opened it, and began to work at the lock. But in the darkness she could not see and made no progress. After fifteen minutes she gave up the task in disgust.

"It's no use," she decided dejectedly. "I—I guess I'm in here for good."

She began to think of her father, of Hannah Gruen, of Helen Corning, and other dear friends. Would she ever see them again? As despondency claimed Nancy, she was dangerously near tears.

"This will never do," she reprimanded herself sternly. "I must keep my head and try to think of some way to escape."

The trapped girl began to rummage in the closet, hoping that by some lucky chance she might find a tool which would help her force the lock of the door. Nancy searched carefully through the pockets of every garment which hung from the hooks. She groped over every inch of the floor.

She found nothing useful, however, and the cloud of dust which she had stirred up made breathing more difficult than before. The closet had become uncomfortably warm by this time. Longingly she thought of the fresh air and cool lake water from which she was closed off.

Then, unexpectedly, Nancy's hand struck something hard. Quickly investigating with her fingers, she discovered a wooden rod suspended high overhead. It was fastened to either side wall and ran the length of the closet. Evidently it had once been used for dress and coat hangers.

"I might be able to use that rod to break out a panel of the door," Nancy thought hopefully. "It feels strong and it's about the right size."

She tugged at the rod with all her might. When it did not budge, she swung herself back and forth on it. At last, amid the cracking of plaster, one side gave way. Another hard jerk brought the rod down.

To Nancy's bitter disappointment, she found that unfortunately the rod was too long to use as a ram in the cramped space. But after further examination, she discovered that it had pointed ends.

"I might use this rod as a wedge in the crack," she thought hopefully.

The young sleuth inserted one end in the space between the hinges and the door, and threw all her weight against the rod. At first the door did not move in the slightest.

"That old Greek scientist, Archimedes, didn't know what he was talking about when he said the world could be moved with a lever," Nancy murmured. "I'd like to see him move this door!"

As she applied steady pressure to the rod a second time, she saw that the hinges were beginning to give. Encouraged, Nancy again pushed full force on the "lever."

"It's coming!" she cried.

Once more she threw her weight against the rod. A hinge tore from the casing and the door sagged. It was now easy to insert the wedge, and Nancy joyously realized that success would soon be hers. With renewed strength she continued her efforts.

Then, just as another hinge gave way, she was startled to hear footsteps. Someone came running into the study, and a heavy body hurled itself against the door of the closet.

For a moment Nancy was stunned. Could this be one of the thieves who had heard the noise she had made and had returned to make sure that she did not escape? She discarded the theory quickly. Surely the three men would want to get far away as quickly as possible. But who was this new-comer? One of the Tophams?

"So, one o' you ornery robbers got yourself locked up, did you?" came an indignant male voice. "That'll teach you to try puttin' one over on old Jeff Tucker. You won't be doin' any more pil-ferin'. I got you surrounded."

The caretaker! Nancy heaved a sigh of fervent relief. "Let me out!" she pleaded. "I'm not one of the thieves! If you'll only let me out of here, I'll explain everything!"

There was silence for a moment. Then the voice on the other side of the door said dubiously, "Say, you aimin' to throw me off, imitatin' a lady's voice? Well, it won't do you any good! No, sir. Old Jeff Tucker's not gettin' fooled again!"

Nancy decided to convince the man beyond doubt. She gave a long, loud feminine scream.

"All right, *all right,* ma'am. I believe you! No man could make that racket. This way out, lady!"

Expectantly Nancy waited. But the door did not open. Then she heard to her dismay:

"If that ain't the limit. The key's gone and I've left my ring o' extra keys somewhere. It's not in my pockets."

Nancy groaned. "Oh, Mr. Tucker, you must find it. Have you looked in every one of your pockets? Please hurry and get me out."

"Hold on, ma'am," the caretaker said soothingly. "I'll just check again."

Nancy was beginning to think she would still have to break down the door, when she heard Jeff Tucker exclaim, "Found it! You were right, ma'am. Key was in my back pocket all the time. It—"

"*Please* open the door!" Nancy broke in desperately.

A key turned in the lock and the bolt clicked. Joyfully Nancy pushed the door open and stepped out. For a moment the bright sunlight in the room almost blinded her. When her vision adjusted, she saw a very tall, thin, elderly man in blue shirt and overalls. He stared at her with concern and amazement.

"Mr. Tucker," she explained quickly, "I'm Nancy Drew. I was here looking for you when those awful thieves came and locked me in the closet." She paused and gazed at the caretaker. "I'm glad to see that you're all right. Their leader told me they'd locked you up too." She then asked the elderly man to tell his story.

Jeff Tucker seemed embarrassed as he began to speak. "I was plain hornswoggled by those critters, Miss Drew. They pulled up here in a movin' van, and told me I'd better get after some trespassers they'd seen nearby. So," the elderly man went on with a sigh, "I believed 'em. One of the men went with me down to the lake and locked me in a shed. I just got out." He shook his head sadly. "And all this time they was robbin' the place. Guess I'll be fired."

Secretly Nancy was inclined to agree, knowing the Tophams. But aloud she said reassuringly:

"Don't worry, Mr. Tucker. We'll report this robbery to the State Police immediately. Perhaps the troopers can catch the thieves before they get rid of the stolen furniture."

The caretaker looked somewhat relieved. "And I can sure give a good description o' those crooks. I'd never forget their ugly faces!"

"Fine," said Nancy. A sudden thought struck her. "Oh, before we go, Mr. Tucker, tell me, was there an old clock in this house? A tall, square-faced mantel clock?"

Jeff Tucker's bright blue eyes squinted. "Mantel clock? Hm. Why, sure enough!" He pointed to the mantel over the living-room fireplace. "Sat right up there. Got so used to seein' it, I couldn't remember for a minute. Don't know how come they took that too. Never thought it was worth much. The Tophams never bothered windin' the thing."

Nancy's pulse quickened. Knowing that the clock had been stolen, she was more eager than ever to have the thieves apprehended. She urged Jeff Tucker to hurry out to her car.

"Where's the nearest State Police headquarters?" she asked him as they climbed into the convertible.

"There's none till you get to Melborne, Miss Drew."

"We'll hurry."

Nancy headed as fast as possible for the highway. Would she succeed in heading off the thieves and recovering the old Crowley clock, so she could learn its secret?

CHAPTER XIV

A Tense Chase

"WHICH way is Melborne?" Nancy asked the care-taker when they reached the highway.

"Down there." He pointed.

"That's the direction the thieves took," Nancy told him, noting the dust and tire marks which revealed the van's exit onto the highway. "But," she added, glancing at the dashboard clock, "they're probably too far away by this time for us to catch them."

"Yes, ding it," Jeff muttered.

Nancy drove as rapidly as the law permitted toward Melborne. All the while, Jeff Tucker peered from one side of the road to the other.

"Those rascal thieves might just have nerve enough to stop an' count their loot," he said to Nancy. "So I'm keepin' a sharp eye peeled."

Nancy smiled in spite of the gravity of the situation. "Maybe," she replied. "Though I doubt that those men would be so reckless."

"Oh, I don't mean out in plain sight. They might have pulled off the road, back o' some o' these closed-up summer places."

"We'll watch for their tire marks on any dirt side road," the young sleuth said.

Jeff became so absorbed in looking for the van's tire marks that he never asked Nancy why she had come to see him at the Topham house.

"Those fake movers," he said, as they neared the outskirts of Melborne. "I wonder how far they went."

Nancy did not reply until they came to a crossroad, then she pointed. "They turned north here on this dirt road. How much farther is it to Melborne?"

"Only a mile."

As they came into the little town, Nancy asked her companion, "Which way to State Police headquarters?"

"Go right down Central Avenue to Maple Street. Turn left, and there it is."

Reaching headquarters, Nancy parked the car and hopped out. Jeff Tucker followed as she walked briskly into the office.

"I want to report a robbery," she told the desk sergeant after identifying herself.

For a moment the officer, taken aback, looked in astonishment at Nancy. "You've been robbed?" he asked. "In *our* town?"

"No, no!" Nancy cried out. She then gave a

*Nancy reported what had taken place at the
Tophams' cottage*

quick but complete resume of what had taken place at the Tophams' cottage. Jeff Tucker added his account.

The police officer needed no further urging. Immediately he summoned four men and issued orders. "Now," he said, turning to Nancy, "have you any idea which road the thieves took?"

"Yes, Officer. When we passed the road crossing a mile outside of town, I saw their truck tracks on the dirt road leading north. I'll be glad to show you."

"Good. Lead the way. But first I'll send out a general alarm."

"Hurry!" Nancy begged as she started out. "Those thieves have at least an hour's head start!"

Jeff Tucker had been advised to return to his home. Accordingly he telephoned his son to come and pick him up in his car.

"Good luck!" he called, as the others pulled away. "I sure don't know how I'm goin' to break this to the Tophams."

Nancy was sorry for him, but she felt a thrill of excitement as she proceeded up the street, the police car following close behind.

Beyond the town, Nancy chose the road which she felt certain the thieves had used. The two cars sped along until Nancy unexpectedly came to a fork. Both branches were paved and no tire marks were visible. Nancy stopped. The police car pulled up alongside.

"What's the matter?" asked the officer in charge, whose name was Elton.

"I'm not sure which way to go now."

The policemen sprang from their automobile and began to examine the road. Officer Elton said that if a moving van had passed that way, its tire marks had been obliterated by other vehicles. It was impossible to tell which route the thieves had traveled.

"It'll be strictly guesswork from here," Officer Elton said to Nancy.

"In that case," replied Nancy, "it's my guess that the van went to the left." She pointed to a sign which read: *Garwin, 50 miles.* "Isn't Garwin a fairly large city?" she queried.

"Yes."

"Perhaps the thieves headed that way to dispose of the stolen furniture."

The officer nodded approvingly. "Sounds reasonable," he said. "Well, in any case, we can't go much farther, because we're near the state line."

Nancy had another thought. "I'll take the road to Garwin and swing around toward River Heights." She smiled. "If I see those thieves, I'll let you know."

"Well, you watch out, young lady. Those men may lock you up again!"

"I will. Anyhow, there'll be plenty of traffic as soon as I reach the main highway."

Without giving the policemen an opportunity

for further objection, Nancy started up and swung her car to the left. She noted in her rear-view mirror that the squad car had turned onto the right-hand road.

"The officers must have picked up a clue," Nancy said to herself. "But I certainly wish I could spot that van and maybe find a chance to look in the old clock!"

Nancy soon reached the main road. As mile after mile of highway spun behind her, Nancy's hopes grew dim. There were a number of side roads, any one of which the moving van might have taken to elude pursuers.

The young sleuth decided to adhere to her original theory—that Sid and his pals had headed for Garwin—and kept on the main highway.

"Those thieves think Jeff and I are still locked up and won't suspect they're being followed," she assured herself. Smiling, she thought hopefully, "In that case they won't be on their guard!"

About ten minutes later Nancy stopped at a service station to have her car refueled, and on impulse asked the attendant, "Did you by any chance see a moving van pass here recently?"

"Sure did, miss," was the prompt answer. "About half an hour ago. I noticed it because the driver was going at a terrific speed for a van."

Heartened, Nancy thanked him and resumed her pursuit, going past the turn for River Heights. "If only I can overtake the truck and somehow

examine the Crowley clock before I have to report
to the police!" she thought.

Again time elapsed and Nancy still saw no sign of
a moving van on the highway. It was growing
dusk and she decided that she would have to admit
defeat.

"I never caught up to them." She sighed in disappointment, and turning into the opposite lane,
headed back for the River Heights road.

Just then Nancy recalled that a little beyond the
service station where she had stopped, she had
noticed a rather run-down old inn. It was a slim
hope, she knew, but the thieves might have put
their van behind it while having a meal there.

"I'll go in and ask, anyhow," she decided.

Nancy increased her speed as much as she dared
and within a few minutes came in sight of the inn.
It stood back from the road a short distance and
was half-hidden by tall trees. In front of the building a battered sign bearing the name *Black Horse
Inn* creaked back and forth from a post. There
was no sign of the van. Beyond the inn Nancy
glimpsed a garage and a large barn. The doors to
both were closed.

"I wonder," mused Nancy, "if the moving van is
parked inside either one."

At the far side of the inn was a small woods with
a narrow road leading into it. For safety's sake,
Nancy thought it best to park her car on this little-
used road.

She turned off the car lights, pocketed the key, and walked back to the curving driveway leading to the inn. As Nancy made her way forward, her heart pounded. There were tire marks which could belong to Sid's van! They led to the barn!

"Maybe those thieves are eating," she thought. "I'll look."

As Nancy stepped onto the porch, the sound of raucous laughter reached her ears. She tiptoed to a window and peered inside. What the young sleuth saw made her gasp, but she felt a glow of satisfaction.

In a dingy, dimly lighted room three men were seated about a table, eating voraciously. They were the thieves who had robbed the Topham bungalow!

CHAPTER XV

Nancy's Risky Undertaking

"I MUST notify the police at once!" Nancy told herself as she recognized the three thieves.

Turning away from the window, she crept noiselessly from the porch. She was about to make a dash for her car when a sudden thought occurred to her.

"If the gang have parked their van in the barn, now's my chance to look for the Crowley clock. I'm sure those men will be eating for a while, or they may even be staying overnight."

Acting on the impulse, Nancy sprinted to her car. Hastily she snatched a flashlight from the compartment, since it was now dark outside.

She made her way cautiously to the rear of the inn. Reaching the barn, she tried the closed doors, her heart pounding. They had not been locked!

As she slid back one of the doors, it squeaked in an alarming fashion. Anxiously Nancy glanced toward the inn, but so far as she could tell, her actions were unobserved. There was no one in sight.

Focusing her flashlight, she peered hopefully into the dark interior. A cry of satisfaction escaped her lips.

In front of her stood the moving van!

"What luck!" she exclaimed, snapping off her light.

With a last cautious glance in the direction of the inn, she hastily stepped inside and closed the barn door. With it shut, the interior of the barn was pitch dark.

Nancy switched on her flashlight again and played it over the moving van. She saw that its rear doors were closed.

Securing a firm grip on the handle, she gave it a quick turn. To her dismay the door did not open. The thieves had locked the van!

"Oh dear! Now what shall I do?" she wondered frantically. "I'll never be able to break the lock."

Desperately Nancy glanced about. She dared not remain many minutes in the barn, lest the thieves return and find her there. But she had to find out whether the Crowley clock was in the van.

"Perhaps the keys were left in the ignition," Nancy thought hopefully.

She rushed to the front of the van and clambered into the driver's seat. But there were no keys hanging from the ignition lock.

Nancy's mind worked frantically. She must find the keys! Perhaps the men had not taken them into the inn but had concealed them in the truck. Suddenly she remembered that people sometimes hide automobile keys under the floor mat. It was barely possible that the thieves had done this.

Hastily she pulled up a corner of the mat. Her flashlight revealed a small ring of keys!

"Luck was with me this time," she murmured, and quickly snatching up the ring, she ran back to the rear of the van.

After trying several of the keys, she at last found one which fitted the lock. Turning it, she jerked open the door. Nancy flashed her light about inside the truck. To her joy she recognized the van's contents as the furniture stolen from the Topham cottage!

"What will I do if the clock is on the bottom of the load?" Nancy wondered as she surveyed the pile of furniture. "I'll never find it."

Dexterously she swung herself up into the truck and flashed the light slowly about on chairs, tables, rugs, and boxes. There was no sign of the Crowley clock.

Then the beam rested for a moment on an object in a far corner. With a low cry of delight, Nancy saw that her search had been rewarded. Protected by a blanket, an old-fashioned mantel clock rested on top of a table in the very front of the van!

The young sleuth scrambled over the pieces of furniture as she tried to reach the clock. Her dress caught on something sharp and tore. Finally she arrived within arm's reach of the blanket. She grasped it and carefully pulled the clock toward her.

One glance at the timepiece assured her that it fitted the description Abby Rowen had given her. It had a square face and the top was ornamented with a crescent.

"The Crowley clock at last!" Nancy whispered almost unbelievingly.

But as she stood staring at it, her keen ears detected the sound of voices. The thieves!

"I'll be caught!" flashed through her mind. "And I won't be able to escape a second time!"

Clutching the blanket and the clock tightly in her arms, Nancy scrambled over the piled-up furniture as she struggled to get out of the truck before it was too late.

Reaching the door, she leaped lightly to the floor. She could now hear heavy footsteps coming closer and closer.

Nancy shut the truck doors as quickly as possible, and searched wildly for the keys.

"Oh, what did I do with them?" she thought frantically.

She saw that they had fallen to the floor and snatched them up. Hurriedly inserting the correct key in the lock, she secured the doors.

But as Nancy wheeled about she heard men's angry voices directly outside. Already someone was starting to slide back the barn door!

"Oh, what shall I do?" Nancy thought in despair. "I'm cornered!"

She realized instantly that she could not hope to run to the front of the car and place the keys under the mat where she had found them. "I'll just put them on the floor," she decided quickly. "Maybe the men will think they dropped them."

Then, glancing frantically about for a hiding place, Nancy saw an empty grain bin. Running to it, still holding the clock, she climbed inside and dropped the blanket over her head just as one of the barn doors slid open.

One of the men was speaking loudly. Nancy recognized the voice instantly. It belonged to Sid, the ringleader of the thieves.

"You had enough to eat," he growled. "We're goin' to get out of here before we have the cops down on our heads."

He climbed into the cab and turned on the headlights. Nancy held her breath. Would her hiding place be discovered? But the men apparently did not even look toward the bin.

In a moment Sid cried out, "What did you do with those keys? Thought you put 'em under the floor mat."

"I did."

"Well, they ain't here."

"Honest, boss, I—"

"Then come and find 'em, and don't be all night about it either!"

"All right. Get out of the way and give me a chance!"

As Jake went to the truck and began a careful search for the keys, Nancy listened fearfully from her hiding place.

"Say, if you've lost 'em—" the leader did not finish the threat, for at that moment the third man announced:

"Here they are on the floor! You must have thought you'd put 'em in your pocket, Jake, and dropped 'em instead."

"I didn't!" the other retorted.

The thieves were obviously in a quarrelsome mood. Just then the leader interposed:

"Cut out the yaking! We ain't got no time for a fight unless we want to land behind bars!"

"And if we do, it'll be your fault, Sid Sax. You left that girl to starve—"

"Shut up!" the leader snarled.

After a few more angry words, the three thieves climbed into the front seat and in a moment the engine started.

In relief Nancy heard the men go. The moment they were a safe distance from the barn, she climbed out of the bin.

Nancy watched long enough to make certain that the van had taken the road to Garwin. Then, snatching up her flashlight and clutching the precious clock in her arms, she turned and ran. "I'd better cut through the woods," she decided.

As Nancy darted among the trees, she cast an anxious glance over her shoulder, but to her intense relief she saw that she was not being followed. There seemed to be no one in the vicinity of the Black Horse Inn.

"I had a narrow escape that time," the young sleuth told herself as she ran. "I hate to think what might have happened if I had been discovered!" She clutched the mantel clock more tightly in her arms. "But it was worth the risk I took! I found the clock and maybe the secret of Josiah Crowley's will!"

Reaching the car, Nancy sprang inside. She took the key from her pocket and inserted it in the ignition lock.

"I'll notify the police as fast as I can," she decided. "Perhaps the state troopers can catch those men before they dispose of the furniture."

Then, just as Nancy was about to start the motor, her glance fell upon the Crowley clock which she had placed on the seat beside her. Did it contain old Josiah's mysterious notebook as she suspected?

"Oh, I must find out!" She got her flashlight.

Since the clock was too unwieldy to open inside the car, Nancy stepped out and laid it on the ground. She unfastened the glass door and ran her

hand around the walls.   There was nothing inside.   She tried the back.   Only the mechanism of
the timepiece was there.

"Gone!" Nancy groaned.   "Oh dear!   Has my
luck run out?"

Could it be, she wondered, that the Tophams
had discovered the notebook only to destroy it?
Nancy discarded this thought as quickly as it came
to mind, for she recalled the conversation she had
overheard between Ada and Isabel.   No, the Tophams were as ignorant as herself concerning the
location of a later will.

It was more likely that Abby Rowen had been
confused in her story.   After all, she had not declared that the notebook would be found inside
the clock.   Nancy herself had made the deduction.

"I was almost certain I'd find the notebook," she
murmured in disappointment.   But a moment
later she took heart again.   "It *must* be here somewhere," she told herself.

Turning the clock upside down, Nancy gave it a
hard shake.   Something inside moved.   Hopefully she repeated the action.

"Unless I'm wrong," Nancy thought excitedly,
"there's something inside this clock besides the
works!"   She examined it more closely.   "An extra piece of cardboard back of the face!   And something in between the two!   The notebook maybe!"

After a vain attempt to remove the heavy cardboard face with her fingers, Nancy took a small

screw driver from the glove compartment. With the tool it required but an instant to remove the two hands of the clock and jerk off the face.

As the cardboard fell to the floor, Nancy peered inside and gave a low cry of joy.

There, at one side of the clock, attached to a hook in the top, dangled a tiny dark-blue notebook!

CHAPTER XVI

The Capture

EAGERLY Nancy removed the little notebook from the hook. By holding the book directly under the beam of her flashlight, she could make out the words on the cover:

Property of Josiah Crowley.

"I've found it at last!" she thought excitedly.

Quickly turning the first few pages, she saw that they were yellowed with age. The writing was fine and cramped, and the ink had faded. The pages were crowded with business notations, and it was difficult to make out the words.

Nancy was thrilled, for she was positive that the notebook would disclose what Josiah Crowley had done with his last will. Yet, she realized that she could not hope to read through the book without a considerable loss of precious time. She must not delay another instant in reporting to the police.

"I'll read the notebook later," she decided, and

tucked it into her pocket. Then she put the clock together.

Hurriedly laying the timepiece back on the car seat, Nancy covered it with her coat and slid behind the wheel. Starting the engine, she swung the convertible onto the highway. Nancy cast an anxious glance in the direction the thieves had taken, and watched for side roads down which the men might turn to avoid the main highway.

"Perhaps I'd better phone the State Police from the first service station or store I come to."

Then suddenly she noticed a sign: *Alternate route to Garwin. Main road under repair.*

Reaching the intersection, she stopped to see if the familiar tire marks of the van indicated it had turned onto this dirt road. It had!

"Now what shall I do?"

As Nancy debated, she saw a car coming toward her. Her hopes soared. She could not be mistaken—it was a police prowl car with a red revolving roof light!

Instantly Nancy grabbed her own flashlight and jumped from the car. Standing at the side of the road, she waved her light and in a few minutes the police sedan stopped.

"I'm Nancy Drew," she said hurriedly to the two men inside. "Are you looking for the furniture thieves in the van?"

"Yes, we are. You're the girl who reported them?"

Nancy nodded, then pointed down the side road. "I think those are their tire marks. The men were at the Black Horse Inn, but left."

"You can identify them?" the driver asked.

"Oh, yes."

"Then please follow us. I'll radio for a car to approach the thieves' van from the other end of the road."

The police car sped down the bad road to Garwin, with Nancy following closely behind. They rode for several miles.

"Oh dear," thought Nancy, "I must have been wrong! We should have overtaken the van by this time."

Another ten minutes passed. Then, unexpectedly, she caught a glimpse of a red taillight on the road far ahead.

"It must be the van!" Nancy told herself hopefully. "The light doesn't appear to be moving fast enough for an automobile."

Evidently the police were of the same opinion, for at that moment their car slowed down. Nancy figured they would not stop the van until they saw the other police car arriving from the opposite direction. A few moments later she could see headlights in the distance.

The squad car in front of Nancy now sped ahead and pulled up alongside the van. "Pull over!" one of the officers shouted to the man in the cab.

Instead of doing so, the van put on a burst of

speed. But in order to avoid smashing into the oncoming squad car, the driver pulled too far to the right. The van swerved sharply. Its two right wheels went off into a deep ditch, and the vehicle toppled over.

In an instant the officers were out of the car and had the fugitives covered.

By this time Nancy, who had stopped her car at the side of the road, came running up. One of the officers turned to her and asked, "Can you identify these men?"

As a light was flashed upon each of the thieves in turn, Nancy nodded. "This one is Sid, who locked me in the closet," she declared, pointing to the leader. "The others are Jake and Parky."

The prisoners stared in complete disbelief. They were astounded to see Nancy Drew standing there. When it dawned on Sid that she evidently was responsible for their capture, he started to say something, then changed his mind and remained silent. The prisoners were quickly identified from licenses and other papers as wanted criminals.

One of the other officers opened the rear of the van and asked Nancy if she could identify the stolen furniture.

"Some of it," she replied. "That desk was taken from the room in which I was locked in the closet."

"Good enough," said the trooper. "These men will get long sentences for this. They'll be held

on several charges.   Are you willing to go with us
and prefer charges against them?"

"Yes, if it's necessary," Nancy promised reluctantly.   "But I don't live in this county and I'm
eager to get home right away.   Don't you have
enough evidence against them?   I think they're
the same men who stole several silver heirlooms
from the Turner sisters."

Sid and his companions winced, but did not
speak.

"I see," said the trooper.   "Well, I guess there's
no need for you to go to headquarters now," the
officer admitted.   "I'll take your address, and if
your testimony should be required, I'll get in
touch with you."

When Nancy showed her driver's license as identification, the policeman glanced at her with new
interest.   Taking her aside, he said, "So you're the
daughter of Carson Drew!   I see you're following
in his footsteps.   Starting rather young, aren't
you?"

Nancy laughed.   "It was only by accident that I
arrived at the Topham bungalow at the critical
moment," she protested modestly.

"Not many girls would have used their wits the
way you did," the officer observed.   "Unless I'm
mistaken, these fellows are old hands at this game.
They're no doubt the men who have been stealing
various things from around Moon Lake for a number of seasons.   The residents will be mighty

grateful for what you've done. And that Mrs. Topham you spoke of—she ought to give you a liberal reward for saving her household goods."

Nancy shook her head. "I don't want a reward, really I don't."

"Just the same you've earned one," insisted the officer, who said his name was Cowen. "If you'd like, I'll tell my chief the whole story and he'll take the matter up with this Mrs. Topham."

"You don't know her," Nancy remarked, "and I do. She'd never offer a reward. Even if she did, I wouldn't accept it." After a slight pause, she added, "In fact, I prefer that my name not be mentioned to her at all."

Officer Cowen shook his head in disbelief. "Well, all right, then. If you're sure you don't want any credit for capturing the thieves, I won't say anything. You're certain?"

"I am," Nancy replied firmly, "for a particular reason of my own."

The trooper smiled. "It must be a mighty good one."

"There *is* one favor you might do me," said Nancy. "Ask your chief to put in a good word for the caretaker, Jeff Tucker, to the Tophams. Perhaps then he won't lose his job."

"Be glad to," Officer Cowen promised. "And if you're really anxious not to figure in the case, I'll see if we can get along without your testimony."

Nancy thanked him, then suddenly thought of

the old clock. At the moment it was lying on the front seat of her car, less than a dozen yards away. Should she reveal this information? She decided against doing so in front of the thieves, who,. though they could not hear what she had been saying, could see everything plainly. "I'll wait until a more opportune time," Nancy concluded.

It was agreed among the state policemen that one of them would stay to guard the van and keep a radio car standing by there. The other three troopers would take the captive thieves to headquarters.

The three prisoners, their faces sullen, were crowded into the car. One of the troopers took the wheel, while the one beside him kept the handcuffed trio closely covered.

Officer Cowen, a strapping, husky man, turned to Nancy. "I'll ride with you," he said. "You're going past headquarters on the main road?"

"I'm on my way to River Heights," she responded.

"Then the station is on your route. You can drop me off if you will."

"Why—why, of course," Nancy stammered. "I'll be glad to."

At once she had thought of the Crowley clock. What if Officer Cowen should not accept her explanation as to why she had helped herself to the heirloom and its strange contents? If this happened, her progress in solving the mystery might receive a serious setback! Even as these disturbing ideas raced through her mind, the trooper started toward the blue convertible.

Nancy braced herself. "I'll just have to 'fess up," she said to herself, "and take the consequences!"

CHAPTER XVII

Strange Instructions

FOR THE next few seconds Nancy's mind worked like lightning as she rehearsed what she would say to Officer Cowen. One idea stood out clearly: the police were concerned in the theft of the furniture, so she would hand over the clock. But they were not involved in locating Mr. Crowley's missing will. For this reason the young sleuth felt justified in keeping the notebook. She would turn it over to her father, and let him decide what disposition should be made of it.

"After all," Nancy told herself, "Dad is handling the Crowley case for the Hoovers, and even the Turners and Mrs. Rowen, in a way."

By this time she and the trooper had reached her car. "Would you like me to drive?" he asked.

"Why—er—yes, if you wish," Nancy replied. "But first I want to show you something," she added, as he opened the door for her. "I have some stolen property here."

"What!"

Quickly Nancy explained that she had taken the responsibility of trying to learn whether or not the van held the stolen furniture. "I recognized a few of the pieces, and possibly this clock which the Tophams had told me about. I took that out to examine it. Then I never had a chance to get it back without being caught. I'm sure the Tophams will identify the old clock as their property."

Nancy's explanation seemed to satisfy the officer. "I'll take it to headquarters," he said. "Let's go!"

He laid the clock on the rear seat, then slid behind the wheel and drove off.

It was nearly midnight when Nancy, tired and worn from her long ride, reached the Drew home in River Heights. As she drove into the double garage, she noticed that her father's car was gone. A glance at the house disclosed that the windows were dark, with the exception of a light in the hall. Hannah Gruen must be in bed.

"Of course she's not expecting me," Nancy reasoned. "I wonder where Dad can be? Oh, I hope he'll get home soon. I want to tell him about my discovery right away."

After locking the garage door, she went to the kitchen entrance and let herself in.

Her eyes lighted on the refrigerator and suddenly Nancy realized she was very hungry. Many hours had passed since she had eaten. "Um, food!" she thought.

Just as Nancy opened the refrigerator door, she heard steps on the stairs and Hannah Gruen, wearing a sleepy look, appeared in robe and slippers.

"Nancy!" cried the housekeeper, instantly wide awake.

"Surprise, Hannah darling!" Nancy gave the housekeeper an affectionate hug and kiss. "I'm simply starved. Haven't had a bite since lunchtime."

"Why, you poor dear!" the housekeeper exclaimed in concern. "What happened? I'll fix you something right away."

As the two prepared a chicken sandwich, some cocoa, and Hannah cut a large slice of cinnamon cake over which she poured hot applesauce, Nancy told of her adventures.

The housekeeper's eyes widened. "Nancy, you might have been killed by those awful men. Well, I'm certainly glad they've been captured."

"So am I!" declared Nancy fervently as she finished the last crumb of cake. "And I hope the Turners get back their silver heirlooms."

"How about the Tophams?" Hannah Gruen questioned teasingly.

"Somehow," said Nancy with a wink, "that doesn't seem to worry me." Then she asked, "Where's Dad?"

"Working at his office," Hannah Gruen replied. "He phoned earlier that something unexpected had come up in connection with one of his cases."

"Then I'll wait for him," said Nancy. "You go back to bed. And thanks a million." The sleepy housekeeper did not demur.

Left alone, Nancy tidied the kitchen, then went to the living room.

"Now to find out what became of Josiah Crowley's last will," she thought excitedly, as she curled up in a comfortable chair near a reading lamp.

Carefully she thumbed the yellowed pages, for she was afraid they might tear. Evidently Josiah Crowley had used the same notebook for many years.

"He certainly knew how to save money," she mused.

Nancy read page after page, perusing various kinds of memoranda and many notations of property owned by Mr. Crowley. There were also figures on numerous business transactions in which he had been involved. Nancy was surprised at the long list of stocks, bonds, and notes which apparently belonged to the estate.

"I had no idea Josiah Crowley was worth so much," she murmured.

After a time Nancy grew impatient at the seemingly endless list of figures. She skipped several pages of the little notebook, and turned toward the end where Mr. Crowley had listed his possessions.

"Why, what's this?" she asked herself. Fastened to one page was a very thin, flat key with a tag marked 148.

Suddenly a phrase on the opposite page, "My last will and testament," caught and held Nancy's attention. Eagerly she began to read the whole section.

"I've found it!" she exclaimed excitedly. "I'm glad I didn't give up the search!"

The notation concerning the will was brief. Nancy assumed the cramped writing was Josiah Crowley's. It read:

To whom it may concern: My last will and testament will be found in safe-deposit box number 148 in the Merchants Trust Company. The box is under the name of Josiah Johnston.

"And this is the key to the box!" Nancy told herself.

For several moments the young sleuth sat staring ahead of her. It seemed unbelievable that she had solved the mystery. But surely there could no mistake. The date of the entry in the notebook was recent and the ink had not faded as it had on the earlier pages.

"There *is* a later will!" Nancy exclaimed aloud. "Oh, if only it leaves something to the Turners, and the Mathews, and Abby Rowen, and the Hoover girls! Then Allison could take voice lessons and little Judy would be taken care of, and—"

Nancy hurriedly read on, hoping to learn something definite. But although she carefully examined every page in the book, there was no other mention of the will, nor any clue to its contents.

"No wonder the document didn't come to light," Nancy mused. "Who would have thought of looking for it in a safe-deposit box under the name of Josiah Johnston? In his desire for safekeeping, Josiah Crowley nearly defeated his own purpose."

Her thoughts were interrupted as she heard a car turn into the driveway. Rushing to the window, Nancy saw her father pull into the garage. She ran to meet him at the kitchen door.

"Why, hello, Nancy," he greeted her in surprise. "If I had known you were here, I'd have come home sooner. I was doing some special work on a case. Back from Moon Lake ahead of schedule, aren't you?"

"Yes," Nancy admitted, trying to hide her excitement. "But for a good reason."

Before her father could hang up his hat in the hall closet, she plunged into the story of her adventures and ended by showing him the notebook which she had found inside the mantel clock. When she had finished, Carson Drew stared at his daughter with mingled pride and amazement.

"You're a good detective, Nancy. You've picked up an excellent clue," he said.

"Dad, I thought it best not tell the police about

the notebook. We don't want to reveal the secret of another will to the executor mentioned in the old one."

"You mean Mr. Topham. I agree," the lawyer replied. "The new will may name someone else as executor." He smiled. "I think you and I should try to see this will. But," he added, "which Merchants Trust Company is it in? There must be dozens of banks by that name."

Nancy suddenly snapped her fingers. "Dad, I believe I know. You recall that Judge Hart and his wife told me they had seen Josiah Crowley in Masonville a couple of times. And there's a Merchants Trust Company there."

Mr. Drew looked at his daughter admiringly. "I believe you have the answer, Nancy. And Judge Hart is just the man to help us. I'll phone him in the morning. Well, I guess we both need some sleep."

As the lawyer kissed his daughter good night, he added, "My dear, you were in serious danger when you encountered those thieves. I don't like to have you take such risks. I am very grateful indeed that you are back home safe."

"The Tophams aren't going to thank me when they find out what I have done," Nancy said, as she went up the stairs ahead of her father. "In fact, we may have a battle on our hands, Dad."

"That's right, Nancy. And it will be just as well that they don't learn the details of how the will was found until the matter is settled beyond a doubt."

"I'm certainly curious to find out if the new will left anything to the Tophams," said Nancy.

"If not," her father put in, "your discovery will strike them at an especially awkward time."

Nancy paused on the stairs and turned to face her father. "What do you mean?"

"Well, there's talk about town that Richard Topham has been losing heavily in the stock market this past month. He has been getting credit at a number of places on the strength of the inheritance, and I suspect he is depending on Crowley's money to pull him through a tight spot. He's making every effort to speed up the settlement of the estate."

"Then we'd better hurry," said Nancy, resuming the climb.

"Don't build your hopes too high," Mr. Drew advised her wisely. "There may be a slip, you know."

"How?"

"We may fail to find the will in the safe-deposit box."

"Oh, I can't believe it, Dad. The notebook says it's there!"

"Then," the lawyer continued, "there is a chance that Josiah Crowley didn't dispose of the fortune as the Turners and the Hoovers and others expected he would."

"But he promised all those people—"

"I know, Nancy. But there's just the possibility that the notation in the notebook was wishful thinking and Mr. Crowley never got around to making the new will."

"You can discourage me all you want to, Dad, but I'm not going to stop hoping!" Nancy said. "Oh, I can scarcely wait for morning to come!"

Her father laughed. "You're an incurable optimist! Now put Josiah Crowley out of your mind and get a good night's sleep."

At the door of her bedroom Nancy hesitated, then turned back toward the stairs.

"What's up?" Mr. Drew asked.

Without answering Nancy ran down to the living room, picked up the notebook which lay on the table, and hurried back up the carpeted steps.

"After all I've gone through to get my hands on this," she told her father, "I'm not going to take any chances!" Nancy laughed. "Tonight I'll sleep with it under my pillow!"

CHAPTER XVIII

A Suspenseful Search

WHEN Nancy awoke the following morning, bright sunlight was streaming through her open bedroom window. As her eyes turned toward the clock on her dresser, she was alarmed to see that it was a little after nine o'clock.

"How could I have overslept on a morning like this?" she chided herself.

Quickly running her hand under the pillow, she brought out the Crowley notebook and surveyed it with satisfaction.

"What a surprise the Tophams are going to get!" she murmured softly.

After hastily bathing and dressing, Nancy hurried downstairs looking very attractive in a blue summer sweater suit. She kissed Hannah Gruen, who said a cheery good morning and told Nancy that Mr. Drew had already left for his office.

"Oh dear," Nancy said, "I wonder if he forgot our date?"

"No indeed," the housekeeper replied. "He phoned Judge Hart and expects word from him by ten o'clock. He'll let you know the result. My goodness, Nancy, you've really made a big discovery. I do hope everything turns out for the best."

She went into the kitchen but returned in a moment with a plate of crisp, golden waffles.

"Better eat your breakfast," she advised. "Your dad may call any minute."

Nancy ate a dish of strawberries, then started on the waffles. "These are yummy," she stated, pouring maple syrup over a second one.

She had just finished eating when the phone rang. Mr. Drew was calling to say Judge Hart had made arrangements at the bank. "Come to my office with the notebook and key, Nancy. We'll start from here."

"I'll be right down, Dad."

Nancy went upstairs for her purse, then drove to her father's office.

"I have the notebook with me," she told the lawyer. "Do you want it?"

"We'll take the book along. I want to show it to the head of the trust department at the bank," Mr. Drew said. "It's our proof we have good reason for taking a look in Mr. Crowley's box."

After leaving a number of instructions with his private secretary, Carson Drew followed his daugh-

ter from the office. He took his place beside her
in the convertible.

"I'll never get over it if we don't find a newer
will," Nancy declared, as they drove along. A
flush of excitement had tinted her cheeks and her
eyes were bright.

"You must remember one thing, Nancy," returned her father calmly. "Crowley was an odd
person and did things in an odd way. A will may
be there, and again it may not. Perhaps he only
left further directions to finding it.

"I remember one case in Canada years ago. An
eccentric Frenchman died and left directions to
look in a trunk of old clothes for a will. In the
pocket of a coat were found further instructions
to look in a closet of his home. There his family
found a note telling them to look in a copper
boiler.

"The boiler had disappeared but was finally located in a curiosity shop. Inside, pasted on the
bottom, was what proved to be a word puzzle in
Chinese. The old Frenchman's heirs were about
to give up in despair when a Chinese solved the
puzzle and the old man's fortune was found—a bag
of gold under a board in his bedroom floor!"

"At least they found it," said Nancy.

The trip to Masonville was quickly accomplished, and Nancy parked the car in front of the
Merchants Trust Company.

Father and daughter alighted and entered the

bank. Mr. Drew gave his name and asked to see the president. After a few minutes' wait they were ushered into a private conference room. An elderly man, Mr. Jensen, arose to greet them.

The introductions over, Mr. Drew hastened to state his mission. Before he could finish the story, the bank president broke in.

"Judge Hart has told me the story. I'll call Mr. Warren, our trust officer."

He picked up his desk phone and in a few minutes Mr. Warren appeared and was introduced. Nancy now brought out the notebook, opened it to the important page, and handed it to the men to read.

When they finished, Mr. Jensen said, "What a mystery!"

Mr. Warren pulled from his pocket the file card which the owner of Box 148 had filled out in the name of Josiah Johnston. The two samples of cramped handwritings were compared.

"I would say," Mr. Drew spoke up, "that there is no doubt but that Crowley and Johnston were the same person."

"I agree," asserted Mr. Jensen, and his trust officer nodded.

"Then there's no reason why we shouldn't open the box?" Mr. Drew asked.

"None," Mr. Warren replied. "Of course nothing may be removed, you understand."

"All I want to see," Nancy spoke up, "is whether

there is a will in the box, the date on it, who the executor is, and who the heirs are."

The bankers smiled and Mr. Jensen said, "You're hoping to solve four mysteries all at once! Well, let's get started."

With Mr. Warren in the lead, the four walked toward the rear of the bank to the vault of the trust department. A guard opened the door and they went through. Mr. Jensen took the key from Mr. Crowley's notebook, while Mr. Warren opened the first part of the double safety lock with the bank key. Then he inserted the key from the notebook. It fitted!

In a moment he lifted out Deposit Box Number 148. It was a small one and not heavy, he said.

"We'll take this into a private room," Mr. Jensen stated. He, Nancy, and Mr. Drew followed the trust officer down a corridor of cubbyhole rooms until they reached one not in use.

"Now," said Mr. Jensen, when the door was closed behind them, "we shall see how many—if any—of the mysteries are solved."

Nancy held her breath as he raised the lid of the box. All peered inside. The box was empty, except for one bulky document in the bottom.

"Oh, it must be the will!" Nancy exclaimed.

"It is a will," Mr. Jensen announced, after a hasty glance at the first page. "Josiah Crowley's last will and testament."

"When was it written?" Nancy asked quickly.

"In March of this year," Mr. Jensen told her.

"Oh, Dad," Nancy cried, "this was later than the will the Tophams submitted for probate!"

"That's right."

"Let's read it right away," Nancy begged.

Mr. Jensen handed the sheets to Mr. Drew. "Maybe you can decipher this. The handwriting is too much for me."

The lawyer took the will. Then, as Nancy looked over his shoulder, he haltingly read aloud, giving an interpretation rather than a word by word account.

"Mr. Jensen—Mr. Warren, your bank has been named as executor," he said.

"Very good." The president smiled. "But I expect Mr. Topham won't be happy to hear this."

Mr. Drew had turned to the last page. "The signature of Josiah is in order," he remarked, "and there are two witnesses—Dr. Nesbitt and Thomas Wackley. No wonder this will didn't come to light. Both those men died in April."

As Nancy tried to decipher the handwriting, she noticed to her delight that the Hoover girls and Abby Rowen were mentioned.

At this moment the president said, "Mr. Drew, the bank's regular lawyer had just left for Europe on an extended vacation. Since you and your daughter have solved the mystery and are so vitally interested in it, would you handle this case for us?"

*Nancy held her breath as Mr. Jensen opened the
safe-deposit box*

Nancy's eyes sparkled and Mr. Drew smiled. "I'd certainly be very glad to," he said.

"What instructions have you for us?" Mr. Warren asked.

Mr. Drew thought a moment, then said, "Because of the unusual aspects of this case, I believe that first of all I'd like you to have photostats of the will made, so I can study the contents carefully."

"We'll be happy to do that," Mr. Jensen replied. "And then?"

"After I'm sure everything is legal," Mr. Drew went on, "I'll deliver the original will for probate and notify the people who will benefit from Mr. Crowley's estate."

"Fine," said Mr. Jensen. "We have photostating equipment right here. I'll have a couple of copies made while you wait. Or shall I send them to your office?"

Mr. Drew glanced at his daughter. "We'll wait," he said, smiling.

While the photostats were being made, Nancy's mind was racing. "Oh, I hope Allison receives enough money to pay for singing lessons, and the other deserving people get nice amounts," she whispered to her father, who nodded.

The wait seemed interminable to Nancy, who could not sit still. She walked back and forth until finally her father remarked teasingly, "You're like a caged lion."

Nancy pretended to pout. "At least I'm not growling," she said, and Mr. Drew grinned.

Soon a messenger brought back the will, together with two photostats of the document.

"Thank you," said Mr. Jensen, who handed the photostatic copies to Mr. Drew.

"I'll work on this at once," the lawyer promised as he put the papers in his brief case. Then he and his daughter left the bank.

Mr. Drew insisted that he and Nancy stop for lunch and refused to let her look at the will while they were waiting to be served. "Relax, young lady," he warned. "There's no point in letting any prying eyes know our secret."

As he saw his daughter's animation fading, Mr. Drew said, "Suppose you come to my office with me and we'll work on the problem together. I'll have the will typed. In this way its full meaning can be understood more easily."

"Oh, thanks, Dad," said Nancy.

In the lawyer's office the young sleuth sat down beside his typist, Miss Lamby. As each page came from the machine, Nancy read it avidly.

"Mr. Crowley certainly seemed to know the correct phraseology for drawing up a will," she remarked.

Finally, when the typing had been completed, Nancy said to the secretary, "I have a lot of questions to ask Dad."

Miss Lamby smiled. "If they're legal ones, he'll

know all the answers," she said.   "There's no better lawyer in River Heights than your father."

Nancy smiled as she dashed into her father's office.   The two Drews sat down to study Josiah
Crowley's last will and testament.

"If this does prove to be legal," said Nancy, "it
will certainly be a blow to the Tophams."

"I'm afraid so."

"Dad, when you call a meeting of all the relatives and read the will aloud," Nancy said, "please
may I be there?"

Mr. Drew laughed.   "I'll humor you this time,
Nancy.   You may be present when the Tophams
get the surprise of their lives!"

CHAPTER XIX

Startling Revelations

"DAD, it's nearly two o'clock now. Mr. Crowley's relatives should be here in a few minutes! I'm so excited!"

Carson Drew, who stood in the living room of the Drew home with Mr. Warren from the bank, smiled at his daughter as she fluttered about, arranging chairs.

"I believe you're more thrilled than if you were inheriting the fortune yourself," he remarked.

"I am thrilled," Nancy admitted. "I can scarcely wait until the will is read aloud. Won't everyone be surprised? Especially the Tophams. Do you think they will come?"

"Oh, yes, the Tophams will be here. And, unless I am mistaken, they will bring a lawyer with them. Just as soon as they learned that another will had come to light, they began to worry. They will certainly want to hear what is in this one."

"Are you certain the will we found can't be broken?" Nancy inquired anxiously.

"Of course I can't be certain, Nancy. But I have gone over it carefully, and so far as I can tell, it is technically perfect. I also asked a couple of lawyer friends and they agree. Josiah Crowley was peculiar in some ways, but he was a very smart man. I'll promise you the Tophams will have a difficult time if they try to contest this will."

"The bank will help you fight," Mr. Warren put in.

With the exception of Abby Rowen, who was still confined to bed, all the old gentleman's relatives had promised to be present. Grace and Allison Hoover, although not relatives, had also been invited.

"It's too bad Mrs. Rowen can't come," said Nancy. "But I'll take the news to her this very afternoon."

"The size of the fortune will probably be a great surprise to everyone but the Tophams," said her father with a smile. "Nancy, you did a remarkable piece of detective work."

"It was fun," she said modestly. "And I can hardly wait to have it all cleared up."

"We may have some trying minutes with the Tophams, Nancy," her father warned.

"Yes, I suppose so. I expect anybody would be sorry to see a fortune slip away. . . . Dad, I see

Grace and Allison coming up the walk now," Nancy announced, glancing out the window.

She greeted them with kisses and escorted the sisters into the living room, where she introduced them to Mr. Warren. As Allison sat down, she whispered to Nancy:

"Is it true a later will has been found?"

"You and Grace have no cause to worry," Nancy assured her with a mysterious smile.

The doorbell rang. This time Nancy admitted Edna and Mary Turner, who were dressed as if for a party. With them was little Judy, who threw herself into Nancy's arms. A few minutes later the Mathews brothers, William and Fred, arrived.

"I guess everyone is here except the Tophams," Mr. Drew commented. "We had better wait for them a few minutes."

There was no need to wait, for at that moment the bell rang sharply. Nancy opened the door and the four members of the Topham family walked in haughtily, merely nodding to the others in the room. As Mr. Drew had predicted, they were accompanied by a lawyer.

"Why have we been called here?" Mrs. Topham demanded, addressing Mr. Drew. "Have you the audacity to claim that another will has been found?"

"I have a will written only this past March, Mrs. Topham," Carson Drew replied evenly. "And I'd like to introduce to all of you Mr. John Warren, trust officer of the Merchants Trust Company, of Masonville, which has been named as executor."

"It's preposterous!" Mrs. Topham stormed. "Josiah Crowley made only one will and in that he left everything to us with my husband as executor."

"It looks like a conspiracy to me," Ada added tartly, as she gazed coldly upon the relatives and friends who were seated about the room.

Isabel did not speak, but tossed her head contemptuously. Richard Topham likewise did not offer a comment, but uneasily seated himself beside his own attorney.

"If you will please be seated, Mrs. Topham, I will read the will," Mr. Drew suggested.

Reluctantly Mrs. Topham sat down.

"As I have said," Mr. Drew began, "a recent will of the late Josiah Crowley was found in a safe-deposit box in the Masonville bank. The will is unusually long, and with your permission I will read from a typed copy only the portions which have to do with the disposal of the property. But first I want to ask Mr. Topham what value he puts on the estate."

"A hundred thousand after taxes," the man replied.

"Oh!" the Turners exclaimed, and Mary said, "I had no idea Josiah had that much money."

"Nor I," Edna agreed.

Mr. Drew picked up several typewritten sheets from the table, and began to read in a clear voice:

" 'I, Josiah Crowley, do make this my last will and testament, hereby revoking all former wills by me at any time made. I give and bequeath all my property, real and personal, as follows:

" 'To my beloved friends and neighbors, Grace and Allison Hoover, a sum equal to twenty per cent of my estate, share and share alike.' "

"I must be dreaming!" Grace gasped.

"You mean I'm going to get ten thousand dollars?" Allison cried out. She burst into tears. "Oh, Nancy, you did this for me! Now I can have my voice lessons."

Isabel Topham eyed her disdainfully. "It would take more than ten thousand dollars to make a singer out of you!" she said maliciously.

"Quiet!" commanded her father. "Let's hear what else this will says."

His daughter subsided, but his wife exclaimed spitefully, "The will is a fraud. The Hoovers aren't even relatives."

"It is no fraud," Mr. Drew told her quietly. Again he picked up the will and began to read:

" 'To Abby Rowen, my late wife's cousin, in consideration of her kindness to me, a sum equal to ten per cent of my estate.' "

"Oh, I'm so glad," Grace murmured. "Now she'll be able to get the medical and other attention she needs."

"And have someone live at her house to take care of her," said Nancy.

"That old lady gets ten thousand dollars?" Ada Topham said harshly. "What did she ever do for Cousin Josiah?" Angrily she turned to her mother. "We took care of him for years—she didn't!"

"I'll say not," Isabel echoed, her voice tart.

" 'To my cousins, Fred and William Mathews, a sum equal to twenty per cent of my estate, share and share alike,' " Mr. Drew read.

"We didn't expect that much," Fred Mathews declared in genuine surprise. "Josiah was very kind." Fred smiled. "Now we can take a trip like we've always wanted to do, William."

"That's right. I just can't believe it. A long trip on an ocean liner or a plane."

" 'To my cousins, Edna and Mary Turner, twenty per cent of my estate, share and share alike.' "

"Oh, how generous!" Edna murmured. "Now little Judy can have the things we've always wanted to give her."

"Yes," said Mary Turner. "Oh, I feel so relieved."

"Aren't we mentioned at all?" Mrs. Topham broke in sharply.

Mr. Drew smiled. "Yes, you are mentioned. I'm coming to that now. 'To Richard Topham, five thousand dollars. To Grace and Allison Hoover—' "

"Hold on!" cried Mrs. Topham. "What about me and the girls?"

"No money was left to you," the lawyer stated simply.

Isabel gave a shriek. "Oh, no! Oh, no! Oh, Mother, all those bills! What'll we do?"

Ada too had cried out. "I'll have to go to work! Oh, I can't bear the thought of it!"

When the furor died down, Mr. Drew read on, " 'To Grace and Allison Hoover my household furniture now in the possession of Mrs. Richard Topham.' "

There was a gasp of surprise from everyone in the room, and Mrs. Topham half arose from her chair. It was generally known in River Heights that she had practically confiscated Josiah Crowley's furniture at the time he had been induced to make his home with the Tophams.

"How insulting!" the woman cried. "Does Josiah Crowley dare hint that I took his furniture?"

"I'm sure I don't know what was in his mind at the time he wrote the will," Mr. Drew told her with a smile.

Grace Hoover interposed quickly, "We have enough furniture without Josiah Crowley's."

Allison nodded. "We'll not take any of it from you, Mrs. Topham."

Mr. Drew carefully folded the document he had been reading, and after placing it in his pocket, he said to the people in the room:

"That is all, except that there is a proviso for the executor to pay all Mr. Crowley's just debts, including his funeral expenses, and that what balance is left in the estate goes to the Manningham Old Men's Home. I understand Josiah Crowley kept his assets in a liquid state. It will not be difficult to convert the estate into cash. For that reason I should think it would be possible to draw on your inheritances at once."

Ada wheeled upon Nancy, her face convulsed with anger. "You engineered this whole thing, Nancy Drew!" she accused bitterly.

"Any good I've done I'm happy about," Nancy answered.

"We'll break the will!" Mrs. Topham announced firmly.

CHAPTER XX

A Happy Finale

"OF COURSE you may take the matter into court if you like," Mr. Drew responded to Mrs. Topham's threat. "But I warn you it will be a waste of your time and money. If you don't wish to accept my judgment, ask your own lawyer."

"Mr. Drew is right," the other lawyer said, after arising and looking carefully at the legal document which Mr. Drew took from his pocket.

"Oh, he is, is he?" Mrs. Topham retorted. "If that's all you know about law, you're discharged! We'll get another lawyer and we'll fight to the last ditch!"

With that she arose and stalked from the room. Isabel and Ada followed, after bestowing a withering glance upon Nancy. Mr. Topham brought up the rear. As soon as the door had closed behind them, their lawyer arose and picked up his brief case.

"Well, I can't say I'm sorry to be taken off the case," he remarked as he, too, took his leave. "But I advise you to be on your guard. That woman is certainly belligerent."

At once the atmosphere in the Drew living room became less strained, though each person was fearful Mrs. Topham would make trouble. Everyone began to talk at once.

"Oh, Nancy, I can hardly believe it yet!" Allison declared happily. "The money means so much to Grace and me! And we owe it all to you, Nancy Drew! You haven't told us how you came to find the will, but I know you were responsible."

When the Hoover girls and Mr. Crowley's relatives begged her for the details, Nancy told of her adventure with the thieves at Moon Lake. After she had finished the story, they praised her highly for what she had done.

"We'll never be able to thank you enough," Grace said quietly. "But after the estate has been settled, we'll try to show our appreciation."

It was on the tip of Nancy's tongue to say that she did not want a reward, when Mr. Drew turned the conversation into a different channel.

"Mrs. Topham will not give up the money without a fight," he warned. "My advice would be to go along as you have until the court has decided to accept this will as the final one. However, if Mrs. Topham and her daughters bring the matter into court, I'll give them a battle they'll never forget!"

After thanking Mr. Drew and Nancy for everything they had done, the relatives and friends de-
parted. Allison and Grace were the last to leave.
On the porch, Allison paused to hug Nancy and
say, "Please let us know what develops. I'm so
eager to start taking voice lessons."

Nancy wanted to set off at once to see Abby
Rowen and tell her the good news. But upon sec-
ond thought she decided to wait. Suppose the
Tophams succeeded in upsetting the whole case!

For a week Nancy waited impatiently to hear
the result of the battle over the will. As she and
her father had anticipated, Mrs. Topham was fighting bitterly for the Crowley estate. She had put
forth the claim that the will Nancy had unearthed
was a forged document.

"This suspense is just awful," Nancy told her
father one morning. "When are we going to get
final word?"

"I can't answer that, Nancy. But apparently
Mr. Topham thinks it's a losing battle. I suppose
you've heard about the family."

"Why, no, what about them?"

"They're practically bankrupt. Richard Topham has been losing steadily on the stock market
of late. After his failure to recover the Crowley
fortune, the banks reduced his credit. He's been
forced to give up his beautiful home."

"No, really? How that must hurt Mrs. Topham
and the two girls!"

"Yes, it's undoubtedly a bitter pill to swallow. They are moving into a small house this week, and from now on they'll have to give up their extravagant way of living. Both girls are working. Personally, I think it will be good for them."

Word came that the three furniture thieves had finally confessed to many robberies and their unsold loot was recovered. Among the pieces were all the heirlooms they had stolen from the Turners.

One evening Mr. Drew came home wearing a broad smile. Facing Nancy and laying both hands on her shoulders, he said:

"We've won, my dear. The will you located has been accepted as the last one Mr. Crowley wrote."

"Oh, Dad, how wonderful!" she cried, whirling her father about in a little dance. "First thing tomorrow morning, may I go and tell Allison and Grace and the others?"

"I think that would be a fine idea. Of course the bank and I will formally notify them later."

The following morning Nancy was the first one downstairs and started breakfast before Hannah Gruen appeared.

"My goodness, you're an early bird, Nancy," the housekeeper said with a smile. "Big day, eh?"

"*Very* big," Nancy replied.

As soon as the family had eaten, Hannah said,

"Never mind helping me today. You run along and make those people happy as soon as possible."

"Oh, thank you, Hannah. I'll leave right away."

Nancy, dressed in a simple green linen sports dress with a matching sweater, kissed her little family good-by and drove off. Her first stop was at the Mathews brothers. They greeted her affably, then waited for Nancy to speak.

"I have good news," she said, her eyes dancing. "Mrs. Topham lost her case. The will Dad and I found has been accepted for probate. You will receive the inheritance Mr. Crowley left you!"

"Praise be!" Fred cried. "And we never would have received it if it hadn't been for you." His brother nodded in agreement.

To cover her embarrassment at their praise, Nancy reached into a pocket and pulled out a handful of travel folders and airline schedules. "I thought you might like to look at these. Now I must hurry off and tell the other heirs."

As she drove away, the two men smiled, waved, then immediately began to look at the folders. "I hope they have a grand trip," Nancy thought.

Half an hour later she pulled into the driveway of the Turner home. Before the car stopped, Judy came racing from the front door. As Nancy stepped out, the little girl threw herself into the young sleuth's arms. "Nancy, guess what! My

aunties found an old, old doll that belonged to
my mommy and they gave it to me. Come and see
her. She's pretty as can be."

Judy pulled Nancy by the hand up the steps and
into the house. "There she is," the child said
proudly, pointing to a blond, curly-haired doll
seated in a tiny rocking chair.

"Why, she's darling," Nancy commented.
"And, Judy, she looks like you, dimples and all."

Judy nodded. "And Aunt Mary says she looks
like my mommy did when she was a little girl, so
I'm always going to take very good care of my
dolly."

At this moment her great-aunts came from the
rear of the house to greet their caller.

"I see," said Nancy, "that you have made Judy
very happy. Now it's my turn to pass along good
news to you," and she told about their inheritance.

The women smiled happily and tears came
to their eyes. Then suddenly Edna Turner gave
Nancy an impulsive hug. "You dear, dear girl!"
she half sobbed with joy. "Now Judy will always
be well taken care of and receive the kind of
schooling we think she should have!"

Mary kissed Nancy and thanked the young
sleuth for her untiring efforts to see justice done.
Judy, meanwhile, looked on in puzzlement at the
scene. But sensing that it called for her participa-
tion, she grabbed up her new doll and began to
dance around with it.

"Now you can go to school too, Carol," she told her doll.

It was hard for Nancy to break away from the Turners, but she reminded them that she still had two calls to make.

"But come back soon," Judy said.

When Nancy arrived at Abby Rowen's she was delighted to find her seated by the window in a chair. Her kind neighbor, Mrs. Jones, was there preparing food for the invalid. To this Nancy added a jar of homemade beef broth and a casserole of rice and chicken which Hannah Gruen had insisted upon sending.

"Can you stay a little while?" Mrs. Jones asked. "I ought to run home for half an hour, then I'll come back."

"She's been so kind," Abby Rowen spoke up. "Today she took my laundry home to wash and iron." After the woman had left, Abby went on, "The folks around here have been very thoughtful of me, but I just can't impose on them any longer. Yet I haven't any money—"

Nancy took the invalid's hand in hers and smiled. "I came to tell you that now you have lots of money, left to you by Josiah Crowley."

"What! You mean I won't have to depend on just my little pension any longer? Bless Josiah! Nancy, I never could believe that my cousin would go back on his word."

Nancy ate some broth and crackers with Abby

Rowen and told the whole story. The old woman's eyes began to sparkle and color came into her cheeks. "Oh, this is so wonderful!" she said. Then she chuckled. "It does my heart good to know you outwitted those uppity Topham women!"

Nancy grinned, then said soberly, "If I hadn't become involved in this mystery, I might never have met several wonderful people—and their names aren't Topham!"

Abby Rowen laughed aloud—the first time Nancy had heard her do this. She laughed again just as the neighbor returned. Mrs. Jones, amazed, had no chance to exclaim over the elderly woman's high spirits. Abby launched into an account of her inheritance.

As soon as Mrs. Rowen finished the story, Nancy said good-by and left. She now headed straight for the Hoover farm. The two sisters were working in a flower bed.

"Hi!" Nancy called.

"Hi, yourself. How's everything?" Allison asked, as she brushed some dirt off her hands and came forward with Grace.

"Hurry and change your clothes," Nancy said. "I have a surprise for you."

"You mean we're going somewhere?" Grace inquired.

"That's right. To Signor Mascagni's so Allison can sign up for lessons."

"Oh, Nancy, you mean—?"

"Yes. The inheritance is yours!"

"I can't believe it! I can't believe it!" Allison cried out ecstatically. She grabbed the other two girls and whirled them around.

"It's simply marvelous," said Grace. "Marvelous. Oh, Nancy, you and Mr. Crowley are just the dearest friends we've ever had." Then, seeing Nancy's deep blush, she added, "Come on, Allison. Let's get dressed."

Nancy waited in the garden. Fifteen minutes later the sisters were ready to leave for River Heights. "But before we go," said Grace, "Allison and I want to give you something—it's sort of a reward."

"Something very special," her sister broke in.

"Oh, I don't want any reward," Nancy objected quickly.

"Please take this one," Allison spoke up.

She led the way to the living-room mantel. There stood the Crowley clock. "We received it this morning from the Tophams," Grace explained.

Allison added, "We think you earned this heirloom, Nancy, and somehow Grace and I feel Mr. Crowley would want you to have it."

"Why, thank you," said Nancy.

She was thrilled, and gazed meditatively at the old clock. Though quaint, it was not handsome, she thought. But for her it certainly held a special significance. She was too modest to explain to Allison and Grace why she would prize the heirloom, and besides, her feeling was something she could not put into words. Actually she had become attached to the clock because of its association with her recent adventure.

"This is the first mystery I've solved alone," she thought. "I wonder if I'll ever have another one half so thrilling."

As Nancy stood looking wistfully at the old clock she little dreamed that in the near future she would be involved in *The Hidden Staircase* mystery, a far more baffling case than the one she had just solved. But somehow, as Nancy gazed at the timepiece, she sensed that exciting days were soon to come.

Nancy ceased daydreaming as the clock was handed to her and looked at the Hoover girls. "I'll always prize this clock as a trophy of my first venture as a detective," she said with a broad smile.

The Hidden Staircase

Both girls froze in their tracks

CHAPTER I

The Haunted House

NANCY DREW began peeling off her garden gloves as she ran up the porch steps and into the hall to answer the ringing telephone. She picked it up and said, "Hello!"

"Hi, Nancy! This is Helen." Although Helen Corning was nearly three years older than Nancy, the two girls were close friends.

"Are you tied up on a case?" Helen asked.

"No. What's up? A mystery?"

"Yes—a haunted house."

Nancy sat down on the chair by the telephone. "Tell me more!" the eighteen-year-old detective begged excitedly.

"You've heard me speak of my Aunt Rosemary," Helen began. "Since becoming a widow, she has lived with her mother at Twin Elms, the old family mansion out in Cliffwood. Well, I went to see them yesterday. They said that many strange,

mysterious things have been happening there recently. I told them how good you are at solving
mysteries, and they'd like you to come out to Twin
Elms and help them." Helen paused, out of
breath.

"It certainly sounds intriguing," Nancy replied,
her eyes dancing.

"If you're not busy, Aunt Rosemary and I would
like to come over in about an hour and talk to you
about the ghost."

"I can't wait."

After Nancy had put down the phone, she sat
lost in thought for several minutes. Since solving
The Secret of the Old Clock, she had longed for
another case. Here was her chance!

Attractive, blond-haired Nancy was brought out
of her daydreaming by the sound of the doorbell.
At the same moment the Drews' housekeeper,
Hannah Gruen, came down the front stairs.

"I'll answer it," she offered.

Mrs. Gruen had lived with the Drews since
Nancy was three years old. At that time Mrs.
Drew had passed away and Hannah had become
like a second mother to Nancy. There was a deep
affection between the two, and Nancy confided all
her secrets to the understanding housekeeper.

Mrs. Gruen opened the door and instantly a
man stepped into the hall. He was short, thin,
and rather stooped. Nancy guessed his age to be
about forty.

"Is Mr. Drew at home?" he asked brusquely. "My name is Gomber—Nathan Gomber."

"No, he's not here just now," the housekeeper replied.

The caller looked over Hannah Gruen's shoulder and stared at Nancy. "Are you Nancy Drew?"

"Yes, I am. Is there anything I can do for you?"

The man's shifty gaze moved from Nancy to Hannah. "I've come out of the goodness of my heart to warn you and your father," he said pompously.

"Warn us? About what?" Nancy asked quickly.

Nathan Gomber straightened up importantly and said, "Your father is in great danger, Miss Drew!"

Both Nancy and Hannah Gruen gasped. "You mean this very minute?" the housekeeper questioned.

"All the time," was the startling answer. "I understand you're a pretty bright girl, Miss Drew —that you even solve mysteries. Well, right now I advise you to stick close to your father. Don't leave him for a minute."

Hannah Gruen looked as if she were ready to collapse and suggested that they all go into the living room, sit down, and talk the matter over. When they were seated, Nancy asked Nathan Gomber to explain further.

"The story in a nutshell is this," he began. "You know that your father was brought in to do legal work for the railroad when it was buying property for the new bridge here."

As Nancy nodded, he continued, "Well, a lot of the folks who sold their property think they were gypped."

Nancy's face reddened. "I understood from my father that everyone was well paid."

"That's not true," said Gomber. "Besides, the railroad is in a real mess now. One of the property owners, whose deed and signature they claim to have, says that he never signed the contract of sale."

"What's his name?" Nancy asked.

"Willie Wharton."

Nancy had not heard her father mention this name. She asked Gomber to go on with his story.

"I'm acting as agent for Willie Wharton and several of the land owners who were his neighbors," he said, "and they can make it pretty tough for the railroad. Willie Wharton's signature was never witnessed and the attached certificate of acknowledgment was not notarized. That's good proof the signature was a forgery. Well, if the railroad thinks they're going to get away with this, they're not!"

Nancy frowned. Such a procedure on the part of the property owners meant trouble for her father! She said evenly, "But all Willie Wharton has to do is swear before a notary that he did sign the contract of sale."

Gomber chuckled. "It's not that easy, Miss Drew. Willie Wharton is not available. Some of us have a good idea where he is and we'll produce him at the right time. But that time won't be until the railroad promises to give the sellers more money. Then he'll sign. You see, Willie is a real kind man and he wants to help his friends out whenever he can. Now he's got a chance."

Nancy had taken an instant dislike to Gomber and now it was quadrupled. She judged him to be the kind of person who stays within the boundaries of the law but whose ethics are questionable. This was indeed a tough problem for Mr. Drew!

"Who are the people who are apt to harm my father?" she asked.

"I'm not saying who they are," Nathan Gomber retorted. "You don't seem very appreciative of my coming here to warn you. Fine kind of a daughter you are. You don't care what happens to your father!"

Annoyed by the man's insolence, both Nancy and Mrs. Gruen angrily stood up. The housekeeper, pointing toward the front door, said, "Good day, Mr. Gomber!"

The caller shrugged as he too arose. "Have it your own way, but don't say I didn't warn you!"

He walked to the front door, opened it, and as he went outside, closed it with a tremendous bang.

"Well, of all the insulting people!" Hannah snorted.

Nancy nodded. "But that's not the worst of it, Hannah darling. I think there's more to Gomber's warning than he is telling. It seems to me to imply a threat. And he almost has me convinced. Maybe I should stay close to Dad until he and the other lawyers have straightened out this railroad tangle."

She said this would mean giving up a case she had been asked to take. Hastily Nancy gave Hannah the highlights of her conversation with Helen about the haunted mansion. "Helen and her aunt will be here in a little while to tell us the whole story."

"Oh, maybe things aren't so serious for your father as that horrible man made out," Hannah said encouragingly. "If I were you I'd listen to the details about the haunted house and then decide what you want to do about the mystery."

In a short time a sports car pulled into the winding, tree-shaded driveway of the Drew home. The large brick house was set some distance back from the street.

Helen was at the wheel and stopped just beyond the front entrance. She helped her aunt from the car and they came up the steps together. Mrs. Rosemary Hayes was tall and slender and had graying hair. Her face had a gentle expression but she looked tired.

Helen introduced her aunt to Nancy and to Hannah, and the group went into the living room to sit down. Hannah offered to prepare tea and left the room.

"Oh, Nancy," said Helen, "I do hope you can take Aunt Rosemary and Miss Flora's case." Quickly she explained that Miss Flora was her aunt's mother. "Aunt Rosemary is really my great-aunt and Miss Flora is my great-grand-mother. From the time she was a little girl everybody has called her Miss Flora."

"The name may seem odd to people the first time they hear it," Mrs. Hayes remarked, "but we're all so used to it, we never think anything about it."

"Please tell me more about your house," Nancy requested, smiling.

"Mother and I are almost nervous wrecks," Mrs. Hayes replied. "I have urged her to leave Twin Elms, but she won't. You see, Mother has lived there ever since she married my father, Everett Turnbull."

Mrs. Hayes went on to say that all kinds of strange happenings had occurred during the past couple of weeks. They had heard untraceable music, thumps and creaking noises at night, and had seen eerie, indescribable shadows on walls.

"Have you notified the police?" Nancy asked.

"Oh, yes," Mrs. Hayes answered. "But after talking with my mother, they came to the conclusion that most of what she saw and heard could be explained by natural causes. The rest, they said, probably was imagination on her part. You see, she's over eighty years old, and while I know her mind is sound and alert, I'm afraid that the police don't think so."

After a pause Mrs. Hayes went on, "I had almost talked myself into thinking the ghostly noises could be attributed to natural causes, when something else happened."

"What was that?" Nancy questioned eagerly.

"We were robbed! During the night several pieces of old jewelry were taken. I did telephone the police about this and they came to the house for a description of the pieces. But they still would not admit that a 'ghost' visitor had taken them."

Nancy was thoughtful for several seconds before making a comment. Then she said, "Do the police have any idea who the thief might be?"

Aunt Rosemary shook her head. "No. And I'm afraid we might have more burglaries."

Many ideas were running through Nancy's head. One was that the thief apparently had no intention of harming anyone—that his only motive had been burglary. Was he or was he not the person who was "haunting" the house? Or could the strange happenings have some natural explanations, as the police had suggested?

At this moment Hannah returned with a large silver tray on which was a tea service and some dainty sandwiches. She set the tray on a table and asked Nancy to pour the tea. She herself passed the cups of tea and sandwiches to the callers.

As they ate, Helen said, "Aunt Rosemary hasn't told you half the things that have happened. Once Miss Flora thought she saw someone sliding out of a fireplace at midnight, and another time a chair moved from one side of the room to the other while her back was turned. But no one was there!"

"How extraordinary!" Hannah Gruen exclaimed. "I've often read about such things, but I never thought I'd meet anyone who lived in a haunted house."

Helen turned to Nancy and gazed pleadingly at her friend. "You see how much you're needed at Twin Elms? Won't you please go out there with me and solve the mystery of the ghost?"

CHAPTER II

The Mysterious Mishap

SIPPING their tea, Helen Corning and her aunt waited for Nancy's decision. The young sleuth was in a dilemma. She wanted to start at once solving the mystery of the "ghost" of Twin Elms. But Nathan Gomber's warning still rang in her ears and she felt that her first duty was to stay with her father.

At last she spoke. "Mrs. Hayes—" she began.

"Please call me Aunt Rosemary," the caller requested. "All Helen's friends do."

Nancy smiled. "I'd love to. Aunt Rosemary, may I please let you know tonight or tomorrow? I really must speak to my father about the case. And something else came up just this afternoon which may keep me at home for a while at least."

"I understand," Mrs. Hayes answered, trying to conceal her disappointment.

Helen Corning did not take Nancy's announce-

ment so calmly. "Oh, Nancy, you just must come.
I'm sure your dad would want you to help us.
Can't you postpone the other thing until you get
back?"

"I'm afraid not," said Nancy. "I can't tell you
all the details, but Dad has been threatened and I
feel that I ought to stay close to him."

Hannah Gruen added her fears. "Goodness
only knows what they may do to Mr. Drew," she
said. "Somebody could come up and hit him on
the head, or poison his food in a restaurant, or—"

Helen and her aunt gasped. "It's that bad?"
Helen asked, her eyes growing wide.

Nancy explained that she would talk to her
father when he returned home. "I hate to disap-
point you," she said, "but you can see what a quan-
dary I'm in."

"You poor girl!" said Mrs. Hayes sympathetically. "Now don't you worry about us."

Nancy smiled. "I'll worry whether I come or
not," she said. "Anyway, I'll talk to my dad tonight."

The callers left shortly. When the door had
closed behind them, Hannah put an arm around
Nancy's shoulders. "I'm sure everything will
come out all right for everybody," she said. "I'm
sorry I talked about those dreadful things that
might happen to your father. I let my imagination run away with me, just like they say Miss
Flora's does with her."

"You're a great comfort, Hannah dear," said Nancy. "To tell the truth, I have thought of all kinds of horrible things myself." She began to pace the floor. "I wish Dad would get home."

During the next hour she went to the window at least a dozen times, hoping to see her father's car coming up the street. It was not until six o'clock that she heard the crunch of wheels on the driveway and saw Mr. Drew's sedan pull into the garage.

"He's safe!" she cried out to Hannah, who was testing potatoes that were baking in the oven.

In a flash Nancy was out the back door and running to meet her father. "Oh, Dad, I'm so glad to see you!" she exclaimed.

She gave him a tremendous hug and a resounding kiss. He responded affectionately, but gave a little chuckle. "What have I done to rate this extra bit of attention?" he teased. With a wink he added, "I know. Your date for tonight is off and you want me to substitute."

"Oh, Dad," Nancy replied. "Of course my date's not off. But I'm just about to call it off."

"Why?" Mr. Drew questioned. "Isn't Dirk going to stay on your list?"

"It's not that," Nancy replied. "It's because—because you're in terrible danger, Dad. I've been warned not to leave you."

Instead of looking alarmed, the lawyer burst out laughing. "In terrible danger of what? Are you going to make a raid on my wallet?"

"Dad, be serious! I really mean what I'm saying. Nathan Gomber was here and told me that you're in great danger and I'd better stay with you at all times."

The lawyer sobered at once. "That pest again!" he exclaimed. "There are times when I'd like to thrash the man till he begged for mercy!"

Mr. Drew suggested that they postpone their discussion about Nathan Gomber until dinner was over. Then he would tell his daughter the true facts in the case. After they had finished dinner, Hannah insisted upon tidying up alone while father and daughter talked.

"I will admit that there is a bit of a muddle about the railroad bridge," Mr. Drew began. "What happened was that the lawyer who went to get Willie Wharton's signature was very ill at the time. Unfortunately, he failed to have the signature witnessed or have the attached certificate of acknowledgment executed. The poor man passed away a few hours later."

"And the other railroad lawyers failed to notice that the signature hadn't been witnessed or the certificate notarized?" Nancy asked.

"Not right away. The matter did not come to light until the man's widow turned his brief case over to the railroad. The old deed to Wharton's property was there, so the lawyers assumed that the signature on the contract was genuine. The contract for the railroad bridge was awarded and work began. Suddenly Nathan Gomber appeared, saying he represented Willie Wharton and others who had owned property which the railroad had bought on either side of the Muskoka River."

"I understood from Mr. Gomber," said Nancy, "that Willie Wharton is trying to get more money for his neighbors by holding out for a higher price himself."

"That's the story. Personally, I think it's a sharp deal on Gomber's part. The more people he can get money for, the higher his commission," Mr. Drew stated.

"What a mess!" Nancy exclaimed. "And what can be done?"

"To tell the truth, there is little anyone can do until Willie Wharton is found. Gomber knows this, of course, and has probably advised Wharton to stay in hiding until the railroad agrees to give everybody more money."

Nancy had been watching her father intently. Now she saw an expression of eagerness come over his face. He leaned forward in his chair and said, "But I think I'm about to outwit Mr. Nathan Gomber. I've had a tip that Willie Wharton is in Chicago and I'm leaving Monday morning to find out."

Mr. Drew went on, "I believe that Wharton will say he did sign the contract of sale which the railroad company has and will readily consent to having the certificate of acknowledgment notarized.

Then, of course, the railroad won't pay him or any of the other property owners another cent."

"But, Dad, you still haven't convinced me you're not in danger," Nancy reminded him.

"Nancy dear," her father replied, "I feel that I am not in danger. Gomber is nothing but a blowhard. I doubt that he or Willie Wharton or any of the other property owners would resort to violence to keep me from working on this case. He's just trying to scare me into persuading the railroad to accede to his demands."

Nancy looked skeptical. "But don't forget that you're about to go to Chicago and produce the very man Gomber and those property owners don't want around here just now."

"I know." Mr. Drew nodded. "But I still doubt if anyone would use force to keep me from going." Laughingly the lawyer added, "So I won't need you as a bodyguard, Nancy."

His daughter gave a sigh of resignation. "All right, Dad, you know best." She then proceeded to tell her father about the Twin Elms mystery, which she had been asked to solve. "If you approve," Nancy said in conclusion, "I'd like to go over there with Helen."

Mr. Drew had listened with great interest. Now, after a few moments of thought, he smiled. "Go by all means, Nancy. I realize you've been itching to work on a new case—and this sounds like a real challenge. But please be careful."

"Oh, I will, Dad!" Nancy promised, her face lighting up. "Thanks a million." She jumped from her chair, gave her father a kiss, then went to phone Helen the good news. It was arranged that the girls would go to Twin Elms on Monday morning.

Nancy returned to the living room, eager to discuss the mystery further. Her father, however, glanced at his wrist watch. "Say, young lady, you'd better go dress for that date of yours." He winked. "I happen to know that Dirk doesn't like to be kept waiting."

"Especially by any of my mysteries." She laughed and hurried upstairs to change into a dance dress.

Half an hour later Dirk Jackson arrived. Nancy and the red-haired, former high-school tennis champion drove off to pick up another couple and attend an amateur play and dance given by the local Little Theater group.

Nancy thoroughly enjoyed herself and was sorry when the affair ended. With the promise of another date as soon as she returned from Twin Elms, Nancy said good night and waved from her doorway to the departing boy. As she prepared for bed, she thought of the play, the excellent orchestra, how lucky she was to have Dirk for a date, and what fun it had all been. But then her thoughts turned to Helen Corning and her relatives in the haunted house, Twin Elms.

"I can hardly wait for Monday to come," she murmured to herself as she fell asleep.

The following morning she and her father attended church together. Hannah said she was going to a special service that afternoon and therefore would stay at home during the morning.

"I'll have a good dinner waiting for you," she announced, as the Drews left.

After the service was over, Mr. Drew said he would like to drive down to the waterfront and see what progress had been made on the new bridge. "The railroad is going ahead with construction on the far side of the river," he told Nancy.

"Is the Wharton property on this side?" Nancy asked.

"Yes. And I must get to the truth of this mixed-up situation, so that work can be started on this side too."

Mr. Drew wound among the many streets leading down to the Muskoka River, then took the vehicular bridge across. He turned toward the construction area and presently parked his car. As he and Nancy stepped from the sedan, he looked ruefully at her pumps.

"It's going to be rough walking down to the waterfront," he said. "Perhaps you had better wait here."

"Oh, I'll be all right," Nancy assured him. "I'd like to see what's being done."

Various pieces of large machinery stood about on the high ground—a crane, a derrick, and hydraulic shovels. As the Drews walked toward the river, they passed a large truck. It faced the river and stood at the top of an incline just above two of the four enormous concrete piers which had already been built.

"I suppose there will be matching piers on the opposite side," Nancy mused, as she and her father reached the riverbank. They paused in the space between the two huge abutments. Mr. Drew glanced from side to side as if he had heard something. Suddenly Nancy detected a noise behind them.

Turning, she was horrified to see that the big truck was moving toward them. No one was at the wheel and the great vehicle was gathering speed at every moment.

"Dad!" she screamed.

In the brief second of warning, the truck almost seemed to leap toward the water. Nancy and her father, hemmed in by the concrete piers, had no way to escape being run down.

"Dive!" Mr. Drew ordered.

Without hesitation, he and Nancy made running flat dives into the water, and with arms flailing and legs kicking, swam furiously out of harm's way.

The truck thundered into the water and sank

The truck seemed to leap toward them

immediately up to the cab. The Drews turned and came back to the shore.

"Whew! That was a narrow escape!" the lawyer exclaimed, as he helped his daughter retrieve her pumps which had come off in the oozy bank.

"And what sights we are!" Nancy remarked.

"Indeed we are," her father agreed, as they trudged up the incline. "I'd like to get hold of the workman who was careless enough to leave that heavy truck on the slope without the brake on properly."

Nancy was not so sure that the near accident was the fault of a careless workman. Nathan Gomber had warned her that Mr. Drew's life was in danger. The threat might already have been put into action!

CHAPTER III

A Stolen Necklace

"WE'D better get home in a hurry and change our clothes," said Mr. Drew. "And I'll call the contracting company to tell them what happened."

"And notify the police?" Nancy suggested.

She dropped behind her father and gazed over the surrounding ground for telltale footprints. Presently she saw several at the edge of the spot where the truck had stood.

"Dad!" the young sleuth called out. "I may have found a clue to explain how that truck started downhill."

Her father came back and looked at the footprints. They definitely had not been made by a workman's boots.

"You may think me an old worrier, Dad," Nancy spoke up, "but these footprints, made by a man's business shoes, convince me that somebody deliberately tried to injure us with that truck."

The lawyer stared at his daughter. Then he looked down at the ground. From the size of the shoe and the length of the stride one could easily perceive that the wearer of the shoes was not tall. Nancy asked her father if he thought one of the workmen on the project could be responsible.

"I just can't believe anyone associated with the contracting company would want to injure us," Mr. Drew said.

Nancy reminded her father of Nathan Gomber's warning. "It might be one of the property owners, or even Willie Wharton himself."

"Wharton is short and has a small foot," the lawyer conceded. "And I must admit that these look like fresh footprints. As a matter of fact, they show that whoever was here ran off in a hurry. He may have released the brake on the truck, then jumped out and run away."

"Yes," said Nancy. "And that means the attack *was* deliberate."

Mr. Drew did not reply. He continued walking up the hill, lost in thought. Nancy followed and they climbed into the car. They drove home in silence, each puzzling over the strange incident of the runaway truck. Upon reaching the house, they were greeted by a loud exclamation of astonishment.

"My goodness!" Hannah Gruen cried out. "Whatever in the world happened to you?"

They explained hastily, then hurried upstairs

to bathe and change into dry clothes. By the time
they reached the first floor again, Hannah had
placed sherbet glasses filled with orange and grape-
fruit slices on the table. All during the delicious
dinner of spring lamb, rice and mushrooms, fresh
peas and chocolate angel cake with vanilla ice
cream, the conversation revolved around the railroad bridge mystery and then the haunted Twin
Elms mansion.

"I knew things wouldn't be quiet around here
for long," Hannah Gruen remarked with a smile.
"Tomorrow you'll both be off on big adventures.
I certainly wish you both success."

"Thank you, Hannah," said Nancy. She
laughed. "I'd better get a good night's sleep.
From now on I may be kept awake by ghosts and
strange noises."

"I'm a little uneasy about your going to Twin
Elms," the housekeeper told her. "Please promise me that you'll be careful."

"Of course," Nancy replied. Turning to her
father, she said, "Pretend I've said the same thing
to you about being careful."

The lawyer chuckled and pounded his chest.
"You know me. I can be pretty tough when the
need arises."

Early the next morning Nancy drove her father
to the airport in her blue convertible. Just before
she kissed him good-by at the turnstile, he said, "I
expect to return on Wednesday, Nancy. Suppose

I stop off at Cliffwood and see how you're making out?"

"Wonderful, Dad! I'll be looking for you."

As soon as her father left, Nancy drove directly to Helen Corning's home. The pretty, brunette girl came from the front door of the white cottage, swinging a suitcase. She tossed it into the rear of Nancy's convertible and climbed in.

"I ought to be scared," said Helen. "Goodness only knows what's ahead of us. But right now I'm so happy nothing could upset me."

"What happened?" Nancy asked as she started the car. "Did you inherit a million?"

"Something better than that," Helen replied. "Nancy, I want to tell you a big, big secret. I'm going to be married!"

Nancy slowed the car and pulled to the side of the street. Leaning over to hug her friend, she said, "Why, Helen, how wonderful! Who is he? And tell me all about it. This is rather sudden, isn't it?"

"Yes, it is," Helen confessed. "His name is Jim Archer and he's simply out of this world. I'm a pretty lucky girl. I met him a couple of months ago when he was home on a short vacation. He works for the Tristam Oil Company and has spent two years abroad. Jim will be away a while longer, and then be given a position here in the States."

As Nancy started the car up once more, her eyes

twinkled. "Helen Corning, have you been engaged for two months and didn't tell me?"

Helen shook her head. "Jim and I have been corresponding ever since he left. Last night he telephoned from overseas and asked me to marry him." Helen giggled. "I said yes in a big hurry. Then he asked to speak to Dad. My father gave his consent but insisted that our engagement not be announced until Jim's return to this country."

The two girls discussed all sorts of delightful plans for Helen's wedding and before they knew it they had reached the town of Cliffwood.

"My great-grandmother's estate is about two miles out of town," Helen said. "Go down Main Street and turn right at the fork."

Ten minutes later she pointed out Twin Elms. From the road one could see little of the house. A high stone wall ran along the front of the estate and beyond it were many tall trees. Nancy turned into the driveway which twisted and wound among elms, oaks, and maples.

Presently the old Colonial home came into view. Helen said it had been built in 1785 and had been given its name because of the two elm trees which stood at opposite ends of the long building. They had grown to be giants and their foliage was beautiful. The mansion was of red brick and nearly all the walls were covered with ivy. There was a ten-foot porch with tall white pillars at the huge front door.

"It's charming!" Nancy commented as she pulled up to the porch.

"Wait until you see the grounds," said Helen. "There are several old, old buildings. An icehouse, a smokehouse, a kitchen, and servants' cottages."

"The mansion certainly doesn't look spooky from the outside," Nancy commented.

At that moment the great door opened and Aunt Rosemary came outside. "Hello, girls," she greeted them. "I'm so glad to see you."

Nancy felt the warmness of the welcome but thought that it was tinged with worry. She wondered if another "ghost" incident had taken place at the mansion.

The girls took their suitcases from the car and followed Mrs. Hayes inside. Although the furnishings looked rather worn, they were still very beautiful. The high-ceilinged rooms opened off a center hall and in a quick glance Nancy saw lovely damask draperies, satin-covered sofas and chairs, and on the walls, family portraits in large gilt frames of scrollwork design.

Aunt Rosemary went to the foot of the shabbily carpeted stairway, took hold of the handsome mahogany balustrade, and called, "Mother, the girls are here!"

In a moment a slender, frail-looking woman with snow-white hair started to descend the steps. Her face, though older in appearance than Rosemary's, had the same gentle smile. As Miss Flora reached the foot of the stairs, she held out her hands to both girls.

At once Helen said, "I'd like to present Nancy Drew, Miss Flora."

"I'm so glad you could come, my dear," the elderly woman said. "I know that you're going to solve this mystery which has been bothering Rosemary and me. I'm sorry not to be able to entertain you more auspiciously, but a haunted house hardly lends itself to gaiety."

The dainty, yet stately, Miss Flora swept toward a room which she referred to as the parlor. It was opposite the library. She sat down in a high-backed chair and asked everyone else to be seated.

"Mother," said Aunt Rosemary, "we don't have to be so formal with Nancy and Helen. I'm sure they'll understand that we've just been badly frightened." She turned toward the girls. "Something happened a little while ago that has made us very jittery."

"Yes," Miss Flora said. "A pearl necklace of mine was stolen!"

"You don't mean the lovely one that has been in the family so many years!" Helen cried out.

The two women nodded. Then Miss Flora said, "Oh, I probably was very foolish. It's my own fault. While I was in my room, I took the necklace from the hiding place where I usually keep it. The catch had not worked well the last time I wore the pearls and I wanted to examine it. While I was doing this, Rosemary called to me to come downstairs. The gardener was here and wanted to talk about some work. I put the necklace in my dresser drawer. When I returned ten minutes later the necklace wasn't there!"

"How dreadful!" said Nancy sympathetically. "Had anybody come into the house during that time?"

"Not to our knowledge," Aunt Rosemary replied. "Ever since we've had this ghost visiting us we've kept every door and window on the first floor locked all the time."

Nancy asked if the two women had gone out into the garden to speak to their helper. "Mother did," said Mrs. Hayes. "But I was in the kitchen the entire time. If anyone came in the back door, I certainly would have seen the person."

"Is there a back stairway to the second floor?" Nancy asked.

"Yes," Miss Flora answered. "But there are doors at both top and bottom and we keep them locked. No one could have gone up that way."

"Then anyone who came into the house had to go up by way of the front stairs?"

"Yes." Aunt Rosemary smiled a little. "But if anyone had, I would have noticed. You probably heard how those stairs creak when Mother came down. This can be avoided if you hug the wall, but practically no one knows that."

"May I go upstairs and look around?" Nancy questioned.

"Of course, dear. And I'll show you and Helen to your room," Aunt Rosemary said.

The girls picked up their suitcases and followed the two women up the stairs. Nancy and Helen were given a large, quaint room at the front of the old house over the library. They quickly deposited their luggage, then Miss Flora led the way across the hall to her room, which was directly above the parlor. It was large and very attractive with its canopied mahogany bed and an old-fashioned candlewick spread. The dresser, dressing table, and chairs also were mahogany. Long chintz draperies hung at the windows.

An eerie feeling began to take possession of Nancy. She could almost feel the presence of a ghostly burglar on the premises. Though she tried to shake off the mood, it persisted. Finally she told herself that it was possible the thief was still around. If so, he must be hiding.

Against one wall stood a large walnut wardrobe. Helen saw Nancy gazing at it intently. She went over and whispered, "Do you think there might be someone inside?"

"Who knows?" Nancy replied in a low voice. "Let's find out!"

She walked across the room, and taking hold of the two knobs on the double doors, opened them wide.

CHAPTER IV

Strange Music

THE ANXIOUS group stared inside the wardrobe.
No one stood there. Dresses, suits, and coats hung
in an orderly row.

Nancy took a step forward and began separating
them. Someone, she thought, might be hiding behind the clothes. The others in the room held
their breaths as she made a thorough search.

"No one here!" she finally announced, and a
sigh of relief escaped the lips of Miss Flora and
Aunt Rosemary.

The young sleuth said she would like to make a
thorough inspection of all possible hiding places on
the second floor. With Helen helping her, they
went from room to room, opening wardrobe doors
and looking under beds. They did not find the
thief.

Nancy suggested that Miss Flora and Aunt Rosemary report the theft to the police, but the older woman shook her head. Mrs. Hayes, although she agreed this might be wise, added softly, "Mother just *might* be mistaken. She's a little forgetful at times about where she puts things."

With this possibility in mind, she and the girls looked in every drawer in the room, under the mattress and pillows, and even in the pockets of Miss Flora's clothes. The pearl necklace was not found. Nancy suggested that she and Helen try to find out how the thief had made his entrance.

Helen led the way outdoors. At once Nancy began to look for footprints. No tracks were visible on the front or back porches, or on any of the walks, which were made of finely crushed stone.

"We'll look in the soft earth beneath the windows," Nancy said. "Maybe the thief climbed in."

"But Aunt Rosemary said all the windows on the first floor are kept locked," Helen objected.

"No doubt," Nancy said. "But I think we should look for footprints just the same."

The girls went from window to window, but there were no footprints beneath any. Finally Nancy stopped and looked thoughtfully at the ivy on the walls.

"Do you think the thief climbed up to the second floor that way?" Helen asked her. "But there'd still be footprints on the ground."

Nancy said that the thief could have carried a plank with him, laid it down, and stepped from the walk to the wall of the house. "Then he could have climbed up the ivy and down again, and gotten back to the walk without leaving any footprints."

Once more Nancy went around the entire house, examining every bit of ivy which wound up from the foundation. Finally she said, "No, the thief didn't get into the house this way."

"Well, he certainly didn't fly in," said Helen. "So *how* did he enter?"

Nancy laughed. "If I could tell you that I'd have the mystery half solved."

She said that she would like to look around the grounds of Twin Elms. "It may give us a clue as to how the thief got into the house."

As they strolled along, Nancy kept a sharp lookout but saw nothing suspicious. At last they came to a half-crumbled brick walk laid out in an interesting crisscross pattern.

"Where does this walk lead?" Nancy asked.

"Well, I guess originally it went over to Riverview Manor, the next property," Helen replied. "I'll show you that mansion later. The first owner was a brother of the man who built this place."

Helen went on to say that Riverview Manor was a duplicate of Twin Elms mansion. The two brothers had been inseparable companions, but their sons who later lived there had had a violent quarrel and had become lifelong enemies.

"Riverview Manor has been sold several times during the years but has been vacant for a long time."

"You mean no one lives there now?" Nancy asked. As Helen nodded, she added with a laugh, "Then maybe that's the ghost's home!"

"In that case he really must be a ghost," said Helen lightly. "There's not a piece of furniture in the house."

The two girls returned to the Twin Elms mansion and reported their lack of success in picking up a clue to the intruder. Nancy, recalling that many Colonial houses had secret entrances and passageways, asked Miss Flora, "Do you know of any secret entrance to your home that the thief could use?"

She said no, and explained that her husband had been a rather reticent person and had passed away when Rosemary was only a baby. "It's just possible he knew of a secret entrance, but did not want to worry me by telling me about it," Mrs. Turnbull said.

Aunt Rosemary, sensing that her mother was becoming alarmed by the questions, suggested that they all have lunch. The two girls went with her to the kitchen and helped prepare a tasty meal of chicken salad, biscuits, and fruit gelatin.

During the meal the conversation covered several subjects, but always came back to the topic of the mystery. They had just finished eating when suddenly Nancy sat straight up in her chair.

"What's the matter?" Helen asked her.

Nancy was staring out the dining-room door toward the stairway in the hall. Then she turned to Miss Flora. "Did you leave a radio on in your bedroom?"

"Why, no."

"Did you, Aunt Rosemary?"

"No. Neither Mother nor I turned our radios on this morning. Why do—" She stopped speaking, for now all of them could distinctly hear music coming from the second floor.

Helen and Nancy were out of their chairs instantly. They dashed into the hall and up the stairway. The music was coming from Miss Flora's room, and when the girls rushed in, they knew indeed that it was from her radio.

Nancy went over to examine the set. It was an old one and did not have a clock attachment with an automatic control.

"Someone came into this room and turned on the radio!" she stated.

A look of alarm came over Helen's face, but she tried to shake off her nervousness and asked, "Nancy, do you think the radio could have been turned on by remote control? I've heard of such things."

Nancy said she doubted this. "I'm afraid, Helen, that the thief has been in the house all the time. He and the ghost are one and the same per-

son. Oh, I wish we had looked before in the cellar
and the attic. Maybe it's not too late. Come on!"

Helen, instead of moving from the room, stared
at the fireplace. "Nancy," she said, "do you suppose someone is hiding up there?"

Without hesitation she crossed the room, got
down on her knees, and tried to look up the chimney. The damper was closed. Reaching her arm
up, Helen pulled the handle to open it.

The next moment she cried out, "Ugh!"

"Oh, Helen, you poor thing!" Nancy exclaimed,
running to her friend's side.

A shower of soot had come down, covering
Helen's hair, face, shoulders, and arms.

"Get me a towel, will you, Nancy?" she requested.

Nancy dashed to the bathroom and grabbed two
large towels. She wrapped them around her
friend, then went with Helen to help her with
a shampoo and general cleanup job. Finally
Nancy brought her another sports dress.

"I guess my idea about chimneys wasn't so
good," Helen stated ruefully. "And we're probably too late to catch the thief."

Nevertheless, she and Nancy climbed the stairs
to the attic and looked behind trunks and boxes to
see if anyone were hiding. Next, the girls went
to the cellar and inspected the various rooms there.
Still there was no sign of the thief who had entered Twin Elms.

After Miss Flora had heard the whole story, she gave a nervous sigh. "It's the ghost—there's no other explanation."

"But why," Aunt Rosemary asked, "has a ghost suddenly started performing here? This house has been occupied since 1785 and no ghost was ever reported haunting the place."

"Well, apparently robbery is the motive," Nancy replied. "But why the thief bothers to frighten you is something I haven't figured out yet."

"The main thing," Helen spoke up, "is to catch him!"

"Oh, if we only could!" Miss Flora said, her voice a bit shaky.

The girls were about to pick up the luncheon dishes from the table, to carry them to the kitchen, when the front door knocker sounded loudly.

"Oh, dear," said Miss Flora, "who can that be? Maybe it's the thief and he's come to harm us!"

Aunt Rosemary put an arm around her mother's shoulders. "Please don't worry," she begged. "I think our caller is probably the man who wants to buy Twin Elms." She turned to Nancy and Helen. "But Mother doesn't want to sell for the low price that he is offering."

Nancy said she would go to the door. She set the dishes down and walked out to the hall. Reaching the great door, she flung it open.

Nathan Gomber stood there!

CHAPTER V

A Puzzling Interview

FOR SEVERAL seconds Nathan Gomber stared at Nancy in disbelief. "You!" he cried out finally.

"You didn't expect to find me here, did you?" she asked coolly.

"I certainly didn't. I thought you'd taken my advice and stayed with your father. Young people today are so hardhearted!" Gomber wagged his head in disgust.

Nancy ignored Gomber's remarks. Shrugging, the man pushed his way into the hall. "I know this. If anything happens to your father, you'll never forgive yourself. But you can't blame Nathan Gomber! I warned you!"

Still Nancy made no reply. She kept looking at him steadily, trying to figure out what was really in his mind. She was convinced it was not solicitude for her father.

Nathan Gomber changed the subject abruptly.

"I'd like to see Mrs. Turnbull and Mrs. Hayes," he said. "Go call them."

Nancy was annoyed by Gomber's crudeness, but she turned around and went down the hall to the dining room.

"We heard every word," Miss Flora said in a whisper. "I shan't see Mr. Gomber. I don't want to sell this house."

Nancy was amazed to hear this. "You mean he's the person who wants to buy it?"

"Yes."

Instantly Nancy was on the alert. Because of the nature of the railroad deal in which Nathan Gomber was involved, she was distrustful of his motives in wanting to buy Twin Elms. It flashed through her mind that perhaps he was trying to buy it at a very low price and planned to sell it off in building lots at a huge profit.

"Suppose I go tell him you don't want to sell," Nancy suggested in a low voice.

But her caution was futile. Hearing footsteps behind her, she turned to see Gomber standing in the doorway.

"Howdy, everybody!" he said.

Miss Flora, Aunt Rosemary, and Helen showed annoyance. It was plain that all of them thought the man completely lacking in good manners.

Aunt Rosemary's jaw was set in a grim line, but she said politely, "Helen, this is Mr. Gomber. Mr. Gomber, my niece, Miss Corning."

"Pleased to meet you," said their caller, extending a hand to shake Helen's.

"Nancy, I guess you've met Mr. Gomber," Aunt Rosemary went on.

"Oh, sure!" Nathan Gomber said with a somewhat raucous laugh. "Nancy and me, we've met!"

"Only once," Nancy said pointedly.

Ignoring her rebuff, he went on, "Nancy Drew is a very strange young lady. Her father's in great danger and I tried to warn her to stick close to him. Instead of that, she's out here visiting you folks."

"Her father's in danger?" Miss Flora said worriedly.

"Dad says he's not," Nancy replied. "And besides, I'm sure my father would know how to take care of any enemies." She looked straight at Nathan Gomber, as if to let him know that the Drews were not easily frightened.

"Well," the caller said, "let's get down to business." He pulled an envelope full of papers from his pocket. "Everything's here—all ready for you to sign, Mrs. Turnbull."

"I don't wish to sell at such a low figure," Miss Flora told him firmly. "In fact, I don't know that I want to sell at all."

Nathan Gomber tossed his head. "You'll sell all right," he prophesied. "I've been talking to some of the folks downtown. Everybody knows this old place is haunted and nobody would give you five cents for it—that is, nobody but me."

As he waited for his words to sink in, Nancy spoke up, "If the house is haunted, why do you want it?"

"Well," Gomber answered, "I guess I'm a gambler at heart. I'd be willing to put some money into this place, even if there is a ghost parading around." He laughed loudly, then went on, "I declare it might be a real pleasure to meet a ghost and get the better of it!"

Nancy thought with disgust, "Nathan Gomber, you're about the most conceited, obnoxious person I've met in a long time."

Suddenly the expression of cunning on the man's face changed completely. An almost wistful look came into his eyes. He sat down on one of the dining-room chairs and rested his chin in his hand.

"I guess you think I'm just a hardheaded business man with no feelings," he said. "The truth is I'm a real softy. I'll tell you why I want this old house so bad. I've always dreamed of owning a Colonial mansion, and having a kinship with early America. You see, my family were poor folks in Europe. Now that I've made a little money, I'd like to have a home like this to roam around in and enjoy its traditions."

Miss Flora seemed to be touched by Gomber's story. "I had no idea you wanted the place so much," she said kindly. "Maybe I ought to give it up. It's really too big for us."

As Aunt Rosemary saw her mother weakening, she said quickly, "You don't have to sell this house, Mother. You know you love it. So far as the ghost is concerned, I'm sure that mystery is going to be cleared up. Then you'd be sorry you had parted with Twin Elms. Please don't say yes!"

As Gomber gave Mrs. Hayes a dark look, Nancy asked him, "Why don't you buy Riverview Manor? It's a duplicate of this place and is for sale. You probably could purchase it at a lower price than you could this one."

"I've seen that place," the man returned. "It's in a bad state. It would cost me a mint of money to fix it up. No sir. I want this place and I'm going to have it!"

This bold remark was too much for Aunt Rosemary. Her eyes blazing, she said, "Mr. Gomber, this interview is at an end. Good-by!"

To Nancy's delight and somewhat to her amusement, Nathan Gomber obeyed the "order" to leave. He seemed to be almost meek as he walked through the hall and let himself out the front door.

"Of all the nerve!" Helen burst out.

"Perhaps we shouldn't be too hard on the man," Miss Flora said timidly. "His story is a pathetic one and I can see how he might want to pretend he had an old American family background."

"I'd like to bet a cooky Mr. Gomber didn't mean one word of what he was saying," Helen remarked.

"Oh dear, I'm so confused," said Miss Flora, her voice trembling. "Let's all sit down in the parlor and talk about it a little more."

The two girls stepped back as Miss Flora, then Aunt Rosemary, left the dining room. They followed to the parlor and sat down together on the recessed couch by the fireplace. Nancy, on a sudden hunch, ran to a front window to see which direction Gomber had taken. To her surprise he was walking down the winding driveway.

"That's strange. Evidently he didn't drive," Nancy told herself. "It's quite a walk into town to get a train or bus to River Heights."

As Nancy mulled over this idea, trying to figure out the answer, she became conscious of creaking sounds. Helen suddenly gave a shriek. Nancy turned quickly.

"Look!" Helen cried, pointing toward the ceiling, and everyone stared upward.

The crystal chandelier had suddenly started swaying from side to side!

"The ghost again!" Miss Flora cried out. She looked as if she were about to faint.

Nancy's eyes quickly swept the room. Nothing else in it was moving, so vibration was not causing the chandelier to sway. As it swung back and forth, a sudden thought came to the young sleuth. Maybe someone in Miss Flora's room above was causing the shaking.

The chandelier suddenly started to sway

"I'm going upstairs to investigate," Nancy told the others.

Racing noiselessly on tiptoe out of the room and through the hall, she began climbing the stairs, hugging the wall so the steps would not creak. As she neared the top, Nancy was sure she heard a door close. Hurrying along the hall, she burst into Miss Flora's bedroom. No one was in sight!

"Maybe this time the ghost couldn't get away and is in that wardrobe!" Nancy thought.

Helen and her relatives had come up the stairs behind Nancy. They reached the bedroom just as she flung open the wardrobe doors. But for the second time she found no one hiding there.

Nancy bit her lip in vexation. The ghost was clever indeed. Where *had* he gone? She had given him no time to go down the hall or run into another room. Yet there was no denying the fact that he had been in Miss Flora's room!

"Tell us why you came up," Helen begged her. Nancy told her theory, but suddenly she realized that maybe she was letting her imagination run wild. It was possible, she admitted to the others, that no one had caused the chandelier to shake.

"There's only one way to find out," she said. "I'll make a test."

Nancy asked Helen to go back to the first floor and watch the chandelier. She would try to make it sway by rocking from side to side on the floor above it.

"If this works, then I'm sure we've picked up a clue to the ghost," she said hopefully.

Helen readily agreed and left the room. When Nancy thought her friend had had time to reach the parlor below, she began to rock hard from side to side on the spot above the chandelier.

She had barely started the test when from the first floor Helen Corning gave a piercing scream!

CHAPTER VI

The Gorilla Face

"SOMETHING has happened to Helen!" Aunt Rosemary cried out fearfully.

Nancy was already racing through the second-floor hallway. Reaching the stairs, she leaped down them two steps at a time. Helen Corning had collapsed in a wing chair in the parlor, her hands over her face.

"Helen! What happened?" Nancy asked, reaching her friend's side.

"Out there! Looking in that window!" Helen pointed to the front window of the parlor next to the hall. "The most horrible face I ever saw!"

"Was it a man's face?" Nancy questioned.

"Oh, I don't know. It looked just like a gorilla!" Helen closed her eyes as if to shut out the memory of the sight.

Nancy did not wait to hear any more. In another second she was at the front door and had yanked it open. Stepping outside, she looked all around. She could see no animal near the house, nor any sign under the window that one had stood there.

Puzzled, the young sleuth hurried down the steps and began a search of the grounds. By this time Helen had collected her wits and come outside. She joined Nancy and together they looked in every outbuilding and behind every clump of bushes on the grounds of Twin Elms. They did not find one footprint or any other evidence to prove that a gorilla or other creature had been on the grounds of the estate.

"I saw it! I know I saw it!" Helen insisted.

"I don't doubt you," Nancy replied.

"Then what explanation is there?" Helen demanded. "You know I never did believe in spooks. But if we have many more of these weird happenings around here, I declare I'm going to start believing in ghosts."

Nancy laughed. "Don't worry, Helen," she said. "There'll be a logical explanation for the face at the window."

The girls walked back to the front door of the mansion. Miss Flora and Aunt Rosemary stood there and immediately insisted upon knowing what had happened. As Helen told them, Nancy once more surveyed the outside of the window at which Helen had seen the terrifying face.

"I have a theory," she spoke up. "Our ghost simply leaned across from the end of the porch and held a mask in front of the window." Nancy stretched her arm out to demonstrate how this was possible.

"So that's why he didn't leave any footprints under the window," Helen said. "But he certainly got away from here fast." She suddenly laughed. "He must be on some ghosts' track team."

Her humor, Nancy was glad to see, relieved the tense situation. She had noticed Miss Flora leaning wearily on her daughter's arm.

"You'd better lie down and rest, Mother," Mrs. Hayes advised.

"I guess I will," Aunt Flora agreed.

It was suggested that the elderly woman use Aunt Rosemary's room, while the others continued the experiment with the chandelier.

Helen and Aunt Rosemary went into the parlor and waited as Nancy ascended the front stairway and went to Miss Flora's bedroom. Once more she began to rock from side to side. Downstairs, Aunt Rosemary and her niece were gazing intently at the ceiling.

"Look!" Helen exclaimed, pointing to the crystal chandelier. "It's moving!" In a moment it swung to the left, then back to the right.

"Nancy has proved that the ghost was up in my mother's room!" Aunt Rosemary said excitedly.

After a few minutes the rocking motion of the chandelier slackened and finally stopped. Nancy came hurrying down the steps.

"Did it work?" she called.

"Yes, it did," Aunt Rosemary replied. "Oh, Nancy, we must have two ghosts!"

"Why do you say that?" Helen asked.

"One rocking the chandelier, the other holding the horrible face up to the window. No one could have gone from Miss Flora's room to the front porch in such a short time. Oh, this complicates everything!"

"It certainly does," Nancy agreed. "The question is, are the two ghosts in cahoots? Or, it's just possible, there is only one. He could have disappeared from Miss Flora's room without our seeing him and somehow hurried to the first floor and let himself out the front door while we were upstairs. I'm convinced there is at least one secret entrance into this house, and maybe more. I think our next step should be to try to find it—or them."

"We'd better wash the luncheon dishes first," Aunt Rosemary suggested.

As she and the girls worked, they discussed the mystery, and Mrs. Hayes revealed that she had talked to her mother about leaving the house, whether or not she sold it.

"I thought we might at least go away for a little vacation, but Mother refuses to leave. She says she intends to remain right here until this ghost business is settled."

Helen smiled. "Nancy, my great-grandmother

is a wonderful woman. She has taught me a lot about courage and perseverance. I hope if I ever reach her age, I'll have half as much."

"Yes, she's an example to all of us," Aunt Rosemary concurred.

Nancy nodded. "I agree. I haven't known your mother long, Aunt Rosemary, but I think she is one of the dearest persons I've ever met."

"If Miss Flora won't leave," said Helen, "I guess that means we all stay."

"That's settled," said Nancy with a smile.

After the dishes were put away, the girls were ready to begin their search for a secret entrance into the mansion.

"Let's start with Miss Flora's room," Helen suggested.

"That's a logical place," Nancy replied, and took the lead up the stairway.

Every inch of the wall, which was paneled in maple halfway to the ceiling, was tapped. No hollow sound came from any section of it to indicate an open space behind. The bureau, dressing table, and bed were pulled away from the walls and Nancy carefully inspected every inch of the paneling for cracks or wide seams to indicate a concealed door.

"Nothing yet," she announced, and then decided to inspect the sides of the fireplace.

The paneled sides and brick front revealed nothing. Next, Nancy looked at the sides and rear of the stone interior. She could see nothing unusual, and the blackened stones did not look as if they had ever been disturbed.

She closed the damper which Helen had left open, and then suggested that the searchers transfer to another room on the second floor. But no trace of any secret entrance to the mansion could be found.

"I think we've had enough investigation for one day," Aunt Rosemary remarked.

Nancy was about to say that she was not tired and would like to continue. But she realized that Mrs. Hayes had made this suggestion because her mother was once more showing signs of fatigue and strain.

Helen, who also realized the situation, said, "Let's have an early supper. I'm starved!"

"I am, too," Nancy replied, laughing gaily.

The mood was contagious and soon Miss Flora seemed to have forgotten about her mansion being haunted. She sat in the kitchen while Aunt Rosemary and the girls cooked the meal.

"*Um,* steak and French fried potatoes, fresh peas, and yummy floating island for dessert," said Helen. "I can hardly wait."

"Fruit cup first," Aunt Rosemary announced, taking a bowl of fruit from the refrigerator.

Soon the group was seated at the table. Tactfully steering the conversation away from the mystery, Nancy asked Miss Flora to tell the group about parties and dances which had been held in the mansion long ago.

The elderly woman smiled in recollection. "I remember one story my husband told me of something that happened when he was a little boy," Miss Flora began. "His parents were holding a masquerade and he was supposed to be in bed fast asleep. His nurse had gone downstairs to talk to some of the servants. The music awakened my husband and he decided it would be great fun to join the guests.

" 'I'll put on a costume myself,' he said to himself. He knew there were some packed in a trunk in the attic." Miss Flora paused. "By the way, girls, I think that sometime while you are here you ought to see them. They're beautiful.

"Well, Everett went to the attic, opened the trunk, and searched until he found a soldier's outfit. It was very fancy—red coat and white trousers. He had quite a struggle getting it on and had to turn the coat sleeves way up. The knee britches came to his ankles, and the hat was so large it came down over his ears."

By this time Miss Flora's audience was laughing and Aunt Rosemary remarked, "My father really must have looked funny. Please go on, Mother."

"Little Everett came down the stairs and mingled with the masqueraders at the dance. For a while he wasn't noticed, then suddenly his mother discovered the queer-looking figure."

"And," Aunt Rosemary interrupted, "quickly put him back to bed, I'm sure."

Miss Flora laughed. "That's where you're wrong. The guests thought the whole thing was such fun that they insisted Everett stay. Some of the women danced with him—he went to dancing school and was an excellent dancer. Then they gave him some strawberries and cream and cake."

Helen remarked, "And then put him to bed."

Again Miss Flora laughed. "The poor little fellow never knew that he had fallen asleep while he was eating, and his father had to carry him upstairs. He was put into his little four-poster, costume and all. Of course his nurse was horrified, and I'm afraid that during the rest of the night the poor woman thought she would lose her position. But she didn't. In fact, she stayed with the family until all the children were grown up."

"Oh, that's a wonderful story!" said Nancy.

She was about to urge Miss Flora to tell another story when the telephone rang. Aunt Rosemary answered it, and then called to Nancy, "It's for you."

Nancy hurried to the hall, grabbed up the phone, and said, "Hello." A moment later she cried out, "Dad! How wonderful to hear from you!"

Mr. Drew said that he had not found Willie Wharton and certain clues seemed to indicate that he was not in Chicago, but in some other city.

"I have a few other matters to take care of that will keep me here until tomorrow night. How are you getting along?"

"I haven't solved the mystery yet," his daughter reported. "We've had some more strange happenings. I'll certainly be glad to see you here at Cliffwood. I know you can help me."

"All right, I'll come. But don't try to meet me. The time is too uncertain, and as a matter of fact, I may find that I'll have to stay here in Chicago."

Mr. Drew said he would come out to the mansion by taxi. Briefly Nancy related her experiences at Twin Elms, and after a little more conversation, hung up. When she rejoined the others at the table, she told them about Mr. Drew's promised visit.

"Oh, I'll be so happy to meet your father," said Miss Flora. "We may need legal advice in this mystery."

There was a pause after this remark, with everyone silent for a few moments. Suddenly each one in the group looked at the others, startled. From somewhere upstairs came the plaintive strains of violin music. Had the radio been turned on again by the ghost?

Nancy dashed from the table to find out.

CHAPTER VII

Frightening Eyes

WITHIN five seconds Nancy had reached the second floor. The violin playing suddenly ceased.

She raced into Miss Flora's room, from which the sounds had seemed to come. The radio was not on. Quickly Nancy felt the instrument to see if it were even slightly warm to prove it had been in use.

"The music wasn't being played on this," she told herself, finding the radio cool.

As Nancy dashed from the room, she almost ran into Helen. "What did you find out?" her friend asked breathlessly.

"Nothing so far," Nancy replied, as she raced into Aunt Rosemary's bedroom to check the bedside radio in there.

This instrument, too, felt cool to the touch.

She and Helen stood in the center of the room, puzzled frowns creasing their foreheads. "There *was* music, wasn't there?" Helen questioned.

"I distinctly heard it," Nancy replied. "But *where* is the person who played the violin? Or put a disk on a record player, or turned on a hidden radio? Helen, I'm positive an intruder comes into this mansion by some secret entrance and tries to frighten us all."

"And succeeds," Helen answered. "It's positively eerie."

"And dangerous," Nancy thought.

"Let's continue our search right after breakfast tomorrow," Helen proposed.

"We will," Nancy responded. "But in the meantime I believe Miss Flora and Aunt Rosemary, to say nothing of ourselves, need some police protection."

"I think you're right," Helen agreed. "Let's go downstairs and suggest it to the others."

The girls returned to the first floor and Nancy told Mrs. Hayes and her mother of the failure to find the cause of the violin playing, and what she had in mind.

"Oh dear, the police will only laugh at us," Miss Flora objected.

"Mother dear," said her daughter, "the captain and his men didn't believe us before because they thought we were imagining things. But Nancy and Helen heard music at two different times and they saw the chandelier rock. I'm sure that Captain Rossland will believe Nancy and send a guard out here."

Nancy smiled at Miss Flora. "I shan't ask the captain to believe in a ghost or even hunt for one. I think all we should request at the moment is that he have a man patrol the grounds here at night. I'm sure that we're perfectly safe while we're all awake, but I must admit I'd feel a little uneasy about going to bed wondering what that ghost may do next."

Mrs. Turnbull finally agreed to the plan and Nancy went to the telephone. Captain Rossland readily agreed to send a man out a little later.

"He'll return each night as long as you need him," the officer stated. "And I'll tell him not to ring the bell to tell you when he comes. If there is anyone who breaks into the mansion by a secret entrance, it would be much better if he does not know a guard is on duty."

"I understand," said Nancy.

When Miss Flora, her daughter, and the two girls went to bed, they were confident they would have a restful night. Nancy felt that if there was no disturbance, then it would indicate that the ghost's means of entry into Twin Elms was directly from the outside. "In which case," she thought, "it will mean he saw the guard and didn't dare come inside the house."

The young sleuth's desire for a good night's sleep was rudely thwarted as she awakened about midnight with a start. Nancy was sure she had heard a noise nearby. But now the house was quiet. Nancy listened intently, then finally got out of bed.

"Perhaps the noise I heard came from outdoors," she told herself.

Tiptoeing to a window, so that she would not awaken Helen, Nancy peered out at the moonlit grounds. Shadows made by tree branches, which swayed in a gentle breeze, moved back and forth across the lawn. The scent from a rose garden in full bloom was wafted to Nancy.

"What a heavenly night!" she thought.

Suddenly Nancy gave a start. A furtive figure had darted from behind a tree toward a clump of bushes. Was he the guard or the ghost? she wondered. As Nancy watched intently to see if she could detect any further movements of the mysterious figure, she heard padding footsteps in the hall. In a moment there was a loud knock on her door.

"Nancy! Wake up! Nancy! Come quick!"

The voice was Miss Flora's, and she sounded extremely frightened. Nancy sped across the room, unlocked her door, and opened it wide. By this time Helen was awake and out of bed.

"What happened?" she asked sleepily.

Aunt Rosemary had come into the hall also. Her mother did not say a word; just started back toward her own bedroom. The others followed, wondering what they would find. Moonlight brightened part of the room, but the area near the hall was dark.

"There! Up there!" Miss Flora pointed to a corner of the room near the hall.

Two burning eyes looked down on the watchers!

Instantly Nancy snapped on the wall light and the group gazed upward at a large brown owl perched on the old-fashioned, ornamental picture molding.

"Oh!" Aunt Rosemary cried out. "How did that bird ever get in here?"

The others did not answer at once. Then Nancy, not wishing to frighten Miss Flora, remarked as casually as she could, "It probably came down the chimney."

"But—" Helen started to say.

Nancy gave her friend a warning wink and Helen did not finish the sentence. Nancy was sure she was going to say that the damper had been closed and the bird could not possibly have flown into the room from the chimney. Turning to Miss Flora, Nancy asked whether or not her bedroom door had been locked.

"Oh, yes," the elderly woman insisted. "I wouldn't leave it unlocked for anything."

Nancy did not comment. Knowing that Miss Flora was a bit forgetful, she thought it quite possible that the door had not been locked. An intruder had entered, let the owl fly to the picture molding, then made just enough noise to awaken the sleeping woman.

To satisfy her own memory about the damper, Nancy went over to the fireplace and looked inside. The damper was closed.

"But if the door to the hall was locked," she reasoned, "then the ghost has some other way of getting into this room. And he escaped the detection of the guard."

"I don't want that owl in here all night," Miss Flora broke into Nancy's reverie. "We'll have to get it out."

"That's not going to be easy," Aunt Rosemary spoke up. "Owls have very sharp claws and beaks and they use them viciously on anybody who tries to disturb them. Mother, you come and sleep in my room the rest of the night. We'll chase the owl out in the morning."

Nancy urged Miss Flora to go with her daughter. "I'll stay here and try getting Mr. Owl out of the house. Have you a pair of old heavy gloves?"

"I have some in my room," Aunt Rosemary replied. "They're thick leather. I use them for gardening."

She brought them to Nancy, who put the gloves on at once. Then she suggested that Aunt Rosemary and her mother leave. Nancy smiled. "Helen and I will take over Operation Owl."

As the door closed behind the two women, Nancy dragged a chair to the corner of the room beneath the bird. She was counting on the fact that the bright overhead light had dulled the owl's vision and she would be able to grab it without too much trouble.

"Helen, will you open one of the screens, please?" she requested. "And wish me luck!"

"Don't let that thing get loose," Helen warned as she unfastened the screen and held it far out.

Nancy reached up and by stretching was just able to grasp the bird. In a lightning movement she had put her two hands around its body and imprisoned its claws. At once the owl began to bob its head and peck at her arms above the gloves. Wincing with pain, she stepped down from the chair and ran across the room.

The bird squirmed, darting its beak in first one direction, then another. But Nancy managed to hold the owl in such a position that most of the pecking missed its goal. She held the bird out the window, released it, and stepped back. Helen closed the screen and quickly fastened it.

"Oh!" Nancy said, gazing ruefully at her wrists which now showed several bloody digs from the owl's beak. "I'm glad that's over."

"And I am too," said Helen. "Let's lock Miss Flora's door from the outside, so that ghost can't bring in any owls to the rest of us."

Suddenly Helen grabbed Nancy's arm. "I just thought of something," she said. "There's supposed to be a police guard outside. Yet the ghost got in here without being seen."

"Either that, or there's a secret entrance to this

mansion which runs underground, probably to one of the outbuildings on the property."

Nancy now told about the furtive figure she had seen dart from behind a tree. "I must find out right away if he was the ghost or the guard. I'll do a little snooping around. It's possible the guard didn't show up." Nancy smiled. "But if he did, and he's any good, he'll find me!"

"All right," said Helen. "But, Nancy, do be careful. You're really taking awful chances to solve the mystery of Twin Elms."

Nancy laughed softly as she walked back to the girls' bedroom. She dressed quickly, then went downstairs, put the back-door key in her pocket, and let herself out of the house. Stealthily she went down the steps and glided to a spot back of some bushes.

Seeing no one around, she came from behind them and ran across the lawn to a large maple tree. She stood among the shadows for several moments, then darted out toward a building which in Colonial times had been used as the kitchen.

Halfway there, she heard a sound behind her and turned. A man stood in the shadows not ten feet away. Quick as a wink one hand flew to a holster on his hip.

"Halt!" he commanded.

CHAPTER VIII

A Startling Plunge

NANCY halted as directed and stood facing the man. "Who are you?" she asked.

"I'm a police guard, miss," the man replied. "Just call me Patrick. And who are you?"

Quickly Nancy explained and then asked to see his identification. He opened his coat, pulled out a leather case, and showed her his shield proving that he was a plain-clothes man. His name was Tom Patrick.

"Have you seen anyone prowling around the grounds?" Nancy asked him.

"Not a soul, miss. This place has been quieter than a cemetery tonight."

When the young sleuth told him about the furtive figure she had seen from the window, the detective laughed. "I believe you saw me," he said. "I guess I'm not so good at hiding as I thought I was."

Nancy laughed lightly. "Anyway, you soon nabbed me," she told him.

The two chatted for several minutes. Tom Patrick told Nancy that people in Cliffwood regarded Mrs. Turnbull as being a little queer. They said that if she thought her house was haunted, it was all in line with the stories of the odd people who had lived there from time to time during the past hundred years or so.

"Would this rumor make the property difficult to sell?" Nancy questioned the detective.

"It certainly would."

Nancy said she thought the whole thing was a shame. "Mrs. Turnbull is one of the loveliest women I've ever met and there's not a thing the matter with her, except that once in a while she is forgetful."

"You don't think that some of these happenings we've heard about are just pure imagination?" Tom Patrick asked.

"No, I don't."

Nancy now told him about the owl in Miss Flora's bedroom. "The door was locked, every screen was fastened, and the damper in the chimney closed. You tell me how the owl got in there."

Tom Patrick's eyes opened wide. "You say this happened only a little while ago?" he queried. When Nancy nodded, he added, "Of course I can't be everywhere on these grounds at once, but I've been round and round the building. I've

never stopped walking since I arrived. I don't see
how anyone could have gotten inside that mansion without my seeing him."

"I'll tell you my theory," said Nancy. "I believe
there's a secret underground entrance from some
other place on the grounds. It may be in one of
these outbuildings. Anyway, tomorrow morning
I'm going on a search for it."

"Well, I wish you luck," Tom Patrick said.
"And if anything happens during the night,
I'll let you know."

Nancy pointed to a window on the second floor.
"That's my room," she said. "If you don't have a
chance to use the door knocker, just throw a stone
up against the screen to alert me. I'll wake up
instantly, I know."

The guard promised to do this and Nancy went
back into the mansion. She climbed the stairs and
for a second time that night undressed. Helen
had already gone back to sleep, so Nancy crawled
into the big double bed noiselessly.

The two girls awoke the next morning about
the same time and immediately Helen asked for
full details of what Nancy had learned outdoors
the night before. After hearing how her friend
had been stopped by the guard, she shivered.

"You might have been in real danger, Nancy,
not knowing who he was. You *must* be more careful. Suppose that man had been the ghost?"

Nancy laughed but made no reply. The girls

went downstairs and started to prepare breakfast. In a few minutes Aunt Rosemary and her mother joined them.

"Did you find out anything more last night?" Mrs. Hayes asked Nancy.

"Only that a police guard named Tom Patrick is on duty," Nancy answered.

As soon as breakfast was over, the young sleuth announced that she was about to investigate all the outbuildings on the estate.

"I'm going to search for an underground passage leading to the mansion. It's just possible that we hear no hollow sounds when we tap the walls, because of double doors or walls where the entrance is."

Aunt Rosemary looked at Nancy intently. "You are a real detective, Nancy. I see now why Helen wanted us to ask you to find our ghost."

Nancy's eyes twinkled. "I may have some instinct for sleuthing," she said, "but unless I can solve this mystery, it won't do any of us much good."

Turning to Helen, she suggested that they put on the old clothes they had brought with them.

Attired in sport shirts and jeans, the girls left the house. Nancy led the way first to the old icehouse. She rolled back the creaking, sliding door and gazed within. The tall, narrow building was about ten feet square. On one side were a series of sliding doors, one above the other.

"I've heard Miss Flora say," Helen spoke up, "that in days gone by huge blocks of ice were cut from the river when it was frozen over and dragged here on a sledge. The blocks were stored here and taken off from the top down through these various sliding doors."

"That story rather rules out the possibility of any underground passage leading from this building," said Nancy. "I presume there was ice in here most of the year."

The floor was covered with dank sawdust, and although Nancy was sure she would find nothing of interest beneath it, still she decided to take a look. Seeing an old, rusted shovel in one corner, she picked it up and began to dig. There was only dirt beneath the sawdust.

"Well, that clue fizzled out," Helen remarked, as she and Nancy started for the next building.

This had once been used as a smokehouse. It, too, had an earthen floor. In one corner was a small fireplace, where smoldering fires of hickory wood had once burned. The smoke had curled up a narrow chimney to the second floor, which was windowless.

"Rows and rows of huge chunks of pork hung up there on hooks to be smoked," Helen explained, "and days later turned into luscious hams and bacon."

There was no indication of a secret opening and Nancy went outside the small, two-story, peak-roofed structure and walked around. Up one side of the brick building and leading to a door above were the remnants of a ladder. Now only the sidepieces which had held the rungs remained.

"Give me a boost, will you, Helen?" Nancy requested. "I want to take a look inside."

Helen squatted on the ground and Nancy climbed to her shoulders. Then Helen, bracing her hands against the wall, straightened up. Nancy opened the half-rotted wooden door.

"No ghost here!" she announced.

Nancy jumped to the ground and started for the servants' quarters. But a thorough inspection of this brick-and-wood structure failed to reveal a clue to a secret passageway.

There was only one outbuilding left to investigate, which Helen said was the old carriage house. This was built of brick and was fairly large. No carriages stood on its wooden floor, but around the walls hung old harnesses and reins. Nancy paused a moment to examine one of the bridles. It was set with two hand-painted medallions of women's portraits.

Suddenly her reflection was interrupted by a scream. Turning, she was just in time to see Helen plunge through a hole in the floor. In a flash Nancy was across the carriage house and looking down into a gaping hole where the rotted floor had given way.

"Helen!" she cried out in alarm.

"I'm all right," came a voice from below. "Nice and soft down here. Please throw me your flash."

Nancy removed the flashlight from the pocket of her jeans and tossed it down.

"I thought maybe I'd discovered something," Helen said. "But this is just a plain old hole. Give me a hand, will you, so I can climb up?"

Nancy lay flat on the floor and with one arm grabbed a supporting beam that stood in the center of the carriage house. Reaching down with the other arm, she assisted Helen in her ascent.

"We'd better watch our step around here," Nancy said as her friend once more stood beside her.

"You're so right," Helen agreed, brushing dirt off her jeans. Helen's plunge had given Nancy an idea that there might be other openings in the floor and that one of them could be an entrance to a subterranean passage. But though she flashed her light over every inch of the carriage-house floor, she could discover nothing suspicious.

"Let's quit!" Helen suggested. "I'm a mess, and besides, I'm hungry."

"All right," Nancy agreed. "Are you game to search the cellar this afternoon?"

"Oh, sure."

After lunch they started to investigate the store-rooms in the cellar. There was a cool stone room where barrels of apples had once been kept. There was another, formerly filled with bags of whole-wheat flour, barley, buckwheat, and oat-meal.

"And everything was grown on the estate," said Helen.

"Oh, it must have been perfectly wonderful," Nancy said. "I wish we could go back in time and see how life was in those days!"

"Maybe if we could, we'd know how to find that ghost," Helen remarked. Nancy thought so too.

As the girls went from room to room in the cellar, Nancy beamed her flashlight over every inch of wall and floor. At times, the young sleuth's pulse would quicken when she thought she had discovered a trap door or secret opening. But each time she had to admit failure—there was no evidence of either one in the cellar.

"This has been a discouraging day," Nancy remarked, sighing. "But I'm not giving up."

Helen felt sorry for her friend. To cheer Nancy, she said with a laugh, "Storeroom after storeroom but no room to store a ghost!"

Nancy had to laugh, and together the two girls ascended the stairway to the kitchen. After changing their clothes, they helped Aunt Rosemary prepare the evening dinner. When the group had eaten and later gathered in the parlor, Nancy reminded the others that she expected her father to arrive the next day.

"Dad didn't want me to bother meeting him,

but I just can't wait to see him. I think I'll meet all the trains from Chicago that stop here."

"I hope your father will stay with us for two or three days," Miss Flora spoke up. "Surely he'll have some ideas about our ghost."

"And good ones, too," Nancy said. "If he's on the early train, he'll have breakfast with us. I'll meet it at eight o'clock."

But later that evening Nancy's plans were suddenly changed. Hannah Gruen telephoned her to say that a man at the telegraph office had called the house a short time before to read a message from Mr. Drew. He had been unavoidably detained and would not arrive Wednesday.

"In the telegram your father said that he will let us know when he will arrive," the housekeeper added.

"I'm disappointed," Nancy remarked, "but I hope this delay means that Dad is on the trail of Willie Wharton!"

"Speaking of Willie Wharton," said Hannah, "I heard something about him today."

"What was that?" Nancy asked.

"That he was seen down by the river right here in River Heights a couple of days ago!"

CHAPTER IX

A Worrisome Delay

"You say Willie Wharton was seen in River Heights down by the river?" Nancy asked unbelievingly.

"Yes," Hannah replied. "I learned it from our postman, Mr. Ritter, who is one of the people that sold property to the railroad. As you know, Nancy, Mr. Ritter is very honest and reliable. Well, he said he'd heard that some of the property owners were trying to horn in on this deal of Willie Wharton's for getting more money. But Mr. Ritter wouldn't have a thing to do with it—calls it a holdup."

"Did Mr. Ritter himself see Willie Wharton?" Nancy asked eagerly.

"No," the housekeeper replied. "One of the other property owners told him Willie was around."

"That man *could* be mistaken," Nancy suggested.

"Of course he might," Hannah agreed. "And I'm inclined to think he is. If your father is staying over in Chicago, it must be because of Willie Wharton."

Nancy did not tell Hannah what was racing through her mind. She said good night cheerfully, but actually she was very much worried.

"Maybe Willie Wharton *was* seen down by the river," she mused. "And maybe Dad was 'unavoidably detained' by an enemy of his in connection with the railroad bridge project. One of the dissatisfied property owners might have followed him to Chicago."

Or, she reflected further, it was not inconceivable that Mr. Drew had found Willie Wharton, only to have Willie hold the lawyer a prisoner.

As Nancy sat lost in anxious thought, Helen came into the hall. "Something the matter?" she asked.

"I don't know," Nancy replied, "but I have a feeling there is. Dad telegraphed to say that he wouldn't be here tomorrow. Instead of wiring, he always phones me or Hannah or his office when he is away and it seems strange that he didn't do so this time."

"You told me a few days ago that your father had been threatened," said Helen. "Are you afraid it has something to do with that?"

"Yes, I am."

"Is there anything I can do?" Helen offered.

"Thank you, Helen, but I think not. There isn't anything I can do either. We'll just have to wait and see what happens. Maybe I'll hear from Dad again."

Nancy looked so downcast that Helen searched her mind to find something which would cheer her friend. Suddenly Helen had an idea and went to speak to Miss Flora and Aunt Rosemary about it.

"I think it's a wonderful plan if Nancy will do it," Aunt Rosemary said.

Helen called Nancy from the hall and proposed that they all go to the attic to look in the big trunk containing the old costumes.

"We might even put them on," Miss Flora proposed, smiling girlishly.

"And you girls could dance the minuet," said Aunt Rosemary enthusiastically. "Mother plays the old spinet very well. Maybe she would play a minuet for you."

"I love your idea," said Nancy. She knew that the three were trying to boost her spirits and she appreciated it. Besides, what they had proposed sounded like fun.

All of them trooped up the creaky attic stairs. In their haste, none of the group had remembered to bring flashlights.

"I'll go downstairs and get a couple," Nancy offered.

"Never mind," Aunt Rosemary spoke up.

"There are some candles and holders right here. We keep them for emergencies."

She lighted two white candles which stood in old-fashioned, saucer-type brass holders and led the way to the costume trunk.

As Helen lifted the heavy lid, Nancy exclaimed in delight, "How beautiful the clothes are!"

She could see silks, satins, and laces at one side. At the other was a folded-up rose velvet robe. She and Helen lifted out the garments and held them up.

"They're really lovelier than our formal dance clothes today," Helen remarked. "Especially the men's!"

Miss Flora smiled. "And a lot more flattering!"

The entire trunk was unpacked, before the group selected what they would wear.

"This pale-green silk gown with the panniers would look lovely on you, Nancy," Miss Flora said. "And I'm sure it's just the right size, too."

Nancy surveyed the tiny waist of the ball gown. "I'll try it on," she said. Then laughingly she added, "But I'll probably have to hold my breath to close it in the middle. My, but the women in olden times certainly had slim waistlines!"

Helen was holding up a man's purple velvet suit. It had knee breeches and the waistcoat had a lace-ruffled front. There were a tricorn hat, long white stockings, and buckled slippers to complete the costume.

"I think I'll wear this and be your partner, Nancy," Helen said.

Taking off her pumps, she slid her feet into the buckled slippers. The others laughed aloud. A man with a foot twice the size of Helen's had once worn the slippers!

"Never mind. I'll stuff the empty space with paper," Helen announced gaily.

Miss Flora and Aunt Rosemary selected gowns for themselves, then opened a good-sized box at the bottom of the trunk. It contained various kinds of wigs worn in Colonial times. All were pure white and fluffy.

Carrying the costumes and wigs, the group descended to their bedrooms, where they changed into the fancy clothes, then went to the first floor. Miss Flora led the way into the room across the hall from the parlor. She said it once had been the drawing room. Later it had become a library, but the old spinet still stood in a corner.

Miss Flora sat down at the instrument and began to play Beethoven's "Minuet." Aunt Rosemary sat down beside her.

Nancy and Helen, dubbed by the latter, Master and Mistress Colonial America, began to dance. They clasped their right hands high in the air, then took two steps backward and made little bows. They circled, then strutted, and even put in a few steps with which no dancers in Colonial times would have been familiar.

Aunt Rosemary giggled and clapped. "I wish President Washington would come to see you," she said, acting out her part in the entertainment. "Mistress Nancy, prithee do an encore and Master Corning, wilt thou accompany thy fair lady?"

The girls could barely keep from giggling. Helen made a low bow to her aunt, her tricorn in her hand, and said, "At your service, my lady. Your every wish is my command!"

The minuet was repeated, then as Miss Flora stopped playing, the girls sat down.

"Oh, that was such fun!" said Nancy. "Some time I'd like to— Listen!" she commanded suddenly.

From outside the house they could hear loud shouting. "Come here! You in the house! Come here!"

Nancy and Helen dashed from their chairs to the front door. Nancy snapped on the porch light and the two girls raced outside.

"Over here!" a man's voice urged.

Nancy and Helen ran down the steps and out onto the lawn. Just ahead of them stood Tom Patrick, the police detective. In a viselike grip he was holding a thin, bent-over man whom the girls judged to be about fifty years of age.

"Is this your ghost?" the guard asked.

His prisoner was struggling to free himself but was unable to get loose. The girls hurried forward to look at the man.

"Is this your ghost?" the police guard asked

"I caught him sneaking along the edge of the grounds," Tom Patrick announced.

"Let me go!" the man cried out angrily. "I'm no ghost. What are you talking about?"

"You may not be a ghost," the detective said, "but you could be the thief who has been robbing this house."

"What!" his prisoner exclaimed. "I'm no thief! I live around here. Anyone will tell you I'm okay."

"What's your name and where do you live?" the detective prodded. He let the man stand up straight but held one of his arms firmly.

"My name's Albert Watson and I live over on Tuttle Road."

"What were you doing on this property?"

Albert Watson said he had been taking a short cut home. His wife had taken their car for the evening.

"I'd been to a friend's house. You can call him and verify what I'm saying. And you can call my wife, too. Maybe she's home now and she'll come and get me."

The guard reminded Albert Watson that he had not revealed why he was sneaking along the ground.

"Well," the prisoner said, "it was because of you. I heard downtown that there was a detective patrolling this place and I didn't want to bump into you. I was afraid of just what did happen."

The man relaxed a little. "I guess you're a pretty good guard at that."

Detective Patrick let go of Albert Watson's arm. "Your story sounds okay, but we'll go in the house and do some telephoning to find out if you're telling the truth."

"You'll find out all right. Why, I'm even a notary public! They don't give a notary's license to dishonest folks!" the trespasser insisted. Then he stared at Nancy and Helen, "What are you doing in those funny clothes?"

"We—are—we were having a little costume party," Helen responded. In the excitement she and Nancy had forgotten what they were wearing!

The two girls started for the house, with the men following. When Mr. Watson and the guard saw Miss Flora and Aunt Rosemary also in costume they gazed at the women in amusement.

Nancy introduced Mr. Watson. Miss Flora said she knew of him, although she had never met the man. Two phone calls by the guard confirmed Watson's story. In a little while his wife arrived at Twin Elms to drive her husband home, and Detective Patrick went back to his guard duty.

Aunt Rosemary then turned out all the lights on the first floor and she, Miss Flora, and the girls went upstairs. Bedroom doors were locked, and everyone hoped there would be no disturbance during the night.

"It was a good day, Nancy," said Helen, yawning, as she climbed into bed.

"Yes, it was," said Nancy. "Of course, I'm a little disappointed that we aren't farther along solving the mystery but maybe by this time tomorrow—" She looked toward Helen who did not answer. She was already sound asleep.

Nancy herself was under the covers a few minutes later. She lay staring at the ceiling, going over the various events of the past two days. As her mind recalled the scene in the attic when they were pulling costumes from the old trunk, she suddenly gave a start.

"That section of wall back of the trunk!" she told herself. "The paneling looked different somehow from the rest of the attic wall. Maybe it's movable and leads to a secret exit! Tomorrow I'll find out!"

CHAPTER X

The Midnight Watch

As soon as the two girls awoke the next morning, Nancy told Helen her plan.

"I'm with you," said Helen. "Oh, I do wish we could solve the mystery of the ghost! I'm afraid that it's beginning to affect Miss Flora's health and yet she won't leave Twin Elms."

"Maybe we can get Aunt Rosemary to keep her in the garden most of the day," Nancy suggested. "It's perfectly beautiful outside. We might even serve lunch under the trees."

"I'm sure they'd love that," said Helen. "As soon as we get downstairs, let's propose it."

Both women liked the suggestion. Aunt Rosemary had guessed their strategy and was appreciative of it.

"I'll wash and dry the dishes," Nancy offered when breakfast was over. "Miss Flora, why don't you and Aunt Rosemary go outside right now and take advantage of this lovely sunshine?"

The frail, elderly woman smiled. There were deep circles under her eyes, indicating that she had had a sleepless night.

"And I'll run the vacuum cleaner around and dust this first floor in less than half an hour," Helen said merrily.

Her relatives caught the spirit of her enthusiasm and Miss Flora remarked, "I wish you girls lived here all the time. Despite our troubles, you have brought a feeling of gaiety back into our lives."

Both girls smiled at the compliment. As soon as the two women had gone outdoors, the girls set to work with a will. At the end of the allotted half hour, the first floor of the mansion was spotless. Nancy and Helen next went to the second floor, quickly made the beds, and tidied the bathrooms.

"And now for that ghost!" said Helen, brandishing her flashlight.

Nancy took her own from a bureau drawer.

"Let's see if we can figure out how to climb these attic stairs without making them creak," Nancy suggested. "Knowing how may come in handy some time."

This presented a real challenge. Every inch of each step was tried before the girls finally worked out a pattern to follow in ascending the stairway noiselessly.

Helen laughed. "This will certainly be a

memory test, Nancy. I'll rehearse our directions.
First step, put your foot to the left near the wall.
Second step, right center. Third step, against
the right wall. I'll need three feet to do that!"

Nancy laughed too. "For myself, I think I'll
skip the second step. Let's see. On the fourth
and fifth it's all right to step in the center, but on
the sixth you hug the left wall, on the seventh,
the right wall—"

Helen interrupted. "But if you step on the
eighth any place, it will creak. So you skip it."

"Nine, ten, and eleven are okay," Nancy recalled. "But from there to fifteen at the top we're
in trouble."

"Let's see if I remember," said Helen. "On
twelve, you go left, then right, then right again.
How can you do that without a jump and losing
your balance and tumbling down?"

"How about skipping fourteen and then
stretching as far as you can to reach the top one
at the left where it doesn't squeak," Nancy replied.
"Let's go!"

She and Helen went back to the second floor
and began what was meant to be a silent ascent.
But both of them made so many mistakes at first
the creaking was terrific. Finally, however, the
girls had the silent spots memorized perfectly and
went up noiselessly.

Nancy clicked on her flashlight and swung it
onto the nearest wood-paneled wall. Helen

stared at it, then remarked, "This isn't made of long panels from ceiling to floor. It's built of small pieces."

"That's right," said Nancy. "But see if you don't agree with me that the spot back of the costume trunk near the chimney looks a little different. The grain doesn't match the other wood."

The girls crossed the attic and Nancy beamed her flashlight over the suspected paneling.

"It does look different," Helen said. "This could be a door, I suppose. But there's no knob or other hardware on it." She ran her finger over a section just above the floor, following the cracks at the edge of a four-by-two-and-a-half-foot space.

"If it's a secret door," said Nancy, "the knob is on the other side."

"How are we going to open it?" Helen questioned.

"We might try prying the door open," Nancy proposed. "But first I want to test it."

She tapped the entire panel with her knuckles. A look of disappointment came over her face. "There's certainly no hollow space behind it," she said.

"Let's make sure," said Helen. "Suppose I go downstairs and get a screw driver and hammer? We'll see what happens when we drive the screw driver through this crack."

"Good idea, Helen."

While she was gone, Nancy inspected the rest

of the attic walls and floor. She did not find another spot which seemed suspicious. By this time Helen had returned with the tools. Inserting the screw driver into one of the cracks, she began to pound on the handle of it with the hammer.

Nancy watched hopefully. The screw driver went through the crack very easily but immediately met an obstruction on the other side. Helen pulled the screw driver out. "Nancy, you try your luck."

The young sleuth picked a different spot, but the results were the same. There was no open space behind that portion of the attic wall.

"My hunch wasn't so good," said Nancy.

Helen suggested that they give up and go downstairs. "Anyway, I think the postman will be here soon." She smiled. "I'm expecting a letter from Jim. Mother said she would forward all my mail."

Nancy did not want to give up the search yet. But she nodded in agreement and waved her friend toward the stairs. Then the young detective sat down on the floor and cupped her chin in her hands. As she stared ahead, Nancy noticed that Helen, in her eagerness to meet the postman, had not bothered to go quietly down the attic steps. It sounded as if Helen had picked the squeakiest spot on each step!

Nancy heard Helen go out the front door and suddenly realized that she was in the big mansion all alone. "That may bring the ghost on a visit," she thought. "If he is around, he may think I went outside with Helen! And I may learn where the secret opening is!"

Nancy sat perfectly still, listening intently. Suddenly she flung her head up. Was it her imagination, or did she hear the creak of steps? She was not mistaken. Nancy strained her ears, trying to determine from where the sounds were coming.

"I'm sure they're not from the attic stairs or the main staircase. And not the back stairway. Even if the ghost was in the kitchen and unlocked the door to the second floor, he'd know that the one at the top of the stairs was locked from the other side."

Nancy's heart suddenly gave a leap. She was positive that the creaking sounds were coming from somewhere behind the attic wall!

"A secret staircase!" she thought excitedly. "Maybe the ghost is entering the second floor!"

Nancy waited until the sounds stopped, then she got to her feet, tiptoed noiselessly down the attic steps and looked around. She could hear nothing. Was the ghost standing quietly in one of the bedrooms? Probably Miss Flora's?

Treading so lightly that she did not make a sound, Nancy peered into each room as she reached it. But no one was in any of them.

"Maybe he's on the first floor!" Nancy thought. She descended the main stairway, hugging the

280 THE HIDDEN STAIRCASE

wall so she would not make a sound. Reaching the first floor, Nancy peered into the parlor. No one was there. She looked in the library, the dining room, and the kitchen. She saw no one.

"Well, the ghost didn't come into the house after all," Nancy concluded. "He may have intended to, but changed his mind."

She felt more certain than at any time, however, that there was a secret entrance to Twin Elms Mansion from a hidden stairway. But how to find it? Suddenly the young sleuth snapped her fingers. "I know what I'll do! I'll set a trap for that ghost!"

She reflected that he had taken jewelry, but those thefts had stopped. Apparently he was afraid to go to the second floor.

"I wonder if anything is missing from the first floor," she mused. "Maybe he has taken silverware or helped himself to some food."

Going to the back door, Nancy opened it and called to Helen, who was now seated in the garden with Miss Flora and Aunt Rosemary. "What say we start lunch?" she called, not wishing to distress Miss Flora by bringing up the subject of the mystery.

"Okay," said Helen. In a few moments she joined Nancy, who asked if her friend had received a letter.

Helen's eyes sparkled. "I sure did. Oh, Nancy, I can hardly wait for Jim to get home!"

Nancy smiled. "The way you describe him, I can hardly wait to see him myself." Then she told Helen the real reason she had called her into the kitchen. She described the footsteps on what she was sure was a hidden, creaking stairway, then added, "If we discover that food or something else is missing we'll know he's been here again."

Helen offered to inspect the flat silver. "I know approximately how many pieces should be in the buffet drawer," she said.

"And I'll look over the food supplies," Nancy suggested. "I have a pretty good idea what was in the refrigerator and on the pantry shelf."

It was not many minutes before each of the girls discovered articles missing. Helen said that nearly a dozen teaspoons were gone and Nancy figured that several cans of food, some eggs, and a quart of milk had been taken.

"It just seems impossible to catch that thief," Helen said with a sigh.

On a sudden hunch Nancy took down from the wall a memo pad and pencil which hung there. Putting a finger to her lips to indicate that Helen was not to comment, Nancy wrote on the sheet:

"I think the only way to catch the ghost is to trap him. I believe he has one or more microphones hidden some place and that he hears all our plans."

Nancy looked up at Helen, who nodded silently. Nancy continued to write, "I don't want to worry

Miss Flora or Aunt Rosemary, so let's keep our plans a secret. I suggest that we go to bed tonight as usual and carry on a conversation about our plans for tomorrow. But actually we won't take off our clothes. Then about midnight let's tiptoe downstairs to watch. I'll wait in the kitchen. Do you want to stay in the living room?"

Again Helen nodded. Nancy, thinking that they had been quiet too long, and that if there was an eavesdropper nearby he might become suspicious, said aloud, "What would Miss Flora and Aunt Rosemary like for lunch, Helen?"

"Why, uh—" Helen found it hard to transfer to the new subject. "They—uh—both love soup."

"Then I'll make cream of chicken soup," said Nancy. "Hand me a can of chicken and rice, will you? And I'll get the milk."

As Helen was doing this, Nancy lighted a match, held her recently written note over the sink, and set fire to the paper.

Helen smiled. "Nancy thinks of everything," she said to herself.

The girls chatted gaily as they prepared the food and finally carried four trays out to the garden. They did not mention their midnight plan. The day in the garden was proving to be most beneficial to Miss Flora, and the girls were sure she would sleep well that night.

Nancy's plan was followed to the letter. Just

as the grandfather clock in the hall was striking midnight, Nancy arrived in the kitchen and sat down to await developments. Helen was posted in a living-room chair near the hall doorway. Moonlight streamed into both rooms but the girls had taken seats in the shadows.

Helen was mentally rehearsing the further instructions which Nancy had written to her during the afternoon. The young sleuth had suggested that if Helen should see anyone, she was to run to the front door, open it, and yell "Police!" At the same time she was to try to watch where the intruder disappeared.

The minutes ticked by. There was not a sound in the house. Then suddenly Nancy heard the front door open with a bang and Helen's voice yell loudly and clearly:

"Police! Help! Police!"

CHAPTER XI

An Elusive Ghost

By THE time Nancy reached the front hall, Tom Patrick, the police guard, had rushed into the house. "Here I am!" he called. "What's the matter?"

Helen led the way into the living room, and switched on the chandelier light.

"That sofa next to the fireplace!" she said in a trembling voice. "It moved! I saw it move!"

"You mean somebody moved it?" the detective asked.

"I—I don't know," Helen replied. "I couldn't see anybody."

Nancy walked over to the old-fashioned sofa, set in the niche alongside the fireplace. Certainly the piece was in place now. If the ghost had moved it, he had returned the sofa to its original position.

"Let's pull it out and see what we can find," Nancy suggested.

She tugged at one end, while the guard pulled the other. It occurred to Nancy that a person who moved it alone would have to be very strong.

"Do you think your ghost came up through a trap door or something?" the detective asked.

Neither of the girls replied. They had previously searched the area, and even now as they looked over every inch of the floor and the three walls surrounding the high sides of the couch, they could detect nothing that looked like an opening.

By this time Helen looked sheepish. "I—I guess I was wrong," she said finally. Turning to the police guard, she said, "I'm sorry to have taken you away from your work."

"Don't feel too badly about it. But I'd better get back to my guard duty," the man said, and left the house.

"Oh, Nancy!" Helen cried out. "I'm so sorry!"

She was about to say more but Nancy put a finger to her lips. They could use the same strategy for trapping the thief at another time. In case the thief might be listening, Nancy did not want to give away their secret.

Nancy felt that after all the uproar the ghost would not appear again that night. She motioned to Helen that they would go quietly upstairs and get some sleep. Hugging the walls of the stairway once more, they ascended noiselessly, tiptoed to their room, and got into bed.

"I'm certainly glad I didn't wake up Miss Flora and Aunt Rosemary," said Helen sleepily as she whispered good night.

Though Nancy had been sure the ghost would not enter the mansion again that night, she discovered in the morning that she had been mistaken. More food had been stolen sometime between midnight and eight o'clock when she and Helen started breakfast. Had the ghost taken it for personal use or only to worry the occupants of Twin Elms?

"I missed my chance this time," Nancy murmured to her friend. "After this, I'd better not trust what that ghost's next move may be!"

At nine o'clock Hannah Gruen telephoned the house. Nancy happened to answer the ring and after the usual greetings was amazed to hear Hannah say, "I'd like to speak to your father."

"Why, Dad isn't here!" Nancy told her. "Don't you remember—the telegram said he wasn't coming?"

"He's not there!" Hannah exclaimed. "Oh, this is bad, Nancy—very bad."

"What do you mean, Hannah?" Nancy asked fearfully.

The housekeeper explained that soon after receiving the telegram on Tuesday evening, Mr. Drew himself had phoned. "He wanted to know if you were still in Cliffwood, Nancy. When I told him yes, he said he would stop off there on his way home Wednesday."

Nancy was frightened, but she asked steadily, "Hannah, did you happen to mention the telegram to him?"

"No, I didn't," the housekeeper replied. "I didn't think it was necessary."

"Hannah darling," said Nancy, almost on the verge of tears, "I'm afraid that telegram was a hoax!"

"A hoax!" Mrs. Gruen cried out.

"Yes. Dad's enemies sent it to keep me from meeting him!"

"Oh, Nancy," Hannah wailed, "you don't suppose those enemies that Mr. Gomber warned you about have waylaid your father and are keeping him prisoner?"

"I'm afraid so," said Nancy. Her knees began to quake and she sank into the chair alongside the telephone table.

"What'll we do?" Hannah asked. "Do you want me to notify the police?"

"Not yet. Let me do a little checking first."

"All right, Nancy. But let me know what happens."

"I will."

Nancy put the phone down, then looked at the various telephone directories which lay on the table. Finding one which contained River

Heights numbers, she looked for the number of the telegraph office and put in a call. She asked the clerk who answered to verify that there had been a telegram from Mr. Drew on Tuesday.

After a few minutes wait, the reply came. "We have no record of such a telegram."

Nancy thanked the clerk and hung up. By this time her hands were shaking with fright. What had happened to her father?

Getting control of herself, Nancy telephoned in turn to the airport, the railroad station, and the bus lines which served Cliffwood. She inquired about any accidents which might have occurred on trips from Chicago the previous day or on Tuesday night. In each case she was told there had been none.

"Oh, what shall I do?" Nancy thought in dismay.

Immediately an idea came to her and she put in a call to the Chicago hotel where her father had registered. Although she thought it unlikely, it was just possible that he had changed his mind again and was still there. But a conversation with the desk clerk dashed this hope.

"No, Mr. Drew is not here. He checked out Tuesday evening. I don't know his plans, but I'll connect you with the head porter. He may be able to help you."

In a few seconds Nancy was asking the porter what he could tell her to help clear up the mystery of her father's disappearance. "All I know, miss, is that your father told me he was taking a sleeper train and getting off somewhere Wednesday morning to meet his daughter."

"Thank you. Oh, thank you very much," said Nancy. "You've helped me a great deal."

So her father had taken the train home and probably had reached the Cliffwood station! Next she must find out what had happened to him after that!

Nancy told Aunt Rosemary and Helen what she had learned, then got in her convertible and drove directly to the Cliffwood station. There she spoke to the ticket agent. Unfortunately, he could not identify Mr. Drew from Nancy's description as having been among the passengers who got off either of the two trains arriving from Chicago on Wednesday.

Nancy went to speak to the taximen. Judging by the line of cabs, she decided that all the drivers who served the station were on hand at the moment. There had been no outgoing trains for nearly an hour and an incoming express was due in about fifteen minutes.

"I'm in luck," the young detective told herself. "Surely one of these men must have driven Dad."

She went from one to another, but each of them denied having carried a passenger of Mr. Drew's description the day before.

By this time Nancy was in a panic. She hurried inside the station to a telephone booth and called the local police station. Nancy asked to speak to the captain and in a moment he came on the line.

"Captain Rossland speaking," he said crisply.

Nancy poured out her story. She told of the warning her father had received in River Heights and her fear that some enemy of his was now detaining the lawyer against his will.

"This is very serious, Miss Drew," Captain Rossland stated. "I will put men on the case at once," he said.

As Nancy left the phone booth, a large, gray-haired woman walked up to her. "Pardon me, miss, but I couldn't help overhearing what you said. I believe maybe I can help you."

Nancy was surprised and slightly suspicious. Maybe this woman was connected with the abductors and planned to make Nancy a prisoner too by promising to take her to her father!

"Don't look so frightened," the woman said, smiling. "All I wanted to tell you is that I'm down here at the station every day to take a train to the next town. I'm a nurse and I'm on a case over there right now."

"I see," Nancy said.

"Well, yesterday I was here when the Chicago train came in. I noticed a tall, handsome man—such as you describe your father to be—step off the train. He got into the taxi driven by a man named Harry. I have a feeling that for some reason the cabbie isn't telling the truth. Let's talk to him."

Nancy followed the woman, her heart beating furiously. She was ready to grab at any straw to get a clue to her father's whereabouts!

"Hello, Miss Skade," the taximan said. "How are you today?"

"Oh, I'm all right," the nurse responded. "Listen, Harry. You told this young lady that you didn't carry any passenger yesterday that looked like her father. Now I saw one get into your cab. What about it?"

Harry hung his head. "Listen, miss," he said to Nancy, "I got three kids and I don't want nothin' to happen to 'em. See?"

"What do you mean?" Nancy asked, puzzled.

When the man did not reply, Miss Skade said, "Now look, Harry. This girl's afraid that her father has been kidnaped. It's up to you to tell her all you know."

"Kidnaped!" the taximan shouted. "Oh, good-night! Now I don't know what to do."

Nancy had a sudden thought. "Has somebody been threatening you, Harry?" she asked.

The cab driver's eyes nearly popped from his head. "Well," he said, "since you've guessed it, I'd better tell you everything I know."

He went on to say that he had taken a passenger who fitted Mr. Drew's description toward Twin

Elms where he had said he wanted to go. "Just as we were leaving the station, two other men came up and jumped into my cab. They said they were going a little farther than that and would I take them? Well, about halfway to Twin Elms, one of those men ordered me to pull up to the side of the road and stop. He told me the stranger had blacked out. He and his buddy jumped out of the car and laid the man on the grass."

"How ill was he?" Nancy asked.

"I don't know. He was unconscious. Just then another car came along behind us and stopped. The driver got out and offered to take your father to a hospital. The two men said okay."

Nancy took heart. Maybe her father was in a hospital and had not been abducted at all! But a moment later her hopes were again dashed when Harry said:

"I told those guys I'd be glad to drive the sick man to a hospital, but one of them turned on me, shook his fist, and yelled, 'You just forget everything that's happened or it'll be too bad for you and your kids!'"

"Oh!" Nancy cried out, and for a second everything seemed to swim before her eyes. She clutched the door handle of the taxi for support.

There was no question now but that her father had been drugged, then kidnaped!

CHAPTER XII

The Newspaper Clue

MISS SKADE grabbed Nancy. "Do you feel ill?" the nurse asked quickly.

"Oh, I'll be all right," Nancy replied. "This news has been a great shock to me."

"Is there any way I can help you?" the woman questioned. "I'd be very happy to."

"Thank you, but I guess not," the young sleuth said. Smiling ruefully, she added, "But I must get busy and do something about this."

The nurse suggested that perhaps Mr. Drew was in one of the local hospitals. She gave Nancy the names of the three in town.

"I'll get in touch with them at once," the young detective said. "You've been most kind. And here comes your train, Miss Skade. Good-by and again thanks a million for your help!"

Harry climbed out of his taxi and went to stand at the platform to signal passengers for his cab. Nancy hurried after him, and before the train came in, asked if he would please give her a description of the two men who had been with her father.

"Well, both of them were dark and kind of athletic-looking. Not what I'd call handsome. One of 'em had an upper tooth missing. And the other fellow—his left ear was kind of crinkled, if you know what I mean."

"I understand," said Nancy. "I'll give a description of the two men to the police."

She went back to the telephone booth and called each of the three hospitals, asking if anyone by the name of Carson Drew had been admitted or possibly a patient who was not conscious and had no identification. Only Mercy Hospital had a patient who had been unconscious since the day before. He definitely was not Mr. Drew—he was Chinese!

Sure now that her father was being held in some secret hiding place, Nancy went at once to police headquarters and related the taximan's story.

Captain Rossland looked extremely concerned. "This is alarming, Miss Drew," he said, "but I feel sure we can trace that fellow with the crinkly ear and we'll make him tell us where your father is! I doubt, though, that there is anything you can do. You'd better leave it to the police."

Nancy said nothing. She was reluctant to give up even trying to do something, but she acquiesced.

"In the meantime," said the officer, "I'd advise you to remain at Twin Elms and concentrate on solving the mystery there. From what you tell me about your father, I'm sure he'll be able to get out of the difficulty himself, even before the police find him."

Aloud, Nancy promised to stay on call in case Captain Rossland might need her. But in her own mind the young sleuth determined that if she got any kind of a lead concerning her father, she was most certainly going to follow it up.

Nancy left police headquarters and strolled up the street, deep in thought. "Instead of things getting better, all my problems seem to be getting worse. Maybe I'd better call Hannah."

Since she had been a little girl, Nancy had found solace in talking to Hannah Gruen. The housekeeper had always been able to give her such good advice!

Nancy went into a drugstore and entered one of the telephone booths. She called the Drew home in River Heights and was pleased when Mrs. Gruen answered. The housekeeper was aghast to learn Nancy's news but said she thought Captain Rossland's advice was sound.

"You've given the police the best leads in the world and I believe that's all you can do. But wait—" the housekeeper suddenly said. "If I were you, Nancy, I'd call up those railroad lawyers and tell them exactly what has happened. Your father's disappearance is directly concerned with that bridge project, I'm sure, and the lawyers may have some ideas about where to find him."

"That's a wonderful suggestion, Hannah," said Nancy. "I'll call them right away."

But when the young detective phoned the railroad lawyers, she was disappointed to learn that all the men were out to lunch and none of them would return before two o'clock.

"Oh dear!" Nancy sighed. "Well, I guess I'd better get a snack while waiting for them to come back." But in her worried state she did not feel like eating.

There was a food counter at the rear of the drugstore and Nancy made her way to it. Perching on a high-backed stool, she read the menu over and over. Nothing appealed to her. When the counterman asked her what she wanted, Nancy said frankly she did not know—she was not very hungry.

"Then I recommend our split-pea soup," he told her. "It's homemade and out of this world."

Nancy smiled at him. "I'll take your advice and try it."

The hot soup was delicious. By the time she had finished it, Nancy's spirits had risen considerably.

"And how about some custard pie?" the counterman inquired. "It's just like Mother used to make."

"All right," Nancy answered, smiling at the solicitous young man. The pie was ice cold and proved to be delicious. When Nancy finished eating it, she glanced at her wrist watch. It was only one-thirty. Seeing a rack of magazines, she decided to while away the time reading in her car.

She purchased a magazine of detective stories, one of which proved to be so intriguing that the half hour went by quickly. Promptly at two o'clock Nancy returned to the phone booth and called the offices of the railroad lawyers. The switchboard operator connected her with Mr. Anthony Barradale and Nancy judged from his voice that he was fairly young. Quickly she told her story.

"Mr. Drew being held a prisoner!" Mr. Barradale cried out. "Well, those underhanded property owners are certainly going to great lengths to gain a few dollars."

"The police are working on the case, but I thought perhaps your firm would like to take a hand also," Nancy told the lawyer.

"We certainly will," the young man replied. "I'll speak to our senior partner about it. I know he will want to start work at once on the case."

"Thank you," said Nancy. She gave the address and telephone number of Twin Elms and asked that the lawyers get in touch with her there if any news should break.

"We'll do that," Mr. Barradale promised.

Nancy left the drugstore and walked back to her car. Climbing in, she wondered what her next move ought to be.

"One thing is sure," she thought. "Work is the best antidote for worry. I'll get back to Twin Elms and do some more sleuthing there."

As she drove along, Nancy reflected about the ghost entering Twin Elms mansion by a subterranean passage. Since she had found no sign of one in any of the outbuildings on the estate, it occurred to her that possibly it led from an obscure cave, either natural or man-made. Such a device would be a clever artifice for an architect to use.

Taking a little-used road that ran along one side of the estate, Nancy recalled having seen a long, grassed-over hillock which she had assumed to be an old aqueduct. Perhaps this was actually the hidden entrance to Twin Elms!

She parked her car at the side of the road and took a flashlight from the glove compartment. In anticipation of finding the answer to the riddle, Nancy crossed the field, and as she came closer to the beginning of the huge mound, she could see stones piled up. Getting nearer, she realized that it was indeed the entrance to a rocky cave.

"Well, maybe this time I've found it!" she thought, hurrying forward.

The wind was blowing strongly and tossed her hair about her face. Suddenly a freakish gust swept a newspaper from among the rocks and scattered the pages helter-skelter.

Nancy was more excited than ever. The newspaper meant a human being had been there not too long ago! The front page sailed toward her. As she grabbed it up, she saw to her complete astonishment that the paper was a copy of the *River Heights Gazette*. The date was the Tuesday before.

"Someone interested in River Heights has been here very recently!" the young sleuth said to herself excitedly.

Who was the person? Her father? Gomber? Who?

Wondering if the paper might contain any clue, Nancy dashed around to pick up all the sheets. As she spread them out on the ground, she noticed a hole in the page where classified ads appeared.

"This may be a very good clue!" Nancy thought. "As soon as I get back to the house, I'll call Hannah and have her look up Tuesday's paper to see what was in that ad."

It suddenly occurred to Nancy that the person who had brought the paper to the cave might be inside at this very moment. She must watch her step; he might prove to be an enemy!

"This may be where Dad is being held a prisoner!" Nancy thought wildly.

Flashlight in hand, and her eyes darting intently

about, Nancy proceeded cautiously into the cave. Five feet, ten. She saw no one. Fifteen more. Twenty. Then Nancy met a dead end. The empty cave was almost completely round and had no other opening.

"Oh dear. another failure," Nancy told herself disappointedly, as she retraced her steps. "My only hope now is to learn something important from the ad in the paper."

Nancy walked back across the field. Her eyes were down, as she automatically looked for footprints. But presently she looked up and stared in disbelief.

A man was standing alongside her car, examining it. His back was half turned toward Nancy, so she could not see his face very well. But he had an athletic build and his left ear was definitely crinkly!

CHAPTER XIII

The Crash

THE STRANGER inspecting Nancy's car must have heard her coming. Without turning around, he dodged back of the automobile and started off across the field in the opposite direction.

"He certainly acts suspiciously. He must be the man with the crinkly ear who helped abduct my father!" Nancy thought excitedly.

Quickly she crossed the road and ran after him as fast as she could, hoping to overtake him. But the man had had a good head start. Also, his stride was longer than Nancy's and he could cover more ground in the same amount of time.

The far corner of the irregular-shaped field ended at the road on which Riverview Manor stood. When Nancy reached the highway, she was just in time to see the stranger leap into a parked car and drive off.

The young detective was exasperated. She had

had only a glimpse of the man's profile. If only she could have seen him full face or caught the license number of his car!

"I wonder if he's the one who dropped the newspaper?" she asked herself. "Maybe he's from River Heights!" She surmised that the man himself was not one of the property owners but he might have been hired by Willie Wharton or one of the owners to help abduct Mr. Drew.

"I'd better hurry to a phone and report this," Nancy thought.

She ran all the way back across the field, stepped into her own car, turned it around, and headed for Twin Elms. When Nancy arrived, she sped to the telephone in the hall and dialed Cliffwood Police Headquarters. In a moment she was talking to the captain and gave him her latest information.

"It certainly looks as if you picked up a good clue, Miss Drew," the officer remarked. "I'll send out an alarm immediately to have this man picked up."

"I suppose there is no news of my father," Nancy said.

"I'm afraid not. But a couple of our men talked to the taxi driver Harry and he gave us a pretty good description of the man who came along the road while your father was lying unconscious on the grass—the one who offered to take him to the hospital."

"What did he look like?" Nancy asked.

The officer described the man as being in his early fifties, short, and rather heavy-set. He had shifty pale-blue eyes.

"Well," Nancy replied, "I can think of several men who would fit that description. Did he have any outstanding characteristics?"

"Harry didn't notice anything, except that the fellow's hands didn't look as if he did any kind of physical work. The taximan said they were kind of soft and pudgy."

"Well, that eliminates all the men I know who are short, heavy-set and have pale-blue eyes. None of them has hands like that."

"It'll be a good identifying feature," the police officer remarked. "Well, I guess I'd better get that alarm out."

Nancy said good-by and put down the phone. She waited several seconds for the line to clear, then picked up the instrument again and called Hannah Gruen. Before Nancy lay the sheet of newspaper from which the advertisement had been torn.

"The Drew residence," said a voice on the phone.

"Hello, Hannah. This is Nancy."

"How are you, dear? Any news?" Mrs. Gruen asked quickly.

"I haven't found Dad yet," the young detective replied. "And the police haven't either. But I've picked up a couple of clues."

"Tell me about them," the housekeeper requested excitedly.

Nancy told her about the man with the crinkly ear and said she was sure that the police would soon capture him. "If he'll only talk, we may find out where Dad is being held."

"Oh, I hope so!" Hannah sighed. "Don't get discouraged, Nancy."

At this point Helen came into the hall, and as she passed Nancy on her way to the stairs, smiled at her friend. The young sleuth was about to ask Hannah to get the Drews' Tuesday copy of the *River Heights Gazette* when she heard a cracking noise overhead. Immediately she decided the ghost might be at work again.

"Hannah, I'll call you back later," Nancy said and put down the phone.

She had no sooner done this than Helen screamed, "Nancy, run! The ceiling!" She herself started for the front door.

Nancy, looking up, saw a tremendous crack in the ceiling just above the girls' heads. The next instant the whole ceiling crashed down on them! They were thrown to the floor.

"Oh!" Helen moaned. She was covered with lath and plaster, and had been hit hard on the head. But she managed to call out from under the debris, "Nancy, are you all right?" There was no answer.

The whole ceiling crashed down on them!

The tremendous noise had brought Miss Flora and Aunt Rosemary on a run from the kitchen. They stared in horror at the scene before them. Nancy lay unconscious and Helen seemed too dazed to move.

"Oh my! Oh my!" Miss Flora exclaimed.

She and Aunt Rosemary began stepping over the lath and plaster, which by now had filled the air with dust. They sneezed again and again but made their way forward nevertheless.

Miss Flora, reaching Helen's side, started pulling aside chunks of broken plaster and lath. Finally, she helped her great-granddaughter to her feet.

"Oh, my dear, you're hurt!" she said solicitously.

"I'll—be—all right—in a minute," Helen insisted, choking with the dust. "But Nancy—"

Aunt Rosemary had already reached the unconscious girl. With lightning speed, she threw aside the debris which almost covered Nancy. Whipping a handkerchief from her pocket, she gently laid it over Nancy's face, so that she would not breathe in any more of the dust.

"Helen, do you feel strong enough to help me carry Nancy into the library?" she asked. "I'd like to lay her on the couch there."

"Oh, yes, Aunt Rosemary. Do you think Nancy is badly hurt?" she asked worriedly.

"I hope not."

At this moment Nancy stirred. Then her arm

moved upward and she pulled the handkerchief from her face. She blinked several times as if unable to recall where she was.

"You'll be all right, Nancy," said Aunt Rosemary kindly. "But I don't want you to breathe this dust. Please keep the handkerchief over your nose." She took it from Nancy's hand and once more laid it across the girl's nostrils and mouth.

In a moment Nancy smiled wanly. "I remember now. The ceiling fell down."

"Yes," said Helen. "It knocked you out for a few moments. I hope you're not hurt."

Miss Flora, who was still sneezing violently, insisted that they all get out of the dust at once. She began stepping across the piles of debris, with Helen helping her. When they reached the library door, the elderly woman went inside.

Helen returned to help Nancy. But by this time her friend was standing up, leaning on Aunt Rosemary's arm. She was able to make her way across the hall to the library. Aunt Rosemary suggested calling a doctor, but Nancy said this would not be necessary.

"I'm so thankful you girls weren't seriously hurt," Miss Flora said. "What a dreadful thing this is! Do you think the ghost is responsible?"

Her daughter replied at once. "No, I don't. Mother, you will recall that for some time we have had a leak in the hall whenever it rained. And the last time we had a storm, the whole ceiling was soaked. I think that weakened the plaster and it fell of its own accord."

Miss Flora remarked that a new ceiling would be a heavy expense for them. "Oh dear, more troubles all the time. But I still don't want to part with my home."

Nancy, whose faculties by now were completely restored, said with a hint of a smile, "Well, there's one worry you might not have any more, Miss Flora."

"What's that?"

"Mr. Gomber," said Nancy, "may not be so interested in buying this property when he sees what happened."

"Oh, I don't know," Aunt Rosemary spoke up. "He's pretty persistent."

Nancy said she felt all right now and suggested that she and Helen start cleaning up the hall.

Miss Flora would not hear of this. "Rosemary and I are going to help," she said determinedly.

Cartons were brought from the cellar and one after the other was filled with the debris. After it had all been carried outdoors, mops and dust cloths were brought into use. Within an hour all the gritty plaster dust had been removed.

The weary workers had just finished their job when the telephone rang. Nancy, being closest to the instrument, answered it. Hannah Gruen was calling.

"Nancy! What happened?" she asked. "I've

been waiting over an hour for you to call me back.
What's the matter?''

Nancy gave her all the details.

"What's going to happen to you next?'' the
housekeeper exclaimed.

The young sleuth laughed. "Something good,
I hope.''

She asked Hannah to look for her copy of the
River Heights Gazette of the Tuesday before. In
a few minutes the housekeeper brought it to the
phone and Nancy asked her to turn to page fourteen. "That has the classified ads,'' she said.
"Now tell me what the ad is right in the center of
the page.''

"Do you mean the one about used cars?''

"That must be it,'' Nancy replied. "That's not
in my paper.''

Hannah Gruen said it was an ad for Aken's, a
used-car dealer. "He's at 24 Main Street in Hancock.''

"And now turn the page and tell me what ad is
on the back of it,'' Nancy requested.

"It's a story about a school picnic,'' Hannah told
her. "Does either one of them help you?''

"Yes, Hannah, I believe you've given me just
the information I wanted. This may prove to be
valuable. Thanks a lot.''

After Nancy had finished the call, she started to
dial police headquarters, then changed her mind.
The ghost might be hiding somewhere in the

house to listen—or if he had installed microphones at various points, any conversations could
be picked up and recorded on a machine a distance
away.

"It would be wiser for me to discuss the whole
matter in person with the police, I'm sure," Nancy
decided.

Divulging her destination only to Helen, she
told the others she was going to drive downtown
but would not be gone long.

"You're sure you feel able?" Aunt Rosemary
asked her.

"I'm perfectly fine," Nancy insisted.

She set off in the convertible, hopeful that
through the clue of the used-car dealer, the police
might be able to pick up the name of one of the
suspects.

"They can track him down and through the man
locate my father!"

CHAPTER XIV

An Urgent Message

"EXCELLENT!" Captain Rossland said after Nancy had told her story. He smiled. "The way you're building up clues, if you were on my force, I'd recommend a citation for you!"

The young sleuth smiled and thanked him. "I must find my father," she said earnestly.

"I'll call Captain McGinnis of the River Heights force at once," the officer told her. "Why don't you sit down here and wait? It shouldn't take long for them to get information from Aken's used-car lot."

Nancy agreed and took a chair in a corner of the captain's office. Presently he called to her.

"I have your answer, Miss Drew."

She jumped up and went over to his desk. The officer told her that Captain McGinnis in River Heights had been most co-operative. He had sent two men at once to Aken's used-car lot. They had just returned with a report.

"Day before yesterday an athletic-looking man with a crinkly ear came there and purchased a car. He showed a driver's license stating that he was Samuel Greenman from Huntsville."

Nancy was excited over the information. "Then it will be easy to pick him up, won't it?" she asked.

"I'm afraid not," Captain Rossland replied. "McGinnis learned from the Huntsville police that although Greenman is supposed to live at the address he gave, he is reported to have been out of town for some time."

"Then no one knows where he is?"

"Not any of his neighbors."

The officer also reported that Samuel Greenman was a person of questionable character. He was wanted on a couple of robbery charges, and police in several states had been alerted to be on the lookout for him.

"Well, if the man I saw at my car is Samuel Greenman, then maybe he's hiding in this area."

Captain Rossland smiled. "Are you going to suggest next that he is the ghost at Twin Elms?"

"Who knows?" Nancy countered.

"In any case," Captain Rossland said, "your idea that he may be hiding out around here is a good one."

Nancy was about to ask the officer another question when his phone rang. A moment later he said, "It's for you, Miss Drew."

The girl detective picked up the receiver and said, "Hello." The caller was Helen Corning and her voice sounded frantic.

"Oh, Nancy, something dreadful has happened here! You must come home at once!"

"What it it?" Nancy cried out, but Helen had already put down the instrument at her end.

Nancy told Captain Rossland of the urgent request and said she must leave at once.

"Let me know if you need the police," the officer called after her.

"Thank you, I will."

Nancy drove to Twin Elms as fast as the law allowed. As she pulled up in front of the house, she was startled to see a doctor's car there. Someone had been taken ill!

Helen met her friend at the front door. "Nancy," she said in a whisper, "Miss Flora may have had a heart attack!"

"How terrible!" Nancy said, shocked. "Tell me all about it."

"Dr. Morrison wants Miss Flora to go to the hospital right away, but she refuses. She says she won't leave here."

Helen said that the physician was still upstairs attending her great-grandmother.

"When did she become ill?" Nancy asked. "Did something in particular bring on the attack?"

Helen nodded. "Yes. It was very frightening. Miss Flora, Aunt Rosemary, and I were in the kitchen talking about supper. They wanted to have a special dish to surprise you, because they knew you were dreadfully upset."

"That was sweet of them," Nancy remarked. "Please go on, Helen."

"Miss Flora became rather tired and Aunt Rosemary suggested that she go upstairs and lie down. She had just started up the stairway, when, for some unknown reason, she turned to look back. There, in the parlor, stood a man!"

"A caller?" Nancy questioned.

"Oh, no!" Helen replied. "Miss Flora said he was an ugly, horrible-looking person. He was unshaven and his hair was kind of long."

"Do you think he was the ghost?" Nancy inquired.

"Miss Flora thought so. Well, she didn't scream. You know, she's really terribly brave. She just decided to go down and meet him herself. And then, what do you think?"

"I could guess any number of things," Nancy replied. "What did happen?"

Helen said that when Mrs. Turnbull had reached the parlor, no one was in it! "And there was no secret door open."

"What did Miss Flora do then?" Nancy asked.
"She fainted."

At this moment a tall, slender, gray-haired man, carrying a physician's bag, walked down the stairs to the front hall. Helen introduced Nancy to him, then asked about the patient.

"Well, fortunately, Miss Flora is going to be all right," said Dr. Morrison. "She is an amazing woman. With complete rest and nothing more to worry her, I believe she will be all right. In fact, she may be able to be up for short periods by this time tomorrow."

"Oh, I'm so relieved," said Helen. "I'm terribly fond of my great-grandmother and I don't want anything to happen to her."

The physician smiled. "I'll do all I can, but you people will have to help."

"How can we do that?" Nancy asked quickly.

The physician said that no one was to talk about the ghost. "Miss Flora says that she saw a man in the parlor and that he must have come in by some secret entrance. Now you know, as well as I do, that such a thing is not plausible."

"But the man couldn't have entered this house any other way," Helen told him quickly. "Every window and door on this first floor is kept locked."

The doctor raised his eyebrows. "You've heard of hallucinations?" he asked.

Nancy and Helen frowned, but remained silent.

They were sure that Miss Flora had not had an hallucination. If she had said there was a man in the parlor, then one had been there!

"Call me if you need me before tomorrow morning," the doctor said as he moved toward the front door. "Otherwise I'll drop in some time before twelve."

After the medic had left, the two girls exchanged glances. Nancy said, "Are you game to search the parlor again?"

"You bet I am," Helen responded. "Shall we start now or wait until after supper?"

Although Nancy was eager to begin at once, she thought that first she should go upstairs and extend her sympathy to Miss Flora. She also felt that a delay in serving her supper while the search went on might upset the ill woman. Helen offered to go into the kitchen at once and start preparing the meal. Nancy nodded and went up the steps.

Miss Flora had been put to bed in her daughter's room to avoid any further scares from the ghost, who seemed to operate in the elderly woman's own room.

"Miss Flora, I'm so sorry you have to stay in bed," said Nancy, walking up and smiling at the patient.

"Well, I am too," Mrs. Turnbull replied. "And I think it's a lot of nonsense. Everybody faints once in a while. If you'd ever seen what I did—that horrible face!"

"Mother!" pleaded Aunt Rosemary, who was seated in a chair on the other side of the bed. "You know what the doctor said."

"Oh, these doctors!" her mother said pettishly. "Anyway, Nancy, I'm sure I saw the ghost. Now you just look for a man who hasn't shaved in goodness knows how long and has an ugly face and kind of longish hair."

It was on the tip of Nancy's tongue to ask for information on the man's height and size, but recalling the doctor's warning, she said nothing about this. Instead, she smiled and taking one of Miss Flora's hands in her own, said:

"Let's not talk any more about this until you're up and well. Then I'll put you on the Drew and Company detective squad!"

The amusing remark made the elderly woman smile and she promised to try getting some rest.

"But first I want something to eat," she demanded. "Do you think you girls can manage alone? I'd like Rosemary to stay here with me."

"Of course we can manage, and we'll bring you exactly what you should have to eat."

Nancy went downstairs and set up a tray for Miss Flora. On it was a cup of steaming chicken bouillon, a thin slice of well-toasted bread, and a saucer of plain gelatin.

A few minutes later Helen took another tray upstairs with a more substantial meal on it for Aunt Rosemary. Then the two girls sat down in the dining room to have their own supper. After finishing it, they quickly washed and dried all the dishes, then started for the parlor.

"Where do you think we should look?" Helen whispered.

During the past half hour Nancy had been going over in her mind what spot in the parlor they might have overlooked—one which could possibly have an opening behind it. She had decided on a large cabinet built into the wall. It contained a beautiful collection of figurines, souvenirs from many places, and knickknacks of various kinds.

"I'm going to look for a hidden spring that may move the cabinet away from the wall," Nancy told Helen in a low voice.

For the first time she noticed that each of the figurines and knickknacks were set in small depressions on the shelves. Nancy wondered excitedly if this had been done so that the figurines would not fall over in case the cabinet were moved.

Eagerly she began to look on the back wall of the interior of the cabinet for a spring. She and Helen together searched every inch of the upper part but found no spring to move the great built-in piece of furniture.

On the lower part of the cabinet were two doors which Nancy had already opened many times. But then she had been looking for a large opening.

Now she was hoping to locate a tiny spring or movable panel.

Helen searched the left side, while Nancy took the right. Suddenly her pulse quickened in anticipation. She had felt a spot slightly higher than the rest.

Nancy ran her fingers back and forth across the area which was about half an inch high and three inches long.

"It may conceal something," she thought, and pushed gently against the wood.

Nancy felt a vibration in the whole cabinet.

"Helen! I've found something!" she whispered hoarsely. "Better stand back!"

Nancy pressed harder. This time the right side of the cabinet began to move forward. Nancy jumped up from her knees and stood back with Helen. Slowly, very slowly, one end of the cabinet began to move into the parlor, the other into an open space behind it.

Helen grabbed Nancy's hand in fright. What were they going to find in the secret passageway?

CHAPTER XV

A New Suspect

THE GREAT crystal chandelier illuminated the narrow passageway behind the cabinet. It was not very long. No one was in it and the place was dusty and filled with cobwebs.

"There's probably an exit at the other end of this," said Nancy. "Let's see where it goes."

"I think I'd better wait here, Nancy," Helen suggested. "This old cabinet might suddenly start to close itself. If it does, I'll yell so you can get out in time."

Nancy laughed. "You're a real pal, Helen."

As Nancy walked along the passageway, she looked carefully at the two walls which lined it. There was no visible exit from either of the solid, plastered walls. The far end, too, was solid, but this wall had been built of wood.

Nancy felt it might have some significance. At the moment she could not figure it out and started to return to the parlor. Halfway along the narrow corridor, she saw a folded piece of paper lying on the floor.

"This may prove something," she told herself eagerly, picking it up.

Just as Nancy stepped back into the parlor, Aunt Rosemary appeared. She stared in astonishment at the opening in the wall and at the cabinet which now stood at right angles to it.

"You found something?" she asked.

"Only this," Nancy replied, and handed Aunt Rosemary the folded paper.

As the girls looked over her shoulder, Mrs. Hayes opened it. "This is an unfinished letter," she commented, then started to decipher the old-fashioned handwriting. "Why, this was written way back in 1785—not long after the house was built."

The note read:

My honorable friend Benjamin:

The disloyalty of two of my servants has just come to my attention. I am afraid they plan to harm the cause of the Colonies. I will have them properly punished. My good fortune in learning about this disloyalty came while I was at my listening post. Every word spoken in the servants' sitting room can be overheard by me.

I will watch for further—

The letter ended at this point. Instantly Helen said, "Listening post?"

"It must be at the end of this passageway," Nancy guessed. "Aunt Rosemary, what room would connect with it?"

"I presume the kitchen," Mrs. Hayes replied. "And it seems to me that I once heard that the present kitchen was a sitting room for the servants long ago. You recall that back in Colonial days food was never cooked in a mansion. It was always prepared in another building and brought in on great trays."

Helen smiled. "With a listening post the poor servants here didn't have a chance for a good chit-chat together. Their conversations were never a secret from their master!"

Nancy and Aunt Rosemary smiled too and nodded, then the young sleuth said, "Let's see if this listening post still works."

It was arranged that Helen would go into the kitchen and start talking. Nancy would stand at the end of the corridor to listen. Aunt Rosemary, who was shown how to work the hidden spring on the cabinet, would act as guard if the great piece of furniture suddenly started to move and close the opening.

"All ready?" Helen asked. She moved out of the room.

When she thought Nancy was at her post, she

began to talk about her forthcoming wedding and asked Nancy to be in the bridal party.

"I can hear Helen very plainly!" Nancy called excitedly to Aunt Rosemary. "The listening post is as good as ever!"

When the test was over, and the cabinet manually closed by Nancy, she and Helen and Aunt Rosemary held a whispered conversation. They all decided that the ghost knew about the passageway and had overheard plans which those in the house were making. Probably this was where the ghost disappeared after Miss Flora spotted him.

"Funny that we seem to do more planning while we're in the kitchen than in any other room," Aunt Rosemary remarked.

Helen said she wondered if this listening post was unique with the owner and architect of Twin Elms mansion.

"No, indeed," Aunt Rosemary told her. "Many old homes where there were servants had such places. Don't forget that our country has been involved in several wars, during which traitors and spies found it easy to get information while posing as servants."

"Very clever," Helen remarked. "And I suppose a lot of the people who were caught never knew how they had been found out."

"No doubt," said Aunt Rosemary.

At that moment they heard Miss Flora's feeble

voice calling from the bedroom and hurried up the steps to be sure that she was all right. They found her smiling, but she complained that she did not like to stay alone so long.

"I won't leave you again tonight, Mother," Aunt Rosemary promised. "I'm going to sleep on the couch in this room so as not to disturb you. Now try to get a little sleep."

The following morning Nancy had a phone call from Hannah Gruen, whose voice sounded very irate. "I've just heard from Mr. Barradale, the railroad lawyer, Nancy. He lost your address and phone number, so he called here. I'm furious at what he had to say. He hinted that your father might be staying away on purpose because he wasn't able to produce Willie Wharton!"

Nancy was angry too. "Why, that's absolutely unfair and untrue," she cried.

"Well, I just wouldn't stand for it if I were you," Hannah Gruen stated flatly. "And that's only half of it."

"You mean he had more to say about Dad?" Nancy questioned quickly.

"No, not that," the housekeeper answered. "He was calling to say that the railroad can't hold up the bridge project any longer. If some new evidence isn't produced by Monday, the railroad will be forced to accede to the demands of Willie Wharton and all those other property owners!"

"Oh, that would be a great blow to Dad!" said

Nancy. "He wouldn't want this to happen. He's
sure that the signature on that contract of sale is
Willie Wharton's. All he has to do is find him
and prove it."

"Everything is such a mess," said Mrs. Gruen.
"I was talking to the police just before I called you
and they have no leads at all to where your father
might be."

"Hannah, this is dreadful!" said Nancy. "I
don't know how, but I intend to find Dad—and
quickly, too!"

After the conversation between herself and the
housekeeper was over, Nancy walked up and down
the hall, as she tried to formulate a plan. Something must be done!

Suddenly Nancy went to the front door, opened
it, and walked outside. She breathed deeply of
the lovely morning air and headed for the rose
garden. She let the full beauty of the estate sink
into her consciousness, before permitting herself
to think further about the knotty problem before
her.

Long ago Mr. Drew had taught Nancy that the
best way to clear one's brain is to commune with
Nature for a time. Nancy went up one walk and
down another, listening to the twittering of the
birds and now and then the song of the meadow
lark. Again she smelled deeply of the roses and
the sweet wisteria which hung over a sagging
arbor.

Ten minutes later she returned to the house and sat down on the porch steps. Almost at once a mental image of Nathan Gomber came to her as clearly as if the man had been standing in front of her. The young sleuth's mind began to put together the various pieces of the puzzle regarding him and the railroad property.

"Maybe Nathan Gomber is keeping Willie Wharton away!" she said to herself. "Willie may even be a prisoner! And if Gomber is that kind of a person, maybe he engineered the abduction of my father!"

The very thought frightened Nancy. Leaping up, she decided to ask the police to have Nathan Gomber shadowed.

"I'll go down to headquarters and talk to Captain Rossland," she decided. "And I'll ask Helen to go along. The cleaning woman is here, so she can help Aunt Rosemary in case of an emergency."

Without explaining her real purpose in wanting to go downtown, Nancy merely asked Helen to accompany her there for some necessary marketing. The two girls drove off, and on the way to town Nancy gave Helen full details of her latest theories about Nathan Gomber.

Helen was amazed. "And here he was acting so worried about your father's safety!"

When the girls reached police headquarters, they had to wait a few minutes to see Captain Rossland. Nancy fidgeted under the delay. Every moment seemed doubly precious now. But finally the girls were ushered inside and the officer greeted them warmly.

"Another clue, Miss Drew?" he asked with a smile.

Nancy told her story quickly.

"I think you're on the right track," the officer stated. "I'll be very glad to get in touch with your Captain McGinnis in River Heights and relay your message. And I'll notify all the men on my force to be on the lookout for this Nathan Gomber."

"Thank you," said Nancy gratefully. "Every hour that goes by I become more and more worried about my father."

"A break should come soon," the officer told her kindly. "The minute I hear anything I'll let you know."

Nancy thanked him and the girls went on their way. It took every bit of Nancy's stamina not to show her inmost feelings. She rolled the cart through the supermarket almost automatically, picking out needed food items. Her mind would say, "We need more canned peas because the ghost took what we had," and at the meat counter she reflected, "Dad loves thick, juicy steaks."

Finally the marketing was finished and the packages stowed in the rear of the convertible. On the way home, Helen asked Nancy what plans she had for pursuing the mystery.

"To tell the truth, I've been thinking about it continuously, but so far I haven't come up with any new ideas," Nancy answered. "I'm sure, though, that something will pop up."

When the girls were a little distance from the entrance to the Twin Elms estate, they saw a car suddenly pull out of the driveway and make a right turn. The driver leaned out his window and looked back. He wore a smug grin.

"Why, it's Nathan Gomber!" Nancy cried out.

"And did you see that smirk on his face?" Helen asked. "Oh, Nancy, maybe that means he's finally persuaded Miss Flora to sell the property to him!"

"Yes," Nancy replied grimly. "And also, here I've just asked the police to shadow him and I'm the first person to see him!"

With that Nancy put on speed and shot ahead. As she passed the driveway to the estate, Helen asked, "Where are you going?"

"I'm following Nathan Gomber until I catch him!"

CHAPTER XVI

Sold!

"Oh, NANCY, I hope we meet a police officer!" said Helen Corning. "If Gomber is a kidnaper, he may try to harm us if we do catch up to him!"

"We'll have to be cautious," Nancy admitted. "But I'm afraid we're not going to meet any policeman. I haven't seen one on these roads in all the time I've been here."

Both girls watched the car ahead of them intently. It was near enough for Nancy to be able to read the license number. She wondered if the car was registered under Gomber's name or someone else's. If it belonged to a friend of his, this fact might lead the police to another suspect.

"Where do you think Gomber's going?" Helen asked presently. "To meet somebody?"

"Perhaps. And he may be on his way back to River Heights."

"Not yet," Helen said, for at that moment Gomber had reached a crossroads and turned sharp right. "That road leads away from River Heights."

"But it does lead past Riverview Manor," Nancy replied tensely as she neared the crossroads.

Turning right, the girls saw Gomber ahead, tearing along at a terrific speed. He passed the vacant mansion. A short distance beyond it he began to turn his car lights off and on.

"What's he doing that for?" Helen queried. "Is he just testing his lights?"

Nancy was not inclined to think so. "I believe he's signaling to someone. Look all around, Helen, and see if you can spot anybody." She herself was driving so fast that she did not dare take her eyes from the road.

Helen gazed right and left, and then turned to gaze through the back window. "I don't see a soul," she reported.

Nancy began to feel uneasy. It was possible that Gomber might have been signaling to someone to follow the girls. "Helen, keep looking out the rear window and see if a car appears and starts to follow us."

"Maybe we ought to give up the chase and just tell the police about Gomber," Helen said a bit fearfully.

But Nancy did not want to do this. "I think it will help us a lot to know where he's heading."

She continued the pursuit and several miles farther on came to the town of Hancock.

"Isn't this where that crinkly-eared fellow lives?" Helen inquired.

"Yes."

"Then it's my guess Gomber is going to see him."

Nancy reminded her friend that the man was reported to be out of town, presumably because he was wanted by the police on a couple of robbery charges.

Though Hancock was small, there was a great deal of traffic on the main street. In the center of town at an intersection, there was a signal light. Gomber shot through the green, but by the time Nancy reached the spot, the light had turned red.

"Oh dear!" she fumed. "Now I'll probably lose him!"

In a few seconds the light changed to green and Nancy again took up her pursuit. But she felt that at this point it was futile. Gomber could have turned down any of a number of side streets, or if he had gone straight through the town he would now be so far ahead of her that it was doubtful she could catch him. Nancy went on, nevertheless, for another three miles. Then, catching no sight of her quarry, she decided to give up the chase.

"I guess it's hopeless, Helen," she said. "I'm going back to Hancock and report everything to the police there. I'll ask them to get in touch with Captain Rossland and Captain McGinnis."

"Oh, I hope they capture Gomber!" Helen

said. "He's such a horrible man! He ought to be put in jail just for his bad manners!"

Smiling, Nancy turned the car and headed back for Hancock. A woman passer-by gave her directions to police headquarters and a few moments later Nancy parked in front of it. The girls went inside the building. Nancy told the officer in charge who they were, then gave him full details of the recent chase.

The officer listened attentively, then said, "I'll telephone your River Heights captain first."

"And please alert your own men and the State Police," Nancy requested.

He nodded. "Don't worry, Miss Drew, I'll follow through from here." He picked up his phone.

Helen urged Nancy to leave immediately. "While you were talking, I kept thinking about Gomber's visit to Twin Elms. I have a feeling something may have happened there. You remember what a self-satisfied look Gomber had on his face when we saw him come out of the driveway."

"You're right," Nancy agreed. "We'd better hurry back there."

It was a long drive back to Twin Elms and the closer the girls go to it, the more worried they became. "Miss Flora was already ill," Helen said tensely, "and Gomber's visit may have made her worse."

On reaching the house, the front door was opened by Aunt Rosemary, who looked pale.

"I'm so glad you've returned," she said. "My mother is much worse. She has had a bad shock. I'm waiting for Dr. Morrison."

Mrs. Hayes' voice was trembling and she found it hard to go on. Nancy said sympathetically, "We know Nathan Gomber was here. We've been chasing his car, but lost it. Did he upset Miss Flora?"

"Yes. I was out of the house about twenty minutes talking with the gardener and didn't happen to see Gomber drive up. The cleaning woman, Lillie, let him in. Of course she didn't know who he was and thought he was all right. When she finally came outside to tell me, I had walked way over to the wisteria arbor at the far end of the grounds.

"In the meantime, Gomber went upstairs. He began talking to Mother about selling the mansion. When she refused, he threatened her, saying that if she did not sign, all kinds of dreadful things would happen to me and to both you girls.

"Poor mother couldn't hold out any longer. At this moment Lillie, who couldn't find me, returned and went upstairs. She actually witnessed Mother's signature on the contract of sale and signed her own name to it. So Gomber has won!"

Aunt Rosemary sank into the chair by the telephone and began to cry. Nancy and Helen put their arms around her, but before either could say a word of comfort, they heard a car drive up in front of the mansion. At once Mrs. Hayes dried her eyes and said, "It must be Dr. Morrison."

Nancy opened the door and admitted the physician. The whole group went upstairs where Miss Flora lay staring at the ceiling like someone in a trance. She was murmuring:

"I shouldn't have signed! I shouldn't have sold Twin Elms!"

Dr. Morrison took the patient's pulse and listened to her heartbeat with a stethoscope. A few moments later he said, "Mrs. Turnbull, won't you please let me take you to the hospital?"

"Not yet," said Miss Flora stubbornly. She smiled wanly. "I know I'm ill. But I'm not going to get better any quicker in the hospital than I am right here. I'll be moving out of Twin Elms soon enough and I want to stay here as long as I can. Oh, why did I ever sign my name to that paper?"

As an expression of defeat came over the physician's face, Nancy moved to the bedside. "Miss Flora," she said gently, "maybe the deal will never go through. In the first place, perhaps we can prove that you signed under coercion. If that doesn't work, you know it takes a long time to have a title search made on property. By then, maybe Gomber will change his mind."

"Oh, I hope you're right," the elderly woman replied, squeezing Nancy's hand affectionately.

The girls left the room, so that Dr. Morrison could examine the patient further and prescribe for her. They decided to say nothing of their morning's adventure to Miss Flora, but at luncheon they gave Aunt Rosemary a full account.

"I'm almost glad you didn't catch Gomber." Mrs. Hayes exclaimed. "He might have harmed you both."

Nancy said she felt sure that the police of one town or the other would soon capture him, and then perhaps many things could be explained. "For one, we can find out why he was turning his lights off and on. I have a hunch he was signaling to someone and that the person was hidden in Riverview Manor!"

"You may be right," Aunt Rosemary replied.

Helen suddenly leaned across the table. "Do you suppose our ghost thief hides out there?"

"I think it's very probable," Nancy answered. "I'd like to do some sleuthing in that old mansion."

"You're not going to break in?" Helen asked, horrified.

Her friend smiled. "No, Helen, I'm not going to evade the law. I'll go to the realtor who is handling the property and ask him to show me the place. Want to come along?"

Helen shivered a little but said she was game. "Let's do it this afternoon."

"Oh dear." Aunt Rosemary gave an anxious

sigh. "I don't know whether or not I should let you. It sounds very dangerous to me."

"If the realtor is with us, we should be safe," Helen spoke up. Her aunt then gave her consent, and added that the realtor, Mr. Dodd, had an office on Main Street.

Conversation ceased for a few moments as the threesome finished luncheon. They had just left the table when they heard a loud thump upstairs.

"Oh, goodness!" Aunt Rosemary cried out. "I hope Mother hasn't fallen!"

She and the girls dashed up the stairs. Miss Flora was in bed, but she was trembling like a leaf in the wind. She pointed a thin, white hand toward the ceiling.

"It was up in the attic! Sombody's there!"

CHAPTER XVII

Through the Trap Door

"LET's find out who's in the attic!" Nancy urged as she ran from the room, Helen at her heels.

"Mother, will you be all right if I leave you a few moments?" Aunt Rosemary asked. "I'd like to go with the girls."

"Of course. Run along."

Nancy and Helen were already on their way to the third floor. They did not bother to go noiselessly, but raced up the center of the creaking stairs. Reaching the attic, they lighted two of the candles and looked around. They saw no one, and began to look behind trunks and pieces of furniture. Nobody was hiding.

"And there's no evidence," said Nancy, "that the alarming thump was caused by a falling box or carton."

"There's only one answer," Helen decided. "The ghost *was* here. But how did he get in?"

The words were scarcely out of her mouth when the group heard a man's spine-chilling laugh. It had not come from downstairs.

"He—he's back of the wall!" Helen gasped fearfully. Nancy agreed, but Aunt Rosemary said, "That laugh could have come from the roof."

Helen looked at her aunt questioningly. "You —you mean that the ghost swings onto the roof from a tree and climbs in here somehow?"

"I think it very likely," her aunt replied. "My father once told my mother that there's a trap door to the roof. I never saw it and I forgot having heard of it until this minute."

Holding their candles high, the girls examined every inch of the peaked, beamed ceiling. The rafters were set close together with wood panels between them.

"I see something that might be a trap door!" Nancy called out presently from near one end of the attic. She showed the others where some short panels formed an almost perfect square.

"But how does it open?" Helen asked. "There's no knob or hook or any kind of gadget to grab hold of."

"It might have been removed, or rusted off," Nancy said.

She asked Helen to help her drag a high wooden box across the floor until it was directly under the suspected section and Nancy stepped up onto it. Focusing her light on the four edges of the panels, the young sleuth finally discovered a piece of metal wedged between two of the planks.

"I think I see a way to open this," Nancy said, "but I'll need some tools."

"I'll get the ones I found before," Helen offered. She hurried downstairs and procured them. Nancy tried one tool after another, but none would work; they were either too wide to fit into the crack or they would not budge the piece of metal either up or down.

Nancy looked down at Aunt Rosemary. "Do you happen to have an old-fashioned buttonhook?" she asked. "That might be just the thing for this job."

"Indeed I have—in fact, Mother has several of them. I'll get one."

Aunt Rosemary was gone only a few minutes. Upon her return, she handed Nancy a long, silver-handled buttonhook inscribed with Mrs. Turnbull's initials. "Mother used this to fasten her high button shoes. She has a smaller matching one for glove buttons. In olden days," she told the girls, "no lady's gloves were the pull-on type. They all had buttons."

Nancy inserted the long buttonhook into the ceiling crack and almost at once was able to grasp the piece of metal and pull it down. Now she began tugging on it. When nothing happened, Helen climbed up on the box beside her friend and helped pull.

Presently there was a groaning, rasping noise and the square section of the ceiling began to move downward. The girls continued to yank on the metal piece and slowly a folded ladder attached to the wood became visible.

"The trap door's up there!" Helen cried gleefully, looking at the roof. "Nancy, you shall have the honor of being the first one to look out."

Nancy smiled. "And, you mean, capture the ghost?"

As the ladder was straightened out, creaking with each pull, and set against the roof, Nancy felt sure, however, that the ghost did not use it. The ladder made entirely too much noise! She also doubted that he was on the roof, but it would do no harm to look. She might pick up a clue of some sort!

"Well, here I go," Nancy said, and started to ascend the rungs.

When she reached the top, Nancy unfastened the trap door and shoved it upward. She poked her head outdoors and looked around. No one was in sight on the roof, but in the center stood a circular wooden lookout. It occurred to Nancy that possibly the ghost might be hiding in it!

She called down to Aunt Rosemary and Helen to look up at the attic ceiling for evidence of an opening into the tower. They returned to Nancy in half a minute to report that they could find no sign of another trap door.

"There probably was one in olden days," said Aunt Rosemary, "but it was closed up."

A sudden daring idea came to the girl detective. "I'm going to crawl over to that lookout and see if anybody's in it!" she told the two below.

Before either of them could object, she started to crawl along the ridgepole above the wooden shingled sides of the deeply slanting roof. Helen had raced up the ladder, and now watched her friend fearfully.

"Be careful, Nancy!" she warned.

Nancy was doing just that. She must keep a perfect balance or tumble down to almost certain death. Halfway to the tower, the daring girl began to feel that she had been foolhardy, but she was determined to reach her goal.

"Only five more feet to go," Nancy told herself presently.

With a sigh of relief, she reached the tower and pulled herself up. It was circular and had openings on each side. She looked in. No "ghost"!

Nancy decided to step inside the opening and examine the floor. She set one foot down, but immediately the boards, rotted from the weather, gave way beneath her.

"It's a good thing I didn't put my whole weight on it," she thought thankfully.

"Do you see anything?" Helen called.

"Not a thing. This floor hasn't been in use for a long time."

"Then the ghost didn't come in by way of the roof," Helen stated.

Nancy nodded in agreement. "The only places left to look are the chimneys," the young sleuth told her friend. "I'll check them."

There were four of these and Nancy crawled to each one in turn. She looked inside but found nothing to suggest that the ghost used any of them for entry.

Balancing herself against the last chimney, Nancy surveyed the countryside around her. What a beautiful and picturesque panorama it was,

she thought! Not far away was a lazy little river, whose waters sparkled in the sunlight. The surrounding fields were green and sprinkled with patches of white daisies.

Nancy looked down on the grounds of Twin Elms and tried in her mind to reconstruct the original landscaping.

"That brick walk to the next property must

have had a lovely boxwood hedge at one time," she said to herself.

Her gaze now turned to Riverview Manor. The grounds there were overgrown with weeds and several shutters were missing from the house. Suddenly Nancy's attention was drawn to one of the uncovered windowpanes. Did she see a light moving inside?

It disappeared a moment later and Nancy could not be sure. Perhaps the sun shining on the glass had created an optical illusion.

"Still, somebody just might be in that house," the young sleuth thought. "The sooner I get over there and see what I can find out, the better! If the ghost is hiding out there, maybe he uses some underground passage from one of the outbuildings on the property."

She crawled cautiously back to the trap door and together the girls closed it. Aunt Rosemary had already gone downstairs to take care of her mother.

Nancy told Helen what she thought she had just seen in the neighboring mansion. "I'll change my clothes right away. Then let's go see Mr. Dodd, the realtor broker for Riverview Manor."

A half hour later the two girls walked into the real-estate office. Mr. Dodd himself was there and Nancy asked him about looking at Riverview Manor.

"I'm sorry, miss," he said, "but the house has just been sold."

Nancy was stunned. She could see all her plans crumbling into nothingness. Then a thought came to her. Perhaps the new owner would not object if she looked around, anyway.

"Would you mind telling me, Mr. Dodd, who purchased Riverview Manor?"

"Not at all," the realtor replied. "A man named Nathan Gomber."

CHAPTER XVIII

A Confession

NANCY DREW's face wore such a disappointed look that Mr. Dodd, the realtor, said kindly, "Don't take it so hard, miss. I don't think you'd be particularly interested in Riverview Manor. It's really not in very good condition. Besides, you'd need a pile of money to fix that place up."

Without commenting on his statement, Nancy asked, "Couldn't you possibly arrange for me to see the inside of the mansion?"

Mr. Dodd shook his head. "I'm afraid Mr. Gomber wouldn't like that."

Nancy was reluctant to give up. Why, her father might even be a prisoner in that very house! "Of course I can report my suspicion to the police," the young sleuth thought.

She decided to wait until morning. Then, if there was still no news of Mr. Drew, she would pass along the word to Captain Rossland.

Mr. Dodd's telephone rang. As he answered it, Nancy and Helen started to leave his office. But he immediately waved them back.

"The call is from Chief Rossland, Miss Drew," he said. "He phoned Twin Elms and learned you were here. He wants to see you at once."

"Thank you," said Nancy, and the girls left.

They hurried to police headquarters, wondering why the officer wanted to speak to Nancy.

"Oh, if only it's news of Dad," she exclaimed fervently. "But why didn't he get in touch with me himself?"

"I don't want to be a killjoy," Helen spoke up. "But maybe it's not about your father at all. Perhaps they've caught Nathan Gomber."

Nancy parked in front of headquarters and the two girls hurried inside the building. Captain Rossland was expecting them and they were immediately ushered into his office. Nancy introduced Helen Corning.

"I won't keep you in suspense," the officer said, watching Nancy's eager face. "We have arrested Samuel Greenman!"

"The crinkly-eared man?" Helen asked.

"That's right," Captain Rossland replied. "Thanks to your tip about the used car, Miss Drew, our men had no trouble at all locating him."

The officer went on to say, however, that the prisoner refused to confess that he had had anything to do with Mr. Drew's disappearance.

"Furthermore, Harry the taxi driver—we have him here—insists that he cannot positively identify Greenman as one of the passengers in his cab. We believe Harry is scared that Greenman's pals will beat him up or attack members of his family."

"Harry did tell me," Nancy put in, "that his passenger had threatened harm to his family unless he forgot all about what he had seen."

"That proves our theory," Captain Rossland stated with conviction. "Miss Drew, we think you can help the police."

"I'll be glad to. How?"

Captain Rossland smiled. "You may not know it, but you're a very persuasive young lady. I believe that you might be able to get information out of both Harry and Greenman, where we have failed."

After a moment's thought, Nancy replied modestly, "I'll be happy to try, but on one condition." She grinned at the officer. "I must talk to these men alone."

"Request granted." Captain Rossland smiled. He added that he and Helen would wait outside and he would have Harry brought in.

"Good luck," said Helen as she and the captain left the room.

A few moments later Harry walked in alone. "Oh hello, miss," he said to Nancy, barely raising his eyes from the floor.

"Won't you sit down, Harry," Nancy asked, indicating a chair alongside hers. "It was nice of the captain to let me talk to you."

Harry seated himself, but said nothing. He twisted his driver's cap nervously in his hands and kept his gaze downward.

"Harry," Nancy began, "I guess your children would feel terrible if you were kidnaped."

"It would cut 'em to pieces," the cabman stated emphatically.

"Then you know how I feel," Nancy went on. "Not a word from my father for two whole days. If your children knew somebody who'd seen the person who kidnaped you, wouldn't they feel bad if the man wouldn't talk?"

Harry at last raised his eyes and looked straight at Nancy. "I get you, miss. When somethin' comes home to you, it makes all the difference in the world. You win! I *can* identify that scoundrel Greenman, and I will. Call the captain in."

Nancy did not wait a second. She opened the door and summoned the officer.

"Harry has something to tell you," Nancy said to Captain Rossland.

"Yeah," said Harry, "I'm not goin' to hold out any longer. I admit Greenman had me scared, but he's the guy who rode in my cab, then ordered me to keep my mouth shut after that other passenger blacked out."

Captain Rossland looked astounded. It was evident he could hardly believe that Nancy in only a few minutes had persuaded the man to talk!

"And now," Nancy asked, "may I talk to your prisoner?"

"I'll have you taken to his cell," the captain responded, and rang for a guard.

Nancy was led down a corridor, past a row of cells until they came to one where the man with the crinkled ear sat on a cot.

"Greenman," said the guard, "step up here. This is Miss Nancy Drew, daughter of the kidnaped man. She wants to talk to you."

The prisoner shuffled forward, but mumbled, "I ain't goin' to answer no questions."

Nancy waited until the guard had moved off, then she smiled at the prisoner. "We all make mistakes at times," she said. "We're often misled by people who urge us to do things we shouldn't. Maybe you're afraid you'll receive the death sentence for helping to kidnap my father. But if you didn't realize the seriousness of the whole thing, the complaint against you may turn out just to be conspiracy."

To Nancy's astonishment, Greenman suddenly burst out, "You've got me exactly right, miss. I had almost nothing to do with takin' your father away. The guy I was with—*he's* the old-timer. He's got a long prison record. I haven't. Honest, miss, this is my first offense.

"I'll tell you the whole story. I met this guy

only Monday night. He sure sold me a bill of goods. But all I did was see that your pop didn't run away. The old-timer's the one that drugged him."

"Where is my father now?" Nancy interrupted.

"I don't know. Honest I don't," Greenman insisted. "Part of the plan was for somebody to follow the taxi. After a while Mr. Drew was to be given a whiff of somethin'. It didn't have no smell. That's why our taxi driver didn't catch on. And it didn't knock the rest of us out, 'cause you have to put the stuff right under a fellow's nose to make it work."

"And the person who was following in a car and took my father away, who is he?"

"I don't know," the prisoner answered, and Nancy felt that he was telling the truth.

"Did you get any money for doing this?" Nancy asked him.

"A little. Not as much as it was worth, especially if I have to go to prison. The guy who paid us for our work was the one in the car who took your father away."

"Will you describe him?" Nancy requested.

"Sure. Hope the police catch him soon. He's in his early fifties—short and heavy-set, pale, and has kind of watery blue eyes."

Nancy asked the prisoner if he would dictate the same confession for the police and the man nodded. "And I'm awful sorry I caused all this worry, miss. I hope you find your father soon and I wish I could help you more. I guess I am a coward. I'm too scared to tell the name of the guy who talked me into this whole thing. He's really a bad actor—no tellin' what'd happen to me if I gave his name."

The young sleuth felt that she had obtained all the information she possibly could from the man. She went back to Captain Rossland, who for the second time was amazed by the girl's success. He called a stenographer. Then he said good-by to Nancy and Helen and went off toward Greenman's cell.

On the way back to Twin Elms, Helen congratulated her friend. "Now that one of the kidnapers has been caught, I'm sure that your father will be found soon, Nancy. Who do you suppose the man was who took your father from Greenman and his friend?"

Nancy looked puzzled, then answered, "We know from his description that he wasn't Gomber. But, Helen, a hunch of mine is growing stronger all the time that he's back of this whole thing. And putting two and two together, I believe it was Willie Wharton who drove that car.

"And I also believe Wharton's the one who's been playing ghost, using masks at times—like the gorilla and the unshaven, long-haired man.

"Somehow he gets into the mansion and listens to conversations. He heard that I was going to be

asked to solve the mystery at Twin Elms and told
Gomber. That's why Gomber came to our home
and tried to keep me from coming here by saying
I should stick close to Dad."

"That's right," said Helen. "And when he
found that didn't work, he had Willie and Greenman and that other man kidnap your dad. He figured it would surely get you away from Twin Elms.
He wanted to scare Miss Flora into selling the
property, and he thought if you were around you
might dissuade her."

"But in that I didn't succeed," said Nancy a bit
forlornly. "Besides, they knew Dad could stop
those greedy land owners from forcing the railroad to pay them more for their property. That's
why I'm sure Gomber and Wharton won't release
him until after they get what they want."

Helen laid a hand on Nancy's shoulder. "I'm
so terribly sorry about this. What can we do
next?"

"Somehow I have a feeling, Helen," her friend
replied, "that you and I are going to find Willie
Wharton before very long. And if we do, and I
find out he really signed that contract of sale, I
want certain people to be around."

"Who?" Helen asked, puzzled.

"Mr. Barradale, the lawyer, and Mr. Watson
the notary public."

The young sleuth put her thought into action.
Knowing that Monday was the deadline set by the

railroad, she determined to do her utmost before that time to solve the complicated mystery. Back at Twin Elms, Nancy went to the telephone and put in a call to Mr. Barradale's office. She did not dare mention Gomber's or Willie Wharton's name for fear one or the other of them might be listening. She merely asked the young lawyer if he could possibly come to Cliffwood and bring with him whatever he felt was necessary for him to win his case.

"I think I understand what you really mean to say," he replied. "I take it you can't talk freely. Is that correct?"

"Yes."

"Then I'll ask the questions. You want me to come to the address that you gave us the other day?"

"Yes. About noon."

"And you'd like me to bring along the contract of sale with Willie Wharton's signature?"

"Yes. That will be fine." Nancy thanked him and hung up.

Turning from the telephone, she went to find Helen and said, "There's still lots of daylight. Even though we can't get inside Riverview Manor, we can hunt through the outbuildings over there for the entrance to an underground passage to this house."

"All right," her friend agreed. "But this time you do the searching. I'll be the lookout."

Nancy chose the old smokehouse of Riverview Manor first, since this was closest to the Twin Elms property line. It yielded no clue and she moved on to the carriage house. But neither in this building, nor any of the others, did the girl detective find any indication of entrances to an underground passageway. Finally she gave up and rejoined Helen.

"If there is an opening, it must be from inside Riverview Manor," Nancy stated. "Oh, Helen, it's exasperating not to be able to get in there!"

"I wouldn't go in there now in any case," Helen remarked. "It's way past suppertime and I'm starved. Besides, pretty soon it'll be dark."

The girls returned to Twin Elms and ate supper. A short time later someone banged the front-door knocker. Both girls went to the door. They were amazed to find that the caller was Mr. Dodd, the realtor. He held out a large brass key toward Nancy.

"What's this for?" she asked, mystified.

Mr. Dodd smiled.

"It's the front-door key to Riverview Manor. I've decided that you can look around the mansion tomorrow morning all you please."

CHAPTER XIX

The Hidden Staircase

SEEING the look of delight on Nancy's face, Mr. Dodd laughed. "Do you think that house is haunted as well as this one?" he asked. "I hear you like to solve mysteries."

"Yes, I do." Not wishing to reveal her real purpose to the realtor, the young sleuth also laughed. "Do you think I might find a ghost over there?" she countered.

"Well, I never saw one, but you never can tell," the man responded with a chuckle. He said he would leave the key with Nancy until Saturday evening and then pick it up. "If Mr. Gomber should show up in the meantime, I have a key to the kitchen door that he can use."

Nancy thanked Mr. Dodd and with a grin said she would let him know if she found a ghost at Riverview Manor.

She could hardly wait for the next morning to

arrive. Miss Flora was not told of the girls' plan to visit the neighboring house.

Immediately after breakfast, they set off for Riverview Manor. Aunt Rosemary went with them to the back door and wished the two good luck. "Promise me you won't take any chances," she begged.

"Promise," they said in unison.

With flashlights in their skirt pockets, Nancy and Helen hurried through the garden and into the grounds of Riverview Manor estate.

As they approached the front porch, Helen showed signs of nervousness. "Nancy, what will we do if we meet the ghost?" she asked.

"Just tell him we've found him out," her friend answered determinedly.

Helen said no more and watched as Nancy inserted the enormous brass key in the lock. It turned easily and the girls let themselves into the hall. Architecturally it was the same as Twin Elms mansion, but how different it looked now! The blinds were closed, lending an eerie atmosphere to the dusky interior. Dust lay everywhere, and cobwebs festooned the corners of the ceiling and spindles of the staircase.

"It certainly doesn't look as if anybody lives here," Helen remarked. "Where do we start hunting?"

"I want to take a look in the kitchen," said Nancy.

When they walked into it, Helen gasped. "I guess I was wrong. Someone has been eating here." Eggshells, several empty milk bottles, some chicken bones and pieces of waxed paper cluttered the sink.

Nancy, realizing that Helen was very uneasy, whispered to her with a giggle, "If the ghost lives here, he has a good appetite!"

The young sleuth took out her flashlight and beamed it around the floors and walls of the kitchen. There was no sign of a secret opening. As she went from room to room on the first floor, Helen followed and together they searched every inch of the place for a clue to a concealed door. At last they came to the conclusion there was none.

"You know, it could be in the cellar," Nancy suggested.

"Well, you're not going down there," Helen said firmly. "That is, not without a policeman. It's too dangerous. As for myself, I want to live to get married and not be hit over the head in the dark by that ghost, so Jim won't have a bride!"

Nancy laughed. "You win. But I'll tell you why. At the moment I am more interested in finding my father than in hunting for a secret passageway. He may be a prisoner in one of the rooms upstairs. I'm going to find out."

The door to the back stairway was unlocked and the one at the top stood open. Nancy asked

Helen to stand at the foot of the main staircase, while she herself went up the back steps. "If that ghost is up there and tries to escape, he won't be able to slip out that way," she explained.

Helen took her post in the front hall and Nancy crept up the back steps. No one tried to come down either stairs. Helen now went to the second floor and together she and Nancy began a search of the rooms. They found nothing suspicious. Mr. Drew was not there. There was no sign of a ghost. None of the walls revealed a possible secret opening. But the bedroom which corresponded to Miss Flora's had a clothes closet built in at the end next to the fireplace.

"In Colonial times closets were a rarity," Nancy remarked to Helen. "I wonder if this closet was added at that time and has any special significance."

Quickly she opened one of the large double doors and looked inside. The rear wall was formed of two very wide wooden planks. In the center was a round knob, sunk in the wood.

"This is strange," Nancy remarked excitedly. She pulled on the knob but the wall did not move. Next, she pushed the knob down hard, leaning her full weight against the panel.

Suddenly the wall pushed inward. Nancy lost her balance and disappeared into a gaping hole below!

Helen screamed. "Nancy!"

Trembling with fright, Helen stepped into the closet and beamed her flashlight below. She could see a long flight of stone steps.

"Nancy! Nancy!" Helen called down.

A muffled answer came from below. Helen's heart gave a leap of relief. "Nancy's alive!" she told herself, then called, "Where are you?"

"I've found the secret passageway," came faintly to Helen's ears. "Come on down."

Helen did not hesitate. She wanted to be certain that Nancy was all right. Just as she started down the steps, the door began to close. Helen, in a panic that the girls might be trapped in some subterranean passageway, made a wild grab for the door. Holding it ajar, she removed the sweater she was wearing and wedged it into the opening.

Finding a rail on one side of the stone steps, Helen grasped it and hurried below. Nancy arose from the dank earthen floor to meet her.

"Are you sure you're all right?" Helen asked solicitously.

"I admit I got a good bang," Nancy replied, "but I feel fine now. Let's see where this passageway goes."

The flashlight had been thrown from her hand, but with the aid of Helen's light, she soon found it. Fortunately, it had not been damaged and she turned it on.

The passageway was very narrow and barely high enough for the girls to walk without bending over. The sides were built of crumbling brick and stone.

"This may tumble on us at any moment," Helen said worriedly.

"Oh, I don't believe so," Nancy answered. "It must have been here for a long time."

The subterranean corridor was unpleasantly damp and had an earthy smell. Moisture clung to the walls. They felt clammy and repulsive to the touch.

Presently the passageway began to twist and turn, as if its builders had found obstructions too difficult to dig through.

"Where do you think this leads?" Helen whispered.

"I don't know. I only hope we're not going in circles."

Presently the girls reached another set of stone steps not unlike the ones down which Nancy had tumbled. But these had solid stone sides. By their lights, the girls could see a door at the top with a heavy wooden bar across it.

"Shall we go up?" Helen asked.

Nancy was undecided what to do. The tunnel did not end here but yawned ahead in blackness. Should they follow it before trying to find out what was at the top of the stairs?

She voiced her thoughts aloud, but Helen urged that they climb the stairs. "I'll be frank with you. I'd like to get out of here."

Nancy acceded to her friend's wish and led the way up the steps.

Suddenly both girls froze in their tracks.

A man's voice from the far end of the tunnel commanded, "Stop! You can't go up there!"

CHAPTER XX

Nancy's Victory

THEIR initial fright over, both girls turned and beamed their flashlights toward the foot of the stone stairway. Below them stood a short, unshaven, pudgy man with watery blue eyes.

"You're the ghost!" Helen stammered.

"And you're Mr. Willie Wharton," Nancy added.

Astounded, the man blinked in the glaring lights, then said, "Ye-yes, I am. But how did you know?"

"You live in the old Riverview Manor," Helen went on, "and you've been stealing food and silver and jewelry from Twin Elms!"

"No, no. I'm not a thief!" Willie Wharton cried out. "I took some food and I've been trying to scare the old ladies, so they would sell their property. Sometimes I wore false faces, but I never took any jewelry or silver. Honest I didn't. It must have been Mr. Gomber."

Nancy and Helen were amazed—Willie Wharton, with little urging from them, was confessing more than they had dared to hope.

"Did you know that Nathan Gomber is a thief?" Nancy asked the man.

Wharton shook his head. "I know he's sharp—that's why he's going to get me more money for my property from the railroad."

"Mr. Wharton, did you sign the original contract of sale?" Nancy queried.

"Yes, I did, but Mr. Gomber said that if I disappeared for a while, he'd fix everything up so I'd get more money. He said he had a couple of other jobs which I could help him with. One of them was coming here to play ghost—it was a good place to disappear to. But I wish I had never seen Nathan Gomber or Riverview Manor or Twin Elms or had anything to do with ghosts."

"I'm glad to hear you say that," said Nancy. Then suddenly she asked, "Where's my father?"

Willie Wharton shifted his weight and looked about wildly. "I don't know, really I don't."

"But you kidnaped him in your car," the young sleuth prodded him. "We got a description of you from the taximan."

Several seconds went by before Willie Wharton answered. "I didn't know it was kidnaping. Mr. Gomber said your father was ill and that he was

going to take him to a special doctor. He said
Mr. Drew was coming on a train from Chicago and
was going to meet Mr. Gomber on the road halfway between here and the station. But Gomber
said he couldn't meet him—had other business
to attend to. So I was to follow your father's taxi
and bring him to Riverview Manor."

"Yes, yes, go on," Nancy urged, as Willie Wharton stopped speaking and covered his face with
his hands.

"I didn't expect your father to be unconscious
when I picked him up," Wharton went on. "Well,
those men in the taxi put Mr. Drew in the back
of my car and I brought him here. Mr. Gomber
drove up from the other direction and said he
would take over. He told me to come right here
to Twin Elms and do some ghosting."

"And you have no idea where Mr. Gomber
took my father?" Nancy asked, with a sinking
feeling.

"Nope."

In a few words she pointed out Nathan Gomber's real character to Willie Wharton, hoping
that if the man before her did know anything
about Mr. Drew's whereabouts which he was not
telling, he would confess. But from Wharton's
emphatic answers and sincere offers to be of all
the help he could in finding the missing lawyer,
Nancy concluded that Wharton was not withhold-
ing any information.

"How did you find out about this passageway and the secret staircases?" Nancy questioned him.

"Gomber found an old notebook under a heap of rubbish in the attic of Riverview Manor," Wharton answered. "He said it told everything about the secret entrances to the two houses. The passageways, with openings on each floor, were built when the houses were. They were used by the original Turnbulls in bad weather to get from one building to the other. This stairway was for the servants. The other two stairways were for the family. One of these led to Mr. Turnbull's bedroom in this house. The notebook also said that he often secretly entertained government agents and sometimes he had to hurry them out of the parlor and hide them in the passageway when callers came."

"Where does this stairway lead?" Helen spoke up.

"To the attic of Twin Elms." Willie Wharton gave a little chuckle. "I know, Miss Drew, that you almost found the entrance. But the guys that built the place were pretty clever. Every opening has heavy double doors. When you poked that screw driver through the crack, you thought you were hitting another wall but it was really a door."

"Did you play the violin and turn on the radio —and make that thumping noise in the attic— and were you the one who laughed when we were up there?"

"Yes, and I moved the sofa to scare you and I even knew about the listening post. That's how I found out all your plans and could report them to Mr. Gomber."

Suddenly it occurred to Nancy that Nathan Gomber might appear on the scene at any moment. She must get Willie Wharton away and have him swear to his signature before he changed his mind!

"Mr. Wharton, would you please go ahead of us up this stairway and open the doors?" she asked. "And go into Twin Elms with us and talk to Mrs. Turnbull and Mrs. Hayes? I want you to tell them that you've been playing ghost but aren't going to any longer. Miss Flora has been so frightened that she's ill and in bed."

"I'm sorry about that," Willie Wharton replied. "Sure I'll go with you. I never want to see Nathan Gomber again!"

He went ahead of the girls and took down the heavy wooden bar from across the door. He swung it wide, pulled a metal ring in the back of the adjoining door, then quickly stepped downward. The narrow panel opening which Nancy had suspected of leading to the secret stairway now was pulled inward. There was barely room alongside it to go up the top steps and into the attic. To keep Gomber from becoming suspicious if he should arrive, Nancy asked Willie Wharton to close the secret door again.

"Helen," said Nancy, "will you please run downstairs ahead of Mr. Wharton and me and tell Miss Flora and Aunt Rosemary the good news."

She gave Helen a three-minute start, then she and Willie Wharton followed. The amazed women were delighted to have the mystery solved. But there was no time for celebration.

"Mr. Barradale is downstairs to see you, Nancy," Aunt Rosemary announced.

Nancy turned to Willie Wharton. "Will you come down with me, please?"

She introduced both herself and the missing property owner to Mr. Barradale, then went on, "Mr. Wharton says the signature on the contract of sale is his own."

"And you'll swear to that?" the lawyer asked, turning to Willie.

"I sure will. I don't want anything more to do with this underhanded business," Willie Wharton declared.

"I know where I can find a notary public right away," Nancy spoke up. "Do you want me to phone him, Mr. Barradale?" she asked.

"Please do. At once."

Nancy dashed to the telephone and dialed the number of Albert Watson on Tuttle Road. When he answered, she told him the urgency of the situation and he promised to come over at once. Mr. Watson arrived within five minutes, with his notary equipment. Mr. Barradale showed him the contract of sale containing Willie Wharton's name and signature. Attached to it was the certificate of acknowledgment.

Mr. Watson asked Willie Wharton to raise his right hand and swear that he was the person named in the contract of sale. After this was done, the notary public filled in the proper places on the certificate, signed it, stamped the paper, and affixed his seal.

"Well, this is really a wonderful job, Miss Drew," Mr. Barradale praised her.

Nancy smiled, but her happiness at having accomplished a task for her father was dampened by the fact that she still did not know where he was. Mr. Barradale and Willie Wharton also were extremely concerned.

"I'm going to call Captain Rossland and ask him to send some policemen out here at once," Nancy stated. "What better place for Mr. Gomber to hide my father than somewhere along that passageway? How far does it go, Mr. Wharton?"

"Mr. Gomber says it goes all the way to the river, but the end of it is completely stoned up now. I never went any farther than the stairways."

The young lawyer thought Nancy's idea a good one, because if Nathan Gomber should return to Riverview Manor and find that Willie was gone, he would try to escape.

The police promised to come at once. Nancy had just finished talking with Captain Rossland when Helen Corning called from the second floor.

"Nancy, can you come up here? Miss Flora insists upon seeing the hidden staircase."

The young sleuth decided that she would just about have time to do this before the arrival of the police. Excusing herself to Mr. Barradale, she ran up the stairs. Aunt Rosemary had put on a rose-colored dressing gown while attending her mother. To Nancy's amazement, Mrs. Turnbull was fully dressed and wore a white blouse with a high collar and a black skirt.

Nancy and Helen led the way to the attic. There, the girl detective, crouching on her knees, opened the secret door.

"And all these years I never knew it was here!" Miss Flora exclaimed.

"And I doubt that my father did or he would have mentioned it," Aunt Rosemary added.

Nancy closed the secret door and they all went downstairs. She could hear the front-door bell ringing and assumed that it was the police. She and Helen hurried below. Captain Rossland and another officer stood there. They said other men had surrounded Riverview Manor, hoping to catch Nathan Gomber if he did arrive there.

With Willie Wharton leading the way, the girls, Mr. Barradale, and the police trooped to the attic and went down the hidden staircase to the dank passageway below.

"I have a hunch from reading about old passage-ways that there may be one or more rooms off this tunnel," Nancy told Captain Rossland.

There were so many powerful flashlights in play now that the place was almost as bright as daylight. As the group moved along, they suddenly came to a short stairway. Willie Wharton explained that this led to an opening back of the sofa in the parlor. There was still another stone stairway which went up to Miss Flora's bedroom with an opening alongside the fireplace.

The searchers went on. Nancy, who was ahead of the others, discovered a padlocked iron door in the wall. Was it a dungeon? She had heard of such places being used for prisoners in Colonial times.

By this time Captain Rossland had caught up to her. "Do you think your father may be in there?" he asked.

"I'm terribly afraid so," said Nancy, shivering at the thought of what she might find.

The officer found that the lock was very rusty. Pulling from his pocket a penknife with various tool attachments, he soon had the door unlocked and flung it wide. He beamed his light into the blackness beyond. It was indeed a room without windows.

Suddenly Nancy cried out, "Dad!" and sprang ahead.

Lying on blankets on the floor, and covered with others, was Mr. Drew. He was murmuring faintly.

"He's alive!" Nancy exclaimed, kneeling down to pat his face and kiss him.

"He's been drugged," Captain Rossland observed. "I'd say Nathan Gomber has been giving your father just enough food to keep him alive and mixing sleeping powders in with it."

From his trousers pocket the officer brought out a small vial of restorative and held it to Mr. Drew's nose. In a few moments the lawyer shook his head, and a few seconds later, opened his eyes.

"Keep talking to your dad," the captain ordered Nancy.

"Dad! Wake up! You're all right! We've rescued you!"

Within a very short time Mr. Drew realized that his daughter was kneeling beside him. Reaching out his arms from beneath the blankets, he tried to hug her.

"We'll take him upstairs," said Captain Rossland. "Willie, open that secret entrance to the parlor."

"Glad to be of help." Wharton hurried ahead and up the short flight of steps.

In the meantime, the other three men lifted Mr. Drew and carried him along the passageway. By the time they reached the stairway, Willie

Wharton had opened the secret door behind the sofa in the parlor. Mr. Drew was placed on the couch. He blinked, looked around, and then said in astonishment:

"Willie Wharton! How did you get here? Nancy, tell me the whole story."

The lawyer's robust health and sturdy constitution had stood him in good stead. He recovered with amazing rapidity from his ordeal and listened in rapt attention as one after another of those in the room related the events of the past few days.

As the story ended, there was a knock on the front door and another police officer was admitted. He had come to report to Captain Rossland that not only had Nathan Gomber been captured outside of Riverview Manor, and all the loot recovered, but also that the final member of the group who had abducted Mr. Drew had been taken into custody. Gomber had admitted everything, even to having attempted to injure Nancy and her father with the truck at the River Heights' bridge project. He had tried to frighten Miss Flora into selling Twin Elms because he had planned to start a housing project on the two Turnbull properties.

"It's a real victory for you!" Nancy's father praised his daughter proudly.

The young sleuth smiled. Although she was glad it was all over, she could not help but look forward to another mystery to solve. One soon came her way when, quite accidentally, she found herself involved in *The Bungalow Mystery*.

Miss Flora and Aunt Rosemary had come downstairs to meet Mr. Drew. While they were talking to him, the police officer left, taking Willie Wharton with him as a prisoner. Mr. Barradale also said good-by. Nancy and Helen slipped out of the room and went to the kitchen.

"We'll prepare a super-duper lunch to celebrate this occasion!" said Helen happily.

"And we can make all the plans we want," Nancy replied with a grin. "There won't be anyone at the listening post!"

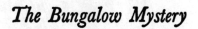

The Bungalow Mystery

The man chained to the bench was Jacob Aborn!

CHAPTER I

A Blinding Storm

"Look at those black storm clouds!" Nancy Drew pointed out to her friend, Helen Corning, who was seated beside her in the bow of the small red motorboat.

Nancy, blue-eyed, and with reddish-gold glints in her blond hair, was at the wheel. She gazed anxiously across a long expanse of water to the distant shores of Twin Lakes. The Pinecrest Motel, where the eighteen-year-old girl and her older friend were staying, was almost two miles away on the smaller of the two lakes.

Helen Corning, dark-haired and petite, looked at Nancy with concern. "I think we're in for a cloudburst," she said, "and Twin Lakes becomes as rough as the ocean in a storm."

A few minutes later angry waves began to beat against the sides of the boat.

"Are there life preservers aboard, Helen?" Nancy asked.

"No," Helen answered fearfully.

Nancy set her chin grimly. Although it was only four o'clock in the afternoon, the sky was becoming increasingly dark. The pleasant summer breeze, which had been blowing earlier, was turning into a stiff wind.

"It's getting harder to keep on course," Nancy remarked, gripping the wheel more tightly.

As she increased the boat's speed to the maximum, the craft fairly leaped through the water, dashing spray into the girls' faces.

"I wonder if there are any raincoats in the lockers," said Helen.

"Please look," Nancy requested. "We'll be drenched by the time we reach the motel dock."

Luckily Helen found two plastic coats. She slipped into one, then helped Nancy into the other.

A streak of forked lightning cut across the sky, momentarily disclosing a thick mass of ugly clouds. The lightning was followed by an ominous crack of thunder, which caused the girls to jump.

"This is terrible!" Helen wailed.

A moment later the wind began to howl. It struck the boat with a force which made Helen grasp the railing next to her for support. Another dazzling flash of lightning illuminated the sky, and simultaneously a deluge of rain began to descend.

Nancy peered ahead into the dimness. The shore line had vanished and the blinding rain made it impossible for her to see more than a few feet beyond the bow of the boat.

"At least we have half a tank of fuel," Nancy announced, trying to sound optimistic. "We'll reach shore soon, I'm sure."

"I wouldn't bet on that," Helen said nervously.

A worried expression furrowed the young pilot's brow. The boat was making little progress against the wind. If anything happened to the motor they would be at the mercy of the waves.

A few minutes later the rain came down even harder. The wind continued to blow a raging gale and the waves, seemed higher.

The girls leaned forward, trying to get their bearings. As a jagged ribbon of lightning illuminated the path ahead, Helen screamed, "About!"

Nancy froze with horror. A tremendous log was floating directly into the path of the motorboat!

Her heart pounding, the young skipper gave the wheel a vicious turn, but not quickly enough. With a splintering crash, the bow of the boat struck the log!

The impact sent Helen sprawling to the deck. Nancy clung to the steering wheel, but was thrown forward violently.

"Helen, are you hurt?" she asked.

"I— I'm all right. Are you?" she stammered, as Nancy helped Helen to her feet. Both girls were breathing heavily.

By now the small boat was listing sharply to starboard. Nancy saw instantly that the log had torn a jagged hole in the side of the craft. Water was pouring in rapidly.

"Quick, Helen!" Nancy ordered tersely. "You bail and I'll try to stop the leak!"

She sprang forward, tore off her raincoat, and stuffed it into the hole. Helen, meanwhile, found a rusty can and began to bail. Despite their efforts, water continued to pour through the opening.

"Let's shout for help!" Nancy cried above the wind, but she doubted that there was any other craft on the lake.

The girls cupped their hands to their lips and shouted frantically. Their only answer was the howl of the gale and the steady beat of rain.

"Louder!" Helen urged, and they screamed until they were hoarse.

"It's no use," Nancy said at last. "We'll have to think of something else."

Just then Nancy saw a giant wave bearing down on them. She met it head on, hoping to ride the crest, but a deluge of water almost inundated the girls. They were flung overboard and the motorboat sank to the bottom of the lake!

An excellent swimmer, Nancy managed to get her head above water almost immediately. Her first thought was for Helen. What had become of her?

Treading water, Nancy glanced about. Helen was not in sight.

"I must find her!" Nancy thought desperately. "She may have been injured!"

Then, several yards away, Nancy saw a white hand flash above the water. With powerful crawl strokes she plowed through the waves to the spot. The hand had vanished!

Nancy made a neat surface dive. Opening her eyes, she tried to see through the clouded water but to no avail. At last, she surfaced and drew in a deep breath.

Clearing her eyes, Nancy was relieved to spot her friend several feet ahead. Helen was floating on her back. Strong strokes brought Nancy directly behind her friend.

"My arms feel numb," Helen said weakly. "Guess I hit them on the boat."

"Don't worry," said Nancy. "Just lie still and I'll tow you to shore."

Nancy, however, had grave misgivings regarding her ability to accomplish this in the turbulent water. She needed every ounce of strength to swim the distance alone. *Could* she manage to save Helen? The storm had made the water very cold. Nancy prayed that she would not get a cramp and both girls go down.

"Hold your breath when you see a wave coming," she instructed Helen, as they started off.

At frequent intervals Nancy shouted for help, although she felt it was wasted energy. On and on they went.

Helen noticed finally that Nancy's breathing showed the great strain on her. "Save yourself," she begged. "Go on to shore without me."

"Never!" said Nancy, as a huge wave bore down upon the two girls, smothering them in its impact.

Feebly, Nancy struggled back to the surface with her burden. "One more like that and I'll be through," she said to herself.

Just then Nancy thought she detected a voice above the roar of the wind. Was it her imagination or had she really heard someone call?

"Help!" she screamed.

This time there could be no mistake, for she distinguished the words:

"Hold on! I'm coming!"

Through the blinding rain Nancy caught a glimpse of a dark object. A rowboat! If only she could hold out until it reached her!

"Over here!" Nancy cried loudly, waving.

As the boat approached, she fully expected to see it swamped. The boat swept safely toward the two girls, barely avoiding a crash, however. To Nancy's surprise, there was only one occupant in the boat—a slender, auburn-haired girl of about sixteen.

Twice she tried to bring the boat alongside the swimmers, but failed. The third time, as the craft swept past, Nancy lunged forward and caught the side of it. She dragged Helen along, supporting her with one hand until she, too, secured a hold.

"Can you climb aboard?" their rescuer asked. "I'll balance the boat while you get in."

Nancy explained about the submerged motorboat and Helen's useless arms.

With the strange girl and Nancy working together, they managed to get Helen into the craft. Then Nancy pulled herself over the side.

"Safe!" Helen said in relief. "I don't know how to thank you," she told their rescuer.

"Are you both all right?" asked the strange girl. "We're not far from the beach—otherwise, I couldn't have heard your cries for help in this wind."

"You were very brave to come for us," said Nancy. "I'm Nancy Drew and this is Helen Corning."

The girl at the oars stared at Nancy with keen interest. "I'm Laura Pendleton," she said. "I read in a newspaper about one of the mysteries you solved. I may need your help some day soon, Nancy."

Without another word Laura bent over her oars again.

"I'll help you row," Nancy offered, snatching up an extra oar from the bottom of the rowboat, and wondering what Laura Pendleton's mystery was.

Using the oar like a paddle, Nancy attempted to keep the boat on course. As she and Laura made some progress against the wind and waves, Helen took new hope.

"I think we're going to make it!" she said in relief. "Oh!"

A vivid flash of lightning illuminated the water. Directly ahead, through the rain, she and Nancy caught a glimpse of the rocky shore line.

"The rocks. Laura! Be careful or we'll be dashed against them!" Helen cried out, as the rowboat was tossed and slapped by the crashing waves.

Another zigzag streak of lightning disclosed the shore line more distinctly. A short distance out from the land and directly in front of their boat stood the ugly protruding nose of a jagged boulder!

CHAPTER II

Uninvited Guests

FOR an instant Nancy panicked. Would the girls be able to steer clear of the menacing rocks? A collision seemed unavoidable!

"We'll be killed!" gasped Helen.

"Row to the left, Laura!" Nancy commanded. "It's our only chance."

With a burst of energy the rowers turned the boat and deftly avoided the jagged boulder. An oncoming wave pushed them farther out of danger.

"There's a cove ahead!" Laura shouted above the wind. "We'll try to make it."

In another five minutes they reached the cove. Here the water was comparatively quiet.

"Thank goodness!" Helen murmured. "Oh, you girls are wonderful!"

As Nancy's oar struck a sand bar, she dropped it and quickly stepped out into water up to her knees. Laura followed and the two girls pulled the boat up onto the beach. Then they helped Helen Corning step onto firm sand.

"How do your arms feel now?" Nancy asked her.

"Better," Helen replied. "But I'm freezing." Her teeth were chattering.

Nancy herself was cold. She squinted through the darkness and rain, trying to see where they were. It seemed to be a desolate spot.

"Where are we?" she asked Laura. "Is there some place nearby where we can sit out the storm and get warm?"

"The only place I know," Laura replied, "is a bungalow I passed a while ago as I was walking along the beach. It's to our right, secluded among the trees."

"Sounds fine," Nancy said. "Let's hurry!"

The three bedraggled girls stumbled along the beach. Water oozed from Laura's sandals. Nancy and Helen had kicked theirs off in the lake and now slipped and slid in their soggy socks.

Presently the girls reached a small, concealed building, a one-and-a-half-storied weather-beaten bungalow which stood a short distance from the water's edge. The upper level nestled into the steep, wooded hillside. Since there was no light inside, Nancy assumed no one was there. She knocked. No answer. Nancy tried to open the door. It was locked.

"Looks as if we're out of luck," said Helen.

But Nancy was not easily discouraged, and she knew it was imperative for the girls to get warm. Her father, a well-known lawyer, had trained her to be self-reliant. He frequently handled mystery cases, and Nancy had often helped him in unearthing valuable clues.

In addition, Nancy had solved some mystery cases on her own—one involving an old clock and another a haunted house. There, Nancy had aided its owners to discover a hidden staircase which led to the capture of the mansion's "ghost."

"I'm sure that the owner of this bungalow will forgive us for going in," Nancy said.

There was a small window to the right of the door. She tried it and found to her relief that it was unlocked.

"That's a lucky break," said Helen, as Nancy opened the window.

Fortunately, it was low enough to the ground for the girls to hoist themselves through easily.

"Whew!" Laura exclaimed, as the wind almost blew them inside. She helped Nancy close the window.

It was pitch dark inside the building. Nancy groped around for a light switch, finally found one, and flicked it on. A small bulb in the ceiling disclosed nothing except two canoes and a wooden bench which stood against one wall.

"Maybe it's only a boathouse," said Helen, flopping wearily onto the bench.

The girls noticed a narrow flight of stairs leading to the second floor.

"I wonder," Nancy mused, "if we might find something up there to wrap around us. Or maybe even some towels to dry ourselves off with. Let's see."

Laura followed Nancy to the rear of the building. Seeing a light switch for the upper story, Nancy turned it and the two girls climbed the steps. To their surprise, the second floor of the bungalow was furnished with two cots and blankets, a table and chairs, tiny refrigerator, a sink, and a two-burner electric stove.

"We're in luck!" Nancy exclaimed happily. "Come on up, Helen," she called.

Laura spotted an open closet in a corner of the room. It was well stocked with food. She held up a can of prepared cocoa.

"Under the circumstances," she said, "I doubt that the owner of this place would object if we made something warm to drink."

Helen and Nancy agreed. Within a short time the three girls had taken off their wet clothing and were wrapped in blankets. Laura had turned on one burner of the stove and made hot chocolate.

"Umm, this is good," Nancy said contentedly.

Both she and Helen again thanked Laura profusely for coming to their rescue, and said they had been trying to get back to the Pinecrest Motel.

"Are you staying there?" Laura questioned.

"For a week," Helen replied. "My Aunt June is coming tomorrow. She was supposed to ride up with us Thursday from River Heights where we live, but was detained. She's going to help design my dress for my marriage to Jim Archer. He's in Europe now on business for an oil company. When he returns to the States, we'll be married."

Nancy Drew asked Laura if she, too, was a summer visitor at the resort. When her question met with silence, Nancy was surprised to see tears gathering in Laura's eyes.

"I'm sorry, Laura," Nancy said instantly. "You've been through a terrible ordeal. You should be resting instead of talking."

"Of course," Helen agreed.

Laura blinked her eyes, then said soberly, "You don't understand. You see, my mother passed away a month ago and—" She could not continue.

Nancy impulsively put an arm around Laura's shoulders. "I do understand," she said, and told of losing her own mother at the age of three.

Helen added, "Nancy lives with her father, a lawyer, and Hannah Gruen, their housekeeper."

"I'm an orphan," Laura stated simply. "My father was in a boat accident nearly six years ago." She explained that Mr. Pendleton's sailboat had capsized during a storm. He had been alone and no one had been near enough to save him.

"That's why," Laura added, "I knew I had to save whoever was crying for help on the lake today. I love to walk in a storm."

Nancy and Helen felt their hearts go out to the parentless girl. Not only was Laura brave, but also she showed great strength of character.

"With whom are you staying now?" Nancy asked Laura.

The girl looked troubled. "I'm alone at the moment. I checked in at the Montewago Hotel just this morning. But my guardian Jacob Aborn and his wife Marian are to arrive some time this evening. They're taking me to their summer home at Melrose Lake. I believe it's near here."

"Yes, it is," Nancy said.

"Do you know the Aborns?" Helen asked.

Laura said that she did not remember the couple. Her mother had frequently spoken of them, however.

"Mr. Aborn is distantly related to my mother, and it was her request that he become my legal guardian in case of her death."

Laura gave a slight sob, then went on, "But no answer came from our lawyer's letter to Mr. Aborn, who was traveling."

"How strange!" Nancy remarked.

"Finally I wrote to Mr. and Mrs. Aborn myself at the Melrose Lake address," Laura said. "The truth was I needed some money as a down payment on tuition at the boarding school I attend."

"And they replied?" Nancy asked.

"Yes. Mr. Aborn told me to come here and he and his wife would meet me."

Helen interrupted. "Then everything's settled, so you should be happy."

The girl shook her head. "I feel I'm not wanted. The letter wasn't cordial. Oh dear, what shall I do?"

Nancy gave Laura a hug. "You'll be at school and during vacations you can visit friends. And you have a new friend named Nancy Drew!"

"Oh, Nancy, you're sweet." Laura smiled for the first time, but in a moment her mood became sad again. "Living that way isn't like having your own home. Mother and I had such wonderful times together." She brushed away a few tears.

Nancy wanted to learn more but saw by her waterproof watch that it was six o'clock. Laura would have to hurry off to meet her guardian. The sky was getting lighter and the rain had almost stopped.

"We'd better leave," she suggested to Helen and Laura.

The girls washed the cups and saucepan, dressed, and put the blankets where they had found them. Before leaving the bungalow, Nancy wrote a note of thanks to the owner, signing it "Three grateful girls."

As they were parting, Laura said, "If my guardians don't arrive I'll call you and arrange a date for tomorrow."

"Please do!" Nancy and Helen urged, and waved good-by.

When they reached the Pinecrest Motel, the two girls went at once to talk to Mr. Franklin, the manager. They told him about the sunken motorboat, expressing extreme regret, and assured him that their parents would pay for the craft.

"Don't worry about that," the manager said. "We have insurance which takes care of such accidents. I'm just glad you girls are all right."

At that moment a short, thin woman swaggered into the office. Her print dress was mud-splattered and she had lost the heel to one shoe. Her wet, bleached hair clung to her head in an unbecoming fashion.

Ignoring Nancy and Helen, who were still conversing with Mr. Franklin, the woman said bluntly, "Is there anyone here who can change a tire for me? I just had a flat half a mile away."

"I'm afraid not," Mr. Franklin apologized. "I'm busy in the office and most of the help are off this evening."

"That's great!" the woman said angrily. "What am I supposed to do—walk to the Montewago Hotel? I'm late already!"

Although Nancy thought the stranded motorist was being extremely rude, she, nevertheless, suggested that the woman telephone a nearby service station. "I'm sure they'll send someone out to help you."

This idea was received with a snort as sparks of annoyance flashed in the woman's pale-blue eyes. "I'll think about that!" she said sarcastically, and, turning, limped toward the telephone booth. She banged the door shut behind her.

The three spectators looked after her with disgust and Helen said, "Some people don't deserve a helping hand."

The irate stranger was still in the booth when Nancy and Helen went off to their room on the ground floor. After a bath and change of clothes the girls felt better. A tasty dinner in the restaurant restored their energy and they played shuffleboard under the floodlights.

The next morning, as the two friends dressed, Helen asked, "Do you think Laura Pendleton will call us?" Helen was putting on Bermuda shorts and a candy-striped blouse.

"I imagine so," said Nancy, "unless her guardian and his wife took her to Melrose Lake last night."

"How far is that from here?" Helen inquired.

Nancy consulted a road map. "About twenty-five miles," she replied. Then, as she was putting on loafers, someone knocked on the door. Nancy went to see who it was.

Laura Pendleton stood in the doorway. She looked very pretty in a becoming pink cotton dress. But the girl's eyes were shadowed and she seemed highly distressed.

"Oh, Nancy—Helen!" Laura exclaimed. "I just had to come see you as soon as I could!"

"We're glad you did," Nancy said. "Come in." Before she could continue, Laura flung herself on Helen's bed and started to sob.

"What's wrong, Laura?" Nancy asked in concern, going over to her.

Slowly the girl sat up and wiped away her tears with a handkerchief. She apologized for her behavior, then said, "I don't think I'm going to be happy living with the Aborns—at least not with Mrs. Aborn!"

Troubled, Nancy asked Laura whether the guardian and his wife had arrived the evening before.

"Only Mrs. Aborn," Laura replied. "She came to my room about an hour after I left you girls.

She was wet and in a very nasty mood. Apparently she'd had a flat tire on the road and was delayed in getting help from some gasoline station."

Nancy and Helen exchanged significant glances. Mrs. Aborn sounded like the woman they had met in Mr. Franklin's office!

"What does your guardian's wife look like, Laura?" Helen asked with interest.

"She's blond, small, and thin. And I guess she was terribly upset about all the trouble she'd had. I understood this and tried to make her comfortable in the extra bedroom, but—"

Laura went on to say that Mrs. Aborn, instead of calming down, had become even more unpleasant, blaming the girl for making it necessary for her to drive to Twin Lakes in the bad storm.

"She said that Mary, my mother, had spoiled me and that I was going to have to toe the mark in her home— Oh, what will I do?" Laura asked.

Nancy did not know, but said Mrs. Aborn's behavior was inexcusable. Then she asked whether Laura's mother had known the guardian's wife well.

Instead of replying to the question, Laura said absently, "Mrs. Aborn called my mother 'Mary.' But, Nancy, Mother's name was Marie!"

CHAPTER III

Strange Guardians

NANCY was almost certain now that she and Helen had met the unpleasant Mrs. Aborn the night before. The woman's quarrelsome mood had extended to Laura.

Aloud Helen said, "But don't forget it's no fun to have car trouble on a bad night. That is apt to make anyone cross."

"I suppose so," Laura conceded.

"How was Mrs. Aborn this morning?" Nancy asked.

Laura's face brightened somewhat as she admitted that the woman had been pleasant and charming. "Mrs. Aborn apologized for her actions last night and said both she and her husband could hardly wait for me to come and live with them."

"I see," said Nancy, but with inward reservations.

"I guess I'm being foolish to worry." Laura smiled. "Mrs. Aborn did say she had met Mother only once, so that could explain the name mix-up."

"Where is Mr. Aborn?" Helen asked.

"He's arriving after lunch today. He was detained on business."

Nancy was puzzled. The Aborns' behavior was unusual and thoughtless, she felt.

"Mrs. Aborn is having her hair set at the beauty parlor in the hotel," Laura explained. "She suggested that I take a taxi here this morning if I felt I had to see you two—which I insisted I did," Laura said, grinning cheerfully.

Suddenly Nancy smiled. "I'm starved." She asked Laura to have a second breakfast with her and Helen in the motel restaurant.

"And afterward," Helen went on, "let's ask Marty Malone—the girl we met yesterday, Nancy —to make a foursome in tennis."

"Great!" said Laura to both suggestions.

When the three girls stepped outside, Nancy took a deep breath of air. She loved the earthy smell of the forests surrounding the lake resort, particularly the scent of the tall pines.

"What a day!" she exclaimed. Only a few fleecy white clouds broke the clear blue sky.

"The weatherman must be on our side." Helen chuckled.

A little later Nancy lent Laura tennis clothes, and the girls went to meet Marty Malone. Soon the four were playing a lively set on the courts located behind the motel. Laura and Nancy, who were partners, won. Helen and Marty took the second set.

"You're a terrific player, Nancy!" Laura exclaimed, as she scored a point during set three.

"Thanks," Nancy said, as they changed courts for service. "Where did you learn to play so well?"

"Private lessons." Laura grimaced. "At boarding school. Mother insisted. Before her illness she was a great sportswoman."

When Nancy and Laura had won the third set, Laura called for time out. "I must go back to the hotel now," she said. "It's almost noon."

After Laura had changed her clothes, Nancy offered to drive her to the hotel. The three girls piled into Nancy's blue convertible. Ten minutes later they drew up in front of the spacious Montewago Hotel. It was several stories high and stood a long distance back from the main road. In front stretched a green lawn bordered by beds of multicolored gladioli, dahlias, and giant asters.

"It's beautiful!" Nancy commented, as Laura stepped from the car.

Helen pointed to an attractive outdoor swim-

ming pool to the right of the hotel. It was filled
with bathers. Laura said that there was also a
riding stable behind the Montewago.

"There are a lot of families here," Laura said
wistfully. "I wish I could stay." Then hastily she
thanked Nancy for driving her over.

"I loved doing it," Nancy replied. "I hope we
see each other again, Laura."

"So do I," Helen added.

Laura snapped her fingers. "I have a wonderful
idea! Why don't you girls come back around three
o'clock? You can meet my guardians. And if
there's time, we can join the other young people
at a tea dance scheduled for four."

"Fine!" Nancy said at once.

"Come directly to my room." Laura waved
good-by.

Nancy detected a worried expression on Laura's
face, and knew she hated the thought of meeting
her strange new guardian.

The young sleuth was so quiet on the return
trip that Helen said, "Penny for your thoughts,
Nancy."

Her friend smiled. "I've concluded that the
Pendletons must have been wealthy."

"What gives you that idea?"

"It's very expensive to live year round in New
York hotels where Laura lived and she also mentioned boarding school. In addition," Nancy enu-

merated, "Laura's clothes have that simple but expensive look—you know what I mean."

"Yes," said Helen. "Well, if you're right, Mr. Aborn will control a great deal of money while he's managing Laura's affairs."

"In the case of a minor," said Nancy, "an inheritance is held in trust until she is twenty-one, Dad says. That's five years for Mr. Aborn. I hope he'll be a wise guardian."

She turned onto Lakeview Lane, a long, straight road bordered by woods. There were no homes along the way but a sign ahead advertised Sterling's real-estate office. Suddenly Nancy stopped.

"I think I'll run in here for a minute," she said, "and ask who owns that bungalow we helped ourselves to."

She walked into the office, introduced herself to Mr. Sterling, an elderly man, and told him the purpose of her call. The realtor grinned. "Any port in a storm is all right, I'm sure."

He said that the bungalow was owned by one of his clients. He had rented it a week before to a Mrs. Frank Marshall from Pittsburgh.

"I guess she fixed up the second floor," Mr. Sterling added. "She and her husband plan to use the place week ends. I'll pass the word along to Mrs. Marshall that you were there."

"I left a note but didn't sign it," Nancy said.

"Perhaps some time I'll stop in person and thank the Marshalls."

Returning to the car, she told Helen what she had learned. "Just for fun let's go out to the bungalow now."

A quarter of a mile farther on Nancy made a right-hand turn which brought them out on the lake drive. Below them, the girls could see the bungalow they had visited.

Suddenly a black foreign car pulled out of the lane that led down to the bungalow. Gaining speed, the automobile came toward Nancy's convertible.

"Watch out!" Helen yelled, jerking to attention as the vehicle passed and nearly sideswiped them.

Nancy slowed down and stopped. She looked back at the car which was almost out of sight. "Some drivers don't deserve a license," she said. "Do you suppose that was Mr. Marshall?"

Helen shrugged. "He wore a straw hat pulled low over his forehead. All I could see was the sleeve of his tan-and-white jacket."

"That's quite a bit," Nancy teased, "in so short a time."

Helen laughed. "Close association with you is making me more observant," she said.

When the girls reached the Pinecrest Motel, Helen exclaimed, "There's Aunt June!" While

Nancy parked, the dark-haired girl slipped from the convertible and hurried to the porch outside the room they occupied.

"Hello, Helen dear." The slim, stylishly dressed woman, with softly waved black hair, smiled at her niece.

Helen returned the greeting and gave her father's younger sister a kiss. "When did you arrive?" she asked. "Have you been waiting long?"

"No. I got here half an hour ago."

The attractive-looking woman was a buyer for a River Heights department store. She told Helen of a retailing problem which had prevented her departure with the girls, then turned to greet Nancy with enthusiasm.

"Isn't this a lovely spot?" Nancy remarked, and Aunt June Corning agreed that the view of the lake was superb.

After learning that Aunt June had not had lunch, the three went into the tearoom. When they had given their order, Miss Corning said, "I have some slightly bad news for you, Nancy."

"What's happened?"

"Well, just before I left River Heights, I phoned your housekeeper to see if she had any messages for you. To my surprise Dr. Darby answered. He said that Mrs. Gruen had sprained her ankle early this morning, and she must not walk for a couple of days."

"I'll call Dad right away and talk to him," said Nancy with concern.

"Wait!" Aunt June said. "Dr. Darby mentioned that your father left on a business trip today before the accident occurred."

"That means Hannah is all alone," Nancy said, rising. "I'll have to go home at once. Will you both excuse me for a minute, please?"

She went to a telephone booth and dialed the Drews' next-door neighbor, Mrs. Gleason. Nancy was relieved to hear that the woman's sister was taking care of Hannah for the afternoon. The housekeeper was in no pain and resting comfortably.

The young sleuth did some rapid thinking. If she left for River Heights late that afternoon she could still fulfill her promise to Laura to meet her guardian and arrive home in time to cook Hannah's supper.

"Will you please tell Mrs. Gruen I'll see her at six o'clock," Nancy requested, and Mrs. Gleason agreed to do this.

When Nancy returned to the others, Helen was telling her aunt of the adventure on the lake and Laura Pendleton's story.

"How dreadful for the girl!" exlaimed Miss Corning. "I feel very sorry for her."

Nancy now told of her plans to return home, and although Helen and her aunt were disap-

THE BUNGALOW MYSTERY

pointed, they agreed that it was the right thing to do.

"But before I leave," said Nancy, "I want to meet Mr. and Mrs. Aborn."

After lunch Nancy packed her suitcase, put it in the car, and paid her motel bill. Soon it was time for her and Helen to leave for the Montewago Hotel.

"Are you sure you won't accompany us, Aunt June?" asked Helen.

Miss Corning shook her head. "I'm a little tired," she said, "and besides, I must unpack."

A short while later the two girls entered the Montewago lobby. Nancy made her way directly to the desk and after a brief wait was informed that Miss Pendleton would receive the girls in her suite. An elevator took them to the third floor.

Scarcely had they knocked on the door when Laura opened it. "Oh, I'm so glad you came," she cried out, smiling with relief.

Laura led the girls into a well-appointed living room with a bedroom on either side. As Nancy stepped inside, she saw a man and a woman seated in chairs near a picture window. In a glance Nancy realized that she and Helen had been right about Mrs. Aborn being the woman they had met the night before. Right now she looked more friendly.

Jacob Aborn arose and smiled graciously. He

was a well-built, somewhat stocky man in his early fifties. His face was square, and his small brown eyes were shifty.

When Laura introduced the girls, Mrs. Aborn rushed toward them. "Darlings!" she said, giving Helen and Nancy a butterfly peck on their cheeks. "You've been so good to poor Laura."

"Perfect bricks!" Mr. Aborn said gruffly. He extended a hand first to Nancy, then to Helen. "The reason I'm late in getting Laura is that I want everything to be perfect for her arrival at our Melrose Lake house."

Nancy was sure Mrs. Aborn recognized the callers and was embarrassed to admit it. They said nothing. There was an awkward silence until Laura said, "Well, let's all sit down."

For a few minutes everyone chatted generally, then Helen asked, "When are you leaving, Mr. Aborn?"

"In half an hour," was the reply. "Laura is tired and I want to get her settled before suppertime."

Mrs. Aborn broke in, "Yes, the poor child needs a lot of rest and good care."

Laura Pendleton seemed annoyed to be treated as a child and an invalid. "I'm fine," she stated defiantly. Turning to Nancy, she said quietly, "I'm afraid that we can't attend the hotel tea dance."

"That's all right," Nancy replied. She told of Hannah's accident and the fact that she must soon head for home.

"Are you all packed, Laura?" Mr. Aborn asked.

"Yes, except to get Mother's jewelry from the hotel safe."

"I'll do that for you, dear," Mrs. Aborn volunteered, rising. She smoothed her skirt restlessly.

Laura said, "Thank you, but I must present the receipt in person." She excused herself, saying she would be right back.

As Laura left the suite, Mr. Aborn turned to the two guests. "I wish Marie Pendleton had been a little more cautious with her inheritance from her husband," he confided.

"What do you mean?" Nancy asked.

"Laura is practically penniless," her guardian explained. "Mrs. Pendleton's illness and the way she lived took almost all her funds."

Nancy and Helen were surprised and dismayed to hear this.

"It doesn't matter, though," Mrs. Aborn said. "We have ample means to provide for Laura. She'll have everything she needs."

Nancy was confused by the woman's seemingly dual personality. She could be crude as on the evening before, or sweet as she appeared now. Perhaps, at heart, she meant well. Nancy hoped so for Laura's sake, but a strange feeling of distrust persisted.

When Laura returned, Helen and Nancy said they must be on their way. The friends shook hands.

"We never can thank you enough, Laura, for coming to our rescue yesterday," Helen said gratefully.

"That's right," Nancy agreed. "If you hadn't come along at that moment we'd probably be at the bottom of the lake!"

Laura shuddered. "Oh, I'm sure you would have reached shore some way! But I am glad I could help and it's been such fun knowing you. I hope you'll come to see me while I'm at Melrose Lake."

"We will," Nancy promised. "What is your address there?"

"Anyone can direct you to my house," Mr. Aborn said heartily. "It's well known in that section."

His wife tapped her foot on the floor. "Jacob, it's getting late," she hinted.

Nancy and Helen hastily bade the Aborns good-by and walked toward the door of the suite with Laura. Suddenly Helen turned around.

"It's lucky you brought two cars!" she called back. "Laura has a lot of luggage."

Without another word, Helen gave Laura a quick kiss and walked into the corridor. Nancy followed a moment later.

"Why did you say that?" Nancy questioned Helen as they rode down in the elevator.

The dark-haired girl signaled for silence. There were several other people in the car. When they stepped out into the lobby Nancy repeated her question.

Helen grabbed her chum's arm excitedly. "I couldn't resist it!" she exclaimed. "Jacob Aborn was the driver in the tan-and-white sports jacket I saw coming out of the road by the bungalow this morning! The driver of the black foreign car!"

CHAPTER IV

The Tree Crash

IF HELEN was right about Mr. Aborn's being the driver of the foreign car, then it should be in the hotel parking lot, Nancy thought.

"Let's take a look," she suggested.

The girls walked to the rear of the hotel where Nancy had left her own convertible. They scouted the lot. There was no sign of a black foreign car. Helen asked the attendant if one had been driven in that day. The man said no.

Helen was puzzled. "I was so sure I was right."

"You still could be," said Nancy. "The car may be parked somewhere else. Mrs. Aborn may have picked up her husband at some other point."

Puzzled, she and Helen climbed into the convertible and Nancy started the engine. As she drove back to the Pinecrest Motel, Helen remarked:

"I don't care for either Mr. or Mrs. Aborn. Their friendliness seems forced, and their promises don't ring true."

"I agree." Nancy nodded. "By the way, did you notice how Laura's guardian went out of his way to tell us she was penniless? And we were total strangers."

"I certainly did," Helen replied. "It was in very bad taste, I'd say."

"As soon as Hannah's ankle is better," Nancy declared, "I'm coming back here. Let's pay Laura a visit together at Melrose Lake. I feel very uneasy about her."

"A wonderful idea!" Helen exclaimed.

When they reached the motel, she got out. "I hope Hannah's foot improves quickly," she said, and waved Nancy out of sight.

A minute later Nancy was on the main highway which paralleled Twin Lakes for some distance. Presently, as she left the lake area, Nancy cast a speculative glance toward the sky. Did she imagine it or was it beginning to cloud over?

Nancy glanced at the speedometer. She was nearly halfway to River Heights. "Maybe I can get home before the storm breaks," she told herself.

A quarter of a mile farther on Nancy saw an obstruction in the road and brought the convertible to a halt. A huge sign read:

DETOUR. BRIDGE OUT. TAKE MELROSE LAKE ROAD. An arrow pointed to the left.

"Just when I'm in a hurry!" Nancy fumed, knowing she would have to go miles out of her way before reaching the River Heights road.

Another anxious glance at the sky told her there was no time to be lost. Already huge storm clouds were appearing.

"I'll be caught in another cloudburst like the one on the lake," she thought.

Hastily she headed the car down the Melrose Lake detour, a narrow, rutty road bordered with tall pines and thick shrubbery. Nancy was forced to reduce her speed to ten miles an hour, and even then it seemed as though the car would shake to pieces.

Within a few minutes it grew so dark that Nancy snapped on the headlights. Giant raindrops began to strike the windshield. In a short time they were followed by a blinding downpour, and the deep ruts in the road filled up like miniature streams.

"I'm in for it now," Nancy groaned, as the car crept up a hill.

Before she could reach a level stretch on the other side of the hill, the storm broke in all its fury. Trees along the roadside twisted and bent before the onslaughts of the rushing wind.

It was difficult for Nancy to see the road ahead.

She crawled along, endeavoring to keep the convertible's wheels out of deep ruts. As she swerved to avoid a particularly large puddle, a blinding tongue of lightning streaked directly in front of the car.

There was a flash of fire and simultaneously a deafening roar. For an instant, Nancy thought the car had been struck.

Almost blinded, the girl jammed on the brakes in time to hear a splintering, ripping noise. Before her horrified eyes a pine tree fell earthward. The convertible seemed to be directly in its line of fall!

"Oh!" Nancy gasped, as the tree missed her car by inches, landing directly in front of it.

Nancy felt as though she were frozen in her seat. How closely she had escaped possible death! When she was breathing normally again, Nancy ruefully surveyed the tree which blocked the road. What was she to do?

"I can't go back because the bridge is out," she told herself. "And there probably isn't anyone within miles of this place." She suddenly realized she had not seen another car going in either direction.

As Nancy continued to gaze at the fallen tree, she decided it could be moved by two people.

"Too bad I'm not twins," she thought. "I won-

der how long it will be before someone comes
past here."

Finally Nancy decided to try pulling the tree
aside. She reached in the back seat for plastic
boots and a raincoat with a hood. After putting
these on, she stepped outside.

Gingerly picking her way through the mud and
heavy rain, she walked to the fallen pine. She
grasped the branches and tugged with all her
might. The tree did not budge. Nancy next tried
rolling it. This, too, she found was impossible.

"Oh, this is maddening," she thought, feeling
completely frustrated.

As another low roll of thunder broke the quiet-
ness of the woods, Nancy was delighted to see
headlights approaching. A moment later a small
jeep pulled up behind her car.

The driver's door opened and a young man's
voice said, "Hello there! Having trouble?"

"I sure am," said Nancy, as he walked toward
her and stood outlined in the convertible's headlights. He appeared to be about seventeen, had
dark hair, and twinkling eyes. Quickly Nancy explained about the fallen tree.

"Wow! You were lucky that it missed you!"
the boy cried, then added, "It will be easy for the
three of us to move the tree."

"Three?" Nancy questioned.

He laughed. "My sister's in the jeep," he explained, then called out, "Come on out, Cath!"

They were joined by a pretty girl, whom Nancy guessed to be fourteen years old. Introductions were exchanged. The brother and sister were Jim and Cathy Donnell. They lived off the next main highway and were returning home from visiting friends.

"I'm glad we came by," Cathy said. "There's only one house on this road and the people haven't moved in yet for the summer."

After Jim had pulled some tangled pine branches away from the convertible, he and the two girls were able to lift the trunk. Little by little they moved the tree far enough aside so that the cars could drive ahead.

"I'll report this to the highway patrol when we get home," said Jim.

"Thanks so much for your help," Nancy told the brother and sister. "By the way, do you know a Mr. and Mrs. Aborn who live at Melrose Lake?"

"We certainly do," said Cathy. "They're the ones whose house is on this route. It's a lovely place, with a lane leading to the house. You passed it about a mile back. The Aborns just bought the place."

"It's a small world," Nancy observed. She told the Donnells, however, that they were wrong

Nancy tried to pull the fallen tree aside

about the Aborns not being at their home, and explained about meeting the couple and Laura Pendleton at Twin Lakes.

"That's funny," said Jim. He explained that his parents had known the Aborns for years. "They used to have a place on the other side of the larger lake, and bought this new house only a month ago. They mentioned that Laura Pendleton was coming to visit them, but said they were taking an extensive trip first."

"I see," said Nancy, thinking, "Another strange angle to this thing!" Aloud she asked, "Is Mrs. Aborn a blond-haired woman, rather small and slight, Cathy?"

"Yes."

Jim said that he and Cathy must say good-by. Their parents would be worried if they did not arrive home soon.

"We'll tell Mother and Dad about the Aborns and Laura," said Jim. "We're all keen to meet Laura. The Aborns think she must be tops!"

"And we want to introduce Laura to our friends here at the lake," Cathy added.

"Grand!" Nancy said enthusiastically. "Laura has had a pretty sad time recently. She needs friends."

The three said good-by and got into their own cars. As Nancy drove on, she kept mulling over the Aborn-Pendleton enigma. She inferred from the Donnells' remarks that the man and his wife were very acceptable people. But Nancy certainly had not received this impression of them.

"I can't wait to meet them again," she thought, "and see how they're treating Laura."

By the time Nancy reached the end of the detour, the storm was over. A little later she turned into the Drews' driveway and parked near the front porch of the large red-brick house. She climbed from the car and made a dash for the porch with her suitcase.

As she inserted her key in the lock and pushed the front door open, a voice called out from the living room, "Nancy? Is that you?"

"Yes, Hannah. Be right in."

Nancy took off her raincoat and boots and put them in the vestibule closet. Then she hurried into the living room and hugged the motherly-looking woman, who was reclining on the sofa.

"Hannah! I'm so sorry about your ankle. How are you feeling?"

A worried expression faded from the house-keeper's face as she said, "I'm fine, now that you're home. This storm has been dreadful and I was concerned about you being on the road. Helen phoned that you were on your way."

Nancy told of the fallen tree at Melrose Lake, and how it had taken her longer than she had planned to make the trip.

"Goodness!" the housekeeper exclaimed. Then she smiled. "Nancy, you're like a cat with nine lives, the way you so often just miss being injured."

Nancy laughed. Then, becoming serious, she asked, "Where did Dad go?"

"To the state capital," Hannah replied, "and that reminds me, dear—you're to call Mr. Drew at eight tonight—" She gave Nancy a slip of paper with a telephone number on it.

"Did he say what he wanted?" Nancy inquired.

A look of concern appeared on Hannah's face as she said, "Mr. Drew wishes you to help him with an embezzlement case he's investigating!"

CHAPTER V

The Unexpected Prowler

AN EMBEZZLEMENT case! Nancy was excited. What, she wondered, did her father want her to do? The young detective longed to place a call to him immediately, but knew she must wait until eight o'clock.

"Where is Mrs. Gleason's sister?" she asked.

Hannah said that the woman had left a short while before, after hearing that Nancy would be home by suppertime.

"But first she fixed a chicken casserole dish for us," Hannah added. "It's all ready to pop in the oven. My dear, I hate to bother you—"

Nancy grinned mischievously and teased, "You mean you hate to have anyone else but you reign in your kitchen. Don't worry, Hannah, I'll be neat."

"Oh posh!" said Hannah. She blushed and gave Nancy a loving glance.

Humming softly, Nancy went to the modern pink-and-white kitchen. The casserole, which looked tempting, stood on one of the gleaming counter tops. After lighting the oven, Nancy placed the dish inside to heat.

She set two wooden trays with doilies, napkins, and silver. Then, after placing bread and butter on each, Nancy poured two glasses of milk. Lastly, she made a crisp salad of lettuce and tomatoes and marinated it with a tangy French dressing.

While waiting for the casserole, Nancy went back to the living room. Hannah was reading the evening paper.

"You're a wonderful help, dear," the housekeeper said gratefully, looking up. "Tell me, did you enjoy your vacation?"

"It was lovely," said Nancy, and described the resort. She then told Hannah of the adventure on Twin Lakes and of Laura Pendleton and the Aborns.

"Hannah, wouldn't it be nice if Laura could visit us sometime soon?"

"It certainly would."

By now their supper was ready and Nancy brought it in on the trays. After they had eaten, she put the dishes in the washer, then helped Hannah, who was using crutches, upstairs to bed.

Nancy then went out to put her car in the garage, and returned to the house just as the clock was striking eight. She went to place the call to Carson Drew.

Nancy looked at the series of numbers on the slip of paper Hannah had given her:

942 HA 5–4727

She dialed the long-distance number, and after one brief ring the phone on the other end was picked up.

"Hotel Williamston," the switchboard operator answered.

"May I speak with Mr. Carson Drew?" his daughter requested.

"One moment, please."

There was a pause, then the operator's voice said, "I'm sorry but Mr. Drew checked out this evening."

"Did he say where he was going?" Nancy inquired in amazement.

The desk clerk said no. Nancy thanked him and hung up, feeling oddly upset. It was unlike her father to change his plans without calling home to tell where he would be. Could anything have happened to him? she wondered.

Since Hannah was asleep, Nancy did not awaken her to discuss the matter. Leaving on a light in the lower hall, she went to her own room and unpacked, deep in thought. As she hung up her dresses in the closet the young sleuth wondered if her father might be following a new clue in another city.

Deciding that this probably was what had happened and that she would hear from her father the next morning, Nancy felt reassured, took a bath, and went to bed. She fell asleep almost immediately.

Several hours later Nancy was awakened by the sound of a dull thud. She sat up and groped for the bedside light. Turning it on, she got out of bed and slipped into her robe and slippers.

"I hope Hannah hasn't fallen out of bed," Nancy thought worriedly, and hurried down the carpeted hall to the housekeeper's room.

Peering in the bedroom door, Nancy saw that Hannah was sound asleep. Puzzled, Nancy went back to her own room. The girl detective had almost decided she had been dreaming, then she heard an even louder noise.

The creaky window in the ground-floor library was being opened! Someone was entering the house!

Alarmed, Nancy decided to call the police and tiptoed to the bedside telephone in Mr. Drew's room. When the sergeant answered, she told him she would unlock the front door.

Nancy tiptoed quietly down the stairs. Upon reaching the ground floor, she eyed the closed door of the library, located at the far end of the living room. Not a sound came from the library which Mr. Drew used as a study.

With bated breath Nancy moved toward the front door and opened it. At that instant the library door was flung open. A man's dark figure was outlined in the doorway. Nancy's heart skipped three beats.

As Nancy debated whether to run outdoors or upstairs, she heard a loud chuckle. At the same time, a table lamp was turned on.

"Dad!" cried Nancy in disbelief, as color flooded back into her face. "Is it really you?"

"Of course!" said Carson Drew, a tall, distinguished-looking man who right now seemed a little sheepish.

He placed the brief case he was carrying on a table, then walked toward Nancy with outstretched arms. His daughter rushed into them and gave Mr. Drew a loving kiss.

"You're the best-looking burglar I've ever seen!" Nancy declared, and told her father of fearing the house was being entered. Then she clapped a hand to her face. "The police! I notified the police when I heard the window creaking open."

At that very moment father and daughter heard a car stop outside. Two policemen rushed in.

"Where's the burglar?"

"Right here," Mr. Drew confessed. "I forgot my house key. Sorry to put you to this trouble."

The policemen grinned and one said, "I wish all our burglary cases were solved this easy!" A few minutes later the officers left.

Mr. Drew explained to Nancy that he had hesitated about ringing the doorbell and disturbing Mrs. Gruen and Nancy. Recalling that one of the windows in the library did not close completely and needed repair, he removed the screen and opened the window.

"I'm sorry I scared you. I flew home tonight rather unexpectedly and didn't have a chance to let you know, Nancy."

"Has there been a new development in your embezzlement case, Dad?" she inquired.

Mr. Drew nodded. "Yes, but since it's late I suggest we both go to bed. We can talk about it in the morning."

Nancy stifled a yawn. "Good idea," she agreed.

Father and daughter turned off the lights and went upstairs. Both slept soundly until eight o'clock the following morning when Nancy was awakened by Hannah.

"Get up, sleepyhead!" said the housekeeper. Teasingly she prodded Nancy's foot with the tip of a wooden crutch while leaning on another one. "It's a beautiful day!"

Nancy jerked awake, rubbing her eyes. "Hannah!" she gasped. "What are you doing up?"

The housekeeper smiled. "One day of staying off my feet will keep me well for a year," she declared. "Besides, I feel fine this morning."

"But Dr. Darby said—" Nancy began.

"Stuff and nonsense!" Hannah replied tartly. "He left me these crutches to use and that's what I intend to do with them. Nancy, is your father home? I noticed his door is closed."

"Yes, Hannah." Nancy related the burglar scare.

The housekeeper smiled in amusement. Then, with a swish of her skirt, she turned and clumped out of the room. She paused at the door, winked at Nancy, and said:

"Pancakes and sausage at eight-thirty—and you tell your dad that I'm going to squeeze some extra-juicy oranges."

Mr. Drew was awake also. Nancy could hear the buzz of his electric razor! It was good, she thought, for the little family to be home again.

In half an hour they were seated in the cheerful breakfast room. As they began to eat, Mr. Drew caught up on the latest news and listened with concern to the story of Nancy's two storm adventures.

"I'm grateful that you're here safely beside me," he said gravely.

When the lawyer heard about Laura Pendleton and the Aborns, he frowned. "I agree with you, Nancy, it does sound strange," he said. "But you should not interfere with Laura and her guardians unless she asks you to. They may turn out to be very nice people."

"I agree," said Hannah, then added pointedly, "But if things should prove otherwise, Mr. Drew?"

"Then I'd be happy to help Laura have another guardian appointed by the court," the lawyer replied. "In the meantime, Nancy, let's invite Laura to spend a few days with us very soon."

Nancy beamed. "Thanks, Dad. That's just what I wanted to do."

When the meal was finished and the dishes had been put in the washer, Mr. Drew and Nancy went to his study, a comfortable room with book-lined shelves, deep-seated leather chairs, and a wide, highly polished mahogany desk.

Nancy sat down in a yellow club chair, then said eagerly, "Come on, Dad, don't hold out on me any longer about this case of yours."

Mr. Drew smiled, and absently fingered a glass paperweight. Sitting down, he began to talk.

Mr. Drew's client, a Mr. Seward, was the president of the Monroe National Bank in Monroe. It had branches throughout the country, including one in River Heights. During a recent audit, many valuable securities had been discovered missing from the main bank's vault. Most of the securities were bonds which read "Payable to Bearer."

"How dreadful!" said Nancy. "It means that whoever has the bonds can cash them."

"That's right." Mr. Drew said that the bonds belonged to various bank clients throughout the country. In all cases the clients had inherited money and had asked the bank as custodian to invest it for them. A Mr. Hamilton was put in charge. This was a very common bank procedure: the bank made the investments and paid the dividends to the individual, thus relieving the person of handling his own transactions.

"I was called in on the case," Carson Drew said, "by Mr. Sill, manager of our River Heights branch, when Mr. Seward advised him that a number of the missing securities belong to residents in our community. Mr. Seward felt this was an odd coincidence."

"It is," Nancy agreed. "Have you any idea who might have taken the property?"

Mr. Drew said no. So far the evidence pointed to Mr. Hamilton, although the man was a highly trusted officer.

"What about the people who work in the vault?" Nancy asked, wrinkling her forehead.

"They're being checked on now. Most of these

employees have worked for the bank a long time, however. At present two of them are on vacation, so the investigation may take some time."

"Couldn't you find out where they went?" Nancy asked.

"We've tried that," her father replied, "but they're not at their homes and the neighbors don't know where they're vacationing. We'll just have to wait until the men get home."

"I see," Nancy agreed.

"The main thing is," said Mr. Drew, "that Mr. Seward doesn't want any publicity about the theft. The bank will continue to pay dividends to the security holders, of course. My assignment is to find the missing property and the guilty person."

"A big order," said Nancy. "How are you going to do this?"

Carson Drew said he was presently checking on employees other than Hamilton who worked in the custodian department. Also, he was trying to find out if there might be a tie-in between the thief and one or more of the persons whose property was missing.

"There must be several people behind this theft," the lawyer explained. "It's pretty difficult in these times to rob a bank, with all the security measures they employ. Nothing is impossible, however, if a plan is well worked out."

"Sounds like an exciting case, Dad," said Nancy. "What can I do to help?"

In reply Mr. Drew gave Nancy a slip of paper with four names on it and their corresponding River Heights addresses. They were: Mrs. William Farley, Mr. Herbert Brown, Mrs. John Stewart, Mr. Stephen Dowd. None of the names was familiar to the young detective.

"These are the local people whose securities are missing," Mr. Drew said. "Think of some reason to meet these people," he directed. "See what kind of homes they have, and try to get an insight into their characters. This is a very vague assignment, but I feel you may find out something incriminating about one of them—you see, we have to be very careful not to arouse suspicion in a case of this type."

"I'll do my best," Nancy assured him.

"The out-of-town names I'll check myself," her father explained. "They live in various large cities around the country, so I'll have to be away a good bit during the next few weeks."

"I'll get busy on these names right away," Nancy said. She gave her father a quick hug. "You're an old dear to let me help you!"

"Promise me you'll be careful," the lawyer warned. "An embezzler can be a dangerous person. And in this case whoever is behind the thefts is playing for big stakes."

The young sleuth said she would take every precaution. As Nancy stood up, the telephone rang.

"I'll get it, Dad," she offered, and hurried to pick up the receiver of the hall phone.

A low-pitched feminine voice said tersely, "Nancy? Nancy Drew?"

"Yes. This is Nancy speaking."

As she held on, waiting for the caller's identification, she heard sounds of a scuffle on the other end of the receiver. This was followed by a cry of pain and a loud *crash!*

CHAPTER VI

An Invitation to Sleuth

"Who is this?" Nancy asked.

But the caller had cut off the connection. What had happened to her? Nancy wondered. Certainly she had sounded very distressed. Nancy hung up and waited for a second call, but the phone did not ring.

"Who was it?" Mr. Drew asked, coming into the hall.

Nancy told what had occurred.

"You didn't recognize the voice?" he remarked.

"No, so I can't call back. Oh dear, someone is in trouble, I just know it. And here I stand helpless to do a thing! It's maddening!"

"It certainly is," her father said. "Well, dear, I must run down to the office." Presently he left the house.

After seeing that Hannah was comfortable, Nancy went to her bedroom and thoughtfully opened the closet door.

"This is as good a day as any to start Dad's investigation," she thought.

Nancy took out a two-piece navy-blue dress which made her look older than her eighteen years. Next, she found a pair of comfortable low-heeled pumps.

For several minutes Nancy experimented with various hair styles. She finally chose a simple off-the-face arrangement. Nancy put on tiny pearl earrings, dusted her nose lightly with powder, and finally added a dash of lipstick.

After she had changed her clothes and given herself a final appraisal, Nancy went to Hannah's room to tell her she was going out for a while.

"Gracious, Nancy," said the housekeeper, giving the girl a sharp glance, "you look awfully businesslike today. Where are you going?"

"Dad asked me to look up something for him," she said. "I'll be back in time for lunch."

"Don't worry about that," said Hannah. "I can get around. Have a good time, dear."

When Nancy left the house she consulted the list Mr. Drew had given her. Mrs. William Farley, the first name on the paper, lived on Acorn Street, seven blocks from the Drew residence.

Nancy set out at a brisk pace, rehearsing in her

mind the approach on which she had decided. One of the girl's favorite community projects was a recreational youth center located in downtown River Heights. The center always needed volunteer helpers as well as entertainers for the children.

"A good way to find out something about Dad's suspects," Nancy decided, "is to see how they will respond to a needy cause. And I'll be telling the truth when I say that I'm working for the organization."

This resolved, Nancy soon reached a modest white house which was set back from the street a short distance. The front walk was outlined with pink and white petunias and the grass was well tended.

Nancy rang the bell. The door was opened almost immediately by an elderly woman with wavy white hair and the greenest, most alert, eyes Nancy had ever seen.

"Yes?" she inquired pleasantly.

Nancy introduced herself, then explained the purpose of her call. She was invited inside.

"Please be seated," said the woman, sitting down herself. Nancy chose a Duncan Phyfe rocking chair covered with a black floral print.

The hostess smiled. "I'd be glad to help you with your project, my dear," she said, "although I have no talent. Also, I don't leave this house very much. I'm a recent widow, you see, and I haven't been too well lately."

Nancy expressed sympathy and said she understood completely. She liked this friendly little woman on first sight.

"Would a small check help your cause?" the widow asked. "Perhaps you could buy some equipment for the children."

"That would be wonderful," Nancy said. "But I'm not soliciting funds."

Mrs. Farley smiled shyly. "I realize this," she said. "But there's so little I can do to help others. Mr. Farley left most of his estate, which was modest, in trust. And I have only a tiny income to live on."

The woman arose, and despite Nancy's protests, went to the desk where she wrote out a check.

Nancy thanked her profusely, for she realized that this was a sacrifice on the widow's part.

"I'm glad I can help," said Mrs. Farley. "Please come see me again and tell me how the youth center is coming along."

Nancy promised to do this. After a few more minutes of conversation, she bade Mrs. Farley good-by and left the house.

"If I'm a judge of human nature," thought Nancy, "that woman never did a mean thing in her life!"

When she reached the sidewalk, Nancy took out Mr. Drew's list from her handbag. Thoughtfully she crossed out Mrs. Farley's name.

Herbert Brown, the next suspect, lived in River Heights Estates, a rather exclusive housing area located on the outskirts of the city.

"It's kind of a long walk," Nancy told herself. "But it will do me good."

As Nancy strolled along, she was so engrossed with her thoughts that she failed to notice a tan sedan whose driver cruised by, honked the horn, then pulled over to the curb.

As the door opened, a good-looking young man about eighteen called, "Hi, Nancy!"

To her surprise, she saw Don Cameron, who had been a fellow student in River Heights High School. Nancy had, in fact, gone to the Spring Prom with the tall, black-haired boy.

"Hello, Don," she said. "What are you doing home? I thought you were working on your uncle's farm this summer before going to college."

Don grinned engagingly. "I've been picking string beans and berries and hoeing potatoes for nearly a month," he replied. "But I have a leave of absence to attend my sister's wedding this Friday."

Nancy had read of Janet Cameron's wedding plans in the *River Heights Gazette* two weeks before. "Jan must be excited!" she exclaimed.

"Everyone at home is going 'round in circles," Don stated, laughing. "Bill Bent, my brother-in-law-to-be, is no better.

"By the way, Nancy," Don continued, "I intended calling you later today. If you're free Thursday afternoon and evening I'd like to have you go to a barbecue party with me. It's being given in honor of Jan and Bill."

"I'd love to," said Nancy. "Where will it be?"

"At the Herbert Browns' home in River Heights Estates," Don said. "Their daughter, Lynn, is Jan's maid of honor."

Herbert Brown! One of the possible suspects in the bank security theft! Nancy could scarcely conceal her excitement. Although she did not like the idea of spying on a host, here was an excellent chance for her to find out what Mr. Brown was like.

"What time does the barbecue begin?" Nancy asked.

"I'll call for you at four," said Don.

He offered to drive Nancy home, and she hopped in beside him. When the young sleuth entered the house, she found Hannah in the living room.

"My goodness," the housekeeper exclaimed, "you haven't solved the mystery already!"

"I gave up," Nancy teased.

"What!"

With a grin Nancy told why she had postponed her trip. "I'll get some lunch for us," Nancy offered, "and then drive to the other two places on the list."

Hannah chuckled. "Since you said you'd be home," she said, "I prepared a fresh fruit salad— it's in the refrigerator. And rolls ready to pop into the oven."

"You're a fine patient!" Nancy scolded.

"I feel better keeping busy," Hannah countered.

Nancy asked whether there had been any telephone calls in her absence.

"No. But you did get a post card in the mail."

Nancy went to the mail tray in the hall and recognized Helen Corning's writing. The message read:

Dear Nancy:

Aunt June and I have decided to take a week's automobile trip up North. Will return directly to River Heights. Plan to stop and see Laura Pendleton on our way. Hope Hannah is better.

Love,
Helen

Nancy read the card aloud and commented, "I hope Helen lets me know how everything is at the Aborns' home. Anyway, I'm going to call

Laura myself in a few days to find out how she is and make a date with her to come here."

"Do you think her guardian will let her leave his care so soon?" the housekeeper asked, as she reached for her crutches.

When there was no reply, Hannah looked out toward the hall. Nancy's normally rosy complexion was deadly white. She looked as if she were about to faint!

CHAPTER VII

A Startling Assignment

"NANCY! Nancy! What's wrong with you?" Hannah cried out, as she tried to hurry to the girl's side.

As the housekeeper limped toward her, Nancy snapped to attention. "I'm all right, Hannah," she said. "But Helen's post card—it brought back the phone call I had this morning—"

Nancy told Mrs. Gruen about the call which had ended so abruptly with a cry of pain. "The caller's voice sounded vaguely familiar, but I couldn't place it," she explained. "Now I think I know who it was."

"Who?" said Hannah.

"Laura Pendleton! I believe someone was trying to stop her from talking to me!"

"Mercy!" Hannah exclaimed, sinking weakly into a soft chair. "Do you think it was one of the

Aborns, Nancy? And why would they do such a thing?"

Nancy shrugged. "I'm going to call the Aborn home right now."

While Hannah listened nervously, Nancy picked up the phone and dialed Information. When the operator replied, Nancy asked for Jacob Aborn's number.

The operator cut off for a minute, then reported, "I'm sorry, miss, but that number has been temporarily disconnected!"

"Can you tell me when this was done?" Nancy requested tersely.

"I'm sorry. I have no further information."

Nancy thanked the operator and hung up.

"It sounds suspicious," Hannah remarked, "but, Nancy, the Aborns may have changed their plans and gone away with Laura for a vacation somewhere else."

"I know one way to find out," said Nancy with determination. She reminded Hannah of the young couple, Cathy and Jim Donnell, who had helped move the fallen tree at Melrose Lake.

"I'll ask them if they've seen Laura or the Aborns," Nancy explained.

Hannah sighed. "You're just like your father," she said, "and he certainly is astute. But I'm worried that you're becoming involved in another complicated mystery."

Nancy tweaked Hannah's cheek. "The more there are, the better I like them!"

The housekeeper smiled. She said that while Nancy was calling Cathy and Jim she would put lunch on the table.

"Fine. I'll help you in a moment."

As Hannah hobbled to the kitchen, Nancy got the Donnells' number and dialed it. After two rings a girl's voice said, "Hello!"

"Cathy?" Nancy inquired.

"Yes."

Nancy gave her name. "Do you remember me?" she asked.

"Of course," said Cathy. "My family and I were talking about you just a short while ago. Jim and I told them about the Aborns' being home and we all went over this morning to say hello and meet Laura. But the house was closed. Nobody's staying there."

"Oh!" said Nancy, disappointed. She explained that this was her reason for calling, and told of the Aborns' telephone having been disconnected.

Cathy already knew this, and added, "Dad found a note on the back porch telling the milkman to discontinue deliveries until further notice."

"Cathy, does Mr. Aborn own a foreign make of car?" Nancy queried.

"Why, no," Cathy replied. She added that her

parents thought the Aborns might have planned suddenly to take a short trip somewhere. "I'm sure that we'll hear from them in a few days. If we do, I'll call you, Nancy."

"Fine," said the young detective. "Remember me to Jim. Good-by."

Deeply troubled, Nancy went to the kitchen and told Hannah what Cathy had said.

"Chances are," said the housekeeper, "the call you received this morning was not from Laura at all. You know a lot of people, dear."

Nancy replied that usually when someone had to break a telephone conversation in an abrupt manner the person called back as soon as possible to explain what had happened.

"That's true," Hannah admitted. "It's very strange."

After lunch Hannah said she was going next door to visit with Mrs. Gleason. Nancy helped her to the neighbor's front porch. Then Nancy backed her convertible from the garage and headed for Mr. Drew's downtown office.

"I'll report my progress so far regarding his suspects."

Nancy parked the car in a lot adjoining a large building where lawyers, doctors, and other professional people had offices. Mr. Drew's suite was on the fifth floor. A few minutes later Nancy greeted her father's secretary, Miss Hanson.

"My, how pretty you look, Nancy!" said the efficient young woman, who had been with Carson Drew for the past five years.

"Thank you." Nancy blushed a trifle. "You look lovely yourself."

When the lawyer learned that his daughter had arrived, Carson Drew at once asked Nancy to come into his office.

"I can see by the gleam in your eyes, Nancy, that you have some information for me."

Nancy told him of her interview with Mrs. Farley. "In my opinion, she's a woman of very fine character." Then Nancy mentioned the invitation to the barbecue party at Mr. Herbert Brown's home.

Mr. Drew raised his eyes and chuckled. "Better than I expected."

"My main reason for coming was to tell you something else," Nancy said.

She quickly reviewed the latest developments in the Laura Pendleton case. Mr. Drew listened quietly. Finally he said:

"There's something odd about all this. Nancy, I must leave River Heights on the three-o'clock plane this afternoon for Cincinnati, but I'll be home by Sunday. Why don't we plan to drive to the Aborns' home later that afternoon and see for ourselves what the story is? They may have returned by then."

"That's a grand idea!" Nancy exclaimed. Then, knowing that he was busy, she kissed her father good-by and wished him a successful trip.

"I'll call you every night at eight!" Mr. Drew promised, and Nancy left the office.

On the way down in the elevator, Nancy asked Hank, the operator, if he knew where Hilo Street was located. Mrs. John Stewart, the third suspect, lived in an apartment at this address.

"I know the general area," Nancy added. "It's about three miles from here on the eastern side of the city."

"That's right," Hank said. "It's a classy neighborhood! All high-priced apartment buildings. I believe Hilo Street runs off East Main."

Nancy thanked him, then went to her convertible. She drove carefully through the city traffic and finally reached Hilo Street. Mrs. Stewart's apartment house was Number 76.

Nancy scanned the buildings and found that this one was the largest on the street. It was ultramodern in design and about twenty stories high. After parking her car, she smoothed her hair and got out.

A red-coated doorman nodded pleasantly to the young detective as she entered the building a minute later. Nancy checked the directory and saw that Mrs. Stewart was in Apartment Three on the fourth floor. She rang the elevator button.

Almost instantly, aluminum doors slid open noiselessly, and Nancy stepped inside the carpeted elevator. It was self-operated, and Nancy pushed the fourth-floor control.

Her heart was pounding with excitement. Would Mrs. Stewart prove to be a link in the embezzlement case? Nancy hoped to find a clue this time!

When the elevator stopped at the fourth floor, Nancy got out and easily located Apartment Three. She pressed the doorbell.

A trim-looking maid, a rather harassed expression on her pretty face, opened the door immediately. "Oh, hello!" she said. "You must be the walker."

"Why, no—" Nancy began, but before she could explain, the maid went into the living room, leaving the door ajar.

As Nancy, speechless, glanced hastily into the apartment beyond, the maid reappeared. She was leading a pair of frisky black-and-white French poodles by a gold-linked leash.

"Here!" she said abruptly, thrusting the leash into Nancy's hand. "Their names are Irene and Frederika. Mrs. Stewart says to take them for a nice, long walk!"

Before Nancy could utter a word, the door was closed with an emphatic bang!

CHAPTER VIII

The Frightened Runaway

NANCY DREW, dog tender! This was a new title, the young detective thought. As she burst into laughter, the two poodles began to yap excitedly and dance around in little circles.

"Hello, girls," Nancy said to them, and bent down to pat the friendly animals. She then rang the doorbell with determination.

This time the door was opened by a tremendously stout woman whose chubby face was framed by a mass of fuzzy brown curls.

"Yes?" she inquired coyly. "Have you had some trouble with the babies? I told Collette to give you explicit instructions."

Nancy smothered a giggle. "Are you Mrs. Stewart?" she asked briskly.

"Of course," the woman said impatiently.

Nancy introduced herself and said that a mistake had been made. She was not the dog walker, but had come to solicit Mrs. Stewart's aid for the River Heights Youth Center.

"Oh dear!" Mrs. Stewart blushed, obviously flustered. "Collette's made a mistake. I'm sorry." She jerked the leash from Nancy and gave the poodles a loving glance. "Mama will give you both cookies while we wait for your real walker."

Nancy cleared her throat and Mrs. Stewart's glance returned to the caller. "Oh, yes—your project. I'm afraid that we'll have to discuss it another time. I'm having an afternoon musicale featuring the most divine violinist—Professor Le Bojo. He is expected any moment—"

"I understand," Nancy nodded. "Perhaps I can return later when Mr. Stewart is home?"

"He left today for a fishing trip in Maine," Mrs. Stewart replied. She added somewhat angrily, "I simply don't understand Gerald—he doesn't appreciate our home life here with the children!" Her glance swept toward the poodles.

Nancy managed to keep a straight face, said good-by to Mrs. Stewart, and left. When she returned to her car Nancy reached the conclusion that Mrs. Stewart was hardly the type to plan a bank swindle!

"Her poor husband," Nancy thought with a laugh.

There was only one more name for Nancy to check today—Mr. Stephen Dowd. She drove out Hilo Street and headed across the city. The man's address was in a business zone which was partly residential, although most of the homes were two-family dwellings.

After a little difficulty, Nancy found the house she sought—a brown duplex situated between a gasoline station and a tailor shop. She parked and went up the walk. Mr. Dowd's half of the house was on the right-hand side.

The young sleuth rang the bell and waited. No answer. She pushed the button again. Still no one came to the door.

"Maybe I can find out something from his next-door neighbor," Nancy thought hopefully.

As she was about to ring the bell on the left, the door was opened by a young woman, a shopping bag in her hand. She appeared startled to see Nancy.

The young sleuth smiled pleasantly. "I came to call on Mr. Dowd," she explained. "He's probably at work?"

"No. Mr. and Mrs. Dowd are both away now—on tour with a show, they said. They board here. I'm Mrs. Wyman."

"Are they entertainers?" Nancy inquired with interest, and explained about the youth center.

Mrs. Wyman said the couple were actors, but

she did not know what parts they played. "Since moving here two months ago, they've been away a great deal of the time."

Nancy thanked Mrs. Wyman and said she would call again. "They sound like the type of people I'm looking for to help amuse the children," she explained.

Nancy drove away, but told herself they would bear further investigation. It seemed unnatural that they would not have told what parts they were playing.

Nancy felt a little discouraged about her findings so far. She realized that she could do nothing else until she met Herbert Brown the next afternoon.

"I think I'll go home, get my bathing suit, and head for the club," she decided. The day was becoming very warm.

Fifteen minutes later Nancy parked in her driveway. As she was about to insert her key in the front lock, the door was opened from inside.

Laura Pendleton, wan and disheveled, stared at the young detective!

"Laura!" Nancy gasped. She could hardly believe her eyes.

"Hello, Nancy," her friend said, as Hannah Gruen came into view, walking slowly on her crutches.

"Come in, Nancy," the housekeeper invited

urgently. "Laura's been waiting for you over an hour. She's terribly upset—"

The three went into the living room and Nancy sat down on the couch beside the visitor. Before Nancy could ask why she was in River Heights, Laura burst into tears.

"Oh, I'm so unhappy!" she sobbed. "That's why I ran away!"

Nancy gently stroked Laura's hair and waited for the hysterical girl to calm down. Then she said quietly, "Tell me everything that has happened since I saw you last."

Slowly Laura started to speak. After Nancy and Helen had left the hotel suite, Mr. Aborn said he had to attend to some business for a short while. He had left the hotel. Meanwhile, Laura and Mrs. Aborn had checked out and waited for the guardian in his blue sedan, which was parked in the hotel lot.

"Where did Mr. Aborn go?" asked Nancy.

"I don't know, but when he met us a short while later he was carrying a brief case. As we started toward Melrose Lake, Mrs. Aborn asked what I had done with Mother's jewelry. When I said it was in my handbag she asked me to give it to her for safekeeping. I said I would when we got home."

"Then you *did* go directly to Melrose Lake?" Nancy questioned.

"Yes," Laura replied. She hesitated, then went on with her story. "The Aborns showed me to my room and I started to unpack.

"I found I needed more hangers," the girl went on, "but when I went to the door to ask Mrs. Aborn for them, I discovered it was locked on the outside."

"Locked!" Hannah gasped and Nancy was shocked.

Laura nodded. "I was so frightened," she said, "that at first I didn't know what to do. Then I heard voices coming from the Aborns' room. I lay down on the floor so I could hear them better and listened.

"Marian Aborn said, 'What did you lock her in for—she doesn't know anything!' and my guardian replied, 'Not yet, but she's a smart kid. See if you can gain her confidence and get hold of the jewels.' "

As Laura paused, a terrible thought came to Nancy. Were the Aborns *thieves?* But they could not be, she argued, if Marie Pendleton had trusted the couple to take care of her daughter. "And besides, I gather the Donnells think they are nice people." Aloud she asked, "What happened next?"

"I thought I must have heard them wrong," the auburn-haired girl said slowly, "but I suddenly remembered Mother telling me always to take good care of her jewelry. So I took it from my handbag and hid it underneath the mattress of the bed.

"Just as I finished doing this, the door to my room opened. Mrs. Aborn stood there, looking very friendly. She offered to help unpack my bags, and admired several dresses as I hung them in the closet—"

"And then—" Nancy pressed.

Laura said that she and Mrs. Aborn had prepared a tasty dinner, then she and the couple had watched television for a while.

"Just before we went upstairs to bed, Mrs. Aborn said it would be a good idea for me to put my mother's jewels in the wall safe in the living room. I agreed and said that I would give them to her in the morning."

"What was Mrs. Aborn's reaction to this?" Hannah asked.

"Oh, both she and her husband became very angry. They said that apparently I didn't trust them to take care of a few insignificant gems, while they in turn had the responsibility of caring for a penniless orphan! Oh, Nancy, I thought Mother had a lot of money! Mrs. Aborn yelled at me and said I was ungrateful and a big burden to them. They were sorry they had ever agreed to take me!

"I can't explain how I felt," Laura went on, her

hands shaking with nervousness. "I was just numb. Then I burst into tears and rushed to my room."

Laura said that finally she had fallen asleep and awakened this morning to find she was again locked in.

"At eight o'clock Mrs. Aborn opened the door, acting very friendly, and said breakfast was ready in the kitchen."

"Was anything said about last night?" Nancy asked.

Laura said no, that the Aborns had acted as though nothing had happened. "But a strange thing occurred after breakfast," Laura stated. "Mr. Aborn took a small package from the refrigerator and left the house, saying he would be back later. Before he went he said I would be sorry if I didn't co-operate with them!"

"I presume he meant to hand over the jewels," Hannah guessed, and Laura nodded.

"I knew then that I had to leave their house and also get word to Nancy. While Mrs. Aborn was emptying the rubbish I tried to use the phone, but she caught me and twisted my arm, then hung up the receiver!"

"You see, I was right, Hannah!" Nancy exclaimed, and told Laura her theory about the call.

"Were you locked up again?" Hannah asked.

Laura explained that before Mrs. Aborn could do this she had run past her and barricaded herself inside the bedroom, not wanting the jewels to be unguarded. At that moment the doorbell had rung. Apparently Mrs. Aborn had not answered it, for the woman had kept quiet for a long while on the first floor.

"So I quickly took my handbag and the jewels, and climbed down a trellis outside my window," Laura said. "Once I was on the detour I was lucky enough to get a ride to the highway and there I caught a bus to River Heights. I took a taxi to your house."

As Laura sat back with an exhausted sigh, Hannah stood up. "You're worn out, dear," the housekeeper said. "I'm going to get you a cup of hot tea and you're not to say another word until you've drunk it!"

With that, she bustled out of the room and returned shortly with a small tray on which was a cup of hot tea and a piece of toast. By the time Laura had finished the snack, color had returned to her cheeks and she looked more relaxed.

"I wonder if we should report your experience to the police," Nancy mused.

"What could we tell them?" Laura quavered.

"That's the point," Nancy continued. "We could tell them that the Aborns tried to get your jewels, but of course they would deny it all. It would be their word against yours."

"And I don't have definite proof!" Laura said dejectedly.

Nancy patted the girl's hand. "We'll do everything we can to help you, Laura. You've really had a terrible experience, you poor girl."

"Nancy, you're a real friend," Laura said. Tears came into her eyes. "Mr. Aborn is my legal guardian—I saw the papers—but what am I going to do?"

"You'll stay with us," Hannah said quickly, "and when Mr. Drew comes home he'll know how to handle the situation."

Nancy was quiet, but she was doing a lot of figuring. Something mysterious was going on at Melrose Lake. She intended to find out for herself what it was.

CHAPTER IX

A Valuable Inheritance

IF IT had been possible Nancy would have started out for Melrose Lake at once, but she felt that Laura needed her. Besides, there was a job to do for her father at the Browns' barbecue next day.

"Helping Dad comes first," Nancy decided.

Laura spoke again of her mother's affairs. "She used to say I'd always be financially independent if anything happened to her."

"We'll find out," Nancy said, and then took Laura upstairs so she might shower and rest.

In the meantime, Nancy selected some of her own clothes for the visitor. When she appeared at the dinner table, Hannah declared that Laura looked pretty as a picture and much more relaxed.

"I am—thanks to both of you," their guest said gratefully.

When the meal was finished the two girls sat out on the Drews' porch. To cheer up her guest, Nancy told Laura of her funny experience with the French poodles, while trying to get volunteers for the youth center. The young detective did not mention her real reason for calling at the apartment.

Laura giggled. "I wish I could have been with you," she said. "Tell me, Nancy, have you any souvenirs of the mysteries you've solved?"

"Two trophies." Nancy displayed a mantel clock and a valuable silver urn. Laughingly she told Laura that her father often said she would have the house cluttered before she finished her career!

Just then the telephone rang and Hannah called from upstairs that Mr. Drew was on the line. Nancy hurried to talk with him.

"Nancy, I've come across some evidence that indicates Mr. Hamilton, or some person working for him in the trust department, was behind the security thefts. A detective is tailing Hamilton, and if he tries to leave town, the Monroe police will be notified."

"How about the others in his department?" Nancy asked.

"They're being watched, too, but not so steadily. Of course we don't want to arrest an innocent man."

Nancy said she hoped the guilty person would make a misstep soon so the case might be solved, and told her father what she had learned of the River Heights suspects since she had seen him.

He suggested that she keep trying to contact the Dowds. "And that reminds me," the lawyer said. "You can forget about Mr. Herbert Brown being suspicious." He explained that Brown was a personal friend of the bank president's and had been cleared.

Nancy was relieved to hear this. "I'll keep trying to get in touch with the Dowds," she promised.

Next, she told her father about Laura Pendleton's flight from the Aborns' home. "Do you think we should report her experience with them to the police?" she asked.

Mr. Drew said no, that so far the two girls had only their suspicions of the couple's dishonesty, even though Laura had overheard them talking about her jewels. "You need some concrete evidence before calling in the authorities," he stated.

"I thought I'd run up to Melrose Lake and do some sleuthing," she said.

"All right, but keep out of danger," he warned. "I'll be eager to hear what you find out. We'll have a conference when I get home and decide what we can do for Laura."

"Thanks, Dad." A moment later they bade each other good night and hung up.

As the teen-aged detective started for the porch, she had an inspiration. It was not essential now for her to meet Herbert Brown. If Don Cameron would agree to take Laura as a substitute to the barbecue party, it would leave Nancy free to go to Melrose Lake the next day!

"I'll ask Don if he'd mind. If he does—well, that's that."

Hopefully Nancy dialed the Cameron house. Don answered and the girl detective told him the problem.

"Wow! A real mystery!" he remarked. "If I didn't know what sleuthing means to you, Nancy, I'd say you were just trying to brush me off. But you have me feeling sorry for this Laura Pendleton, too. Okay. If she's willing to go with me, I'll be glad to take her. But I'm sure sorry you can't make it. See you another time."

"Thanks, Don. I shan't forget this. Of course if Laura won't go, I'll keep the date. 'By now."

As Nancy walked toward the porch, she smilingly crossed her fingers, hoping that Laura would agree to the plan. Stepping outside, Nancy asked, "How would you like to go to a barbecue tomorrow, Laura?"

The girl's face glowed with anticipation. "It would be fun!" she exclaimed. "Where, Nancy?"

When the plan was explained, Laura said, "Oh, but I don't want to take your date away from you."

"Don and I have already arranged everything," Nancy assured her. Then she told of her desire to do some sleuthing at Melrose Lake.

At once Laura said she was afraid to have Nancy go to the Aborns' home. "There's no telling what my guardian might do to you," she said fearfully. "He has a terrible temper, and if he learns you're helping me—"

"He won't learn that," Nancy said determinedly.

Reluctantly Laura agreed to Nancy's whole scheme. "But if anything should happen to you, I— I'd just want to die!" she declared.

Before the girls went to bed, Hannah suggested that Laura's jewelry be put into the wall safe in Mr. Drew's study.

"Dad, Hannah, and I are the only persons who know the combination," Nancy told Laura.

"It would be a good idea," the brown-eyed girl replied. "First, I'd like to show you some of Mother's treasures. She gave them to me before her last illness."

"Do you have this in writing?" Hannah asked.

"Yes, I do. Why?"

"Then the jewelry wouldn't be part of your

mother's estate," Mrs. Gruen answered, "and there'd be no tax on it."

Laura took a package from her handbag and opened it. She displayed a string of priceless matched pearls, a gorgeous diamond clip and earrings, several jeweled pins set with rubies, pearls, and emeralds, and six rings, including one with a brilliant star sapphire.

Nancy and Hannah were astounded. "Why, this is the most beautiful collection I've ever seen!" Nancy exclaimed. She pointed to a ring set with a perfect aquamarine. "I love this!"

Laura smiled. "That was Mother's favorite," she said. "My father gave it to her on their first wedding anniversary."

"Thank goodness your guardian didn't find these things!" Hannah declared.

Finally the jewels were put into the safe and everyone went to bed.

Nancy awoke at seven o'clock the next morning. After taking a shower, she decided to wear a forest-green cotton dress and flat-heeled brown play shoes.

Laura was still sleeping when Nancy joined Mrs. Gruen at breakfast. The housekeeper was using a cane.

"My ankle feels almost as good as new," Hannah announced. "I've discarded the crutches."

Nancy was delighted to hear this. As they ate, she and the housekeeper talked about the young sleuth's trip.

"I'll worry about you every second until you return home," Mrs. Gruen declared. "If you're not here by ten thirty, I'll notify the police."

Nancy grinned. "I'll try to be here by suppertime. If not, I'll call you."

A short while later Nancy battled the early-morning traffic through the city. Reaching the outskirts, she took the road to Melrose Lake.

"Poor Laura," she thought, wondering what the day would disclose about the girl's strange guardian and his wife.

If Laura were really penniless, maybe the man thought he had a legitimate right to take and sell the jewelry for the girl's support. But his wife had bragged about having plenty of money to take care of their ward.

After a time Nancy came to the Melrose Lake detour. Laura had told her there was a sign marked "Eagle Rock" in front of the lane leading to her guardian's property.

Presently Nancy approached the spot where the pine tree had fallen. Fortunately, it had been removed.

She drove more slowly, afraid of inadvertently missing the Eagle Rock sign. Then, sighting the turnoff, Nancy left the detour.

"This ring was Mother's favorite," Laura said

She had gone but a few hundred feet along the Aborns' road when she decided it might be safer to walk. After parking along the side of the roadway, she started off. In a few minutes Nancy suddenly caught sight of a man walking rapidly through the woods. He carried a small bundle under his arm.

"Jacob Aborn!" she thought, recognizing his profile and the peculiar stoop of his shoulders.

Nancy recalled Laura's story of her guardian taking a small package from the refrigerator and leaving the house with it. What was in the bundle and where was he taking it?

"I'm going to find out!" Nancy declared. Without hesitation, she quietly plunged into the thicket. Following at a safe distance she managed to keep the man in sight.

"He doesn't seem to be worried about being followed," Nancy thought. "He must not have heard my car when I turned into the lane." She continued her musing. "I'm glad I wore this green dress. It's good camouflage!"

Just then a twig crackled under her foot, breaking the stillness of the woods. Jacob Aborn turned and looked back, frowning. He stood a minute, listening intently. Only by ducking quickly behind a large bush had Nancy avoided detection.

"I'd better be more careful if I don't want to get caught," she warned herself.

As the man continued through the forest Nancy followed, painstakingly avoiding twigs or loose stones. She kept well behind him.

"Wouldn't it be a joke on me if he's just a bird watcher!" She giggled at the thought. "And maybe that package has his lunch in it!"

Laughing to herself, Nancy picked her way through the woods as she trailed Laura Pendleton's guardian. Suddenly he disappeared behind a clump of high blueberry bushes. Nancy hurried forward. When she reached the spot the girl detective looked about in all directions.

"Which way did he go?" she asked herself.

Jacob Aborn seemed to have vanished into thin air!

CHAPTER X

The Danger Sign

ALERT for possible danger, Nancy moved forward with the utmost caution. It occurred to her that possibly Aborn had become aware he was being followed and had hidden in the bushes to watch the pursuer.

"I'll walk into a trap!" Nancy thought with alarm. "Mr. Aborn will learn I'm spying on him and everything will be ruined!"

With great caution she moved from one bush and tree to another. Laura's guardian was not hiding behind any of them.

"That's funny," Nancy said to herself.

She examined the ground, almost expecting there would be a cave or secret tunnel in the vicinity. But the earth was firm and in many places very rocky.

Finally Nancy came to a tiny clearing. On the far side attached to a large oak was a crudely printed wooden sign which read:

PRIVATE PROPERTY. KEEP OUT. DANGER!

"I wonder if that's where Mr. Aborn went and why?" the young detective asked herself.

She waited several minutes, then decided to cross the clearing. She was not stopped. Entering the woods again, she saw a dilapidated shack. The windows had been boarded up, and the roof sagged.

"One good gust of wind would blow the place over," Nancy said to herself.

She stepped from among the bushes and stood in the shadow of the trees, curiously surveying the building. Was it possible that Jacob Aborn had entered it?

Nancy's eyes searched the ground for footprints. Directly ahead, in the soft earth, she saw the fresh mark of a man's shoe. Instantly her suspicions were confirmed.

Jacob Aborn had come this way!

"I'll just have a look at this shack," the young sleuth decided.

After quickly glancing about to make certain she was not being watched, Nancy hurried forward. Tiptoeing across the front porch, she quietly tried the door. It was locked. Nancy walked around to the rear door and found that it likewise was securely fastened.

Although disappointed, Nancy was unwilling to give up. Making a complete circuit of the shack, she saw a window from which several boards had fallen. It was too high for her to peer through. Nancy returned to the rear of the building to get an old box that she had seen. She set it beneath the window and mounted it.

Pressing her face against the glass, she gazed inside. The room, apparently a kitchen, was bare of furniture and covered with dust and cobwebs.

"I wish I could get inside," Nancy thought.

She was about to climb down from the box when a strange feeling came over her. Though she had heard no sound, Nancy sensed that unfriendly eyes were watching her every move.

Before she could turn around and look over her shoulder, a coarse, angry voice barked into her ear:

"What are you doing here, young lady?"

Nancy wheeled and faced Jacob Aborn!

With as much dignity as she could muster, the girl detective stepped to the ground and regarded the man with composure. His eyes burned with rage.

"I was merely curious," Nancy replied. "And may I ask why *you* are here?"

"Yes, I'll tell you. I'm looking for my ward."

"You mean Laura Pendleton?"

"Yes. Who else? I thought maybe she was hiding here. But nobody's in the shack."

"Why in the world would Laura hide in this ramshackle place?" Nancy asked, trying to show as much surprise as possible.

"Search me," Mr. Aborn said, then added angrily, his eyes boring Nancy's, "Laura has run away!"

"*Run away?*" Nancy repeated.

"Yes. Yesterday. I'll tell you something about that ward of mine—" A crafty light came into Jacob Aborn's eyes as he went on, "At times she acts unbalanced—thinks folks don't treat her right."

"Indeed?" said Nancy, pretending to be shocked.

By now Laura's guardian had calmed down. When he spoke again he was once more the pleasant man Nancy had met at the Montewago Hotel.

"It's for Laura's own good that she ought to return home," he said. "Mrs. Aborn is dreadfully upset. She loves Laura just like a mother. Miss Drew, have you heard from Laura by any chance?"

Nancy was on her guard. "Why should I hear from her?" she countered. "We never met until that accident on the lake and she came to rescue my friend Helen and me."

Mr. Aborn did not pursue the subject. Instead, he said, "Laura's a nervous, high-strung girl. Why, do you know she locked herself in her room the entire time she was with us—wouldn't eat, or even let us try to help her?"

"Terrible!" Nancy said, pretending to be shocked. "Laura does need help."

Secretly Nancy felt that Jacob Aborn was telling this version of the locked-door story to cover his own actions, in case they came to light.

"Have you notified the police, Mr. Aborn?" she asked, probing for further information.

"We have a private detective working on the matter," the man stated. "We don't want any bad publicity because of dear Marie Pendleton's memory. She entrusted Laura to my care because she knew how much my wife and I would love the girl."

Nancy suddenly was finding it hard to concentrate on what Mr. Aborn was saying. Was she wrong or had she heard a sound inside the shack?

"This is very strange," she told herself. "But I don't dare pursue the subject or Mr. Aborn will really become suspicious." Aloud she said, "I certainly hope Laura is all right. Well, I must go now. I have some friends here at Melrose Lake I plan to call on." She paused, then added lightly, "In fact, I believe you know them, Mr. Aborn— the Donnell family."

The man looked startled, then recovered himself. "Oh, yes. Fine family. Say hello to them for me, please."

Nancy promised that she would. Since Mr. Aborn made no move to accompany her, she said good-by and walked rapidly back to the spot where her convertible was parked.

As Nancy climbed into it, she cast a glance over her shoulder. There was no sign of Mr. Aborn. Had he gone into the shack? Was someone there? Had he been delivering packages to the person?

Nancy started the car's motor and backed out to the main road. As she drove along, her thoughts were entirely on Mr. Aborn. She had no doubt but that the man had been lying about Laura's behavior.

"I must find out more about that man," Nancy decided.

Reaching the highway, she stopped at a service station, had the gas tank of her car filled, and asked directions to the Donnell home. The attendant told her how to reach the place, and a short while later Nancy drew up before a lovely redwood house located well off the road.

She got out and rang the front doorbell. There was no answer. Nancy walked around to the back of the house. A gardener was there, trimming the flower beds.

"Howdy, miss!" the elderly man hailed her. "Looking for the Donnells?"

"Yes. Are they away?" Nancy inquired.

"Yep. They're visiting relatives in Crescent Gardens 'til tonight. Any message?"

Nancy said no, that she would call again, and thanked the man. As she drove away Nancy was disappointed that she had been unable to pick up any information regarding Mr. Aborn.

"I don't want to leave Melrose Lake until I have learned *something* to help Laura," she thought. "Mr. Aborn may trace her whereabouts to our home and force Laura to return with him before Dad gets back to town. I suppose he has a legal right to do it."

At last an idea came to Nancy. "I'll go to one of the hotels on the lake and engage a room. Then, after it gets dark, I'll do a little more investigating."

Fortunately, Nancy always carried an overnight case in her car trunk. It contained pajamas and robe, two changes of clothing, toilet articles, and, this time of year, a bathing suit.

Presently she saw a large white building ahead of her. Its green lawn sloped down to the sandy beach. On the stone pillar at the side of the driveway was the sign: *Beach Cliff Hotel.*

"I think I'll stop here," Nancy decided. She parked her car and entered the pleasant lobby. In a few minutes she had registered and been taken to a comfortable room overlooking the lake.

"I'll telephone home," Nancy said to herself, "and tell Hannah where I am."

As Nancy placed the call, a chilling thought suddenly popped into her mind. Perhaps the detective whom Aborn had engaged had already traced the runaway girl, and knew Nancy had not told all she knew about Laura. If so, Nancy might find that her guest had already been whisked away from the Drew home!

CHAPTER XI

Trapped!

WHEN Hannah Gruen answered the telephone at the Drew residence, Nancy at once asked, "Is Laura all right?"

"Why, of course," Hannah answered in surprise. "She's upstairs setting her hair for the party this afternoon."

"Well, tell her to be very careful," Nancy urged. "Mr. Aborn has a detective looking for her!"

"Oh dear!" exclaimed Mrs. Gruen. "And when will you be home, Nancy?"

The young detective explained where she was and that she planned to stay at Melrose Lake and do more sleuthing.

"I think I may be on the trail of something big."

"I don't like the idea of you prowling around the Aborns' home in the dead of night," the housekeeper objected.

"I'll be careful," Nancy promised. "I may even get home tonight."

"Well, all right," Hannah consented reluctantly. "By the way, Nancy, I had a repairman fix the window in Mr. Drew's study this morning, and also requested the police to keep a lookout for anything suspicious going on in this neighborhood."

"Wonderful!" Nancy said, feeling relieved. "Any more news?"

"Everything's quiet here," Hannah reported. "And Laura seems happy."

Laura came to speak to Nancy and was alarmed when she heard that a detective was looking for her. "But I won't go back to those awful Aborns! They can't make me! If they try it, I'll—I'll run right to the police!"

"That's a good idea," said Nancy. "By the way, I'd like to do some sleuthing at the Aborn house. I may want to get inside without ringing the bell." The young sleuth chuckled. "Since it's now your house too, may I have permission to go in and look around?"

"You certainly may," said Laura with a giggle. "If no doors are unlocked, try my bedroom window. I left it open a crack and there's a sturdy rose trellis right alongside it."

"Terrific!" said Nancy elatedly.

After she completed the call, Nancy went to

the hotel coffee shop for a hearty lunch. Since it was now almost one thirty, the room was empty.

After eating, Nancy put on her bathing suit and wandered down to the beach. A boy in attendance gave her a towel and Nancy stretched out on the sand, unaware of the steadfast glance of a couple hidden behind a large green-and-white striped umbrella not far away. They nodded to each other, then when Nancy was not looking, they quickly left the beach.

"Guess we're safe," the woman muttered. "She's here to stay and have a good time."

As the strong rays of the sun beat down on the unsuspecting girl, she rehearsed her plan for the evening. When it was dark she would visit both Jacob Aborn's home and also the shack in the woods, if time permitted.

"I'll miss Dad's call tonight," Nancy reflected.

Standing up half an hour later, Nancy put on her bathing cap and walked to the water. She stuck her toe in. The lake water felt icy cold, and Nancy noticed that there were more people on the beach than in swimming. Nevertheless, she waded out to where it was deep enough to make a surface dive and plunged in. Once she was wet, the water was invigorating.

After swimming for a while, Nancy came back to her beach towel and dried off. Then she returned to her room, showered, and slept for two hours, realizing that the rest would give her more endurance for the evening ahead.

Awakening at six o'clock, Nancy put on the simple black cotton dress from her suitcase and pumps. After brushing her hair until it snapped with electricity, she was ready for supper.

"What will it be this evening, miss?" asked the friendly waitress.

Nancy selected steak, a baked potato, and tossed salad, then sat back to enjoy the soft dinner music playing in the background. The orchestra was in an adjoining lounge.

Nearby diners regarded the lone girl with interest, for the prospect of the daring adventure had brought a becoming flush to her cheeks.

"If I'm wrong in suspecting Jacob Aborn of being dishonest," thought Nancy, "then I guess I'd better give up sleuthing!"

Upon leaving the dining room an hour later, she lingered on the porch for a few minutes, watching couples dance. As a red-haired young man began to walk toward Nancy with an invitation in his eyes for her to dance, she hastily went to her room.

Chuckling to herself, Nancy said aloud, "Romance and detective work won't mix tonight!" Then she changed to walking shoes, sweater, and skirt.

The moment it became dark enough for her

purpose, Nancy left the hotel in her car. As she drew near the Aborns' lane a short while later, she turned the convertible off the road and ran it into a clump of bushes where it would not be seen.

Switching off the engine and locking the doors, Nancy started down the lane leading to the house, holding her flashlight securely. She found the windows of the house dark.

"The Aborns are out, I guess," she told herself. "Well, that means I can do some looking around."

Circling the structure cautiously, Nancy noted that the second-floor wing, where the bedrooms apparently were located, was in the back. She found the trellis easily.

"I'll try the doors first," Nancy decided, and darted to the front. Gently turning the handle, she found the door locked.

An investigation of two other doors revealed that they, too, were securely fastened.

"I guess I'll have to climb after all," Nancy said to herself.

As quietly as possible, she climbed the trellis. It wobbled and creaked a little but did not give way. When Nancy reached the window ledge of Laura's bedroom, she found to her delight that the window raised easily. She crawled through and switched on her flashlight.

As Nancy tiptoed across the room, which was in

disorder, she heard a noise. Halting, she listened. A car was approaching the house. Looking out the window she could barely make out the figures of a man and a woman who alighted. Who were they and what should Nancy do?

"I'll stay right here," she determined.

As Nancy waited tensely she realized someone was walking up the stairs. Quickly Nancy closed the window without a sound. As she looked around for a hiding place she saw a closet, and darted inside it, switching off her flashlight. Crouched in a far corner behind some of Laura's dresses, Nancy scarcely dared to breathe.

The door to the room was opened a moment later and the boudoir lamps switched on. Cautiously Nancy peered out through the keyhole in the closet door. She saw Jacob Aborn!

The man went directly to Laura's dressing table. Apparently he had not heard Nancy, for he did not glance toward the closet.

Ruthlessly he jerked out drawers from the dressing table and emptied their contents upon the bed. As he surveyed the assortment of tiny bottles, boxes, and other paraphernalia, Laura's guardian gave a disgusted grunt.

"Last place to look!" he said, as if addressing someone out in the hall, probably his wife. "Guess Laura really took the jewels with her. Well, I'll soon have them back!"

Nancy's heart leaped. There was no longer any doubt in her mind as to the character of this man. She was now certain that his sole interest in Laura was to get possession of her property! Only the girl's opportune escape from the house had prevented him from seizing the valuable jewelry collection!

"Laura's mother couldn't have known his true character, or she wouldn't have entrusted her daughter to Aborn's care," Nancy pondered.

Her thoughts came to an abrupt end as the man moved toward the closet. Fearfully, Nancy ducked down behind Laura's dresses again and fervently hoped that she would not be discovered.

Suddenly, as Nancy's legs began to grow cramped, the closet door was jerked violently open. Jacob Aborn looked in!

CHAPTER XII

A Black Abyss

As JACOB ABORN stared into the closet where Nancy was hiding, the girl detective wished wildly that she were invisible. There was no telling what harm the man might inflict if he saw her!

"He has such a violent temper," Nancy realized.

But Aborn's glance did not stray to the dress section. Instead, he reached up for two large suitcases which were on a shelf above the clothes. He set them on the floor outside and shut the closet door.

Beads of perspiration trickled down Nancy's neck as she relaxed. Presently she heard the man leave the room and shut the hall door with a loud bang.

Nancy waited a moment, then left her hiding

place. "I suppose I'd better leave while I can," she advised herself.

But running away from a chance to pick up a clue was not in Nancy's nature. As she heard Laura's guardian descending the stairs to the first floor, she became aware of a woman's voice somewhere below. Nancy decided, "I'll stay and see what's going on."

Before leaving Laura's bedroom she gave it a final searching look and shook her head, puzzled. The room was one which Nancy would be happy to call her own. The feminine furnishings and good colonial pieces showed evidence of discerning taste. They did not fit the Aborns' character. Perhaps an interior decorator had planned it!

"One could believe from this room that the Aborns really wanted Laura," Nancy pondered.

It just did not make sense. Many criminals, Nancy knew, laid the groundwork to lull any suspicion on the part of their victim, then cornered him. But Laura had not even been settled in her new home when the Aborns had begun to persecute her.

Soundlessly Nancy opened the bedroom door, and keeping her flashlight low to the floor, tiptoed along the carpeted hall. Step by step, she edged down the stairway to the floor below. Here there was no sign of activity but Nancy saw a light shining through louvered doors to her left.

"That's probably the kitchen. The Aborns are in there," she thought.

A moment later the woman said, "Here's the combination. I'll pack this stuff while you open the safe."

Quickly Nancy stole into the living room and hastily ducked out of sight behind a large sofa. She was just in time. One of the louvered doors opened and Laura's guardian came into the living room carrying a suitcase. He flicked on a table lamp.

Near it hung the small oil painting of a ship. Aborn lifted it from the wall and set the picture against a chair.

Nancy's eyes widened as she saw that the painting had concealed a wall safe. Aborn deftly twirled the dial to the left, then several notches to the right, and back to the left again. He swung the safe door open.

With a grunt of satisfaction, the man removed several packages of bank notes and some papers which looked like stock certificates. Mr. Aborn chortled and called to his wife:

"When we get the rest of these cashed, you and I will be set for life—thanks to Laura and a few others."

Nancy, startled, almost gave herself away. So Laura did have a sizable inheritance other than the jewelry! But how had the securities reached the safe? Had Aborn brought them here or was he stealing them from someone else? Nancy felt more confused by the moment.

As her thoughts raced, Aborn replaced the loose papers in the safe and closed it. Then he put the money and securities into the suitcase. Giving a tired yawn, he switched off the lamp and left the room.

"Guess I'll turn in," he called to his wife. "Got to be up early tomorrow and get Fred. You ready?"

"Yes."

Marian Aborn came from the kitchen carrying the other bag. Together the couple ascended the stairs. Nancy heard a bedroom door above close.

"Now I must get the police," the girl detective thought.

She paused for several seconds, after coming from behind the couch, to stretch her cramped limbs. "I'd better go out the front door," she decided. "The bedrooms don't overlook that."

Noiselessly Nancy slipped outside and started for her hidden car. Then a temptation came to her. "Why don't I investigate that shack in the woods first? I may have an even bigger story to tell the police! I'll do it!"

Taking a deep breath of air, Nancy hurried toward the path leading to the dilapidated building. Had she been right about having heard someone inside? Was he a friend or an enemy of Aborn's? Were the packages being carried there and what did they contain? Loot?

"Maybe just food," Nancy concluded. "But being taken to whom?"

Beaming her flashlight on the ground, the young detective soon picked up the trail she had taken earlier in the day. It was quiet and eerie as she stumbled along the uneven ground. Nancy became apprehensive once or twice as she heard scuffling noises of forest creatures in the underbrush, but went on.

"I wish Dad were here now," she thought fervently.

Nancy reached the shack without mishap and paused in front of it. A sixth sense seemed to tell her there was someone inside who needed help. No person would stay in such a place unless forced to.

"This is no time for me to hesitate," she told herself.

As Nancy moved toward the rear of the tumbledown building, she glanced at her flashlight and was alarmed to see that it was beginning to grow dim.

"Just my luck when I need it the most!"

In an attempt to save the battery, Nancy switched off the light. As her eyes became accustomed to the darkness, she moved toward the window she had looked through earlier that day. Appraising it, the young sleuth realized that the window ledge was too high from the ground for her to climb through unassisted, even when standing on the box.

Undaunted, she began to examine the other windows. On the south side of the shack she found one which opened from the rickety porch. It was boarded up.

"This is my entry," Nancy determined.

She began searching the yard for something with which to pry off the boards, and finally found a stout stick. Nancy began wedging it between the boards with all her might.

The first board offered stubborn resistance. Then, with a groan and a squeak, it gave way. The remaining boards were removed with less difficulty.

To Nancy's joy, the window was unlocked! Pushing it up, she beamed her flashlight inside. The room beyond was bare and quiet as a tomb.

"Well, here comes Nancy Drew, housebreaker and spy!" Nancy thought with amused determination. "It's certain now no one lives here."

When she was halfway through the window the young sleuth hesitated without knowing just why. She glanced back over her shoulder. A queer sensation made Nancy quiver as she turned searching eyes toward the woods.

"How silly!" she scolded herself. "No one's there. It's just nerves."

Bravely Nancy swung herself through the window. Hastily she moved toward an adjoining room, noting that her flashlight was growing dimmer. Soon she would be left in total darkness! She must hurry!

Her light revealed a small room, also empty, its walls and floor dusty from long lack of any occupant's care. Nancy was disappointed to find nothing of interest.

"I'd better leave and drive to police headquarters," she thought.

Just then Nancy's flashlight revealed a trap door in the floor. Quickly she moved over toward it. But she had taken only a few steps when an unusual sound arrested her attention. Had she heard a board creak behind her, or was it a night sound from the woods?

After hesitating a second, Nancy again started for the trap door. As she reached down to grasp the ring in it, her body became tense.

This time there was no mistake. She had heard a peculiar sound which seemed to come from beneath the floor.

"It sounded like a groan!" Nancy decided. She felt cold all over.

Someone was imprisoned in the cellar! Who? And why?

As Nancy tugged at the ring, another idea came to her. This might be a trap laid for her!

"Oh, what should I do?" she thought, hesitating. There was still time to run away from danger.

But the fear that some person was in distress gave her the courage to open the trap door. As it swung upward, Nancy saw before her a flight of stone steps, leading down into complete darkness. A gust of damp, musty air struck her in the face and momentarily repulsed her.

Nancy glanced nervously at her flashlight. The battery could not last much longer. Already the light was so weak that she could barely see the steps in front of her. Did she dare investigate the cellar?

"It won't take long," she thought.

She descended the steps and came to a landing. The rest of the stairway went toward the left. Nancy peered anxiously into the black abyss below.

To her horror, she saw a man stretched out full length on a bench. His face was turned upward and Nancy caught a full glimpse of the countenance.

He was Jacob Aborn!

CHAPTER XIII

An Actor's Ruse

SPELLBOUND, Nancy stood like a stone image, gazing down into the face of Jacob Aborn. How had the man reached the bungalow ahead of her? What was he doing sleeping in the musty cellar of the old shack?

As these thoughts flashed through Nancy's mind, the beam of her flashlight flickered again. Then it went out, leaving her in total darkness.

Sheer panic took possession of the girl detective. Something very strange was going on! She must not be caught in a trap!

Turning, she gave a low cry and stumbled up the stairway and toward the window through which she had entered. Her flight was abruptly checked as she banged one foot on something metallic that moved ahead of her. In a second she smelled kerosene.

"A lantern!" she decided.

The thought of a light gave her hope. She felt around and discovered an old-time oil lantern.

Collecting her wits, she stopped and listened for any sounds of pursuit. There were none. The shack appeared as deserted and silent as before.

"I'm sure that was Jacob Aborn down in the cellar," Nancy thought in perplexity. "I didn't imagine it. But how did he get here so fast? After I left his house I didn't waste much time."

Suddenly an amazing thought came to Nancy. Was the man she had seen by chance a brother, even a twin, of Jacob Aborn? He might be honest and Jacob had found him in the way!

"I'm going to find out!" Nancy declared excitedly.

Eagerly she reached into the pocket of her dress, recalling that at dinner she had taken a pack of matches from the hotel dining table for her souvenir collection. Good! The pack was still there!

Striking a match she was pleased to discover that the lantern was half full of oil. Someone had used it recently, for the glass was clean. Nancy lighted the wick and a flame spurted up. Carrying the lantern, she returned to the trap door.

Suddenly, from below, Nancy heard a moan of pain. This was followed by a pitiful cry of "Help!"

"That settles it," the worried girl thought.

As she descended the steps, the lantern's flick-

From below came a pitiful cry of "Help!"

ering glow revealed that the cellar was dungeon-like, with solid stone walls and no windows.

She held the light high above the figure on the bench. A man, deathly pale, was lying where she had first seen him.

But he was not Laura's guardian!

"There's certainly a startling resemblance, though," Nancy thought, her heart filled with pity for this unfortunate stranger.

Dropping to her knees, she felt his pulse. It was faint but regular.

"He's just unconscious," she told herself in relief.

At the same time, Nancy saw with horror a large chain around the man's waist. It was attached to the prisoner in such a way that it allowed him some freedom of motion and yet held him captive. Was Jacob Aborn responsible for this atrocity? Nancy wondered angrily.

"I must do something to revive this man," she decided, "and get him away from here."

Picking up the lantern, Nancy mounted the cellar steps two at a time. She headed for a small sink in one corner of the room above, where she had seen a pump.

After a search through the cupboard she at last found a battered tin cup. Quickly pumping water into it, she returned to the cellar.

Nancy wet her handkerchief and applied it

gently to the prisoner's forehead. Then she sprinkled a little of the water on his face and chafed his
wrists. The man stirred slightly and moaned.

As she gazed anxiously into his face, Nancy wondered how she could have mistaken him for Jacob
Aborn. Although the two men were of the same
age, and had similar facial characteristics, the
prisoner was gaunt and thin. His features, con-
trary to Mr. Aborn's, were gentle and relaxed.

Now Nancy saw that the man was slowly regaining consciousness. As his eyes fluttered open he
cried "Help!" feebly, then stared into Nancy's
face, amazed.

"Help has come," Nancy said quietly.

The man attempted to raise himself to a sitting
position with Nancy's aid. "Didn't—think—help
—would—ever come," he murmured. Then he
saw the cup in Nancy's hand and asked for water.

Nancy steadied the cup while he drank. Finally
the man leaned against the wall. "First water I've
had in twenty-four hours," he said more clearly.

The young sleuth was horrified. She introduced
herself, then asked, "Who are you—and who did
this terrible thing to you?"

A bitter expression passed over the prisoner's
face. "I'm Jacob Aborn," he said. "A crook by the
name of Stumpy Dowd took over my house, imprisoned me here, and somehow or other arranged
for my new ward, Laura Pendleton, to come to my

home earlier than she was expected. Yesterday he told me that he had the girl's inheritance in his possession—and showed bonds to prove it."

"You're Jacob Aborn!" Nancy repeated, as the prisoner, exhausted by these words, leaned against the wall.

Quickly Nancy's mind flashed back to everything that had happened since she had met Laura. The puzzling questions that had bothered her about the girl's guardian now became clear. Most of all, it was a relief to know that the person to whom Marie Pendleton had entrusted her daughter's care was not a criminal.

Equally important, Nancy realized that Stephen Dowd—alias Stumpy—used his talent as an actor and skill with make-up to fool other people, and then probably swindled them. The young sleuth wondered if there was a tie-in between Laura's inheritance and the Monroe National Bank thefts of stocks and bonds. She must find out from Jacob Aborn, but the police should be notified immediately, as well as her father.

Aloud Nancy said, "I want to hear the whole story of what has happened to you, Mr. Aborn, but first—"

Briefly, she told of having met the man who had impersonated him and of seeing Laura at Twin Lakes. Nancy was about to add that Laura was now at her home when Mr. Aborn said:

"If Stumpy caught you here once today we'd better get out right now!" He told Nancy that Dowd kept the key to the padlock on his chains on a hook near the stairway.

"This is a lucky break," said Nancy. She snatched the lantern from the floor and started toward the stairs.

"Please hurry," Mr. Aborn said faintly. "Stumpy Dowd is a dangerous criminal! He boasted to me that he and his accomplices have victimized several people besides Laura!"

Nancy anxiously moved the lantern up and down, illuminating the dingy walls. Just above her head to the left she finally saw the hook, with a key dangling from it.

"I have it!" she exclaimed triumphantly.

As Nancy hurried back to Mr. Aborn's side she speculated on how the Dowds had found out about Mr. Aborn, his wife, and Laura.

"I'll have you free in a minute, Mr. Aborn," Nancy said, as she stooped over the bench.

While she worked on the rusty lock, Nancy asked if he had known the Dowds previously.

"Yes," he replied. "Mrs. Dowd was hired by my wife as a maid to come when we arrived. Soon after I reached the house her husband came. He grew quite loud and abusive and when I objected he knocked me unconscious. When I came to, I was chained in this cellar."

"How dreadful!" Nancy exclaimed. "But where is your wife?" she asked.

"She had to go to Florida unexpectedly. Her mother, who lives there, had an emergency operation. Marian went down to be with her and I moved into our new home." Mr. Aborn sighed. "Of course I haven't heard a word from her since I've been tied up here!"

"You'll be able to find out about her now," Nancy assured him. "Do you know how many people are working with Stumpy Dowd?"

"One or two others besides his wife, I believe. Stumpy Dowd is secretive about some things, although he boasted a lot. I did hear him mention the name Fred, but I don't know who he is."

When the padlock finally snapped open Nancy's spirits soared. Now the suitcase of securities that Stumpy Dowd had packed could be retrieved. The criminals could be apprehended and her father's case perhaps solved!

Meanwhile, neither Nancy nor Mr. Aborn had noticed a dark figure creeping slowly down the steps. Near and nearer the man came, a stout cane gripped tightly in his right hand.

"That's wonderful, Nancy!" Mr. Aborn exclaimed. "Now if I just knew where Laura is." As he spoke Mr. Aborn glanced up. A look of horror froze his face.

"Look out, Nancy!" he shouted.

CHAPTER XIV

A Desperate Situation

THE WARNING came too late. Before Nancy could turn, the end of the cane crashed down on her head. With a low moan of pain, she sagged to the floor and lay still.

How long she remained unconscious, the young sleuth did not know. When at last she opened her eyes Nancy found herself stretched out on the cold floor of the cellar. Bewildered, it was a full minute before she could account for the splitting pain in her head.

Then, with a shudder, the young sleuth remembered what had happened. She had been struck down from behind. Who was her assailant?

Nancy became aware that someone was standing over her, but objects whirled before her eyes and she could not distinguish the face. Then, gradually, her vision cleared. She saw Stumpy Dowd gazing down upon her, a satisfied leer on his face.

"Well, Miss Drew," he said mockingly, "we meet again. You've gotten in my way once too often!"

As Nancy started to speak, Dowd reached down. Catching Nancy by an arm, he jerked her roughly to her feet. Nancy was so weak that she nearly fell over.

Nevertheless, with a show of spirit, she said, "You'll regret this, I promise you!"

"Let the girl go," Jacob Aborn pleaded from the other side of the room. "Do anything you like to me, but set her free." Nancy saw that he was again padlocked.

Stumpy Dowd glared at his other prisoner. "It's quite impossible for me to release either of you," he said calmly. "You see, you both know too much."

Nancy was aware that resistance would be useless. Right now she did not have the strength to make a break for the stairs. But as the criminal began to unwind a long rope, Nancy realized that unless she thought of something the situation would be desperate. There would be no way to escape!

As Stumpy began to bind Nancy's feet together he said sarcastically, "Mr. Aborn will enjoy having company. And you two have so much to talk about."

An idea suddenly came to Nancy. She remembered that a detective who had called on her father a few months before had told her how it was possible to hold one's hands while being bound so as to slip the bonds later. He had given a demonstration.

"If I can only remember the correct position," Nancy prayed fervently.

When Dowd began to bind Nancy's wrists she tried to follow the detective's instructions. As the ropes cut into her flesh it seemed to Nancy that she must have made a mistake. Certainly there was little space between her wrists and the bonds.

"And now, just to make sure you won't get away—" Stumpy muttered with a sneer.

He took the end of the rope and ran it through a ring in the wall, knotting the rope fast.

"I guess that will hold you for a while and teach you not to meddle in affairs that are none of your business!" the man added.

Nancy Drew had never been so angry in her life, but she realized that any argument she might give would only provoke the man to further torture. So she set her jaw grimly and kept still.

"You'll pay for this, Dowd!" Jacob Aborn spoke up in a quavering voice. "When I get free—"

"When you get free!" Stumpy Dowd taunted.

"That's a laugh. Why, you fool, how do you propose to get help? If it hadn't been for this meddle-
some Drew girl only the rats would have known
you were here!"

Nancy could not help but remark quietly,
"The police will catch you in the end."

"I doubt it," Dowd said with confidence. "I've
covered my trail thoroughly. I've made plans to
leave the country and I'd like to see the police or
anyone else catch me!" He turned to Laura's
guardian. "First, of course, we'll have to get the
jewels away from Laura."

"How do you propose to do that," Nancy asked
quickly, "when you don't know where she is?"

Stumpy Dowd laughed. "That's what you think.
Laura is at your home in River Heights, Nancy
Drew!"

As Nancy blinked, a look of horror came into
Mr. Aborn's eyes. Nancy knew he was wondering
why she had not mentioned Laura's being at her
home. Also, he realized that his last hope of keeping Laura's whereabouts unknown was gone.

Nancy, too, was worried. What did Stumpy
plan to do? Right now, he looked pleased at his
prisoners' reactions.

"My wife overheard Laura placing a call to
Nancy Drew in River Heights yesterday morning.
When Laura ran away, we had a hunch she would
go there. I asked my detective to find out."

Dowd said the sleuth had seen Laura leaving the house that afternoon with a young man. "I presume she left her jewels behind," he added. "But we'll get them before we leave this area!"

"Don't try anything foolish," Nancy warned.

"All my plans are well made," Dowd said coolly. "Too bad you aren't more cautious, Miss Drew."

He said that his wife had felt a draft in the house and gone downstairs to find the front door part way open. Then she had seen a girl heading into the woods and had awakened him. Dowd had figured out that it might be Nancy.

"That's the end of my story," he said, "except to tell you, Aborn, I sold your blue sedan this morning. The money helped pay for my new foreign car."

Jacob Aborn was so furious he almost choked. "You robber! You kidnaper!" he cried out.

"Tut, tut, none of that!" Dowd said. "You'll get your blood pressure up."

"Laura's not in your clutches, and she won't get there!" Aborn stormed. "And I can support her without any inheritance!"

Dowd shrugged. "It won't do any good to threaten me. You're my prisoner and don't forget it! After the jewels are mine—"

Nancy felt as if she would choke with rage. Mr. Aborn closed his eyes and seemed to have fainted.

Meanwhile, Stumpy Dowd had replaced the key on the wall—the hook supporting it, Nancy saw, was far out of the two prisoners' reach.

"You can think of this in the days ahead," the crook taunted. "And now—good-by!"

Turning, he ambled up the steps. Nancy heard mocking laughter as the trap door was slammed shut. Soon a deathlike quiet fell on the shack.

"Mr. Aborn!" Nancy called.

There was no answer. Nancy's heart beat wildly. Was the man only in a faint or had something worse happened to him?

Holding her breath, she strained her ears to see if she could detect any sign of life. A few seconds later Nancy caught faint sounds of inhaling and exhaling.

"Thank goodness," she thought.

Presently the man stirred, and regaining consciousness, looked about. Seeing Nancy, he exclaimed, "Now I remember! We were so near freedom."

"Yes, we were, Mr. Aborn. And we may get out of here yet. I'm trying to slip this rope off my wrists. In the meantime, I want to tell you why I didn't mention that Laura is at my home. I was about to do so when you urged that we leave the shack as fast as possible."

"I see and I forgive you," said Mr. Aborn. "Never having met you, Dowd's announcement gave me a momentary feeling of distrust in you. But that's gone now."

"Then would you mind telling me about Laura's mother and the estate she left?" Nancy requested, as she worked to free her hands.

"I'll be glad to. Mrs. Pendleton appointed the Monroe National Bank executor of her estate and me as Laura's guardian. During Mrs. Pendleton's long illness she had all her securities taken from her private safe-deposit box and put in care of the bank. They were turned over to the custodian department and kept in the bank's personal vault."

"Then how could Stumpy Dowd get them?" Nancy asked.

"That's the mystery. He didn't say."

Nancy was convinced now that a good portion of Laura's inheritance must be among the securities stolen from the bank. She asked whether Mrs. Pendleton had left a large estate.

Mr. Aborn nodded. "Laura is a very wealthy young woman," he said, then went on to explain that at the time of Mrs. Pendleton's death, the Aborns were abroad. Upon their arrival in New York, Mrs. Aborn had received word of her mother's illness. It was then that Laura had been asked to postpone coming to Melrose Lake until his wife's return.

"Laura was staying on at her boarding school

with the headmistress until our trip to Melrose."

"She never received your letter," Nancy told him. "The Dowds must have intercepted it. Soon they told her to come."

Just then Nancy thought she had found the trick to freeing her hands, but a moment later she sighed in discouragement. The rope still bound her wrists.

"At least we have a light," she said. Fortunately, Stumpy Dowd had forgotten the lantern.

"Yes, but the oil is burning low," Mr. Aborn remarked quietly. "When it's gone we'll be in the dark—as I have been for the past two weeks."

Nancy shuddered. "Did Stumpy bring you food in little packages?"

"Yes, when he thought of it. He kept me alive just to pump me for information, and threatened to harm Laura if I didn't tell him what he wanted to know."

Suddenly Nancy felt the rope which chafed her wrists slacken. At the same time the light went out. The cellar was plunged into darkness.

CHAPTER XV

Plans for Rescue

BACK in River Heights, meanwhile, Hannah Gruen had spent a restless and worried evening, expecting to hear Nancy's convertible pull into the driveway at any moment. Moreover, Mr. Drew had failed to call at the appointed hour and Hannah had no knowledge of how to contact the lawyer.

At ten thirty, when the front doorbell rang, the housekeeper limped hurriedly to answer it. Instantly she felt a sense of keen disappointment.

"Oh, hello, Laura," she said, and turned to greet Don Cameron. "Did you have a good time at the barbecue?"

"It was wonderful!" Laura exclaimed happily, as she and Don entered the house.

"Certainly was fun," Don agreed. "Too bad Nancy wasn't with us. Where is she, Mrs. Gruen?"

At these words tears welled up in Hannah's eyes. She told of not hearing from either Nancy or Mr. Drew that evening. "I'm so upset," she said. "What will we do? Call the police?"

"Probably Nancy decided to stay overnight at the Beach Cliff Hotel," Laura said at once. "Have you called there to find out?"

"No, because Nancy always calls when she changes her plans."

Don, greatly concerned, went at once to the telephone. Impatiently the young man waited for a response to his ring.

The hotel telephone operator answered. When Don asked for Nancy Drew, the girl said, "Just a moment." It was nearly five minutes before she told him:

"We are unable to reach your party. Miss Drew is not in the hotel."

"Then she didn't check out earlier this evening?" Don inquired.

"No. Miss Drew is still registered."

Don Cameron hung up, a drawn expression on his face. He told the others what he had learned.

"Oh, I just know something has happened to Nancy!" Laura cried, her lower lip quivering with nervousness. "And it's all my fault."

Hannah took the girl into her arms. "You must not feel this way," she said gently. "Nancy is trying to help you because she wants to."

Don spoke up, "I don't know whether we should notify the police or drive to Melrose Lake ourselves."

As the three hesitated, they heard an automobile stop in front of the house. Then a door slammed. Don looked out the window.

"It's a man," he said. "He's coming to the door."

Don opened the door to Carson Drew, who came inside immediately. He greeted Hannah and Don. Then, after being introduced to Laura Pendleton and bidding her welcome to his home, the lawyer asked:

"Where's Nancy? Upstairs?"

When told that his daughter had not returned from her investigation at Melrose Lake, the lawyer was gravely concerned.

"I don't like the sound of this at all," he said. "I had no idea that Nancy was planning to sleuth in Mr. Aborn's home at night."

"She mentioned something about wanting to pay another visit to a mysterious shack in the woods, Mr. Drew," Hannah volunteered. "But I don't know where it's located."

Carson Drew's anxiety deepened. "It would be just like Nancy to follow up a good clue," he said, "particularly if she thinks there is something odd about the shack. She never gives up until she figures out the solution to whatever the problem is."

Despite his worry, Nancy's father uttered these words proudly. He had often admired the initiative his daughter displayed when she was trying to unravel a mystery.

"I think you're on the right track, Mr. Drew," Don Cameron said thoughtfully. "Since Nancy hasn't returned to the hotel, there are three possibilities—she's had car trouble, something has happened to her in the woods—"

"Or the Aborns have discovered Nancy prowling about their house," Laura put in fearfully. "And if that is the case, there's no telling what they may do to her!"

The girl quickly mentioned a few of the things which had happened in her brief stay at the Aborns.

"I'll leave for Melrose Lake immediately," Mr. Drew announced. "If I don't find Nancy in a very short time, I'm going to notify the police that she's missing!"

The others begged Mr. Drew to let them accompany him. The lawyer thought it best for Hannah to remain at home in case Nancy should call.

"But I'll be glad to have you accompany me, Laura and Don," he added.

Don hurried to the telephone to notify his parents of the plan, while Laura went for a coat.

Then they went outside and got into Mr. Drew's car.

"Be sure to call me as soon as you've found out something!" Hannah called.

"Don't worry, we will!"

Nancy's father was a skillful driver and right now he was intent upon reaching the lake as soon as possible. He could barely restrain himself from breaking the speed limits.

"This is one time I wish I had a helicopter," he told the two young people.

"It wouldn't do you much good at Melrose Lake, Mr. Drew," said Laura. "It's a pretty thickly wooded area. I doubt that you'd find a landing strip."

Don realized that this remark, although unintentional, heightened Carson Drew's worry about Nancy being lost in the woods. He changed the subject quickly.

"I thought you weren't due home until Sunday, sir," Don said.

"That's right," the lawyer replied, his eyes intent on the highway ahead. "In Cincinnati late this afternoon I had a call from Chief McGinnis of the River Heights police. He thought it was imperative for me to return home immediately."

Mr. Drew proceeded to tell Don and Laura the complete story of the embezzlement case.

Laura looked worried. "The Monroe National Bank had my mother's securities!" she exclaimed. "You don't suppose—"

"Maybe," Don put in, "Nancy learned something in connection with this at the Aborn house and is staying to get more information."

"Oh, she shouldn't have done it!" Laura cried out fearfully.

"Now there may not be anything to your theory," Mr. Drew remarked. "Don't borrow trouble."

Don patted Laura's shoulder. "Sure. We have enough worries as it is. Mr. Drew, you were telling us why you came back early."

"Yes. Although I'm making a private investigation for Mr. Seward, the bank president, Chief McGinnis has been helping me on an unofficial basis. We're old friends, you see.

"When Nancy told me that two of the suspects —the Dowds—were in the acting profession and had been out of town recently, I had a hunch they might tie in with the case. I asked the chief to check on any past records the couple might have, and call me in Cincinnati."

At this point Carson Drew explained that Chief McGinnis had learned that the Dowds both had records for theft and embezzlement. Each had served prison terms. Using various aliases, they had either acted or worked in theaters in several states and among other crimes had robbed the ticket offices.

"When the chief told me this," said Carson Drew, "I asked him to take the list of missing securities to various brokerage offices in the River Heights area. He did this and found that during the past few days all of them had been sold by a woman."

"The same woman?" Don asked.

"Apparently not," Mr. Drew replied. "At least when Chief McGinnis asked for the woman's description it was different every time."

"How odd!" Laura exclaimed. "Could it have been Mrs. Dowd? Since she's an actress she must be good at disguise."

"You may be right," Mr. Drew acknowledged. "Anyway, the chief sent two officers to their house to pick up the Dowds for questioning."

"Did they find them?" Don asked eagerly.

The lawyer shook his head. "When the police got to the house they learned that the actor and actress had had a man caller earlier in the day and that the three had left together. Mr. Dowd said they would not be back."

"How discouraging for you"—Laura sighed in sympathy—"but I'm sure you'll find them."

"There's a state alarm out for the couple," Mr. Drew said. "They shouldn't be able to get very far."

"What do the Dowds look like?" Laura asked.

In reply, the lawyer took two photographs from his breast pocket and handed them to her.

Laura held the pictures toward the light on the dashboard. She shook her head in disbelief. "These are the Dowds?" she repeated.

"Yes, why? Have you seen them before?"

Laura said in a tense voice, "I know them as Mr. and Mrs. Aborn. Oh, Mr. Drew, if they've caught Nancy, she's in real danger!"

CHAPTER XVI

A Speedy Getaway

UNAWARE that help was coming, Nancy worked feverishly to slip her hands out of the ropes in the dark cellar of the shack.

"How are you doing?" Jacob Aborn asked her.

"The bonds are becoming looser," Nancy replied.

Suddenly she recalled Hannah's promise to send the police to the Aborns' home if she had not returned at a reasonable hour. When she told the imprisoned man about this, it seemed to give him courage.

However, to herself Nancy said, "By that time those criminals will have escaped. They may even prevent Hannah from carrying out her plan! And both Laura and Hannah may be harmed!"

As if to offset this alarming possibility, the ropes around Nancy's hands suddenly pulled free.

"I did it!" she exclaimed, and Mr. Aborn sprang from his bench, crying, "We'll be able to escape!"

Nancy did not respond, for she was working grimly at the ropes which bound her feet. "If I could only see!" she muttered.

Then she remembered the packet of matches in her skirt pocket. She took it out and lighted a match, which she stuck in a crack in the wall. As the light burned she worked to untie the knots that bound her ankles. Several more matches were used before she was free.

"Miss Drew, you're the most ingenious girl I've ever met!" Mr. Aborn said admiringly. "I wish I could think that fast. It just occurred to me that there's a can of kerosene under the stairs. You might fill the lantern."

Nancy found the can and in a few seconds the place was aglow with light.

"Now I'll open the padlock again," Nancy told Mr. Aborn.

After getting the key she hurried to the side of Laura's guardian. A minute later the chains fell to the floor with a loud thud.

"At last!" Jacob Aborn cried in relief.

"Our next step," said Nancy, "is to get out of here as fast as we can and then try to alert the police."

"It's my bet," her companion said, "that Dowd has already skipped town."

Nancy was inclined to agree, but since the swindler had not expected his two prisoners to escape, he might still be at the Aborn house with his wife.

"We'll head for my car," Nancy said, "and decide what we'll do when we reach it."

Jacob Aborn moved forward several steps, then his knees began to tremble. "My legs will be all right after I've used them for a few minutes," he apologized.

But try as he would, the man was unable to climb the stairway unassisted. Nancy reached out a strong arm to help him. At last they reached the top of the stairway.

The young sleuth led the way to the door, unbolted it, and the two stepped outside.

"What a relief!" Jacob Aborn gasped, filling his lungs with pure air.

In the east, the moon had risen over the woods and the sky was peppered with stars. The route among the trees would be easy to find in the clear night. Yet Nancy glanced uneasily at her companion, wondering if he would be able to walk to the car.

As if reading her thoughts, Aborn said, "I'm fine now. Let's go!"

Nancy offered her arm again, and at a slow pace they walked across the clearing and entered the woods. They had gone but a short way when Mr. Aborn sank down on a log, breathing heavily.

"You go on without me, Nancy," he said in a voice shaky with fatigue. "I can't do it."

"Just rest here for a moment," Nancy said encouragingly, unwilling to leave the man.

Shortly, Mr. Aborn felt he could continue. Leaning heavily on Nancy, he moved forward, refusing to pause again even for a brief rest.

"You're a very kind girl to help me," he said hoarsely.

Nancy replied modestly, "I'm *so* glad I found you. Think of what it means to Laura to have her real guardian found! I know she will be happy living with you and your wife."

At the mention of his wife's name Mr. Aborn said he was grateful that she had gone away before the Dowds invaded their home. "She might have been made a prisoner too!" he declared.

Presently, with a feeling of relief, Nancy caught sight of her convertible standing among the bushes where she had left it. After she had helped Mr. Aborn into the front seat, Nancy took her place behind the steering wheel.

"Now we'll drive to the nearest police station," she announced. "You direct me."

She inserted the key and tried the starter. To Nancy's surprise, the motor did not turn over.

"That's funny," she said, and tried again. Nothing happened. Next, Nancy glanced at the fuel gauge. It registered half full.

"I wonder if your battery's dead," Mr. Aborn said in a faint voice.

"I think not," Nancy replied, as she reached into the glove compartment and took out an extra flashlight she kept there for emergencies.

She got out of the car, lifted the hood, and flashed her light inside. She had taken a course in automobile mechanics and knew the possible sources of trouble.

"I see what the trouble is," Nancy called. "The distributor has been uncapped and the rotor's missing! This is sabotage!" Without this necessary part the car could not start. "I'm sure that Mr. Dowd is the saboteur," she added angrily.

Mr. Aborn sighed resignedly. "Stumpy Dowd leaves no stones unturned," he said in a tired voice. "Just in case we might escape he wanted to make certain we'd have no transportation. I'm afraid, Nancy, that we'll have to go to the main highway for help."

As Mr. Aborn spoke, Nancy heard a car motor not far away. Eagerly she looked to right and left but saw no approaching headlights.

"Quick! Duck down!" Mr. Aborn whispered, and Nancy crouched in the bushes alongside her car.

A dark foreign sports car emerged from the Eagle Rock lane, then made a left-hand turn in the direction of Twin Lakes!

"It's the Dowds making a getaway!" Mr. Aborn said. "We're too late!"

Nancy was alarmed by this turn of events. She wondered why Stumpy Dowd was not heading toward River Heights. Had he given up the idea of going to the Drews' residence and forcing Laura Pendleton to give him the jewels? Or was he taking an alternative route there?

"Oh dear! I wish there were a telephone nearby!" Nancy moaned. She told Mr. Aborn that his had been disconnected.

Jacob Aborn spoke up. "Nancy, I'm sure that Dowd and his wife have left my house for good. I think the best plan is for us to go there."

"Yes," Nancy agreed. "After you're safely inside I'll go for help."

"I can't let you do that," Jacob Aborn protested. "Few cars come along this road at night. You'll have an extremely long walk before you reach the main highway."

Silently Nancy agreed, but she also noted that the man's strength was almost spent. She helped him from the car, and the two slowly approached the lane that led to Mr. Aborn's house.

"Oh, if I could only get my hands on that scoundrel!" the man muttered.

The thought gave him new strength, and he moved forward again. Cautiously the two crept toward the house, approaching it from the rear.

"We'd better make certain that no one's here," Nancy whispered.

As they drew near the back door she saw that it stood ajar, as though someone had left hurriedly without taking time to shut it.

With Jacob Aborn close behind her, Nancy stepped cautiously into the kitchen. There was profound silence. The place appeared deserted.

Crossing the room on tiptoe, Nancy and Mr. Aborn walked toward the living room. He clicked on a light. Everything was in disorder. A chair had been overturned and papers were scattered about.

"The Dowds certainly made a thorough search," Nancy remarked.

Just then Mr. Aborn's eyes fell upon the wall safe which stood open. With a cry of alarm he tottered across the room to look inside. Everything had been taken out.

Mr. Aborn groaned. He told Nancy that a sizable sum of his own money had been in the safe, along with shares of negotiable stock. Stumpy Dowd had forced him to tell the safe's combination on threat of harming Laura.

Mr. Aborn, white as starch, sank into a nearby chair and buried his head in his hands. "Nearly all my securities were in there," he said. One quick glance at him told Nancy that the man was on the verge of a complete collapse. She could not leave him alone, yet how could she get help without doing so?

A second later she and Mr. Aborn were startled to hear a car driving up the lane. Were the Dowds returning? Had the couple merely gone out for a while, or had they forgotten something in their hasty flight?

Nancy's next thought was far worse than either of these. Had Stumpy Dowd somehow learned that his two prisoners had escaped?

CHAPTER XVII

Two-way Detecting

As THE automobile pulled to a halt, Mr. Aborn slumped to the floor in a faint. Evidently he had shared Nancy's thought that the Dowds were returning, and would force their way in. The terrifying thought that he might become a prisoner again had been too much for the exhausted man.

"Oh!" Nancy cried out.

From the window Nancy saw four people hurriedly alighting from the car. A moment later the bell rang and a woman's voice cried, "Mr. Aborn —Mr. Aborn—please let us in. It's the Donnells!"

Nancy hurried to the front door and flung it open. "Cathy! Jim!" she cried out. "Oh, you don't know how glad I am to see you!"

The two young people introduced Nancy to their parents, a good-looking couple in their forties. Then they stepped inside.

"What are you doing here, Nancy?" Jim Donnell asked, puzzled at the girl's disheveled appearance. "What's going on?"

Nancy replied by saying Mr. Aborn was ill, and there was no time for further explanation right now. She hastily led the family into the living room. When they saw their unconscious friend on the floor, Mrs. Donnell rushed forward with an excited cry.

"How dreadful!" she exclaimed.

As she knelt down, the kindly woman said she was a registered nurse. After a brief examination of the patient she reported that Mr. Aborn appeared to be suffering from malnutrition and shock.

While Jim and his father lifted him onto the couch, Nancy told what had happened to him. The Donnells were stunned.

Before they could discuss it, however, Nancy turned to Jim. "Two phone calls must be made right away," she said. "Would you be able to take care of them for me?"

"Glad to," the boy said. "I suppose you want me to notify the police to pick up Stumpy Dowd—"

"Yes," Nancy said tersely, and described the black foreign car.

She next asked Jim to call Chief McGinnis at River Heights and tell him to have extra men patrol the Drew home. "Find out if Mrs. Gruen and

Laura are all right," she requested, "and see if our housekeeper knows where to get in touch with Dad."

Jim said he would do all of these things. As soon as he returned, he would try to fix Nancy's car.

After Jim left, Nancy turned to the others. Mr. Aborn had regained consciousness and said he felt better and able to talk.

"Lillian," he said, giving Mrs. Donnell a wan smile, "the angels must have sent you. How did you know we were in trouble here?"

"We didn't for sure," Mr. Donnell replied gravely, "until tonight—it's a long story."

The gray-haired man said that he and his wife had been amazed to hear on Tuesday from their children that Marian Aborn had returned from Florida and that she and Jacob had met Laura Pendleton at Twin Lakes.

"We were sure you would have told us of your change of plans, if this were true, Jacob," he said to his old friend. "Anyway, we came over here yesterday morning to say hello and meet Laura. No one answered the bell."

"We concluded," said Mrs. Donnell, "that Nancy Drew had been mistaken in thinking that you were coming back here—anyway, we remembered you saying that due to the illness of Marian's mother you would not be able to come here with Laura until after your wife's return."

"That's right," said Mr. Aborn. He explained to Nancy that first there had been legal technicalities regarding his appointment as the orphan's guardian, since he had been living in another state. That was why his ward had remained at her boarding school.

Mrs. Donnell went on to say that this evening they had received a telephone call from Mrs. Aborn who was still in Florida. "Marian had tried several times to get you and was upset to learn that the phone here was disconnected. She called us to see why."

"My wife hadn't heard from me in over two weeks," Mr. Aborn stated.

Mrs. Donnell said, "But Marian thought she had. Mrs. Aborn sent telegrams here and replies came to her in Florida."

Mr. Donnell said that when the family heard that Marian Aborn was indeed in Florida, they were fearful something was terribly wrong.

"We told Marian what we knew, suggested she come home immediately, and said we would come over here right away to see what we could uncover."

"Thank goodness you did," Nancy sighed, and Mr. Aborn gave his friends a grateful smile. Then he asked, "How is Marian's mother?"

"Getting along very well."

"When will my wife arrive?" Mr. Aborn asked anxiously.

"She's taking a night plane from Miami to the Hamilton airport," Mrs. Donnell replied. "My husband will meet her."

Cathy's mother then went to the kitchen to prepare a light meal for Mr. Aborn. Nancy excused herself and went to wash her face, legs, and grimy hands. Refreshed, she returned to the living room, wondering what was keeping Jim so long.

"He'll be here soon, Nancy," said Cathy.

"I'll feel much better when I know everything's all right at home," Nancy replied.

While Mr. Aborn ate, the pretty detective told the others of Stumpy Dowd's connection with Mr. Drew's case.

"What a story!" Mr. Donnell exclaimed.

Nancy excused herself for a moment and went to the front door to listen for Jim's car. As she stood on the steps her heart suddenly leaped. A tall figure stood up from behind a bush near the front steps.

"Nancy?" a man's voice called softly.

Nancy knew who it was. "Dad!" she cried out.

Carson Drew leaped the steps and gave his daughter a resounding kiss. "Are you all right?" he whispered.

When Nancy said yes, and that it was safe to

talk aloud, Don Cameron and Laura emerged from some shrubbery.

"We saw lights and heard voices," Laura explained. "We thought it was the Aborns. What's going on here, Nancy?"

"Yes, tell us!" Don urged.

Once again Nancy explained what had happened. Carson Drew listened to his daughter's story of her encounter with the thief, a stern expression on his face.

"You were lucky to come out of this so well," he remarked.

"Yes," Laura agreed. "And it's so wonderful to have a guardian whom you say is nice!"

"Mr. Aborn is a fine person, Laura," Nancy said. "I'll take you in to meet him in a minute."

Carson Drew now brought Nancy up to date on his news, and ended by saying, "We were so worried we drove here immediately, not even taking time to call the police."

Don added that they had left Mr. Drew's car at the end of the lane and were scouting the house to see if Nancy were inside when she had appeared on the front steps.

"How many times I wished you were here!" said Nancy. She now suggested that everyone come into the house to meet the others. "Jim Donnell," she added, "should return any minute."

"I'll wait for the young man out here and act

as guard in case the Dowds show up," Carson Drew said, sitting down on a step. "The rest of you run along—"

As Nancy walked inside with Don and Laura she saw that Mr. and Mrs. Donnell were helping Mr. Aborn up the stairs to his bedroom. Hearing voices, the guardian turned, looked at his ward, and exclaimed:

"Laura dear—at last—I'd know you anywhere! You look just like your mother!"

"Mr. Aborn!" Laura cried out. She raced up the steps and gave her guardian a big kiss.

Introductions were quickly made, and when Mr. Aborn was settled in his bed, he had a visit with Laura and Nancy. But after they had chatted for a few minutes the girls could see that the man needed sleep badly.

"We'll say good night now," said Nancy. "Sweet dreams." She turned off the light, and they went downstairs.

When Nancy and Laura reached the first floor, they found Mr. Drew and Jim Donnell talking in the hall with a state trooper. While Cathy took Laura aside, Nancy walked toward the group.

She was introduced to Sergeant Murphy, then Carson Drew explained to her that the state police were putting all available cars on the chase and hoped to round up the Dowds and their accomplice shortly.

"Good!" Nancy exclaimed. "But what about Mrs. Gruen?"

Sergeant Murphy said that he had talked with Chief McGinnis. The River Heights official had immediately sent a patrol car and four men to the Drews' home.

"Your housekeeper was relieved to hear that you, Miss Drew, had been found," he reported. "Nothing unusual has happened at your home to-night. But it will be closely guarded until the Dowds and their accomplice are caught."

"Oh, I'm glad," said Nancy. Sergeant Murphy left, after saying he would check back later.

Nancy and Mr. Drew walked into the living room, and she introduced her father to Mr. and Mrs. Donnell and Cathy. After a few minutes of excited conversation, the young sleuth said:

"Dad, I have a hunch that the man 'Fred' whom Stumpy Dowd mentioned is someone employed at the Monroe National Bank. Tell me, was Mrs. Pendleton's name ever mentioned in connection with the missing securities?"

Mr. Drew shook his head. "No, Nancy, it wasn't."

"Then," said Nancy, "I think we're going to find that Laura's bonds were never deposited in the bank's vault. Whoever took them and passed them on to Stumpy Dowd must be someone who works in the custodian department of the bank."

"That's good reasoning, Nancy," her father agreed, "but we have checked almost all the employees and they've been given a clean bill of health. One man, Mr. Hamilton's assistant, has been on vacation and we won't be able to interview him for another week or so."

"What's the man's name?" Nancy asked.

Mr. Drew consulted a list of names which he took from his pocket. "William Frednich."

Nancy snapped her fingers. "Frednich! Maybe *he's* the 'Fred' the Dowds were talking about. And if he is," she continued excitedly, "I think they're together and I believe I know where the Dowds are hiding out with this man!"

Carson Drew looked at his daughter in amazement. "Where?" he asked.

"Not far from here," Nancy said mysteriously. Then she jumped up from her chair. "Let's find out, Dad!"

CHAPTER XVIII

Night Trail

CARSON DREW, startled, looked at his daughter.

"Where do you think the Dowds and Fred are hiding, Nancy?"

"In a bungalow on Twin Lakes—the one I told you we stayed in after Laura rescued us," she explained. "My main reasons for thinking so are these: I saw a black foreign car come from there, and the place was well-stocked with food. Fred may have been living there."

"Go on. This is interesting," the lawyer said.

Nancy's hunch was that the thieves had first planned the bank theft, then the Dowds had rented the bungalow under an assumed name.

"Makes sense." Carson Drew nodded.

"Fred," Nancy continued, "knew of Laura's large estate and jewelry, and got the idea of having Stumpy Dowd impersonate Mr. Aborn. In order to get the jewelry they had to have Laura with them, so they decided to take her to the Melrose Lake house."

"Good logic," said Mr. Drew. "Then, when the real Mr. Aborn appeared, they had to kidnap him temporarily. Well, we'll follow your hunch. Shall we go?"

The others offered to go, but Mr. Drew thought that the Donnells should stay with Mr. Aborn and Laura.

"Please do," Nancy added. "After all, my hunch could be wrong. The Dowds may return here."

"We'll nab 'em if they do!" Jim said determinedly.

A few minutes later Mr. Drew's car was on the detour again, heading for the Twin Lakes road. When they reached it, there were no other cars in evidence.

"That's odd," said Nancy, knowing that this was the only road which connected the two resorts.

"Oh, oh!" said Don. "Look!"

Mr. Drew had also seen a small red light a few hundred feet distant. He slowed up. Ahead was a gate obstruction across the highway. On it was nailed a sign which read:

ROAD UNDER CONSTRUCTION
Travel at your own risk

"This is great!" Mr. Drew remarked unhappily.

"Maybe it won't be too bad," Nancy said. "I came this way the other day and I think I know all the turns."

"Why don't we try it, sir?" Don spoke up.

"All right."

Don got out of the car and moved the barrier enough so Mr. Drew could drive through. They went slowly, because of the steam shovels, bulldozers, and equipment parked along the road.

To make matters worse, the pavement was gone in places where repairs were being made. The car tires wallowed in soft dirt.

Soon, however, they reached the end of the construction section and Carson Drew stepped on the accelerator. The car responded with a burst of speed.

"We're not far from Twin Lakes now," Nancy said as she spotted a few familiar landmarks.

Don wanted to know what the plan would be when they reached the bungalow. Mr. Drew said they would first check to see if the foreign car were in the vicinity. "Of course it will be hidden."

"Next," Nancy added, "we'll have to make sure Fred and the Dowds are there, and not some innocent people. But if Stumpy's there, we'll notify the police. Right, Dad?"

"Unless Dowd sees us first," he said grimly.

Nancy said she hoped this would not happen.

"But I suppose they probably will have someone acting as a lookout."

"As I understand it, Nancy," said her father, "the bungalow is in an isolated spot."

"Yes, and there are a lot of trees around it."

"Could anyone inside the house make a getaway by boat?" Don asked.

"Not easily," Nancy answered. "The bungalow is not built over the water. It's some distance from the lake and there's no dock where a boat could be tied." Presently she said, "We're about a mile from the bungalow."

Carson Drew's face tensed. He drove to a point about a tenth of a mile from the lane leading down to the bungalow, then stopped the car in a clearing off the road.

"We'll cover the rest of the distance on foot," he announced.

As Nancy got out the right-hand side of the car after Don she glanced at the luminous dial on the clock. It was three o'clock in the morning!

Walking three abreast, the sleuths saw the bungalow below. It was in darkness.

"I don't see any sign of a car," Don whispered to Nancy, as he guided her by the arm.

Carson Drew was silent, but suddenly he jerked to attention. A twig had snapped. Now they saw a man walking toward the trio through the woods!

As Don, Nancy, and Mr. Drew ducked behind

some shrubbery, they noticed that the man approaching them was carrying a fishing pole and a box of the type ordinarily used for bait.

Passing by the watchers, he walked unhurriedly toward the beach. At this moment the moon chose to show itself brilliantly, and Nancy observed that the man was tall and heavy.

"Hello, Sam," he said, and now the watchers could see a rowboat and passenger gliding out of the shadows.

"I hope the fish are biting well this morning." His voice carried clearly in the stillness.

The fisherman deposited his gear in the boat, and the two companions shoved off. They were barely out of sight when Don whispered hoarsely, "A light in the bungalow."

From the second-story window had come a flash of light. It did not reappear.

"Someone's up there!" Nancy whispered. "Maybe the fisherman alerted him."

"Let's circle the house," said Carson Drew, and suggested that he take the left half of the circle while Nancy and Don took the right. They would meet back at this same spot in a few minutes.

"Be careful now," he warned the young people.

"You too, Dad," Nancy said.

The route Nancy and Don took led past the door into the first floor of the boathouse bungalow. Cautiously they listened at the exit. There was no sound from within. They went on to the beach side.

The two tiptoed among the shadows as far as the center of the rear of the building without incident, then quietly returned to the meeting place. When they arrived, Mr. Drew was not there.

"That's funny," said Nancy, a little alarmed. "Where *is* Dad?"

Just then she and Don heard a low groan. It seemed to come from behind a tree about twenty feet away. Forgetting caution, the couple rushed to the spot. Behind its broad trunk a man lay sprawled on the ground. Mr. Drew!

"Dad!" Nancy exclaimed, kneeling down. She felt the lawyer's pulse. It was steady.

"I think he was knocked out," said Don angrily. "Nancy, you're right about this being a hide-out. We must get the police!"

"And right away!" Nancy agreed, as Carson Drew sat up groggily. In a moment he could talk.

The lawyer said that after leaving Nancy and Don he had started around the bungalow. Someone had come from behind and struck him. "I suppose he dragged me here."

"Stumpy Dowd, I'll bet!" Nancy exclaimed. "And this may mean that he and his wife made a getaway while Don and I were on the other side of the bungalow! Dad, do you feel well enough to try to follow them?"

"Yes, but where did they go?" he asked. "And how? By boat, car, or on foot?"

As if in answer to his question, the three suddenly saw in the clear moonlight the figures of two men and a woman running up the bungalow lane toward the road. Each man carried a big suitcase. Laura's inheritance and Mr. Aborn's little fortune!

"After them!" Don cried.

But Mr. Drew could not make it. He tottered unsteadily and leaned against the pine. "Go on!" he said.

"No!" Nancy replied quickly. "Don, bring Dad's car here, will you?"

As the boy started off, the trio heard the muffled backfire of an automobile coming from the direction of the woods across the main road.

"Hurry, Don!" Nancy urged. "They had a car hidden there."

By the time Don returned, Carson Drew felt better. He suggested that Nancy drive, since she was more familiar with the road. When everyone was in the car, with the lawyer in the rear seat, they took off.

Upon reaching the road, the young sleuth turned right. "I think this is the direction the other car took," she said. "Anyway, it leads to Stamford, where I know there's a state police headquarters."

Carson Drew sat up groggily

The road became rough and was full of sharp turns. Nancy drove fast but carefully, slowing at each curve. There was no sign of another car until Don suddenly cried out:

"I think we're approaching a car!"

Nancy peered forward intently. She saw nothing but the road ahead.

"It's hidden now by that hill in front of us," Don told her.

There was a long moment of suspense, then Nancy exclaimed, "I see it!"

"Do you think it's the Dowds?" Don asked.

"It could be," Mr. Drew replied.

As the car reached a smooth, straight piece of road, Nancy put it to a faster and faster pace.

"We're gaining on them!" Don said exuberantly.

Little by little the Drew sedan crept up on the car ahead. Soon its headlights spotlighted the rear of the other vehicle—a black foreign car! Three figures were silhouetted inside it!

At the same moment Nancy caught sight of a huge black-and-white checkerboard sign at the side of the road. A bad curve ahead! With well-timed precision, Nancy eased up on her speed and gradually used her brake, knowing that abrupt pressure might cause a bad skid.

"That other driver isn't paying any attention to the warning!" Don exclaimed.

The snakelike curve was only a few hundred feet ahead on a steep downgrade. The occupants of the Drew sedan held their breath. Would the others make the turn? There came a violent screech of brakes.

"Oh no!" Nancy cried out in horror.

As she and her companions watched, the foreign car shot off the edge of the road and plunged down a steep cliff!

CHAPTER XIX

Missing Property

STUNNED by the accident to the speeding car, Nancy brought the sedan to a halt at the curve. Everyone inside was reluctant to look down into the ravine below, from which there was not a sound.

But only for an instant. Then Carson Drew urged, "Out, everyone, quickly! We must do what we can for those people!"

Nancy and Don sprang from the car and rushed to the edge of the road. The lawyer was close behind them.

As the three gazed down into the ravine, the first light of dawn revealed that the foreign car had rolled nearly to the bottom of it and overturned against a boulder. A wheel had been torn loose from its axle and the body had been smashed in. There was no sign of any of the three occupants.

A silence held the trio above. It was inconceivable that anyone in the wreck could be alive!

At last Carson Drew found his voice. "I guess we'd better notify the police and emergency squad," he said.

Don agreed, but Nancy thought they should first see if by chance any of the accident victims were alive.

Mr. Drew and Don nodded, and followed Nancy as she scrambled down the incline. Nancy, in the lead, gasped as she saw the body of a strange man, apparently not the driver, which had been flung out of the car into a clump of bushes near the wreck. She also noticed gasoline spilling from a hole in the tank. Vaguely she thought of fire and an explosion.

"Hurry!" she urged.

As the three drew closer they saw a man's leg and a woman's high-heeled shoe protruding from beneath the left-hand side of the car.

With frantic haste Don and Mr. Drew dragged the man out, while Nancy tugged at the woman's body. Stumpy Dowd and his wife! Both were breathing, but unconscious. The victims, cut and badly bruised, were carried to a safe place on the grass.

"Now let's see about the other man, Mr. Drew," urged Don.

As they headed for the bushes where he lay,

Nancy stared at the car. "The suitcases!" she thought. "Laura's inheritance and Mr. Aborn's little fortune! I must get them out before they may be burned up!"

Crawling under the wreck, she began to grope about frantically. Her hand struck a suitcase and she dragged it out.

At that instant Nancy realized how hot the metal was. There might be spontaneous combustion at any second. She must work fast to save the second suitcase!

"It's the only way I can ever repay Laura for saving my life on Twin Lakes!" Nancy thought.

By feeling around she found the bag and triumphantly brought it out, only to be jerked from the scene by Carson Drew and Don.

"Nancy!" Carson Drew cried, white-faced and horror-stricken. "Are you mad? Those suitcases aren't worth your life!"

There was a sudden explosion. Then flames enveloped the car and the dry grass in the immediate vicinity began to burn.

Don Cameron shuddered, but looked at Nancy, admiration showing in his eyes. "You're the most courageous girl I've ever met," he said slowly. "Nancy, you might have been killed!"

As she herself realized what a narrow escape she had had, Nancy breathed a prayer of thanksgiving.

She was shaken and silent as the men threw dirt on the flames to keep them from spreading. When they finished, Don told Nancy that he and Mr. Drew thought the third man would be all right, although the stranger as well as the Dowds were injured, perhaps seriously.

"Now I suppose we must get the three of them to a hospital as fast as we can," he said.

At that moment they all heard the low whine of an ambulance alarm. This was followed by a police siren.

Nancy, Mr. Drew, and Don looked at one another hopefully. "Do you suppose—" Nancy began.

She was right. Help had come! A moment later police and emergency squad cars stopped at the top of the ravine. Four officers, two stretcher-bearers, and an intern, clad in white, hurried down to the group.

"Thank goodness," said Mr. Drew. Introductions were quickly made, then he asked, "How did you know about the accident?"

An officer, Lieutenant Gill, told him that a farmer living not far away had seen the speeding car go off the road and notified headquarters.

"When we heard it was a black foreign car, we were suspicious immediately," he said. "Can you identify these people as the Dowds?"

"From pictures, yes," said Mr. Drew, and briefly told the whole story of the Dowd affair up to the present moment.

"And I can testify that they were impersonating the Aborns," Nancy added.

"Anybody know who the other man is?" Lieutenant Gill inquired.

"I believe," Mr. Drew replied, "that he's William Frednich, assistant to the president of the River Heights branch of the Monroe National Bank. He's suspected of removing certain securities from the bank."

During this conversation the intern had been examining the accident victims and the attendants had laid them on stretchers. The doctor reported that the victims had been given first aid and had revived. They would be in good shape after a short stay in the hospital.

"They'll get a nice long rest after that," said Lieutenant Gill, "in the state pen. I shan't try to question them now."

As the prisoners were carried up to the ambulance, with the others following, Lieutenant Gill explained to the Dowds how Nancy had saved them from being burned in the wreckage.

"I don't believe it," said Stumpy ungratefully.

His wife was more gracious. "Thanks, Miss Drew. And I want to tell you I'm tired of this whole business. You're only a kid but you've really taught me a lesson."

Nancy did not answer. She found herself choking up, and tears came into her eyes.

As the ambulance moved away, Nancy, quickly brushing her moist eyes dry with the backs of her hands, turned toward the east. She observed that a beautiful sunrise was beginning to flood the sky with brilliant color.

Don yawned. "What do you say we head for home?" he suggested. "Otherwise, I'll never be able to make my sister's wedding this evening."

"Oh dear!" Nancy exclaimed. "I forgot all about it. Please forgive us for keeping you up all night."

Don grinned. "I wouldn't have missed this excitement for anything!"

"I suggest," said Mr. Drew, "that we go back to Nancy's hotel and the Drews will get some sleep. Don, you take my car and return to River Heights. Later, Nancy and I will take a taxi and pick up her convertible at the Aborns'."

"Thank you, sir. I'll do that."

While the three had been talking, Lieutenant Gill had been wedging open one of the two locked suitcases which Nancy had taken from the wrecked car. Mr. Drew and the others walked over as he lifted the lid.

The bag was jammed with feminine clothing. There were several dresses, a large make-up kit, pieces of lingerie, shoes, and several wigs—a gray one, a black hairpiece, and one which was decidedly auburn.

"That clinches it, Dad!" Nancy exclaimed. "Mrs. Dowd must have gone around in disguise to cash the bonds."

"But where's the money she got?" Don asked.

"It must be in the other bag," Nancy suggested, "together with securities and money belonging to Laura Pendleton, Mr. Aborn, and River Heights bank clients."

Lieutenant Gill opened the second suitcase. It contained men's clothing and toilet articles.

"Nancy, you risked your life for this!" Don exclaimed.

Nancy Drew could not believe her eyes. Had she been mistaken in believing that Stumpy Dowd had put the contents of Mr. Aborn's safe in the bags? Quickly she glanced down at the foreign car. Had Laura's inheritance and other people's money burned in it?

The thought stunned the young sleuth. But in a moment an idea came to her.

"There's just a possibility the papers *are* here," she said.

All eyes turned on the girl detective, as the group awaited a further explanation.

CHAPTER XX

A Surprise Gift

"I'M SURE," said Nancy, "that Mr. Dowd not only put the money and securities in one of these suit-cases, but never removed them!"

"Then *where* are they?" Don asked.

Nancy smiled. "These bags may have false bot-toms!"

Lieutenant Gill said, "Why, of course. I should have thought of that."

Kneeling down, he soon found that Nancy was right. The bottom of each bag opened up, dis-closing packages of thousand-dollar bills and se-curities.

"Good thinking, Nancy," said Don admiringly. "You're a whiz of a detective, all right."

It took Mr. Drew and the officers several min-utes to count the large sum of money and make a rough estimate of the value of the stocks and bonds. When they finished, the officer gave Carson Drew a receipt to turn over to the president of the Monroe National Bank. Meanwhile, he would take the stolen property to police headquarters and send on a detailed report.

A few minutes later Nancy's group said good-by to the officers, and returned to Mr. Drew's car. When they reached the Beach Cliff Hotel, Nancy and Mr. Drew got out. They thanked Don for all he had done.

"Don't mention it." The young man grinned. Turning to Nancy, he added, "I kept my date with you yesterday after all!"

As he got into the driver's seat Don said that when he returned the car to the Drews' home he would tell Hannah Gruen what had happened.

It was now very light. Nancy and her father, exhausted, could hardly wait to get a few hours sleep. They tumbled into their beds and slept until noon, then met in the hotel dining room for a hearty brunch.

"How's your head, Dad?" Nancy asked.

"Sound as ever!" Carson Drew said, grinning. "I don't even have a bump."

"Then we have a date," Nancy told him, waving a note. "This was at the desk. I picked it up. The clerk said Jim Donnell left it a little while ago."

"The date's with him?" Mr. Drew asked.

"No. Laura Pendleton. She says she and the

Aborns are thrilled by the news which the police relayed and would like us to come to their house as soon as possible. What do you say, Dad?"

"We'll go."

As Nancy finished her pancakes and sausages she remarked that she could hardly wait to start for the Aborns' home. "I wonder if the Dowds have confessed everything and what Mr. Frednich had to say."

"In my opinion it's an open and shut case," the lawyer replied.

While Mr. Drew paid the hotel bill, Nancy called a taxi and soon the Drews were heading for Eagle Rock Lane. Reaching it, they got out of the cab and the lawyer paid the driver.

Nancy slid in behind the steering wheel of her convertible, as Mr. Drew got in on the other side. The motor started at once. "Good old Jim," Nancy said with a smile, and drove up the lane to the Aborn home.

As she parked, the front door was opened by a woman of about forty-five. Her pretty face showed humor, kindness, and intelligence.

After the Drews had introduced themselves, the woman said she was Marian Aborn and had reached home "in the wee small hours" because her plane was late. "I've been most eager to meet you two," she added, smiling. "How can I ever thank you for all you've done?"

As the callers went inside, Laura Pendleton hurried down from the second floor. After greeting Mr. Drew she gave Nancy a kiss and exclaimed, "Everything is so wonderful—you've captured the thieves and recovered all the money—and I have the nicest guardians anyone could ever hope for!"

"And Jacob and I have a daughter to love!" said Marian Aborn, smiling fondly at Laura.

Nancy asked how Mr. Aborn felt. His wife said, "Come see for yourselves," and led the way to a small study at the rear of the house.

She knocked, then opened the door, and Nancy heard the steady drum of typewriter keys. Jacob Aborn was seated behind the machine.

The erstwhile cellar prisoner already looked like a new man. His face was flooded with color, and his eyes were alert and happy. Now he stood up, greeted the Drews, and expressed his great appreciation for all they had done in recovering his and Laura's property.

He grinned at Nancy. "First time a girl ever risked her life for me!" he said. "To show my appreciation I'm writing my adventure. You know, writing is my business. If I sell this one to a magazine, I'm going to give the proceeds to Nancy's favorite charity—the River Heights Youth Center!"

"Why, that's terrific!" Nancy exclaimed.

Mrs. Aborn's face sobered. She said that she

had not yet heard the entire story of what had happened. Before anyone had a chance to tell her, the doorbell rang. Lieutenant Gill walked in with Chief McGinnis of River Heights and another man. While Nancy greeted the officers, her father hurried to shake hands with the stranger.

"This is Mr. Seward, president of the Monroe National Bank," he announced a moment later, and introduced the dignified white-haired man.

The president's glance included the policemen as he said, "I want to thank all of you in person for the splendid job you did in capturing the Dowds and the two bank employees involved in the thefts."

"There is a fourth man?" Nancy asked in amazement.

Mr. Seward explained that Alma Dowd's brother, Joe Jackson, had been employed by the Monroe National Bank in their vault department for some time. He and Frednich had cooked up the scheme of taking the securities. They had done this between audits of the bank's holdings. Frednich, in his job as assistant custodian, had known exactly how to place his hands on the valuable stocks and bonds.

"Frednich overheard Mrs. Pendleton's discussion with me about Laura and the large estate she would inherit some day," Mr. Seward said, "and also that Mr. Aborn would be her guardian.

When Frednich learned that Laura Pendleton had a valuable jewelry collection, he instantly thought of a swindle scheme. Frednich had chanced to meet Mr. Aborn one time while vacationing at Melrose Lake. He had been amazed by the strong resemblance between Aborn and Stumpy Dowd, whom Alma's brother had introduced to Frednich. He asked Dowd to impersonate Mr. Aborn and to move up the date when Laura would come to the guardian's home. He even deposited some securities with the bank in Stumpy's name, so there would be no question of Dowd's having anything to do with the thefts."

"Where is Joe Jackson now?" Nancy asked.

Chief McGinnis said he would answer this question. "We caught him cruising by the Drews' home. When we stopped the car, he tried to escape. After the whole story broke, we got a confession from him. He was going to burglarize your home, Nancy, to find the jewels."

"There's one thing I don't understand," said Mrs. Aborn. "Why did the Dowds rent the bungalow when they had helped themselves to this house?"

Nancy grinned. "I'm sure I know," she said. "Dowd was smart enough not to want either Frednich or Jackson to stay here—just in case anyone from the bank traced the thefts to them before Dowd could make a getaway. So he had Alma

Dowd rent the bungalow and convinced Frednich that it was a good hide-out."

After Mr. Aborn and Laura had signed statements for the police, the officers and Mr. Seward left. Nancy suddenly felt a sense of loneliness and realized it was because her work on the case was at an end. Would another mystery come her way to solve? she wondered. And it did. In less than a week, Nancy was facing up to the challenge of *The Mystery at Lilac Inn.*

Nancy and her father now said good-by to the family at Eagle Rock. As Nancy gave Laura a farewell hug, she asked, "When will you come to get your jewelry?"

Laura consulted her guardian, who said the next day would be convenient for them to drive to River Heights. "Will three o'clock be all right?"

"Yes indeed."

The following afternoon Laura Pendleton and the Aborns arrived promptly. After iced tea and some of Hannah's delicious open-faced sandwiches, Laura whispered to Mr. Drew that she would love to get her jewelry from the safe. Excusing himself, Nancy's father left the room and returned in a few minutes with the package, which he handed to Laura.

Nancy, meanwhile, was listening to Jacob Aborn's surprising news that he had finished his story and was sending it to a leading magazine.

"Wonderful!" said Nancy. As she said this, she looked up to see Laura standing before her. In the girl's hand was the beautiful aquamarine ring Nancy had admired earlier in the week.

"I'd like you to wear this," Laura said shyly, "as a reminder that our friendship began on the water." Quickly she slipped the ring on the third finger of Nancy's right hand.

The pretty detective gave an exclamation of delight and admired the gift for a long moment. Then she showed it to the others. At last she turned to Laura and said with genuine sincerity:

"The ring is priceless and I'll always treasure it as a reminder of you—although no one can place a value on a true friendship like ours."

Seeing tears in Laura's eyes, Nancy added quickly with a grin, "Even if we had to be ship-wrecked to get an introduction!"

SWEET TALK

MORE TITLES BY JULIE GARWOOD

The Ideal Man
Sizzle
Fire and Ice
Shadow Music
Shadow Dance
Slow Burn
Murder List
Killjoy
Mercy
Heartbreaker
Ransom
Come the Spring
The Clayborne Brides
The Wedding
For the Roses
Prince Charming
Saving Grace
Castles
The Secret
The Prize
The Gift
Guardian Angel
The Bride
The Lion's Lady
Honor's Splendour
Rebellious Desire
Gentle Warrior
A Girl Named Summer

JULIE GARWOOD

SWEET TALK

DOUBLEDAY LARGE PRINT HOME LIBRARY EDITION

DUTTON

This Large Print Edition, prepared especially for Doubleday Large Print Home Library, contains the complete, unabridged text of the original Publisher's Edition.

DUTTON
Published by Penguin Group (USA) Inc.
375 Hudson Street, New York, New York 10014, U.S.A.

Penguin Books Ltd, Registered Offices: 80 Strand, London WC2R 0RL, England

Published by Dutton, a member of Penguin Group (USA) Inc.

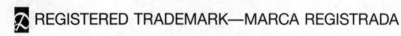 REGISTERED TRADEMARK—MARCA REGISTRADA

ISBN 978-1-62090-253-0

Printed in the United States of America

PUBLISHER'S NOTE

To Aaron Michael Hass Garwood,
for your thoughtfulness, your
generosity, and your love.
Welcome to the family.

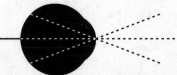

This Large Print Book carries the
Seal of Approval of N.A.V.H.

SWEET TALK

PROLOGUE

The Pips were at it again. The four girls had vanished from the unit dragging thousands of dollars' worth of equipment with them and causing quite a commotion. The staff was frantic, desperate to find them before word of their disappearance leaked out. The only person not concerned was the man who held their futures in his hands. He insisted that the restless, mischievous adolescents had not escaped. They were pulling just another silly prank, no doubt orchestrated by Olivia MacKenzie, the ringleader. From the minute he'd looked into those gorgeous, sparkling blue eyes, he'd known she was going to be a troublemaker and a fighter.

He couldn't have been more pleased. Olivia gave the other Pips—Samantha Pearson, Jane Weston, and Collins Davenport—strength and a voice. Until she'd entered the program, the girls had been sullen, lethargic, and even borderline suicidal. And who could blame them? They spent most of their days in forced isolation, locked away from family and friends and the rest of the world. Members of the staff were constantly telling them how fortunate they were to have been chosen for the experimental program. Nurse Charlotte even insisted they were blessed.

The girls scoffed at the notion. All of them had a disease that, thus far, no drug had been able to conquer, and none of them felt the least bit fortunate to be human pincushions, subjected to a tremendous and sometimes unbearable amount of agony. The Pips were forbidden to call the wonder drug cocktail that was pumped into their veins poison, but that's what all of them believed it was. Excruciating pain followed each infusion, and by evening their bodies were covered with blisters from the tops of their heads to the bottoms of their feet. No, none of them felt blessed.

Though the youngest of the group, Olivia was the strongest and the toughest, and she had quickly stepped into the role of protector. Once she had gained her new friends' trust, she began to chip away at the boredom and, more importantly, the anger and the fear.

Pranks were Olivia's specialty. Within two weeks of her arrival, the nurses and the doctors grew hesitant to open their lockers for fear of what was going to jump out at them. Nurse Charlotte developed a twitch in her left eyelid after a rubber snake sprang at her, delighting the Pips to no end.

As the girls became more fearless, their repertoire of mischief grew. Each had a favorite trick.

Jane, the artistic one in the group, had a flare for design. She could sit for hours with a notepad and pencil drawing shapes, then connecting them into beautiful mosaics. She loved symmetry and color, so when the others suggested they TP the nurses' station, she objected. She thought that would be too crass. Instead, she decorated the space from ceiling to floor with streamers of every color of the rainbow.

Samantha, or Sam as she was called by her friends, was the adventurer. She was unafraid of risk, but she wasn't reckless. She went about each of the pranks methodically. Every situation was patiently examined and carefully planned to achieve the desired result. It took her a week to collect enough lime Jell-O to fill all the specimen cups. After warming them in the nurses' microwave for a few seconds, she slipped the little beakers of green liquid onto the lab cart and sent them downstairs for analysis. The girls laughed for days remembering the sight of the red-faced nurse on the phone apologizing and trying to explain the mishap to the lab tech.

Olivia had found it easy to bring Jane and Sam into the fun, but Collins had been more of a challenge. Because she was the most sensitive, it took her the longest to conquer her depression; but

once she did, she was game for anything. Olivia designated her to be the
decoy in their adventures. When the
girls wanted to slip by the staff unno-
ticed, Olivia would send Collins to distract them. She was blessed with a
sweet nature and a soft Southern accent that drew people to her, so when a
teardrop or two would fall down her
cheek, everyone would rush to console
her. Once the tears began to flow, they'd
huddle around her and give her their full
and undivided attention. A couple of
faint sobs, and she had them—especially the men—eating out of her hands.
Little did her sympathetic audience
know, the other three Pips were behind
them, strategically placing furry fake
spiders in unexpected spots.

In an attempt to keep the Pips calm
and in their beds, their specialist, Dr.
Andre Pardieu, gave each of them a
deck of cards and took the time one afternoon to teach them how to play poker.
They were quick learners. By the end of
the month the Pips had taken him for
more than three hundred dollars. They
used the cash to buy pizzas and cake

for Nurse Kathleen's birthday and a few other fun items to torment the staff.

After spending several weeks in the hospital, the Pips fell into a routine. Monday was poison cocktail day, and they were too sick to play any pranks. Tuesday, they were still too ill to do more than lift their heads off their pillows, but by nightfall the blisters would disappear, and they would begin to feel human again. They decided that Wednesday would be orange wig day; Thursday would always be freak-out-the-nurses day, and on Friday, as a compliment to their doctor—they all had a crush on him—they would speak his native tongue, French, which was a real trick considering the fact that only Olivia understood the language. Weekends were spent on target practice with their water guns, working jigsaw puzzles, and doing crosswords. Olivia's aunt Emma was what Dr. Pardieu called a coconspirator. She sent Olivia the water guns and wigs and other novelties. Whatever her niece requested, she got.

Dr. Pardieu also had a routine. Each morning when he walked into the unit,

he greeted the girls the same way: "Bonjour, mes petites pipsqueaks."

And they responded, "Bonjour, Docteur Pardieu."

Olivia came up with a new idea one
Thursday. After the doctor had made his
rounds, she suggested a game of hide-
and-seek to torment the nurses. She
had broken into an empty storage closet
the week before and discovered the
rectangular room had enough space to
fit all of them. It was at the end of the
newly constructed south wing, which
would be dedicated and opened for patients the next month.

The girls crept down the hall behind
Olivia and slipped into the dark closet.
They sat on the floor with their backs
against the walls, two facing two, and
stayed quiet while they strained to listen
for every sound. The scent of disinfec-
tant hung in the air around them. They
could hear the supervisor calling their
names as she clipped along the gray-
and-white tile floor, her rubber-soled
shoes squeaking with each step. When
the sound faded, Olivia reached up and
switched on the light.

All of them squinted against the sudden brightness.

"She's gone," Sam whispered, trying to stifle her laughter.

"Maybe we shouldn't stay here," Collins said. "We don't want her to keep looking for us."

"Are you kidding?" Olivia said. "Of course we want her to look for us. That's how we roll."

Jane was the most law-abiding of the four and whispered, "What if she calls the police? We could get into serious trouble." She was twisting the tube on her IV while she fretted.

Sam rolled her eyes. "She won't call the police," she said. "You worry too much."

"She could call our parents," Jane suggested then.

Olivia shrugged. "My mother has caller ID. As soon as she sees it's the hospital calling, she won't pick up. My disease is too stressful for her."

"You're joking, right?" Sam asked.

"No, I'm not. Mom has trouble coping."

"What does your father think?" Collins asked the question. "He's never come to visit you," she remarked, a tinge of sympathy in her voice as she reached over and patted Olivia's hand. The girls could always count on Collins for emotional support.

"None of her family has visited," Sam said.

"They're busy," Olivia answered with an indifferent shrug. "Mom flies back and forth between our homes in San Francisco and New York City. My parents have a strange marriage," she added, sounding very grown-up. "Mom adores him. She's . . . dramatic about it. I don't know how else to explain it. She doesn't have room for anything else in her life."

"Or *anyone* else," Collins said. Like daughters, she silently added.

"What about your father?" Sam asked again.

"Oh, he likes the adoration. At least he used to."

"No, I mean how does he cope with your illness? Is it too stressful for him, too?"

"Not really. He ignores it. Sometimes

I think he pretends I'm at a sleepover. He used to call every week to see how I was doing. The last time I talked to him he asked me if I was having a nice time."

"Seriously?" Sam asked. She couldn't comprehend anyone being so oblivious. Her own family had taken her illness pretty hard, especially her four older brothers. Though they constantly reminded her that she was tough and could whip this thing, she knew on the inside they were worried.

"Seriously," Olivia insisted. "He loses track of time. At least that's what my sister, Natalie, tells me. She's always defending Mom and Dad. Nat would come see me if she could, but she's finishing college, and by the time she got off the plane here, she'd have to turn around and go back. She's ten years older than I am," she added.

"She hasn't called here in a while, has she?"

"She's very busy, too," Olivia responded.

"I talked to your sister once," Collins

said. "You were getting x-rayed and couldn't come to the phone."

"Do you know this is the first time you've talked so openly about your family?" Jane remarked.

"Why is that?" Collins asked.

"Because it's embarrassing. I'm tired of making excuses for them," she blurted. "My family's dysfunctional. You're right, Sam. None of them has come to see me, and I don't think that's normal. Do you?"

All three girls shook their heads. "Exactly," Olivia said. "Aunt Emma is the only normal one. She doesn't like my father much, but I think it's because of the way my mother acts around him. Emma tries to hide how she feels when she talks to me, but I know. Once I heard her tell my mother she thought my father was shrewd with money but he was a nincompoop when it came to his family. She also said he was one of the most charismatic men she'd ever met."

"What does that mean?" Collins asked. "That he's smooth?"

"Polished, charming," Jane suggested. "Charismatic isn't a bad thing."

"My aunt made it sound bad. I wasn't supposed to be listening to the conversation, so I couldn't ask her what she meant."

"I don't know any charismatic men or women," Sam said. "At least, I don't think I do."

Olivia decided to change the subject. She wanted to talk about something else for a while. "If I get to grow up, I think I'd like to catch criminals. No matter how talented and clever they might be, eventually they all make mistakes," she said. "And they always get caught."

If-I-get-to-grow-up was a morbid game the girls played every now and then, though never in front of Dr. Pardieu, because they knew he would make them stop. Each time Olivia played, she changed what she wanted to become if she got to grow up. Last week she thought she wanted to become a chef. The week before that she was certain she wanted to become a physician just like Dr. Pardieu. The week before that she was determined to become a newscaster.

"You could become a detective or an

FBI agent," Collins said enthusiastically. "It would be cool to carry a gun. Maybe I'll become an agent."

"You're a klutz, Collins," Jane said. "You'd shoot yourself. And besides, you'd probably cry every time you had to talk to a crime victim."

Her friend wasn't offended. "I probably would," she admitted.

"If I get to grow up, I'm going to become—" Sam began.

"A pilot," the other three Pips said in unison.

"Yes, a pilot," Sam agreed.

"Honestly, Sam, don't you ever think about any other careers?" Jane asked, clearly exasperated. "Why are you so stuck on being a pilot?"

"Let's see," Sam began. "My grandfather was a pilot; my father is a pilot; my four brothers are pilots . . ."

"And that means you have to be a pilot?" Collins asked.

"It's in my blood," she said with a shrug. "I have to fly."

No one argued with her. Then Jane said, "If we didn't have this horrible disease, we probably would never have met. Each one of us lives on a different side of the United States. Sam lives in Alaska; Olivia lives in California; Collins lives in Louisiana, and I live in upstate New York."

"I think fate would have pulled us together, no matter what," Sam said.

"It would have been nice if it hadn't been a terminal disease that brought us together," Olivia said.

Collins drew her knees to her chest. "My bum's getting cold."

"Mine, too," Olivia said.

The girls shifted to get closer to one another for warmth.

They didn't speak for a few minutes, and then Olivia broke the silence. "Aunt Emma thinks my father is going to leave my mother. She thinks that's the real reason he purchased the apartment in Manhattan." She had been worrying about the possibility that her parents would split up, and now that she'd told her friends about her family, she decided to tell them the rest. She felt closer to the Pips than anyone. Maybe it was because of what they were all going through together: shared laughter and shared pain.

"Divorce?" Collins asked in a bare whisper, as though the word would sting if she said it any louder.

Olivia nodded. "It will be a real nightmare if it happens."

"Why would your aunt give you such a worry?" Sam wanted to know. "You have enough to deal with. You don't need any more problems."

"Before I came here I made my aunt promise me she wouldn't keep anything from me, but I know she does sometimes. I want to know what's going on back home . . . the good and the bad."

"Divorce isn't such a big deal," Jane commented with a shrug. "You'll get through it."

"That's kind of callous," Sam told her.

"I'm being honest. My parents fought all the time. Everything got better once the divorce was final."

"What did they fight about?" Collins wanted to know.

"My big brother, Logan, mostly," she

said. "Logan was getting into all sorts of trouble with drugs and alcohol. It's a miracle he graduated from high school. Mom protected him, made excuses for him. Dad cut him off, refused to give him any more money, but Mom would sneak some to him. Dad got sick of fighting all the time and left. That gave Logan the freedom to do what he wanted, and my mom would just give in. He even talked her into trying to up the value on my life insurance policy. Ghoulish, right?"

"Depends," Olivia said. "Who gets the money if you die?"

"Logan."

"Then, yes, it's ghoulish."

"The insurance company wouldn't do it. I'm a bad risk," Jane said.

"You should stay alive just to spite your brother," Sam said.

"I plan to," she replied, smiling. "So, you see, Olivia, my family is as wacked as yours."

"I don't think so," Olivia argued. "I could tell you stories that would turn your hair gray."

"We don't have any hair, remember? The wonder drugs made it all fall out," Sam said.

"We were already bald from the chemo when we got here," Collins reminded them. She gently brushed her fingertips across her bare forehead as though sweeping a stray lock into place. Exaggerating the lilt of her Southern accent, she said, "So you're going to have to take my word when I tell you I had the most fabulous blond hair."

"You, Olivia, and Sam could all be movie stars," Jane said.

"So could you," Olivia countered.

"I'm so thin and pale. I have these dark circles under my eyes and—"

Olivia wouldn't let her continue. "The medicine has just been rougher on you than the rest of us. When it's over, you'll see your beautiful self again."

Jane wasn't convinced. "But Collins has blond hair and blue eyes—"

"Fabulous blond hair," Collins interrupted, smiling.

Jane rolled her eyes, then continued on. "Olivia, your eyes are such an intense, brilliant color of blue, so I'm guessing your hair is blond, too."

"Nope," she said. "Dark auburn," she corrected. "You've got pretty hazel eyes, I'll bet your hair is light brown, Jane."

"You're right."

"Sam, you're the easy one," Collins said. "Your eyes are green, so I think you're a natural redhead."

"I used to have dark brown hair, almost black," she said.

"When this is over . . . if we make it . . ." Jane began.

"We'll make it." Olivia's voice was emphatic.

"I'm not ready to die yet," Sam said.

"Neither am I," Collins whispered. "I have too much living to do, and I haven't even gotten started."

"But will you three still be my best friends?" Tears sprang into Jane's sunken eyes. There was no question that she was the most frail member of the group. Her pale skin looked almost translucent. Her voice was weak as she added, "No matter where we end up, no matter what we're doing . . . okay?"

"Absolutely," the others responded.

They made fists and gently tapped one another's knuckles to seal the promise.

"Friends forever," Sam whispered.

Olivia nodded. "Till death do us part."

ONE

TWELVE YEARS LATER

Olivia MacKenzie was certain she would have been offered the job if she hadn't punched the boss during the interview. But knocking the man senseless turned out to be a real deal breaker.

The CEO of one of the largest investment firms in the country, Eric Jorguson, was now being questioned by an FBI agent. He wasn't cooperating. The agent had taken Jorguson to the opposite side of the terrace and was trying to get him to calm down and answer his questions. Jorguson was busy screaming at Olivia, threatening to have her killed and also to sue her because she'd broken his jaw. She hadn't done any such thing, of course. The man was ex- aggerating. She'd smashed his nose in, not his jaw. A waiter wearing the name tag TERRY pinned to his black vest stood next to her trying to soothe what he re- ferred to as her extreme case of nerves. She wanted to punch him, too.

"You're in shock," he told her. "That's why you look so calm. The guy tears your dress and gropes you, and it's only natural for you to go into shock. Don't you think? That's why you're not crying and carrying on."

Olivia looked at him. "I'm fine, really." Now *please* leave me alone, she silently added.

"Hey, look," Terry said. "They're ar- resting Jorguson's bodyguard. What's the guy doing with a bodyguard, I won- der." A few seconds later he answered his own question. "He must need one. Especially if he attacks other women the way he attacked you. You think you'd like to go out with me sometime?"

She smiled to ease the rejection. "I don't think so."

"You're still in shock, aren't you?"

Olivia was angry, not hysterical. She stood by the table with her arms folded across her waist as she patiently waited for the FBI agent to get to her. She had been told it wouldn't take long.

Terry tried twice more to engage her in conversation. She was polite but firm each time he attempted to get personal.

She watched the agents while she tried to figure out how she had gotten into this bizarre situation. Job hunting wasn't supposed to be dangerous. She had already interviewed with three other Fortune 500 companies without incident. Before she had gone to those interviews, however, she had done quite a bit of research. She didn't have that luxury with Jorguson Investments. Because the position had just become available, she'd had less than a day to study the company's prospectus. She should have looked more closely before she agreed to the preliminary interview. Should have, could have, she lamented.

She hated job hunting and all the inane interviews, especially since she really liked her current job and the people she worked with. But there was talk of cutbacks. Serious talk, and according to some of the other employees, Olivia didn't have seniority. She would be one of the first laid off. It was important to her that she stay in her current job until she accomplished what she had set out to do, but it didn't look like that was going to happen. The only constant in Olivia's life right now was the mortgage. It had to be paid, no matter what, which was why she had to have job options.

She had gone to the office an hour earlier than usual this morning, finished two case files by noon, and headed over to Seraphina, a lovely restaurant with a stunning view. The five-star restaurant overlooked a manicured terrace, with tables strategically placed under a canopy of tree branches. Beyond was the river. Lunch was going to be a treat. She'd never dined at Seraphina because of the expense, but she'd heard that the food was wonderful. Grossly overpriced, but wonderful. No peanut butter and jelly sandwich today.

The hostess showed her to a table on

the south side of the terrace. It was such a beautiful day with just a slight nip in the air, perfect for lunch outside.

The preliminary interview with Xavier Cannon, the company's lead attorney, had gone well, she thought, but he hadn't answered some of her more pressing questions and had suggested instead that she ask Jorguson. Cannon also mentioned that, if Jorguson liked her, he would offer her the job during lunch.

Jorguson was waiting for her. She spotted him across the busy terrace. He held an open folder in his hand and was reading a paper inside it. As she drew closer she could see that it was her résumé.

For about twenty seconds she thought he was quite a charmer and a rather distinguished-looking man. He was tall and thin and had a bright, white smile.

He stood and shook her hand. "Bring the lady a drink," he snapped impatiently to a passing waiter.

"Iced tea, please," she said.

The waiter had already moved her chair for her, and she sat before Jorguson could come around the table to assist her.

Jorguson's cell phone rang, and without offering an apology or an excuse for the interruption, he turned his back to her and answered. His voice was low and angry. Whoever he was talking to was getting a dressing-down. His vocabulary was crude.

So much for charming, she thought. She tried to focus on her surroundings while she waited. The linen tablecloth draped all the way to the ground, and in the center of the round table was a crystal bowl of fresh-cut flowers in every color. She looked around her and smiled. It was a really pretty day.

Jorguson finished his call. He slipped the phone into his suit jacket and gave her his full attention, but the way he was staring at her quickly made her uncomfortable. She was about to ask him if something was wrong when he said, "You're stunning. Absolutely stunning."

"Excuse me?"

"You're very beautiful," he said then. "Xavier mentioned how pretty you were, but I still didn't expect . . . that is to say, I wasn't prepared . . ."

Olivia was horrified by his close scrutiny. His leering inspection made her skin crawl. Jorguson wasn't just unprofessional; he was also creepy. She opened her linen napkin and placed it in her lap. She tried to turn his attention so he would stop gawking at her.

Typically she would have waited for him to lead the questioning, but the awkward silence and his inappropriate behavior compelled her to speak first.

"This morning I had a few minutes, and I pulled up your prospectus. Your company is quite impressive," she said. "But there was a note that last year you were investigated by the FBI—"

He rudely cut her off with a wave of his hand. "Yes, but of course nothing came of it. It was simple harassment." He continued, "They didn't like some of my clients and wanted to make trouble, which was ridiculous. I should have sued, but I didn't have the time."

Sue the FBI? Was he serious or just trying to impress her with his power. His arrogance was overwhelming.

"You're a brand-new attorney, aren't you?" he asked.

"Yes, that's correct."

"Only two people ranked higher than you on the bar. I cannot tell you how remarkable that is. Still, you don't have much experience with contracts."

"No, I don't," she agreed. "How did you find out about my scores? That's confidential—"

He waved his hand in the air again, dismissing her question. The gesture irritated her. She admitted then that pretty much everything about the man irritated her.

"There were quite a few others who applied for the position, and most of them have more experience than you, but when I discovered you were Robert MacKenzie's daughter, I moved you to the top of the list."

"You know my father?" She couldn't hide her surprise.

"Everyone who's anyone knows who your father is," he replied. "I know people who have invested in your father's Trinity Fund and have made a handsome profit. Very impressive," he stated with a nod. "I'm considering adding the fund to my own portfolio. No one plays the market like your father does. He seems to have a knack for choosing the right investments. If you're half as clever as he is, you'll go far, young lady."

Olivia wasn't given time to respond. He'd already moved on. "You'll be wonderful working with our clients. With that smile of yours, you could get them to sign anything. Oh yes, they'll be as dazzled by you as I am," he gushed. "And I have several powerful clients. Xavier will guide you. Now then, what questions do you have for me? I have a potential client meeting me here at one, so this will have to be a quick lunch."

"Did the SEC investigate when—"

He interrupted. "No, the SEC will never investigate me," he boasted. "I'm protected there."

"You're protected? How?"

"I have a friend, and he has assured me . . ."

Her eyes widened. "You have a friend at the Securities and Exchange Commission?"

Color crept up his neck. His eyes

darted to the left, then to the right. Was he checking to make sure no one was listening to the conversation?

He leaned into the table and lowered his voice. "I don't have any worries there. As I just said, I won't be investigated, and since you're going to be working closely with me, I don't want you to be concerned."

Working closely with him? That thought made her cringe.

"About this friend . . ." she began.

"No more questions about the SEC," he snapped. He wasn't looking into her eyes now. He was staring at her chest. The longer he stared, the more indignant she became. She considered snapping her fingers several times in front of his eyes to get his attention but, wanting to remain composed and professional, decided to ask a question about the investments he'd made.

Jorguson was slick; she'd give him that much. He danced around each question but never really gave her any satisfactory answers.

The topic eventually returned to the SEC. "Who is your contact?" she asked, wondering if he would tell her. He was so smug and arrogant, she thought there was a good chance he might. She also wanted him to assure her that everything he did was legal, and she thought it was odd that he hadn't offered any such affirmation.

"Why do you want to know? That's confidential information."

He was staring at her chest again. She folded her napkin, smiled at Terry the waiter when he placed her iced tea in front of her, and handed him her menu.

"I won't be staying for lunch."

The waiter hesitated, then took her menu, glanced at Jorguson, and walked away.

Olivia was disheartened. The salary at Jorguson Investments was good, really good, but it had taken less than five minutes to know she couldn't work for this man.

What a waste of time, she thought. And money. She could have worn one of her old suits, but she'd wanted to stand out, so she bought a new dress. It was expensive, too. She loved the fit and the color, a deep emerald-green silk. It had a high V-neck, so there was no need to wear a necklace. Diamond stud earrings, which were so tiny you could barely see the sparkle, and a watch were her only jewelry. She wore her hair down around her shoulders and had taken the time to use a curling iron.

Olivia looked at Jorguson. The degenerate was still staring at her chest. And for this she had curled her hair?

"This isn't going to work," she said.

She tried to stand. Jorguson suddenly bolted upright, grabbed the top of her dress, and ripped it apart. The silk material tore, exposing her collarbone and part of her black bra.

Appalled, she slapped Jorguson's hands away. "What do you think—"

"Are you wearing a wire? You are, aren't you? That's why you asked me who my contact was. That investigation stalled, sweetheart. It's not going anywhere. The FBI's been after me for two years now, and they've got nothing. I know for a fact they're following me. They won't ever get anything on me. They like to go after successful entrepreneurs. I'm an honest businessman," he shouted into her chest. "Now where's the damn wire? I know it's in there somewhere."

Olivia was so shocked by his behavior, she bounced between disbelief and outrage. She shoved his hands away, pulled her top together, and said, "If you try to touch me again, you'll regret it."

He tried again, and she retaliated. She heard a crunching sound when she punched him and felt a good deal of satisfaction. It was short-lived. A giant of a man with a thick neck and bald head appeared out of nowhere. He was wearing a tailored black suit, but he looked like a thug. He was at the other end of the terrace and heading toward her. As Jorguson was screaming and holding his nose with one hand, he was waving to the big man and pointing at Olivia with the other.

"Martin, see what she did to me?" he howled. "Get her, get her."

Get her? Was he twelve? Olivia could feel her face turning red. She kept her attention centered on the bodyguard as she jumped to her feet. His suit jacket opened, and she saw a gun. He hadn't reached for it, though, and was glancing around to see how many people were watching.

She was in trouble, all right. She thought about taking off one of her stiletto heels and using that as a weapon, but she decided she could do more damage with it on. She spied Terry watching from the doorway with a cell phone to his ear. She hoped he was calling the police.

"Do you have a permit to carry that gun?" she demanded of the bodyguard, trying to make her voice sound as mean as possible. Now, why, in God's name, had she asked that? What did she care if he had a permit or not? She was slowly slipping her hand inside her purse to get to her pepper spray. She couldn't find it and realized then that, when she'd changed purses, she'd left the spray at home on her bedside table. A lot of good it would do her there.

The thug named Martin, zigzagging around the tables, was getting closer. The man was built like a sumo wrestler. Olivia figured she was on her own. The

other diners were already beginning to
scatter. She stepped back from the table, dropped her purse into the chair,
and waited for the man to reach her. If
he touched her, she'd kick him where it
mattered most, and if he blocked her,
she'd go for his knee or his midsection.

Jorguson, holding his bloody nose,
was backing away but still pointing at
her and shouting. "How dare you touch
me. You're going to be sorry. I know
people who will hurt you. You don't hit
me and get away with it. Don't you know
who I am and what I can do? One phone
call is all it will take," he screamed.
"You're a dead woman, Olivia MacKenzie. Do you hear me? A dead woman."

Of course she'd heard him. She
thought everyone within a ten-block
area had heard him. She refused to give
him any satisfaction by reacting, though,
and that was probably why he was becoming more outrageous with his
threats.

Her attention remained centered on
the bodyguard. She thought he would
do his best to intimidate her in front of
his employer, maybe even try to get her

to apologize to Jorguson—hell would freeze before she'd do that—but he surely wouldn't touch her. Not in front of all these people.

Or maybe he wouldn't care who was watching. Jorguson had shouted his intent to have her killed. Would this bodyguard try to top that crazy threat?

There was a wall of windows in the restaurant facing the river, and diners were crammed together, their faces plastered to the glass. Some had their cell phones glued to their ears; others were using the cell phone cameras to record the incident . . . for YouTube, no doubt. Certainly, most of them had witnessed Jorguson ripping her dress and then screaming after she'd punched him. The man had howled like an outraged hyena. Surely they'd heard his ridiculous threats, too.

The bodyguard took Jorguson's orders to "get her" to heart. He lunged. He grabbed her upper arm and twisted as he jerked her toward him. Pain shot up into her neck and down to her fingers. His grip was strong enough to break her bone.

He glanced over his shoulder at the crowd before turning back to her. "You're coming with me," he ordered.

A woman rushed out of the restaurant shouting, "You leave her alone." At the same time, two men in business suits ran past the woman to help Olivia.

"Let go of me," she demanded as she slammed the heel of her shoe into the top of his foot.

He grunted and let go. Olivia got in a solid kick, and he doubled over. But not for long. He quickly recovered and, roaring several grossly unflattering names at her, straightened and reached for his gun. His face was now bloodred.

Good Lord, was he going to shoot her? The look in his eyes suggested that he might. Apparently, Martin had forgotten his audience, or he no longer cared he was being watched. His impulse control had vanished. He had the most hateful look on his face as he pulled the gun from the waistband of his pants. The two businessmen coming to her aid stopped when they spotted the weapon.

"I said you're coming with me," he snarled as he lunged.

"No, I'm not." She threw a twelve-dollar glass of iced tea at him. He ducked.

"Bitch." He spit the word and tried to grab her again.

"I'm not going anywhere with you. Now get away from me."

The gun seemed to be growing in his hand. She backed away from him, and that infuriated him even more. He came at her once more, and before she could protect herself, he backhanded her. He struck the side of her face, his knuckles clipping her jaw. It was a hard hit and hurt like hell. The blow threw her backward, but even as she was falling, she didn't take her eyes off the gun.

She landed on her backside, winced from the impact on her tailbone, and quickly staggered to her feet.

She understood what the expression "seeing stars" meant. Dazed, she tried to back away.

The thug raised his gun again, and suddenly he was gone. Olivia saw a blur fly past her, tackling the bodyguard to the ground. The gun went one way, and the thug went the other, landing hard. Within seconds her rescuer had the man facedown on the grass and was putting handcuffs on him while reading him his rights. When he was finished, he motioned to another man wearing a badge and gun who was rushing across the terrace.

With one of his knees pressed against the bodyguard's spine, the rescuer turned toward her. She suddenly felt lightheaded. She could have sworn she saw an ethereal glow radiating all around him and the sound of a singing choir echoing overhead. She closed her eyes and shook her head. The blow to her jaw must be making her hallucinate. When she opened her eyes again, the vision and the choir were gone, but the man was still there, looking up at her with beautiful hazel eyes.

"Who are you?" he asked as he hauled the bodyguard to his feet.

"Olivia MacKenzie," she answered. She sounded bewildered, but she couldn't help that. The last few minutes had been hair-raising, and she was having trouble forming a clear thought.

"Who are *you*?" she asked.

"Agent Grayson Kincaid. FBI. Are you all right?"

"I've been better."

"Maybe you should sit down."

The bodyguard finally found his voice. "I was protecting my boss."

"With a Glock?" Kincaid asked. "And against an unarmed woman?"

"She kicked me."

A hint of a smile turned his expression. "Yeah, I saw."

"I'm bringing charges."

"You attacked her," Kincaid snapped. "If I were you, I'd be real quiet right now."

The bodyguard ignored the suggestion. "Mr. Jorguson has known for a long time that the FBI has been tailing him and listening in on his private conversations. What you're doing is illegal, but you people don't play by the rules, do you?"

"Stop talking," Kincaid said.

Another agent grabbed hold of the bodyguard's arm and led him away. He didn't go peacefully. He was shouting for a lawyer.

"Hey, Ronan," Kincaid shouted.

The agent dragging the bodyguard away turned back. "Yeah?"

"Did you see it?"

Ronan smiled. "Oh yeah, I saw it all. After I put this clown in the back of the car, I'll go get Jorguson."

Olivia glanced around the terrace. In all the commotion she hadn't seen him slip away.

Kincaid nodded, then turned back to her.

"The gun is under the table," she offered.

"I'll get it," Kincaid said.

He walked over to her, and she flinched when he reached out to touch her. Frowning, he said, "I'm not going to hurt you. I just want to see how bad it is."

"It's fine," she insisted. "I'm fine."

He ignored her protest. He gently pushed her hair away from the side of her face. "Your cheek's okay, but he really clipped your jaw. It's already starting to swell. You need to put ice on it. Maybe I should take you to the emergency room, have a physician look at your arm, too. I saw the way he twisted it."

"I'll be all right. I'll ice it," she promised when he looked like he wanted to argue.

He took a step back and said, "I'm sorry I couldn't get to him faster."

"You got here before he shot me. He really was going to shoot me, wasn't he?" She was still astounded by the possibility and getting madder by the second.

"He might have tried," he agreed.

She frowned. "You're awfully nonchalant about it."

"I would have taken him down before he shot you."

Her cell phone rang. She checked the number, then sent the call to voice mail. Out of the corner of her eye, she saw a man rounding the corner of the building and glaring at her. He stormed toward her, just as Kincaid bent to retrieve the bodyguard's gun.

"What the hell's the matter with you?" the man shouted.

Since he was wearing a gun and badge, she knew he was also FBI. "Excuse me?"

"You ruined a perfectly good sting.

Were you wearing a wire? Did you get anything we could use? No, I didn't think so. You weren't supposed to be here until one. We weren't ready."

The agent screaming at her was an older man, late fifties, she guessed. His face was bright red, and his anger could light fires.

He moved closer until he was all but touching her, but she refused to be intimidated. "Stop yelling at me."

"She's not with the FBI," Kincaid said.

"How . . ." The confused agent took a step back. He looked at Olivia, then at Kincaid.

"I'd know if she was. Your undercover woman hasn't shown up yet."

"Two months' planning," the agent muttered. He pointed at Olivia. "Are you wearing a wire? Jorguson seems to think you are. Are you with a newspaper or—"

"Poole, leave her the hell alone," Kincaid said.

Poole was staring at her chest. Uh-oh. Olivia knew where this was going.

"If you think you're going to look for a wire, be advised. I'll punch you, too," she warned.

Distraught to have his investigation fall apart, Agent Poole stepped closer and said, "Listen, you. Don't threaten me. I could make your life a nightmare." He put his hand in front of her face and unfolded three fingers as he said, "I'm F . . . B . . . I."

She smiled. It wasn't the reaction he expected. "You want to talk nightmares?" she said. She put her hand up to his face and unfolded her three fingers. "I'm I . . . R . . . S."

TWO

Olivia was still waiting with Terry the waiter by her side. He tried several more pickup lines, and when none of them worked, he finally shrugged and went back into the restaurant.

Agent Kincaid had told Olivia to stay put until he and the other agents dealt with Jorguson and his bodyguard. He hoped by the time they returned to her Agent Poole would have calmed down. Unfortunately, that didn't happen. Poole's expression bordered on homicidal. His eyes bulged, his jaw dropped, and his face contorted in a scowl. Had

Kincaid not been so angry with him for deliberately ignoring orders, he might have laughed.

It was apparent that Poole still didn't want to believe that Olivia was just an innocent bystander. He planted his hands on the table and leaned forward. "Someone tipped you off that we were running this operation, right? You're with a newspaper or one of those trashy television shows, aren't you? Are you doing an exposé on Jorguson or something? If you are, I'll shut you down," he threatened.

"IRS," she quietly repeated.

"I want proof."

She reached into her purse and pulled out an oblong laminated card. "Here you go."

Kincaid thought she sounded almost cheerful, which didn't make any sense considering what she had just been through. She should have been on her last nerve, but Olivia MacKenzie's calm demeanor was impressive . . . not to mention her stunning beauty. Her eyes were a clear violet blue. Her complexion was flawless, and her lips were lush and full. From what he could see, her body was just about perfect, too. Full breasts, narrow waist, and long, shapely legs. It was one hell of a challenge not to stare at her. He hadn't experienced a reaction like this since he was a teenager.

"Okay, then," Olivia said. She snatched her ID from Agent Poole and slipped it into her purse. Then she tried to leave. "Good luck with Jorguson and Martin." She turned toward the parking lot, but Kincaid stopped her by grabbing hold of her hand. "Not yet."

"Not yet?" she repeated, looking up at him. "I really should return to work, and I'm going to have to go home and change clothes first."

Ignoring her protest, he gave Poole his full attention. "Shut this down and go back to the office," he said, his voice decisive and abrupt. "You and I need to have a word as soon as I'm finished here."

"How long will that take?" Poole demanded.

"As long as it takes."

"Yes, sir." Poole gave Olivia one last glare and took off.

"He looks like I just ruined his life," Olivia remarked.

"Isn't that what you do at the IRS?"

She could hear a smile in his voice. "Pretty much," she agreed. She tugged her hand away from his and asked, "Where exactly are we going?"

"Inside."

She stopped. "Oh, I don't think . . ."

He took her hand again and pulled her along toward the restaurant doors. She gave up on protesting. She could have argued, but she didn't think anything she said would matter. Agent Kincaid looked like the kind of man who was used to getting his way. The air of authority about him was a bit daunting, and she had the feeling he wasn't going to let her go anywhere until he was finished with her.

He was being awfully familiar with her, holding her hand. Was he making sure she wouldn't bolt? The onlookers who were beginning to return to their tables parted to let them pass.

Five minutes later she was sitting alone at a table in a private dining room, waiting for Agent Kincaid to come back.

A waiter had brought her a glass of ice water. She reached into her purse and retrieved her inhaler. All the commotion on the terrace had made her a little short-winded. She had been treated with some powerful drugs when she was a child, and one of the side effects was a touch of asthma. She never went anywhere without her inhaler.

She decided to call her boss, Royal Thurman, to let him know she was going to be late. He wouldn't really care, she knew, but it was the courteous thing to do. His phone went to voice mail, and she had just finished leaving a message when another call came in. She didn't recognize the number, but as soon as she heard the loathsome voice, she thought she knew who it was. Carl Simmons, her father's attorney, was on the line threatening her again.

"You were told to stop interfering," he said in a muffled whisper. "This is your last warning."

"Who is this?" she demanded, knowing full well Carl wouldn't tell her. Still, there was always the hope his temper would get the better of him, and he'd let it slip.

"You're forcing us to silence you. Do you want to get hurt?"

"You can threaten me all you want. I'm not going to stop."

Olivia didn't wait for a response. She ended the call and placed her phone on the table just as Agent Kincaid walked into the room. He had a small plastic bag with him.

Her hands were shaking. The phone call had gotten to her, but she didn't want the agent to notice, so she put her hands in her lap. He pulled out a chair, sat down facing her, and handed her the bag of ice. Then he asked her to tell him what led up to Jorguson's attack.

She held the bag against the left side of her jaw while she talked. Twice during her explanation she put the bag down, and each time, he picked it up and put it back in her hand.

"Did you happen to hear any of Jorguson's threats, Agent Kincaid?" she asked.

"Call me Grayson," he said. "And, no, I didn't hear the threats. Tell me."

She repeated what Jorguson had shouted and added, "He was furious and out of control. 'One phone call and you're a dead woman.' He actually shouted that. He didn't seem to care who was listening. You and the other agents were planning to catch him to-day, weren't you? I'm guessing I was in the wrong place at the wrong time, and somehow that really botched up your plan."

"It wasn't the right plan to begin with," Grayson admitted.

She could hear the irritation in his voice and surmised that the fault for the fiasco lay at the feet of Agent Poole, though Grayson wasn't going to say it.

"What happens to Jorguson now?" she asked.

"We're taking him in. We're not through talking to him."

"I'm sure his lawyers are already on their way."

"It doesn't matter how many lawyers he has circling him. Jorguson isn't going anywhere until I'm finished with him. Can you recall what he said to you?"

She repeated everything she remembered of the conversation and added, "You might want to ask him who his friend at the SEC is. I doubt he'll tell you, but it's worth a shot. I'm not even sure he was telling the truth. He's a braggart and very full of himself."

"Jorguson knew you worked for the IRS?"

"Yes. Maybe he thought I was out to get him."

"Are you?"

"No."

"Would you tell me if you were?"

She didn't answer the question, but said, "Do you think I would have interviewed for a position in his company if I were investigating him?"

He laughed. "Good point."

"Any other questions, Grayson?"

"No, I think that's it," he said. "I have your phone number. If I think of anything else, I'll call you." He handed her his card and added, "And if you remember anything pertinent, you call me."

"Yes, I will," she agreed. She laid the bag of ice on the table and stood to leave. With a sigh she said, "Too bad

Jorguson couldn't have waited until after lunch to attack me."

"That is a shame," he said with a smile. He handed the ice back to her. "Let's eat."

She laughed. "I was just kidding. I should go. I've got so much to—"

"Aren't you hungry? I'm sure you must be, and I am, so let's eat. You took a hit for the FBI. The least we can do is offer you lunch. If you like seafood, the chowder's great."

"Do you eat here often?"

"Every once in a while."

Olivia was torn. She loved seafood chowder. Really loved it. If the iced tea was twelve dollars a glass, she could only imagine what the chowder cost. She would insist on paying for her own meal, so the question was, did she want to spend a small fortune on lunch? No, she should go home, change her clothes, and eat a peanut butter sandwich. It would be dry because she was out of strawberry jam. Come to think of it, she was out of bread, too. And she really wanted chowder, now that Grayson had mentioned it.

Nope, she was going to be practical. Money didn't grow on trees, according to her mother, even though as a child, Olivia never once thought that it did.

It didn't take much coaxing to get her to stay, especially after Grayson argued that it would be a professional courtesy.

Grayson removed his suit jacket, and she couldn't help but notice how broad his shoulders were and how muscular he was. He was certainly in shape, and she wondered how often he worked out to stay so fit. Dark brown hair and deeply tanned skin, he looked as though he'd just stepped out of an ad in a sports magazine. She also noticed how impeccably dressed he was. His suit was definitely designer label. The cut and fit were perfect. Probably Armani or Prada, she guessed. His shirt was crisp, and his tie had a subdued design in a dark hue. For such a big man, he certainly wore his clothes well.

By comparison she was a mess. After she gave the waiter her order, she went to the ladies' room to freshen up and got a good look at herself in the mirror. She had grass in her hair and a gaping tear in the top of her dress. If that weren't enough, the left side of her jaw was already turning purple. She looked as though she'd been in a barroom brawl.

There wasn't much she could do to improve her appearance. She brushed her hair, put on some lip gloss, and tried to stop feeling embarrassed. Why did she care what Grayson thought about her appearance? After today, she probably would never see him again. She already knew he was out of her league. She had very little experience with men, but she had a feeling that Agent Grayson Kincaid was the James Bond of the FBI: a gorgeous man who loved women. Olivia knew she had no business judging him without knowing anything about him. She'd bet a month's salary she was right, though.

She returned to the table, and while they waited for their orders, they talked about living in D.C., and he asked her several questions about her work. He seemed genuinely interested. By the end of lunch she was over her bout of nerves and was glad she had stayed. Once she tasted the chowder, she stopped obsessing about the cost. It was worth the price. She sat back, crossed one leg over the other, and asked, "Did you grow up around here?" She was curious to know if he would share any personal information.

"No, the family lived in Boston until I was in my teens. Then, because of my father's business, we moved to Washington, D.C."

"You travel a lot, don't you?"

"I used to, before I joined the FBI."

"Ever been to Europe?"

He smiled. "Yes. What about you? Have you traveled much?"

She shook her head. "I've lived in San Francisco and D.C. Except for a few business trips, that's it. No, wait," she added. "I went to Colorado."

"To ski?"

"No. One of my best friends went through the Air Force Academy. I attended her graduation. Samantha's a pilot. She flies those sleek little jets now."

A waiter cleared the table while another placed fresh glasses of iced tea and dessert menus in front of them. His eyes were on Olivia, and he nearly knocked her glass over. She grabbed it before it spilled.

Grayson understood. It was difficult not to stare at her. He waited until they were alone again and then asked, "What about you? Where did you grow up?"

"San Francisco until I was eleven. Then I moved to D.C. I've been here ever since."

When he frowned, she realized the little slip she'd made. She hadn't included her family when she told him she'd moved. Maybe he hadn't noticed and was frowning about something altogether different. She hoped so. She didn't want to talk about those first years in D.C. It was too personal and too painful to relive, and she certainly didn't want to talk about her odd family.

Grayson's phone beeped, indicating he had a message. Olivia smiled. The distraction was just what she needed. "Why don't you check it? I don't mind."

He shook his head. "It can wait. You said you moved to D.C. Just you?"

She pretended not to understand. "D.C.'s my home now. The crime's a problem and you have to be so careful, but I love the energy. Don't you?"

"You didn't mention family. You moved alone?"

So much for distracting him. Grayson was an FBI agent, she reminded herself. Guess he was trained not to be distracted.

"Yes, I moved here without family."

"And you were just eleven years old."

"Yes."

She suddenly felt as though she was being interrogated, and she didn't like it one bit.

"Boarding school?" he asked.

Sure. Why not? "Something like that."

Grayson knew he was making her uncomfortable, but he couldn't figure out why. What was she hiding? Olivia checked the time and reached for her purse. He didn't want her to leave just yet. He took a drink and casually asked, "Married?"

The question surprised her. "No. You?"

"No. Ever gotten close?"

She smiled and relaxed. "No. You?"

"No."

She laughed. "You're FBI. You could find out anything you wanted to know about me."

"Yes. It wouldn't be as much fun, though."

Grayson had a beautiful smile. She thought he might be flirting with her now, but she couldn't be sure. She wasn't good at this. It was peculiar. Less than two minutes ago she couldn't wait to get out of here, and now she wanted to stay.

"You're with the IRS," he said. "You could find out all about *me.*"

"You know I can't do that. I can only work on the cases I'm assigned," she said, and before he could pose another question, she asked, "How did you end up in the FBI?"

"I finished law school and didn't know what I wanted to do. None of the offers appealed to me. My cousin, Sam Kincaid, worked for the FBI. His specialty is languages," he added. "He's also an attorney, and he thought I'd be a good fit. Turns out he was right."

"A law degree would certainly give you a leg up in the FBI."

"Yes," he agreed. "Okay, now it's my turn. How did a nice girl like you end up working for the IRS?"

"During my third year of law school, I worked as a law clerk for Judge Bowen because I wanted to get as much experience as I could in family law. After I passed the bar, my goals changed, and I decided to learn about investigative work and tax law. I'm now an attorney with the IRS."

"An attorney, huh?" He didn't know why he was surprised, but he was. He had pictured her sitting in a cubicle somewhere checking tax returns.

"Isn't everyone in Washington an attorney? I think it's a prerequisite to living here."

He laughed. "That's about right."

The waiter presented the check inside a black leather folder. When she argued that she should pay the bill, Grayson slipped his American Express card inside.

"Next time you're attacked during an interview, you can pay for lunch."

The likelihood of such a thing happening was ridiculous, but she decided to be gracious and thanked him.

"Why were you interviewing with Jorguson's company?" he asked.

"Cutbacks, and since I'm one of the newer employees, I have to assume I'll be one of the first to go. I was exploring other options," she explained. "I hope I can stay with the IRS a little longer, though. I have a goal to accomplish there. I'm learning so much about how to investigate financial crimes. I hound the investigators with all my questions. They've been very patient with me."

"Would you stay with the IRS permanently if you could?"

"Yes, I would. When I first started, I wanted to learn and then move on. My primary interest is children's advocacy, but I now know I can't do that full-time because I'd burn out too quickly. Working for the IRS is a nice balance. I had assumed the work would be boring, but as it turns out, it isn't."

"So what's your goal at the IRS?"

"It's not important," she dismissed with a shrug.

Grayson tilted his head and studied

her, wondering what he was missing. Olivia was being evasive, and he felt that she was leaving out an important detail. She reminded him of his nephew, Henry. Talking to the eight-year-old took endurance, and getting the full story was nearly impossible.

He leaned forward. Olivia instinctively folded her hands in her lap and waited. She hoped he hadn't noticed how tense she was. She knew he wasn't through questioning her, and she also knew she was confusing him. Too late, she realized she shouldn't have mentioned anything personal, especially her goal.

"Let me recap," he began, sounding very much like a professor now.

"You want to recap?"

He ignored the laughter in her voice. "Yes, I do. You said you enjoy working at the IRS. Is that correct?"

She slowly nodded. "Yes."

"Assuming the cutbacks don't come, you'd stay with the IRS."

"That's right."

"Even after you accomplish your goal?"

"Yes."

"What about children's advocacy?"

"I'm doing some work on weekends and evenings when necessary for Judge Bowen and Judge Thorpe. It can get intense."

"Is this goal of yours legal?"

She laughed. "Yes."

Grayson suddenly realized how much he was enjoying this bizarre conversation. He liked being with her. When she smiled, a dimple appeared in her right cheek, and her eyes fairly sparkled. Damn, she was pretty. Everything about her appealed to him. Whatever perfume she was wearing was a real turn-on. It was so feminine and sexy. So were her legs.

"Aren't you going to tell me what your goal is?" he asked.

She gave him the sweetest smile she could muster. "No, not really."

THREE

To his credit, Grayson didn't pressure her to explain. She wondered how he would have reacted if she'd oh-so-casually said, "My goal? I want to put my father in prison . . . or die trying."

Okay, maybe the "or die trying" was a little over the top, but she was more certain than ever that she had to do something to stop him.

Everyone has a breaking point, and Olivia would never forget the night several months ago when she'd reached hers. She had just passed the bar and wanted to celebrate with her aunt Emma.

The day hadn't started out great. In fact, it was hellish. It was a Saturday, she remembered, and there were a hundred things she'd wanted to get done before nightfall. Unfortunately the best-laid plans . . .

She had overslept a full hour because she forgot to set her alarm on her iPhone; her right front tire had blown out while she was driving sixty miles per hour on the highway; she had tripped over a small pothole she hadn't noticed when she was crossing the street, skinning both knees; and the strap on her favorite purse had snapped. The most upsetting offense of all: the leather on her brand-new shoes got scuffed. Needless to say, by five o'clock she wasn't in the best of moods.

Emma would fix that. Just being around her aunt made everything better. Olivia changed her clothes and headed over to Emma's gorgeous colonial house to have dinner with her. Her aunt was such a sweet, loving woman; she had a knack for making everyone she was with feel good. Olivia would leave her frustrations and worries at the door, and she knew that by the time she sat down to a delicious dinner prepared by Emma's longtime cook, Mary, she'd be laughing and having a fine time, listening as Emma regaled her with the most wonderful stories about her travels around the world. Whenever she spoke of her late husband, Daniel, her voice would soften and sometimes her eyes would get misty with her memories. After all these years, Emma's love hadn't waned, and some of the stories she told were so romantic.

Olivia missed her uncle very much. He was a kind and generous man, and though he was an extremely successful businessman with tremendous demands on his time, he never left any doubt that Emma came first. It was obvious to everyone who knew them that they were crazy about each other. While Olivia knew better than to wish for marriage and happily ever after, she loved listening to her aunt talk about him and their life together.

Olivia arrived at Emma's house at dusk. She drove through the gates and up the long driveway that circled in front of the three-story Georgian mansion. A dark sedan sat parked near the steps that led to the main door. Olivia didn't recognize the car, and as she got closer she could see the figure of a man sitting in the driver's seat. She had to pass the car to reach her usual parking space behind the house, and when she was a few yards away, she recognized the man. He was Carl Simmons, her father's attorney. He was looking down at his phone and didn't turn his head or look in her direction. Olivia felt a knot forming in her stomach. If Carl Simmons was here, that meant her father was inside with Emma. She hadn't counted on running into her father tonight, and she didn't look forward to the encounter. She pulled around the house and parked outside the garage as was her habit when she had lived with Emma. She entered through the back door, and as soon as she walked into the kitchen, she could hear raised voices. The house-keeper, a robust woman named Harriet, looked relieved to see her.

"What's going on?" Olivia asked.

Harriet put her finger over her lips in an unspoken command to keep silent, then motioned for Olivia to follow her into the laundry room. She pulled the door shut behind her and whispered, "I'm so thankful you're here. Mary certainly got hold of you quickly, didn't she? She only just went upstairs to get her phone so she could text you."

As if on cue, Olivia's phone beeped, indicating she had just received a text.

"No, I stopped by to have dinner with all of you. I heard shouting when I came into the kitchen."

"It's a fight," Harriet said, nodding for emphasis. "A big one. Your father and your aunt are having it out. Something terrible happened and Emma is enraged. Mary and I have never seen her like this. And your father is getting meaner and meaner. He threatened her, Olivia, and he's saying such terrible things about your mother."

"The fight's about my mother?" she asked, trying to understand.

Harriet shook her head. "I don't think so, but your father dragged your mother into it. From what I overheard, it's about some charity that lost money."

The poor housekeeper was beside

herself with worry. She kept folding and refolding a dish towel. "Emma never raises her voice," she whispered. "So you can see how serious this situation is."

"Yes," Olivia agreed. "Harriet, you said my father threatened Emma?"

"He did. Something to do with your mother. Whatever it was upset Emma."

Olivia opened the door. "All right. I'll go in now and see what I can do."

"May I offer a suggestion?"

"Yes, of course."

"If I were you, I'd listen at the door to find out what's going on. Once Emma sees you, she'll stop the argument, and you'll never know what it was about."

Harriet was right. Since Olivia was a little girl, Emma had tried to shield her from any unpleasant family conflicts. Even though Olivia was an adult now, Emma continued to protect her.

Olivia didn't like the idea of eaves-dropping on a private conversation, but she thought she just might linger at the door for a few minutes to get the gist of the argument. That wouldn't be consid-ered eavesdropping, would it? Of course it would, she admitted. But right or wrong, she was still going to do it.

As it turned out, she couldn't lean against the door because Mary had gotten there first. That didn't matter, though. Olivia could hear every word from down the hallway.

Her father's voice was furious. "If you try to make trouble, I'll leave Deborah, and you know what that will do to her. She says she can't live without me. Shall we find out?"

"Do it," Emma challenged. "Leave my sister. You've made the threat to divorce her how many times now? I'm not giving you any more money to stay with her. I made that mistake years ago, and I won't make it again. My sister may be a fool but she deserves better, and if she can't see it, then she'll have to wallow in self-pity when you leave."

"If Deborah does anything crazy, it will be on your hands."

"Are you suggesting she might harm herself? What do you suppose that will do to your reputation, Robert? Investors want stable managers, and they don't like scandal. Tell me," she continued, "did you ever love Deborah?"

Olivia stopped a few feet from the door. Mary, Emma's cook for the past twelve years, a sturdy German woman who always wore her silver-gray hair pulled back in a tidy bun, stood in front of her, unaware that she'd approached. Looking embarrassed to be listening in on a conversation that had become so personal, Mary turned to leave and saw Olivia standing behind her. After giving her a sympathetic smile and a pat on the arm, Mary went down the hall toward the kitchen. Olivia stepped up to the door. It was open a crack and the voices were loud and clear. She waited for her father's answer to Emma's question, but she didn't hear one.

Then Emma asked, "Are you capable of loving anyone but yourself?"

"The question's ridiculous. You still haven't told me what you plan to do—"

"About Jeff Wilcox?" Emma asked. "That depends on you. Are you going to stand by and do nothing while Jeff goes to prison because of your lies?"

Olivia leaned forward and peeked into

her aunt's study through the tiny opening in the doorway. She saw her father
pick up a magazine from the desk and
flip through it nonchalantly as he responded. "Yes, that's exactly what I'm
going to do. Stand by and do nothing. I
didn't put a gun to his head and force
him to give me the money and make the
investments for his charity."

"Believe me, if I had known that he
was going to do that, I would have put
a stop to it immediately. If Daniel were
alive, he would never have let Jeff get
involved with you."

Olivia recognized the name. Jeff Wilcox had been her uncle Daniel's pro-
tégé. He was the son of close personal
friends of her aunt and uncle, and when
he had graduated from college, he had
gone to work for Daniel. Olivia was away
at school at that time, but she remembered seeing Jeff at a couple of gather-
ings. She'd heard her aunt and uncle
speak of him many times. From what
they said, he was a courteous and easy-
going young man who often expressed
his gratitude for the opportunity her uncle had given him and the kindnesses

shown to him by her aunt. Shortly after her uncle died, she'd heard that Jeff had taken a position with a charitable organization.

"He knew there were risks," she heard her father say.

"You set him up," Emma cried. Olivia had never heard her aunt so upset. "You lied to him. He would never have invested the charity's funds if he had any inkling that they weren't safe. I know Jeff. He's honest and decent. He has a wife and a new baby now. He wouldn't risk that. Have you no conscience?"

"I only did what he asked," her father answered. "It's not my fault if his board of directors thought he misappropriated the funds. I offered him several investment strategies, and he made the final decision."

"Decisions based on the lies you told him," Emma countered.

"Wilcox isn't such an upstanding citizen," he snapped. "Greed was his downfall. He demanded a fee from me for investing the charity's funds, and I've got the signed papers to prove it."

"Lies, all lies," she cried out. "Jeff would never—"

"It's his word against mine," her father snapped. "And when the authorities investigate, they'll see that the evidence is on my side. The documents clearly show that there were risks with the investments and no guarantees. Documents that he signed, I might add."

Olivia had heard enough. She took a deep breath, opened the door, and walked inside. Neither Emma nor her father noticed her. They stood with their backs to the door. The window was on her father's right and she could see his reflection. His eyes were cold and his jaw was clinched.

"How much did Jeff Wilcox give you?" Olivia asked.

Robert MacKenzie turned to her, the contemptuous scowl gone, replaced by a dazzling smile. She'd been told that women adored him and that, if he hadn't decided to go into the Wall Street world, he could have made millions as a movie star. Tall and fit, with thick silver-tipped hair and eyes as blue as hers, he was considered devastatingly handsome, but it was his charm that captured his clients. Men believed they were in his inner circle, and women thought he wanted them in his bed. He had never cheated on his wife, though, for to do so would diminish his carefully constructed persona. He had learned to use all of his attributes to captivate and to hypnotize. Besides, money was far more important and arousing than sex. Very few people knew the real Robert MacKenzie, the devil hiding beneath the angel's wings.

"Hello, darling. How long have you been standing there?" he asked.

"Not long," she lied. "I just heard you talking about Jeff Wilcox. What have you done to him?"

"Nothing. Your aunt was misinformed," he said, shaking his head and never letting the smile fade. "As usual," he added. He walked over to her, put his hands on her shoulders, and leaned down to kiss her on her cheek. "How are you feeling? Are you taking your medicine every day?"

It always came back to her health. She believed it was her father's way of reminding her that she was flawed in his eyes. He knew how to manipulate her and make her feel inferior. When she was younger, it had worked, but no longer.

Olivia looked at Emma to gauge her reaction. Her aunt's gaze was locked on Robert, and her face was flushed with anger.

Olivia stepped back, then walked over to stand next to her aunt in a show of loyalty. "Father, I haven't had to take medicine for years. You know that." Turning to Emma, she said, "Tell me about Jeff Wilcox."

"Don't answer that," Robert ordered. "Olivia doesn't need to concern herself with business matters, especially in her weakened condition."

"Will you stop—" Olivia began to protest.

Her father cut her off when he said to Emma, "My daughter is so starved for affection, she'll believe anything you say, Emma, and she'll try to help because you've shown her that you care. If you get her involved in this, the stress could prove to be too much for her."

"For God's sake, Robert, your daughter has grown up and is quite healthy. Stop trying to make her an invalid."

"Tell me about Jeff," Olivia repeated. She folded her arms and leaned back against the desk, leaving no doubt that she wasn't going to budge until she got an explanation.

Her father refused to respond. Emma didn't have any such qualms. "Jeff became the manager of the Walden Foundation. They help the indigent and the homeless by providing housing and job programs. They've had a tremendously successful track record. The man who started the charity had, himself, been homeless and had been helped by a kind stranger. When Walden's luck turned, he vowed he would help others, and he started the charitable foundation. He died several years ago, but he left thirty-two million dollars for his charity to continue, and Jeff was brought in as its director. The position was perfect for Jeff. He always wanted to do work that would make a real difference in the world. And he was doing a great job I understand . . . until he met your father."

"Jeff gave him the money to invest," Olivia said.

"That's right."

"And now it's gone," she concluded.

"Yes," her aunt said. "All of it squandered in risky investments."

"The risks were clearly explained," her father argued.

Emma ignored his protest and continued, "The board of directors had allowed Jeff autonomy to make these investments because he had given them assurances that everything was in secure funds. Of course, when the investments went under, they called for an investigation. Your father had guaranteed that all of the investments were protected and had the highest ratings possible, and Jeff, being the trusting and decent man that he is, believed him." She shot Robert a look of contempt.

Olivia's father shook his head and smiled condescendingly at her. "He was lying, Emma. The papers he signed clearly show he was made aware of the risks."

Emma turned back to Olivia. "The prosecutors are involved now. They're claiming that Jeff not only mishandled the money but also that he did it knowingly and with the intent of lining his own pockets. If there's a trial and he's convicted, he could go to prison and be taken away from his wife and his baby— all for something I know he didn't do."

Olivia turned to her father. "How much did you make on these investments?"

Her father gave a slight shrug and answered, "It's not my responsibility to keep people from making stupid decisions. If Wilcox had chosen to invest in my Trinity Fund, he wouldn't be in this mess, but he insisted on another route."

"How much?" Olivia insisted.

"My five percent commission for the transactions was a low fee, considering the circumstances."

"So you walked away with over a million and a half, and Jeff Wilcox faces prison—not to mention the charity that is destroyed."

"I've wasted enough time talking about this," her father said as he began making his way to the door. "I have to be back in New York for an event tonight."

Olivia could barely control her anger. Her chest was tight, and she desperately needed to use her inhaler, but she didn't dare in front of him. It would be one more thing to mock, and it would prove to him that she was, indeed, inferior.

She had known that her father's business activities were suspect in the past, but it was as though she was seeing him without a filter for the first time. Even his attire seemed disingenuous, with his hand-tailored suit and his handsome cashmere scarf draped around his neck. Olivia watched him slip on a black wool coat that was impeccably cut and a perfect fit.

"Father?"

"Yes?" He said as he put on one leather glove and reached for the doorknob.

"This has to stop. You can't continue to hurt people this way."

Her father turned back to her with a compassionate smile. "Get some rest, Olivia. You look pale. That terrible disease you have . . . it's lurking under your skin . . . waiting. You never know when it could come back." He left without saying good-bye.

Monday morning, Olivia applied for a job with the IRS.

FOUR

"I don't know what I was thinking," Olivia told Jane. "Agent Kincaid asked me how I ended up working for the IRS, and once I started explaining . . . it got away from me."

"Did you tell him you're investigating your father?"

"No," she replied. "But I went on and on about reaching my goal, and he naturally wanted to know what the goal was. I wouldn't tell him, of course. I barely know the man. He has to think I'm crazy."

The two women were sitting side by

side in beige leather recliners in what they called the Dracula room of St. Paul's Hospital. Olivia was giving blood her friend would receive the following afternoon.

Dressed in black silk pajamas and a hot-pink robe, birthday gifts from Sam and Collins, Jane had come down from her hospital room to keep Olivia company. Jane's long honey-brown hair was up in a ponytail and she looked pale, terribly pale. Dr. Pardieu had ordered the blood transfusion and had told Jane that it would help immensely. It had in the past, he reminded her, and there was no reason to think it wouldn't help now.

"You shouldn't care what other people think."

"I know," Olivia agreed. "But Grayson's . . . different. I do care what he thinks about me, and honest to Pete, I don't have the faintest idea why." She sounded bewildered.

"Grayson?"

"Agent Grayson Kincaid. He told me to call him Grayson."

"Do you think you'll ever see him again?"

"Probably not," she said and was surprised by the stab of disappointment she felt. "Let's talk about something else. Did I mention that Jorguson told me he admires my father and that he knows people who have done quite well investing in his fund?"

"He must not have heard that you're trying to stop him."

"How could he have heard? Every time I make an inquiry or lodge a complaint, it's squelched. No one's calling me back, the SEC . . ." She took a breath. "It's frustrating, but I'll keep trying."

"Tell me everything that happened at the interview," Jane said. "Start at the beginning."

Since Jane was looking so sickly, Olivia decided to accommodate her, and by the time she was finished, Jane had a stitch in her side from laughing so hard.

"Let me get this straight. You asked Jorguson's bodyguard if he had a permit to carry a gun? The man's pointing a . . . what did you call it?"

"A Glock. Agent Kincaid called it a Glock."

"Okay then, he's pointing a fancy Glock at you, and you want to know if he has a permit?" Jane thought, given the circumstances, the question was hilarious, and she couldn't stop laughing.

Olivia handed her a tissue to wipe the tears from her cheeks. "I watch way too much television, don't I? On all those police shows the detectives ask the criminals if they have permits. I was trying to think of something to say to get him to stop coming toward me. It's illegal for him to even carry the gun. I don't know why I didn't point that out."

"Weren't you scared?"

If an outsider had asked her that question, she probably would have pretended that it was no big deal, she hadn't been scared at all. She wanted people to think she was a tough, no-nonsense kind of woman. Only Jane and the other Pips knew the real Olivia. They understood her vulnerability because they were just like her.

"Oh yes, I was scared," she said. "But I was also so astonished by his behavior I could barely think what to do, and I was angry, really angry. People shouldn't bring guns to five-star restaurants."

"Is that a rule?"

Olivia laughed. "It sounded like one, didn't it? I guess I just didn't want to die in such a lame way."

"Getting shot during an interview *is* a lame way to die."

She shrugged. "I can think of better ways. Don't laugh at me. I'm giving you my blood, which happens to have antibodies you need, so be nice to me."

A nurse came into the room to check Olivia's IV. After saying hello, Jane switched to French as she continued the conversation. Because of their crush on Dr. Pardieu, all the Pips eventually had become fluent in his language. It was their way of saying thank you to him for saving them.

"I'm always nice to you," Jane said. Then, in the blink of an eye, she became melancholy. "What if the transfusion doesn't work this time? What if I don't feel better and I have to start chemo again?"

"The transfusion will work," Olivia assured her.

"You're a real contradiction, you know that?" Jane said. "You're such an optimist with everyone, but when it comes to yourself, you only see the negative."

Dismissing her criticism, Olivia responded, "The transfusion helped in the past, and there's no reason to think it won't help now. You're just a little anemic, that's all. Don't stop trusting Dr. Pardieu. He's taken good care of all of us."

Jane was in the mood to feel sorry for herself. "But you and Collins and Sam have all been cured. I'm the only one struggling after all this time. I don't understand it. I was feeling great until a few weeks ago."

"We're in remission," she corrected. "Not cured."

"Dr. Pardieu said you're safe now," she said. "And none of you have had any symptoms for years. I'm the difficult one." Jane knew she sounded pitiful, but she didn't care. She usually tried to be the positive, upbeat one, but she knew she didn't have to put up any shields with Olivia or the other Pips. She could cry like a three-year-old if she wanted to and not worry that any of them would think less of her.

"You've always been difficult," Olivia said, smiling. "Sam says you can be a real pain in the . . ."

Jane burst into laughter. "I guess I'm not going to get any 'there, there, you poor thing' from you."

"When did you ever get any of that from me?" She shifted position in the recliner and winced when the needle moved ever so slightly.

"Never."

"If Dr. Pardieu isn't worried . . ."

"He says he isn't."

"Has he ever lied to any of us?"

"No. In fact, he's been brutally honest."

"So, if he isn't worried . . ."

Jane smiled because she realized she was actually feeling much better. A little whining wasn't such a bad thing after all. "If I don't have to do another round of chemo, I'm going to participate in the

art show at the Scripts Gallery. The art-
ists have to be there," she explained. "I'll
have four paintings on display. Maybe
I'll get lucky and sell one or two."

"Are you low on funds? I could give
you—"

"I've got more money than I know
what to do with from my mom's life insurance. I'm just saying, getting paid for
my work is validation. I want you to
come to the gallery, okay?"

"Let me know when and where, and
I'll be there."

"Logan's going to try to come to the
show, too."

"Your brother's out of rehab?" Olivia's
surprise was evident in her voice.

"Yes," she replied. "And he's doing
really well this time. He seems serious
about his sobriety. He's going to meetings every single day, and he's trying to
make amends."

"Like?"

"He comes to see me every evening
on his way home from work."

"Logan has a job?"

"He's working as a mechanic at Rog-
er's Rent-A-Car company. He helps out

at the counter, too. Logan says the owner is giving him more responsibility, and he doesn't want to let him down. He worries about me. He never used to."

"He was too drunk and too stoned to worry about anyone." She saw Jane's expression and hurriedly said, "I'm sorry. I shouldn't have said that."

"No, it was true, but not any longer. He brings me carryout and told me that when I get home, he'll come over and cook for me."

"Maybe rehab worked this time," Olivia said, though she didn't hold out much hope. Jane was an eternal optimist. Olivia wasn't. Logan hadn't gone willingly; rehab had been court mandated. Jane's older brother had been a mess for as long as Olivia had known Jane. He drank alcohol like water, and his drug of choice was cocaine.

She hoped for Jane's sake that Logan had decided to change his life. She was about to ask another question about Logan when he walked into the room. He was tall, gaunt, and painfully thin, but there was a light in his eyes Olivia hadn't seen before. He put his finger to his lips to let Olivia know he didn't want her to say anything, then quietly snuck up behind Jane. He leaned down and whispered, "Boo."

Jane jumped. "Logan, will you stop doing that," she demanded. "Why you think it's funny to scare people is beyond me."

He laughed. "Hi, Olivia. How are you doing?"

"I'm fine," she answered.

He turned to Jane then. "I've been all over this hospital looking for you. What are you doing here?"

"Olivia's giving me her blood," Jane said. "She's keeping me alive with her antibodies." She realized she shouldn't have joked when she saw Logan's expression. He looked stricken. "I'm going to be fine."

"Don't try to protect me," he said. "I know you're sick. Always tell me the truth, okay? I can handle it."

"Jane's anemic, that's all," Olivia said, trying to help Jane downplay her illness.

"And your blood will make her better?"

"Yes, that's right," Jane said and then hastened to change the subject. "What about the art show? Did you get permission?" Turning to Olivia she explained, "Logan has a nine o'clock curfew at the halfway house."

Logan grinned. "Yes, I got permission. I can stay out until ten thirty." He leaned down and kissed Jane on the cheek. "I've got to go. I've got a meeting in thirty minutes."

Jane waited until Logan had left the room and then said, "What do you think?"

Olivia smiled. "I think he's on the right track."

"I do, too. He's different now in a good way. He's been clean and sober over a hundred and twenty days. That's the longest he's ever gone," she added. "And he isn't hanging out with all those losers anymore. I wish Mom were alive to see his recovery."

Jane took a breath. "Okay, we're through talking about my brother. I've got really funny news to tell you. You'll never guess what Collins did. I'm not supposed to tell you because she wants to, but you need to be warned so you won't laugh the way I did. She was furious with me. I couldn't help it," she added. "I swear you'll never, ever guess."

"Is she in trouble?"

"No."

"Just tell me."

"She took the exam and she passed. Aced the interviews, too. In fact, they actually recruited her."

"They?"

"FBI," Jane said. "Collins has decided to become an FBI agent. It's kind of ironic, don't you think? This news coming on the same day you have a run-in with the FBI?"

"It wasn't a run-in. It was a mistake," Olivia argued. "Collins in the FBI—that's a good one." She laughed. Miss Sensitivity an agent? Not possible.

"I'm not joking. Can you picture it? Collins carrying a gun?"

"Dibs on telling Sam."

"I already tried," she said. "I got voice mail. She'll get back to me when she can."

Olivia's cell phone rang, interrupting their conversation. Before she looked at the iPhone screen, she checked her watch.

"Talk about a pain in the backside," Olivia said. "Natalie's right on time."

"Your sister's on time? On time for what?"

"She's been calling every night for the past five nights at exactly seven o'clock."

"You better answer it. You may explain after you talk to her . . . if you want to explain . . . unless it's private . . ."

Exasperated, Olivia said, "You know I tell you everything."

Jane nodded. "I know. I was being sensitive. It's a new thing I'm trying. Now answer your damned phone. I want to hear what's going on."

Olivia didn't want to talk to her sister, but she knew that, if she didn't answer the call now, Natalie would continue to phone her every fifteen minutes until she got hold of her. Her sister was as tenacious as a junkyard dog, and in some instances just as mean.

"Hello, Natalie. What's new?"

Her sister wasn't in the mood to be chatty. "Did you talk to Aunt Emma yet?"

Olivia counted to five before she an-

swered the question, hoping to get rid
of some of her anger before she spoke.
It didn't help. "No, I did not." Her voice
was emphatic.

"She's home from London."

"Yes, I know."

She could hear Natalie's long, drawn-
out sigh over the phone. "Don't you care
about our mother?"

Here comes the drama, Olivia thought.
She really wasn't in the mood to put up
with Natalie's antics tonight. She'd had
enough drama today.

"Is Mother there with you?" she asked.

"Yes."

"May I speak with her?"

"She's on the other line talking to our
father . . . you know, Robert MacKenzie,
the man you've been ignoring."

Olivia couldn't resist a bit of sarcasm.
"I thought I was ignoring our mother."

"Don't be rude," Natalie snapped.

Olivia vowed she wouldn't let her sister goad her into an argument, no matter how abrasive she became, and so
she remained silent.

Another sigh, then Natalie said, "All
I'm asking is that you talk to Aunt Emma

and convince her to come to our father's birthday party."

"His birthday isn't for several months," Olivia stated.

"These big celebrations take time. It's going to be an amazing event," she said, enthusiasm lacing her words. "One of Dad's assistants booked the grand ballroom at the Morgan Hotel over a year ago, and we're expecting as many as three hundred guests."

"Three hundred for a birthday party?"

"It's amazing, isn't it?"

Amazing was obviously Natalie's word of the day. "Yes," she said. "Amazing. But here's my question. Dad lives in Manhattan. Why is he having a birthday party in Washington, D.C.?"

"Oh, there's going to be another party in New York."

"Two birthday parties?" she asked and began to laugh. "Isn't that a little narcissistic?"

"Dad didn't want to exclude anyone, and all those men and women who invested in the MacKenzie Trinity Fund want to celebrate with him. He's made them all rich."

"I'm betting they were already rich."

"Yes, but Dad's a financial genius, and he has more than doubled their investments. So many of his investors live in D.C., and that's why he decided to throw a party there, too. There's going to be at least three senators and twice that many congressmen attending the party and a couple of ambassadors, too." Natalie sounded starstruck.

"Was every investor invited?"

"No. That would have made the number of guests well over a thousand. Just the high-income investors were invited. I'm telling you, it's going to be amazing."

"It sounds like it will be," she said to placate her sister.

"So you understand."

"Understand what?"

"Aunt Emma has to be there," she cried out. "For God's sake, pay attention. You know how important Emma is. And powerful. How many boards do you think she's on? And she's a huge patron of the arts."

"She's on three boards."

"She's an influential member of society," Natalie said. She sounded calmer now, more in control. "If she doesn't attend the birthday party, it will be noticed. People will talk, and Mother will be embarrassed."

"I don't think Aunt Emma cares what people say."

"But Mother does," she snapped. "This is tearing her apart. She can't stand the rift. It's terrible that Emma won't talk to her."

"I believe it was our mother who started the silent treatment when Emma told her she'd changed her trust. Our mother and father aren't getting any of her money."

"Mother doesn't care about that," Natalie insisted. "She's just happy that you and I are still beneficiaries. We'll both get large sums when Emma's gone, and I will gladly hand it over to our father to invest. Unlike you, I'm loyal."

Her sister's callous and mercenary attitude was making Olivia sick. "Wasn't the money you got from Uncle Daniel's trust enough, Natalie? Now you can't wait to get your hands on more?"

Olivia heard Natalie's husband, George,

in the background telling her to hand him her phone. Then he was on the line.

"Olivia, George Anderson here."

"For God's sake, George. She knows your last name," Natalie said.

"We understand your aunt Emma joins you for dinner every Sunday."

"When she's in town," Olivia said.

"Yes, and you cook for her."

"I don't cook, George. We go out." She knew she was irritating him with her interruptions, and she couldn't help smiling.

"At one of the dinners, perhaps you could mention your father's birthday party and request that she attend. Is that so difficult?"

"Apparently it is," Olivia said.

"Don't be sarcastic," he chided. He turned away from the phone. "There's no reasoning with her, Natalie."

Her sister came back on the line. "Who cares who started the silent treatment. Emma needs to do the right thing and call Mother," she said in a near shout. "And by the way," she continued on a rant now, "shame on you, Olivia.

Do you realize how cruel you're being to the family? If you don't show up for the party either, how would it look? It wouldn't just be hurtful, it would be disloyal."

Olivia muted the phone. "Natalie wants to know if I realize how hurtful I'm being to the family."

Jane put her hand out, palm up, and wiggled her fingers. "Let me talk to her. Come on, give me the phone." Jane's face wasn't pale now. In the space of a few seconds, her complexion turned bright pink. "I'll set the record straight."

Olivia smiled. Jane had always been her champion. She hit the mute button again and said to Natalie, "Aunt Emma has a mind of her own. You know that."

"But she'll do anything for you because she feels . . ."

Natalie had suddenly stopped. Olivia's determination not to get pulled into an argument flew out the window. "She feels what?" she demanded angrily. "Go ahead, say it."

"Okay, I will," she said defiantly. "She feels sorry for you. She always has, ever since you got sick. Why do you think she moved to D.C.?"

"Oh, I don't know. Maybe because she loved me and knew the rest of you had pretty much written me off."

"We did no such thing."

"Emma wanted me to have a home to go to when I was released from the hospital. And she wanted me to have at least one visitor when I got out of isolation."

"You do like to dredge up the past, don't you?"

Olivia closed her eyes. She couldn't do this anymore.

"Natalie, do me a favor."

"What?"

"Stop calling me."

She didn't give her sister time to argue. She disconnected the call, dropped her phone into her purse, and turned to Jane to tell her what Natalie wanted.

"Why is she so hell-bent on getting your aunt Emma to attend the party?"

"According to Natalie, everyone who matters in D.C. society knows who Emma is, and if she isn't at the party, it will be noticed, and that will embarrass my mother."

"Is Natalie working for your father now?"

"No," she answered. "She's just helping out with the birthday parties. She and her husband, George, still run that Internet company. From what I understand, it's doing quite well. They sell everything from shoes to kitchen sinks. They have so many people working for them, they can afford to take time off."

"Is George a believer, too?" she asked.

Olivia laughed. "A believer? Do you mean under my father's charismatic spell?"

"Yes, that's what I mean."

"Yes, he is. According to Natalie, our father has doubled their money. She boasts that they could retire now if they wanted."

The nurse walked into the room carrying a glass of orange juice. She handed the drink to Olivia and unhooked the IV.

"You know the drill," she said. "Drink all the orange juice, sit back, and relax. If you feel dizzy, push the call button."

Olivia's cell phone rang. Certain it was

Natalie calling again with a renewed attack, she didn't bother to look at the screen.

Her greeting wasn't very polite. "You're driving me crazy. You know that? Absolutely crazy."

A deep male voice responded. "Yeah? Good to know."

Agent Grayson Kincaid was on the line.

FIVE

Grayson had spent the rest of his afternoon putting out fires caused by the Jorguson debacle, but as busy as he was, he couldn't get Olivia MacKenzie out of his head, and that irritated the hell out of him. His response to her didn't make any sense. After all, he'd been with the woman for only an hour. It was purely a physical reaction, he reasoned. She had a beautiful face, an amazing smile, an incredible body. He would have to be a eunuch not to notice or react.

He sat at his desk reading through a file and cross-checking it with the data on his computer screen, but every now and then she'd pop into his thoughts. Disgusted with his lack of focus, he shook his head in an attempt to clear it and started over again on page one.

Agent Ronan Conrad knocked on his door, opened it, and leaned in. "Have you got a minute?"

"Sure. Come in."

The office was claustrophobic. Ronan had to shut the door in order to pull out the one chair so that he could sit. In the process he banged his knee on the metal desk.

It was a cold, uninviting space. The gray walls were bare, and there weren't any personal items, like family photos or mementos, on the desk. The only window was the size of a postage stamp.

"I like what you've done with the place," Ronan said, grinning.

The two men were good friends. They had gone through training together and had been assigned to the same team now for four years. Their work ethic and dedication were very similar, though their backgrounds couldn't have been more different. Ronan grew up in a large working-class family in the inner city. He attended a state university on an athletic scholarship and upon graduation entered the Marines. After serving several years on a special ops team, he returned home to attend graduate school and was recruited by the FBI.

Grayson, on the other hand, had been dealt a different hand. He was born into a family of wealth and prestige, and in the D.C. area was considered a blue blood. He entered the academy after earning his law degree at Princeton. His inheritance from a trust fund handed down by his grandfather was substantial, but Grayson had made several wise investments and had turned a large fortune into an even larger fortune. If the truth be known, he didn't need to work for a living.

Coming from two such dissimilar circumstances, one would assume that the two men would be worlds apart, but the opposite was true. They had bonded after the first couple of weeks of training. Ronan initially had his doubts when he'd learned of Grayson's privileged background, but his opinion quickly changed. There wasn't anyone in their class who trained harder or studied longer. Grayson excelled at every test the academy threw at him, and soon a friendly rivalry developed between the two friends, each one pushing the other to a higher level. By the time they graduated from the academy, both men had won the admiration and respect of the instructors and all the other trainees.

"How do you like filling in for Pensky?" Ronan asked, crossing his arms and leaning his chair back on two legs.

"She's back Monday, thank God. I hate being cooped up in this office. I feel like I'm in a tomb."

Ronan looked around the room. "I think the utility closet is bigger," he remarked. "Maybe you'll get to use it."

"Why would I want to do that?" Grayson asked. He rolled his shoulders to work out the stiffness. He'd been leaning over the file folders for hours now.

"Word is, the job is yours if you want it. Pensky's going to retire next year. Maybe sooner."

Grayson shook his head. "I don't want it."

"If you end up getting custody of your nephew, you probably won't want to be running all over the country. Pensky's job would be perfect for you."

"I'm hoping my brother will step up and start acting like a father."

"Come on, Grayson. You know that's not gonna happen. At least not anytime soon."

Ronan had known Grayson's brother, Devin, almost as long as he'd known Grayson. He'd met him shortly after graduating from the academy. Devin had the same upbringing as Grayson, but the two brothers were polar opposites. Grayson had a strong work ethic and a fierce sense of duty and loyalty to family, but Devin was irresponsible and self-centered. Since his wife's death several years ago, he had become quite the jet-setter. He liked the action in Monte Carlo and Dubai, and he loved women. He was the ultimate playboy and, sadly, often forgot he had a son.

Ronan knew it was difficult for his friend to talk about his family, and he doubted anyone else in the office knew about the situation.

"You're lucky your brother isn't dragging Henry all over Europe."

"I wouldn't let that happen."

"Is Henry still living with your father?"

"Yes," he answered and then abruptly changed the subject. "What's happening with the Harrison investigation?"

"That's what I wanted to report. Those brothers are crazy, plain crazy. I enjoyed arresting them, and I have to admit I wish they had resisted. I would have loved to punch all three of them."

"Are they in lockup?"

Ronan nodded. "And they're not going anywhere. They were denied bail."

"No bail? That's good."

"After you dropped the case in my lap—why are you smiling?"

"Because that's exactly what I did. It's called payback."

Ronan looked surprised, then conceded. "Yeah, okay. I guess I deserved it after the Brody case."

"You guess? Do you know how many interviews I had to do with those freaky cult members?"

"I heard it was hilarious," Ronan said.

"I still don't know how you did it. One

day you're running the investigation, and the next it's on my desk."

"It took finesse," Ronan boasted. "Someday I'll teach you a few of my tricks." Turning serious, he asked, "What about Poole? Have you talked to him yet?"

"Yes, and he agreed to a transfer."

"He agreed?"

"Yeah, well, I didn't really give him a choice."

"And in return?"

"I won't detail his latest screwup in his personnel file. Of course, his superior will, but I won't. I won't add fuel to the fire."

"You're too soft, Grayson," Ronan said with feigned disgust. "I almost got that out with a straight face. You're a hard-ass, just like me."

"Maybe," he allowed. "What's going on with Jorguson? Have you heard anything?"

"No, not yet. The only reason we got dragged into the middle of the investigation was because of that hothead, Poole," he remarked.

Grayson disagreed. "We weren't

dragged into the investigation. We were doing a favor for Agent Huntsman."

"Poole was told to shut down the operation, and he completely ignored the order. That's about the third or fourth time he's disregarded Huntsman's instructions, right?"

"Right," Grayson said.

"He should be fired or forced to retire."

"That's Huntsman's call, not ours, but I agree with you. Poole needs to get out."

"It's a good thing we made it to the restaurant when we did," Ronan said. "I don't think Poole would have gotten to the bodyguard before he hurt Olivia MacKenzie."

"You remembered her name."

Ronan nodded. "I remember everything about her," he admitted. "And I didn't even speak to her. You interviewed her. What's she like?"

"Smart," he said.

"And?"

"And what?"

"And drop-dead gorgeous."

Grayson smiled. "That, too."

"So you did notice."

"Of course I noticed," he said. "I'm not blind."

"Huntsman doesn't have the evidence to prove Jorguson is laundering money for some of his clients, so he's decided to do some pushing. I helped him get statements from six strong witnesses who saw Jorguson attack MacKenzie at the restaurant, and we have the cell phone video. Huntsman hasn't contacted her yet to find out if she'll testify. He's charging him with battery. It's not much but—"

Grayson interrupted. "If that's the only charge, Huntsman has to know it will never get to court. Jorguson's attorneys will either get it thrown out or plea it down."

"Of course they will," he agreed. "But Huntsman is going to keep them busy, flood them with paper. I honestly don't know what he hopes to accomplish," he said.

"He's frustrated."

"Yes, he is," Ronan agreed.

"I just finished my report and sent it over to him, and when he reads it, he'll realize there's a better way to go after Jorguson."

"What better way?" Ronan wanted to know.

"Apparently Poole didn't mention Olivia's occupation to Huntsman. He was probably embarrassed because he couldn't intimidate her." Thinking about it made him smile.

"What am I missing?" Ronan asked.

"Olivia MacKenzie works for the IRS. Therefore, Jorguson attacked . . ."

"An IRS agent." He laughed. "Oh, that's sweet. Huntsman's going to love it. Did Jorguson know? Of course he did. He was interviewing her, right?"

"Right."

"I'll contact MacKenzie—"

"No, I'll do it." Grayson heard how eager he sounded and quickly added, "I want to get out of this office. I can't breathe in here."

He thought he'd been smooth, but Ronan wasn't fooled. "So you are, in fact, interested in her?"

"I'm interested in helping Huntsman nail Jorguson. I already interviewed Olivia, and I think I should finish it up."

"A phone call would probably—"

"No, I should do it in person."

Ronan stood. "Okay, I'll get her phone number for you, and you can set up a time to meet."

Without thinking, Grayson said, "I've already got it programmed in my phone."

"But you're not interested," Ronan said as he strolled out of the office.

Grayson could hear his laughter through the door.

SIX

Grayson wanted to meet with Olivia to discuss the Jorguson investigation, at her convenience, he insisted, as long as it was Saturday at five o'clock. It was the only time he had available, he explained, and he wanted to get this all tied up before Monday.

"There are some discrepancies I'd like to go over as soon as possible regarding the incident with Jorguson."

"Discrepancies? How could there be any discrepancies? There were at least twenty people watching," she said. "Some of those people were recording

with their phones. And just for the record, Agent Kincaid, it wasn't an incident. It was an attack."

"I know," he said, placating her. "Jorguson's attorneys are calling it the alleged incident, and Jorguson's version
of what happened is quite different from
yours."

"You're joking."

"Sorry, no." He heard her sigh. "Olivia?"
he said after a long minute of silence.

"I'm thinking, Grayson."

He liked the way she said his name.
She dragged it out so he'd hear her
frustration. He smiled in reaction. "Five
o'clock. I can either come to you, or we
could meet somewhere."

"You want to meet Saturday night?"
she questioned. Didn't the agent have a
life outside of the office?

"Early Saturday night," he corrected.

Ah, so he did have plans, probably a
late date, she speculated as she took
another sip of the orange juice the nurse
had given her.

Jane was checking messages on her
phone and wasn't paying any attention
to the conversation.

"Three o'clock works better for me," she told him.

"No, that won't work for me. I'm tied up until four thirty."

"Then it will have to wait until Monday."

"No."

"No? Can't you be a little flexible? I have plans, and I can't change them."

"What plans?"

He sounded suspicious. Was he simply curious, or didn't he believe her? Olivia pictured Grayson tackling that horrible bodyguard, saving her from certain harm, and she decided the least she could do in return was cooperate.

"I'm going to a formal affair," she said. "I have to get ready and be at the Hamilton Hotel by seven thirty. If clearing up discrepancies will only take ten or fifteen minutes, then fine, we'll meet at five."

"It could take longer than that. What's the formal affair?"

"The Capitol League Benefit."

"That's Saturday night? I thought it was next weekend." Grayson had received an invitation and had respectfully

declined, but he had also made a substantial donation to the charity because
he believed it was a good cause.

"Then you're planning to attend?"

He thought about it for a second or
two, then said, "Yes."

She felt a little burst of pleasure that
took her by surprise.

"Then perhaps we could meet at the
hotel. It shouldn't take all that long to
discuss Jorguson's blatant lies, should
it? Unless you have plans . . . or if you
have a date and it would be rude to
leave her while you discussed . . ."

"Jorguson's lies?"

She could hear the amusement in his
voice. "Yes. Do you have a date?"

"No."

"Really?"

He laughed. "Really. I'm working, remember? The Jorguson investigation."

"That's right."

"What about you? Do you have a
date?"

"No," she said. "I sound boring, don't
I?"

"Olivia, there isn't anything boring
about you," he said, and before she

could respond to the compliment, he asked, "Were you planning to go alone?"

"Yes. My aunt is being honored at the event, and I promised her I'd attend. I was planning to meet her there. Unlike us, she has a date."

"Who is your aunt?"

"Emma Monroe."

"Why don't I drive you to the hotel? We can talk on the way there."

"Yes, all right."

"Listen . . . I might as well . . ."

"Yes?" she asked when he hesitated.

"I might as well take you home after . . ."

"That would be lovely."

"What time?"

"Seven."

"I'll see you then."

He ended the call, turned back to his desk, and noticed Ronan standing in the doorway. He didn't ask him if he had listened to the awkward conversation. The look on his face told Grayson he had.

"Man, that was painful," Ronan said. "What happened to you?"

Grayson shrugged. "Damned if I know."

Olivia told Jane about her conversation with Grayson while she wheeled her friend back up to her hospital room.

Always the artist, Jane asked, "Give me a visual. What does he look like?"

"He's tall, well over six feet, and he has dark hair, a really great mouth, and a firm jaw. Good bone structure . . . you know, patrician," she explained. "His eyes are intriguing. Now that I think about it, he's very sexy and quite hand-some."

"You sound surprised. Didn't you think he was handsome when you met him?"

The elevator doors opened, and she backed the wheelchair in, then waited for Jane to push the eighth-floor button. "Yes, I did think he was nice-looking, but . . . you know . . . he's FBI . . ."

"Would I want to paint him?"

"Oh yes, you would. He wouldn't let you, though. From the little I know about him, I think he'd be mortified if you even suggested it. He's an agent, very strait-laced and professional. So, of course, a relationship is out of the question. He's interesting, though. Very sophisticated. No rough edges. Aunt Emma would like him."

"And you're going out with him tomorrow night."

"No, I'm going to the Capitol League Benefit. He's going to drive me there and drive me back home."

"Will he go inside with you?"

Olivia laughed. "Of course he will."

"Then you've got yourself a date."

"It isn't a date," she argued. "It's work related. We'll be discussing the Jorguson investigation."

"How romantic."

Olivia pushed the wheelchair into Jane's room and parked it in the corner while Jane got back into bed. There were two thick books on her bedside table, a biography and a book about addiction recovery. On top of the volumes was an AA pamphlet. Jane was obviously taking her brother's new sobriety seriously, and Olivia knew that her friend would do anything she could to help Logan stay on the right path.

Olivia didn't want her to be disappointed again. She decided not to mention the reading material or bring up the fact that Logan's addiction wasn't just alcohol but also cocaine. Maybe AA would work for that recovery, too. For Jane's sake, she hoped it would.

Olivia stood at the foot of the bed and waited for Jane to get settled. Her arms folded across her chest, she was frowning at her friend as her thoughts went back to their conversation about Grayson Kincaid.

"What?" Jane asked when she noticed how serious Olivia looked.

"I don't want tomorrow night to be romantic. How crazy would it be for me to get involved with him? Even assuming he would be interested . . ."

"Of course he would be interested. How could he not? You're fairly intelligent, somewhat sweet when you aren't being bitchy, and beautiful."

"Bitchy? Fairly intelligent?"

Jane laughed. "Only *you* would focus on the negatives. I did say beautiful."

She shrugged. "It doesn't matter, because as soon as my father is arrested . . . if I ever find the evidence to get him arrested . . . I'll become a leper. No one in this city will want to be seen with a MacKenzie. My family will call me a traitor, and, in fact, that's what I am. They can't be surprised by what's coming, though. I've pleaded with Natalie and her mule-headed husband, George, and my mother—who, by the way, is a completely lost cause—to get their money out of my father's investment firm, but no one will listen to me. I don't want to hurt them, but I don't know what else to do. If he continues, he'll not only ruin them, he'll destroy the lives of hundreds of other innocent people."

"Do you have any solid evidence yet?" Jane asked.

"No," Olivia admitted. "But I know I'm right. My entire life I've seen how my father operates. He's very charming. He has a way of getting people to believe he's the most sincere and candid person they've ever met, and he looks very successful, so when he presents an investment opportunity, they trust him. Sometimes I think he actually believes what he tells them. It's almost like a compulsion and he can't help himself."

Olivia wished she could look away and let things play out, but she couldn't. She knew what was coming and she couldn't just stand by as more and more people got sucked in. She'd seen it happen before. When she was young, she knew her father was different from other dads, but it wasn't until she was older that she realized what he was and finally could see what he'd been doing.

One of his first ventures was in oil. He had convinced hundreds of people that geologists had discovered incredibly rich oil deposits off the coast of Texas. All he needed was enough money to invest in the drilling equipment to extract it. People gave him millions because he assured them that they were taking a small risk. He made them believe they were going to make a hundred times what they'd put in. People were greedy. No one knew how much drilling actually went on, but within a year he announced that the wells had come up dry; the geologists were mistaken. The investors walked away with a loss, but somehow Olivia's father moved on to bigger and better.

He formed another company a couple of years later. This time he invested in technology. He managed to find enough people to believe that he had collected a group of engineers who were on the verge of developing a revolutionary battery, one that would solve all the country's energy problems. That turned out to be a flop, too, but while the investors lost every dime and the company went under, her father's lifestyle became more lavish.

Those were just a couple of his so-called business ventures. Now he'd gotten even bigger. With his new firm, he'd collected massive amounts of capital from investors, big and small, with promises of phenomenal returns. Somehow he'd convinced them that their money was safe, but there was no way he could maintain the big profits he'd been claiming.

"Is there any way he could be legitimate this time?" Jane wondered.

Olivia thought about Jeff Wilcox facing prison because of her father's lies. How many more were there? She shook her head. "No, it just doesn't make any sense. I try to warn people, but until I find proof, no one will pay any attention to me." She took a breath. "Actually, that's not quite true. My father's law firm, Simmons, Simmons and Falcon—or as I like to call them, Slimeball, Slimeball and Slimeball—did get wind of what I'm trying to do, and they're trying to stop me. They sent a nasty threatening letter. If I don't desist with what they called my insane and inflammatory accusations, they'll have me arrested."

"On what charges?"

"They don't have any. It's all bogus. I haven't done anything illegal. They're just trying to scare me. If they were to try to sue me, they'd have to let me see my father's financials, and trust me, Jane, they'd kill me before they'd let that happen."

"Good God, Olivia. Don't talk like that."

"They should all be in prison."
"Then go after them. Just don't . . ."
"Don't what?"
"Don't get killed."
Olivia laughed. "That's the plan."

SEVEN

Olivia was ready by six thirty Saturday night and spent the next half hour catching up on e-mails. She wore a black floor-length gown. The silk hugged the curves of her body, but it wasn't obscene, by any means. The scooped neck showed a little cleavage, nothing that would have men ogling, she thought. Her neck was bare, and her only jewelry was a pair of teardrop diamond earrings that her aunt Emma had given her for her birthday. Her hair was swept up in a cluster of curls. A few tendrils escaped at the base of her neck.

Grayson was five minutes early. She opened the door and stood there staring up at him, speechless. The man was even more sexy in a tux. James Bond, all right, she thought. No, she corrected. Better.

Neither of them moved for a few seconds, and then Grayson said, "You look nice." He sounded hoarse.

"Thank you. So do you," she said as she stepped back. "Please, come inside. I'll just get my purse and wrap."

He stepped into a small foyer and followed her into the living room. Olivia lived in an upscale neighborhood on the edge of Georgetown. The building was old, the third-floor apartment was spacious and comfortable. Tall arched windows and worn hardwood floors were the backdrop for her overstuffed sofa and two matching chairs. The walls had been painted a pale blue, the windows were trimmed in white, and the furniture was a soft yellow color. A black square coffee table sat in front of the sofa with a stack of books on one side and a white vase filled with fresh daisies in the center. Colorful rugs brightened the area.

He noticed a pair of worn tennis shoes under the coffee table and a pair of flats in the doorway of a small room off the living area that Olivia obviously used as an office. Her laptop sat on an old, dark cherrywood desk that had been beautifully restored. Bookcases flanked the desk, the shelves bowed from the heavy books.

Grayson was an armchair architect at heart and appreciated the unique features of these older buildings. He would have loved to see the rest of the apartment.

Olivia came back into the living room and noticed Grayson staring at her ceilings. He caught her watching and said, "I like the moldings."

"I do, too. That's one of the reasons I bought the apartment."

"Ten-foot-high ceilings? That's rare."

"Yes."

"Bet it gets cold in here in the winter, doesn't it?" he asked when he noticed the old-fashioned radiators.

She pointed to the afghan draped over a chair. "I wrap up in that."

He nodded. "How many bedrooms?"

"Two."

"One large, one small?"

"No, both are quite spacious."

"Has the kitchen been remodeled?"

Puzzled by his interest, she answered. "Yes, the whole building was remodeled a few years ago."

"How long have you lived here?"

"A little over two years. Are you interested in the neighborhood? Thinking about moving?"

Grayson didn't explain that he bought buildings, renovated them, and either sold them or rented them out. It was an expensive, yet profitable, hobby.

"Just curious. Are you ready?"

He took the key from her and locked the deadbolt on their way out. Neither said another word until they were in his car and on their way.

"Tell me what Jorguson is saying happened," she began.

He glanced at her. "You attacked him."

She was properly outraged. "That is absolutely not true."

"Special Agent Huntsman has been after Jorguson for some time. He wants to know if you'll testify should he take him to court."

"Yes," she said without hesitation. "But do you really think it will get that far?"

He grinned. "Those were the exact words my partner, Agent Conrad, said. Jorguson knew you worked for the IRS, so, in fact, he attacked a representative of the IRS, didn't he? It's my understanding the Internal Revenue Service doesn't like it when one of their own is assaulted."

She laughed. "No, they don't."

"Huntsman wants to push this."

"I'll help in any way that I can," she promised.

"How much research did you do before your interview with Jorguson?"

"Very little," she admitted. "I didn't have the time. A big mistake on my part. I never should have gone to the interview."

"Jorguson's client list is filled with real

bad . . ." He started to say "asses" but substituted "people" instead.

She laughed. "Bad people? You sound like one of my kids."

"One of your kids?"

"The kids I represent. When we had lunch, I thought I mentioned I do some work on the side for Judge Bowen and Judge Thorpe."

"Yes, you did mention it. It just jarred me to hear you call them your kids."

"When they're in trouble, they are my kids. In most cases, I'm all they have." Her voice had turned serious, passionate.

"I've got a feeling it's enough."

"Tell me more about these bad people."

"Jorguson Investments is legit as far as Huntsman can tell; however, some of his clients have brought in copious amounts of cash. One in particular, Gretta Keene, was very active. Her base was in Belgium but she operated in the United States for several years. The federal government took action a few months ago to have her deported. She disappeared before that happened."

"Where's all the money coming from? Drugs?"

"Among other endeavors, we suspect."

"So let me go out on a limb here. If and when I talk to Agent Huntsman, he's going to tell me Jorguson is money laundering for either the mob or perhaps one of the drug cartels."

He smiled. "Maybe."

She switched gears. "Did you talk to Jorguson about his threat to have me killed? 'One phone call and you're a dead woman.' I believe those were his very words."

"He denied threatening you. When I mentioned the number of people who heard him, he said they were all mistaken. While he was spewing his ridiculous lies, his two attorneys' heads were nodding up and down like they were bobbing for apples. We happened to have a video from one of the waiters' cell phones and played it for him." He grinned as he added, "His expression was priceless."

"Bet he changed his story then."

Grayson nodded. "As a matter of fact,

he did. The alleged incident was all a big misunderstanding, and he was bluffing when he pretended to threaten you."

"He actually said he pretended to threaten me?"

"I can't make this stuff up," he said, laughing.

"What else did he say?"

"He'd love it if you would come work for him."

"The thought of seeing that pervert every single day sends shivers down my spine."

"Then that's a 'no'?"

They'd stopped at a red light, and Grayson glanced over at her with a warm smile. Olivia was suddenly tongue-tied, and her heart skipped a beat. She didn't know what to make of her physical reaction to him. She was usually so professional and composed, and this was a business evening, wasn't it?

"You're blushing," Grayson said. "How come?"

She didn't answer his question.

The light turned green, but Grayson didn't notice. When Olivia had turned in her seat to face him, the slit in her gown exposed part of her thigh. Her skin was golden, and he wondered if the rest of her was as flawless. The driver behind them honked, and Grayson's gaze was pulled back to his driving.

"Have you ever been to the Hamilton?" he asked.

"No, I haven't. It only just opened a couple of months ago. I've stayed at the one in Boston. It's beautiful and quite elegant. Have you been to this one?"

"Yes, I have. Aiden Hamilton threw a party a couple of weeks before the grand opening. I've known Aiden and his family for some time now. My cousin, Sam, helped on a case for Aiden's brother-in-law, Alec, and he introduced us. Sam and Alec are both FBI."

"How was the party?"

"Good," he said. "I ran into a lot of old friends I hadn't seen in a while. I was ready to take my date home when Alec suggested we play a little poker. I got home at six the next morning."

"And your date?"

"I took her home and came back for the game. She wasn't happy about that."

"Did you win any money?"

"Aiden decided to join us, so, no. When he plays, he wins. I lost the girl-friend and a lot of money. Had fun, though."

"You don't sound too broken up about the girlfriend."

"The relationship wasn't going any-where," he said. "And, hey, it was poker."

"And she didn't understand. I do," she said. "I love poker."

He raised an eyebrow. "Yeah? You really like to play?"

"I do."

"Any good?"

"I think I am."

He grinned. "We'll have to see about that."

They pulled into the circle drive in front of the hotel, ending the conversa-tion. Two attendants rushed forward to open their doors. Grayson's BMW was whisked away by the valet, and he took hold of Olivia's arm and walked by her side up the wide steps to the entrance.

The Hamilton Hotel faced Pennsylva-nia, a busy and noisy street, but as soon as they walked through the doors, Olivia felt as though she'd entered another world. There was a perfect blend of old-world charm and sleek contemporary touches. Massive columns stretched to the ceiling of a soaring lobby, and grand curved staircases on either side led to a wide mezzanine overlooking the main reception area. The polished brass balusters on the steps were topped with a carved railing of rich mahogany. Every table and chest was adorned with fresh flowers. Beautiful marble floors were covered in rich Oriental rugs, and the luxuriously upholstered furniture was overstuffed, inviting guests to linger and relax in this elegant and quiet setting, forgetting the turmoil and demands of the outside world.

All seven Hamilton Hotels were known for unparalleled luxury, absolute discretion, and impeccable service. The hotels catered to discriminating clientele and were dedicated to protecting privacy. Because of the chain's reputation for pampering guests and taking care of their every whim, dignitaries, politicians, lobbyists, and celebrities had already booked the four ballrooms in this hotel well into the future.

The Capitol League gala was being held in the largest ballroom, which was located on the first floor at the end of a long, wide corridor. Outside the large double doors leading into the ballroom was an open area with a magnificent fountain. Directly beyond were tall windows overlooking the serenity gardens.

Two Capitol League attendants stood side by side at the doors. Olivia pulled her invitation from her beaded clutch and handed it to one of them. Grayson noticed the man was so preoccupied staring at her, he barely glanced at the card.

There was already a crowd gathered inside, but the flow was good, and it was surprisingly easy to get from one side of the ballroom to the other.

Olivia hadn't attended many of these events. When she could afford it, she donated to causes that were close to her heart, most having to do with children in need, yet she rarely went to the parties, and for that reason she knew very few people attending the celebration.

Grayson, on the other hand, was the

man of the hour. He seemed to know everyone, or rather, most of the guests seemed to know him. He was immediately surrounded by friends and donors. A senator on the finance committee stopped to talk about his reelection campaign and to ask what Grayson thought about a certain stock. Olivia wasn't sure what to do. This wasn't exactly a date, so she didn't think she should stay and listen to his conversations with friends. Or should she? Feeling a bit awkward, she decided to find her aunt Emma, but when she tried to step away, Grayson took hold of her hand and pulled her into his side. He wasn't at all subtle. She gave him a disapproving frown. He responded by winking at her.

Olivia decided to be accommodating and humor him, and as it turned out, she was very happy she did. She soon lost count of the number of powerful men and women he introduced her to. She patiently stayed beside him for a good twenty minutes, smiling until her face felt frozen, and chatting amicably with the CEO of a cereal conglomerate, a Nobel Prize winner for physics, a real estate tycoon, an Internet software whiz, two art gallery owners, a couple of ambassadors, and a congresswoman. She even had a brief, though surreal, conversation with a senior adviser to the president of the United States. The topic was yoga, of all things.

The second there was a lull, Grayson suggested they go find her aunt. Then James Crowell stopped Grayson to say hello. Olivia recognized him from the cover of *Time*.

Crowell was Person of the Year and she believed it was a well-deserved honor. He was a genius and a self-made billionaire and, like Bill Gates and Warren Buffett, had donated most of his fortune to charity. Olivia was starstruck. Crowell was one of her heroes because of all of his humanitarian efforts. How did Grayson know him? It was obvious that Crowell liked Grayson, and from their conversation and their ease with each other, she concluded they had been friends for some time.

Just who was Agent Grayson Kincaid? The real Bruce Wayne?

Grayson watched Olivia as Crowell shook her hand and walked away.

"Your face is flushed," he remarked.

"I admire Mr. Crowell. He's done a lot for the poor in this country." She turned to Grayson and said, "May I ask you a question?"

"If it will get you to quit frowning, sure."

"I'm not frowning. This is my puzzled expression."

"Yeah? Good to know. What's the question?"

"You are with the FBI, aren't you? It isn't just a hobby, is it?"

He laughed. "Yes, I'm with the FBI, and no, it isn't a hobby."

"So if I were to look in your garage, I wouldn't find a Batmobile?"

He looked at her as though he thought she was crazy. Shaking his head and looking very serious, he said, "Of course not."

She felt foolish for making the comparison and for asking such a silly question.

Grayson put his arm around her waist and pulled her close so that an elderly couple could get past. Then he leaned down and whispered into her ear.

"I keep it in my cave."

EIGHT

Was there anyone Grayson didn't know?

"It's so good to see you again, Grayson," Aunt Emma said when they found her.

He took her hand and bent down so that she could kiss his cheek. "It's always good to see you, Emma."

"How is your father?"

"Doing well, thank you. He's sorry he couldn't be here tonight to celebrate with you, but he had another engagement he couldn't cancel. He sends you his best wishes."

Emma turned to Olivia. "I had no idea

you knew Grayson," she said to her niece, who was standing there with her mouth open in astonishment. Olivia gave Grayson a scolding glare for not telling her he was acquainted with her aunt, but before she could say anything, Emma continued, "You look lovely, dear." She kissed her on both cheeks. "I'm so pleased you're here."

Olivia thought her aunt looked radiant. She was a petite woman, just five feet three inches, and Olivia, at five feet six inches and in stilettos, towered over her. Emma had never had any face work done, but with her genes and her bone structure had aged beautifully. She had silver hair, cut short with just a hint of curl. She wore a silver floor-length gown, the cut simple and elegant. Her crystal clear eyes never missed anything, and her smile could melt the coldest of hearts.

Another acquaintance asked for a minute with Grayson, and while he was turned away, Olivia whispered to her aunt, "Are any of the others coming tonight?"

"The family? No," Emma answered. "They're all in New York."

"Have you spoken to my mother yet?"

"No, dear, I haven't. Now go and find your seats. The ceremony is about to start. I've been told that there won't be any long-winded speeches tonight, thank heavens. Three of us are receiving the Brinkley Humanitarian Award, and none of us feels we deserve it. It's . . . humbling," she admitted. "I tried to talk my way out of this, but the committee said this event could raise a lot of money, so here I am." She stepped closer and whispered, "Tomorrow I expect to hear all about how you met Grayson Kincaid. I always thought you and he would make a good match, but you're so stubborn about letting anyone interfere—"

She abruptly stopped when Grayson joined them. A few minutes later the ceremony began.

Olivia was so proud of her aunt. She was being honored for her contributions to the community, specifically for creating a medical scholarship for cancer research and for funding a new pediatric oncology ward at the children's hospital. Olivia knew how pleased Emma's late husband would be. When he died, Uncle Daniel left her with a large fortune, and she had put it to good use. From the response the audience gave after her considerable accomplishments were listed, it was apparent that Emma was well loved and appreciated by everyone.

As soon as the music started and couples headed to the dance floor, Olivia asked Grayson if he was ready to leave. He draped her wrap around her shoulders and followed her out of the ballroom.

Aiden Hamilton intercepted them just as they were crossing the lobby. He reminded Olivia of a model in *GQ*. Was everyone in Grayson's life perfection? Impeccably dressed, Aiden looked as though the tuxedo had been invented with him in mind. He was tall and terribly fit, and he approached them with a wide smile. The greeting between the two men was a bit humorous. Grayson slapped Aiden on his shoulder, and

Aiden retaliated in kind. Then they shook hands like gentlemen.

Grayson introduced Olivia to his friend, and after pleasantries were exchanged, Grayson asked him, "How long are you in town?"

"Just overnight," he answered. "I leave for Sydney first thing in the morning."

"Are you building another hotel?"

Aiden nodded. "Hopefully," he said. "We built one in Melbourne and didn't run into any problems, but we're having trouble with permits in Sydney. It will work out," he added. "What about you, Grayson? Still working twenty-four/ seven?"

He shrugged. "Pretty much."

"I wish we had time for a poker game," Aiden said. "I'm sure you still have a few dollars left for me to win."

"Your luck is bound to run out some-day, Hamilton," Grayson countered. "I'll get my revenge."

Aiden turned to Olivia. "Sorry to bore you with this chatter," he apologized. "I'm sure you don't want to hear about our poker games."

"Actually, Olivia is quite a poker player, too," Grayson said.

Aiden looked at her admiringly. "Is that so?"

"I learned when I was a little girl," she explained. "My friends and I loved to play. We haven't had much opportunity lately."

"Then perhaps the next time I'm in town, you can join us," Aiden offered. He smiled warmly and took her hand. "It was a pleasure meeting you."

Grayson pulled her hand away. "We were just leaving," he said abruptly. He put his arm around Olivia's shoulder and turned her toward the door. She nearly tripped, trying to keep up with him.

Olivia thought that Aiden Hamilton was one of the most attractive men she'd ever met. He was a real charmer who, no doubt, could have any woman he wanted, whenever he wanted, but she didn't see a reason for Grayson to be jealous. In her mind, he was much sexier.

Once they were in the car and on their way, she asked, "Tonight . . . how did you know all those people?"

"I run into them now and then at different events, and I don't know all of them, just some."

But you do run in their circle, she thought. He was so at ease with the movers and shakers in D.C., and she realized, there wasn't any question, she was completely out of his league.

"Thank you for introducing me to James Crowell. It was the highlight of the night for me."

Grayson thought about all the people he had introduced her to, including several A-list celebrities, and yet she was most impressed by a short, skinny, balding man who, without seeking publicity or fanfare, had made a real difference in the world. The fact that she recognized what Crowell had done made Grayson like her all the more.

"The men and women who met you tonight, including James Crowell, won't forget you because, frankly, you're pretty unforgettable, Olivia, and if there are cutbacks and you have to leave your current job, you have a connection with all of them."

"You were networking," she said.

He shook his head. "No, *you* were networking. You just didn't realize it."

She didn't know how to react. She wasn't used to people doing nice things for her, at least not lately. "Then tonight was about helping me."

He nodded. "And clearing up a few details about your interview with Jorguson."

"Right, Jorguson. Our discussion could have been done over the phone, couldn't it?"

"Yes," he admitted. "But this was more fun."

She agreed. "Then thank you. I did have fun tonight. Meeting James Crowell was a dream come true."

He laughed. "Yeah?"

Grayson loosened his tie as he steered the car into traffic. He didn't say anything for several minutes and seemed perfectly relaxed. He was a real enigma, a man who was just as comfortable tackling thugs as he was socializing with the rich and powerful.

Olivia wasn't good at small talk, and the silence was making her feel uneasy. She took a breath and blurted, "You make me nervous, but you know that, don't you?"

"Uh-huh."

She expected him to ask her why he made her nervous and wondered what she would tell him, but he didn't ask. Maybe he knew why and could explain it to her. She really had enjoyed herself tonight. It had been a long time since she had gotten all dressed up and gone out with such a handsome man. A long, long time.

She should get into the game, she thought. Then she remembered her father and what was coming, and she pushed the notion of getting involved with any man aside.

Her cell phone rang. She didn't recognize the number.

"This is Olivia MacKenzie."

One of her clients was on the line. "Olivia, it's Tyler." The voice was hushed and brimming with fear. He had said her name once, and so she put up one finger. "Everything's fine, Olivia." Two fingers up. "I just wanted you to know that I'm back home with my uncle and aunt, Olivia, and everything is okay."

She heard someone speaking in the background, and then Tyler said, "They don't want you to worry and have to look for me. You won't, will you?"

"Now that I know you're okay, Tyler," she said, deliberately saying his name so he would know she understood the threat, "I won't worry."

"I've got to hang up now." His voice dropped to a whisper. "He just went into the kitchen. There are two other men here, and they're really mad. They say my uncle wants too much money. They have guns, Olivia. I'm so scared . . . should I hide? I'm going to hide."

"I'm on my way."

The line went dead. Olivia quickly found the address recorded in her phone and rattled it off to Grayson. "A little boy is in danger," she said and then repeated what Tyler had told her. "I'm sorry, there isn't time for you to take me home so I can get my car. Besides, I'm going to need your help. We have to get there quickly."

"Call nine-one-one and request a squad car to meet us."

Grayson had pulled onto the ramp

and was now blazing down the expressway. He also called for backup and was patched through to his partner, Agent Ronan Conrad.

"Ronan, where are you?"

"On my way home. What do you need?"

Grayson told him where he was headed and filled him in on the situation. "I'm on my way," Ronan answered.

"We'll be there in five minutes," Grayson said.

"Make it faster," Olivia urged, her voice strained. "Five minutes might be too long."

He pushed the accelerator. "Tell me about Tyler."

"He's ten years old and was removed from his uncle's house and put in a safe house. The Purdys—the uncle and the aunt—are drug dealers, and they were using Tyler to deliver the product."

"Which is?"

"Cocaine and meth. Mostly meth these days," she added. "The aunt and uncle are twisted. The aunt has this thing about blood and family. Inside that sick mind of hers she believes she owns Tyler now that his parents are in prison."

"It doesn't sound like the kid ever had a chance," he remarked.

"Judge Bowen was his savior. He put Tyler with a good family and severed all parental rights. The aunt and uncle were never given custody, and there's a restraining order, but that means nothing to them."

"Why did you hold up three fingers?"

"That's the number of times he said my name. It's a code the kids and I have. If he says my name once, I know he's in trouble. The more times he says it, the more dangerous the situation. I never know who might be there with him listening or coaxing him when he's talking to me."

"Have you ever been called when it wasn't an emergency?"

"No, never," she said emphatically. "These kids understand real danger, and they wouldn't exaggerate. There's too much at stake to cry wolf."

The neighborhood they drove into was in the heart of gang territory. A few of the owners of the cookie-cutter houses had at one time tried to keep up maintenance, but the vast majority had let their homes go to seed. Half of them had already been abandoned and condemned. Grayson drove past a house that was falling apart. One side of the porch had collapsed, and the front lawn had been turned into a junkyard. There was a rusted-out washing machine and a stripped-down motorcycle blocking the broken sidewalk. It was impossible to tell if there was any grass because every inch of the yard was layered with trash. The air smelled of mildew, rotting garbage, and despair.

Three blocks west was the Purdy house. Grayson slammed on the brakes, threw the car in park, and said, "Stay in the car, Olivia." His voice was calm, almost soothing.

He pulled his tie off and tossed it on the seat as he got out of the car. His jacket followed. Opening the trunk, he reached for his bulletproof vest and slipped it on. He was adjusting the Velcro straps when Ronan arrived. He took the corner on two wheels and came to a hard stop inches from Grayson's car.

Grabbing his vest, he walked over to Grayson, saw Olivia, and nodded to her.

"How many inside?"

"Four adults, but there could be more."

They could hear sirens wailing in the distance. "Are we waiting for additional backup?"

"No, there's a boy inside. We can't wait."

Grayson bent down to look at Olivia and once again ordered her to stay inside the car.

"Be careful," she said. "I've been to court with these people. They're . . . sadistic."

His nod indicated he'd heard her. He pulled his gun free, and with Ronan at his side headed to the house.

The streetlights were dim, but Olivia could see that the Purdy house should have been condemned years ago. At least half of the shingles were missing from the sagging roof, and the aluminum siding had been torn off both sides. The wood on the front porch looked as though it had been torched, and there were holes in the porch floor. In the shadows, she could just make out Grayson kicking in the front door.

Olivia didn't realize she was holding her breath until her chest started to hurt. Two shots were fired in rapid succession, then another and another. A man came running around the side of the house. He had a gun in his hand and was glancing over his shoulder. He appeared to be young, in his late teens. Dressed in a filthy tank top and jeans, he had a crazed look in his eyes.

He headed to the street but didn't make it. Ronan came at him from one direction, and Grayson from the other. The man fired wild, and a second later they had him facedown in the dirt.

Two squad cars arrived. The policemen ran to Grayson, and after he filled them in, they rushed into the house.

Where was Tyler? Was he safe? He knew to hide, but would he come out for the FBI or the police?

Olivia glanced in the rearview mirror and saw three men she was pretty sure were gang members. They were half a block away and were walking toward her. One of them picked up a board from the gutter, but an older man in the middle of the three shook his head, and the board was immediately tossed back into the street. Were the three simply curious to know what was going on, or were they wanting a fight?

The police brought out two of the most frightening-looking men Olivia had ever seen. They were handcuffed and shouting for lawyers. Odd how even the most drugged degenerates with burned-out brains still understood the law and knew how to manipulate it. Odd and disgusting.

Grayson and Ronan were both talking to a policeman, but she noticed their gazes were locked on the group that had stopped in the street a couple of houses away. Their number had in-creased from three to six. A child, no older than six or seven, ran down the street to join them.

Olivia watched as the leader of the group grabbed the little boy by the arm and pivoted him in the opposite direc-tion, yelling, "Marcus, I told you to stay inside. Now, go home."

The boy started to protest, but when

the older man gave him a hard shove, he reluctantly walked away with slouched shoulders, dragging his feet.

Olivia turned back to the house and saw something moving on the roof. Oh God, it was Tyler. In the moonlight she could see him creeping along the ridge.

She flew out of the car and called to Grayson. "Tyler's on the roof."

Grayson rushed back inside, and a minute later he was reaching for Tyler from the second-story window. The boy wouldn't budge, but when Grayson pointed to Olivia, he began to inch his way down the slope.

While she waited for them, yet another squad car arrived. When one of the policemen asked how many bodies were inside, Ronan answered, "Two in the kitchen, one male, one female."

The front door opened, and Tyler flew across the porch and down the stairs. He ran to Olivia and nearly knocked her off her feet when he threw himself into her arms.

She hugged him tight. "Are you all right? They didn't hurt you, did they?"

His head was tucked under her chin,

his voice muffled when he answered. She could feel him trembling, and he was crying softly.

"I did it the right way, didn't I?" he asked. "I said your name when I called you on the phone, just like you told me to if I was in trouble."

"Yes, you did it just the way we practiced. You're very brave, Tyler."

"I knew you'd come for me."

"Of course. Are you ready to let go of me yet?"

He stepped back. "You smell good. How come you're all dressed up?"

As she walked to Grayson's car and opened the back door for him, she explained that her aunt had received a special award.

One of the gang members who had been watching shouted to Tyler. "Is she going to put you in juvie?"

Another yelled, "What'd you do, kid?"

Tyler turned to the group. "I'm not going to juvie, and I didn't do anything wrong." He pointed to Olivia and said, "She's my lawyer. I called her, and she came right away. She's taking me back to my new home." His voice was filled with pride.

The leader of the group, a hard-looking man who was probably still in his twenties but looked fifty, motioned to his friends to stay where they were as he walked over to Olivia. Grayson was suddenly standing in front of her.

The man stepped to the side so that he could see Olivia and asked, "Are you really his lawyer?"

"Yes," she answered. "I'm Tyler's attorney."

The man glanced warily at Grayson, then said, "Uh . . . do you have any cards on you with your phone number in case one of us needs a lawyer? I didn't like my last one. He didn't do anything to help me."

She didn't know how to answer him. The thought of representing a gang member made her shudder.

Although he didn't realize it, Tyler came to her rescue. "You have to go through court to get her," he said, sounding very grown-up. "The judge gave her to me."

The explanation seemed plausible to the man. He nodded and headed back to his friends. He suddenly stopped, then turned to Grayson. "You got the kid out just in time. Another couple of hours would have been too late. Those fools decided they would make their own meth. Cut out the middleman," he added. "They were going to start cooking tonight. They would have blown themselves up and taken the kid with them."

Grayson wanted to get the boy away before the bodies were carried out. He and Ronan had surprised the aunt and the uncle when they burst into the house. Startled, the woman had thrown a meat cleaver at them and then she and the uncle reached for their guns and began shooting. Grayson heard Ronan mutter, "Son of a bitch," a scant second before he shot her.

Olivia waited while Grayson and Ronan wrapped up things with the police. She had put Tyler in the backseat. After he'd snapped on the seat belt, she'd covered him with Grayson's jacket.

Clearly exhausted, the child was sound asleep minutes later.

She called the foster mother and filled her in on what had happened, assured her that Tyler was all right, and estimated that she'd have him back home within an hour.

When they were finally on their way, Grayson said, "One of the policemen told me they'd been to the aunt and uncle's house this evening looking for Tyler. They searched the house but couldn't find him. The foster mother reported him missing when he didn't come home in the carpool from soccer practice."

"The aunt was probably waiting to grab him," she said. She looked back at Tyler to make sure he was sleeping and then asked in a whisper, "Are they both dead?"

"Yes."

She was pleased he didn't embellish. "I shouldn't feel relieved, should I? It's just that they were such vicious people, and they wouldn't have left Tyler alone. The drugs made them evil."

He shook his head. "No, they were already evil. Drugs made them bolder. Does Tyler like where he's living now?"

"Oh yes, very much," she said. "The foster mother is a loving woman. He's very comfortable there."

"Would he tell you if he weren't?"

"We've got a secret code for that, too."

As they drove toward Tyler's new home, Olivia was thinking how fortunate it was that Grayson had been with her tonight.

"I'm glad you were with me. It made it so much easier. Thank you."

He pulled onto the expressway and cut over to the middle lane. "You're welcome. Tell me, what would you have done if you'd been home when Tyler called? You told me there wasn't time for me to take you home to get your car. Would you have driven into that neighborhood alone?"

She knew he wouldn't like the answer. "I always call for backup," she said. "And usually the squad car beats me to the address."

"But not always?"

"No, not always."

His frown was fierce. "What about to-night? What would you have done?"

"Tyler was on the roof. I would have signaled to him not to move because the roof wasn't stable. Then I would have figured out a way to get him down."

"What if he was inside the house, and you heard him screaming?" he asked. "Then what?"

She didn't hesitate to answer. "I would have gone in after him."

Even though Grayson knew that's what she was going to say, it still infuriated him.

"No training, no weapon . . . what would you have done? Shout at them?"

"If I heard Tyler scream, I would have gone in," she insisted. "And so would you."

Only after she made that statement did she realize how foolish it was.

"Of course I would have," he snapped. "I've been trained for situations like this, and I carry a weapon."

"This conversation is ridiculous. Tyler's

safe, and that's all that counts. It all worked out."

He wasn't ready to let it go. "It's amazing you're still alive."

He had no idea how truthful that remark was. "Yes, it is," she agreed.

"You've never been close to death, and maybe that's why you're such an optimist."

Never been near death? Try two years' worth, she thought. And optimistic? Her friends were constantly telling her she was too negative. What would Grayson think if he knew this about her?

The discussion finally ended when they reached the foster home. Grayson carried Tyler inside and put him in his bed. The child never opened his eyes.

It was three in the morning by the time they reached Olivia's apartment. Unaccustomed to such late hours, Olivia was exhausted. Grayson, on the other hand, looked as though he'd just started the evening.

He parked in front of her building. The doorman rushed outside to tell him he had to move his car, but then he saw

the weapon at his side and stepped
back.

"It's all right, John. He's with the FBI,"
Olivia said.

"Is everything okay, Miss MacKenzie?"

"Yes. Everything's fine," she said. She
stopped at the elevator and turned to
Grayson. "You don't have to come up
with me."

"Sure I do."

He pinned her to the wall when he
reached around her to push the button.

"You're still nervous with me, aren't
you?"

She looked up into his eyes. She was
barely inches away from him. All she
had to do was tilt her head ever so
slightly and lean in, and she'd be kissing
him. She didn't give in to the urge.

"No. I'm no longer nervous with you."
It was a blatant lie, but she thought she'd
told it well.

He wasn't buying it. He flashed that
adorable smile again. He could get anything he wanted with that smile, she
thought. And probably did. That reminder helped. She knew women threw

themselves at him, but she wouldn't be one of them. He wasn't her type.

She laughed. Talk about a whopper of a lie. That was the big daddy of them all.

The elevator doors opened on three. He stepped back to let her out first, then followed.

"What's so funny?"

"I was just thinking you're not my type, and that was funny to me because . . ."

"Yes?"

"Because you are."

He frowned. "Your type?"

You're every woman's type, she thought. She didn't tell him that, thank God. Instead, she said, "I'm tired. I'm not making much sense."

Her apartment was at the end of the hall. She got her keys out of her purse and unlocked the door. Grayson pushed it open and backed her inside. His eyes never left hers as he put his arms around her.

"I had a lovely time tonight," she said, remembering the awards gala. "It was really nice . . ." She realized what she was saying. "Except for the two people you had to shoot and except for . . . Oh God, Grayson, just kiss me. I won't stop talking until you do."

He pulled her closer, and his lips brushed over hers. It was a quick middle-school kind of kiss, a prelude, she quickly realized, to driving her out of her mind. As soon as she put her arms around his neck, he stopped teasing her. His mouth opened and his tongue delved inside to rub against hers. She tightened her hold. His mouth was doing magical things to her, and every nerve in her body reacted. It was the most erotic kiss she'd ever experienced, and she never wanted it to end. He made love to her with his tongue, and when he lifted his head he could have taken anything he wanted.

She sagged against him. Taking a deep breath, she let go of him and stepped back so he could leave, even though she wanted him to kiss her again. She wanted . . . him.

"Be sure to lock the door," he said in parting. His voice was a rough whisper.

And he was gone. Her hand shook as she flipped the deadbolt. She kicked her shoes off, walked into the bedroom, and dropped down on the bed.

She knew she was going to be thinking about that kiss for a long time, and she wondered . . . had it meant anything to him?

NINE

Olivia was having a lazy Sunday afternoon. She read *The Washington Post* and *The New York Times,* did two crossword puzzles, played three games of Words with Friends on her iPhone, and was now talking to Samantha and Collins on a conference call to give them an update on Jane. It had been two months since her last transfusion, and she was back in the hospital again.

Although she didn't mention Grayson Kincaid to them, Olivia couldn't stop thinking about him. She wasn't sure why she didn't tell them about him. Maybe it was because she didn't want to make a big deal of their relationship. Besides, there really wasn't anything to tell, was there? In the two months since the awards gala, he hadn't called her. Of course, he never said he would. In fact, his last words to her were a reminder to lock her door. How romantic was that?

At the very least, he owed her an update on Jorguson. She hadn't heard a word about the investigation.

For the first full week after their alleged date, she was certain he'd get in touch with her. The second week she convinced herself that he was too busy to call but that he would eventually get around to it. After three full weeks had passed and not a word, she decided hell would freeze over before she went out with him. She had wasted enough time thinking about him and vowed she wouldn't spend one more second remembering that amazing kiss. Yeah, right. That was pretty much still all she could think about.

Would he have kissed her if she hadn't asked him to? Now that was the million-dollar question.

Olivia realized she was daydreaming again while she was still on the conference call. Sam and Collins were discussing Jane's medical issues, and she forced herself to pay attention.

"Why didn't the last transfusion help?" Collins asked.

"How do you know it didn't?" Olivia said.

"Because she's back in the hospital," Sam pointed out.

"Dr. Pardieu told Jane he wanted to run a couple of tests, that's all. He insists he's not worried, and we trust him, don't we?"

"Of course we do," Sam said. "We wouldn't be here if it weren't for him. I'm sorry I can't give her blood."

"We all have the same blood type," Collins reminded. "That's why we were put in the experimental program. I don't understand why Dr. Pardieu won't take some of ours, Sam."

"Mine just happens to work better for her," Olivia answered. "You know, if you're so worried, you could talk to Jane about this."

"Isn't it too soon for you to give blood again?" Sam asked.

"No," Olivia assured. "It's been almost eight weeks. If she needs it again, there wouldn't be a problem."

"I wish I were there. I can tell how Jane's feeling just by looking at her."

"She's going to be fine," Collins insisted. "But you know the last thing she needs now is stress. Olivia, Sam told me that creepy brother of hers is hanging around again."

"Actually, Logan is really trying this time. I think he might make it. He lives in a halfway house, and he's working. Jane says he hasn't missed a single day."

"That's different," Collins admitted.

"He cares about Jane, and he's trying to make up for all the pain he's caused."

"That will take a lifetime," Sam said.

"If Jane can forgive him, we can, too," Olivia said. "She went back into the hospital last week, and Logan has been there every day. He comes to see her on his lunch hour and after work. When she's home, he brings her dinner. He's trying, Sam."

"Okay, I'll give him another chance," Sam said. "Listen, I've got to go. Quickly, Olivia, tell me how your search is going."

"I can't get access to my father's records, so I've run into another dead end," she answered. "I have been able to get copies of some of the statements for his fund, though, and reading them is like gazing at the stars and trying to identify each one. There are lists of thousands of investments. Some of them I recognize as legitimate but the rest are really obscure. It appears that there are a great many in foreign countries. It also appears that the portfolio changes constantly. I swear he's Houdini. He might be committing the perfect crime because I can't find the fraud."

"You can't find it *yet*," Collins said. "There's no such thing as a perfect crime. At least that's what they tell me."

"Are you still determined to become an FBI agent?" Olivia asked.

"Yes," she answered emphatically. "And I think I'll be a good one."

"When do you begin your training?" Sam asked.

"I'm still waiting to hear. I know the academy will be a challenge, so I've decided to get a head start. I've been going to a firing range to get some practice."

"Have you shot anyone yet?" Sam asked with feigned alarm.

"Of course not," Collins answered indignantly, "but there have been a couple of close calls."

She shared a few stories about her first experiences with a firearm. By the time the friends ended their conversation, she had them laughing uproariously.

Olivia had just disconnected the call when another came in. Her boss, Royal Thurman, was on the line. He had never called her at home before, and an alarm was sounding inside her head. Something bad was coming, she thought.

"There's a problem I need to discuss with you," he began in his deep baritone voice. "Do you have any time this afternoon? My wife and daughters are shopping at Tysons Corner, but they're going to meet me for dinner at Neeson's Café at six. My girls love their macaroni and cheese. The restaurant is quite close to you, isn't it?"

"Yes, sir, it is."

"Could you stop by the café at five? It's important, Olivia, or I wouldn't bother you at home."

She didn't ask him to explain what the problem was or even to give her a hint. She was supposed to have dinner with her aunt, but Emma had decided to go to Palm Springs early for a seminar to get away from the cold.

"I'll be there," she told him.

Don't borrow trouble, she warned herself. The nurses used to say that to her when she was worried about the results of one of her tests. And for a long while, the results had been bad. It didn't seem to matter if she borrowed trouble or not. She took a deep breath. This wasn't the chemo isolation unit, and she was now an adult. If Thurman was going to fire her or let her go because of cutbacks, so be it. She'd find another job. But wouldn't he do it during office hours?

Olivia had told her boss about her horrid interview with Jorguson. He hadn't laughed, but she could tell he wanted to. He'd assured her that, when the cut-backs came, he would do everything he could to protect her.

Maybe that had changed.

Fortunately, she didn't have long to stew about all the possibilities for the meeting. It was already three thirty. She jumped into the shower, washed and dried her hair, and pulled it back in a ponytail. She dressed in a heavy, dark green sweater, skinny jeans, and knee-high boots. She even took time to put on some makeup and dab perfume on her wrists.

She pulled on her heavy sheepskin coat, a bright red wool scarf, a knit cap, and gloves. The inside of her coat had a large pocket, so she put a credit card in it, added her driver's license, three twenty-dollar bills, her cell phone, and her keys. She zipped the pocket closed and headed to the elevator.

John was on duty in the lobby. "It's awful cold out there," he warned.

"I'm going to Neeson's to meet my boss," she said. "It's close."

"I love Neeson's. They've got the best

mac and cheese in the city. My stomach's grumbling just thinking about it."

"Would you like me to bring you some?"

"Oh no, no. I wasn't hinting." He opened the door for her.

"I'll get you some," she promised as she walked past.

The blast of frigid air entering her lungs as she stepped outside reminded her that she'd left her inhaler in her apartment. She turned to run back up to get it but changed her mind. Neeson's Café was six short blocks away from her building, and if she took her time, she'd be fine. She didn't want to keep Mr. Thurman waiting.

By the time she was halfway to the restaurant, she was frozen solid. It was bitterly cold, and there was a wet, blustery wind. The lighted display on the bank across the street said it was eighteen degrees. She increased her pace the last two blocks. When she walked into the tiny vestibule, the warm air stung her cheeks, and her lungs felt like they were burning.

Although she was ten minutes early,

Mr. Thurman was already there in a large booth in the back of the nearly empty restaurant. He looked relieved to see her. It was bad, all right. She reminded herself not to borrow trouble and almost laughed at the notion.

Mr. Thurman, the ultimate gentleman, helped her with her coat and hung it up for her, then waited until she was seated before he slid into the booth across from her. He pushed his empty coffee cup to the side and stacked his big hands on the table. When a waitress came over with a coffeepot and refilled his cup, Olivia requested hot tea and an order of mac and cheese to go.

"I'll get right to it," Thurman said. "I was about to sit down for Sunday breakfast when I received a call from Carl Simmons of Simmons, Simmons and Falcon. You're familiar with the law firm?"

"Oh yes."

"I wasn't," he said. "I mean to say, I'd heard of the firm, but I'd never had a conversation with any of them until today. You can guess what the topic was."

She smiled. "Me."

"Exactly so," he said. "You must also

know that the firm represents your father."

"Yes, I know. But why would he call
you?"

"Carl . . ." He paused to smile and
said, "He insisted I call him by his first
name because he's certain we will become good friends who—according to
him—will help each other. I could almost
hear him winking over the phone," he
added. "I didn't care for the man one
little bit."

"What did he want?"

"He felt it was his duty to warn me
about you. He believes you may be
abusing your position as counsel for the
IRS. I asked him what proof he had,
knowing full well there wasn't any, and
he hemmed and hawed. Then he got to
his obvious agenda. He specifically
mentioned your father. Simmons believes you're trying to manufacture evidence to discredit him. If that happens,
his investors will lose faith in him, and
before you know it, they'll remove their
money, and his fund will go belly up."

"And it will be all my fault."

"Exactly so."

"I'm not manufacturing evidence, sir."

"I know that, Olivia," he said, his voice kind and sympathetic. "I'm merely repeating what he said to me."

"I've worked on cases I've been assigned and only those cases," she assured him. "I certainly haven't looked at my father's file. That would be illegal, and besides, what would be the point? It's all a fairy tale. I came to the IRS to learn."

"You told me about your father before I hired you, remember? You do exceptional work. Researching your father's dealings outside of your job hasn't interfered with that."

"But?"

"But I want you to be ready for what's coming. Simmons hinted . . . strongly hinted," he stressed, "that you were mentally unstable and needed help. He also suggested that your family is determined to see that you get it. He kept saying 'in my opinion' and seemed to think slandering you is perfectly okay if he's only giving his opinion."

"That's a new tactic."

"He didn't come right out and say that

you're unfit, but I'll tell you, Olivia, he's going to try to get you fired. He'll go over my head, but I don't think he'll be successful. If what you say is true about your father's investment fund, I'm guessing that Simmons is raking in profits right along with him. He isn't going to let you ruin it for him. He's shrewd, all right. He'll get out right before the bubble bursts. I've seen it before, and it saddens me to say I know I'll see it again. Greed has a way of overtaking morals."

The hot tea was placed in front of her along with a carryout bag. She thanked the waitress and handed her a twenty-dollar bill.

She stared out the window and wasn't surprised to see snow falling. "I can't find anything," she whispered.

"Could your judgment be impaired because of past experiences with your father? Could you be wrong about him now? What if he's innocent? Have you considered that he might have learned some valuable lessons over the years and has made up his mind to be honest in his dealings? Your father is thought by many to have a special knack when it comes to picking stocks. His portfolio performance is quite impressive."

She wondered if he realized how naive he sounded. "No, I don't believe he's learned any lessons. I think he's just gotten better at hiding his crimes."

"From what I've heard, his fund has gone through the roof," he pointed out. "His clients have made enormous profits."

"Oh, sir, you aren't one of his clients, are you?"

He laughed. "And suffer your wrath? No, of course not. I just want you to consider the possibility that your father might be a changed man."

Mr. Thurman wasn't familiar with the details of her father's history. He, therefore, wasn't convinced that her father was doing anything wrong, and she didn't have any evidence to prove that he was. Still, her boss was loyal to her. After pointing out the possibility that she could be mistaken, he let it go.

His family arrived promptly at six. They asked her to have dinner with them, but she declined, explaining she had made plans to see her friend who was in the hospital.

"We're supposed to get snow tonight," Mr. Thurman said. "If you have to drive, be careful."

Olivia counted herself lucky to have such a great boss. He genuinely cared about her. She knew he was trying to protect her from being laid off, and now he was trying to help her with the Carl Simmons situation.

She had just left the restaurant when her cell phone rang. She stepped back inside the warm entry to answer.

Judge Bowen was on the line. "Olivia, I just received a call from an attorney named Carl Simmons . . ."

"Oh no. What did he say?" she asked. "No, let me guess. In his opinion, I'm unstable and making things up."

The judge chuckled. "Yes, he did say something like that, though he did coat it with his concern for you and the well-being of any children who may be in your charge. He was playing me, Olivia, and you know how much I hate that. He didn't come right out and say it, but he implied that you were unfit, and he felt it was his duty to caution me. He said the occasional case I give you involves vulnerable children, and I should be aware that, because of your fragile state of mind, if anything were to happen to one of the children, I could be held responsible. Did you know you're about to have a nervous breakdown?"

"No, I didn't," she replied.

"Of course, Simmons insisted that he was telling me this in the strictest of confidence," he said with obvious disgust. "He added that your father is being urged to have you committed for a seventy-two-hour evaluation."

Olivia was shaking with anger. "I'm so sorry you were dragged into this."

"I know what this is all about. Simmons's firm represents your father . . ."

"That's right."

"And you're probing."

"Yes, I am."

"I warned Simmons you could sue him for slander, and he assured me that it would never happen. He said he was only trying to protect the innocent, and that he had proof of your irrational acts. He brought up a couple of names. Just a second . . . I wrote them down." He paused and she heard papers rustling. "Here they are: a Frank Greeley and a Kimberly Mills . . ."

She had to think for a second. "Yes," she said. "They were involved in two different cases I handled for Judge Thorpe. Greeley was a real hothead. He claimed that I had manufactured lies that he was an abusive father. 'Crazed with power' I believe were his words. Of course, the bruises and welts on his four-year-old little girl didn't give him much credibility. Mills also called me crazy. She had been called to the office for a meeting about an abuse charge. I happened to walk in just as she'd grabbed her little boy and was about to backhand him. I knocked her down, and she began screaming that I was a lunatic. In both instances, the parents filed a complaint, but nothing came of them. It would take some fancy footwork for Simmons to create a case."

"There's more, Olivia."

She rubbed her temple and took a deep breath to calm down. "Yes?"

"He also alluded to drugs you had taken in the past that may have had a lasting effect on your mental state and impaired your judgment."

She was speechless.

"Olivia?"

"Yes?"

"I know you're a private person, and I hate asking, but was there ever a time . . ."

"The drugs?"

"Yes."

"When I was a child, I went through chemotherapy."

The judge was outraged on her behalf. "If you can find grounds to sue him, I'll testify," he said. "I'd love to see you tie up all his firm's assets and paralyze them."

"I don't know if that will happen, but thank you for your support," she responded.

"I think I'll give Judge Thorpe a call and give him a heads-up. He'll probably get a real kick out of the drug accusation."

Once she got past her anger, Olivia realized she shouldn't have been surprised that Carl Simmons had contacted Mr. Thurman and Judge Bowen. The slimeball had been calling her on a regular basis and threatening her. The scare tactics weren't working, though, and that must have been exceedingly frustrating for Carl. It was a natural progression to go to her employers. Poke the bear, he's bound to attack. And she'd certainly been poking and prodding. Of course they would retaliate.

It was a pity he hadn't come right out and slandered her. According to Judge Bowen, Simmons came close a couple of times, but the creep knew what he was doing. Olivia understood his plan. He would try to discredit her, destroy her reputation, and attack her character. She also knew that the next attack would be even more despicable but within the law.

Slimeball was smart, but she was smarter, she told herself. Eventually she would nail him for his part in ripping off innocent people, stealing their life savings, while he was living the high life. His day in court was coming.

She pulled her coat collar up around her neck, adjusted the scarf, and started walking home. The snow was coming down in sheets, and there was already more than an inch on the sidewalk. Had the temperature dropped? She couldn't make out the numbers on the bank, but she thought it felt colder because her face was stinging, and her lungs struggled to take in the frozen air. She tugged on her scarf and pulled it up over her mouth and nose. Why hadn't she gone back for her inhaler? She would love to sprint home, but she couldn't. Her chest was already tight, and she was wheezing. She had to slow the pace.

There wasn't any traffic, and she was the only person on the street. The snow was swirling down all around her, and the only sound was the gushing wind. The streetlights looked like they were covered in gauze. As bitterly cold as it was, she thought it was beautiful. Her street looked like a holiday greeting card. Everything was so clean and white, and all the little lights in the windows of the apartments were glowing. It was almost magical.

Being the pessimist that she was, she reminded herself that tomorrow it would all be a mess. Slush from cars would splatter against the windows, and the snow would turn brown and gray from being trod upon. But tonight it was pretty.

No way she was going to drive to the hospital, though. She had already slipped twice crossing streets, and people—including her—were crazy when they drove in snow. Olivia decided she'd make herself a cup of hot tea and call Jane to check on her. She didn't feel guilty. She was going to see her friend tomorrow after work when she donated more blood for her. They'd have a nice chat then.

There was an SUV illegally parked at the end of the block. Though she couldn't see him, she knew the driver was inside because the motor was running and the windshield wipers were moving. Must be waiting for someone, she thought as she crossed the street and hurried on. She switched the carryout bag from one arm to the other and tried to take a deep breath. She could really use her inhaler now. The green awning over the entrance of her building was weighed down by the snow. She could tell the walkway had been shoveled, but it was quickly filling up with fresh flakes.

She was almost home when she heard an odd popping sound. She pictured a giant champagne bottle being uncorked. Out of the corner of her eye, she saw the SUV coming toward her. Then she saw John through the window of her apartment building. He was standing behind his desk. He smiled when he spotted her and hurried to unlock the door.

All of a sudden there was rapid gunfire, bullets whizzing all around her. She understood what was happening and knew she needed to get to safety, but her legs wouldn't cooperate. She felt an excruciating jolt of pain in her thigh, then another jolt near her shoulder that was so forceful it knocked her back. The third jolt sent her spinning into the wall. Her head slammed against the brick, and her body crumpled to the ground.

The world began to reel in a chaotic blur, with images of snow and lights and brown bags flying through the air. She tried to get up, but a dizzying fog rolled over her, and everything went black.

TEN

She made the ten o'clock news.

Grayson had the television on and was half listening to the end of a *Dateline* interview with a congressional lobbyist while he finished his third report on his laptop. He hit the "send" button and closed the lid. It was Sunday evening, and he was only now finishing work.

He put the laptop back in his briefcase on the table next to his nephew's school backpack. In the two months since Henry had come to live with him, Grayson's apartment had lost all semblance of order. The backpack was lying open; papers were sticking out every which way, and the report on volcanoes that was due tomorrow wasn't there. Grayson searched the living room, then went back into the den. He tripped over some Legos and a remote-control robot Henry was building, and found the report on the sofa, half hidden under Henry's tennis shoes.

Grayson made sure the entire report was there, then put it back in the yellow folder and added it to the papers he'd already straightened inside the backpack. The child would probably still lose at least one assignment before he got to class if history was any indication, but he was getting better at organization. He no longer left his backpack in the car.

Grayson went into his bedroom and was about to change out of his jeans and sweater when he heard the newscaster say that a young woman had been gunned down in front of her apartment building. A conversation about the city came back to Grayson. Washington, D.C., could be a dangerous place to live, and one had to be careful, but the energy here made the city irresistible. Hadn't Olivia said that? He smiled remembering.

A day didn't go by that he didn't think about her, and if his life hadn't gotten so damned complicated, he thought he'd most likely be with her right now.

He picked up the remote to turn up the volume. The lead into the news was over and a commercial was playing. He stood in front of the flat screen and waited. He assumed the shooting had something to do with the gang war going on, and he was curious to know where it happened.

Then Ted on Channel 12 announced that he was reporting live from Georgetown. Grayson stopped breathing. "Ah, hell," he whispered. "Don't let it be Olivia." The sick feeling in his gut contradicted the hope. He told himself he was overreacting. It had been two months since Jorguson had threatened her, but he had calmed down since then.

The newscaster said the name of the street, then the camera switched to the chaotic scene in front of an apartment building. Her apartment building. Grayson recognized the doorman. What was his name? John, he remembered. The man's face was gray. Grayson could see his hands shaking as he clutched something that looked like a paper bag against his chest. He was standing in the background talking to a couple of detectives. Grayson didn't recognize either one of them.

It was Olivia. Had to be. Even though he had spent only one evening with her, she had made a lasting impression. She was a beautiful, smart, and caring woman, and the way she handled that terrified little boy was something to see. The world needed Olivia MacKenzie.

His cell phone rang. Ronan's greeting was brisk. "Are you watching the news? Olivia MacKenzie was shot multiple times, and she—"

"Is she alive?"

"Yes," he answered, reacting to the fury in Grayson's voice.

"Where is she?"

"They took her to St. Paul's. It's the closest trauma center," he explained. "I talked to Detective Cusack, and he told me Olivia's in surgery now."

"How bad is it?"

"She got hit three times."

"I'm going over to the hospital."

"I'll meet you there."

Grayson had just put his gun in his safe. He got it out and shoved it back in its holster, then picked up his badge. His hands shook. That surprised him, and he realized he needed to get his anger under control.

He went down the hall and quietly opened the door to one of his spare rooms to check on Henry. His nephew was sleeping soundly. He pulled the door closed and went into the kitchen. The housekeeper, Patrick, was sitting at the table making a grocery list. Grayson told him where he was going and headed out.

The snow was still coming down hard, and the roads were like an ice rink. There were car accidents everywhere. Grayson drove his SUV and took as many side streets as he could to avoid getting slammed by other drivers. He parked the car in the doctors' lot close to the hospital door. The security guard didn't give him any argument once he showed him his badge.

He got directions to the surgical floor, and in a hurry, he took the stairs. The floor was nearly deserted. A scrub nurse was rushing by. He stopped her and asked where Olivia MacKenzie was.

"She's still in the OR," she said. "Are you family?"

"FBI," he answered. "Where are the guards?" he asked then.

"I'm sorry? There aren't any guards on this floor."

He didn't show any reaction to that news but asked, "Could you find out her condition and how much longer she'll be in there?"

"Yes, of course. The surgical waiting room is right down that hallway," she said motioning to her left.

"Which OR is Olivia in?"

She pointed to the doors at the end of the hallway on the right.

"I'll wait here." No one could get past him as long as he blocked access to the OR.

The nurse promised to be right back.

She rushed down the corridor, then picked up a wall phone directly outside the OR doors.

He pulled out his cell phone and started making calls. Within minutes he'd arranged twenty-four-hour protection for Olivia.

He refused to even consider the possibility that she might not make it. The idea was simply untenable. It was bizarre, this connection he felt, but he didn't try to reason through it.

Ronan arrived a few minutes later. His dark hair was covered with snow. He brushed it off as he walked down the hallway.

"How is she?" he asked.

"Still in surgery. A nurse is checking on her condition."

Ronan looked around. "There's no one here. No police, no hospital guards . . . what the hell?"

"I've got agents on the way."

"This is our case then?"

"Oh hell yes."

"Good," Ronan said, nodding. "Do you think Jorguson's responsible? He did boast that he was going to have her killed."

"That was two months ago. He's threatened a couple of other attorneys since then. He's a hothead, and I know he's got some badasses for clients, but I still don't think this was his work."

"I'm not marking him off."

"I'm not either," Grayson agreed. "I'm just saying I don't think it's him."

"Who besides Jorguson would want her out of the way?"

"She works for the IRS. That could open up all sorts of possibilities. Who knows what some disgruntled taxpayer might do."

"I don't believe they've released her name yet, which means they haven't notified the family. Probably still trying to locate them." Ronan walked down to the surgical waiting room to see if anyone was there. He returned a minute later. "It's empty."

"After I get an update, I'll call Olivia's aunt."

The nurse he'd asked to check on Olivia interrupted. She was smiling. "The patient is on her way to recovery. She's

going to be all right. The surgeon said
he would be out in a few minutes to talk
to you. He also said she's a very lucky
young lady."

Grayson felt as though he could take
a deep breath again, so great was his
relief. Ronan noticed. He waited until the
nurse had left, then asked, "You only
had one date with Olivia, right?"

"Right."

"Did you . . ."

Grayson knew what he was asking.
"What the hell, Ronan."

"So that's a no, you didn't."

They both heard the bell indicating
the elevator doors were about to open.
Each put his hand on the grip of his
weapon and waited. Two detectives
stepped out. The younger one was the
spitting image of the actor Tom Cruise,
down to the thick brown hair and square
jaw.

"Doesn't that guy look like . . ." Ronan
whispered.

"Yeah, he does," Grayson agreed.

Both detectives were eating sandwiches and chatting. They stopped
when they saw Grayson and Ronan. The

older one, wearing part of his sandwich on his mustache, called out, "Who are you?"

"FBI," Ronan answered.

"You don't need to be here. We've got this."

"No, you don't." Grayson didn't raise his voice, but the look in his eyes showed he was in charge.

"This is our case," the Tom Cruise look-alike snapped. He had a definite swagger as he walked toward Grayson.

Grayson wasn't impressed with his rooster tactics. Neither was Ronan who said, "No, this isn't your case. It's ours."

"We were assigned this at the scene," Mustache told them. "Didn't see either of you there."

"So you knew this woman was gunned down, that it was a hit, right?" Grayson asked.

"Yeah, of course," Mustache replied.

"But you didn't think to post guards?"

The two detectives glanced at each other. Then Mustache said, "She's in surgery. We were going to wait and see if she made it . . ."

Grayson spotted the surgeon at the

end of the hall. He was talking to the nurse.

"You deal with them," he told Ronan as he walked toward the OR doors.

He heard Cruise say, "I'm gonna make some calls."

Ronan responded, "You do that."

After Grayson talked to the surgeon, he made the dreaded call to Emma Monroe, Olivia's aunt. It hadn't taken him long to get her cell phone number and to find out she was in Palm Springs for a seminar.

Emma knew something was wrong as soon as she answered the phone and heard Grayson's voice.

"Olivia's going to be fine," he began.

"What happened?" she demanded before he could continue. "Was there an accident?"

"No, there wasn't an accident," he said and then explained what had happened to her. He also told Emma what the surgeon had said and ended by repeating once again that Olivia was going to be fine.

Emma was beside herself. "Three gunshots? Someone shot her three times? Who would do such a thing to a lovely, kind . . . she's been through so much . . . she's had so much pain and now this. You find out who did this, Grayson." She went from shock to fury.

"I will," he promised.

"Where was she shot?"

"Right hip, left shoulder, and left side," he said. He'd already given her that information, but he knew she was having trouble taking it all in.

"Someone needs to contact Dr. Pardieu. I hope the surgeon has already called him," she said.

"Dr. Pardieu?"

"Andre Pardieu. He's her physician. Grayson, I'm going to get on the first flight I can find . . . no, I'll charter a jet," she decided. "I should be there—"

Grayson interrupted. "The city's snowed in, Emma. No flights in or out."

"She shouldn't be alone. She needs someone to watch out for her."

"There will be someone with her at all times," he promised. "No one's going to get to her."

"Has anyone called her parents and her sister?"

"I'll check," he said.

"I'll call them. They're all in Miami, celebrating with some new investors. Olivia's father purchased a mansion overlooking the ocean."

Grayson could hear the disapproval in her voice, which told him there were family issues. He didn't care about that. His total focus was on finding out who wanted Olivia MacKenzie dead.

Little did he know just how high that number would be.

ELEVEN

Olivia could have sworn Tom Cruise stopped by to say hello. Then Grayson appeared and shooed him away.

She floated in and out of consciousness. Everything was a blur, and visions swirled around in her head: snow and paper bags flying through the air and John's face at the window and a thin crimson line streaming across the white earth. Then, out of the fog, Grayson's face appeared. Why was he there? Did he want to kiss her again? She couldn't focus enough to find out, and she drifted away once more.

The next time she came to, she felt something cold on her head. She forced her eyes open and saw Grayson leaning over her. She closed them again. She was hallucinating. Focus, she told herself. She knew she was dreaming and needed to make herself wake up. Yet, when she looked again, he was there. He was no illusion.

When he moved the cold pack on her head, she felt the throbbing pain. She opened her mouth to complain but nothing came out. Her throat was so sore.

Finally in a raspy voice she managed to whisper, "What is it with you and ice?"

"What is it with you getting hit in the head?" He smiled as he added, "The nurse wants you to keep this on your bump."

"Bump?"

"I think you slammed your head into the brick wall outside your building."

"Why would I want to do that?"

He didn't have a ready answer to her question. She struggled to sit up and felt pain all the way down to her toes.

"Be useful. Help me sit up."

"You are sitting up."

She closed her eyes. "Go away." She wanted to stay awake, but the fog was descending again and she couldn't fight it.

The next time she woke up, she was lucid and feeling half human. She looked around. She was in a room filled with vases of flowers, and Dr. Andre Pardieu was standing at the foot of the bed reading her chart.

"Bonjour, Docteur."

"Ah, you're back with us," he said.

"I have to give Jane some blood."

"No, not now. You need to rebuild your strength, then you can help her."

Their conversation continued in rapid French. Grayson stood in the doorway listening. It was apparent the physician had great affection for Olivia. Grayson could have sworn he heard him call her Pipsqueak.

At the end of their talk, Dr. Pardieu switched back to English. "Now that I see you're all right, I'll keep my plans to go to France. I'll be in Paris for a conference, and then I'll be going on a holiday with my family. If you need me, you know how to get hold of me." He kissed her on the forehead before he left the room.

Olivia was looking out the window when Grayson walked in, and she hadn't noticed him watching her. He wondered how anyone could look that good after being shot three times. Her face was pale, but she was still beautiful. Her dark auburn hair spilled out on the pillow behind her.

She caught him staring at her. Those clear blue eyes locked on his. Then he walked over to the window ledge and leaned against it. He folded his arms across his chest and said, "How are you feeling?"

"All things considered, pretty good," she replied.

What was he doing here? she wanted to ask. How did he get involved in this? One silly kiss, then two months without a word. Message received, she thought. He obviously hadn't wanted to have anything to do with her and had moved on. Damn it, so had she.

"Are you ready to answer some questions?" he asked.

"Yes."

"Do you remember what happened?"

"I do remember," she said, surprised that she did. "But it won't help much. There was a black SUV parked at the end of the block. The motor was running, and I remember thinking that he was waiting for someone. Guess he was waiting for me, wasn't he?"

"Apparently so."

The topic of the conversation was horrific, she thought, yet they were both acting and sounding so casual about it. Olivia knew Grayson must be used to dealing with attempted murders and all sorts of other awful happenings. He was a pro at this sort of thing. Nothing much seemed to faze him. She, on the other hand, was a novice.

"Could you see anyone in the SUV?"

"No, the windows were tinted, and it was snowing. Visibility wasn't good. The driver was on my side of the street. And that's it, Grayson. That's all I know." She smiled and waited for his next question.

"That's it, huh?" he said.

"I should call my aunt. I don't want her to worry."

"I talked to her."

"You did? You didn't upset her, did you?"

"No, of course not. Hearing that you'd been shot three times didn't upset her at all."

She ignored his sarcasm. "She's in Palm Springs."

"No, she's on her way here."

Olivia asked him about her boss and her friend Jane, but she didn't mention her parents or her sister.

"Just a couple of questions, and I'll let you rest while I go talk to Judge Bowen and Judge Thorpe," he said.

"They're here?"

He nodded. "So is your boss, Thurman. They're in the waiting room discussing their contempt for an attorney named Simmons."

"I'd like to see them."

"There are about twenty other people waiting to say hello and make sure you're all right."

"I'll talk to Judge Bowen, and—"

"After I talk to them," he said. "But before I go . . . do you have any idea who might have done this?"

"Don't you mean, who wants me dead?"

"Yes."

She started wiggling fingers on her right hand, then her left, as she counted. Then her right hand again.

"At least fifteen people would like to get rid of me," she said.

"Did you include Jorguson?" he asked.

"No," she answered. "Should I? That makes it sixteen people who would like me to disappear. I'm sure there are more. I'll be happy to write their names down for you."

He thought she was joking. He walked over to the side of her bed, towering over her. "This is a serious matter, Olivia," he said.

"I am being serious, Grayson."

"Your aunt told me she couldn't imagine anyone would want to harm you. She said you're sweet and kindhearted."

"I'm not." She sounded disgruntled.

He wasn't going to argue with her. He turned to leave and stopped, remembering the other question he wanted to ask. "When we were having lunch, you told me you had a goal you wanted to accomplish."

"Yes." She'd hoped he'd forgotten the conversation.

"Does your goal have anything to do with the number of people who would like to get rid of you?"

"Yes."

He waited for her to explain, but she remained stubbornly silent. "We aren't playing twenty questions," he snapped. "What's your goal, Olivia?"

She knew he would eventually find out what she was trying to do. What did she care if he thought she was a vindictive, traitorous daughter? Doing the right thing was more important than the guilt she felt.

"I'm going to put my father in prison."

After talking to Judge Bowen, Judge Thorpe, and Royal Thurman, Grayson understood their contempt for the attorney Carl Simmons. Suggesting that Olivia was a drug addict at a very young age when, in fact, she had gone through chemotherapy was despicable, and Gray-

son personally wanted to throw the bastard into a wall.

He spent the next several hours finding out all he could about Olivia that
wasn't on her résumé. Her aunt Emma
was a great help. Despite the weather,
she had managed to get back to D.C.,
and they sat together in the nearly deserted hospital cafeteria discussing
Olivia's past and her contentious relationship with her immediate family.
Emma began by telling him about the
experimental program Olivia and three
other young girls were part of and a little
of what they had endured.

"Olivia wouldn't be happy I'm telling
you about this," Emma said. "She's a
very private person. Her relationship
with her parents was strained even back
then. I didn't realize for a long time that
none of them—her father, her mother,
nor her sister—ever came to see Olivia
when she was allowed visitors at the
hospital. Olivia was all alone."

Grayson didn't show any reaction to
what she was telling him, but he now
understood why Olivia helped kids who

didn't have anyone to watch out for them. She knew what it was like.

"Tell me about her father."

"Robert MacKenzie is one of the most charismatic men you'll ever meet. He could sell you a beach house in the Arctic. He walks into a room, and he owns it. Do you know what I mean?"

"Yes," he replied.

"In the past Robert has run several companies. Each one ended up going under, yet Robert did quite well. He got his salary and bonus when he resigned. He's always lived extravagantly. When he bought a home in New York, I thought he would divorce my sister, but that didn't happen. She's still with him."

"He was CEO of these companies?"

"Yes. It was all legal," she said.

"Now he runs his own investment firm?"

"That's right, the Trinity Fund, and it's quite successful. On paper anyway. Olivia knows several people who have given her father their retirement funds to invest. They all get quarterly statements showing how well their investments are doing. She's seen how her father works, and she's convinced this is just another one of his scams."

"She thinks he's running a Ponzi scheme?"

"If he is, she hasn't been able to prove it. Shall we head back upstairs? I'd like to say good-bye to Olivia and find out if she needs me to bring her anything."

Grayson walked by Emma's side to the elevator. He was lost in thought. "What do *you* think of Robert MacKenzie?"

"I agree with Olivia. He should be in prison."

The number of people on Olivia's enemy list made sense now. She'd been asking questions and probing, bringing attention to her father's firm. She probably had already gone to the SEC, and the men raking in the money wouldn't like that one little bit.

A woman in a wheelchair was coming out of Olivia's room when they arrived. A slender young man was pushing the chair. Emma introduced Olivia's friend Jane and her brother, Logan, to Grayson.

Logan extended his hand and said, "You're gonna catch this guy, right?"

"Yes," Grayson assured him.

"When are you going home, Jane?" Emma asked.

"Tomorrow," she said. "I'll come back in a month or so when Olivia's strength is back."

"Olivia is giving Jane some of her blood," Logan explained. "It's got anti-bodies she needs. Right, Jane?"

"Yes," she said. "Olivia's worn-out, so I wouldn't stay long. Now, if you'll excuse us, Logan has a meeting to attend."

"And you need rest," he told Jane.

Emma and Grayson watched until they turned the corner. Then Emma said, "Jane doesn't look at all well, does she? She's so pale."

Grayson thought Jane's brother looked just as sickly. When Emma went on into Olivia's room, he stopped to go over the schedule with the agent on duty tonight. After that, he called Ronan to talk about Robert MacKenzie's investment firm and found out that Ronan had already dug into Olivia's family and had come up with all sorts of possibilities for those relatives who might want Olivia out of the way. He wondered if Olivia knew that her brother-in-law, George, had a gambling problem and had recently taken out another mortgage on his home to pay some of his debts.

By the time Grayson ended his conversation with Ronan, Emma had left and Olivia was alone. He checked his watch as he entered her room. He needed to head home soon. Now that his nephew was living with him, he tried to eat dinner with him as often as possible to give him some kind of stable home life.

Olivia was fighting sleep. The television was on, and she was trying to watch the news. Her eyelids kept closing on her. She saw Grayson and asked, "Why are you here? I didn't think I'd ever see you again. Were you assigned to this investigation?"

"No," he answered. "I asked for it."

The pain medication was kicking in, and she was feeling a bit loopy. "Because of Jorguson."

"No, because of you."

She frowned. "Let's get something straight."

"All right," he agreed. "What?"

She looked at him. "What?"

"You wanted to get something straight."

She remembered. "You better understand, Grayson. I'm never going to ask you to kiss me again."

He smiled. "You won't need to."

His cell phone rang, interrupting the moment, which was a good thing, he thought, because he was seriously thinking about kissing her. He knew that he wouldn't give in to the urge, but he didn't like the fact that he wanted her.

His nephew was calling to remind him that he had to build a solar system and that Grayson had promised to help.

"What solar system?"

"*The* solar system," Henry stressed.

"This is the first I'm hearing about this, Henry."

"I was sure I told you, and I thought you said you would help me."

"When is it due?" he asked, thinking that he would make time this weekend to help him.

"Tomorrow."

Ah, come on. "Tomorrow?"

"Yes, and we need stuff."

"What stuff?" Grayson wondered.

"Stuff to make it. Like Styrofoam and string maybe."

Grayson noticed that Olivia's head was back on her pillow and her eyelids were at half-mast, but she was smiling. She obviously thought the conversation was amusing. He didn't. This parent "stuff" was a bitch.

"Okay. I'm on my way home." He ended the call and said, "I guess you got all that."

"How old is he?"

"He turned nine two weeks ago."

"And you need to build a solar system?"

"Apparently so. I'll be driving all over town looking for supplies. I better get going."

"Good luck," she whispered and fell sound asleep.

TWELVE

The night before Olivia was released from the hospital, her aunt Emma came to visit and insisted that Olivia move into her home to recuperate. Olivia refused. She told her aunt she wanted to sleep in her own bed and not be fussed over. In truth, she didn't want to put Emma in any danger, and as long as the shooter was still out there, everyone around Olivia was at risk.

As Emma was leaving, Grayson and Ronan walked in. Emma smiled at the agents and said, "Grayson, in all this

confusion I forgot to ask about your father. How is he doing?"

"Better," he answered but didn't ex-
pound.

Olivia was curious to know what had
happened to his father but thought it
would be intrusive to ask. She'd have to
wait until she and Emma were alone to
find out the details. Not that it was any
of her business, she reminded herself.
She had made up her mind to maintain
a professional relationship with Grayson
and not to ask any personal questions.

"Please give him my best," Emma
said. She turned to Olivia. "I'll be here
early tomorrow to drive you home."

Grayson stepped forward. "I . . . we
feel it would be best if I took Olivia
home . . . for security reasons," he said.

"All right," Emma responded. She
gave Olivia a kiss on the forehead and
left.

Grayson had a list of questions he
wanted to ask Olivia, particularly about
her brother-in-law and the debt he had
incurred. Did she know about it? Did
her sister? From what he had discovered thus far, Olivia's relationship with

her family was strained at best. In the days she had been in the hospital, he hadn't seen any member of Olivia's immediate family come to visit.

Unfortunately, he didn't get the chance to ask any of his questions. A constant stream of visitors, several phone calls, and her exhaustion overrode his agenda. He decided to wait until tomorrow to talk about her family.

The following morning, he drove her home from the hospital but didn't bring up the obviously uncomfortable subject of her relatives. When Grayson announced that an off-duty policeman would be arriving soon to keep watch outside her door, she protested. As long as she stayed inside her apartment, she insisted, she was safe. Grayson listened to her argument and ignored it, stating emphatically that the guard was not negotiable.

They had just reached her apartment and Olivia was fishing through her purse for her key when a door at the end of the hall opened and an elderly woman wearing a pink chenille bathrobe stepped out. Her thin white hair was held away from her bony face by two bobby pins, and her lips were pursed to give a breathy whistle. When Olivia looked in her direction, the woman crooked her finger and motioned for her to come closer.

"Hello, Mrs. Delaney," Olivia said as she approached the woman.

"Olivia, dear, I need milk." As she spoke, Mrs. Delaney was peering around Olivia and looking suspiciously at Grayson.

"I'm sorry," Olivia said, "I'm afraid I won't be going to the store for a few days, but I'll be happy to get you some milk when I shop again."

Mrs. Delaney looked perturbed. "All right," she said. "I'll call down to John and have him bring me some when he comes to work tomorrow, but he always buys the wrong kind. I specifically ask for two percent, and he inevitably brings me whole milk. That's just too rich for me. My nervous stomach won't tolerate it."

"I understand," Olivia answered patiently. "I'll be sure to let you know when

I'm going to the supermarket, and you can give me a list."

"Good," Mrs. Delaney said and turned to go back into her apartment. "Get me some of those lemon cookies, the ones with the icing on top, not the plain ones like you got me last time." Grayson and Olivia could hear her adding to her list even as she was closing the door.

"She doesn't like to go out in the cold," Olivia explained.

"Sounds like she's rather particular."

"A little," Olivia laughed. "She's all alone, and I don't mind helping out when I can."

Grayson took the key from Olivia's hand and inserted it into the lock. "You may act tough, but you have a soft heart, Olivia MacKenzie." He pushed the door open and stepped back so she could go inside.

Olivia was happy to be home. Her aunt had sent her staff over to clean the apartment, restock the refrigerator and pantry, and do Olivia's laundry. There were fresh apples and oranges in a wooden bowl on the kitchen island,

chicken noodle soup ready to be warmed
up, and fresh baked bread.

"If you aren't too tired, I'd like to talk
to you about your family," Grayson said.

"Okay, but I don't know what I can tell
you that would help." She was emptying
her purse looking for her cell phone.
She finally found it and went into her office to plug it into her charger.

When she returned, Grayson had removed his suit jacket and was tugging
at his tie. She noticed what he was doing but didn't comment. If he wanted to
get comfortable, that was fine with her.
She would still be able to maintain her
distance. He wasn't a friend; he was her
protector.

That reminder should have helped
keep it all in perspective, but he looked
great in a suit, and with the jacket off,
he looked even better. She had forgotten what a muscular frame he had. Her
side was throbbing, her shoulder stung,
and her hip felt as though there was still
a bullet inside the bone. She was a
wreck, and yet she could still lust after
him. She could have blamed her thoughts
about ripping his clothes off on her pain

medication, but she hadn't taken any today.

"I'd like to discuss your brother-in-law," he continued.

"George? There's not much to say about him. I haven't been with him all that much. I've usually just talked to him on the phone, and it's always been superficial. You know, 'How are you?' . . . 'Fine' . . . 'How are you?' Then he'd hand the phone to my sister. George isn't much of a talker. He's a bit . . . stiff," she said. "He makes Natalie happy, though."

"How long have you known him?"

"Almost ten years. I met him several months after they were married."

"You didn't go to their wedding?"

"No, it was in San Francisco, and I was here in D.C. It wasn't possible for me to leave."

Olivia never talked about her illness, and he wondered if she knew that he had found out all about her time in the experimental program. According to her aunt, Olivia only discussed those years with her other family, the three girls who went through the program with her. He also knew that her surrogate father was Dr. Andre Pardieu.

He forced himself to finish his questions so she could rest. "Do you know anything about their financial situation?"

Olivia sat on the easy chair and put her head back on the cushions. "He and Natalie started an Internet company several years ago, and they're doing very well. Natalie invested most of their profits with our father, God help her. I tried to talk to her, make her understand what a scam it all was, but she's sipped the Kool-Aid and is a believer. Like my mother," she added. "She likes to paint a picture of the perfect family. She thinks Natalie is the perfect daughter; George is the perfect son-in-law . . ."

"And you?"

She closed her eyes and smiled. "Imperfect," she said very matter-of-factly. "So she usually doesn't include me when she talks about her family. Natalie has become an only child. These days my mother considers me a traitor."

"A traitor to the family?"

"Yes," she answered. "And I guess I am. I have to stop him. He can't go on ruining lives and destroying families. I used to think he couldn't help himself, that it was all just a game to him, but now I know better. Money is everything to him. He's obsessive about bringing in more and more. He lures his rich friends to give him their savings and their trusts to invest, and he also targets large pensions and charities.

"The more difficult the potential client, the more my father thrives. My aunt Emma won't let him near her money, and it's making him frantic. He hates losing, and he's determined to find a way to force her to give him everything she has. It won't happen, but he'll go to prison still trying."

Olivia struggled to get up. Surprised by how much that action drained her, she headed to her bedroom. "I'm going to change clothes," she said. "Help yourself to something to eat and drink."

"Want me to warm up some soup for you?"

"That would be nice."

She walked down the hall but stopped at her bedroom door and looked back at him. "My mother idolizes my father, and she only has room in her heart for him. She can't help the way she is. It's like he has this mind control over her."

"Does she know what he's doing? Is she part of it?"

"No." She was emphatic. "And if you showed her absolute proof, she wouldn't believe it or see it. Honest to God, I think she'd throw anyone under the bus to protect him."

"Including you?"

She didn't answer. "I think, once my father is behind bars, my mother might open her eyes. Then again, she might not. She might want to crawl in the cell with him."

"Olivia?" he called when she walked into her bedroom.

She stepped back into the hallway. "Yes?"

"Why would your mother think you're imperfect?"

She sighed. "I got sick, Grayson. That made me imperfect."

She really hoped he was through asking questions about her family tonight. He was dredging up all sorts of emotions she didn't want to feel. She shut her bedroom door and changed into a pair of blue-and-white flannel pajama bottoms and a blue T-shirt. That little bit of effort exhausted her, and she sat down on the side of the bed. She fell back, rolled to her side, and closed her eyes. She would just rest for a few minutes and then have some soup, she told herself. After that, she'd send Grayson home and get a little work done on her computer.

Fifteen minutes passed and Olivia hadn't come back to the living room. Grayson opened the bedroom door a crack and looked in. Her hair covered the side of her face, and her arms were crossed over her chest. Grayson pulled the covers back on the king-size bed, then lifted Olivia into his arms. He held her close against his chest for a minute, liking the feel of her warm body against his. He gently placed her between the sheets and covered her. He brushed her hair back and stroked her cheek. Her skin was so soft, so smooth.

"There's nothing imperfect about you, Olivia."

THIRTEEN

Ronan thought Olivia's brother-in-law, George Anderson, looked good for the shooting and wanted to put him at the top of the list.

Grayson wasn't convinced.

Ronan opened his desk drawer, pulled out a Nerf football, and tossed it across the office to Grayson. Throwing the football while they brainstormed had become a ritual, providing the cavernous office was empty.

"I'll put Anderson in the top five," Grayson said. "But there are others who look better, like Carl Simmons and his crew, and unfortunately, Olivia's own father. Any one of them could have hired men to silence her. Did you know she was calling the SEC?"

Ronan smiled. "Good for her."

Grayson tossed the football back to Ronan. "Olivia's been asking a lot of questions about the Trinity Fund. There could be someone connected with the SEC who doesn't want an investigation."

Ronan nodded agreement. "Let's talk about Anderson."

"Yeah, okay. He owes three hundred thousand to a bookie named Subway, and every week the interest escalates."

"Every week?"

"Every week," Grayson repeated. "If Anderson continues to let the loan ride, in six months he could owe as much as, what . . . six hundred thousand?"

Ronan tossed the football as he answered, "Right. So I'm gonna go out on a limb here and suggest that Subway isn't a bookie. He's a loan shark."

Grayson nodded. Then Ronan asked, "Does Olivia know about her brother-in-law's gambling problem?"

"I doubt it. I'm going over there in a

little while to talk to her about him. She mentioned that George is in town and wants to stop by tonight."

"And what did you say?"

They were throwing the football faster and faster until it was rocketing across the office.

"I said he's not getting in unless I'm there. The guard knows," he added.

"What about Anderson's wife, Natalie? Do you think she's aware of her husband's gambling problem?"

"I don't think so," he said. "He could get some money out of the Trinity Fund to pay off the loan—they have close to four million in an account with her father—but he hasn't taken any."

"Because she'd find out."

"That's what I'm thinking. She's put a great deal of her own money in the account. Her uncle, the late Daniel Monroe, was very wealthy. He set up trust funds for his two nieces so that they'd each get a large sum. The minute Natalie got her money, she turned it over to her father to invest."

"What about Olivia's fund?"

"She gets hers next year."

He then told Ronan what he'd discovered about Simmons, Simmons and Falcon. He'd looked into their banking practices and their accounts and had uncovered that Carl Simmons was a silent partner to Robert MacKenzie.

"Carl Simmons is slandering her, spreading lies about her to get her to stop asking questions. How much do you want to bet her father knows what he's doing?"

Grayson nodded. "If things work out, I'll get to see him in action in a few weeks at the Morgan Hotel."

"The big birthday party?"

Grayson nodded. "I haven't crashed a party in a while. It should be interesting." He tossed the football back to Ronan and stood. "I'm leaving."

"You're going over to Olivia's now?"

"Yeah. Henry's sleeping over at a friend's tonight."

"Not that I'm keeping tabs," Ronan said, "but it appears you've been spending an awful lot of time at Miss Mac-Kenzie's apartment."

"What can I say," Grayson answered

with a grin, "I take my investigations seriously, and I'm very thorough."

"Uh-huh," Ronan drawled with a good
deal of skepticism.

The fact of the matter was, Grayson
had looked for excuses to see Olivia.
Even when a question could be answered with a simple phone call, he'd
insist that it needed to be done in person. He couldn't resist being with her.
What he was feeling was so new to him,
he couldn't explain it. The only thing he
knew for certain was that Olivia Mac-
Kenzie was different from any other
woman he had ever met, and the more
time he spent with her, the more he
wanted.

He was walking toward the stairs
when Ronan asked, "Are you still being
a gentleman?"

"With Olivia?" he said, pretending not
to understand.

"No, with her dog."

He laughed. "She doesn't have a dog,
and, yes, I'm still being a gentleman."

And it was killing him.

It had been three weeks since Olivia had been shot, and the only time she had left her apartment was to go to the doctor to have her stitches removed. She was beginning to feel like a caged animal. Her routine was so boring. She got up early every morning, dressed, then went into her office and logged on to her computer with her password. Since there weren't any distractions, she got caught up with her cases fairly quickly.

The only exercise equipment she owned was a treadmill, and since she couldn't go to the gym and use the elliptical trainer like she used to, she got on her treadmill twice a day to break up the boredom. Some days, when her asthma wasn't bad, she would run; other days she walked so slowly she felt as though she was crawling.

Collins came over two Sundays in a row and stayed for a couple of hours each time. Then she'd go back to the firing range to work on accuracy. Olivia still trembled thinking about Collins carrying a gun.

Jane stayed at home because of the weather. Washington was having an unusual winter. It was bitterly cold, and snow kept blasting the city. She lived in a townhouse near Dupont Circle and was busy renovating it to be a studio for her painting. Olivia had missed her art show, but Jane told her all about it. She'd sold three paintings and felt validated and invigorated.

Sam called only a few times, but then she was in Iceland, so she kept in touch by e-mail. She wrote long, rambling letters about the jets she was flying and didn't complain at all about where she was stationed.

All three of Olivia's friends dated, but none of them had ever been in a serious relationship. Though they were healthy today, they lived with the fear that their luck would change. And how could they put a man they loved through that kind of worry? They had decided to be practical. Happily ever after wasn't in the cards for them.

Olivia had just finished answering a couple of e-mails. She closed her laptop and checked her watch. Remembering that Grayson was coming over, she went to her bedroom to change clothes. She stayed casual in a pair of fitted jeans and a white blouse she didn't bother to tuck in. She brushed her hair and dabbed on a little perfume and lipstick.

George would also be arriving soon. He'd said he wanted to have a serious talk with her. Olivia wondered if Natalie would be with him. She was positive she knew what George wanted to talk about: getting Aunt Emma to invest in Trinity Fund to show her loyalty and support to the family. Olivia's response wasn't going to change, no matter what George said. Invest in Trinity? Absolutely not.

How could Natalie and George be so blind?

Grayson arrived just after she straightened up her living room. She'd gathered up all her newspapers and magazines, put them in a recycle bag, and was folding her afghan when she heard the doorbell. She tossed the afghan on the back of the sofa.

She always felt a little catch in her throat whenever she saw him. Tonight was no different. He wasn't wearing a suit. He was as casually dressed as she was, in jeans and a camel-colored sweater. His gun was at his side. That hadn't changed.

He looked wonderful, she thought, but then he always did. She stepped back and waited while he hung up his coat in her hall closet.

"You're early," she said. "George won't be here until eight."

"I wanted to talk to you before he got here."

He went to the sofa and sat down. She followed. "Talk about George?"

"Did you know he had a gambling problem?"

Her expression confirmed she hadn't known. She looked shocked, then shook her head. "He doesn't seem the type. He's so . . . stuffy."

She sat down next to him and listened in growing astonishment as he described the hole George had dug himself into.

"He owes that much?"

Grayson repeated the amount. He thought her reaction to the news was comical. Her cheeks turned pink, and she was sputtering. "How could anyone . . . he borrowed from . . . how stupid is he?"

"Are you asking me?"

"A loan shark? He really went to a loan shark?"

"Yeah, he did," he said, smiling. "And, yeah, it was stupid. People do stupid things all the time. It's why I have a job. You work for the IRS . . . don't you deal with stupid all the time?"

She laughed. "Yes, I guess I do." She thought about George for a second. "Natalie's going to kill him."

"You don't think she knows?"

"George is still breathing, so, no, I don't think she has any idea."

Olivia hadn't meant to sit so close to him. She didn't want to move, though. She loved the way his eyes crinkled at the edges when he smiled. She stared into those eyes and said, "May I ask you a question?"

"Sure. What do you want to know?"

"It's not about the investigation," she said.

"Okay. Shoot," he told her.

"Do you ever think about kissing me?"

He smiled at her again, and she felt

as though she was melting. "Yeah, I do. All the time," he said as his hand moved to the back of her neck.

"All the time, Grayson?" she asked, her tone teasing.

He pulled her toward him, and his lips covered hers in a kiss that was outrageously carnal. His mouth was hot, and his tongue stroked hers until she was desperate for more. She could have stopped him, but that was the last thing on her mind.

For Grayson, the kiss was consuming and extremely arousing. When he came to his senses and realized what was happening, he took her by the shoulders and gently pushed her away. "We can't do this now." His voice was harsh.

Olivia was feeling dazed. One kiss and she was shaking. What would happen if he made love to her? She'd probably disintegrate. She threaded her fingers through her hair and took a breath. Grayson had disappeared into her kitchen. She needed to apologize. She knew she was putting him in an awkward position. He was an agent investigating a crime, and she was the victim.

Getting personally involved was not a good idea. Their relationship should stay professional . . . shouldn't it? Her head was telling her yes, but her heart was screaming no.

When she entered the kitchen, Grayson was standing at her refrigerator. He had the door open and seemed to be looking for something in particular.

"What would you like?" she asked.

That was a leading question. "I don't know. Something to drink."

She pushed the door closed. "There are all sorts of drinks in the beverage drawer. It's behind you."

It looked like a regular drawer to him; the exterior was the same dark cherry-wood as the cabinets. He opened it, pulled out a bottle of water, then closed it.

"Nice," he said, making a mental note for his next remodel. "I like it. I should put one of these in my kitchen. My nephew is always in the refrigerator."

"Henry?" she asked.

"Yes," he answered.

"He's living with you?"

"Yes, ever since my father's heart attack."

"I'm sorry. Is your father going to be okay?"

"Yes," he replied and said nothing more.

That was it? Just yes? No explanation at all. Okay, she got the message. His personal life was off-limits. She felt like a fool now because she had all but begged him to kiss her. Again.

Olivia leaned against the sink and folded her arms across her waist. She was irritated with herself. She had broken her vow not to ask personal questions, to let him volunteer whatever he wanted to tell her.

"Do you mind if I look at your cabinets?" he asked.

Since he already had opened the door above the sink and was looking at the wood, she didn't bother to answer.

"I rehab houses," he explained. "This wood is nice. I like the grain. Did you choose it?"

"Yes."

"I also like the granite."

He suddenly moved and pinned her

against the sink. Then he leaned down and kissed her. It was quick and very nice.

"What was that for?" she asked, bewildered.

"To get you to quit frowning."

He brushed his mouth over hers again. "Know what else I like?"

"No, what?" she whispered.

He stepped back. "Your sink."

She walked past him. "You're such a flatterer."

He followed. "Hey, I really do like your sink."

She rolled her eyes. "You want to kiss me; you don't want to kiss me. You kiss, then you don't kiss. Make up your mind, for Pete's sake."

He laughed. There was a knock on the door, and his mood changed in a heartbeat. "Go sit down. George is here."

"He's early," she said. "Guess he didn't have any trouble finding the place."

"He's never been here before?"

"No."

He waited until she was seated, then unlocked the door and opened it. George was a big man, almost as tall as Grayson. He needed to lose some weight, at least sixty pounds. He carried most of the extra pounds in his chest and stomach. Heart attack waiting to happen, Grayson thought.

George introduced himself to Grayson but couldn't look him in the eye.

"Are you staying or leaving?" he asked.

"Staying," Grayson said firmly.

"Why? There's a guard right outside the door. She doesn't need one inside, too. He patted me down, which I found a bit insulting."

"Come sit down, George," Olivia called. She wanted to get up and properly greet him at the door, but Grayson had insisted she sit.

"I see no reason why he—"

"I'm staying," Grayson repeated.

"Grayson's with the FBI," Olivia explained. "They're investigating the shooting."

Olivia's brother-in-law stopped arguing. He took his coat off and started to hand it to Grayson. He quickly changed his mind and draped it over a table. It immediately fell to the floor, and George didn't bother to pick it up.

He was used to others taking care of his needs, Grayson thought.

George looked around the living room before taking a seat in one of the chairs facing the sofa. Olivia didn't care if he liked her home or not. After Grayson and she were finished talking to him, he wouldn't be coming back.

"How are you feeling?" he asked Olivia.

"I'm fine," she answered.

He turned to Grayson. "Have you got any leads on who shot Olivia? I'm sure it's one of the people she's going after for not paying their taxes. A lot of people hate her . . . I mean . . . hate the IRS."

Grayson didn't say a word. He simply stared at George until he flinched and looked away.

"Where's Natalie?" Olivia asked.

"In Miami with your parents."

"Does she know you're here?"

"Of course. In fact, she suggested I come talk to you."

Here we go. "Talk to me about what?" she asked innocently.

"You simply have to talk to Emma and convince her to put her money in Trinity," he blurted.

"No. Was there anything else you wanted to talk about?"

"Don't dismiss me," he snapped. "This is important. People . . . influential people . . . know she hasn't invested. When she does, they'll follow suit."

"No."

"This is killing your mother and your sister."

"What's killing them?" she asked. She tried to sound worried but couldn't pull it off.

"This hold you have on Emma. She'll do whatever you tell her to do."

"She will not. She's an intelligent, strong, independent woman." *And you're a moron,* she silently added.

"But you've got this special hold on her, ever since you gained her sympathy when you were sick."

"I gained her sympathy? Are you kidding me?"

"I'm simply stating what I know to be true."

"You know, George, until today I thought you had at least half a brain. I don't think that any longer. You're as blind as Mother and Natalie when it comes to Father's scam."

George huffed and started to get up. He glanced at Grayson, and quickly sat down again. "You're the one who's blind. Do you realize how much money Natalie and I have made?"

Grayson took over. "Why don't you use some of it to pay off your loan?"

Feigning ignorance, he said, "What loan?"

"The loan from your bookie. Subway calls himself a bookie, right?"

"Listen here," he shouted. "That's private . . ."

"Natalie doesn't know about the loan, does she?" Olivia asked.

He seemed to deflate in front of her. His shoulders slumped as he hunched over, and his head dropped.

"No." He sounded as though he wanted to cry. "She'll divorce me if she finds out."

"You're going to have to take that risk. You can't ignore a loan shark—"

"He's a bookie," he snapped. He buried his face in his hands. "I've been such a fool. I started out placing a couple of bets on some college basketball games, and before I knew it, I was in over my head."

"How does getting Emma to invest in Trinity help you?" Olivia asked.

"It doesn't," he answered. "I'm just trying to help your parents and Natalie. It's very important to them that the firm continues to grow, and Emma is so influential. If her friends knew she'd put her faith in the fund, they'd follow suit."

"And you could take some of your money out for your debts?"

"No, I can't do that . . . not without Natalie finding out about the gambling."

She was getting sick to her stomach. "Tell Natalie, and for God's sake, get your money out of that fund before it's too late."

"You're not going to be reasonable, are you?" He paused for a moment, and Olivia could almost see his mind racing.

"Now that you know about my debts . . . what about you?"

"What about me?"

"You could borrow against your trust. Don't you get it in two months?"

"No, a year and two months," she corrected.

"What happens to the trust if Olivia dies before she gets it?" Grayson asked.

Without hesitating, George said, "It all goes to Natalie."

"And you."

"Well, yes, we're married—" He stopped abruptly. "Wait . . . you don't think I would ever harm Olivia."

Grayson didn't answer. He didn't think George had the nerve to shoot anyone. He could see him hiring people, though.

"And once she has the money, if anything were to happen to her, it would go to whomever she's named in her will," Grayson said.

George pretended he didn't know anything about a will.

Grayson continued, "And I'll bet you know how much is in Olivia's trust, down to the last dollar."

"Olivia was given more than Natalie

because of her illness. At least, that's what Natalie and I believe."

"George, it's time for you to leave," Olivia said.

He didn't protest. Once he had his coat on, he said, "You won't talk to Emma?"

How many times did she have to say it? "No."

She didn't walk him to the door. Grayson did. After he locked it, he said, "What does your sister see in him?"

"You haven't met my sister yet, have you? When you do, you'll understand."

"Understand what?"

"He's perfect for her."

"I see."

She touched his arm. "I don't think George would have harmed me, but I'm glad you were here."

"Me too," he said. He took her hand. "You know, if you need anything . . . that is, if you get scared or want to talk, you can call me."

"I know," she answered with a warm smile. "Thank you, Grayson. I don't know that I could have handled all this without you."

He looked away from her and didn't say anything. He seemed preoccupied. "I should get going," he said finally.

She watched him turn off the kitchen light and walk to the closet to get his coat . . . only, he didn't get it. He pulled it off the hanger, then hung it back up. He stood there deep in thought for a few seconds, then he circled the living room and turned off all but one lamp. The room was cast in shadows. He stopped at the fireplace, picked up the remote from the mantel, and pushed the "on" button. Fire licked the logs, the gas feeding it until the flames were high.

The living room was warm and cozy now.

He silently watched the fire for a couple of minutes with his hands in his pockets, and then he began to walk back and forth, staring at the floor as though he were looking for answers to some unsettling question.

Olivia observed his peculiar behavior. She was getting a crick in her neck as he paced in front of her. She thought he might be trying to work something out about the investigation, or he was thinking about her lovely relatives perhaps, maybe even thanking God they weren't in his family. He'd met only George. She wondered how he was going to react when he met the others. She should probably take his gun away before she introduced them.

"Grayson? What are you doing?" she asked, breaking the silence. She'd been sitting too long. She stood and stretched her arms over her head to get the stiffness out of her shoulders and immediately regretted the action. "Ouch," she whispered, grimacing. Her shoulder and side were healing nicely, but stretching wasn't such a good idea yet.

Grayson had stopped pacing. She looked up at him, and the intensity in his eyes made her breathless. She went to him. Stopping just a foot away, she faced him. "What's going on?" she asked softly. "Tell me what you're thinking about. Maybe I can help you."

He almost laughed. "Yeah, okay. I'm thinking I'm not gonna be able to keep my hands off you much longer. Wanna help me with that?"

FOURTEEN

He'd rendered her speechless. Fortunately, the condition didn't last long.

"I thought you were thinking about George."

"Why would I be thinking about him?" he asked, clearly exasperated.

"Because he was just here," she reminded. "And you're angry."

"I'm not angry." His jaw was clenched, and he was frowning at her.

"Yes, you are . . . and so I assumed you were thinking about my brother-in-law. But you weren't."

"No."

His eyes looked deeply into hers, and she suddenly realized what was going on inside him.

"You want me," she said. It was a statement, not a question.

Her surprise irritated him. "Hell yes, I want you. And guess what, sweetheart. You want me, too."

Her hands went to her hips. "You can't know that."

"Sure I can. Are you going to be honest with me and admit it?"

He took a step toward her. He was definitely trying to intimidate her, she thought, and she was having none of it. She stood her ground.

"That isn't the question here."

"Yes, it is."

"There's no need to raise your voice, Grayson."

"You're yelling, Olivia."

She was having trouble catching her breath. She guessed grabbing her inhaler wouldn't be very romantic, but then he was glaring at her now, and how romantic was that?

"Yes, I want you," she admitted. "Does my honesty please you?" She wagged her finger at him. "It doesn't matter, so tuck your ego away. I will not distract you, and having sex with you . . . Stop smiling. Having sex . . ."

"Will distract me?"

"Exactly so."

Grayson wanted to take her into his arms and kiss every inch of her. God, she was beautiful and so damned passionate.

"You will get fired," she said.

He had to force himself to pay attention. "I what?"

"Get fired."

He shook his head. "No."

"This isn't funny, Grayson. You'll get into trouble."

He shook his head again. "I mean . . . if they found out . . . Oh, for the love of God, stop looking like you want to laugh. I'm thinking about you."

"I'm thinking about you, too."

He went back to the hearth, picked up the remote, and turned the gas off. The fire flickered and sputtered, then went out.

Olivia felt a stab of disappointment the second he turned away from her.

Yet she was determined to help him make the right decision, no matter how it affected her.

"You have to think about this, base your decision on logic, not lust."

Grayson turned around, and his eyes never left hers as he walked toward her. He stopped just inches away, and though he wanted to take her into his arms, he forced himself to wait. He needed to hear her say the words first.

"Do you want me to touch you, Olivia?"

His voice was gritty with emotion, and she could see the passion in his eyes. She knew she could end this now. She could lie and he would leave . . . except, she didn't want him to leave, no matter how complicated it became. And so she simply gave him the truth. No coyness, no lies, no games. "Yes," she whispered. "I do want you to touch me."

"Now?"

She sighed. "Oh yes. Now."

He reached for her, pulling her into his embrace. She wrapped her arms around his neck and began to place soft kisses along his jaw and the side of his neck. She teased his earlobe with her tongue and knew he liked what she was doing because he tightened his hold and pulled her against him.

He growled low in his throat as he roughly twisted her hair into his fist and jerked her head back. His open mouth came down on hers and his tongue sank inside to mate with hers. The scorching kiss went on and on until she was shaking with desire and could barely stand up. Her fingers slid into his hair, and she clung to him.

Panting, she stepped back. "Grayson." His name was said with a groan.

He swept her up into his arms and carried her to her bedroom. She put her head on his shoulder and closed her eyes. Her heart was racing; she couldn't catch her breath, but all she could think about was touching him. She loved his scent, so earthy and clean and male. It made her want to get even closer to him.

Grayson lifted her chin so she'd look at him. "Are you sure? Your wounds—"

She silenced him by putting her finger on his lips. "I'm okay," she said.

He slowly put her down, and she

stepped back, her gaze locked on his as she began to unbutton her blouse. She was trembling so, she could barely get her fingers to work. He was quicker. In seconds he pulled off his sweater, then his T-shirt, and was bare-chested.

Her heart beat faster and faster. The dark hair sprinkling his bronzed skin tapered to a V at his waist. His upper arms and chest were all muscle. Grayson was one fit man. One perfect man.

She was suddenly feeling self-conscious.

"Let me," Grayson said. He gently pushed her hands away and finished unbuttoning her blouse. Then he slid it down her arms.

Her bra was lacy and sexy as hell, her breasts full. Grayson reached for the clasp and removed the garment. It dropped to the floor. He was desperate to touch her. He slowly glided his fingers down to the small of her back. "You're so soft everywhere, so beautiful."

Olivia's breasts rubbed against his chest, and an electric sensation coursed through her body. His skin was warm, his muscles hard beneath. She could feel his strength and power under her fingertips, and his dark curly chest hair tickled her breasts when she moved. The erotic feeling intensified when she put her arms around his neck and her breasts rubbed against him again.

Resting the side of her face against his chest, she could hear his pounding heart and knew he was as excited as she was. It had happened so quickly. She wanted to kiss him, to touch him everywhere.

He unbuttoned her jeans and pushed them to the floor so she could step out of them. When he slipped her panties down, she felt a tingle that started at her toes and shot up through her body. Olivia watched as he slipped out of his own clothes. He was so magnificent, so perfectly sculpted, like one of Michelangelo's statues.

She pulled the covers back, and Grayson followed her down onto the sheets. He covered her with his body. Bracing his weight with his arms, he lifted up and stared into her eyes.

"You feel so good," he told her.

He clasped the sides of her face and finally kissed her. He wasn't gentle. His mouth took possession of hers, his tongue forcing her to respond. He couldn't get enough of her.

The kiss went on and on until Olivia was burning in every cell of her body. Her fingers glided over his hot skin, caressing his shoulders and his back while her hips moved erotically against his hard arousal.

Grayson ended the kiss and looked at her. He could see the passion and knew she wanted him as much as he wanted her. He kissed her again, then moved slowly down her body. His lips gently nibbled on her neck and the valley between her breasts.

His thumbs brushed across her nipples, once, then again. Her body responded by arching against him, and she moaned softly, telling him without words how much she liked his touch. He began to caress her breasts, then leaned down and took one nipple into his mouth, sucking hard. She cried out and moved restlessly against him. She couldn't keep still. Her hands stroked his shoulders, and she shifted under him until she was cuddling his arousal and forcefully moving against him. Her toes rubbed against his legs. His skin was hot, and she could feel his strength, but it didn't overwhelm her, for he was being so incredibly gentle, so loving.

His hands were everywhere, stroking, teasing. He was gentle and rough, and he was driving her wild. She wanted to make him as crazed as she was. Her hands slid down between their bodies, and she caressed his arousal. She knew he liked that because he groaned and tightened all around her. He couldn't take the torment long. His mouth claimed hers again in a hot, wet kiss that ignited the fire inside her.

She arched up against him. "Now, Grayson," she demanded. She was close to screaming if he didn't end the teasing and come to her.

He moved between her thighs and looked deeply into her eyes. When he thrust inside, he was immediately surrounded by liquid heat. She was so tight, so perfect for him. She drew her legs up to take more of him, and he groaned again. He began to move, slowly at first, and then with growing need. Losing all control, his mind was consumed with finding release for both of them. It was a blissful, pulsating torture as he reached higher and higher peaks of ecstasy. She dug her nails into his shoulders and arched up against him each time he withdrew, quickening the pace. Suddenly, she tightened and squeezed him, crying out his name with her climax. He couldn't stop his own release. He held her in his arms while he lost himself in her.

Her orgasm overwhelmed her, consumed her. The world seemed to splinter into a million brilliant stars, and she felt as though she had skyrocketed to the heavens and was slowly floating back to Earth. She was stunned by the intensity. She had never lost control like this, and it was terrifying. Yet Grayson had held her, whispered to her, telling her she could let go, she could trust him. And, oh God, how she did.

"Wow."

One word, that was all, but it was enough to tell her how pleased and satisfied he was. She recovered before he did. His breathing was still harsh, and she could feel his heart racing. Then she realized she was having just as much trouble. She was still tingling everywhere and continuing to stroke his back and his shoulders.

Grayson lifted his head and smiled at her. She looked properly ravaged, and that gave him an arrogant satisfaction. Her lips were red, and he could see the passion still there in her beautiful eyes.

"I love your mouth," he whispered before he kissed her again.

Realizing he was probably crushing her, he gathered enough strength to roll away from her. He lay on his back and took a deep breath. He was amazed it was taking him so long to clear his mind. Making love to Olivia was nothing like he'd ever experienced before. It was different. *She* was different.

"You said, 'Wow.'"

He could hear the laughter in her comment. He rolled to his side, propped his head with his arm and said, "No, I didn't."

Her eyes were closed, but she was

smiling. "Oh, but you did, Agent Kincaid. You said, 'Wow.' Is that your sweet talk?"

"Did you want sweet talk?"

"No. 'Wow' pretty much said it all."

He trailed his fingers from her neck to her stomach. "You screamed my name."

"I didn't scream."

"Oh, but you did, Miss MacKenzie."

His mood darkened in the space of a heartbeat. He stared at the scar from the bullet wound on her shoulder and was suddenly enraged. He wanted to kill the man who had hurt her and hoped he got the chance. She was lucky, the surgeon had told him. Both the injury to her shoulder and her side were considered minor. The bullets had gone straight through and hadn't hit anything vital. The hip was more serious because the bullet had lodged in bone.

"Does this still hurt?" he asked as he gently traced a circle around her shoulder.

"No."

"What about this?" He circled the small, raw wound on the side of her waist.

Olivia shivered. He was giving her goose bumps. "No."

He touched her hip. "And this?"

"Better," she admitted.

"What about your throat?"

She frowned. "What about it?"

"Does it hurt from screaming?"

She smiled. "I did not scream."

"Only one way to prove it," he told her.

Suspicious, she asked, "How?"

He pulled her into his arms. "I gotta make you scream again."

Olivia was curled up against his side sound asleep. Grayson wasn't going to spend the night, but he was too comfortable and content to move. He decided he would call Ronan tomorrow and remove himself from the case. He'd still follow what was being done, might even make a couple of suggestions here and there, but that was all. He couldn't sleep with Olivia again and run the investigation at the same time. Actually, he supposed he could; he just wasn't going to.

Maybe he'd stay with Olivia until early morning after all. He'd get up at five and leave. Yeah, that's what he would do. He pulled the covers up and yawned loudly. Olivia scooted closer and put her head on his shoulder.

He had made her scream twice, and he was damned proud of that accomplishment. He was thinking about how aggressive she had become after her second orgasm. She'd pushed him onto his back and proceeded to drive him crazy with her hands and her mouth and her tongue. Her enthusiasm staggered him. He realized he was getting hard again, and was seriously thinking about waking her up, when his cell phone rang. He gently lifted her off him, grabbed his phone from the bedside table where he'd put his gun and holster, and answered.

Henry was calling. "Uncle Grayson. I think I'm sick. Can you come get me?"

Grayson sat up. He heard the worry in Henry's voice but didn't ask for an explanation because he knew what was wrong. Henry was homesick. As much as the boy wanted to sleep over with friends, he couldn't seem to get through an entire night. Grayson had thought about Henry around ten o'clock, and when he didn't call, he had thought Henry had finally gotten over his problem.

He was getting better, though. He'd made it until eleven thirty this time.

"It's okay. I'll come get you."

After he'd dressed, he kissed Olivia on the forehead and nudged her.

"I've got to go. You're okay?"

"I'm fine," she told him. "Good night."

She disappeared under the covers. He stood there for a minute and then began to laugh. Had he been wanting some praise or a testimonial about their time together, he would have been disappointed. Apparently she wasn't much for sweet talk either.

FIFTEEN

Grayson asked Ronan to take over the MacKenzie investigation and to assign another agent to assist. Ronan refused.

The football was flying across the office as the two men argued. It was late, after nine in the evening, and both Ronan and Grayson were sitting at their desks catching up on paperwork. They had already discussed pending investigations, none of which were pressing, and then they began to talk about the progress on Olivia's case. That was when the argument started.

"I'm serious," Grayson insisted. "I'm

going to remove myself from the investigation. I'll talk to Pensky tomorrow."

Ronan hurled the football to Grayson.
"No, don't talk to her. I'll take the lead,
but you're staying on. You can assist.
Or . . ."

"Or what?"

"Distance yourself from Olivia until we
get the shooter."

That was easier said than done. Grayson couldn't get her out of his mind. All
he wanted to think about was taking her
to bed again. "I don't know if I can distance myself."

"Jeez, Kincaid. What happened to
your discipline?"

Ronan feigned disgust, which made
Grayson laugh. "I don't know what the
hell happened to it."

"It's different with her?" Ronan asked,
serious now.

"Yes."

"Okay, so you care about her."

"Of course I care." He was getting irritated. He put a spin on the football and
sent it spiraling back to Ronan.

"Tell me how you can walk away."

"I'm not walking away—"

Ronan interrupted. "Do you think someone else—besides me, of course— could do a better job protecting her and finding the shooter? You'd put her safety in someone else's hands?"

"I trust you to do the job," he snapped, "but no one else."

Ronan was hitting a nerve. Grayson didn't want to leave the case, but he didn't know how he was going to keep his objectivity.

"I'm not working this without you," Ronan said. "Don't talk to Pensky. All right?"

Grayson snatched the football from the air and held on to it as he thought about his options. Finally, he gave in. "Yeah, okay, for now anyway. I'll find a way to keep my distance."

"Good." Ronan swiveled in his chair and picked up a notepad from his desk. "I've got another name to put on the list of suspects."

"Yeah? Who?"

"Jorguson's bodyguard. Remember him?"

"The tank? That's what I felt like I was

hitting when I tackled him. His name is Ray Martin."

"Jorguson fired him, blamed the whole incident on him."

Grayson laughed. "I thought he blamed Olivia. Didn't he say it was all her fault?"

"For a little while he did. Then it became a misunderstanding. Jorguson just found out Olivia's going to testify against him, and now there's a court date set."

"His attorneys will delay, probably keep it out of court for at least a year, maybe two."

Ronan didn't disagree. "Jorguson pointed the finger at Martin. He said after he was fired, Martin ranted to some people that it was all Olivia's fault, actually said he was going to get even with her."

"Who did he say that to?"

"According to Jorguson, Martin made the threat in front of him and his assistant, Xavier Cannon. He claims he said it to a couple of clients. We've checked them out, and these clients have less-than-stellar reputations themselves."

"They're setting up Martin so the heat's off Jorguson."

"Could be," Ronan agreed. "Guess what Martin drives?"

"Tell me." He spun the football with one hand then sent it in a high arc across the room.

"Brand-new black SUV. Ford Explorer, to be exact." Ronan caught the ball and lobbed it back. "There's more," he told him. "I sent two agents over to his place. Martin lives a couple of blocks from that drug house we broke into to get the kid for Olivia."

"Gangland."

"Yes," he said. "The agents showed up to bring him in for questioning, and right there in plain sight on the table was a whole display of weapons. Gave the agents cause to search the rest of the house. They found an arsenal. Turns out Martin has a thriving business on the side selling guns to the neighbors. He said he just wanted to help them protect their homes."

"Now see, that makes him a nice guy."

"That's what I was thinking."

"What about George Anderson?" Grayson asked.

"I did what you suggested and had one of our agents in Las Vegas check out the loan shark, figuring he's like all the others—you know, a real business-man who breaks legs and arms to get his clients to pay up but doesn't see the feasibility in killing them because then he'd never get paid. Anderson's loan shark, Subway, is different. Every now and then one of his clients turns up dead. Looks like he's sending a mes-sage to other slackers. Word is, he gave Anderson a deadline. He's got three months to pay it all back."

"Do you think Anderson would know how to find a shooter?"

"No, but I think Subway would have names, and if Anderson mentioned how much money his wife would get if Olivia were dead, then, yeah, I think he'd help him find a driver and a shooter. He might have hired them for Anderson."

"Anderson's a weasel . . ."

"Is he capable of hiring a hit?"

Grayson didn't have to think about it.

"To save himself, yes. But then, so is Martin."

"Then there's also the possibility it was random. It could be a gang initiation. She was about the only person out during that freakish snowstorm. A blizzard that early in the season is unusual, and weathermen had only predicted flurries, so how does a kid anxious to get in a gang pass the test when there's no one around to kill? Maybe Olivia was just a handy target."

Grayson realized he was holding the football and tossed it back to Ronan. "She's made a lot of people who haven't paid their taxes very angry."

Ronan offered yet another option. "What about the kids she's helped? One of their relatives or guardians could be out for vengeance."

"I've talked to Judge Thorpe and Judge Bowen, and they gave me the names of the boys and girls she's been assigned. I tell you, Ronan, some of the places she's gone into, some of the god-awful situations those kids were in . . . I would have unloaded my gun on all of them once I got the kids out."

"No, you wouldn't have. You would have wanted to, but you would have taken them in."

"I swear I don't know how she does it," Grayson said. "She admitted she likes working for the IRS, partly because it's more mundane and balances out the horrors she sees in the other job."

"Were there any suspects? Relatives of these kids who want her dead?"

Grayson caught the ball, tucked it under his arm, and shuffled through a stack of papers on his desk until he found the one he wanted. He skimmed over it and said, "Two cousins of one little boy. Guess she really nailed them in court. They each got twenty years."

"So we've got motive . . ."

"Neither one of them have the connections outside of prison or the funds to hire a hit. I've got a few others I'm still checking out, but nothing looks promising."

"I want it to be Carl Simmons, her dad's attorney. After I interviewed that son of a bitch, I really wanted it to be him. Listening to all the trash he was talking about Olivia, trying to get her fired, calling her crazy . . ."

"She's been getting threatening phone calls," Grayson said. "She thinks it's Simmons. He disguises his voice, but she's pretty sure it's him. He only calls her cell phone number . . ."

"Were you able to trace the number back?"

"Every call came from a different public phone."

"Every call?"

"Olivia told me there have been four in all."

"Is she scared?"

"No, she's angry."

Ronan nodded. "You know who Simmons reminds me of? A game show host. He's got this phony yellowish-brown tan and these capped teeth that are a little too big for his mouth, and the color is beyond white. Creepy smile, too. He's tall and skinny, and when he opens his mouth, it's freaky."

"A real lady-killer, huh?"

Ronan laughed. "Funny thing is, he could be. I'd like it if he was the shooter," he repeated. "I'd like it a lot. Put his tanned ass in prison."

Grayson tossed the football into an open file drawer and turned his computer off. "Olivia's due to go back to work," he said. "How much longer will there be a protection detail?"

"I'm getting pushed now to end it," Ronan said. "Another week, maybe, but the budget . . ."

"I understand," Grayson said. "I'll take over and pay for it. I don't want her to know that, though. I'll hire some off-duty policemen I know and trust." As he grabbed his coat and put it on, he added, "I'll help out, too."

Ronan was searching for one of his gloves. He knelt on one knee and located it under the desk across from him where he'd tossed his coat. "For how long?" he asked.

"Until we make an arrest."

Ronan followed Grayson outside. "That could take awhile. I look at the list and I ask myself, who doesn't want to kill her?"

It had been two weeks since Olivia had seen Grayson. The last time they were together they had spent several passionate hours making love. Then nothing . . . not even a phone call to say, "Hello, how are you doing?"

She knew she probably should have been furious with him, but she wasn't. After the first time he'd kissed her, she hadn't seen him or heard from him for two long months. It took a shooting to get him to remember her. Maybe this was going to be a long hiatus as well. Grayson was a busy man, she reminded herself, with a nine-year-old he was now raising—though she didn't know if that was a temporary or a permanent situation—and his father, Edward Kincaid, was recovering from a massive heart attack.

Emma had given her the details about his father's condition. She said that the cardiac surgeon had called the heart attack the widow maker, and if Grayson's father hadn't gone to the emergency room when he'd first experienced symptoms, and if the cardiac surgeon hadn't been right there to take over, Edward Kincaid wouldn't have made it.

Olivia understood why Grayson couldn't take time for her. No, she wasn't angry with him, but she was damned irritated. How long would a phone call take? Or even an e-mail or a text? No time at all. Exactly.

It was Friday afternoon, and she was about to do a favor for a coworker so that he and his family could leave early to catch a flight to Miami for a long weekend. She had volunteered to drop off some papers, and she was looking forward to her errand. The company she was going to visit unannounced was called Nutrawonder Works, a vitamin distribution company. It was owned and operated by William Hood, who, according to the notes she'd been given, had raised suspicion that he'd been ripping off the government for several years. The IRS wanted to go through his records to prove it and also to find evidence that he had been ripping off his employees as well by falsely reporting contributions to their pension fund. The word *bully* was underlined in red on the report.

Olivia didn't plan to walk into Nutra-wonder alone. She was going to take an armed IRS agent with her, but as it turned out, that wasn't necessary. Just as she picked up the phone, Grayson walked in.

She put the phone down and watched him walk toward her. Don't stare, she told herself, yet she continued to do just that. Her mind scrambled for ways to get over her nervousness, and the advice she'd once been given before ascending a podium to speak in front of a crowd popped into her head: Think of him naked. She tried that trick, but a picture of his magnificent body appeared and had her suddenly feeling breathless and hot. Okay, that was a bad plan. Don't think of him naked, she told herself.

She could feel her cheeks getting warmer. She opened her desk drawer, took out her inhaler, and used it. God, how telling was that?

Grayson stopped in front of her desk.

"Are you ready to leave?" he asked casually. "I'll drive you home."

She was still too rattled to come up with a witty and stinging reply. She nodded, then shook her head. "The policeman drove me here."

"I've sent him home. Another guard will be at your front door at ten tonight. Until then, you've got me."

No apology, no excuses, and not a hint of embarrassment or guilt. All right. If that was the way he wanted to play it, she'd go along. She could be just as aloof.

"I have to make a stop before I go home. I need to drop off some papers."

"That's fine."

"It's not going to be a pleasant meeting. You might need your weapon."

"Yeah, okay."

He was Mr. Cool, leaning against the desk looking relaxed and . . . mellow. Yes, that was the word to describe him: mellow. Her nerves were raw. She had worried and wondered about him for the last two weeks, but here he stood, calm and collected. Obviously, he hadn't been thinking about her. She wanted to kick him and kiss him at the same time.

She put the papers she was going to take to Nutrawonder in a legal envelope and sealed it. Then she got her purse out of the bottom drawer and started throwing personal items inside. Her cell phone went in first, then her indulgences: M&M's, a protein bar she'd been carrying around for a couple of months but refused to eat because the last one tasted like sawdust, and a cold bottled water she'd just gotten out of the refrigerator.

"You forgot your inhaler," he said. "It's in your middle drawer."

"No, I have one in my purse. I always keep an extra one here."

"You might want to check. I saw two in your drawer when you opened it."

He didn't miss anything, did he? She might have two in her desk, but she always carried one with her . . . except today. She ended up emptying everything in her purse onto her desk and realized then that she had put the one she always carried with her in the drawer.

"Oh . . . I didn't realize . . . I don't do that. Thanks for noticing."

What else had he noticed? How nervous she was? That was a given, she decided. She put the inhaler where it belonged and was ready to leave. Even while she was telling herself she didn't care, she was wishing she'd taken the time this morning to put on something a little fancier. Her pale pink silk blouse, black pencil skirt, and black flats were so ordinary. She could at least have worn high heels or boots. What had she been thinking? That it was freezing outside, that's what. Wearing high heels in this snow was asking for a broken ankle. And when she wore boots, her feet always got hot while she worked at her desk. Still, she should have put a little effort into her appearance. She hadn't even bothered to put her hair up or curl it. The thick mass was down around her shoulders. She nervously pushed a strand away from her face as she walked toward him.

He lifted her coat from the rack and held it out for her. "What happens when you forget it?"

"My inhaler?"

She put her coat on and turned toward him. Grayson took her scarf and wrapped it around her neck, gently lifting her hair out of the way. They stood inches apart.

"Yes, your inhaler," he said. "What happens when you forget it?"

She stared into his eyes. "I get into trouble."

"Olivia?"

She jumped. One of Mr. Thurman's assistants, a sweet, older woman named Violet, stood in the hallway. "Mr. Thurman wanted me to tell you that the team is on their way to Nutrawonder and will wait in their cars until you give them the word."

"Thank you, Violet."

The assistant took a step closer to Olivia. She glanced at Grayson, smiled, and then said, "I hear Billy Hood is a nasty piece of goods, if you know what I mean. Would you like to borrow my pepper spray?"

She smiled. "No thanks. I've got something better." She tilted her head toward Grayson as she walked past Violet. "I've got him."

SIXTEEN

Billy Hood was indeed a nasty piece of goods, though, after meeting him, Grayson had a few more succinct words to describe the bastard.

Nutrawonder's offices were located outside the city and just a mile off the interstate in a run-down industrial area. The building was old and in need of paint. The linoleum floors were cracked and split, and the desks of the employees were crammed together. It was around sixty degrees inside, and Grayson noticed that some of the men and women were wearing their coats as they worked at their computers.

Hood's office was upstairs. Unlike the sterile first floor, the second floor had been remodeled. There was a garish neon-blue carpet, new furniture, and dark paneled wood in the reception area. The temperature was much more pleasant.

The woman sitting behind the desk was wearing enough makeup to spackle an entire wall. She had a fashion magazine open in front of her and was casually turning the pages with unnaturally long, curved, polished nails, completely ignoring Olivia and Grayson.

"We close in five minutes," she said, without looking up. "Besides, Mr. Hood isn't available. He's on the phone in his office, but he isn't available to anyone. You'll have to make an appointment. Mr. Hood doesn't see anyone without an appointment." She finally raised her head. "Do you want to leave your name or your card . . . or something?" she asked. She was staring at Grayson while she twirled a strand of hair in her fingers. "Or your phone number?"

Olivia rolled her eyes. She glanced at Grayson to see how he was reacting to Miss Spackle. He didn't seem affected. He was probably used to getting hit on, she supposed, and for some reason that irked her. She walked past the receptionist, opened the door to Hood's office, and went in. The receptionist didn't notice until Grayson followed Olivia.

"Hey, Billy isn't available," she called out. "I mean Mr. Hood isn't available."

Grayson stopped in the doorway. "You can go home now," he told her as he was pulling the door closed.

Hood was talking on his cell phone. Grayson spotted a suitcase behind the door.

"Just make sure you bring your passport, Lorraine. I'll meet you at the airport." He looked up from his conversation and saw Olivia and Grayson standing there. "Hold on a second." He pointed to the door. "I'm talking on the phone," he snapped. "Get out of my office." He looked at Olivia, lingering on her legs, and said, "I guess you could stay, darling."

Olivia shook her head. "I'm not your darling. Now get off the phone."

Hood was an unpleasant-looking man. There were deep wrinkles in his forehead and above his cheekbones. Olivia attributed them to scowling most of his life. His beady eyes were a little too close together and his jowls hung low like a bulldog's. She knew he was married, and she wondered if his children looked like him—God forbid—or like their mother. She pushed the silly thoughts aside and focused on the task at hand.

Hood ended the call and slipped the cell phone into his pocket.

"Who are you?" he demanded.

Olivia gave him a friendly smile. "Where are you going, Mr. Hood, if you don't mind my curiosity? I noticed the suitcase, and I did happen to overhear you telling Lorraine not to forget her passport."

"California," he answered. "Napa."

"Lorraine doesn't have a driver's license to show at the airport?" she asked in her most pleasant, noncombative voice.

"Of course, she has a driver's license."

She tilted her head and looked puzzled. "You are aware that California is still part of the United States."

"Maybe I don't want to tell you where I'm going. Did you ever think of that? For all I know you could be . . ."

"What?" Grayson asked.

Olivia stood on one side of the desk, and Grayson was on the other, looming over him. Hood swiveled his neck and blurted, "Spies."

Olivia looked at Grayson with mock surprise. "Mr. Hood appears to be a little paranoid. Perhaps it's because Lorraine isn't his wife."

"Ah."

"My personal life is none of your business."

She nodded. "You're right—" she said as she pulled the legal papers out of her envelope.

She was about to tell him that his finances were definitely her business when he interrupted. "You're working for my wife, aren't you? You're spying for her. How dare she not trust me." He pointed to the door again, and just as

Olivia was about to explain who she was and why she was there, he started cursing her. "Get out of my office, you bloodsucking bitch." He added several more gross names before he took a breath.

Olivia pretended to be both shocked and thrilled. Her hand flew to her throat, and she gasped. She sounded excited when she said, "I didn't know we got to use dirty words, Mr. Hood. Let me have a turn." She dropped the papers on his desk in front of him, placed her card with the bold IRS letters visible, leaned in, and said, "Prison."

Grayson listened to the conversation with great amusement. Olivia's handling of Hood was truly impressive. He had seen many sides of her since they'd met. He knew she was loving and gentle. He had seen that side when they'd rescued Tyler from the drug dealers. He had witnessed her steely determination when she stood up to George. He definitely had seen her passionate side with her uninhibited lovemaking. And today, he was getting a glimpse at her wicked sense of humor, a side he thoroughly appreciated.

Hood, on the other hand, wasn't amused. "Go ahead. Do another audit. You won't find anything. I'm still leaving on vacation. I'm going to—"

"California?" she asked, helping him remember the lie he'd just told.

"Yes, bitch, California."

"I'm afraid you're going to have to put that trip off for a while."

He tried to grab her arm. Grayson put a death grip on his shoulder. "Don't touch her unless you want to get hurt. You don't want to get hurt, do you, Billy?"

Hood glared at Grayson before turning to Olivia again. "Lorraine's going to be pissed," he muttered. "How long do I have to postpone my trip?"

"Ten to twenty with good behavior would be my guess."

Olivia texted the leader of the audit team, but there wasn't any need. They were already in the building.

Since Grayson was watching Olivia, Hood made the mistake of assuming that he wasn't paying any attention to him. He slowly reached into his desk drawer.

Grayson slammed the drawer shut, and Hood howled in pain. His fingers were trapped, and Grayson wasn't letting him pull them out.

"Now, see, Billy," Grayson said, his tone mild. "That has to hurt."

"You broke my fingers," he screamed. "You broke my fingers."

Olivia was surprised by Grayson's actions but didn't comment. A moment later she understood the reason behind the brute force.

"Let's see what you keep in your drawer," Grayson said.

"That's private property. You have no right . . ." He stopped protesting when Grayson produced a handgun. "I have no idea how that got there."

"Yeah, right."

"It's not loaded."

"Oh?" Grayson pointed the barrel at Hood. "Then if I pull the trigger . . ."

"Don't!" he shouted. "Okay, okay, it's loaded. It's for protection in case someone tries to rob me. I wasn't going to shoot anyone. I'm telling you I didn't even remember the gun was in my drawer."

Olivia and Grayson were through talking to him, but it took another twenty minutes before they were able to leave Nutrawonder. After refusing to cooperate, Hood was led out in handcuffs, shouting that he'd been set up and a lawyer would prove his innocence.

Once Grayson and Olivia were back in the car, he asked, "Did you know the gun was there?"

"I had a suspicion."

"Then you noticed him reaching for the drawer."

"No, I noticed you noticing him reaching for the drawer."

Olivia saw the muscle in his cheek flex as he clenched his jaw.

"I wouldn't have gone into the office alone," she said. "There would have been at least one armed agent with me. When I'm alone, I'm more observant, and, yes, I know I should always be observant, so stop the scowl."

"You're right. You should always be more observant. You take risks, Olivia. Dangerous risks."

"I beg to differ. I don't normally go

into situations like the one today. I was doing a favor for a colleague."

"Did he warn you about Hood?"

"Yes."

"Damn it, Olivia, you need to be more careful."

"I was being careful."

"Yeah, right."

"Don't take that tone with me."

"What tone?"

"You're snapping at me."

She looked disgruntled. For some reason her expression eased some of his anger away.

"I care about you," he said quietly.

She didn't acknowledge his statement for a long while, and Grayson didn't pressure her. He had just parked the car when she whispered, "I care about you, too. If I didn't care, I never would have . . ."

"Let me touch you?"

"I was going to say I never would have touched you."

She rushed to move the subject away from sex because, from the moment she'd seen him, she'd wanted to rip his

clothes off and have wild, arrest-able
sex.

"Your job is more dangerous than
mine," she said. "I don't have a bulletproof vest in the trunk of my car, and I
don't carry a gun."

"Do you worry about me?"

She didn't answer because they had
just arrived at her apartment building.
Grayson followed her upstairs. When he
got a whiff of her perfume, he instantly
reacted. Her scent had the power to
drive him crazy. It was so damned sexy.

He hung up her coat and then his. His
suit jacket followed. Olivia went into the
kitchen and opened the refrigerator to
search for something she could munch
on. She wasn't really hungry yet; she
was feeling the tension of having Grayson in her apartment again. She decided
on a Jell-O cup. It had zero calories,
and it would keep her hands and her
mouth busy. She pulled out a spoon
and turned around to finally answer him.
She knew he wasn't going to let it go.

He stood in the doorway, waiting. She
pointed the spoon at him and said, "Yes,
I worry about you, but I don't want to.

Besides, what's the point? Worrying is wasted energy. What will happen will happen no matter if I worry or not, and when it does, it's usually bad."

"Interesting," he said. "All this time I thought you were an optimist."

"I don't live in the clouds."

He crossed the kitchen and backed her into the corner. "Here now, gone tomorrow. Is that your attitude?"

She waved the spoon in front of his face and tried to push him away. "Something like that," she said defiantly.

"You're always optimistic with kids, aren't you?"

"Of course."

"What about your friends, Jane and Samantha and Collins? Are they as pessimistic as you are about their futures?"

She was taken aback. "I know you've met Jane, but how do you know about Samantha and Collins?"

"Emma told me about them." He took the Jell-O and spoon from her and put them on the counter. Then he put her hands around his neck.

"She shouldn't have . . . What are you doing?"

"Kissing you," he answered. He tugged on her earlobe with his teeth and knew she liked that. He felt her tremble.

"Stop it." She tried to sound irritated instead of breathless.

"You like it."

Since she'd tilted her head to the side to give him better access to her neck, she couldn't tell him he was wrong. "Yes," she whispered.

"I'm keeping my distance." His fingers slid through her silky hair, and he gently turned her to look up at him. His mouth came down on top of hers. She never wanted the wet and hot sensation to end. As he made love to her with his tongue, she clung to him, and when he tried to end the kiss, she pulled him back to kiss her again.

He was shaking with desire when he finally backed away. "Olivia, it happens so fast with you," he whispered. "All I have to do is get near you, and I want it all. I thought it was your perfume that was such a turn-on, but it isn't. It's you."

She understood. When she got close to him, all she could think about was making love to him. She tucked her head under his chin so she wouldn't be distracted and asked, "What did you mean about keeping your distance?"

His chin dropped down and he rubbed it lightly across the top of her head. "I'm keeping my distance from you until we make an arrest."

"This is your idea of keeping your distance?"

He hugged her. "Apparently so."

He let go of her and walked out of the kitchen. She followed. "Where are you going?"

"To bed."

She opened her mouth to protest, then closed it. Grayson took her hand and started toward the bedroom.

"We have to have sex," he said very matter-of-factly.

"Why?"

"You know why. You're here now, but you could be gone tomorrow. We need to take advantage of the time we have."

"That's not funny," she snapped, pulling on his hand.

"Yeah, it kinda is."

She was furious with him. "I could die tomorrow," she argued.

"Yes, you could." He'd removed his tie and was now working on his shirt. His smile was tender. "But you're here now."

"You're being cruel, Grayson."

"No, I'm not. Take your clothes off, sweetheart."

She couldn't believe his gall. Did he think that all he had to do was snap his fingers and she'd strip for him? she wondered, even as she removed her blouse and reached for the zipper on her skirt.

"This is just lust." She made the statement as her skirt dropped to the floor. She pulled the silky camisole over her head and tossed it behind her. Her bra and panties followed. "Sex is a way to release pent-up tension . . . you know, anxiety. But it's primarily lust. That's all it is."

Saying it out loud didn't make it true. Olivia was already emotionally invested. She wanted Grayson to touch her, yes, but there was another reason besides the physical. Her feelings for him were growing.

Grayson was watching her expressions. In the past minute she'd looked

happy, then angry, and now . . . disgruntled. He was pretty sure he knew
what was going on in that stubborn mind
of hers. He was pushing her and she
was pushing back.

He had already undressed. He
dropped down on the bed, and before
she realized what he was going to do,
he'd pulled her down until she was strad-
dling him.

"No, it isn't just lust. It's much more."

She acted as though she hadn't heard
what he'd said and tried to kiss him. He
wouldn't let her. "Admit it."

"No."

If this was a game of who was more
stubborn, she would win hands-down.
She brushed her lips over his and whispered, "No," once again.

His mouth covered hers, and he
kissed her hard, thoroughly. He fell back
on the bed, forcing her to stretch out on
top of him, then rolled over until he'd
pinned her beneath him.

Her fingers spread upward through
his hair as she kissed his chin, then
lower, until her lips were pressed against
the pulse at the base of his throat. She

could feel his heartbeat under her lips. She rubbed her pelvis against his in an attempt to drive him out of his mind. She wanted him to beg her to stop the erotic torment and come to him. Oh yes, she would make him beg.

The plan backfired. Five minutes later she was begging him. When it came to sex, how could she have thought she was superior to him? My God, he was a master. He knew what she liked, where to touch and stroke and how to make her respond. He made her burn with passion. She was writhing in his arms as she pleaded with him to come to her.

Grayson was determined to make her admit the truth to him before he let her climax. The effort nearly killed him. He used his last shred of discipline as his hands and his mouth moved over her sweet body. His forehead was beaded with perspiration, and he was aching with his need, yet he continued to hold back.

"It's a hell of a lot more than lust between us, isn't it?" he demanded.

His hand slid between her thighs. She

relented. "Yes," she cried out. "Happy now?"

"Damn right," he whispered gruffly. He lifted up and looked at her. Her eyes were misty, and it was his undoing.

"Grayson," she groaned. "Gloat later."

He moved between her thighs and thrust inside her. She arched up against him, taking him deeper. He wanted to make it last, this glorious rapture, but he couldn't control his body any longer. Or his desire. Olivia was as wild to find fulfillment as he was, and both climaxed together.

Long minutes passed while they tried to regain their senses. Olivia couldn't understand how something that was so wonderful could keep getting better.

"Are you okay?" he asked as he tried to find the energy to roll away from her.

She nodded against his shoulder. He moved onto his back and pulled her with him. She felt like a rag doll, a very content rag doll. She probably looked like one, too, with her hair hanging over her face.

"Did you enjoy hearing me plead?"

He smiled. "Yeah, I did."

She rolled on top of him, stacked her hands on his chest, and stared at him. He looked arrogantly pleased with himself. And why wouldn't he? She'd caved and given him a little hint of the truth. She hadn't told him she loved him, but she'd come close.

"I'll get even with you," she whispered. "I'll make you beg."

He laughed. "I look forward to it."

He caressed her back, his touch gentle now, sending shivers down her arms and legs. "I love your scent."

"I thought you loved my mouth."

"That too."

She tried to roll off him, but he wouldn't let her, so she laid her head on his chest and rested her hands on his arms. His biceps were firm and taut, and she marveled at him. He was so powerful, so protective. She had never been this uninhibited with anyone. Yet, when she was with him, all she wanted to do was melt into him and let his courage and strength enfold her. He made her feel safe.

With a contentment she'd never experienced before, she lay quietly, feeling his rhythmic breathing against her cheek.

After a few minutes passed, she said, "Why does Henry live with you?"

The unexpected question jarred him. "His mother died several years ago, and Henry moved in with his grandfather. Then, when he became ill, Henry came to live with me."

"What happened to Henry's father?"

"His father is my brother, Devin. After his wife died, he went a little crazy. She . . . stabilized him, helped him focus. Now he travels a great deal. I guess you could say he's become somewhat of a jet-setter these days."

"Does he love Henry?"

"Yes, he does. He just doesn't like being a father. Since he's out of the country so often, I've gained full custody."

She rolled to her side and her fingertips moved over his skin in feather-light strokes. She circled his navel and moved lower.

"Henry has to come first," she said.

"I know," he said. He grabbed her hand to stop her from tormenting him, then pulled her into his arms. "I'm hungry," he told her.

"Me too," she whispered. "What would you like?"

He tilted her face up toward him, kissed her brow, then her cheek. "You," he answered.

"Me?"

"Yeah. I want you."

No other words were necessary.

SEVENTEEN

What started out to be a lovely, thoroughly satisfying evening ended up in a fight.

They reluctantly left her bed, and because Grayson didn't want the intimacy to end, he followed her into the shower. Olivia was shocked by how quickly she could want him again, and though she was a little clumsy and in jeopardy of drowning, she did get him to beg her to come to him. By the time he gave in, she could barely stand. Grayson lifted her up, wrapped her legs around him, and made love to her again.

The man had far more stamina than she did. He had already dressed and was in the kitchen looking for something to eat before she had dried her hair. She put on jeans and one of her favorite T-shirts. It was old, a little frayed around the bottom, and a little too tight across her breasts, but she loved the feel of the soft fabric against her skin. Besides, after what she'd done in bed and on her knees in the shower, being self-conscious about a tight T-shirt was ridiculous.

Grayson was guzzling a bottle of water, leaning against the kitchen island when she joined him. His gaze was locked on her as he slowly put the bottle down.

"You're beautiful. You know that?"

She shook her head. "Not a lick of makeup on and I'm beautiful. You've overdosed on sex."

He laughed. "That's not possible. I can never get enough of you."

The way he was looking at her, the intensity in his expression as he watched her, indicated he meant what he said. He looked as though he was thinking about dragging her back to bed. She was suddenly embarrassed and didn't have any idea why.

He noticed she was blushing and thought that was hilarious.

"Sweetheart, considering what you just did with that sweet mouth of yours . . ."

She interrupted. "I'd rather not discuss what we did."

She nudged him out of her way so she could open the refrigerator. "Would you like chicken parmesan with pasta?"

"Sure," he said.

She handed him the casserole dish. He lifted the lid and said, "Did you make this?"

"Oh God, no. My aunt's cook, Mary, brings meals over. She thinks I'm wasting away."

"You've got a great body," he remarked, and before she could react to the compliment, he asked, "What can I do to help? I'm starving."

She put him to work making a salad. It didn't take any time at all to warm the chicken and pasta. She sliced hot French bread, and dinner was ready. They sat at the small table in the alcove overlooking the street. Grayson turned the plantation shutters so no one could look in.

He ate like a starving linebacker. "Does your aunt's cook . . ."

"Mary," she supplied.

"Does Mary bring food every day?"

"Sometimes, or she'll bring a week's worth of dinners. She puts all of them in the freezer with instructions on each, and all I have to do is slip one into the oven or the microwave, and dinner's ready. I keep telling her she doesn't need to continue cooking for me, but she's like my aunt Emma. Neither one of them will listen."

"When did she start cooking for you?"

Olivia stared at her plate while she thought about it, twisting the pasta around and around her fork, barely aware of what she was doing.

"When I was finally released from the unit . . . the hospital unit," she explained. "I moved in with Aunt Emma and Uncle Daniel. They'd purchased a house in D.C. about eight months before."

"Why didn't you go back home to San Francisco?"

"I had to continue to see Dr. Pardieu, and I would never leave Jane and Collins and Sam. They were still undergoing treatment."

He nodded to let her know he understood. "You're very loyal."

"They're my sisters." Her voice was emphatic. "We protected one another."

"From what? The outside world?"

She shrugged. "Something like that. Mary had just started working for Emma. At the time I was released, I was weak and thin, and from Mary's horrified expression, I assumed I looked bad. I was suddenly encased in a bear hug, and Mary told me she was going to fatten me up. I remember thinking of the story *Hansel and Gretel.*"

"The witch was going to fatten them up before she cooked them."

She nodded. "Mary wasn't a witch, though. She was and is an angel. Unfortunately, I'm still not fattened up enough to suit her."

"Emma moved here for you, didn't she?"

"Yes." She put her fork down and pushed her plate aside. "I thought when

I went off to university and later when Uncle Daniel died, she would move back to San Francisco, but she loves it here, and she doesn't want to move."

"Mary has a key to your apartment?"

"Yes, of course."

"Who else has a key?"

"Jane and Collins. Neither one of them has ever used her key, though."

"What about Samantha?"

"Jane and Collins live here, and in an emergency they know they can come stay with me. That's why they have keys. Emma's house is always open to all of us, too," she added. "But Sam's in Iceland or somewhere thereabout. She doesn't need a key."

Olivia carried her dishes to the sink. Grayson followed and nudged her out of his way. "I've got this."

She was happy to let him clean up. She sat on a stool at the island watching him. His back was to her so she could stare at him. He could easily overwhelm her, she thought. Can't let that happen. But he was so . . . bigger than life. So wonderful and sweet and sexy and . . . She suddenly wanted to wrap her arms around him and hold tight.

Snap out of it, she told herself.

He turned and saw her watching him. "Is something wrong?" he asked. "You're frowning."

Fortunately, her cell phone rang, and she didn't have to come up with a suitable answer. She wasn't going to tell him the truth, that he scared the hell out of her, making her want things she could never have.

She didn't recognize the phone number, but as soon as she heard the voice, she knew exactly who was calling.

"Olivia, this is Eric Jorguson. Now, don't hang up on me, please. Hear me out."

"What do you want?" she asked quietly. She tapped Grayson on his shoulder, and when he turned to her, she whispered Jorguson's name.

Jorguson continued, "I want to apologize for my behavior at the restaurant."

"That happened some time ago."

"And you're wondering why I'm apologizing now? Is that it? I know it's long overdue. I jumped to the wrong conclusion. I should have reasoned it through. You're Robert MacKenzie's daughter, and if I can trust him with my money, I can certainly trust that you wouldn't be part of anything so underhanded as wearing a wire. I completely overreacted." He paused and then said, "The other reason I'm calling is to offer you a position."

She nearly dropped the phone. "You want me to come work for you?" She shivered with repulsion over the possibility. At least she didn't gag.

"Yes, I most certainly do. Once I understood you weren't working for the FBI, I realized what a catch you would be. I really want you to consider working for me."

He then explained in great detail what the position would be, and when he casually mentioned the starting salary, she nearly dropped the phone again.

Grayson was leaning against the sink, a dish towel in hand, watching her intently. He looked like he was about to grab the phone and throw it against the wall.

"I hope you don't mind, Olivia," Jorguson went on, "but I did have a look at your financials."

"My financials?" she repeated, dumbfounded by his temerity.

He either didn't hear how strained her voice was, or he didn't care. "And I noticed you have never accepted any money from your relatives. You're making your own way on your own terms, and I admire that. Yes, I do," he insisted. "I also found out what your annual salary is, working for the IRS. In one year with me, Olivia, you'll make more than five times that amount.

"Besides salary," he continued, "there are other benefits, and you'll only work with three of my top clients."

He listed their names, and Olivia thought they sounded familiar. Probably from the FBI's Most Wanted List, she surmised. Hmmm. The possibilities were growing. She might be able to help Agent Huntsman nail him. Wouldn't that be lovely?

"I'll have to think about it," she said.

"Yes, think about it. Take all the time you need. Now, one last thing . . ."

"Yes?"

"I want to tell you how sorry I am that Ray Martin, my personal assistant, went after you the way he did."

"Do you mean when he attacked me and hit me?" *And you were yelling, "Get her, get her"?* she thought but didn't add.

"No, I mean when he drove by your apartment building and shot you. I want you to know he was no longer working for me. I had already fired him after the incident at the restaurant, and I believe he blamed you and wanted revenge."

"You're certain it was him?"

"Oh yes. You won't have to worry about thugs like Martin bothering you when you work for me. You'll be pro-tected."

And on he continued, raving about his luxurious offices and how very lucky she was to be one of his chosen.

As soon as the call ended, she looked over at Grayson and said, "I don't know if I want to laugh or throw up. Get this. Jorguson said he's invested in my fa-ther's fund." She laughed. "He's going to lose every penny."

"Huntsman will want to know about

this. I'll tell him. What else did Jorguson say?"

Grayson followed her into the living room, and she plopped down on the sofa. He stood on the other side of the coffee table and asked her to repeat the entire conversation.

Olivia was still flabbergasted when she finished. "How can he do that? Call me as though there weren't still charges pending for the attack?"

"He wouldn't call unless he was convinced his attorneys were making it all go away. They've evidently managed to shift all the blame onto Martin." He thought for a second and said, "He didn't give you any concrete reasons why he thinks Martin is the shooter?"

"Not really," she said. "Other than saying Martin wanted revenge because Jorguson fired him. That's more of a guess on Jorguson's part, isn't it? Could Ray Martin be the shooter?"

"He doesn't have an alibi, said he was home watching *Sixty Minutes*."

"Really?" She didn't know why she thought that was funny, but she did.

"Really," he insisted. "Couldn't re-

member what was on, though. We don't
have proof yet that he was involved with
your shooting, but we can prove he's
been selling guns to his neighbors, and
we found his stash."

"He's got a bad temper," she added.
"I've seen it."

"Yes, he does," he agreed. "He tried
to throw a chair at an agent during questioning. He's got a short fuse, and he
could kill someone. One of the guns we
found, an old .45, was used in a shooting last year. Only prints on it were his.
Martin's going away for a long time."

"What if he has something to offer in
return for a lighter sentence? Maybe he
could give you Jorguson and some of
his clients."

"He'd have to give up Gretta Keene
along with Jorguson to get any consideration, and that's not going to happen."

"I thought you told me Keene vanished right before she was deported."

"We don't think she ever left the country. She's still running her operation here,
and we believe Jorguson is still laundering her blood money."

He sat down next to her and called

Ronan. He was waiting for him to pick up when Olivia said, "You know, I could take a leave from the IRS and maybe use some of my vacation . . ."

Ronan answered. "Hold on," Grayson said. Turning to Olivia he asked, "For what purpose?"

"Do you realize the data I'd have access to if I were to work for Jorguson? You told me Agent Huntsman has been after him for some time now. I'd like to help. This would be an opportunity . . . Stop looking at me like you think I'm crazy."

"Do you actually believe he'd let you near anything illegal?"

"I could snoop around, find out how he communicates with Keene and how he—"

"There's no way in hell you're going to work for that bastard."

"I really think I'm the one who should make that decision."

Thus began what Olivia would later refer to as the blowout. Grayson had a dark side, and she didn't like it one little bit. He thought he could intimidate her and almost did, but she gave as good as she was getting. At least, she thought she did. But in the end, FBI trumped her.

"Are you really that stubborn?" she demanded.

"Apparently I am," he countered.

In the heat of the moment, Grayson had forgotten Ronan was on the line. His friend was on his way to pick up a date. He tried a couple of times to get Grayson to talk to him, then gave up and listened.

Grayson argued, "You can't be that naive, Olivia. The only reason Jorguson wants you working for him is to keep an eye on you, and to keep you from testifying against him. That's also the reason he would pay you an obscene salary."

"I realize—" Olivia began, and that was as far as she got. She didn't get in another word for several minutes while Grayson lectured over the foolishness of her suggestion.

The sharp whistle from the phone reminded him that Ronan was still waiting.

"Jorguson called Olivia," Grayson explained to him.

"I gathered as much," Ronan said. "I

could hear you shouting at her. Olivia's just trying to be helpful," he said in her defense. "It's a stupid idea, going to work for that creep . . ."

"Damn right it is."

"*But*," he said, all but shouting the word, "don't tell her that. She means well."

While Grayson talked to his partner, Olivia went into the kitchen to get a bottle of water. When she returned, she paused to glare at him just for the sheer pleasure of it, then took a drink and sat down next to him.

Grayson finished his call, put his arm around her, and said, "I didn't mean to shout at you."

She rolled her eyes heavenward. "Yes, you did."

"Yeah, you're right. I did."

She made the mistake of looking up at him. He kissed her then, distracting her. He took the bottle out of her hand and gulped down a long swallow before handing it back.

With a calmer voice now, Olivia said, "I was only offering to help."

"I understand," he answered, "but

these are dangerous people who have done terrible things. If you knew more about them, you'd see."

Olivia decided to let Grayson win this battle. So much for her superspy ambitions. She realized she couldn't infiltrate Jorguson's operation or help Agent Huntsman.

Letting the subject of Jorguson drop, she said, "I hope Ray Martin is the man who tried to kill me. He's your main suspect, isn't he?"

"No."

"No? Why not?"

"It doesn't feel right."

"What does that mean?"

He shrugged, which, in her opinion, wasn't much of an answer.

"He had motive," she said. "I got him fired."

"If everyone who got fired—"

"Revenge is a powerful motive."

"There are other powerful motives and other people who stand to gain much more than satisfaction or revenge if you're out of the way. Why do you want it to be Martin?"

"It would make it easy."

"That isn't a reason."

He was gently stroking her arm. She put her head down on his shoulder. "I don't want it to be a relative." The fact that she considered it possible that her father or mother or her sister or brother-in-law could go to such lengths made her sick. "You haven't met my father yet, have you?"

"No, I haven't."

"Why?"

"I wanted to find out all I could about him before I met him. I've talked to a lot of people who know him and have worked with him and for him."

"I'll bet every one of them sang his praises, even the ones who lost money."

"Pretty much," he agreed. "Ronan has taken the lead on the investigation. He's met him. He flew to New York and questioned him."

"But you're trying not to form an opinion until you meet him?"

"No, that's not possible. I know what he's done to you, sweetheart. I've got a real strong opinion."

There was anger in his voice. Grayson had become her champion, and she was a little overwhelmed. A long quiet minute passed before she spoke again. "When will you meet him?" she asked.

"At his birthday party here in D.C. next weekend."

She bolted upright. "You can't go to his party."

"Of course I can," he said. "Want to come with me?"

"Absolutely not. You're not going either," she insisted. "And quit shoving my head down on your shoulder. I mean it."

"Do you know you're even more beautiful when you're mad?" he said.

She wasn't having it. "Saying I'm beautiful isn't going to sway me, Grayson, so you can stop the phony flattery."

"It's not flattery, Olivia. You are beautiful."

She shook her head.

"What do you see when you look in the mirror?" he asked.

The question surprised her. "It depends."

"On what?"

"If I'm all dressed up and everything works, I feel pretty."

"What do you mean, if everything works?"

Before she could stop him, he lifted her up onto his lap and put her arms around his neck.

"I'm not a puppet, Grayson. You can't just put me where you want me."

He ignored her criticism. "What do you mean, if everything works?"

"You men . . ."

"Yes?"

"You have it so easy. Put on a suit and walk out the door. It's far more complicated for a woman. I'll give you an example. If I were to wear my all-time favorite white, wickedly sexy dress—which I happen to love with all my heart, as shallow as that sounds—and if my hair is just right, and my complexion is clear, and the makeup works, then I'd feel and see a pretty woman when I look in the mirror."

"It's kind of complicated, isn't it?" he remarked, trying not to laugh. "What happens when you're not dressed up?"

She didn't tell him the truth, that some days she felt like that ugly twelve-year-old in the hospital, fighting blisters and welts. "I look and feel drab sometimes. Yes, drab," she repeated, jabbing him in his chest. "Don't you dare laugh at me. I'm not so different from other women. We all have insecurities about our appearance."

He laughed anyway. She was primed for a fight. Apparently, he wasn't. She leaned in and kissed him, teasing him with her tongue. She knew he liked that because he tightened his hold around her.

"I'm not above having sex to get what I want," she purred.

He laughed again. "Glad to hear it."

EIGHTEEN

Olivia was going stir crazy. Work kept her busy during the days, but nights were difficult. She became quite the little housekeeper. She organized her kitchen cabinets, painted the guest bathroom a pale pink, decided she didn't like the color, and then painted it a dark blue. That didn't work either, so with her bodyguard at her side, she went back to the paint store a third time and purchased a can of taupe paint. Only after it was on the walls did she realize she'd painted it the original color.

It seemed to her that she was constantly tripping over the bodyguards following her around. She was allowed to go to work or stay home. There were no other options as far as Grayson was concerned. Even Aunt Emma's house was considered out of bounds.

An off-duty policeman drove her to work, then returned at five or six, depending on her schedule, to drive her home.

Another guard sat outside her office.

Olivia put her foot down about the twenty-four-hour protection, insisting that it was ridiculous to have a guard standing outside her apartment door. Once she was inside her home and had locked the deadbolt, she was perfectly safe. Besides, there was a doorman on duty twenty-four hours a day in the lobby. She gave Grayson the same argument about work. There was absolutely no reason for a bodyguard to sit outside her office.

Grayson relented as long as she promised not to go anywhere alone. He gave her five different cell phone numbers to call for the bodyguards. One of

them would always be available to accompany her.

She breathed a sigh of relief when
she got the news that Ray Martin was
behind bars. He had been denied bail—
the prosecutor convinced the judge that
Martin was a flight risk—and Olivia didn't
think it was coincidence that there hadn't
been another attempt on her life since
he was locked up. She pointed out the
obvious fact to Grayson, but every time
she brought it up, Grayson asked the
same question: What did Martin have to
gain by killing her? Revenge apparently
wasn't enough of a motive to suit him.

Monday evening she video-chatted
with Samantha, who couldn't stop raving about her jet.

"I wish you could go up with me,"
Sam said. "You'd love it."

Olivia thought she might like it, too.
"As long as you're the pilot, I don't think
I'd worry."

"Tell me about Jane. How is she doing?"

"Have you talked to her?"

"She was throwing up when I called
and couldn't come to the phone. Logan

answered. He told me he's really worried about her. He said she's losing
weight, and he can't understand why
the doctor can't fix her."

"Fix her?"

"Yes, that's what he said. Olivia, has
it come back?" she asked, fear radiating in her voice.

"Dr. Pardieu says no, there aren't any
signs that our disease has come back,
but her cell count is down, and her
symptoms aren't consistent. He's still in
France. I'll be happy when he gets back
and can take over again."

"When are you giving her blood?"

"Soon," she answered. "The hospital
will let me know."

"Collins is there. She can give her
blood, too."

"Yes," she agreed. "Maybe Jane's just
got a bad case of the flu. Some viruses
stay in your system a long time, don't
they?"

"I think you're reaching," Sam said. "I
feel so helpless. So does Logan," she
added.

"Jane's brother has only just recon-
nected with her, and it's heartbreaking

for him to see her so ill. He was never around when she was in the unit with us."

They continued to talk for another ten minutes. Sam told her there were several good-looking men around her, but she wasn't interested in any of them. "I'm so much younger than most of them," she said.

Olivia told her about Grayson and how she had gotten so involved with him.

"His nine-year-old nephew lives with him."

"How come?" Sam asked.

"The child's mother died, and the father is absent."

"That's too bad," she said. "I know what you're thinking. You're just like me. We're fatalists."

"Yes."

"We can't plan futures. Happy endings don't exist for any of us."

"Maybe we shouldn't live our lives . . . waiting. You know?"

Sam agreed. "I'm going to cram all I can into the time I have."

By the time they said their good-byes,

Olivia was feeling an overwhelming sadness, but she didn't allow herself to wallow in self-pity long. Since she was stuck at home, she decided to catch up on her reading. She had two unread novels and at least twenty-five journals stacked on her desk.

When she couldn't read another article without falling asleep, she went shoe shopping on the Internet. After that, she decided to do a little investigative browsing. She remembered Grayson mentioning a couple of Jorguson clients. One name in particular, Gretta Keene, came to mind first, so she decided to focus on her. She typed her name into the search engine and was surprised by the number of articles she found. As it turned out, the woman had quite a résumé. According to the reports, she was a Belgian emigrant who had become a major player in the American drug scene. After a long investigation by the government, she was finally charged with drug trafficking, but the case never got to court because of a technicality. Shortly after her release, the Belgian government instigated their own attempts to have her extradited. They were anxious to get her back so they could prosecute her for murder. Unfortunately, before any formal action could be taken, Keene disappeared, and she hadn't been heard from since.

In her research, Olivia saw Jorguson's name mentioned several times as a business associate, but he wasn't linked to any criminal activity. If the FBI was so convinced that Jorguson was laundering money for Keene, Olivia surmised they had some pretty good evidence, just not enough to convict him. She now understood their determination to connect the dots and to prove that Keene and Jorguson were working together.

Olivia was really getting into her research and thinking it was kind of fun, that is, until she happened upon photos of a crime scene, bloody bodies amid bags that were to be filled with drugs. The article printed with the pictures stated that Keene was believed to be connected to the killings, but that hadn't been proven either. Olivia found several more references to the same incident, and those led to other articles. After an hour, Olivia couldn't look at another crime scene or read about another bloodbath between rival drug cartels. These people were monsters. If Jorguson was aiding them in any way, Olivia prayed the FBI would catch him soon.

She turned off her computer and looked at the clock. The evening was still young, so she decided to try to make dinner. She chose a recipe from her one and only, new, never-before-opened cookbook and went to work. The result was a disaster. Emma's cook, Mary, saved her from starvation. Olivia pulled one of Mary's chicken-and-noodle casseroles from the freezer and popped it in the microwave. As she sat at her kitchen island eating out of the casserole dish, her thoughts went to Grayson.

She thought about him all the time. Whenever she had a spare minute, there he was. As far as her relationship with him went, she was certain that, when the threat was over and he was convinced that the proper arrests had been made, she wouldn't see him again. And that was for the best, she believed; yet,

whenever she thought about never seeing him again, she'd feel an ache deep
within her chest.

Was this just a fling? Maybe . . . except, she didn't do flings. She knew exactly what had happened and finally
found enough gumption to admit it.
She'd fallen in love with Grayson. What
she didn't understand was how she had
allowed herself to be vulnerable. This
was all her fault. She couldn't blame
Grayson for any of it. He'd never done
anything to lead her on or make her
think he had these feelings for her. She
had likened him to James Bond when
she'd first met him, and she'd seen all
the movies. In every one of them Bond
made love to the woman and moved on.
And so would Grayson. Wasn't that for
the best?

Olivia decided not to think about the
future.

On Friday she left work early—Fridays
were always slow for some reason. She
arrived home, changed into jeans and a
periwinkle-blue sweater, and went to the

kitchen to see what she could microwave.

Grayson changed the plan when he
showed up at her door and told her he
was taking her out.

He looked wonderful. His face was
ruddy from the bitter cold outside. His
coat collar was up, and his hair was
damp from the falling snow.

Olivia hadn't seen him since last Sunday when he'd dropped by unexpectedly. He had been able to stay for only
a few minutes then, but he'd called her
every day, sometimes twice, to check
on her. Now, with him standing in front
of her, she wanted to throw herself into
his arms. Resisting the nearly overwhelming urge, she forced herself to
step back so he could come inside, and
still not trusting herself, she put her
hands behind her back.

"Come on. I'm taking you to dinner,"
he repeated.

"You don't tell me we're going out to
dinner. You ask me. That's how it's done.
And then I decide if I want to go or not."

His hand moved to the back of her
neck, and he jerked her toward him. His

open mouth came down on hers, his tongue penetrating, tasting, teasing, tempting. When he lifted his head, she sagged against him.

She came to her senses and moved away from him. "We can't go out to dinner," she said as she walked into the kitchen. "It wouldn't be safe. Those were your words, Grayson." She opened the refrigerator, then closed it. "You told me I couldn't go to a restaurant or a shopping center or—"

"I remember what I told you. Office and home. I don't recall adding paint store to the list."

The bodyguard had told on her. She said, "We went in at closing and were the only customers."

Grayson noticed the open cookbook on the island. "Did you already make dinner?"

Her chin came up. "Risotto."

He looked around. "Where is it?"

"In the sink . . . soaking."

When he saw the wooden spoon sticking straight up out of the glue-like substance, he began to laugh. He took the spoon handle and attempted to move the congealed goo in the pan, but it wouldn't budge. "When did you make this?"

"Last night," she answered. "Grayson, it's not that funny."

"Yeah, it is."

She opened the refrigerator again. "Thank goodness for Mary."

"You don't want to go out?"

"You were serious? Of course I want to go out. I'm going crazy staying in all the time. I'm getting a vitamin D deficiency, for Pete's sake. I need sun and fresh air. I'm even trying to learn how to cook, and if that doesn't tell you how far gone I am, I don't know what will."

"A vitamin D deficiency?"

She folded her arms. "It's real."

"Where we're going you'll be safe."

Suspicious, she asked, "Where? Your office? No, I've got it. Vending machines at the police station."

"My place."

She shook her head. "I can't be around Henry. It wouldn't be safe for him."

"He isn't home tonight. He went to a movie with his grandfather and then is spending the night. It's the only other place he'll sleep."

Curious to see what his home was like and desperate to get out of her apartment, she agreed. "Okay, but no funny stuff."

He grinned. "Funny stuff?"

Ignoring him, she rushed into her bedroom to get her shoes.

Grayson was holding her coat when she returned. She slipped it on, grabbed her purse and cell phone, and unlocked the deadbolt. Grayson saw her inhaler on the table and picked it up.

"What are we having for dinner? Are we doing carryout?"

"I'm cooking for you."

"You cook?" She sounded shocked.

It was a short ride to Grayson's building, a grand five-story structure at the intersection of two quiet streets in a very exclusive neighborhood.

"I'm guessing you're a minimalist," she remarked.

Grayson used an app on his iPhone to open the iron gates that led to a parking garage below the building.

"How do you figure that?" he asked.

"Your home," she explained. "I'm guessing it's sleek, modern. Everything has a function. Am I right?"

The garage was empty. He pulled into a parking slot next to the elevator. "Have you forgotten I have a nine-year-old living with me?"

"Okay, cluttered minimalist."

"Until Henry moved in, the only furniture I had was my bed and a chest of drawers. The living room was empty. Once I'd finished remodeling, I planned to put it on the market. Everything changed, of course. I ordered furniture, and the last of it just arrived."

"Are you still thinking you'll sell?"

He shook his head. "Henry needs stability, so no more moving."

"Are you the only tenant living in the building?"

"Yes. I bought the building, remodeled the top floor, and the architect I hired is working on plans for the others."

"You should have become an architect."

"No, it's just a hobby."

The elevator doors opened to his foyer, gleaming marble floors and a wide-open space. The living room was straight ahead. Facing them was a wall of windows, and the view was spectacular. Area rugs in muted tones adorned dark hardwood floors. The furniture was sparse and did have the sleek lines she'd imagined. Two mahogany leather club chairs sat adjacent to a taupe over-stuffed sofa. The contemporary fireplace was encased in black granite that went all the way to the ceiling. There were lots of neutrals, and on the wall next to the fireplace was an abstract painting she thought might be a Richter original. Beautiful splashes of color and thick drapes gave the room dimension and texture.

The dining room was surrounded by windows as well. On the round, dark cherry table, she noticed a pad, no doubt to protect it from the Lego kit strewn about.

There was evidence of a nine-year-old everywhere. A handheld video game was on the arm of a chair; a pair of gym socks were under the dining room table, and there were three other Lego kits half completed behind the sofa.

To the left of the foyer was a long hallway. From what she could see, there were at least three bedrooms. To the right was another hallway that led to the kitchen and the pantry beyond. Grayson took her coat and hung it in the hall closet. She followed him, but stopped at the entrance to a gourmet chef's dream come true.

"This kitchen is practically the size of my entire apartment," she said.

Stainless steel, granite, and sleek lacquered cabinets everywhere she looked. All of the appliances appeared to be brand-new: two double-size ovens, a microwave, an espresso machine, a coffeemaker that had so many buttons it looked like it could run NORAD, a huge stove with eight gas burners, and a few other electrical gadgets she had never seen before.

The granite island was twice the size of hers. She pulled out one of the four bar stools and sat.

"Do you know how to work all of these appliances?"

"Sure I do." He was at the sink across from her washing his hands. "But Patrick, our housekeeper, runs the kitchen," he explained.

"Housekeeper?" she asked.

"That's what Patrick calls himself, but he's more like a manager. He runs the house and he also helps with the renovation projects I take on. He needed a place to live at the same time Henry was moving in with me, so it's worked out for everyone. He keeps Henry and me on schedule and somewhat organized. Would you like something to drink? A glass of wine or . . ."

"Just water for now."

He got her a bottle, opened it, and handed it to her. "I'll get dinner started and then go change out of this suit."

"May I help?"

"No, you relax. I've got this."

"So what's your plan?"

He moved to the other side of the island to face her. Then he looked at his watch. "It's six thirty-five. I'll change my clothes and fix dinner. By eight twenty we should be finished. That's when I'll hit on you."

"Oh?"

"Yes. Then, at eight forty I'll hit on you

again. My plan is to wear you down," he
added.

She nodded and very seriously said,
"I see."

"At eight fifty-five you'll give in just to
get me to stop nagging you. Besides . . ."

"Besides what?"

"Let's face it, sweetheart. I'm good.
You've told me so."

"When did I . . ."

"Every time I touch you and you moan
and beg me to—"

She put her hand over his mouth. She
could feel her cheeks warming, knew
she was blushing. "I can't argue with
the truth." She took a calming breath.
"And then?" she asked, trying to maintain a somber expression.

"At approximately one in the morning,
we'll get dressed, and I'll take you home."
He smiled as he added, "And that's my
plan."

She leaned forward. "That's all good
and well, but I was asking you what your
plan was for dinner."

He laughed as he came around the
island and leaned down to kiss her. "You
taste good," he whispered.

"Grayson, you know we can't . . . not here . . ."

He rubbed his lips over hers. "Yeah, I know. Want to hear my secondary plan?"

"You like messing with me, don't you?"

"I kinda do. I like the way you blush."

She nudged him. "Go change your clothes."

"Come with me."

She pushed him again. "Oh no. I'll wait here."

As soon as he left the kitchen, she went to the window to look out. She could see over the rooftops for blocks. Down below, traffic was moving slowly, and there were no pedestrians on the sidewalks. Snow flurries were expected, and the temperature had plummeted.

She turned and surveyed the apartment. There was a rectangular table with four chairs near the window. Henry's backpack was in the center of the table with two action figures. A deck of cards was stacked next to a notepad and pen. On the chair was an iPad.

Grayson returned wearing a pair of jeans and a light-blue cotton shirt, open at the neck with sleeves rolled up. Olivia insisted on helping prepare dinner. He grilled salmon he'd been marinating, made a spicy lemon-pepper sauce, and added steamed vegetables and brown rice. He let Olivia do the microwaving of the vegetable steam bag, but after seeing the result of her attempt to cook risotto, he wouldn't let her near the fish.

She didn't think he'd noticed during dinner, but when they were rinsing the dishes and putting them in the dishwasher later, he said, "You should have told me."

"Told you what?" she asked, handing him a glass to rinse.

"That you don't like salmon."

"It looked delicious."

"You didn't taste it."

"Okay, I don't like salmon. I'm sorry."

"I would have fixed you something else."

"You went to so much trouble, I didn't want to be impolite," she explained. "Does Henry like your cooking."

"My nephew has a very limited palate. Chicken fingers and mac and cheese are his favorites. Patrick can get him to eat vegetables, but I can't."

Grayson's cell phone beeped with a text. He read the message and sighed. "Henry's coming home from the movie. He was supposed to spend the night with his grandfather, but . . ."

"He'd rather sleep here?"

"No, his grandfather . . . my dad . . . has a friend coming over to spend some time with him. She just called him to let him know she's back in town."

"Do you have time to take me home?"

He shook his head. "They're on their way now, but as soon as Patrick gets back, we can leave. It shouldn't take too long."

"I don't mind waiting, and I'd like to meet Henry."

He took a plate from her hand and said, "I'll finish here. You look tired. Why don't you relax, and I'll brew a cup of coffee."

"If you don't mind, I'd prefer tea if you have it," she said.

"Tea coming up," he said.

Olivia sat in one of the club chairs and picked up a comic book from a stack on the side table. As she thumbed through the pages, reading about a su- perhero in a slick purple suit who could teleport himself anywhere in the world, she began to feel a tightness in her chest. She recognized the signs of her asthma immediately and walked to the hall closet to get her purse. She pulled her cell phone out, then her lipstick, comb, billfold, tissues . . . no inhaler.

Grayson saw what she was doing. "Your inhaler is in my coat pocket."

Startled, she asked, "How did it get in your coat?"

"You left it on the table, so I grabbed it."

It was such a thoughtful thing to do. "Thank you."

She was thinking how terribly sweet he was until he started lecturing her.

"You need to pay attention and make certain you've always got an inhaler with you, Olivia. I've done some reading on asthma, and an attack can get out of hand. I don't understand how you can be so cavalier about it."

She used her inhaler and put it in her purse. Then she walked into the living room. She stopped in front of the windows.

"This view is spectacular."

He stood behind her and put his arms around her. "Don't want to talk about inhalers?"

"Not really," she said. "I'll admit I've become a little too careless about my asthma. I'll try to do better."

He turned her around, tilted her face up with his hand under her chin and kissed her. He meant only to give her a quick kiss, but in no time at all it got out of hand, and before he realized what he was doing, he'd lifted her up, her pelvis pressed against his, his mouth ravishing hers.

She didn't hear the bell on the elevator. Grayson did and reluctantly let go of her.

The doors hadn't completely opened when Henry bounded out, shouting, "Uncle Grayson!"

"I'm right here, Henry. You don't need to shout."

Henry remembered the intercom and pressed it. "I'm home, Grandfather."

Turning back to Grayson, he said, "He let me ride up by myself. Who's she?"

"A friend," he answered. "Put your coat away and take your shoes into your bedroom." Henry had already kicked them off. "Then come meet her."

He was back in two seconds, which told Grayson he'd opened his bedroom door and tossed his coat and shoes in. He slid across the marble and walked over to Olivia. Grayson made the introductions.

Olivia thought Henry was a charmer. There were a few similarities to Grayson in bone structure, high cheekbones and square jaw, and he definitely had the same smile. Henry was tall for his age and lanky. He stared up at her with big brown eyes for a good twenty seconds without saying a word. She stared back.

Grayson watched the two with amusement.

Henry broke the staring contest. "Do you work in the FBI?"

"No."

"Why not?"

"I don't want to."

"She's an attorney, Henry," Grayson explained.

"You are, too."

"Yes."

He looked at Olivia again. "Do you go into the court to help good people or bad people?"

"She has two jobs," Grayson said. "She works on taxes for the IRS," he said, trying to simplify it for him.

"I don't know taxes."

"She's also a children's attorney."

Henry was fascinated by the idea. "Kids can have their own lawyers? You could work for me."

"Yes, I guess I could," she said. She walked over to the sofa and sat. He followed and sat beside her.

"How was the movie?" she asked.

"Grandfather didn't buy the premise. That's what he said."

Grayson sat in an easy chair facing them. "Did he explain what premise meant?"

Henry nodded. "He did, and he said he didn't believe a car could turn into a robot."

Transforming one item into another

was the topic of conversation for the next ten minutes, and then the three of them moved to the dining room table. While Grayson caught up on his e-mails on his laptop, she and Henry worked on constructing a filling station with Legos.

She heard, "You're doing it wrong," at least ten times, and she noticed that every time Henry said it, Grayson flashed a smile. Henry thoroughly enjoyed that she was so inept.

"Grandfather says I need a woman," Henry casually remarked.

That statement got Grayson's full attention. Olivia didn't seem fazed. "For what purpose?"

"To boss me probably. Olivia, when we're finished, do you want to see my room?"

She was trying to cram a tiny cube into the base of the attached carwash. She couldn't resist teasing him.

"I already saw your room. It's very nice. I liked your bed. I rolled around in it and tested the pillow. Nice and firm."

Henry was giggling. "No, you didn't."

"Oh yes," she countered. "Then I went through all your stuff, played some video

games, and when I was finished, I went
into your closet and tried on some of
your clothes."

He had a good laugh. Then he told
her she was connecting the Legos all
wrong again. She handed him the tiny
piece and said, "You fix it. I'll watch."

"Olivia, will you write down your phone
number in case I need my own lawyer?"

"Henry, she doesn't—" Grayson began.

She interrupted. "I don't need to write
my number. I'll give you one of my cards."

He followed her to the entry where
she'd left her purse and patiently waited
while she searched for the case with her
cards. She found it and gave him one.

"Are you worried about something?"
she asked.

"No, but I'm going to try out for soccer."

She wanted to ask him to explain why
he thought he'd need an attorney for
soccer and would have if the elevator
bell hadn't sounded. A few seconds later
Patrick arrived.

She had expected a much older man,
but Patrick was in his early forties. He

was very tall, at least six feet five, and
with his lean frame, he had the physical
attributes of an NBA player. He shook
her hand and shot Grayson a sly look of
approval before heading to his room to
change.

"Patrick plays basketball most Friday
nights," Henry told her.

He then asked her to play a card
game with him. Since Henry was having
such a good time with Olivia—he was
clearly winning—Grayson waited until
his nephew had gone to bed to take her
home.

Olivia was quiet in the car, her mind
jumping from one thought to another.

"Do you worry that Henry's father will
come home and take him?"

"No."

"Why not?"

He smiled. "Because my brother
knows what's best for Henry, and right
now he needs stability."

"But what if . . ."

"Olivia?"

"Yes?"

"Do you like to worry?"

She started to say no, of course not,

then decided to think about it. "I guess I'm used to worrying."

"So, you do admit you're a pessimist."

"I'm a realist."

Grayson didn't argue. "Henry likes you."

"That's because I have the sense of humor of a nine-year-old. He gets me."

"What about me? Do you think I get you?"

She turned toward him. "Probably not."

He didn't look at her as he said, "Oh, I know exactly what's going on inside that illogical mind of yours."

She took immediate umbrage. "Excuse me? Illogical?"

"About some things, yes, you're definitely illogical," he said. She opened her mouth to disagree, but he changed the subject. "Ronan told me you're reading up on a couple of Jorguson's old clients."

"I was thinking I might—"

He cut her off. "You aren't still considering going to work for that prick, are you? Because if you are, you should know I'm not gonna let that happen. If you think I'll stand by and watch you put yourself in danger, you're out of your ever-loving mind."

Olivia was surprised by his reaction. In the space of a few seconds, he had worked himself into a lather. "You care that I—"

"Damn right, I care."

She put a hand up. "Don't yell at me."

"I'm telling you, Olivia, I won't let you—"

"I'm not going to work for Jorguson. And don't you dare say, 'Damn right, you're not,'" she rushed to add when he looked as though he was about to say just that. "I made the decision, not you."

"If you want to think—"

"Grayson, I'm not going to argue with you."

He took a breath. "Yeah, okay. Tell me why you were looking at Jorguson's connections."

"I've been stuck at home every night, and I haven't been able to find anything on my father, so out of sheer boredom, a little curiosity, and . . ."

"And what?"

"My ego," she said. "I guess I thought

I might find something that would help the FBI's investigation."

"Did you find anything?" he asked.

"I discovered a great deal about Gretta Keene and some of the horrific crimes she might have committed. If Jorguson is involved with any of them, I hope you can find the proof you need to bring him down."

"We will," he assured her.

Grayson noticed a car parked in a no-parking zone just around the corner from Olivia's apartment and called it in. The plates were registered to a woman who lived one block over. He parked in front of Olivia's building, and she waited until he came around to get her. He was being a gentleman, but he was also pro-tecting her. She noticed he always made himself the target whenever they walked anywhere. It was all part of his job, he'd told her. She'd argued she wasn't the president, and he shouldn't have to take a bullet for her, but he'd simply ignored her.

They entered her apartment building, and when the elevator doors opened on her floor, he walked out first. He took her key from her, unlocked her door, and followed her inside. After he'd checked every conceivable place for someone to hide, he came back into the living room. Just as he was taking off his coat, Ronan called.

"Where are you?" he asked.

"Olivia's."

"Ah."

"Ah? What the hell do you mean by 'ah'?" he asked, inwardly cringing over how defensive he'd sounded. He went into Olivia's study and shut the door so that he would have some privacy and said, "Look, Ronan, I know I said I was going to distance myself from this investigation . . ."

"Yeah, you did say that."

"And you've gotta be thinking it's Friday night. What am I doing in her apartment, right?"

"Actually—"

Grayson didn't let him get any further. "I know I shouldn't have gotten involved with Olivia, but I swear from tonight on I'll distance myself. So stop bringing it up."

"Grayson, what the hell's wrong with you?"

He had the answer, but he didn't say it out loud. Guilt. He knew what he should be doing and what he shouldn't. Yeah, it was plain old guilt.

"Are we done?"

"Depends," Ronan said. "If you've finished ranting, I'll tell you why I called."

Grayson leaned against the desk and closed his eyes. He had been ranting.

"Ray Martin wants a deal."

"That son of a bitch bodyguard punches Olivia and pulls a gun on her, and he wants to deal. The hell with that."

"You're not being reasonable."

Grayson knew he was right. "What does he want to deal with? What's he got to offer?"

"He'll give us the name of the weapons supplier and will testify against him."

"Come on. You can't trust—"

"He says he has proof."

"Like what? A receipt?"

Ronan laughed. "Something like that. What do you think? If it's legit, would you press to make a deal?"

"I can't be objective," he admitted,

and as soon as the words were out of his mouth, he was appalled. He really couldn't be objective, and how in God's name had he allowed that to happen? Hell. "If Martin's the bastard who tried to kill Olivia, there isn't going to be any deal made."

"You weren't convinced he was the shooter," Ronan reminded him. "Have you changed your mind?"

"No, I'm still not convinced, but as long as he remains a suspect . . ."

"Okay, I won't argue." He sounded resigned.

"Ronan, he punched her and pulled a gun on her. He ought to get a firing squad for that."

"Are we still doing firing squads?"

Grayson ended the call a minute later and went into the living room. Olivia had kicked off her shoes and was sitting on the sofa with her feet up on the ottoman, her iPad in her lap. She looked up when Grayson entered the room, saw his dark expression, and asked, "What's wrong?"

He threaded his fingers through his

hair and continued to frown at her. "Listen . . ."

"Yes?"

"I just told Ronan I couldn't be objective, and that's just not acceptable. This can't go on. I need to be able to concentrate on the investigation, but you're messing with my mind, Olivia. I can't allow that to continue."

She put the iPad on the coffee table and sat up. "I'm what?"

"You heard me. You're messing with my mind. I've got to get my focus back, stay away from you while I work. I feel like I'm missing something, some detail that might make a difference, but every time I'm with you I get sidetracked. It's not your fault. You're a very seductive woman."

He thought he was giving her a compliment, but she wasn't pleased. "I distract you."

"Yes. Not on purpose, but, yes, you do," he said firmly.

"What did you mean when you said you feel like you could be missing something?"

"I'm not paying attention, damn it. My

focus is all screwed up. I don't know how else to explain it. This is totally not like me. I've got to get back on track."

"Okay, I'll help."

He almost laughed. "You'll what?"

"I'll help you focus. Why is that funny?"

"Olivia, you're the problem."

She took exception. "And you're not? How about I won't touch you and you won't touch me? I have as much self-control as you do, probably more."

He laughed. That reaction didn't sit well.

"You think you're stronger willed than I am? Really?"

"Of course," he responded, as if there was no doubt.

"I'm not going to argue with you. You believe one thing; I believe another. I'm hungry for something sweet. Would you like something?"

"No," he replied. "Tell me what you found out about Gretta Keene. Anything that might be helpful?"

Olivia got up, tossed her hair over her shoulder in what Grayson thought was a deliberately provocative gesture, and went into the kitchen. She came back a minute later with a cherry Popsicle and a plate. "Are you sure you don't want anything?"

"No," he said curtly. "Now talk to me about Keene and then I'm out of here."

She put the plate on the table, tore the paper off the Popsicle, and said, "I just love these."

"Gretta Keene," he reminded her.

He watched her use the tip of her tongue to lick the side of the Popsicle.

"I'm sure Agent Huntsman knows all there is to know about Gretta, but I did discover she's quite a micromanager. She has to oversee every detail, no matter how small."

Her tongue slowly slid up one side and down the other. Grayson couldn't take his gaze off her mouth. He knew what she was doing, and he was amused. Still, he couldn't look away.

"Gretta has trust issues." She put the tip of the Popsicle in her mouth, her full, luscious lips closing around it. Then she took a bite and chewed. She was savoring the icy cold feeling against her tongue. "She won't move away from the money or underlings."

"She what?" He was having a hell of a time concentrating. She was driving him crazy, and she knew it. How could eating a Popsicle be so sensual, so erotic, and such a turn-on?

She repeated what she'd just said and then took another bite. When a drop of the red juice began to slide downward, she slowly drew her tongue across her lower lip to catch it.

"Gretta wants to keep the men who work for her under her thumb at all times so none of them will branch out on their own and become competitors. There was one employee who went against her orders, and she made an example of him. He was tortured before he was killed. I think she's here because she has to watch Jorguson, especially if a lot of her money is going through his firm."

Olivia sucked the last bit of the Popsicle into her mouth and put the stick on the plate.

Grayson watched her carry her plate back into the kitchen. He loved the way her hips moved when she walked. Reluctantly, he reached for his coat and pulled it on.

"I'll check in every now and then," he said, his voice gruff. "But you don't go anywhere alone. Got that? You call one of the numbers and get one of your guards to go with you."

She walked him to the door. "For how long do I have to—"

"For as long as is necessary," he said. "And by the way, your little seduction didn't work."

His restraint was rapidly shredding, and it was taking all of his concentration to keep from grabbing her.

She didn't act innocent or protest that she didn't know what he was talking about. She stepped out of his way so he could leave, waited until he was closing the door, and then whispered, "Oh, I think it did."

NINETEEN

A week had gone by without a word from Grayson. Olivia kept telling herself she was happy and relieved that he'd stayed away. She was feeling guilty for the seduction game she played with the Popsicle. It wasn't really fair. He was just trying to do his job, and their relationship was getting in the way. They had been acting like horny teenagers who couldn't keep their hands off each other, and it had to stop. It wasn't right for either of them. Grayson had his job to think about, and she had her heart to think about. She was getting too emotionally involved, and since the relationship couldn't go anywhere, separating herself was the only decent thing to do.

She wondered if he would ever get married and decided that, yes, of course he would. He'd probably have children, too. He should, anyway, because he would be such a great father. He was so loving and patient with Henry.

Every time she thought about her bleak future, she'd get depressed, and yet she couldn't seem to stop thinking about it. Others might try to convince her that she could have a normal, happy life with a marriage and a family, but she knew better. She had seen the anxiety and suffering that illness could cause, and just the mere possibility that it could rear its ugly head again, as she feared it had done with Jane, made her determined never to let anyone she cared about go through that heartache and sacrifice.

On Friday evening Emma called and insisted that Olivia have dinner with her. Olivia was delighted to have the chance to get out of her apartment for an evening, but that meant she had to call one

of her guards to drive her. She had
promised. All five guards were nice, polite gentlemen who took their job seriously, but she was getting sick and tired
of having to rely on them. She longed to
be able to get in her car and go wherever she wanted whenever she wanted.
Boring but necessary chores, like grocery shopping or picking up her dry
cleaning, now appealed to her. Even
though she hated shopping for clothes,
she needed a new pair of running shoes,
but a trip to the mall was out of the
question because there was always the
worry of bullets flying all over the food
court while the man who wanted her
dead tried a second time to kill her.

Her patience was running out, yet every time she was close to throwing up
her hands and yelling, "Enough already,"
she'd get a look at herself in the mirror
and see the raw bullet scars. She'd then
decide she needed to be patient a little
longer. Besides, the FBI wouldn't be
paying for protection unless they felt
there was a real threat. Right?

Ronan accidentally let the cat out of
the bag. He called with a question about

Simmons, Simmons and Falcon. He wanted to know how long the firm had been working with Olivia's father. She didn't have the answer but said she'd try to find out for him.

"While I have you on the phone, I'd like to ask you something," she said.

"Okay." Ronan was sure she was going to ask about Grayson.

"The FBI wouldn't be paying for these bodyguards if—"

Before thinking, he said, "They aren't paying. They stopped. . . . I mean to say . . ."

Olivia sat up straight, bristling at what he was trying not to tell her. "Who's paying the bodyguards?" There was no immediate reply, so she asked, "It's either Grayson or Emma, isn't it? Tell me."

Ronan sighed. "Grayson's paying." He rushed to add, "He wants to keep you safe, Olivia."

"Yes, I know. Did you have any other questions?"

Ronan heard the stiffness in her voice. "It doesn't matter who's paying. If you go anywhere, you call for a bodyguard first. Understand?" he said sternly.

"Good night."

"Olivia . . ." he began, but it was too late. She was gone.

She found her car keys, locked the door after her, and took the elevator down to the garage. What an idiot she was, not to have figured it out sooner. If she truly needed a bodyguard, the FBI would have continued to provide the protection. How dare Grayson do this behind her back! She could take care of herself.

By the time she reached her car, she began to calm down. Maybe she was being too hard on Grayson. After all, he'd obviously acted out of concern. He felt there was still a threat out there, and he wanted to protect her. True, his intentions were good, but he should have been honest with her, shouldn't he? She made up her mind to pay him every dollar he'd spent on the bodyguards. Only then would her pride be salvaged.

She would prove that she could be cautious and self-sufficient. She wouldn't allow herself to be blindsided again.

She took caution to a whole new level. She carried her pepper spray in one hand and held her key fob in the other, one finger hovering over the panic button. She even checked to see if there were any red lights blinking under the car or in the backseat. Killing someone with a bomb wasn't all that unusual. She wasn't being paranoid; she was being smart. She even made certain she wasn't being followed and took several side streets to get to her aunt's house. She arrived alive and well.

Mary had set the table in the dining room. She and Harriet stayed in the kitchen, no doubt to eavesdrop because they knew the topic was going to be Olivia's father.

Emma greeted her with a kiss on each cheek. Her aunt always looked so put together. Olivia had never seen her in what she called casual clothes, and the thought of Emma putting on a pair of jeans made her smile. It was such an outlandish picture. Tonight Emma wore a fitted charcoal-gray wool dress with a high round neck. The skirt was straight and ended just below the knees. Her mid-heel shoes matched the dress exactly. They were a beautiful suede. Her

only jewelry was her wedding ring—
she'd never taken it off after Daniel
died—and a jeweled broach in the shape
of a hummingbird. Standing next to her,
Olivia felt like a hobo.

She straightened her sweater and
said, "I should have taken the time to
put on a dress, but I had only just
changed out of my clothes from work
when you called." She realized she was
making excuses and paused. "I should
have changed out of these jeans at
least."

"You're fine, dear. You worry too
much, but then you always have been a
worrier. Come sit and we'll have dinner."

Olivia didn't have much of an appetite. Two fudge bars and a grape Popsicle had dampened it. Olivia loved junk
food, mostly freezing-cold junk food. It
was a dark secret only her friends knew
about. The cold had soothed the sores
in her mouth after the chemotherapy,
and ever since, she craved the icy sweet
comfort. Half of her freezer was stuffed
with Dove bars, Fudgsicles, Popsicles,
and various flavors of ice cream. The

other half was reserved for Mary's healthy casserole dishes.

Tonight, Mary had prepared a roast turkey with root vegetables for dinner. She entered the dining room with a large platter and held it for Olivia to serve herself. Olivia didn't want to hear Mary tell her she was too thin and needed to put some meat on her bones, as she had often done in the past, so she took a portion of everything and said, "This smells wonderful."

After Mary returned to the kitchen, Emma said, "Catch me up. What have you been doing?"

Having sex with Grayson, thinking about having sex with Grayson, and having more sex with Grayson. Emma would be horrified if Olivia blurted out those thoughts.

"I've been doing some research on a few of the names connected to Eric Jorguson." She then explained who and why, and when she was finished, Emma asked several questions.

"It was a wasted effort," Olivia told her. "Aside from the fact that I made myself sick reading all the awful things these monsters have done, I couldn't find anything that might help Agent Huntsman."

"What else have you been up to?"

"Trying to figure out who shot me. And work has been busy." She put her fork down and talked a bit about her job.

Emma asked, "What about your father? What have you done about him?"

"I've sort of put him on the back burner . . . it's so frustrating," she admitted. "Word has gotten out that I'm trying to stop him and . . ." She didn't finish her sentence. Time for some honesty, she decided. "I've been seeing Grayson," she began.

Emma didn't seem surprised. She smiled.

"You knew?" Olivia asked.

"Yes, dear. You were explaining why you've put your larcenous father on the back burner," she reminded.

Olivia felt cowardly because she didn't want to admit to her aunt that she feared the repercussions of the truth, that when it all came out and her father was arrested and charged, life would change dramatically. There was going to be such anger, such hate, and it would all be directed at her family. Her father would be safe behind bars and probably become a celebrity with the other prisoners because of his oh-so-clever scams, but the rest of them would be fair game for the press and for all those people who had lost their life savings. Even though Olivia knew it had to be done, she dreaded what was coming.

"There's a young man sitting in a jail cell waiting to go to trial for a crime your father committed," Emma said.

Olivia was surprised. "Jeff Wilcox? Why is he in jail?"

"He was arrested. The prosecutors feel they have enough to convict him."

"Didn't the court set bail?"

"Yes, but they've revoked it. I asked Mitchell to check into it, and he says they're trying to force Jeff into making a deal, but he's refused, and so they've come up with some excuse to keep him in jail until his court date."

"Who is Mitchell?"

"Mitchell Kaplan is one of my attorneys. He's also a financial adviser and a dear friend. I believe you've met him."

If she did, she didn't remember. "Is he representing Jeff?"

"No. Jeff's attorney is Howard Asher. Mitchell said he's a deal maker. That's all Asher does, make deals, and ninety-nine percent of them are bad deals. He'll do anything to stay out of court. Mitchell told me that Asher doesn't know what he's doing. A public defender would have been a better choice. Jeff doesn't have the resources to fight this. He doesn't have any income, and his poor wife is at home trying to hold on until this is all sorted out." She stared at Olivia a long minute and then said, "And you, young lady, are just the one to sort this all out, aren't you?"

"Yes, ma'am, I am."

"No more back burner . . ."

"No."

Emma nodded. "I feel responsible for what's happened to Jeff. Your father used Jeff's friendship with me to get close to him. Did you know, if it does go to trial, your father is going to testify against Jeff?"

Olivia was beginning to feel the familiar tightness in the pit of her stomach
again. "No, I didn't know."

"Your father won't want it to go to
trial. It would bring too much attention
to him, and heaven forbid, his attorneys
might not be able to keep his records
hidden."

"I promise you, my focus is back
where it should be."

Focus. That was the word of the week.
Grayson had told her he needed focus.
She did, too. He'd also told her he felt
as though he could be missing something because he hadn't been giving the
investigation his full attention. She'd distracted him. Now she felt the same way.
She had allowed Grayson to distract her
from her investigation into her father's
dealings.

"I'm going to help," Emma continued.
"Mitchell Kaplan is one of the best attorneys in the country, and investment
fraud is a specialty. He's agreed to take
this case on, but you have to hire him.
Mitchell made me promise that I would
step back from this. He believes if my
financial assets are in any way con-

nected to this, your father will try to attach them."

Olivia agreed. "He's been trying to get your money into his Trinity Fund for a long time now."

"I would say there's a love/hate relationship between us, but the fact is, there has never been any love." Emma pushed her plate aside and, sitting back in her chair, folded her hands on the table. With a steady voice of authority she said, "I have an unwritten agreement with Mitchell, but you need to give him a small retainer. After this is all over, I'll transfer money into your account to pay his full fee. I can't do that now, though, because—"

"It could come back to you."

"It probably will anyway, dear, but it's best not to have a paper trail leading to my door. I also want you to give Jeff's wife a check, enough to make ends meet. Do you have enough to do that?"

Olivia nodded. "Yes," she said. And if she ran out of money before this was sorted out, she would take out another mortgage on her apartment. Whatever it took, she would make things right.

"You need to go see Jeff as soon as possible, before any deals are made."

"I'll go tomorrow."

"Take a check over to Mitchell on your way. I'll give you his card."

"Tomorrow's Saturday," she reminded. "Will he be in his office?"

"Yes, he will, and he's expecting you at ten o'clock. You could messenger the check over, but I'd like you to meet him, and he certainly wants to meet you."

She didn't ask why. "What about Jeff? Does he know what you're doing?"

"What *you're* doing," she corrected. "And the answer is no. You're going to have to explain it all to him."

"I'm a MacKenzie. How am I going to get him to trust me?"

Emma smiled. "You'll find a way."

TWENTY

For Olivia, Saturday started at four thirty in the morning with a call from a police station across town.

The officer on duty apologized for the early hour. "Judge Bowen told me to call you. We have a little girl here who needs protection . . . your kind of protection. The judge doesn't want her in the system. It has something to do with a trial that's coming up," he told her. "He said you'd help the child disappear for a while."

"I'll be right there."

Thank goodness for GPS, or she

never would have found the police station. The paperwork didn't take as long as usual because the judge had already signed the order. By eight o'clock she had nine-year-old Lily Jackson settled in her new, though temporary, home.

When she got in her car and checked her phone, there was a message from Mitchell Kaplan moving their meeting to eleven. Olivia was thankful for the extra time. She drove back to her apartment, showered, and changed into a dark blue dress. She left her hair down but used a barrette to keep it out of her face, then put on her earrings and watch. Since there was still a little time to spare, she went through her briefcase again to make absolutely certain she had all the necessary papers for Jeff. She'd already written her check to Mitchell Kaplan and tucked it in her purse, along with another one for Jeff Wilcox's wife.

Coat and scarf on, she headed out. The elevator doors opened, and there stood Grayson. She was so surprised to see him, she froze, but only for a second or two. She stepped into the eleva-

tor and pressed the button to the garage.

"Hi." Not very original, but it was the
best she could do.

Grayson didn't look happy to see her.
"What are you doing?"

When she didn't immediately answer,
he pushed the button to stop the elevator. "I said, what are you doing?"

"Errands."

"No."

"No?" She didn't shout the word, but
she wanted to. Instead, she pushed his
hand away from the buttons. "Ronan
told me you've been paying for my bodyguards, and I want you to know I'm going to reimburse you for every dollar you
spent, but, Grayson, you really should
have told me what you were doing."

"I'm going to keep you safe, no matter how much you fight me," he countered. He nudged her chin up so she
would look him in the eye and said,
"Damn it, Olivia. I don't want anything
to happen to you."

She thought he was going to kiss her,
but he suddenly stepped back.

"I am safe," she insisted. "And, of course, I'm being cautious."

"Were you cautious when the elevator doors opened?"

"I usually have my pepper spray at the ready," she countered.

"Usually?"

His voice was deceptively soft, a bad sign she recognized from past experience. Grayson was about to lecture the hell out of her.

"Push the button to the garage. I have an appointment I can't miss."

He started to argue, then changed his mind and pushed the button to the lobby.

"I'll take you."

"I'm perfectly capable—"

"I'll take you. Where are you going?"

"First to an attorney's office, then to jail."

Mitchell Kaplan was going to be a godsend for Jeff Wilcox. Olivia had taken time the night before to look up some of his cases and was impressed. Kaplan's adversaries called him a barracuda, and that was exactly what Jeff needed.

His nickname certainly didn't fit his appearance. Kaplan reminded her of a teddy bear. He was short, a bit round in the middle, and wore thick wire-rimmed glasses. He was also soft-spoken and reserved. Although Olivia and Grayson spent only a short time with the attorney, they both liked him.

"Where are they holding Wilcox?" Grayson asked.

"Mr. Wilcox has been held close to his home in Fairhaven. It's a decent facility, but I had my assistant check this morning before I sent you there to talk to him, and I learned that last night he was moved to Beaumont."

"That's ninety miles from here. Wilcox won't last long there."

Kaplan nodded.

"Why did they move him?" Olivia asked, and then before Grayson or Kaplan could explain, she asked, "Why won't he last long?"

"Fairhaven is to a country club what Beaumont is to Attica," Grayson explained.

"My assistant was told he was moved because of overcrowding. It's a game they're playing, trying to force Mr. Wilcox to take the deal he's been offered. There are serious charges, and I'm sure the federal prosecutor would like to save the taxpayer the expense of a trial."

Kaplan went over the documents he was sending with Olivia and then said, "Please tell Mr. Wilcox I'll get the ball rolling right away to get him released, but I can't do anything until he signs the paper retaining my services. I'll plan on being at the jail to see him later today. By now I imagine Mr. Wilcox is feeling beat down."

"Then you'll be able to get him out of there today?" she asked.

Kaplan nodded. "He'll be under house arrest, but he'll be home."

Olivia handed him an envelope containing the retainer check and pulled the other envelope from her purse. "Would you see that he gets this, as well?" she asked. When Kaplan gave her a questioning look, she continued, "It will help his family get through the next couple of months," she explained.

Smiling, Kaplan took the envelope. "Of course."

Olivia thanked him and was walking out the door with Grayson at her side when Kaplan said, "Mr. Wilcox's useless attorney is meeting with him late this afternoon. I'd try to get there before he does."

Once they were out in the hallway, Olivia whispered to Grayson, "This is going to sound really paranoid. The deal that's being pushed on Wilcox—I've got a feeling my father has something to do with it."

He nodded. "It does sound paranoid, but I'm not dismissing the possibility."

"What if Wilcox's inept attorney has made a deal of his own to pressure Wilcox to cooperate."

"Who would make the deal? Your father?"

"Simmons," she suggested. "He's one of my father's attorneys. I wouldn't put anything past him, and he and my father would have good reasons not to want this to go to trial. Kaplan would bring them into it, and there goes my father's low profile."

As soon as she clipped her seat belt in place, she said, "I'm nervous about meeting him."

"Wilcox?"

"Yes, Wilcox," she said. "I don't know if he'll remember me, but as soon as he hears my last name, he'll probably spit in my face."

"I won't let that happen. Start with 'I'm going to get you out of here,' and I guarantee he'll listen."

"You can't stop him from—"

"If he does anything to you, I'll cold-cock him."

As much as she hated to admit it to herself, she was glad he was so protective. "Can you take the time to go with me?"

"You're not going without me."

"What about Henry?"

"Basketball camp all day with Patrick. As long as I'm back by eight tonight, I'm good."

"Why eight?"

"I've got a date."

Her reaction was instantaneous. She felt as though he'd just coldcocked her and immediately recognized that she was being illogical. She wanted him to move on, so shouldn't she be happy that he had a date?

"That's nice." She tried to sound pleased, but her voice betrayed her, coming out raspy, as though she'd just gargled vinegar.

Grayson pulled onto the highway. "Traffic isn't bad. It shouldn't take us all that long to get there."

"Did you just meet this woman, or is she someone you've known for a while?" she asked. "I'm just curious," she rushed on. "Making conversation."

"What woman?"

"You said you had a date tonight."

"Yes, I do."

"I see."

"Aren't you going to say 'That's nice' again?"

"I was just . . ."

He glanced at her. "Making conversation."

"Exactly. Where are you going?" She hurriedly added, "You don't have to tell me, unless you want to tell me."

"A birthday party."

"A birthday . . ." The light dawned. "Oh no, you aren't."

He started to laugh. "Yes, I am."

"Grayson, we talked about this. You're going to my father's birthday party? Is that what you're saying?"

"That's what I'm saying."

"I don't want you to go." She knew she sounded like a petulant child.

"Really? Why didn't you say something sooner?"

"I did say . . ." She realized he was teasing her. "I mean it."

"What are you so worried about?"

She looked out the side window while she tried to put into words what she was feeling. "I'm related to him."

"Olivia, we all have at least one family member we'd rather not be related to," he said. His brother immediately came to mind.

"Just one? I've got a plethora."

Had she not sounded sincere, he would have laughed again. "I want to see him at work."

At work? She thought about it for a minute and understood. "Yes, he will be working, dazzling people. He'll make sure everyone loves him."

"But I won't."

"I know." *Because of what your father did to you.* She remembered Grayson saying those very words to her. He knew what Robert MacKenzie was all about. He couldn't be swayed.

"Who's going with you?"

"No one," he said. "I'll be working. Did it bother you when I said I had a date?"

"Of course not." It was an outrageous lie, and she was pretty sure he knew it.

"When we go out on a real date—and we will be going out on a real date—"

"I don't think we should—"

He cut her off. "Once I'm convinced we have the right man behind bars and it's safe out there for you, we should celebrate."

She started to object but changed her mind. What could one date hurt? A celebration date, nothing more. "Yes, okay. One date."

"I'd like you to wear the white dress you've told me about. You've made me very curious to see it."

"Oh, I don't know about that. My coveted, one-of-a-kind white dress? If I were to wear the dress, there would be rules you'd have to follow."

"Rules? Like what?"

"Like no red wine. And you couldn't eat any pasta with red sauce. Now that I think about it, I should probably give you a list of what you could and couldn't eat. Maybe it would be better if you didn't eat at all."

"I don't usually fling my food around when I eat."

"One tiny little splat, and the dress is ruined," she warned. "It's vintage, 1960. It can't be replaced."

"I'm not taking you out to dinner and not eat."

"I guess I could wear a raincoat."

He whistled and shook his head. "That dress must be something else."

The banter was fun, and Olivia was beginning to relax, but her lighthearted mood changed with a phone call. Her sister wanted to harass her one last time to make Emma attend the birthday party. Natalie had blocked her phone number on the display so that Olivia would answer the call.

Olivia denied Natalie's request yet again, but her sister was not ready to end the conversation.

"I wanted you to know that all of us have suites at the Morgan Hotel. Mom and Dad are in the presidential suite, and George and I are in a smaller suite on the same floor. The top floor, of course," Natalie bragged.

"What's happened to you?" Olivia asked. "You and George made a lot of money with your Internet company, honest money," she qualified, "and you never acted like this."

"Like what?"

Like a greedy fool, she silently answered, but since she didn't want a fight, she didn't say it aloud. "Is there something else you want, Natalie?"

"Mother would like you to stop by before the party."

"So she can drag me along? No, thank you."

Natalie exploded. "Aren't you ashamed of yourself? You should be," she shouted. "You're so damned selfish."

And on she went. Olivia held the phone away from her ear and waited for the rant to end. She knew Grayson could hear every word. The people in the Ford Explorer in the next lane could probably hear.

Turning to him, Olivia quietly said, "I just realized I haven't had anything to eat since last night. I had to get up at four thirty, and by the time I got back to the apartment, I was in too much of a hurry. Think we could stop for a bagel or something?"

Natalie had gone into warp speed, screeching. The more she ranted, the louder she got.

"You left your apartment at four thirty? What the hell for?" Grayson asked.

Great. Now she was going to have shouting in both ears. "It was closer to four forty-five."

"That makes a big difference. Where did you go?"

Olivia started to answer, but Natalie's voice had just gone up another decibel. She was demanding to know if Olivia knew she was such a bitch.

"Hold on," she told Grayson before putting her phone back to her ear. "Yes, Natalie. I do know I'm a bitch."

Warp-speed screaming again.

"I'm waiting for an explanation," Grayson reminded, ignoring her sweet smile.

"I drove across town to a police station to pick up a nine-year-old little girl. She's a new client," she explained.

He nodded. "Which police station?"

"Oh, you wouldn't know it."

"I know all of them. Which one was it?" he repeated.

She didn't want to tell him because the station was located in such a bad area, and she knew he wouldn't take the news well. He coaxed it out of her, though. Thankfully, Grayson was neither a screamer nor a screecher. She couldn't imagine him ever behaving like her sister. Grayson's voice was soft but firm. Sometimes he could be downright scary, but he was never scary with her. Angry, yes—scary, no. He always got his point across, and when he was displeased with her, she knew it.

He didn't ask her if she knew she was crazy—that was a Natalie move—but his look suggested he thought she might be.

Olivia put her phone to her ear again

and, interrupting her sister's tirade, said, "Good-bye, Natalie." She took great delight in ending the call.

"In the middle of the night . . . What would you have done if your car had broken down?" he asked her.

"I'd stay in the car, keep the doors locked, and call you."

"You'd call me?"

That took a little wind out of his anger. "I'd also call for a tow. Now, can we please stop and get something to eat? We should probably find a drive-through. I want to get there before Wilcox's attorney."

At her insistence, they stopped at a McDonald's. She ate a chicken wrap and drank a Diet Coke and told Grayson it was delicious.

"It doesn't take much to make you happy," he remarked.

She smiled as she sipped the last of her Coke. "I'm a simple girl at heart," she said. Carefully folding the wrapper and napkin so that no crumbs would fall, she placed them in the paper bag.

"Have you figured out what you're going to say to Wilcox?" he asked.

She had given some thought to the conversation, but she couldn't know how Wilcox would react to seeing her. Would he remember her? Would he freak out when he heard her name? She practiced a couple of approaches on Grayson and was feeling pretty good about her plan . . . until she walked into the jail. She was immediately sorry she'd eaten anything because her stomach started doing flips. The rancid smell of what she suspected to be rotting mice in the walls was overwhelming, and everything looked old and decayed. The few pieces of furniture were broken-down and ready for the dump. Grayson told her the jail was going to be closed just as soon as a new facility was finished, but with budget cuts, no one knew exactly when that would be.

The air in the cell block was heavy with sweat. The cells were so crowded, there was barely room to walk around. A jailer with dark circles under his eyes and a weariness to his gait led Jeff Wilcox into a small interrogation room. Wilcox sat on one side of a small wobbly

table. He looked scared and overwhelmed.

He saw Grayson's FBI badge and
said, "Am I being charged with mail
fraud, too?" His voice was flat, with little
emotion.

"No," Grayson answered.

"Shouldn't my attorney be here for
this interrogation?"

"It's not an interrogation. We're having a conversation," Grayson said.

Wilcox was focused on Grayson and
was obviously afraid of him or possibly
what he thought he was going to hear
from the FBI agent. Olivia had time to
study the man. The longer she watched
him, the angrier she became on his behalf. She was seeing one of her father's
victims up close and personal.

"You're going to fire your attorney,"
Grayson said very matter-of-factly. He
stood next to Olivia with his arms folded
across his chest, his stance relaxed.

"Why?"

Grayson looked at Olivia. "Do you
want to start explaining?"

Jeff Wilcox turned to face her then,
and his eyes widened.

"Hi, Jeff," she began. "I don't know if you remember me. I'm Olivia—"

He almost came out of his chair. "MacKenzie," he finished. "I remember you." His demeanor changed immediately to anger. "You're that bastard's—"

She cut him off. "Listen carefully. Yes, I'm that bastard's daughter, and I know what he is. I'm here to help you." She rushed to continue before he could turn away from her. "You have a new attorney. His name is Mitchell Kaplan. Have you heard of him?"

"Of course, I have. He's famous. I can't afford . . ."

"I'm paying for his services," Olivia said.

"Did he agree to take my case? Does he know what I've been charged with?"

Before Olivia could answer, he listed them. "Investment fraud, securities fraud, investment adviser fraud, and my attorney says, if I take the deal, they won't add mail fraud."

"What is the deal?" Grayson asked.

"Twenty-five years. Solid twenty-five years." He put his head in his hands. "I swear to God I didn't do anything wrong.

I swear it, but my attorney said that, given the atmosphere, the prosecutor could add another twenty and get it."

She thought he might start crying. Who could blame him? She put her briefcase on the chair across from him, pulled out a manila folder, and placed it in front of him.

"I know you're innocent, and I know what you're up against. Mr. Kaplan has written you a letter. Please read it, and then if you agree, sign the attached paper authorizing him to take over your defense. You can either choose to let Kaplan prove your innocence or . . . not. It's up to you."

She could see the confusion in his eyes. He wanted to believe but was afraid.

"Why do you want to help me?"

Tears came into her eyes. "I told you why," she said, her voice shaking. "I know what he is, and he has to be stopped. I would like your help to do that, but even if you can't, or won't, I'll still keep trying until I succeed."

"Read the letter," Grayson suggested.

"How do I know this is real?" He

looked at Olivia and said, "Your father showed me investment statements on official letterheads, and it was all a fake."

"Read the letter, Wilcox," Grayson repeated more firmly. "You've got nothing to lose and everything to gain."

His hands shook as he opened the envelope. Olivia's hands were shaking, too. She hadn't realized how anxious she'd been about this meeting. She felt as though she'd just put herself through a wringer. Her nerves were stretched tight, and she could only imagine how Jeff was feeling.

Jeff looked up from the page he was reading. "Mr. Kaplan says he'll have me out of here by tonight. Can he do that?"

"If he says he can, then he can," Olivia replied. "You'll be under house arrest, but you'll be home with your wife and your baby."

Jeff was starting to believe. She could see it in his eyes. She watched him go through the rest of the folder, scouring every page.

"There are copies of all these papers for you to keep."

"Do either of you have a pen?"

Jeff signed two papers, one firing his current attorney, Howard Asher, and another retaining Mitchell Kaplan.

He'd just handed the papers back to Olivia when Asher walked in.

"What's going on here?" he bellowed.

Asher wasn't what she'd expected. Because Olivia had heard how inept the man was, she had made the assumption that he was young and inexperienced and perhaps had only just passed the bar. Asher was in his late thirties or early forties. He was dressed in a business suit and tie, but there was still something disheveled about him. She noticed the expensive Rolex watch he was wearing when he reached out to shake Jeff's hand.

She decided he was also sleazy when he wouldn't stop giving her the once-over. Her chest and legs seemed to captivate him.

"This is for you," Jeff said, reaching out with the signed document in his hand.

Asher was still staring at Olivia when he asked, "What is it?"

"A paper I signed, firing you," Jeff answered.

That got his attention. He whirled around and snatched the paper. "What's this about? You need an attorney, Jeff."

"Mitchell Kaplan will be handling my defense."

Asher's mouth dropped open. "Kaplan? You can't afford Mitchell Kaplan. You've got to be kidding."

"Mr. Kaplan has agreed to represent me."

Asher shook his head. "Prove it."

"I don't have to prove it. You're fired. That's all you need to know."

"It's too late," Asher stammered. "We've made a deal."

Jeff looked to Olivia for help.

"Then you're in trouble, Mr. Asher," she said, "because Jeff hasn't agreed to any deals."

"Exactly who did you make this deal with?" Grayson wanted to know.

Asher looked as though he needed to sit. His face was gray. "This can't be happening. How did you ever get Kaplan interested . . ."

"I think we're done here," Olivia said.

"Wait . . . now, wait here," Asher demanded. "Jeff, you'll get fifty years or more if you don't take the deal. You can't take this to trial. You'll get . . ."

He stopped arguing when Jeff put his hand up. "I'm not taking any deals, and you're no longer my attorney."

Grayson could see the panic in Asher's eyes. The attorney had gotten past his surprise and was now letting his anger control him. His body was rigid and his hands were fisted at his sides.

"Jeff, it's time to go back to your cell," Grayson said as he motioned to the jailer.

"Wait," Asher demanded. "Just wait a minute. We're not finished here."

"Yes, we are finished," Olivia stated emphatically.

Asher turned to her and took a threatening step forward. Grayson pulled Olivia into his side.

"Listen, you," Asher muttered, "go back to your boss and tell him we've already made the deal and it's solid. It's done. Kaplan will just have to step back."

Olivia had had it. She took a step toward Asher and said, "No, you listen.

There isn't any deal. Got that? No deal. And, by the way, I don't work for Mitchell Kaplan."

Asher was obviously scrambling to keep his sinking ship afloat. His eyes darted back and forth between Jeff and Olivia while he tried to think of a way to stop what was happening.

The jailer escorted Jeff out of the interrogation room. Asher didn't move. He seemed rooted to the floor, he was so livid. "I don't know what you think you're doing here, but you're messing with the wrong people," he hissed. "Powerful people."

"Oh, I think I know exactly who I'm messing with," she replied. Her voice was as smooth as a summer breeze. "Allow me to introduce myself. My name is Olivia MacKenzie."

She picked up her briefcase and walked to the door. Grayson pulled it open for her. She looked back over her shoulder and said, "Tell my father I'll see him in court."

TWENTY-ONE

Grayson arrived at the Morgan Hotel a little after nine o'clock. He noticed all the security as soon as he walked inside. Because he'd worn a gun—he never left home without it—he had to show his credentials three separate times before he reached the guarded ballroom doors.

Ronan caught up with him as he was going in.

"Wait up," he called. He showed his identification to another guard and started to walk past. The guard reached out and put his hand on Ronan's arm.

"Do you have an invitation? I don't see one. You can't go inside without an invitation. There's some very important people in there."

One glacial look from Ronan, and the guard immediately pulled his hand back. The antagonism in his voice irritated Ronan. "I'm FBI. I can go wherever the hell I want to go. Got that?"

"Yes, sir." The guard hastily opened the door and stepped away.

"What are you doing here?" Grayson asked.

"I didn't want to miss the show."

"You've met MacKenzie," he reminded. "You interviewed him, remember?"

Ronan grinned. "Of course I remember, but that was one-on-one, and I want to see what he's like in a crowd. I'm betting he's as humble as he was with me. He's a real nice guy," he added. "Just ask anyone."

His sarcasm wasn't lost on Grayson. "Yeah, right. Nice guy. Olivia's worried I'll like him."

Ronan shook his head. "Did you tell her we put a lot of nice guys in prison every damn day?"

"Sure I did."

The two agents moved to the back of the room and tried not to draw any attention as they watched the guests.

Four bars were set up, one in each corner, and people thronged around them as the bartenders rushed to fill their drink orders. Waiters passed among the crowd, offering dainty canapés or glasses of wine from their silver trays. The double doors to the adjacent ballroom were open, and there were stations with every kind of delicacy to eat. The best of everything. Guests were encouraged to help themselves to whatever they wanted.

A man walked past carrying a heaping plate piled with oysters, crackers, and a mound of caviar. The glutton was practically drooling in anticipation of his feast.

"I wonder how these people would react if they knew they were paying for this," Grayson said.

"I think they're going to be real pissed when they find out they paid for his mansion on the beach."

"You're right. No expense spared tonight. Do you know how much a bottle of that champagne costs?" he asked when a waiter offered fluted glasses to a couple in front of them.

"I drink beer, not champagne, but I'm guessing a whole lot."

Grayson laughed. "Yes, a whole lot. It tastes like seawater, too."

Grayson spotted Olivia's brother-in-law, George, and pointed him out. There was a woman next to him, smiling and sipping champagne. She didn't look anything like Olivia, but Grayson was sure she was her sister because she was holding George's hand and occasionally smiling at him. Grayson thought the affection looked forced. George appeared to be miserable.

"I wonder if he paid the loan shark back," Ronan remarked.

"It's easy to check."

"From the look on his face, I'm guessing, no. Is that his wife with him? She's pretty. There's a small resemblance to Olivia."

"I don't see it." But then he knew what a witch Natalie was to her sister.

It took a lot to surprise Grayson, but

he nearly did a double take when he saw who walked in the door.

"Olivia and I went to see one of Mac-Kenzie's victims today," he told Ronan. He then explained everything that had happened with Jeff Wilcox.

Ronan was impressed that Mitchell Kaplan had taken the case. "The prosecutor won't like that."

Grayson shrugged. "Asher's reaction was telling. He went into a panic."

"His reaction to getting fired? From what I know about him, he's got to be used to it. I've heard he's a terrible attorney."

"I'm going to look into his finances. I think he was paid to make the deal and put Wilcox away. The last thing Robert MacKenzie wants is a trial."

"Are you thinking MacKenzie paid Asher?"

"That's what I'm thinking. Not directly, of course. The guy's one shrewd son of a bitch."

"It's going to be tough to prove that Asher even knows MacKenzie," Ronan said.

Grayson smiled. "Not that tough. Asher just walked in the door."

"Are you kidding me? Showing up here . . . not real bright. I'll get some pictures of him with MacKenzie. I'm gonna have to use my cell phone," he said. "And I can't let MacKenzie see me do it. Where's Asher now?"

"At the bar on the left. He's gulping down whiskey."

"From what you've told me, Asher has had one hell of a day. He must need courage before he talks to MacKenzie. Real stupid to talk to him here, though. Speaking of the devil, there he is. The birthday boy. I'll see what I can do about pictures."

The crowd had parted, and Grayson had a clear view of Robert MacKenzie. He was standing by the French doors to the terrace, surrounded by well-wishers. His wife stood just behind him. There was no doubt who the stunning woman was, for Olivia was her spitting image.

Grayson dismissed her and focused on MacKenzie. The man was quite the showman. He had an easy smile and a charming way about him. Self-confidence oozed from his pores. Grayson watched him closely and decided that what made him so charismatic wasn't just his handsome looks or his personality but the way he interacted with other people. It was a talent really. His gaze never left the person he was talking to. He didn't once glance to the left or the right. His concentration couldn't be broken. If he were talking or listening to a woman, he added touch to his repertoire. He would pat her arm or clasp her hand, nodding sagely when the woman paused for a response, and all the while his eyes would be locked on hers. He appeared to be fascinated by whatever his companion was saying. His intelligent eyes reeked sincerity.

MacKenzie reminded Grayson of a sorcerer. He could be all things to all people. He made them feel as though they could whisper their secrets, and he alone would keep them safe. He didn't pretend to be God, just one of His agents.

How could they not trust him? Grayson was impressed. He was watching a master work the crowd, and because

MacKenzie's guests were all so spell-bound, they couldn't see what he really was.

MacKenzie used their greed to lure them in. He didn't go after all the wealthy people, just the ones who coveted more. There were plenty of rich, successful people who were prudent with their money, who used their wealth wisely and generously, but Robert MacKenzie knew how to weed them out. He went after those who were never satisfied. He understood their twisted and pathetic insecurity, and he pounced on it. He knew exactly how to snare them: You're a rich man now, but is it enough? And will it last? With your well-deserved, though admittedly lavish, lifestyle and with rampant inflation? No, of course it won't last. How could it? Can you envision what your life will be like when it's all gone? Do not worry, my friends. Give me your millions, and like a modern-day Midas, I'll double it . . . triple it . . . quadruple it.

He made them believers.

And because they were the superrich, others wanted to emulate them. People who aspired to such wealth looked to these paragons of affluence for examples of what to do. The hopefuls believed the rich had an in, that they were in the know and understood the fluctuating market. If the man who signed their checks invested with MacKenzie's Trinity Fund, shouldn't they take their meager life savings and invest, too?

It was the domino effect, Grayson thought. From the top to the bottom, from the first to the last, they would all fall.

Drink in hand, Asher was weaving his way through the crowd to get to MacKenzie. When he reached him, he motioned to MacKenzie's wife and waited a few feet away. MacKenzie ignored him and everyone else until he finished his conversation, then, with a whispered word from his wife, he excused himself and joined Asher.

The attorney's forehead was beaded with sweat, and as he pulled a handkerchief from his pocket and wiped the sweat away, he talked fast and furiously. Grayson waited to see how MacKenzie would react to Asher's bad news.

Had he not been watching so closely, he would have missed it. For a second or two, but certainly no longer, MacKenzie's expression cracked. Grayson saw real, raw anger. Then—wham bam—Mr. Nice Guy was back. Smiling broadly, he put his arm around Asher's shoulders. He looked like a man who couldn't have been happier to see an old friend and hear the latest news. MacKenzie was good, all right, a pro playing his role.

Grayson thought about Olivia and the hell she'd endured from the time she was just a little older than Henry, and he suddenly wanted to smash his fist into MacKenzie's sparkling white teeth.

Ronan came back carrying a stemmed glass of ice water and a small digital camera. "I got some great photos with this camera and my phone. I've already sent a couple of them on to our computers."

"Where'd you get the camera?"

"I confiscated it." He slipped the camera into his pocket and said, "Hey, isn't that Senator What's His Name?"

Grayson nodded. "Yeah."

"What a schmuck."

"Yeah, he is." He lost sight of Asher and asked Ronan if he knew where he was.

They both spotted him at the same time. Asher was standing by the entrance, guzzling one last drink. He put the glass down and headed for the door.

"Who's that calling out to Asher?" Ronan asked. "I can't see his face."

"Neither can I," Grayson said.

They watched Asher drag his feet as he crossed the ballroom. The man demanding his attention finally separated himself from the crowd.

"Carl Simmons," Ronan said. "Wonder what MacKenzie's top attorney wants to chat with Asher about." He was grinning as he asked the foolish question. "Talk about a schmuck."

"No, Simmons is much worse than a schmuck."

"He's got an alibi for the night of the shooting. While Olivia was taking three bullets, Simmons was with a woman. According to her, they were supposed to attend a party but decided to spend the night in bed instead. Of course, Simmons could have paid someone to shoot Olivia, so, yes, you're right."

"Right about what?"

"He stays on the list." He pulled out the camera he'd lifted and said, "I think I'll get some shots of Asher with Simmons. Look how scared Asher is. Maybe I can capture that expression and show it to him when we pull him in."

Ronan left on his errand, but Grayson stayed where he was and kept his eyes on Simmons. The longer Asher talked to him, the more Simmons's outrage grew.

Olivia was going to get her security guard back whether she wanted it or not. Simmons's expression went way beyond anger, and Grayson knew his hate would be directed at her.

If Simmons was going to do something, it would be soon, and with that possibility in mind, Grayson called two bodyguards on his list and sent both of them to Olivia's apartment. One would stay outside her door, the other in the lobby.

He then phoned Olivia. Hell, what if she wasn't home? He took a breath when she answered.

"Is your door locked?"

"Grayson, where are you? I can barely hear you."

He walked into a back hallway. "Is this better?"

"Much better," she said. "Where are you? I thought you were going to the birthday party."

"I'm at the party . . ."

"Have you seen him?"

He could hear the anxiety. "I'll tell you all about it. You're staying in tonight, right?"

"No, I was just leaving. Jane's back in the hospital, and I thought I'd sit with her for a while."

"Does she know you're coming?"

"No."

"Good. Then you won't have to call and tell her you're staying home." He told her about Asher and Simmons. "I've got a feeling Simmons is going to do something. The look on his face . . . he's going to come after you. Could be as soon as tonight. You have to stay home. Check your door and make sure the deadbolt is in place. I'm sending over a couple of bodyguards, and I'm going to come by as soon as I'm finished here."

"Yes, all right."

"I mean it. Promise me."

"I promise," she said without hesitation.

"Don't let anyone in, no matter who it is. If your sister or your mother knocks on the door, don't answer."

"I understand," she insisted. "Stop worrying. I won't let anyone but you in."

"One more thing," he said. "If one of your kids calls, you don't leave. You call me. I'll leave here in five and be at your apartment in fifteen. If you need to go, I'll drive you."

"Okay."

Her quick agreement pleased him. He checked the time, then went to find Ronan. He spotted Asher leaving the ballroom. The guy was practically jogging, he was in such a hurry to get away. Simmons was on his cell phone and followed Asher at a much slower pace. He wasn't paying any attention to where he was going and nearly knocked a waiter over.

Ronan came up behind Grayson. "Want to say hello to the birthday boy?"

Grayson smiled. "Yeah, I'd like that. Got to make it quick, though. I'm going to stay with Olivia tonight. I've got an uneasy feeling . . . probably nothing, but I want to hang around."

MacKenzie saw them coming. He had just blown out candles on a gigantic birthday cake amid cheers.

"What's the wife's name?" Grayson asked.

"Deborah."

"Olivia looks like her."

"Wait until you get a close look at her father. Same color eyes."

"Ronan." MacKenzie said his name and extended his hand. "Good to see you again. How is your investigation going? Have you arrested the man responsible for shooting my daughter?"

"Not yet," Ronan answered.

"Then what brings you here?" Mac-Kenzie asked pleasantly. He looked at Grayson and then back to Ronan.

"I heard it was your birthday, and I wanted to give my congratulations," Ronan responded.

Without so much as a blink, MacKenzie smiled broadly and said, "I appreciate that. Please . . . have a drink and something to eat. Enjoy yourself." He paused and then turned to his wife. "Where are my manners. Deborah, this is Agent Ronan Conrad. He was assigned to our daughter's investigation."

She greeted Ronan with a warm smile. "Such a terrible ordeal, to get a phone call telling us our daughter had been shot."

"Did you rush to her side?" Grayson asked the question.

Deborah looked at her husband, no doubt hoping he would answer.

"It wasn't possible to go to our daughter," Robert answered. "We were in Florida at the time, and our schedule wouldn't permit deviation."

"She's put us through such worry over the years," Deborah said. "She's been ill most of her life. Hasn't she, Robert?"

"How inconsiderate of her," Ronan drawled.

Grayson didn't show any outward reaction to Deborah's comments, though he was seething inside.

"Allow me to introduce myself. I'm Agent Grayson Kincaid."

"FBI," Robert told his wife.

Deborah's hand went to her throat. It was impossible not to notice the huge diamond ring she wore. "Is there a problem?"

"Are you working on the investigation with Ronan?" Robert asked.

"Yes, but I'm also a friend of Olivia's."

"Then you know . . ." Deborah began.

"Know what?" Grayson asked when she hesitated and looked to her husband again.

Robert answered. "How fragile our daughter is." He suddenly looked quite sad. "Mentally fragile. She's been through so much . . ."

"And put you through so much, Robert," Deborah reminded him.

He showed a flash of impatience for being interrupted and then a quick nod. "Yes, she has."

Grayson couldn't be quiet any longer. "Do you mean when she was in the chemotherapy unit? Was that when she put you two through so much?"

"I see she's talked to you about her past," Deborah said. Her voice had taken on a hard edge.

"She had you to comfort her when she was going through that hell, didn't she?"

Once again Deborah deferred to her husband who said, "The poor thing. She does tend to exaggerate."

"Exaggerate what? The side effects?" Grayson asked.

"It wasn't as bad as she tells people," Deborah explained. "She's got quite the active imagination."

"Then you did stay with her while she was going through the chemo? She was just a child, wasn't she?"

"No, neither one of us stayed with her. It just wasn't possible," Deborah explained.

"Then how do you know that Olivia exaggerated?" Ronan asked the question.

"I don't believe this is the time or the place for this conversation," Deborah said. She was angry and opened her mouth to say something more, but her husband stopped her by putting his hand on her arm.

"You're right. This isn't the time," Grayson agreed.

"You were explaining that Olivia has become mentally fragile," Ronan reminded Robert.

"Yes, indeed she has. It's not her fault," he insisted. "We love her dearly, don't we, Deborah?"

"Oh yes, of course we do. We would have loved to have had her here tonight to celebrate with us, but we couldn't dare include her. She's so unpredictable we couldn't risk a scene and watch her embarrass herself."

Robert looked almost sympathetic. "It's all those poisonous drugs she's taken over the years. They've made her paranoid. She really can't help how she is."

"How exactly is she?" Grayson asked.

"She makes up the most bizarre stories," Robert said. "And no matter how outrageous they are, she can't let them go. Olivia needs medical attention and a safe environment. As her parent it's my responsibility to see that she gets it."

Grayson smiled. "You'd better not let Olivia hear you talk about her like that, or she'll never come see you in prison."

With those parting words Grayson and Ronan left the ballroom.

"He pretty much spelled it out, didn't he?" Ronan said.

"Yeah, he's laying the groundwork."

"How soon do you think they'll come for her?"

"Soon. Maybe tonight."

"That son of a bitch is gonna lock her away somewhere, keep her drugged so she can't make trouble."

"Know what's worse? That son of a bitch is her father."

TWENTY-TWO

Grayson arrived at Olivia's apartment with his gym bag in hand and announced that he was staying over.

"You went home and packed?" she asked.

"I always keep clean clothes and a shaving kit in the trunk of my car."

Frowning, she followed him into the living room. "For sleepovers?"

"No, for the gym," he patiently explained. He dropped the bag on the chair.

He wanted to pull her into his arms, but he wouldn't let himself. It took all the willpower he could muster not to kiss her sweet lips.

"You're sleeping here tonight?" she asked.

"Yes. I'll take the sofa," he answered.

"Why?" she asked, bewildered. "I think you'd better explain what happened at the birthday party, and if you tell me my father's your new golf buddy, you're sleeping on the floor."

"Olivia, sweetheart . . . ?"

"Yes?" she asked, trying not to be worried. Grayson couldn't be fooled. Her father couldn't charm him.

Grayson looked into her eyes for several seconds, then said, "Your parents are god-awful people."

She was thrilled. She threw her arms around him and kissed him on the cheek. "Thank you. That's about the nicest thing you've ever said to me."

The doorbell rang. He took her hand and led her into her bedroom.

"Stay here," he said. He was reaching for his gun as he left the room and pulled the door closed behind him.

She didn't have to wait long. A minute later Grayson told her she could come out, and she emerged to find Ronan removing his coat. He tossed it on the back of a chair near the door, lifted a gun out of the back of his waistband, and handed it to Grayson. "I thought you might need some extra firepower. Never know. There are more clips in my coat pockets."

Grayson turned to Olivia. "Ronan's going to hang out for a while."

Instead of asking why, she simply said, "Okay," and waited for one of them to start talking. Her patience quickly ran out when neither of them spoke. Hands on her hips, she said, "Exactly what are you boys expecting to happen here? A shootout on the third floor? I'll tell you right now, Mrs. Delaney won't like that."

Ronan smiled. "Mrs. Delaney?"

"The tyrant in three-ten," Grayson answered. "She makes Olivia do her grocery shopping for her."

"She does not make me grocery shop. I just pick up a few things for her now and then . . . that isn't important now. What's going on?"

"You didn't tell her?" Ronan asked Grayson.

"I haven't had time."

"Tell me now," she demanded.

Grayson told her about the party and his conversation with her parents. By the time he'd finished, Olivia had dropped down on the sofa and was speechless.

"She seems to be taking this pretty well," Ronan remarked.

"Yeah, right," Grayson said. Then he started counting. "Five, four, three, two . . ."

She bounded to her feet with a roar. Grayson smiled. "There it is," he told Ronan.

"How dare he! If Carl Simmons comes through my door and invades my home, I want you to shoot him, Grayson. You can shoot him, too, Ronan. No, I'll do it. Ronan, give me a gun, and I'll shoot him. I'll be doing the world a favor. That snake, that creepy slimeball, that . . ." She stopped sputtering for a second, searching for more names. "That no good . . ."

"Take a breath, sweetheart," Grayson suggested. She was starting to wheeze as she paced back and forth.

"Yes, you're right. I need to calm down so I can think. That's what I need to do.

That son of a . . . When do you think
this will happen?"

"Soon." Grayson took off his jacket
and began to unbutton his shirtsleeves.

Olivia stopped in the middle of the
room. It was really beginning to sink in,
the lengths her adversaries would go to.
"You really believe Simmons will bring
men here to take me?"

"Yes, that's what I believe. If you'd
seen the look on his face when Asher
was talking to him, you'd be a believer,
too."

"Your father's in this, as well, Olivia,"
Ronan said. "You need to know that."

"Oh, I know."

"I'm going to get out of these clothes,"
Grayson said.

Olivia widened her pacing trail from
the sofa to the kitchen and back. On
one of her trips she noticed another FBI
gym bag on the floor outside her office.
"Are you staying over, too?" she asked
Ronan.

"Maybe."

Olivia walked into her kitchen. It was
dark, and she stood in the shadows
looking out the window, trying desper-

ately to understand how it had come to this and how her father could justify what he was doing. She was suddenly overwhelmed with sadness. How could she miss what she never had?

Oh, snap out of it, she scolded. Feeling sorry for herself wouldn't accomplish anything. Besides, she had a family. She had Jane and Collins and Sam. They were her sisters. But as loving and supportive as they were, she had to admit she needed more. God help her, she needed Grayson in her life.

She took a deep breath and closed her eyes. Concentrate on now. Don't worry about the future; just focus on tonight. Stop thinking like an outcast daughter and start thinking like a smart, strong, independent woman.

Pep talk over, she went back into the living room. Who would come to get her? How many would there be? And where did they think they would take her?

"Wait a minute," she said.

"Yes?" Ronan was carrying his bag into the guest bathroom. He turned back and waited.

"Simmons has to know I would never let him in my apartment."

"Okay."

"Wait . . ."

"Yes?" he asked, trying not to smile. She was so earnest.

"That's it, isn't it? Simmons knows I'll be cautious, and I won't let just anyone in. He'll send someone I know, someone I'll open the door for. That no good . . ."

And she was off on another tirade. Grayson came out of the bedroom just as she was winding down. He'd changed into jeans and a shirt and had his gun and holster back on his hip. He was on his cell phone.

"Yes, I'll tell her." He ended the call and said, "That was Agent Huntsman. He's helping us out with Jeff Wilcox's old attorney, Asher. He said to tell you that you owe him one, Olivia."

"I do? Okay."

Before she could ask what Huntsman was doing to help, Grayson said, "You were right, Ronan. Asher was going to try to disappear. He was getting in his car with a suitcase and files when they picked him up."

"Is he being arrested, and if so, on what charges?" Olivia asked.

"He was taken in for questioning. No charges yet," Grayson said. "He's going to explain where the twenty-thousand-dollar deposit came from."

"What twenty thousand?"

"That was the amount of cash deposited in Asher's account the day before he offered his services to Wilcox."

"How did you get that information so quickly?" Olivia asked.

"Our resources are extensive," Ronan explained.

"Didn't you need a court order or a . . ." She stopped when Grayson gave her the look. She was getting used to seeing that expression, the did-you-really-just-ask-that-question look.

"Never mind." She went into the kitchen and got a grape Popsicle from the freezer. She was about to tear the wrapper off when Grayson grabbed it from her.

"Oh no, you don't. I'm not going to be

distracted tonight." He put the Popsicle back in the freezer.

She followed him. "I wasn't going to . . ." she whispered. "You know."

"Do you mean drive me nuts like you did with the last Popsicle?"

She smiled. "I drove you nuts?"

"You know you did."

She laughed. "Yes, but it's good to hear you admit it."

Olivia realized there was nothing she could do now but wait. Grayson had taken his laptop into her office to write a report, and Ronan had turned on the television. She sat next to him and watched him channel surf. He settled on a station and leaned back when the news came on.

"Does Agent Huntsman know why you're here?" she asked.

"Yes, he does. I told him."

"Is he your superior?"

He flashed a smile. "No, we just help each other out every once in a while."

"What happens if Grayson's wrong?"

"He isn't wrong. He's got this way of reading people. I don't know how else to explain it. It's something he sees in their eyes maybe. He's saved our lives more than once. A couple of years ago we were called in to help on a case with Huntsman. There were five of us and an informant who had worked with Huntsman for over a year. Very trustworthy," he added. "We knew there was a deal going down, and we were waiting for the suspect to show up with his crew. We got there real early and had time to set up the ambush. We had a good two hours to wait. Anyway, Grayson's watching the informant talk to Huntsman, and he goes over to the two of them and chats for a minute, surely no longer. The informant's supposed to leave, but Grayson grabs him and puts him in cuffs. Then he tells all of us we have to get out."

"Why? What happened?" she asked when he hesitated.

"He won't even take the time to explain, so we all hightail it out of that house. We're all in our cars down the street, parked behind an abandoned building, and we're waiting there for maybe ten minutes. No one's saying anything to Grayson, but I know Huntsman and the other agents are thinking, what the . . . has Grayson lost it? We've got a major bust about to happen, and he's screwing it up."

"But you weren't thinking that."

"No, I trusted his instinct. And about five minutes later the house blows up. And I mean blows. It was like a nuclear bomb went off. Even tore out the foundation. From that night on, Huntsman doesn't question Grayson. If he says he's got a feeling or he's read something in the guy's eyes or in the way he's behaving that none of us notice, we listen. Grayson would make a hell of a profiler," he added. "But that doesn't interest him."

"And tonight he saw Simmons's reaction to Asher's news."

"Yeah, but that was easy. Grayson said anyone with half a brain would know Simmons was going to do something crazy. You know those cartoon characters that have fire coming out of their eyes and ears when they get mad? According to Grayson, Simmons looked like that."

"He compared him to a cartoon character?"

He nodded. "He won't admit it, but I'm pretty sure he watches cartoons with Henry."

Olivia imagined Grayson kicking back with his nephew and laughing at some juvenile TV show, and she got a warm feeling. No wonder she loved him.

"Anyway, he knew Simmons was going to do something because you . . ."

"I what?"

He grinned. "You really pissed him off."

She laughed. "Oh, I hope so."

"After we chatted with your father, we knew what the plan was, especially after he said he was going to see that you were put somewhere safe. Grayson's convinced it'll happen tonight."

"Was my mother with him?" she asked. She didn't wait for a response. "Of course she was. She never leaves his side if she can help it."

Grayson joined them. "Huntsman's here with Larson. One will stay in the security room off the lobby watching the garage and the front entrance, and the other will watch the back steps. They won't be seen."

"All the floors are on closed-circuit," Olivia said. "I hope Simmons comes. I'd love to sit down and have a chat."

Grayson shook his head. "He'll stay away and wait to hear."

"What if they're coming here to kill me? Have you considered that possibility? Hide my body where it won't be found. Simmons would like that."

She saw the look on Grayson's face and went to him. She didn't care that Ronan was watching as she moved into his arms. "I'm just saying—"

"No one's going to hurt you ever again," Grayson stated with an unflinching resolve.

Olivia had just looked at the time on Grayson's watch—it was straight up midnight—when a knock sounded at her door. Then the doorbell rang.

Grayson motioned for Olivia to go into the kitchen. Both he and Ronan had their guns drawn. Ronan looked through the peephole. The only man visible was George Anderson, Olivia's brother-in-law.

The banging got louder. George shouted her name. "Come on, Olivia. Open the door. I've got to talk to you. It's important."

It got quiet for a minute while George conferred with the men accompanying him, and then he started banging on the door again. "There's been an accident. Open the door."

Olivia could hear him, of course. She came out of the kitchen and shouted, "All right. I'm opening the door. Hold on." She'd tried to sound sleepy and thought she'd done a good job. She stood there smiling over her performance until Grayson tilted his head toward the kitchen. Nodding, she went back to hide.

Ronan waited just inside the entrance to Olivia's study. Grayson opened the door and moved out of the line of sight.

There were two men with George. They knocked him to his knees as they pushed their way inside. They were in such a hurry they got halfway into the living room before they realized their target wasn't there.

George didn't wait around. He staggered to his feet and ran down the hall to the elevator, frantically hitting the button.

The men Simmons had sent were big and looked like bodybuilders. Dressed alike in black pants and white shirts with identification cards clipped to their pockets, they were obviously trying to look like hospital orderlies. Damned scary orderlies who would give patients nightmares. One was bald and had an eagle tattoo on the back of his head; the other had a scar that cut into his chin. Tattoo held a gun, and Scar carried a small black bag.

Disarming the man with the gun came first. Grayson didn't waste time. He came up behind him and clipped him hard on the back of his neck. The hit didn't seem to faze him, but the barrel of Grayson's gun pressed against the face of the eagle got his attention.

"Drop the gun," Grayson ordered.

"Hey, we're just here to—"

"Drop the gun."

Ronan had his weapon pointed at Scar. "Shoot him," he told Grayson. "We only need to interrogate one."

"Yeah, okay."

Tattoo heard the click of the weapon and quickly dropped his gun. "Don't shoot," he cried out.

Thirty seconds later, both men were handcuffed and sitting side by side at the kitchen table. They'd been read their rights but thus far hadn't asked for a lawyer.

"You've got this all wrong," Tattoo said.

They had been searched and their wallets were now on the table. Grayson found their drivers' licenses, read their names, and said to the tattooed man, "Where did we go wrong, Kline?"

"We were sent here to get Miss Mac-Kenzie and take her to Marydale Hospital, where she can get the treatment she needs."

"Marydale is at least a hundred and fifty miles from here," Ronan pointed out.

Kline shrugged. "It's where we were told to take her."

"Who told you to take her?"

The two men looked at each other. Then Kline said, "I guess her doctor."

"You guess?" Ronan asked.

Grayson opened the black bag and held up two vials of a milky substance. "What were you planning to do with these?"

The other man, whose name was Vogel, answered. "We were going to sedate her because we were told she was violent."

Grayson found a third vial in the bag. "There's enough here to put down a horse."

"Did you know how much to give, or were you just going to guess?" Ronan asked.

"I knew about how much." Vogel was becoming defensive. "And it was going to be a long drive. I didn't want her to wake up."

"*About* how much? You could have killed her." Grayson was trying to keep his temper under control. He was so furious, he wanted to throw both of them out the window.

"I would have been careful," Vogel insisted.

"Oh, then that's all right."

Vogel perked up. He obviously didn't

understand sarcasm. "I didn't want to hurt her, but . . . you know . . . she's . . ." The way Grayson was looking at him broke his concentration. He looked at Kline for help.

"Violent," Kline whispered.

"Right. Violent."

They were following a script, and any deviation rattled them.

"Were you just going to drop her off at the door?" Grayson asked.

"No, we were going to take her in and then . . . you know . . . leave her because . . ." Vogel answered.

"She's violent?" Grayson supplied. He glanced over at Olivia. Had he not known better, he might have given some credence to their claim. She was standing behind Vogel with her lips clinched tightly, looking as though she could strangle the man with her bare hands.

"How come you're dressed like orderlies?" Ronan asked.

"We wanted to look professional," Vogel explained.

"Yes, professional," Kline agreed.

"Cut the BS." Ronan shouted the order. Olivia flinched in reaction.

"I'm going to go get George. I'll be right back," Grayson said.

Olivia couldn't believe he was leaving now. They hadn't gotten Kline and Vogel to tell them anything yet. She followed him into the living room. "You're leaving now? George is long gone. Don't leave." He gave her the look again. "Oh . . ." she said, suddenly understanding. "George isn't gone. Where is he?"

"I imagine he's beating the hell out of the elevator button about now. The elevator is locked on the ground floor."

"He could have taken the steps."

"One of the bodyguards blocked it. George can't open the door."

"Oh. Okay, then. Go get him."

There was a warm glint in his eyes. "You're gonna have to let go of me first."

She had a death grip on his hand. She let go, and turning on her heels, she hurried back into the kitchen.

Grayson was marching down the hallway toward George when the medallion above the elevator doors lit up. George spotted Grayson coming and, in a panic, pounded on the doors, chanting, "Come on, come on . . ."

The doors opened, and for a second George thought he was going to get away. He tried to run inside, but Agent Huntsman stopped him. Without breaking stride, Huntsman grasped George by the back of his neck and dragged him down the hall.

Grayson led the way to Olivia's apartment as Huntsman shoved the blubbering George inside.

"Shut the hell up," Huntsman ordered.

Grayson grabbed George and dropped him into a chair adjacent to Kline and Vogel. With his head in his hands, George began to cry. "I'm sorry, Olivia. I didn't want to be a part of this, but I didn't have a choice."

"The hell you didn't," Grayson snapped.

Ronan caught Huntsman up on what they had learned.

"We'll take these two in," Huntsman said, pointing to Vogel and Kline.

"Where's Larson?"

"He's babysitting the driver. He was sitting in his van in front of the building with a loaded .45 in his lap."

"You can take them just as soon as

they tell me who hired them," Grayson
said.

Kline responded with a defiant smirk
on his face. "You can't make us tell you
anything. You can talk to our lawyer.
Right, Vogel?"

"Right."

Grayson conceded. "You don't want
to talk to us, then don't. We've got you
for attempted kidnapping, and I'm going
to add attempted murder. I'll make it
stick, too."

"Attempted murder? We weren't going to murder her," Vogel protested.

Grayson pointed to the vials. "Sure
you were."

"You're part of this, too, George,"
Ronan interjected. "Attempted kidnapping and—"

In a panic, George began to stammer.
"No, no, that's not right. I . . . I was told
she was mentally ill, and I was only trying to help."

Ronan grinned. "That's pretty good,
George. You got that lie out without
blinking."

"I'm telling the truth. I didn't mean any
harm."

Huntsman stood behind George while he recited his rights. "We need another pair of handcuffs."

"Hey, George, did you ever pay that loan off? It must have tripled by now. If you didn't pay it back, you'll probably be safe in prison," Grayson said.

"And you will be going to prison," Ronan assured him.

"Did you pay the loan off?" Grayson asked again.

George's face was turning white. "Not yet. No."

"Who hired you?" Grayson asked Kline.

He wouldn't answer. Neither would Vogel. George was the weakest link, so Grayson concentrated on him again.

"How did you end up with these two? I know you don't run in the same circles. So how do you know them?"

"They work for Carl Simmons."

"Shut your mouth," Kline demanded.

"You do work for him. Everyone knows it."

"We said shut up," Vogel yelled this time.

"Olivia, do you have any duct tape?" Grayson asked.

"Yes. In the cabinet by the pantry."

Grayson found it. He ripped off a long strip.

"I know my rights. You can't—" The first strip covered Vogel's mouth.

"That might not stick," Grayson said. "I'd better reinforce it." And with that, he taped over Vogel's nostrils, making breathing impossible. "That should do it."

He crossed to the other side of the table, winked at Olivia as he passed her, then pulled out a chair and straddled it. Stacking his arms across the back, he stared at George, completely ignoring the wide-eyed Vogel.

"You were telling us that these two work for Simmons. What do they do for him?"

Vogel's face was turning beet red.

George was gaping at him. "He can't breathe."

"Yes, I know," Grayson said. "What do Kline and Vogel do for Simmons?"

"You're killing him."

"What do Kline and Vogel—"

"I'll tell you. Just get that tape off him and let him breathe."

Grayson reached across the table and ripped the tape off. Vogel gasped for air.

"You keep your mouth shut, George," Kline blurted.

"Hand me the tape," Huntsman said.

"Okay, I'll be quiet. No tape. This isn't right," Kline said. "You can't treat us this way."

"No, it isn't right." Grayson nodded to Huntsman who immediately covered Kline's mouth with the tape. "Know what else isn't right?" he continued. "Kidnapping and attempted murder."

George looked as though, at any moment, he could burst into tears. "Oh God, how did this all get so messed up?"

"This is the last time I'm going to ask . . ."

"All I know is that Kline and Vogel have been working for Carl Simmons for at least a year. He tells people they're his bodyguards. I heard him offer them a big bonus if they could get it done fast."

Kline grunted and shook his head. Grayson raised his hand, and Kline immediately stopped making noise. It was almost a Pavlovian response.

"It?" he asked George.

"Olivia. If they could take care of Olivia fast."

"How did you end up with them tonight?" Ronan asked.

George's shoulders slumped. He looked completely defeated now.

Ronan got down in his face and shouted, "Answer the question."

George flinched. "Something happened during the party. I don't know what set Carl off, but I swear he was shaking. I've never seen him so angry. He dragged me out to the lobby, and when he couldn't see Kline right away, he called him on his cell phone. I heard him tell him what to do."

"And?" Ronan prodded.

"He told me I had to go with them because Olivia wouldn't open her door to two strangers, but she would if she saw me through the peephole. I told him about the doorman, that he could call

Olivia and tell her there were three of us and she'd never let us come up."

"What did he say?" Ronan asked.

"He told me not to worry about it, that Kline would take care of the doorman."

"Did he tell you how Kline would take care of him?"

George shook his head. "No, and I didn't ask. I didn't want to know."

"What a weasel," Grayson said under his breath.

"As it turned out," George continued, "the lobby was empty and the door was unlocked. He must have been on a break. . . . No, he wasn't," he said, finally figuring it out. "You wanted us to come inside. You were waiting for us. How did you know we were coming?"

"What else did Simmons say?" Grayson asked, ignoring the question.

George couldn't look Olivia in the eye. Staring at the table, he said, "The place they were taking her would keep her locked away where she couldn't make any more trouble. She'd be let out in three days. Carl said that was all the time Robert needed."

"Three days?" Ronan asked.

"What's MacKenzie going to get done in three days?" Grayson asked.

"He told Carl he'd have it all cleared out by then."

"You heard him say that?" Ronan asked.

"Yes, I did. Robert came out in the lobby and pulled Simmons over behind some potted plants. Both of them were hopping mad. I don't think my father-in-law cared at that point if I heard him. He was in a rage about some attorney—Mitchell Kaplan—and Olivia hiring him."

Olivia smiled. "He's afraid of Jeff Wilcox's attorney because he knows he'll have to open up his files." She looked at her brother-in-law. "George, tell me what you think 'clearing it out' means." She wanted him to acknowledge what her father was going to do.

"You know . . ."

"Tell me, George."

"The money, the stocks . . . he's going to close it all down."

"He'll hide money," Ronan predicted.

"What were you promised?" Grayson asked. "No, let me guess. Simmons found out about your gambling debts and was going to see that you got enough money to pay them off without Natalie finding out. I'm right, aren't I?"

"Yes. Simmons told me nobody else knew about the loans, and he'd help me out. He said there was no way I could get money out of the fund without the family suspecting."

Olivia couldn't understand George's stupidity. When was he going to pull his head out of the sand? "Aren't you beginning to figure it out?" she said to him. "Simmons wasn't going to give you any money. You have to know."

He looked up at her with weary eyes. "Know what?"

"That it's gone, George. You're never going to get it back."

TWENTY-THREE

Probable cause. The legal term would be a game changer.

Grayson contacted the New York office, which would continue the investigation. Since there was now probable cause, he anticipated it wouldn't take long to get a signed order to stop Robert MacKenzie and Carl Simmons from clearing out any accounts.

Once Kline and Vogel had been removed from the apartment, George became more talkative. To Olivia, he seemed genuinely contrite, but neither

Grayson nor Ronan were buying his re-morse.

Olivia fixed George a cup of coffee, ignoring Grayson's frowns, and sat with him while he talked about all the mistakes he had made. He was certain Natalie would divorce him, and before Olivia realized what was happening, she became his counselor, even suggesting ways he might discuss his problems with her sister.

"I should have told her about the loan, and he's right," George said, tilting his head toward Grayson. "I did borrow the money from a loan shark. I should get it all out in the open, shouldn't I? How will Natalie ever forgive me if I keep secrets? Could I text Natalie?" he asked Ronan, who had taken his cell phone. "I'll tell her now."

"No," Ronan answered.

"George, you can't text that information or e-mail her. You have to sit down with her and explain." Olivia couldn't believe he thought it was okay to drop that bomb in a text. How would he phrase it? Oh, by the way, I owe around five hundred thousand to a man who will break my legs if I don't pay up soon? "She might understand," she told him. *If she had a lobotomy first,* she thought. "I'll help you tell her if you want."

"You would do that?"

She nodded. "Yes."

Grayson was about to drag Olivia into the living room and ask her what the hell she was doing when George whispered, "I can help you, too."

She wanted to nudge Grayson and say, "Ah ha! See what happens when you're patient?" She didn't, though. She kept her attention on George and asked, "How can you help?"

"He keeps files." His voice gained strength, now that he'd made up his mind to share the information. "Your father keeps files hidden."

"Where?" Grayson demanded, his tone surly.

George immediately shut down. Olivia shook her head at Grayson. "Have you seen the files?" she asked softly.

"I shouldn't . . . he's my father-in-law, and every dollar Natalie and I have is tied up in investments he's made for us."

Grayson and Ronan looked as though

they wanted to grab George by the throat. Olivia remained calm and refused to give up.

"It's time for you to get a backbone, George." She put her hand on his and with sincere compassion said, "Do the right thing."

He rubbed his brow and kept silent for another minute. "They're in the wall in his study."

"The New York apartment study?" Ronan asked. "Or are they in San Francisco or Miami?"

"New York. I swear you'd never know the wall moved. There aren't any panels. It looks just like . . . a wall. He doesn't know I saw him, thank God. None of us are allowed to go into his study, even when he's there, and he always keeps the door locked. I made a joke about it once. I think I called it Fort Knox or something, and he exploded. I was in shock. It's the first time I'd ever seen him lose his temper like that. I saw that ugly side of him again tonight."

"When did you see the files?" Olivia asked.

"About a month ago. Natalie and your

mother were in the dining room, and I went down the hall to knock on the study door to tell him dinner was ready. The door was open a crack. I was surprised because that never happened. I almost didn't look in, but . . . you know . . . curiosity."

"And what did you see?" she asked.

"Your father had his back to me, and he was putting a file folder away. I swear the entire wall moved. I got away from the door as fast as I could because I knew he'd kill me if he saw me watching."

Grayson took a call and left the room. Ronan leaned against the wall, going through George's cell phone messages while Olivia and George continued to talk.

"Did my mother know men were coming here tonight?" Olivia asked.

"I don't think so. She usually just repeats whatever your father says. She thinks she's being a supportive wife."

"What about Natalie? Did she know?"

"No. This was all Carl Simmons and your father. Start to finish."

Ronan had just read one of many angry texts from Natalie demanding to know where George was when another text appeared. After he read it, he said, "The son of a bitch is going to try to shred those files."

Grayson had just returned to the kitchen, and Ronan tossed him the phone. He quickly read it, cursed, and said, "Yes, that's exactly what he's going to do."

"What happened?" Olivia asked.

"Natalie sent George a text. Your father has decided to fly back to New York right away. He's on his way to the airport, and you, George, are an ingrate because you bailed on the party. I guess that's still going on."

"He's going home now?" George asked. "He left his own party to go home? He's got his own jet, so he can get back to his apartment in a couple of hours."

"McGraw's the lead on this in New York," Grayson said. "He just called, and I told him about the files in the wall. He's putting an agent on MacKenzie's door just in case he slips past the others."

"What about Simmons?" Ronan asked.

"He left the party right after Olivia's father. We'll find him."

"Are you taking me in?" George asked. He looked frantic.

"Yes," Ronan answered. "In fact, we're leaving now."

"Wait, please," Olivia called. "I'd like to ask George another question."

"Go ahead," Ronan said.

She looked George in the eye and asked, "Do you think Simmons hired someone to shoot me?"

He hesitated several seconds and then nodded. "He's capable of it. I wouldn't have thought that a year ago, but now . . . yes. In fact, I wouldn't be surprised if he tried to shoot you himself. I don't have proof that he's involved, though."

Olivia nodded. "That's okay."

"Except . . ."

"Yes?"

"When Carl was talking to Kline in the lobby, I heard him say he wouldn't be upset if something happened on the drive to Marydale tonight. I thought he was joking because he was smiling, but then he told Kline not to mess up again."

"You left that part out before, didn't you?" Ronan said.

George nodded but insisted it hadn't been on purpose. "That could mean anything, couldn't it?"

Grayson towered over him. "What do you think it meant?" he asked.

George seemed to shrink before their eyes. "I guess it could mean that Simmons had hired Kline to shoot Olivia, and he messed up because . . ."

"I didn't die," Olivia finished.

"Yes, but it could have meant something altogether different, and that's why I didn't mention it." He put both hands up. "I know, I know. I should have told you everything."

He looked at Olivia then. "That's why I was going to ride all the way to the mental facility with you. I wanted to make sure Kline didn't hurt you. I was going to protect you."

"By hurt her you mean kill her," Ronan stated.

"Yes."

"If you were going to protect her, why

did you run the second she opened the door?"

He bowed his head. "I got scared, but I was going to wait in the van. I didn't want to watch them drug her. I didn't want to be a part of that."

"Yeah, right," Ronan said.

"You are part of it," Grayson said.

Olivia could see his anger building and sought to diffuse it before he punched George. She got up from the table and went to Grayson.

"Could I please be there when you question Simmons? I can't wait to hear the spin he puts on this."

Her smile calmed him. "I'll see what I can do."

Grayson suddenly needed to be alone with her, to hold her, to love her. With that thought in mind, he vigorously helped George to his feet. Ronan then gripped his arm and shoved him toward the front door. A minute later, as Grayson was sliding the deadbolt into place behind them, he could hear George blubbering once again that his life sucked. Grayson had to agree.

He returned to Olivia. "I want to go to bed," he said, reaching for her.

She pulled away. "No, Grayson. We can't. You said yourself we have to stay away from each other."

"I know what I said. But damn it, Olivia, staying away is killing me."

She stepped back. "What about Henry?"

"He's already in bed."

"You should go home and be there when he wakes up."

He put his hand on her neck and gently pulled her closer. "I ate dinner with him last night, and he almost fell asleep at the table. He and Patrick go back to basketball camp tomorrow. They'll leave around seven thirty, so it doesn't matter if I'm there or not. He'll tell me all about it tomorrow night."

"I don't want you to ignore him," she said, trying to catch her breath. His body was pressed against hers.

"I don't ignore him." His mouth was now hovering over hers, his warm breath tickling her lips. "It's sweet the way you worry about Henry."

"I don't really worry about him," she whispered. "He has you."

He tilted her chin up so he could look into her eyes and said, "So do you, sweetheart. Like it or not, you've got me."

He didn't give her time to reason or to argue. He sealed his promise with a kiss that let her know how much he wanted her.

Backing her into the living room, he pulled her T-shirt over her head. His hands quickly went to work on the zipper to her jeans, as she struggled to unbutton his shirt and pull it off his shoulders.

She pushed away and gazed up at him for a second. His eyes were filled with such passion. She took his hand and led him toward her bedroom. "Just this once," she said.

"Yes," he agreed. "Just this once."

TWENTY-FOUR

Sunday morning with Grayson was wonderful. And enlightening. He woke Olivia, caressing her as he nuzzled the side of her neck. He was making love to her.

"Shouldn't I be awake for this?" she asked, her voice a sleepy whisper.

"It's not necessary. You can go back to sleep."

As if that were possible. His mouth and his hands were everywhere, and oh, did he know how to drive her out of her mind. She was soon writhing in his arms, demanding that he come to her.

She climaxed twice before he did. He

held her close for several minutes until his breathing calmed and his heart stopped racing. "Each time it's more intense, isn't it? More amazing."

Olivia started to tremble. "Grayson, we need to talk. I . . ."

He wouldn't let her say another word. He kissed her hard, then got out of bed. "We'll talk later. I'm getting in the shower now, and then I'm making breakfast."

"I don't eat breakfast."

He was heading into the bathroom when he said, "Sure you do."

She'd already lost her train of thought because she'd watched him walk away, and all she could think about was how sexy he was. She knew for a fact that he was all muscle because she'd touched every inch of him. That thought led to another, and she was suddenly replaying the different ways they'd made love during the night. Had she really been that uninhibited, that wild?

With an audible sigh, she got out of bed and put on her robe. She should have been exhausted, but she wasn't. Fact was, she'd slept better than she

had in years. She'd felt so safe and protected in his arms.

As it turned out, she did eat breakfast, and Grayson didn't even have to
coax her. He made an omelet with pep-
pers and chives and mushrooms. It was
delicious.

She was sipping hot tea while she
watched him clear the table and stack
the dishes in the dishwasher.

"I'll clean up," she promised. "You
cooked."

"It's done."

She smiled. "I know. That's why I offered." She tapped her forehead. "Always thinking."

She put her teacup in the sink and
followed him into the living room. He
took his laptop out of his bag and sat
on the floor. Leaning against the sofa,
he stretched out his legs, opened the
computer, and pulled up *The Washington Post.*

"The newspapers are in the hall," she
told him. "I'll get them."

After she looked through the peephole, she opened the door, scooped up
the papers, and locked the door again.

"I like reading the actual paper," she explained. "I stare at a computer screen all week. It's a nice change."

Grayson took *The Washington Post,* and she started reading *The New York Times.*

She noticed he read the financial section first, then the sports section.

"Grayson, may I ask—"

"Not yet, sweetheart." He moved the paper so that he could check the time. "We're having a normal, leisurely Sunday morning. At noon you may ask questions."

"But—"

"Noon."

She understood, and she was happy to wait. The world and all the ugly problems could return at noon. Until then, Grayson wanted time for just the two of them.

And it was lovely. Curled up against his side, she read most of the *Times.* There was a particularly interesting article about a renowned Broadway producer she thoroughly enjoyed. She even read the entire editorial page and checked out the new fashions in the style section. At one point she glanced over at Grayson, who was immersed in a story about a new construction project, and she marveled at how comfortable they were in their silence.

At twelve o'clock, Grayson reluctantly let reality intrude. He stacked the papers on the table and tensed in anticipation of what he was pretty sure was coming. Olivia would ask him about the future. His future. She would tell him that he needed to move on, that there could never be a future with her. She'd hinted at it several times already. It didn't matter how she phrased it. Whatever she told him would lead to a quarrel, and as stubborn as she was, it would be a long one. He was stubborn, too, and this was one argument he was determined to win. He wasn't going anywhere, and he wondered how many times he would have to say those words before she believed him.

"Okay, what's the question?" he asked.

She surprised him. She straddled his hips and put her hands on his shoulders. Sighing, she said, "I was going to ask if you wanted to go back to bed. You know, for sex." She leaned forward and ran the tip of her tongue across his lower lip, then she shrugged her shoulders and looked at him with sad, innocent eyes. "But you wouldn't let me ask any questions . . . and now it's too late."

He was laughing as she got up and headed to the kitchen to get them something to drink. A knock on the door changed her direction.

"Ronan's here," she announced as she swung the door open. Please don't let it be more bad news, she prayed.

"It's bad news, isn't it?" she asked before Ronan could step inside. "It's Sunday, and you're here, so it's bad news." So much for taking a stab at optimism.

Ronan smiled at her. "No, it isn't bad news."

"Oh, okay then."

"We're going to New York," Ronan told Grayson, who was already heading to the closet to get his coat.

"Why?" Olivia asked.

Ronan answered. "We want to see what's in that wall."

"They're going to let you?" she asked.

He gave her the look, just like Grayson did, the how-could-you-ask-such-a-dumb-question look.

She found his arrogance amusing. "Of course, you're going in. Why haven't they opened the wall?"

"They're waiting for McGraw, so no one's been inside the apartment yet."

"What about my father?"

"They've been holding him, and he's not too happy about it. He was picked up when he landed in New York. He can't be held much longer. We have to get moving or we'll miss our flight."

Grayson followed Ronan to the door. He stopped, pulled Olivia into his arms, and kissed her passionately. "I'll call," he promised. "Don't go anywhere with-out—"

"Calling one of the bodyguards," she recited as though she'd memorized the rule.

"Call Carpenter," he suggested. "His wife's pregnant. He can use the extra money."

And he was gone.

TWENTY-FIVE

Robert MacKenzie's apartment reeked of wealth. Original artwork hung on every wall, rare antiques blended in with the elegant furnishings, and beautiful rugs covered the gleaming hardwood floors. Grayson walked by a table with a vase he knew cost more than ten thousand dollars. He wondered whose pension paid for that.

A locksmith was working on the door to the study. One of the agents told Grayson he'd been at it for twenty minutes.

The locksmith heard him. "I haven't seen a lock like this before. It's tricky."

Grayson motioned to Ronan. "You want to get this?"

Ronan stepped forward. "Yeah, I've got it."

The locksmith moved out of the way. "I'm telling you, it's tricky."

"Yeah, okay," Ronan said as he reached for the tool the man was holding. He squatted down eye level to the lock and after a couple of maneuvers, turned the door handle, and the door opened wide.

The locksmith's mouth dropped open. "How did you do that?"

How? Ronan had grown up in the inner-city and had learned all sorts of tricks, most of them illegal. That's how. But he wasn't going to talk about his past with a stranger or boast that he could pretty much open any lock by the age of ten. Instead, he said, "Just lucky."

Agents rushed into the study with cameras. While everything was being documented and recorded, Grayson and Ronan turned their attention to the walls. They examined each one carefully

and finally agreed on the one that would
move. It took them a while to figure out
how it worked, but once they pinpointed
the correct spot and gave it a firm push,
a section of the wall, about four feet
wide, swung open, revealing a small
room. File cabinets lined one wall, and a
stack of file folders sat on an immacu-
late desk in the center.

Grayson and Ronan were the first to
have a look. They sifted through some
of the files and called in a couple of investigators who, after several hours of
inspection, verified what the two agents
had concluded: Robert MacKenzie was
running one of the most elaborate Ponzi
schemes they had ever seen.

It was all there. His meticulous record
keeping was impressive. There were
statements for every investor and every
deposit. Transaction records showed
that he made purchases of stocks,
bonds, and other funds, but when these
were cross-referenced with the statements the investors got, it was apparent
that he had bought only a fraction of the
amount he had reported to them. Buying ten shares of a stock and then show-

ing a hundred shares on the investor's statement, he was able to pocket the difference, and the investor never knew. The number of transactions he showed in one month alone was mind-boggling, making it almost impossible for his clients to keep up. The inspectors surmised that some of the companies and funds that appeared didn't actually exist. There were lists of handwritten names crossed off in a ledger book, and these names appeared on statements as a buy, and the very next month they were listed as a sell. If an investor were to ask about any particular security, it would already have disappeared. Like a Ping-Pong ball, MacKenzie had bounced from one to the other, never landing for long in one place.

Investors were sent reports that showed how much money they were making, and even with those, MacKenzie was clever. One month the profit would be slight; the next it would be bigger. He even showed a couple of minor downturns, just to make it realistic.

There were records that indicated some investors had cashed in and taken profits, but these were few and far between. With his charisma and powers of persuasion, Robert MacKenzie had most likely convinced his clients to wait for a bigger payout. How long he could have held on to his deception was the question. The only way he could keep going was to take in more than he returned . . . or spent on his lavish lifestyle.

Without a doubt, it was the most convoluted scam Grayson had ever seen. It was also brilliant. No wonder Olivia was having such trouble finding proof. It was a maze of lies.

A particularly thick file caught Grayson's attention. It had Eric Jorguson's name on it.

He picked it up and thumbed through the papers. Some of the pages showed names of other people whose investments appeared to be linked with Jorguson's. One was Gretta Keene. It didn't take much scrutiny to discover that funds were being moved from one to the other through the account. Grayson could tell that it would take some time to unravel all these figures, but he knew Huntsman was going to be ecstatic when he got his hands on this information.

Jeff Wilcox's file was there, as well. Inside were several signed documents.

Grayson looked through them and held up a couple of pages, comparing them to two pages he had laid on the desk. He called to Ronan. "Look at this."

"What have you found?" Ronan asked.

"Contradictory documents," Grayson said. "And they all have Jeff Wilcox's signature on them."

"Why would MacKenzie keep them?" he asked. "These alone will put him away for years."

"For his signature," Grayson answered. He pulled out a sheet with Jeff Wilcox's name signed at least a dozen times. "When MacKenzie forged his name, he wanted it to look authentic."

"What about the money from the charity Wilcox gave him?"

Grayson gathered the papers and slipped them back in the file. "Looks as though Wilcox gave it to him in good faith, and MacKenzie lost a good deal of it in a risky scheme and kept the rest for himself."

"What a guy," Ronan said, shaking his head.

"Yeah, a real peach," Grayson agreed.

"I'll bet Olivia will be happy, knowing that her suspicions were true. She was right all along."

Grayson thought for a second. "I don't think she'll be celebrating."

"Why? She's been vindicated. Her father won't be able to scam innocent people anymore."

"That's true," Grayson said. "But now all those people who trusted in Robert MacKenzie, the innocent clients who gave him their life savings, are going to find out the truth: They've lost it all."

TWENTY-SIX

Monday was a nightmare. The sins of Olivia's father were being broadcast all over the news channels and the Internet. It was the story of the day. Investors were in shock and disbelief. They awakened to find that they had been duped and that all of their money was gone. Those who had lost their life savings felt helpless. They had no one to turn to, nowhere to go to get their hard-earned money back. Such deceit was simply inconceivable.

Once the initial shock wore off, they were out for blood, and who could blame

them? They couldn't get to Robert Mac-
Kenzie—he was safe behind bars with
guards protecting him—and so they
took their anger out on the other members of his family. Olivia had anticipated
what was coming once the news broke,
and she knew it would be bad. She still
wasn't prepared.

Officer Carpenter drove her to work,
but instead of leaving and returning for
her at the end of the day, he stayed. He
pulled up a chair and sat right outside
her office door—Grayson's instructions,
no doubt.

Working at her desk, she received a
multitude of hateful phone calls. She listened to the comments of the first few
callers, and from then on, she simply
hung up as soon as the irate words began to fly. If she took the time to respond to each one, she'd never get anything done. Mr. Thurman stopped by a
couple of times to check on her.

"Are you worried about me?" she
asked.

"Just a little," he admitted. "There are
some terribly angry people out there
calling and threatening you."

"Sir, I work for the IRS. I'm used to it."

He smiled over her joke and said, "All right, I'll let you get back to work, but I insist you take half the day. Go home at noon, and if you must, work from there."

Olivia didn't argue. She intended to leave at noon as Mr. Thurman had ordered, but it took her longer than expected to finish working on one particularly challenging file. It was after two when Officer Carpenter dropped her at her apartment door.

Safe and sound, she thought and sighed with relief. She actually believed that, once she was inside her apartment, she would have a little peace and quiet.

There were forty-eight extremely hostile messages waiting for her on her home phone and half that many on her cell phone. Both numbers were unlisted and Olivia was surprised that so many people had been able to get hold of them. She wanted to hit the delete button, but she made herself listen to each and every message. By the time the last one played, she felt completely drained.

She was just about to change out of

her black wool skirt and silk blouse when another call came in. The second she heard the voice she picked up.

"Olivia, it's me, Henry Kincaid. Can you come to school?" The little boy's voice trembled.

"Of course I'll come to your school."

"Now? Can you come to Pinebrook now? 'Cause I need a lawyer and you're my lawyer, right?"

"Yes, now," she promised, hoping her quick agreement would calm him. "Henry, can you tell me what's wrong?"

"We have to go to the principal's office 'cause I got into trouble," he whispered. "It's because of soccer. Bobby told me not to try out or I'd be sorry, but I told him I was going to try out anyway. Ralph is going to try out, too."

Olivia checked the time. Two thirty. "Where are you? Shouldn't you be in the classroom?"

"I'm in the nurse's office. Miss Cavit wants to talk to you. Okay? And after we talk to the principal, will you take me home?"

"Henry, I'm not authorized to take you out of the school—"

"But I—"

"I'll sit with you until your grandfather or Patrick gets there."

"You won't leave me alone?"

"No, I'll stay with you. I promise."

The nurse came on the line a second later. She introduced herself and said, "Henry had a little accident. He tripped into a locker and struck his forehead, his nose, and his eye. The nosebleed has stopped, but I'll keep him here until school dismisses at three fifteen. He's resting on a cot," she explained. "The poor lamb's got a bump on his forehead. I've got an ice pack on it now."

"Have you notified his family?"

"I left a message for Grayson Kincaid. Henry told me his uncle is in New York on business. I also left a message for Henry's grandfather, and I just spoke to Patrick, Henry's housekeeper. He was at the dentist and couldn't leave yet. He'll be here at the regular dismissal time, but Henry seems insistent that you come, too."

"May I speak to Henry again?"

"Olivia," Henry whispered, "Miss Cavit says you should come when school is over."

"Henry, let her think that's what I'll do, but I'm really leaving now and should get there in fifteen minutes or less. All right?"

She could hear the anxiety leave his voice. "Okay."

Olivia was out the door minutes later. She said a prayer there wouldn't be any angry people in the garage waiting for her, and blessedly there weren't. Once she was in her car with the key in the ignition, she used her iPhone to get directions to Pinebrook School. It was a cold, rainy day, which worked to her advantage. Few reporters liked waiting outside in the raw elements. There were several cars parked along the street with their motors running. She spotted them before she turned in their direction and quickly drove the other way, even going so far as to drive down an alley on the off chance she was being followed.

She thought about calling Grayson to let him know she was going to the school, then decided to wait until she had the full story from Henry.

The private school was all redbrick and ivy vines. Very Georgetown, she thought to herself. She pulled into one of the visitor's slots and went up the stone steps.

A security guard opened the door for her. He was a man in his late sixties and wore a brown uniform. He had a sincere smile and a wealth of information to impart. "You're here for the Kincaid boy?"

"Yes, sir, I am," she answered. "My name is Olivia MacKenzie."

She put her hand out, and he quickly shook it and introduced himself. His name was Arthur. He motioned to a corner, and she followed. "I didn't see it myself, but I have no doubt what happened," he stated with a nod. "That Deckman boy is a bully, and he's been after Henry and his friend Ralph because they're younger and smaller. I used to be just like those little boys. I was small for my age, and I got picked on. I know what it feels like. I wish Principal Higgins would take a firmer hand."

"Is the Deckman boy's first name Bobby? Henry mentioned that name to me."

"That's right. Bobby Deckman. He's been in trouble before, several times, as a matter of fact, but his father does some fast talking and makes a hefty donation, and bam, the problem goes away. I know I shouldn't be saying this, but I figure, what the heck. I'm retiring in a couple of months, and it's time someone said something."

"Tell me what you suspect."

"The Deckman boy attacked Henry. He smashed his face into the locker. If the custodian hasn't gotten to it, there's blood still on the locker. Poor little Henry's blood."

"Are there cameras in the hallways?"

"Oh my, yes." His eyes widened. "I could make you a disc, but I'd have to hurry. As soon as Bobby's father gets here, I'm afraid the disc will accidentally get wiped."

She smiled. "Could you make me two?"

He nodded and ducked into the security office next to the school's entrance.

Olivia didn't have to stand there long. Arthur reappeared, grinning and waving two discs, just as another security guard rushed down the hall toward them. He explained he had gotten Arthur's page and would take over front door duty.

"Come with me," Arthur told her.

He led her up some stairs to a computer lab. Fortunately it was empty. Arthur used his security code to access the Internet, then stepped back so that Olivia could insert the disc. She quickly sent the file to her e-mail account, and she sent another to Grayson. With Arthur hovering over her, she watched the video. The encounter between the two boys lasted less than a minute, but the video left no doubt who the aggressor was. Olivia felt heartsick. Bobby was twice the size and weight of Henry.

Olivia played it one more time. "What grade is the Deckman boy in? He looks like a senior in high school."

"Fifth. He's quite big for his age," Arthur said. "And mean," he added in a whisper. "Look at his expression as he grabs Henry. He's enjoying himself. It's downright evil, if you ask me. I tell you, there's something missing in that boy's head."

She silently agreed. There wasn't any provocation. Bobby came up behind Henry, half lifted him, and threw him into the locker.

Olivia could feel her anger building. Arthur fueled it when he said, "Do you see? That's what the Deckman boy does. He chooses a kid and goes after him. Then, when he gets bored, he chooses another kid. Always younger so they can't fight back."

"And Principal Higgins?"

"He's never had any concrete proof until now," Arthur said. "The kids Bobby goes after won't tell what happened. They're afraid. Bobby's a bully, all right. The school needs to get rid of him."

Olivia was in wholehearted agreement. She grabbed her phone and called Officer Carpenter, quickly filled him in, and after he gave her his e-mail address, she sent the video to him.

"I'll take care of it," he told her.

After making the promise, Carpenter demanded to know why she had left her apartment without a bodyguard. The man was almost as bossy as Grayson, she thought. She had to listen to a lecture and vow to wait for him to come to her.

Arthur walked her to the nurse's office. "You'll like Miss Cavit. She worked in a hospital for twenty years before she retired from the long hours and took this job. She's real good with kids."

The nurse was sitting at her desk in a tiny room. Beyond was another little room with two cots side by side. Henry was resting on one of them. He lit up when he saw Olivia in the doorway.

Miss Cavit said, "There's a meeting with Bobby Deckman's parents after school. Three forty-five. Henry tells me you're his lawyer."

She smiled. "Yes, that's right."

"I imagine you'll want to be at the meeting, too."

"Oh yes, I will." Olivia walked to the cot and sat down beside Henry. "How are you feeling?"

"Good," he said. "I knew you'd come here 'cause you said you would."

She turned to Miss Cavit. "Could you give us a moment while I confer with my client?"

"I'll be at my desk if you need me," she answered.

When she'd pulled the door closed, Olivia turned to Henry. "Okay, tell me what happened."

He took hold of her hand, surprising her. His expression was so earnest. "Bobby decided Ralph and I couldn't try out for soccer."

"Did he tell you why he didn't want you to try out?"

"He was just being mean 'cause he can. He's like that with other kids, too. Honest," he insisted.

"I believe you, Henry." She reached into her purse and pulled out a small notepad and pen. "Tell me about the other kids he's bullied."

Olivia took copious notes, and when she was finished with her questions and had deciphered Henry's convoluted stories, she asked, "Why didn't you tell your uncle Grayson about Bobby Deckman?"

"'Cause Ralph and me were going to stand up to Bobby together."

"Ralph and I," she automatically corrected.

He grinned. "You're just like my uncle

and Patrick. They're always telling me the right way to talk. How come you do it?"

"It's how I roll." She laughed after using the silly expression she and the other Pips had often used when they were in the unit together. The non-answer always baffled the nurses.

Patrick arrived a few minutes before three fifteen. He sat on the empty cot next to Henry's and his tall frame dwarfed the tiny room. Olivia pulled up the video on her phone and let Patrick watch Bobby throw Henry into the locker.

"Oh man," he whispered. "Has Grayson seen this? He's going to go ballistic."

"Not yet," she answered. "I think we should go to the principal's office now. It's almost three forty-five."

Henry clasped Olivia's hand and walked by her side down the hall until he spotted some of his friends. He let go then and walked behind her with Patrick, imitating his swagger.

The Deckmans were waiting in the reception area. Mr. Deckman looked like an uptight banker with his conservative suit and tie and his rigid stance. His wife looked like one of those reality show housewives of Washington, D.C. She was unattractive, painfully thin, and had had way too much face work. *Brittle* was the word that came to mind. Olivia feared that if she shook her hand a little too vigorously she'd crumble into a thousand pieces.

Mr. Deckman didn't acknowledge them, and his wife kept giving them covert glances but didn't speak.

Bobby was waiting in the principal's office. When they were all ushered in by the receptionist, Olivia was taken aback by the hostility in the boy's eyes. He wasn't looking at her, though. His anger was directed at his father.

Extra chairs were dragged in. On the left of the principal's desk sat Brittle, Uptight, and Bobby. On the opposite side, Henry and she sat in straight-backed chairs. There was a chair for Patrick, but he preferred to stand behind Henry. She could tell he was still hopping mad.

Principal Higgins was a young man, probably in his early to middle thirties,

Olivia estimated. There were stress lines around his mouth and dark circles under his eyes. Running the all-boys school had taken its toll.

Higgins rubbed his jaw. "This is a difficult situation. We know Henry and Bobby were in an altercation, but the boys have given different interpretations of what happened."

"Boys like to fight," Mr. Deckman said.

Had he not shrugged and acted so indifferent, Olivia might have softened her response.

"Your son is a bully."

"He is not," Mrs. Deckman snapped. "He's a normal fifth grader."

"He's a bully," she repeated. "And that won't stand. Principal Higgins, this isn't the first time Bobby's been accused of attacking a student, is it?"

"Now, see here. That's confidential information," Bobby's mother said.

"No, it isn't," Olivia replied. "Your son punched Tom Capshaw. Split his lip open."

"There is absolutely no proof that it was our son who struck Capshaw," Mr. Deckman argued.

Olivia opened her notepad and glanced at it. "What about Will Kaufman or Matt Farrell?"

"Those altercations happened last year," Mrs. Deckman said. "It was all hearsay, one boy's word against another's, and then both Will and Matt changed their stories." She turned to her husband. "They were just roughhousing, weren't they, Sean?"

Her husband nodded. "That's exactly right. No proof of any wrongdoing."

"This time there is proof," Olivia said. She handed the principal one of the discs.

"What is that?" Mr. Deckman asked.

"A security tape," Olivia answered.

Principal Higgins looked surprised. "I don't know how you got this, Miss Mac-Kenzie, but I'm not sure we can . . ."

Olivia turned to Bobby's parents. "You do want to know the truth, don't you? If it was just two boys roughhousing, this will prove it."

Mr. Deckman stammered, "Well, of course I—"

"Good," Olivia said. She nodded to Principal Higgins, who slipped the disc into the computer slot. He adjusted the monitor so they could see it, then came around the desk to watch the video with them.

Not a word was spoken as the event played out on the screen. Mrs. Deckman's face turned white, and she winced when she saw Bobby throw Henry into the locker. Mr. Deckman's face turned red. When Olivia turned to look at Bobby, he was smiling. What was he? A sociopath in the making?

Principal Higgins was appalled, but Olivia could detect a hint of relief as he returned to his chair and removed the disc.

Mr. Deckman grabbed the disc from his hand, slipped it into his pocket, and said, "I'd like to look at this again at home."

Mrs. Deckman smiled at her husband's quick response. Did she think the problem had just gone away?

"That's fine," Olivia said. "I've sent the video to Henry's uncle and to others as well. This isn't going away."

Mr. Deckman sprang to his feet and was all bluster when he said, "That's illegal. I'll sue. You can't confiscate private property. It's an invasion of privacy. It's . . ." He turned his outrage on the principal. "Do something, Higgins. If you want to keep your job, fix this."

Principal Higgins was not intimidated. He looked directly at Deckman and stated, "We do not tolerate violence or bullies in this school."

Mrs. Deckman's smile had disappeared and she now looked worried. "Yes, we understand, but he's just a child. We could get him counseling. We'll do it right away."

"I don't know . . ." Higgins began. "We simply can't have this behavior . . ."

"If we bring charges," Olivia told the principal, "the decision would be out of your hands. This is clearly a case of assault, and I'm confident that any court would see it our way."

Principal Higgins was the one who looked worried now. "I understand your point of view, Miss MacKenzie, but for the sake of our school and its reputation, I hope we can find a way to settle this without a legal battle."

Olivia appeared to consider his concerns and then said, "We suggest that Bobby be expelled from Pinebrook immediately. He should not be allowed to return here or attend any other school until he's gotten the help he needs. He could have broken Henry's neck. Surely, you wouldn't wait until something that serious happened before taking action, Principal Higgins?"

The Deckmans erupted, but Olivia stood her ground. Any threats that the parents hurled at her were met with the sound and logical details she would use in a suit against them and their son.

Until now, Bobby had sat quietly with a smug grin on his face, but he was beginning to see the handwriting on the wall. He rushed to his father, poked him in the chest, and screamed, "Don't you dare let them kick me out. You'll be sorry if you do."

There was no calming the boy. A minute later, as he was being dragged from the office by his mother and father, everyone could hear Mrs. Deckman trying to comfort him with the promise of a new iPad as soon as this mistake was sorted out. Mr. Deckman paused at the door to give Olivia a contemptuous glare before he left.

Olivia spent a few more minutes talking to the principal, and Patrick and Henry waited for her in the reception area. When she came out, Henry hugged her. "Thank you, Olivia," he said.

She leaned down, smiled, and kissed his cheek. "You're very welcome, Henry."

Officer Carpenter was standing by the front door to the school when she walked outside. He held out his hand to take her car keys, but after her protest, he agreed to follow her in his car if she promised to be cautious. Just to make him happy, she drove under the speed limit the whole way home.

He was just about to say good-bye to her at her apartment door when Mrs. Delaney, who must have been listening for Olivia to return, stuck her head out and announced she needed milk. Carpenter waited while Olivia went into her apartment and came back with a quart. The grumpy woman made her stand there while she found her reading glasses and checked the expiration date, then she thanked Olivia and went back inside.

After Carpenter wagged his finger in Olivia's face and told her to stay home, he left. Olivia locked her door and leaned against it. She suddenly felt very tired. She changed into snug jeans and a blouse, put her hair up in a ponytail, and went into the kitchen to find something she could microwave for dinner. Determined to eat something healthy first, she made a salad and ate every bit of it. She thought about what had happened at Henry's school and realized how lucky she'd been that no one had recognized her. Maybe they hadn't seen the news yet or hadn't associated her name with the family. Regardless, she was thankful. She even had the thought that maybe it wasn't going to be as bad as she'd anticipated. Maybe it would go away sooner rather than later.

In her dreams perhaps. Just as she was going to put her frozen dinner in the microwave, another call came in. It was so grossly disturbing, she lost her appetite. She put the dinner back in the refrigerator and curled up on the sofa to watch television.

Her father's face was plastered on all the major channels. The broadcaster on one news network was interviewing a tearful woman who kept saying she'd been promised a triple return on her money. Olivia pushed the button on the remote and turned the television off. The silence brought a few welcome moments of peace.

She decided a Popsicle sounded good so she got one from the freezer, put it on a plate, and went back to the television. Maybe she could find an old classic movie to take her mind off her worries. A knock on the door startled her, and an instant of panic gripped her stomach. Had one of the angry investors gotten inside the building? She walked over and peered through the peephole. When she saw Grayson standing there, she threw the door open and fell into his arms. He looked tired, she thought.

"What are you doing here? It's almost ten. Did you just get back from New York? Shouldn't you be—"

His mouth stopped her. He tightened his hold and kissed the breath out of her. She didn't resist him. She wrapped her arms around his neck and kissed him back passionately. It had been such an awful day, but he was here now, and everything was better.

"I missed you, too." He took off his coat, hung it in the closet, and draping his arm around her, pulled her along to the sofa.

"How's Henry?"

"Fully recovered," he replied. "When I opened the file you sent and saw Henry being slammed into his locker, I wanted to lock that Deckman kid up in solitary for the rest of his life."

"That's a little extreme, don't you think?" she teased.

"Henry and Patrick are singing your praises. Thank you, by the way."

He kissed her on her forehead and pulled her down next to him. They talked about the school for a few more minutes, and then Olivia said, "I want to hear about the files again. Tell me everything. Start at the beginning when you entered the apartment."

She took a bite of the Popsicle and waited. Grayson, she noticed, was staring at her mouth.

"I can't concentrate while you're eating that," he said.

A little bit of the devil in her came out. She put the Popsicle in her mouth and sucked the sweet cherry juice. "How come?" she asked innocently.

His eyes narrowed. "Olivia," he warned, "want to find out how fast I can get your clothes off?"

Smiling sweetly, she stopped tormenting him and took the Popsicle to the sink. Her mood changed immediately when she heard her phone ring.

Grayson went to the door of her study to listen to the incoming call. He obviously didn't like what he heard. "Son of a bitch," he growled. "Did you hear that?" he asked when she came back into the living room.

She shook her head. "Come sit and tell me—"

"How many others are there?" he demanded.

"I'm up to fifty-some now."

"Son of a . . ."

"Grayson, you knew this was coming."

"Did you listen to all of them?" His voice shook, he was so angry.

"Yes," she said. "Trust me. You don't want to. Some of them are sick."

"How many were death threats?"

"Stop snapping at me. I didn't make the calls."

Her retort eased some of the tension, and he gave her a slight smile.

"I should have erased them and turned the phone off," she admitted.

"No, absolutely not. I'm going to have every damned call traced."

"You can't arrest people for saying mean things."

"Death threats? Hell yes, I can arrest them."

"When did you get back from New York?" she asked to keep him from getting worked up again.

"Around five today. I didn't see the video until I got home." He was still glaring as he followed her.

"Did you get to see any Broadway shows?" she asked with a straight face.

The question jarred him; then he

laughed. He dropped down next to her and swung his feet up on the ottoman. "I was in your father's study until after two. Then I went back around nine this morning. Spent most of the day there."

"I've never been to the apartment," she said.

He described the layout but didn't mention the fact that there wasn't a single photo of her anywhere. He went into detail about the secret room and what he had seen in the files.

"Ronan talked to Wilcox's attorney, told him what we found," he said.

"That's wonderful," she said. "Emma will be so relieved."

"There's more," he continued. "And I think you'll really like this."

"What?" she asked.

"You know that Eric Jorguson invested with your father."

"Yes."

"It appears that not all the money Jorguson had flowing through the fund was going into his retirement nest egg. When the auditors sort it all out, I'm pretty sure they'll be able to prove this was one of his money-laundering accounts."

"Wouldn't that be something?" Olivia shook her head. She'd listened intently to all the evidence that was piling up against her father, and the cold reality of the situation was setting in. "This is going to go on for a long while, isn't it?" she asked. "The phone calls and the threats?"

"Depends on the next big story." Grayson could see her wilting before his eyes, so he changed the subject. "Want to know what I did when I got home this evening?"

"What?" she asked, wondering why he suddenly sounded exasperated. "Did you eat dinner with Henry and Patrick?"

"Yes," he replied. "Henry met me at the door and went into a long narration of what happened at school. Then Patrick gave me his summary. Then Henry started over again," he said, smiling. "You impressed the socks off him, Olivia. He's now quoting you."

"He's sweet," she said. "And so is Patrick."

"Uh-huh, sweet. We sat down for dinner when sweet Henry remembered he had another assignment due tomorrow."

She bit her lower lip to keep from laughing. "What was it?"

"He had to memorize all the states in alphabetical order and all the capitals. He was supposed to have been working on it for a couple of weeks, but he just remembered tonight." He shook his head as he added, "When he told me, I swear I was speechless."

"What did you do?"

"It wasn't as bad as I thought. He knew some of them, and Patrick came up with a rap tune. It made it easier for Henry."

"Did you memorize them along with him?"

"Yes . . . and, no, I'm not singing for you."

"Children learn quickly. I'm sure you got through the assignment in no time."

"I haven't told you about the math yet."

The lighthearted conversation ended with the doorbell. Then the banging on the door started. Olivia reluctantly went to answer it. She looked through the peephole and groaned.

"Who is it?" he asked, coming up behind her.

"World War Three," she said. "Natalie and my mother."

"You don't have to let them in."

"Oh yes, I do. Natalie will stand there hitting the door and shouting until tomorrow if she has to. I might as well get it over with now."

Grayson made her step back into the living room before he opened the door. Natalie couldn't storm inside because he blocked her.

"Where is my sister?" she demanded. She pushed against his chest.

"You don't want to do that."

"I know she's here. Let me in," she shouted.

Since she was acting like a child, he decided to treat her like one. "You will behave yourself, or you will leave."

The second he stepped back, Natalie rushed in. Her mother, Deborah, showed more decorum. She nodded to Grayson as she walked past.

Natalie saw Olivia and screamed, "Do you know what you've done?"

Ignoring her sister, Olivia said, "Hello, Mother."

Deborah MacKenzie looked exhausted. Grayson noticed her hands were shaking as she struggled to remove her coat. He took it from her.

She was a beautiful woman. Except for the color of their eyes—Olivia's were blue; Deborah's were brown—Olivia looked just like her.

"Hello, Olivia. How are you feeling?"

"I'm fine. How are you?"

"I'm very distressed," she said. "I don't understand what's happening. Your father's in jail, and he's been accused of stealing money. It's outrageous to think that my husband would do such a thing. It's all a misunderstanding," she whispered. "It has to be."

"No, Mother, it isn't a misunderstanding. This is what I've been trying to tell you, but you wouldn't listen."

"This is all your fault," Natalie yelled. She was pacing around the room with her arms crossed.

Olivia turned to her. "Sit down and wait your turn. I'm talking to Mother. When I'm finished, I'll listen to you."

"You selfish—"

"Don't say it. If you call me names, you're out of here."

Grayson smiled. He was impressed with the way Olivia had taken the upper hand.

"Mother, I know this is a shock."

Olivia could see the anger washing over her mother. She straightened up, her spine rigid. Her voice turned to ice when she said, "A shock? My husband is in jail. It's all a mistake," she insisted. "Because of you, young lady. You started all those rumors. You've ruined your father with your foolish accusations."

Rumors? Olivia didn't know where to start. She looked at Grayson and lifted her shoulders.

"You must fix this," her mother implored. "Show your father the support he needs now. He's all alone in New York, without any family to help him through this humiliation. I wanted to go and stand by his side, but he's been denied bail."

For good cause, Olivia knew. They were sure he would try to run.

"I'm going home with Natalie," she

said then. "I'll stay with her until this is resolved."

Hopeless. Her mother was completely hopeless. Still drinking Robert MacKenzie's poisoned water, Olivia realized. Eventually she would be forced to face reality. And so would Natalie. It wouldn't do any good to try to reason with either of them now. She actually felt sorry for them. Acknowledging the truth was going to be painful.

"Okay, Natalie, it's your turn," Olivia said.

"Did you know George is sitting in a cell? He's been accused of the most heinous crimes."

"Yes, I do know," she replied calmly. She crossed the room to Grayson and leaned against him. She needed comfort.

"This is all such a mess," Natalie railed.

"The time is getting away from us, Natalie. Get the papers out," her mother ordered.

Uh-oh. Olivia didn't like the sound of that.

Natalie opened her purse and pulled

out a stack of papers. She unfolded them and was searching for a pen.

"What are you doing?" Olivia asked.

Natalie finally explained. "Mother and Father's assets have been frozen, and most of my money is unavailable. I have a small account that will get us through, but there isn't enough to pay for George's defense. So, you're going to sign over your trust. I know you don't get the money for another year, but if you sign it over to us now, we can borrow against it and hire the best attorney we can find to clear this up. You got him into this mess. You can damn well help to get him out."

"You must help your father, too," her mother said firmly. She put her purse over her arm and reached for her coat. "You simply must call your aunt Emma and insist that she support your father."

"And by support, Mother, do you mean you want me to ask her to give Father all of her money?"

Her mother's chin came up. "Yes, that's exactly what I mean. His defense will be expensive, and Emma is a member of this family. She must do her part."

"You need to sign these papers," Natalie reminded, shoving them at her. "And we aren't leaving until you do."

Olivia pushed them away. "I'm not signing anything."

"Yes, you are," Natalie cried. "You owe us."

For Olivia, that was the final straw. As she calmly walked out of the room, she turned back and said, "Grayson, please get the door."

TWENTY-SEVEN

Olivia was sitting with Jane and Collins in Jane's hospital room, catching them up on the latest events. The news about her father was still a hot topic on TV, but now the how-could-this-have-happened-again questions had started. Fingers were pointed; and if history were to repeat itself, no one was going to step up and take responsibility for not doing his job.

Olivia wondered how many had ignored all the signs and all the complaints and had simply turned a blind eye.

Collins couldn't understand how Natalie could blame Olivia.

"It's easier to blame me than to admit that she was horribly deceived by her father," Olivia explained. "Natalie trusted him."

"Natalie knows what a Ponzi scheme is, doesn't she?"

"Of course she does," Olivia said.

"What do you think she'll do when she finds out about George's debt to that loan shark?" Jane asked.

"She won't be happy," Collins predicted.

Olivia laughed. "You think?"

"What about your mother?" Collins asked. "Do you think she'll ever figure it out?"

"I doubt it. She's a lost cause."

"No, she's just loyal to a fault," Jane said. "No one's a lost cause. Look at my brother. Logan's completely turned his life around."

Olivia smiled. Jane always looked for the good in people. She wished she could be more like her friend. She had such a sweet disposition and a gentle soul.

"If convicted on all counts, your father will never get out of prison," Collins predicted.

"How do you feel about that?" Jane asked. She sounded like a therapist now. She was sitting up in bed, trying to ignore Collins, who was fluffing her pillows.

"It's for the best," Olivia said. "If he got out, he'd just do it again. He really can't help the way he is."

Collins disagreed. "Your father knows the difference between right and wrong. He set out to steal."

Jane pulled a pillow from behind her and whacked Collins with it. "Go sit down and stop fussing over me."

Laughing, Collins dodged the attack and sat on the edge of the bed. Olivia took the pillow and put it on a chair. She noticed a couple of long strands of Jane's hair. Oh God, it was falling out again. Was she doing chemo and not telling them? She turned the pillow over so Jane wouldn't notice, then went to the window ledge and leaned against it.

"What's the matter?" Collins asked

when she noticed Olivia's stark complexion.

Olivia wasn't going to talk about Jane's illness now, and so she said, "I don't want to talk about family any longer. I'm sick of it. Let's talk about something else."

"Okay," Collins agreed. "Tell us about Grayson."

"Olivia can't keep her hands off him," Jane announced.

Both of her friends had a good laugh. Olivia didn't take exception because it was true. She couldn't keep her hands off him. Jane was simply repeating what she'd told her.

"I don't understand it. I really don't," Olivia said, perplexed. "I make all these resolutions, and the second I see him, I want to . . . you know."

"You're in love with him." Collins stated the obvious.

"Of course I'm in love with him. I wouldn't be so miserable if I weren't. But I'm not going to marry him."

"Has he asked?" Jane wanted to know.

"No."

"Has he told you he loves you?" Collins asked.

"No," she answered. "But I know he cares about me. It's all the little things he does . . ." Her voice trailed off as she thought about him.

"Like?" Collins asked. "Give us an example."

"He carries an extra inhaler for me because he knows I'll forget to put one in my purse," she said. "And he does so many sweet, loving things for me." Tears came into her eyes. "When I first met him, I thought of him as the James Bond type. He was so sophisticated and sexy and . . ."

When she didn't go on, Collins said, "Love 'em and leave 'em, like Bond?"

"Exactly. He isn't like that, though. He's responsible and solid." She thought of him with Henry. Grayson was patient and loving, and she knew he would always be there for his nephew. Henry knew it, too.

"I sometimes think about a future with him, and then I remember what your parents went through, Collins, and your mother, Jane. Sam's family, too. I saw their fear, and I heard them crying. For a while there, when everyone but Dr. Pardieu thought we were dying, your families came and kept vigil. It was awful for them."

Collins nodded. "We all remember, Olivia."

"How can I put Grayson through that?" She shook her head. "I can't do that to him. I won't."

Collins didn't try to convince her that she was wrong. How could she with Jane so ill now?

"You can't live your life waiting for it to come back." Jane made the statement. "What a fatalistic attitude. Olivia, you need to stop being afraid."

"What about you, Jane?" Olivia asked. "What's going on?"

"And don't tell us it's the flu again," Collins warned.

"I'm feeling better again. It's the weirdest thing. I get so sick, and then I bounce back. Since Dr. Pardieu has been away, another doctor has been seeing me. By the way, Logan's going to be here any minute. Please don't talk about my illness in front of him. Okay? He gets so upset. I know he's scared, so keep it upbeat."

They quickly agreed. Then it was Collins's turn to catch her friends up. She told them she was still waiting to hear when she would start at the academy. She couldn't understand why it was taking so long, but she thought it might have something to do with her medical history.

Exasperated, Jane said, "You're just like Olivia. The two of you need an attitude adjustment."

An argument ensued, and Jane deflected it by changing the topic. "I can't believe everything that's happened to you in the last few months, Olivia. You were attacked by the CEO of a major corporation and his goon, and you were rescued by the FBI. You were shot three times, and then you were almost kidnapped and taken to a mental hospital."

"I hope that's the end of it, and I really hope and pray they find whoever shot you," Collins said.

Logan walked in and heard what she'd said. "Jane told me that Martin guy was the shooter."

His eyes were red, and it was obvious he'd been crying. No one mentioned his condition.

"I thought so, too," Olivia said. "But until there's absolute proof, Grayson is going to continue to provide protection for me. He doesn't care if I want a bodyguard following me around or not. He's extremely stubborn."

"What's absolute proof?" Logan asked. He walked to the side of the bed and kissed Jane's forehead.

"A confession would seal it," Jane suggested. "But he obviously isn't talking."

"Finding the weapon would also do it. If they could trace it to Martin, Grayson would be convinced," Olivia said.

"When do you get to go home?" Collins asked Jane.

"Hopefully tomorrow," she answered. "Olivia, will you be around in a couple of weeks?"

"For the Dracula room? Absolutely."

"Why is the doctor waiting so long?" Collins wondered.

"He wants me to finish some meds first."

Olivia yawned again. "I'm exhausted. I'm going home. Come on, Collins. Let Jane visit with her brother."

Olivia waited until she and Collins were in the elevator before talking about Jane's condition. "She's losing her hair."

"I saw it on the pillow," Collins said.

"She doesn't want us to know."

"We could try to talk to the doctor who's covering for Dr. Pardieu, but he has to hold her confidence, and if she wants to keep it secret, he can't tell us anything."

Several heartbeats later, Collins took Olivia's hand and whispered, "It's back, isn't it?"

"Maybe," Olivia allowed. Determined to be more positive, she added, "And maybe not."

TWENTY-EIGHT

Olivia had suffered a week from hell. The phones never stopped ringing; the threats never subsided, and because of the disruption she was inadvertently causing at the office, she'd been forced to work at home. By Friday, she was feeling like a caged orangutan.

She pretty much looked like one, too. She continued to shower and brush her teeth every day, but getting dressed didn't seem all that necessary. Her new uniform was a pair of baggy sweats and an old faded T-shirt. She didn't bother with a bra or shoes and didn't do much of anything with her hair. Every morning she put it up in a ponytail, but by nightfall, most of it was hanging around her face. Her eating habits weren't much better. She walked around with a bag of chips—the unhealthy kind—and a Diet Coke.

She was sitting cross-legged on the floor with her laptop balanced on her knees and a pencil clutched in her teeth. She had just reached for a potato chip when there was an unexpected knock at the door. She stuck the pencil in her hair, popped the chip in her mouth, and went to answer it.

When the door opened, Grayson took one look at her and started laughing.

She dared him to criticize her. "What's so funny?"

He wasn't about to tell her. In her present frame of mind, she wouldn't believe him if he told her that, no matter how she dressed, she was beautiful to him. Her face scrubbed clean and dressed in clothes that could pass for bag lady rejects, Olivia could still grace the cover of any glamour magazine.

The phone was ringing as he shut the

door behind him and locked it. Another caller was leaving a threatening message.

"How many . . ." Grayson began.

She shoved the bag of chips into his hand. "Hold that thought," she said as she rushed into the study to listen to the rest of the message.

The voice was an angry growl. "You got that, bitch? Bill and me are gonna hurt you because you took all that money. We're gonna . . ."

Olivia picked up the phone before Grayson could get to her and yelled, "It's not 'Bill and *me*'—it's 'Bill and *I* are going to hurt you'—dumb ass." She slammed the phone down.

"Okay, sweetheart. I think it's time for you to get out for a little while," Grayson said calmly. He put his hands on her shoulders and guided her out of the study. She was as stiff as an ironing board.

"How can you want to be seen with me?" She sounded pitiful. She realized she was feeling sorry for herself, but the phone calls were getting to her, and so was the isolation. She hadn't stepped outside her apartment since Monday.

"I'm hoping you'll change your clothes and put on shoes," he answered drily, as he pushed her along into her bedroom.

"I'm going to have to change my name," she said, "and move to Europe where no one knows me. That's what I have to do."

"It will get better," he promised.

She scoffed at his prediction. Grayson turned her around and tilted her chin up. "Snorting isn't ladylike, sweetheart."

Ignoring his comment, she said, "Do you know what's really ironic? Natalie and my mother haven't gotten all these hostile calls."

"Have you talked to them?"

"Only once. Natalie's been leaving her own horrible messages for me. I picked up yesterday when she called, and it was more of the same. She and Mother have gone into hiding, so these threatening calls aren't reaching them."

"Do you want them to get the threatening calls?"

"No, of course not. I'm just saying . . ."

The tenderness in his eyes warmed her heart, and suddenly the whining and complaining weren't all that satisfying.

"Why are you here?" she asked.

"I'm taking you out to dinner."

"Do you have your gun with you?"

He smiled. "Yes."

"Okay. If you want to risk it, we'll go to dinner."

The lopsided ponytail was driving him to distraction. He pulled the elastic band free and handed it to her. "That's better," he said. He traced the side of her jaw with his fingers, leaned down, and kissed her.

"Sometimes you overwhelm me," she whispered. How could this gorgeous, sexy man want to be with her? He could have any woman in the world, and yet here he was.

"Overwhelm, huh? I like that."

He looked a little too arrogantly pleased with himself. "Only sometimes, Grayson."

"We have a reservation at Veronique's in ninety minutes. You're wasting time."

She was astounded. Veronique's was

the hottest restaurant in D.C. It had received rave reviews and had been
booked solid every night since it opened.

"It takes six months to get a reservation there. How did you—"

"Olivia?"

"Yes?"

"Wear the white dress."

She gasped. "But that means—"

"I'll explain everything in the car. Get
moving."

He didn't have to tell her again. She
was already stripping out of her clothes
in the bathroom before he pulled the
bedroom door closed behind him. She
showered and washed and dried her
hair in record time. It took her longer to
do her makeup. She was going for the
pouty, sultry look. Her dark, smoky eye
makeup made the color of her eyes
more intense. After applying her red lipstick, she dropped her robe, sprayed
perfume, and slipped into her lacy un-
dergarments. Next came the dress. It
was probably sinful to love a piece of
clothing as much as she loved this dress,
but it was so perfect. It was made in
1960, but it had never been worn . . .

until tonight. She'd paid a fortune for it at a vintage shop, and it was worth every dollar. It had a low-cut square neckline and long tapered sleeves that came just below her wrist. The straight skirt was short, just to her knees, and the fabric clung to every curve of her body. This dress was so spectacular, it would make any woman look and feel like a temptress.

And she was ready. After one last inspection in the full-length mirror, Olivia took a deep breath and opened the door without making a sound.

Grayson was standing by the window. His head was bent, and he was going through his text messages. He glanced up and saw her, and his reaction was instantaneous. His mouth suddenly went dry. He couldn't swallow, and breathing was impossible. She was stunning. He was so aroused, he would have sworn his blood was on fire coursing through his veins.

Olivia didn't need to hear any compliments. His smoldering eyes said it all.

A minute passed and then another, and he still hadn't said a word. He slowly began to walk toward her. The way he was looking at her made her heart race. If he were a panther, she was his prey, and every nerve in her body tensed in anticipation.

For Grayson, the primal need to touch her overrode caution. He stood in front of her, one hand on the small of her back, the other at her neck. He roughly twisted her hair around his fist, forced her head back, and growled, "Open your mouth for me," a scant second before his mouth covered hers. His tongue thrust inside, stroking hers, forcing her to respond. He savored the taste of her. For this moment in time she was completely his. No one else could have her. She belonged to him.

The scorching kiss ended. He lifted his head, and staring into her eyes, he slowly rubbed his thumb across her lips. He took a deep, shuddering breath. "I'll get your coat."

Olivia could barely get her wits about her. She hurried back into the bedroom to collect her evening bag. The kiss so rattled her, she'd almost forgotten it. She caught a glimpse at her reflection in the mirror. Her lipstick had stayed on her lips. Impressive, she thought. Especially considering the way Grayson had tried to devour her. Just thinking about that kiss made her heartbeat quicken.

Grayson helped her with her coat and locked the door for her. He still hadn't said a word about her appearance, and for some reason she was inordinately pleased by that fact.

He had parked illegally in front of her building again. John was standing behind the counter talking to a policeman at the door. She slowed to greet them, but Grayson had her elbow and was in a hurry to get her in the car. Were there angry people outside waiting for her? Sleet was spitting across the windshield. Who would stand outside in this weather? She could feel a dark cloud closing in on her mood and rebelled against it. Not tonight. She was not going to be pessimistic and worry about anything. She was going to have the most wonderful evening with Grayson. No worries. No complications.

Once they were on their way, he finally spoke. "I'm gonna want you to keep your coat on during dinner."

She laughed. He didn't join in. "Oh my . . . you're serious? I am not keeping my coat on while I eat." She laughed again. "So, you like the dress?"

"How about I tell you what I wanted to do to you when I saw you standing in the doorway?"

Her face felt warm, and she knew she was blushing. "The dress isn't inappropriate . . . is it?"

His slow smile caught her by surprise. "No, the dress is beautiful."

"Then what's the problem?"

He decided he might as well tell her the truth. "It's you. You're the problem."

Turning toward him, she folded her arms defensively. "Would you care to explain?"

"It's the way you fill out the dress. It hugs your perfect, voluptuous body, and the sensual way you move in it . . . hell, it should be illegal." His voice was becoming more intense. "You're the sexiest woman I've ever known, and in that dress . . ." He shook his head. "Just keep the coat on."

He thought her body was voluptuous? She fought the urge to look down at her chest. Wait a minute. . . . Was *voluptuous* a code word for "fat"? No, it couldn't be. Grayson wouldn't be looking at her that way if that's what he meant. He was telling her she looked hot. She smiled at him to let him know she appreciated the compliment, but he returned her smile with a frown.

"Now what?" she asked.

"How many other men have seen you in that dress?"

"This dress is a 1960 vintage—"

"How many?"

"None. This is the first time I've worn it. I was waiting for a special occasion, and you did tell me to wear it."

"Yes, I did."

"Remember the promise? As soon as you were convinced you had the right man behind bars for trying to kill me, you'd pull the bodyguards and we'd celebrate."

"We've got the gun—"

She interrupted. "The gun used to shoot me?"

"Yes," he said, smiling. "That gun."

"Where did you find it?"

Grayson promised to tell her everything later. He pulled up to the restaurant entrance. A valet rushed forward to open Olivia's door while another attendant came around to give Grayson a claim ticket. He told the man to keep his car close.

Veronique's was a small bistro with a European flair. Grayson was watching the crowd as they entered. He thought every man there was staring at Olivia, and he didn't like that one little bit. She hadn't taken off her coat yet, but the second she'd walked in, she had their attention.

"Would you like to check your coat?" the maître d' asked her when they stepped up to his podium.

She looked at Grayson. "Would I?"

He muttered something she couldn't quite catch before he helped her remove her coat. He took her hand and headed to the bar. Like the sea parting, men stepped back on either side, making a path for her. It was actually comical, and had he not been feeling so possessive of her, Grayson might have laughed. Instead, he decided a little intimidation was called for, and he unbuttoned his suit jacket so that his badge and gun were visible.

Olivia also noticed the stares. Her reaction was panic. Ever since the scandal with her father had hit the news, various photos of the MacKenzies had been plastered on all the media. There were quite a few pictures of her parents and her sister attending parties, and since Olivia was never with them, she hadn't expected she'd be so easily recognized.

She turned back to Grayson and whispered into his ear. "I'm not so sure this was a good idea. I think some of these people might know who I am. They're staring. Maybe we should leave."

He put his arm around her waist and pulled her close. "It's the dress they're staring at." It wasn't just the dress, of course. They were staring at a beautiful woman.

The maître d' appeared and told them their table was ready. Grayson didn't like the first choice—the table was in the middle of the room—but another was available against the wall near the back. It was more intimate.

Once Olivia was seated with a menu in front of her, she began to relax. Her back was to the other diners, and she decided she would let Grayson handle any problems tonight. If anyone wanted to get in her face and yell at her because of what her father had done, she would let Grayson shoo him away. She was not going to let anyone or anything mar her evening.

She tried to ask Grayson for the details about the gun, but he shook his head and said, "We'll talk after dinner. Every time I think about you getting shot, I get angry, real angry. I don't want to ruin my appetite."

She turned her attention to the menu. Each selection was written in French with the English translation below. Everything sounded wonderful.

"I'm starving," she admitted.

"Potato chips didn't do it for you?"

A waiter placed a silver basket filled with freshly baked bread and a small silver disk with sweet, creamy butter on the table.

"Dr. Pardieu would like this restaurant," she remarked.

Grayson's cell phone vibrated. He pulled it out of his pocket to see who was calling, then quickly got up from the table. "I'll be right back. I've got to take this."

He wasn't gone long. "I'm sorry, Olivia, but we have to leave. Henry's on his way to the emergency room to get stitches. It doesn't sound too bad," he rushed to add when the color left Olivia's face.

She didn't ask questions until they were in the car. "What happened to him?"

"He went to a birthday party at one of those indoor playgrounds. I guess he tried to do a summersault into some kind of ball pit and didn't quite make it. Ralph's father thinks Henry will need about six stitches in his forehead. Ralph is Henry's best friend, and he doesn't have a brain in his head either."

"Henry's a smart little boy."

"Yes, he is," he agreed. "But he also just turned nine, and at that age, *caution* isn't a word he's familiar with."

A few minutes later, they were walking into the emergency room lobby. Ralph and his father were in the waiting area. As soon as they saw Grayson, they hurried over.

"Henry's getting an X-ray to make sure he doesn't have a concussion. Who's this?" the father asked, thrusting his hand out to Olivia.

Grayson made the introductions. "Olivia, this is Dr. Ralph Jones."

The doctor wasn't letting go of Olivia's hand. Staring intently at her, he said, "I'm an ophthalmologist. A divorced ophthalmologist. Would you like to sit with Ralph Junior and me while Grayson checks on Henry?"

What the hell? Grayson thought. Ralph was hitting on her. Grayson put his arm around her shoulder and said, "She works for the IRS."

A pallor came over the doctor, but he quickly recovered. "Someone's got to, I suppose. Why don't you tell me all about your job?"

"She's coming with me," Grayson said. "Let go of her, Jones. You don't need to stay now that I'm here."

Olivia softened the harshness of his command. "I'd like to sit with Henry."

She noticed a nurse waving to her. It was Kathleen from the chemo ward. Olivia excused herself and went to say hello. "What are you doing in the ER?"

"They were short staffed, so I'm filling in," she said. "How are you doing, sweetie?"

"I'm good."

"Yes, you certainly are," she replied, looking past Olivia to Grayson. "That's one fine man you've got there."

Olivia agreed. Grayson was one fine man.

"Has Jane been admitted again?" Kathleen asked. She knew everything that went on inside the hospital, and she'd made it a point to keep up with all the Pips. "Is that why you're here?"

"No," Olivia answered, "not this time."

"Jane certainly has had a rough go of it," Kathleen said.

"She says she's doing better, but I don't believe her. Neither does Collins or Sam."

"Dr. Pardieu is back from his medical conference, and you know what a miracle worker he is. He'll sort it all out. Why are you here then?"

After Olivia quickly explained, Kathleen called radiology to see how much longer Henry would be. "He's on his way up now. Did you have a big evening planned? You're all dressed up."

"Dinner at Veronique's," she answered.

"Oh, that's fancy," Kathleen said. "I don't believe I've ever seen you with makeup on. You look lovely. Let's see what you're wearing."

Smiling, Olivia unbuttoned her coat and held it open. "Gorgeous," Kathleen raved. "The fabric is divine."

Grayson had finished the paperwork and came up behind Olivia. Kathleen introduced herself and asked, "Have you and Olivia been dating long?"

"We're not—" Olivia began. She'd seen the speculative look in Kathleen's eyes and thought she should explain that they weren't actually dating, that the evening was more of an obligation for Grayson because of the investigation.

Grayson cut her off. "For a while now," he said.

"Then you know Olivia's a hellion, don't you?" the nurse said, smiling. "She gave us such trouble when she was about your nephew's age. Made all of us love coming to work just to see what she'd do next."

"Kathleen's being polite," she said. "I was a holy terror back then."

Grayson leaned down and whispered, "Back then?"

"My break's over," Kathleen said. She hugged Olivia. "They'll put Henry back in bay four. It's the second curtain on your left. Why don't you wait in there?"

As soon as Kathleen hurried away, Olivia said, "I should stay out here. Have Ralph and Ralph left?"

"Yes," he replied. "But you're coming with me. Henry will be happy to see you. He asks about you all the time."

"He does?" she asked, smiling.

"Yeah, he does. I have to make up all sorts of terrible stories about you."

They walked to the curtained-off bay Kathleen had pointed out. Henry's shoes were on a chair in the corner with his coat. There was another chair on the opposite side of the bed.

"Why don't you sit here while I go see what's taking so long," Grayson said.

He was on his way to the elevators when the doors opened, and Henry was wheeled out by an orderly. The child had blood all over his face. There was a jagged cut that started at the top of his hairline above his right temple and ended at the tip of his eyebrow. He also had a bloody nose.

Grayson's breath caught when he saw all the blood, but he concealed his appalled reaction because Henry was watching him. "How are you doing, Henry?" he asked, his voice filled with sympathy.

The child was trying hard not to cry. "It hurts," he whispered as he was wheeled past. "Ralph said they're going to put a needle in my head. A big one," he added worriedly.

Henry spotted Olivia just as the orderly stopped the wheelchair. He was so happy to see her, he bolted out of the wheelchair and ran to her. She was getting up when he threw himself into her arms, nearly knocking her off her feet.

"Don't . . ." Grayson called. But it was too late. Henry had his arms around Olivia's waist, and his bloody face was pressed against her chest.

"I'm glad you came to see me," he said.

"You certainly have had more than your share of injuries lately, haven't you?" she said sympathetically. "Let's see what you've done to your face."

He stepped back and looked up at her. "The nurse cleaned it, but it started bleeding again."

"Does it hurt?"

He nodded. "A lot," he admitted. He noticed the front of Olivia's dress was covered in his blood, and he became teary eyed again. "I ruined your pretty dress."

Her smile was filled with tenderness. She brushed his hair out of his eyes and said, "That's okay. It's old."

Henry moved on to his major concern. "They're going to put a needle in my head."

Grayson stood there watching her as she listened to Henry's worries. She couldn't have cared less about the dress now. All she wanted to do was comfort the child.

Grayson's heart swelled with his love for her. He probably should tell her how he felt, he supposed, but he knew what would happen. She would panic and bolt. He understood how her mind worked now. She'd run, all right. She wouldn't get far, though, because he was determined to spend the rest of his life with her. Getting her to agree was going to be a challenge.

Grayson filed the problem away for another time and went to his nephew. He picked him up and placed him on the bed, then tilted his head to the side so he could get a better look at the damage.

"Did you break your nose?"

"No, he didn't, and he doesn't have a concussion." The emergency-room physician gave the news. "He just banged his head. The plastic surgeon on call is already here finishing up with another patient. I thought, because of where the cut is, a plastic surgeon should do the repair. He wants me to go ahead and numb the area and clean it."

A nurse placed a metal tray on the counter. Henry spotted the needle and grabbed his uncle's arm. Grayson calmly assured him that the needle would take away the hurt, and as soon as the area was numbed, Henry relaxed. By the time the plastic surgeon arrived, Henry was laughing at a story Olivia had told him.

They didn't leave the hospital until after ten, and Henry was sound asleep in the back of Grayson's car before they pulled out of the hospital drive.

"Thank you," Grayson said to Olivia as he checked on his nephew in his rearview mirror. "Having you there made it easier on Henry."

"I'm just glad he's okay," she answered. "Henry's a great little boy."

"I'm really sorry about tonight," he continued. "The evening didn't exactly turn out the way I'd planned."

"There are more important things than dinner at a swanky restaurant," she said.

"We'll celebrate another time," he promised.

"You haven't told me about the gun," she reminded him. "Are you sure they've found the gun that shot me?"

"Yes, ballistics confirmed it. It's a match. No question."

"And?"

"Ray Martin's house. They found it inside Martin's house. No fingerprints, though. The weapon had been wiped clean."

"But the police had already gone through that house from top to bottom. How could they have missed anything? And how did they know to search again?"

"A guy called. He didn't give a name, just identified himself as a neighbor. He said his son and some of his friends had gone into the abandoned house and found it."

"So, it was Martin after all. A simple motive: revenge," she said. "I was sort of hoping Simmons had done it. He could have found out about Jorguson and Martin and planted the gun. I was hoping my father's sleazy partner would never see the light of day again."

"Your wish may come true anyway," he told her. "We picked him up at his D.C. office. He was just beginning to shred documents when we got there. We'll not only indict him for his part in your attempted kidnapping, but if we find what we think we'll find in those files, we'll be able to get him for his part in your father's Ponzi scheme as well. Unfortunately, he's already posted bail so he's free for now, but he's got a lot of prison time ahead of him."

"You didn't think it was Martin who shot me, did you?"

"No, I didn't," he admitted. "But finding the weapon . . ." The sentence trailed off, and he shook his head.

"Do you know what this means? With Martin locked up, the case is closed. My case anyway. No more bodyguards."

She was smiling until he reminded, "And all the death threats on your phone?"

"Oh." The burst of optimism was gone. How could she have forgotten the calls?

"That's right," he said. "The bodyguards stay."

"Maybe for a few more days," she conceded. "Surely, all the anger about my father will die down soon."

"It's going to take longer than a few days."

She knew he was right. "I'm paying the bodyguards."

"No, you're not."

She counted to ten. It didn't help. "I'm going to insist."

The set of his jaw told her he was going to be stubborn. "Insist all you want."

She decided to table the discussion since she wasn't winning. Besides, her asthma was kicking up. The cold night air had triggered the wheezing. She opened her purse and only then realized she didn't have her inhaler.

"Grayson . . ."

He reached into his coat pocket and pulled out an inhaler. "Here you go."

She used it and, without thinking, handed it back to him. It wasn't until he drove into his garage that she realized where he was taking her.

"You should have dropped me at my building. There's a guard right inside the door."

"I can't take you home yet. We haven't had dinner."

He parked the car and came around to open her door. "McDonald's is open," she said.

"I'm going to prepare a gourmet dinner for you."

"Really?"

"How do you feel about hot dogs?"

TWENTY-NINE

Olivia tried to say good night to Grayson at her door, but he was having none of it. He backed her into her apartment, kicked the door shut, and jerked her into his arms.

"I want you."

From gentleman to caveman, she thought. The transformation was extremely arousing. She tried to remember why she shouldn't go to bed with him. Oh yes, they needed to talk. "Grayson, I need to tell you—"

"Now. I want you now."

He didn't give her time to argue. He

kissed her hard and then proceeded to tell her in the most graphic detail exactly how he was going to make love to her. By the time he finished, her legs had turned to Jell-O.

He was waiting for her permission. She wrapped her arms around his neck and spread her fingers up into his hair. "You do have a way with words," she whispered.

Just tonight, she promised herself. Just one more night. Then she would make him leave.

Their need for each other was fierce, and their lovemaking was wild. Grayson wasn't gentle, nor was she. Her lips were swollen from his kisses, and his shoulders wore scratches from her demanding touch. When Grayson finally summoned enough strength to move away from her, he was panting for breath, and his body was covered with a fine sheen of perspiration. Her scent mingled with his, clinging to the air around them.

"Oh my." Olivia sighed.

"Your voice is hoarse," Grayson told her.

"I might have screamed."

"Might have?" he asked, grinning. "You were . . . demanding. I got a little rough, didn't I?"

"I got a little rough, too."

Now or never, he thought to himself. It may not be the best timing, but he was going for it regardless, while she was still recovering. He moved so quickly, she didn't have time to react. Pinning her to the bed, he said, "I have something to tell you." He cupped the sides of her face with his hands, holding her captive.

She looked wary. "Yes?"

"I love you."

Tears came into her eyes. "No. You can't love me. I should have—"

"I love you," he repeated firmly.

"Grayson . . ."

He kissed her forehead. "You love me, too."

She pushed against him. "That doesn't matter," she cried out.

"I sure as hell think it does."

He rolled onto his back and stared at the ceiling. She tried to get up, but he grabbed her hand and pulled her back down. She landed on top of him. Holding her prisoner with his arm wrapped around her, he forced her head down on his shoulder and said, "Calm down, sweetheart. It's going to be all right."

The irony in the situation wasn't lost on him. He was having to soothe her because he'd told her he loved her.

Olivia was desperately trying not to cry. "I let this go too far," she whispered against the side of his neck. "I shouldn't have. I knew better. I really did, but you're so irresistible, and I'm weak when I'm with you."

He decided to ignore her ramblings. "I want you in my bed every night," he said gruffly. "I want to wake up with you beside me."

"No, I can't . . ."

"I love you," he repeated. "Will you marry me?"

Her reaction wasn't what he would consider an encouraging one. She bolted upright and in a near shout said, "Oh God, no."

At the very least he should have been insulted. The appalled look on her face did smack at his ego. He didn't get upset, though, because he was pretty sure he knew what was going on inside that wonderful, but decidedly warped, mind of hers.

"Tell me you love me," he demanded. His hand moved to the nape of her neck, and he tugged on her hair, forcing her to look at him. "Tell me. I know you do. I want to hear you say the words."

"It won't matter," she said. A single tear escaped and slowly trailed down her cheek. "I don't understand why you want—"

"I just do," he snapped. "Tell me."

"I love you."

The tightness in his chest immediately eased. Although he already knew how she felt, he needed her to acknowledge it. The rest was up to him.

"I won't marry you, Grayson. I can't marry you. You need to move on without me."

"What about Collins and Jane and Samantha? Can they ever get married? Will they?"

"What do my friends have to do with this conversation?"

"Everything," he answered. "They have everything to do with this. And so does Dr. Andre Pardieu. Your friends were in the same experimental program under his supervision."

She couldn't look at him. She dropped down beside him. "Yes."

He began to stroke her back and could feel how tense she was. "Your aunt told me a little about that period in your life. You were in the hospital a long time, weren't you?" She refused to answer. He wasn't deterred. "I know your family didn't come to see you. You were all alone."

"I was glad of it," she blurted. "I saw what my friends' families went through. It was horrible for them. I can still see their faces, their anguish."

She remembered what Sam had once said after her family had visited. They'd all been crying, and Sam told her that maybe it would be better if she died because then they would be at peace.

"You think it's going to come back," he said very matter-of-factly. "And you don't want anyone you love to go through that agony. Right?"

She kept silent.

"Do your friends share your fatalistic attitude?"

"They're realists like I am."

"I see." His fingers gently trailed down her spine. "So you are willing to live your life waiting for death? What the hell, Olivia? Do you not see how crazy that is?"

She was suddenly furious. She pushed away from him and got out of bed.

"I don't care if you understand or not," she cried. She grabbed her silk robe and put it on. Her hands were shaking so, she could barely get the sash tied. "Fatalist? Ask Jane how she's feeling these days." She threaded her fingers through her hair in agitation. "Of the four of us, she's the most optimistic, but what good does that do? It's come back. I know it has, and oh God, poor Logan. He's only just become her brother again, and now he's going to go through hell. All those years he drank and used drugs, he was so horrible to her, and he's desperately trying to make up for the past, but it's too late. I don't know what will happen to him when she dies." Tears streamed down her face. "And Henry.

What about him, Grayson? He's already lost his mother. Do you want him to watch me die?" She put her hands up. "I'm done talking about this."

Grayson wanted to go to her, to comfort her, but in her nearly hysterical state, he knew she'd fight him. He sat up, casually leaned against the headboard, and said, "Okay. My mistake. Never mind."

His blasé tone confused her. She took a step toward him. "Never mind what?"

"The proposal. Never mind. Forget I mentioned it."

"Oh."

"Come sit with me. I have a favor to ask."

She slowly walked over to the side of the bed. He put his hands on her hips and pulled her onto his lap. A wary look in her eyes, she faced him with her hands on his shoulders.

"I want you to give Dr. Pardieu permission to talk to me," he said.

Her grip on his shoulders tightened. "Why? I thought you understood what I just said. Now that you have the right man locked up, my case is closed. You must move on."

"Yeah, right. I'm moving on," he agreed a bit quickly. "I still want to talk to the doctor, and he can't tell me anything unless you give permission."

"I don't know why you need—"

"You're going to do this, Olivia. First thing in the morning," he ordered, leaving no room for negotiation.

She glared at him.

"Are you going to call me a dumb ass?" he asked.

"No, but I'm thinking it," she muttered. "Why are you smiling?"

"Because we had our talk, and I understand. You aren't going to marry me, and you hope that I'll get on with my life . . . my life without you."

"Yes," she said defiantly. "When you leave here, that's exactly what I want you to do."

"Okay. You give Pardieu permission to talk to me about you, and after that conversation, you'll never see me again. That's my condition."

Never see him again. The thought made her sick.

"Yes, all right."

Grayson untied her belt and opened her robe, uncovering her beautiful breasts. She was so lovely. His fingers caressed her soft, flawless skin.

Olivia was confused. She didn't want him to stop touching her, and yet she wanted him to go.

"Everything will change when I leave here. I know that's what you want," he told her. He pushed the robe off her shoulders. "But I haven't left yet."

THIRTY

Grayson had been up half the night working at his computer. It was amazing how much confidential information was available when one had the right credentials and knew where to look.

Olivia had said that it would have been easy for Simmons to find out about her connection to Jorguson and Martin, and that was true. Her entire life was there with a push of a button, including the names of her employers. Simmons had obviously gained access to that information because he'd called them to try to discredit her.

Yes, it would have been easy for Simmons to plant the gun in Martin's house. He considered the possibility while he showered and got dressed. It was Sunday morning, and he was getting ready to leave for the office. He knew Ronan was already there, catching up on his own reports.

In the kitchen, Henry was having breakfast with his grandfather and Patrick. The two men were getting a blow-by-blow of what had happened the night before. Grayson heard Henry boast that Olivia had come to the hospital and had insisted on holding his hand while he got stitches. He also mentioned once again that she was his very own attorney, which the men knew was his segue into the story of what had happened in the principal's office.

Grayson poured himself a glass of orange juice and pulled out a chair across from his nephew. "Has there been any change in plans?" he asked.

Henry nodded. "Grandfather is going to take Ralph and me to the movie, but Ralph has to go home after because"— he glanced at his grandfather before continuing—"because he can only take so much of Ralph."

"I get that," Patrick said, smiling.

Grayson nodded. Ralph was a little on the wild and loud side, but then, so was Henry. Together they sometimes sounded like a tornado.

"Henry, how would you feel about me marrying Olivia?" Grayson asked.

Henry's eyes clouded with worry. "Will you move away?"

"No, she would move in here with us."

"With me and Patrick?"

"Yes, and with me," he said.

"Will you have a wedding?"

"Yes."

He shook his head. "No, I don't want you to marry her." He bowed his head and stared at his cereal bowl.

"We know you like Olivia," his grandfather said. "You talk about her all the time."

Henry wouldn't look up. "I do like her. I just don't want Grayson to marry her."

"Tell us why," Patrick insisted. "We want to understand."

Henry glanced at his grandfather, received his encouraging nod, and turned to Grayson. "Because if you have a wedding, you have to ask my father, and he'll come back here and take me away."

Grayson was surprised by Henry's response. The child's anxiety was almost palpable. He shouldn't have such a worry, Grayson thought. He sat quietly while his father tried to calm the boy's fears. "We would never let that happen. Never."

Grayson explained that he had full custody, but that didn't make much difference to Henry.

It was Patrick who finally convinced him. "Don't you have your own attorney?"

Henry nodded. "You know I do. It's Olivia."

"Do you think she'll let your father take you away?"

Henry didn't have to think about it long. "No." He smiled then. He looked at Grayson and added, "If I tell her, she won't let you invite my father."

Grayson laughed. "I think you're right."

"Are congratulations in order?" his father asked. "You do know I've yet to meet this woman."

"You will," Grayson said. "And, no, congratulations aren't in order. She's being difficult."

"Do you want me to ask her?" Henry offered.

Patrick gave his opinion. "You might have a better chance with the kid."

It was the last time Grayson smiled the rest of the day. When he got to the office, he told Ronan about Olivia's hope regarding Simmons, and after tossing the football for a few minutes, the two decided on a plan of action.

"It can't hurt," Ronan said.

"Right. Just to be sure," Grayson replied.

For the next several hours, both he and Ronan caught up on their case files. It was late afternoon before Grayson finished his last report. He had just logged off his computer when his cell phone rang.

"Grayson Kincaid?" The voice had a thick French accent.

"Yes."

"This is Dr. Andre Pardieu. Olivia Mac-Kenzie asked that I give you a call. She has authorized me to discuss her medical history and her prognosis with you. What would you like to know?"

"Thank you for calling, Doctor. I know you're a busy man, so I'll get right to the point. I'm in love with Olivia and I want to marry her, but she's a very stubborn woman."

Dr. Pardieu laughed. "Yes, I've known that for quite some time."

"Olivia is afraid to commit. She fears that her cancer will return. She sees her friend Jane so ill, and that has convinced her she can't make plans for the future. I don't know how I'm going to persuade her, but I figure if I got some assurance from you, I'd have a better chance."

"I can't discuss Jane's case specifically, but I can tell you that Olivia should not be concerned. I've been away from the hospital and haven't been able to give this latest development my full attention, but now that I'm back, I'm going to get to the bottom of it. Let me assure you, Olivia has not shown any symptoms of toxemia, so, from what I've seen, she has nothing to worry about."

"Thank you, Doctor," Grayson said.

"Good luck," Dr. Pardieu said. "Olivia

deserves some happiness, and I hope she'll find it with you."

"Yes, sir. That's my plan," Grayson assured him before he ended the call.

Grayson sat back in his chair and thought about what the doctor had said. Something stuck in his mind. Toxemia was a general term for blood poisoning, wasn't it? He booted up his computer again. He began feeding in data, and that only created more questions. When he ended his search, he told Ronan what he had discovered. They knew whom they had to talk to and what information they needed to gather. By late afternoon, their questions had been answered, and he phoned Dr. Pardieu right away. If the doctor confirmed his suspicions—and Grayson was certain he would—he needed to act immediately. Time was critical.

Olivia tried to keep busy so she wouldn't think about Grayson, but that was impossible. Sam called, and even with a horrible connection, she knew something was wrong. She heard it in Olivia's voice. The questions came, one after the other, until Olivia was close to tears.

"I can't talk about him," Olivia said. "Tell me the story again, Sam. It will take my mind off my miserable life."

"No, you've heard that stupid—though amazingly incredible—story at least five times."

"More like twenty, but tell me again. It makes me laugh every time I hear it."

Sam's sigh was loud and clear even with the static. "There I was, minding my own business in seat twenty-eight A on flight—"

"Twenty-seven forty-three," Olivia supplied.

"The plane was packed, and it was noisy, but I'd blocked it all out because I was frantically studying for a final I had to take the next morning at zero eight hundred. The flight was making good time and I, along with everyone else, thought everything was just fine, when a flight attendant tapped me on the shoulder and asked me to come with her."

Olivia added the details she remembered. "You shoved your notebook into your flight bag and dragged it with you. You thought you were being upgraded to first class for some bizarre reason."

"Yes, that's what I thought. Clever deduction."

"You told me."

"Should I go on?" Sam asked.

"You want to, don't you?"

"Okay, yes," she said, her voice eager. "You and Collins and Jane are the only ones I can brag to. My brothers are so sick of hearing this story, they groan whenever I bring it up."

"I'm not groaning," she assured her.

"It was a beautiful plane," she continued. "A jet, of course, with—"

"Don't get technical again. Suffice it to say it was pretty."

Sam laughed and continued, "It wasn't a jumbo jet, but it was still pretty, I suppose. Anyway, I followed the perky flight attendant past first class, noticing that all the seats were occupied. I started to get a bad feeling, but the flight attendant was smiling and acting like nothing was out of the ordinary. She said that she'd heard me tell another passenger that I'd gone through the Air Force Academy. I hadn't said anything to any of the passengers, and I was about to correct her when she said in a rather loud voice that the captain had also gone through the academy and wanted to say hello. That didn't make any sense, and she could tell I was going to argue. She knew the cockpit door was locked while the flight—"

"I know. Don't cite regulations. Get to the good part."

"The attendant whispered 'please,' then tapped on the door—that crazy smile on her face all the while—and the door opened, and she pushed me inside. And I mean pushed me," she reiterated.

"You don't have to go into a long description of this part," Olivia pleaded.

"Oh, I want to. The whole crew was throwing up into these plastic bags, and it began to dawn on me: they must have gone through their passenger list looking for a pilot. It smelled so vile in the cockpit, the attendant gagged. I didn't, of course. I grew up with such gross brothers. That, plus going through chemo . . . nothing really gets to me.

"Anyway, their complexions were lime green and they were throwing up what looked like chunks of bile."

"Oh God, Sam. Don't be so . . . visual."

Sam laughed. "I naturally thought the worst, that they had been poisoned, but the captain told me they had just been on a flight where several passengers became quite ill. It took two of us to get the copilot out of his seat and move him. You know the rest."

"Oh no, you have to tell it."

"In the midst of dry heaving, the captain gave me instructions. As you know, I've flown just about everything with wings," she boasted. "This plane wasn't a challenge. I told him to relax; I'd take over. The attendant came back in with a napkin over her mouth and nose because of the awful smell that I'd kind of gotten used to, and she told me some of the passengers knew something was wrong and were getting nervous. The captain flipped on the intercom to calm them down. He still thought he was going to land the plane."

"But you didn't know the intercom was left on," Olivia interjected.

"No, of course I didn't. I wouldn't have argued with the captain if I'd known passengers were listening, and he was so sick, he forgot. He looked like he was going to pass out any second. I told him to relax, that I could handle it, and I began to familiarize myself with the control panel and do a couple of maneuvers to get the feel of the plane.

"The poor captain's eyes kept closing, and he was struggling to stay conscious. He said that, on final approach to the runway, I must instruct the passengers to get into a crash position. I tried not to take insult, and I asked him why would I want to do that, and we got into a bit of an argument."

Olivia laughed. "A bit of an argument? I heard the recording. It was more than a bit."

"Can you believe passengers recorded the conversation? You can't do anything these days without someone documenting it. I swear, our privacy—"

"You're getting off track, Sam," Olivia reminded.

"Yes, okay. So even though I tried not to take insult, I was insulted. I mean, how could I not be? I tried to explain my position, and I listed all the different planes I'd flown, and I ended my litany by saying that I am a pilot in the United States Air Force, and I have been trained by the finest. Air Force fighter pilots don't crash planes. I also told him I could understand his reticence if I were a crop duster or even a Navy pilot, but come on . . . I'm Air Force. Didn't he realize how superior we are?"

"You also said—and I'm quoting—'We are the best pilots in the world.'"

"We are," she countered, and Olivia could picture her friend shrugging. "So I might have said something like that. Yes, it was ego, but the passengers calmed down. At least, that's what the attendant told me. She also said there were three passengers in the back of the cabin throwing up. Whatever that virus was, it was quick and powerful."

"But you did instruct all of them to get into crash position?"

"Only because the captain insisted."

"Tell me what you said, your exact words."

"Don't make me. It was all over the news."

"Tell me."

"I just explained that the captain and the copilot were under the weather and that I would be landing the plane. I also said that, even though I personally did not believe it was necessary, they all should get into crash position, and I only hoped they were as insulted as I was."

"And?"

"And on approach I saw all the fire trucks and the ambulances, and I might have said something to the tower about getting them the hell off my runway."

"Might have."

"I also told the passengers that the landing would be the smoothest they'd ever experienced. It was, too," she asserted. "Not a single bump."

"That's what I heard on the news," Olivia said.

"The tower thought we should use the chute, but I got them to let us park at the gate because it would be much easier to get all of the sick off the plane that way. Once we opened the door, I got out of the way so the paramedics could get into the cockpit. I waited a long time in the galley while all the passengers filed off, but then I saw what time it was, and I knew my ride was waiting for me at baggage claim. I put on my baseball cap and my jacket, grabbed my flight bag, and headed into the terminal. I was relieved no one stopped me because I had to get back to base before curfew."

"You just left."

"You know I did. I had to," she explained. "Randy was driving three of us back. He'd already picked up the others, and I didn't want them to be late, too."

She sighed before she continued, "I had this stupid hope it would blow over. You know, no big deal, right? Unfortunately, it was all over the news. I got back in plenty of time, and after I dropped my bag in my room, I went to report to my commander. That was mortifying. He was in a bar with some other officers—a sports bar—and there were jumbo screens all over the place. I asked him for a moment alone and quickly explained what had happened. I also told him I thought the newsmen would try to get on base, and if they wanted any interviews, I was going to assume he'd handle them. He didn't like me dumping it in his lap, but I argued I had an exam the next morning, and I needed to concentrate on that. The commander is never in a good mood, but he was that evening, and it was only later that I found out why. He'd heard what I'd said about being superior to the Navy. He liked that."

"Ego," Olivia said. "All of you pilots have major egos." Olivia heard a beep on the line, indicating there was a call waiting. "I've got to go," she said after she looked at the screen.

"Wait. Don't you want to hear about the press conference? It was really hilarious."

"I'm sure it was," she agreed. "Sorry, I can't hear more. Jane's beeping in."

"E-mail me after you talk to her," Sam said, "and tell her I'll call her this week."

Olivia said good-bye and switched to Jane's call. Her friend was phoning to invite Olivia to dinner. She insisted that she come because Logan was making a special roast with fresh herbs. Although Olivia really didn't want to go out—the weather had turned nasty and it was beginning to sleet—she did want to see Jane and make sure she was all right. She would pretend that everything was fine, but Olivia would know the truth as soon as she looked at her face. She told Jane she'd be there in an hour.

The nasty phone calls about her father had subsided—there were only two that morning—and, at Olivia's insistence, Grayson had canceled the guard at her door as long as she promised to call one of them if she chose to leave. Since Jane lived just a short distance away, Olivia decided she'd be safe if she took extra precautions. John, the doorman, kept her informed about the number of reporters trying to get in the building to interview her. He had warned her that some of them sat in their cars, waiting, so, before leaving her apartment, she called down to John. The sleet was working to her advantage, he told her. There weren't any cars on the street tonight.

John escorted her to her car in the

parking garage and watched her pull out onto the street. Olivia drove around in circles until she was convinced she wasn't being followed, then headed over to Dupont Circle where Jane lived.

Jane's three-story townhouse was quite small, but there was an art studio on the top floor. The converted attic was the reason Jane had purchased the space because the light coming in through the windows was perfect for her work.

Logan opened the door. He looked surprised to see her.

"Jane didn't tell you she invited me?" Olivia asked.

Logan stepped back to let her inside. "I'm sure she did. I just forgot. Don't worry. There's plenty of roast."

Olivia followed him into the living room. The room was dark except for the glow from the fire he'd started in the hearth. He switched on a lamp, and she could see how haggard he looked.

"Jane's upstairs resting," he said. "I'll go get her."

"How is she doing?"

"Not good," he replied. He was looking everywhere but at her. "I'm scared," he said.

"Let her rest awhile longer," Olivia said. She nodded toward the kitchen. "Something smells wonderful. Can I help?"

He smiled. "Thanks, but I've got it under control."

"Then don't let me keep you. I'll occupy myself until Jane comes down." She pointed to a stack of magazines on the coffee table. "I can do some reading."

As soon as Logan went into the kitchen, Olivia picked up the magazine on top of the pile and sat down on the sofa. She flipped through the pages. Nothing caught her attention, so she placed it back on the table. She then spotted a laptop sitting on the floor next to an easy chair. She hadn't read the newspaper, and she thought she'd pull up the *Times* and catch up on the latest happenings. She knew Jane wouldn't mind if she used her computer for a few minutes.

Olivia reached for the computer and lifted the lid. The dark screen came to life, and an open page appeared. The title at the top caught her attention: "The Pathological Effects of Arsenic Ingestion." What an odd subject to be reading about, Olivia thought. She hit the key to return to the previous page, and then the page before that. It didn't take long for her to realize she wasn't holding Jane's computer at all. It was Logan's.

Logan's voice called from the kitchen. "When do you give her blood again, Olivia?"

Olivia quickly closed the computer and placed it on the floor where she'd found it.

"I'm not sure," she answered.

Logan walked into the living room, drying his hands on a dish towel. He glanced at the stairs, making sure Jane wasn't there, and lowered his voice. "She's talking crazy. She won't tell you, but she's in a lot of pain." He walked closer and in a whisper said, "I think she might kill herself. That's how depressed she is."

Olivia moved to the side so that Logan would turn his head toward the light and she could see his eyes more clearly. She took a step back. She was so rattled, she couldn't think what to say. Her hand went to her throat. "Oh God," she gasped. His pupils were dilated as big as saucers.

Logan patted her shoulder. "I've moved into the guest room so I can watch her. It will actually work out for the best. My meetings are a few blocks away, and I can go more often. Next to Jane, of course, my sobriety is the most important thing to me."

"Good," she said, trying to stay calm. "And you've been cooking for her so she'll keep her strength. You're doing everything you can."

"I'll go get Jane. Please don't tell her what I said. It will only upset her, and she won't confide in me anymore."

"Of course," she agreed.

He stopped at the bottom of the stairs. "Do you mind if we eat right away? I've got a meeting to get to. They help me stay sober," he explained.

"I don't mind. I'm hungry."

She wanted to call Grayson, but by the time she dug her cell phone out of her purse, Jane and Logan were joining her.

"Go sit at the table," Logan told his sister. "The roast will dry up if I don't get it out of the oven. I'll go ahead and scoop it out on the plates." He disappeared into the kitchen.

"Have you talked to Grayson today?" Jane asked.

"I'm going to call him now," Olivia answered.

Jane smiled. "Good."

Olivia wanted to cry. Jane looked like hell, and she'd lost so much weight. She waited until her friend took a seat at the table, then walked into the living room and called Grayson. He answered on the second ring. His greeting wasn't polite.

"Where the hell are you? I just left your apartment. You were supposed to—"

"I'm at Jane's, Grayson," she said. "Logan's here." She was just about to tell him about her suspicions, but Logan came into the living room. She quickly said, "Grayson, I'll call you back. It shouldn't be long, Grayson." She ended the call quickly. Logan was standing there, listening. Plastering a smile on her face, she went to join her dearest friend and her psychopath brother.

The plates were already on the table. Logan had prepared them, and they all looked the same, except for one thing. Olivia noticed that Jane's plate had a sprig of parsley on the side. Logan's didn't, and neither did hers.

She went to Jane, kissed her on the cheek, and hugged her. She took her place at one end of the table. Logan took the other.

"Logan, do you have any pepper?" she asked.

"Sure. I'll get it for you."

The second he disappeared into the kitchen, Olivia grabbed Jane's plate and switched it with Logan's. She switched the parsley, too.

"What are you doing?" Jane asked.

Olivia put her finger to her lips, a sign to keep silent. Jane nodded but continued to frown.

"What's this orange stuff?" she asked Logan when he returned.

"Mashed sweet potatoes. Jane loves them. Some nights, that's all she eats."

Logan ate his dinner quickly. "I don't want to be late for the meeting," he explained.

Olivia moved the food around on her plate, but didn't eat any of it.

"Not hungry?" Logan asked.

"I thought I was, but I guess I'm not feeling very well. Grayson and I had a fight," she explained.

Olivia didn't know how much longer she could keep silent. Jane was repeating a story Collins had told her, and Olivia noticed she had eaten every bit of the mashed sweet potatoes, and so had Logan.

She dragged dinner out as long as she could, telling two stories about Jane, praying that Grayson would get there soon. She hoped she'd said his name enough times for him to figure out that she was in trouble. Jane's home wasn't far from Olivia's apartment. She had just finished her second story and was frantically trying to think of a third when Jane said, "Okay, Olivia, dinner's over. Tell me why."

"Why what?"

"Why you switched my plate with my brother's."

If Olivia had any doubts, they were all erased in that second. Logan leapt to his feet, overturning his chair.

"You what?" he screamed.

Jane looked thunderstruck by his behavior. "What's going on?"

Olivia kept her attention on Logan. Oh, this was going to be bad, she thought . . . really bad . . . for she could see the rage coming over him.

"Olivia?" Jane asked.

"Logan's been poisoning you."

"That's absolutely ridiculous," he roared. "Why would you tell such a lie?"

"Your eyes are dilated, which tells me you're using again," she began. "You have a very interesting website on your computer, all about arsenic."

"Oh my God . . ." Jane whispered.

"He told me he was worried you would kill yourself, Jane. Laying the groundwork, I suppose. I guess you were taking too long to die."

"Shut up," Logan shouted.

Olivia continued to address Jane.

"That's why you've been so sick. He's been giving you the poison, and he's been clever about it. He makes sure it's no longer in your blood by the time you go to the hospital. I'm guessing he's been giving it to you for a long time. After a few days, arsenic doesn't show up in the blood, but it's everywhere else. Now that we know what to look for, we'll have all the proof we need."

Logan was frantically trying to search for a way out. He grasped his head in his hands. "I can't think," he muttered.

"That's because you're high," Olivia pointed out. "You can't lie as well when you're drugged, can you?"

"You're crazy. You can't prove anything." His agitation was beginning to take over.

"Yes, I can," she said. "You're not as clever as you think."

He turned to his sister. He couldn't seem to control the twitch in his neck that had suddenly appeared. "That's my money sitting in your account. Mother meant it for me, but you convinced her to leave it all to you. I want what's rightfully mine."

"You wouldn't have gotten away with it," Olivia said. "An autopsy would have shown the poison."

"I'm smarter than you think," he boasted. "The arsenic was just supposed to weaken her a little. I figured the cancer or something else would kill her, but she wasn't sick enough, so I decided to speed things up. Since she's been feeling so ill, no one would blame her for wanting to end it all with a bottle of sleeping pills."

Olivia went to Jane and put her hand on her shoulder to keep her in her chair. When she looked up, Grayson was standing in the doorway, his gun trained on Jane's brother. He didn't make a sound. She knew he wanted her to move away from Logan, but she was afraid to leave Jane's side.

"You think that's clever, Logan?" she taunted. She wanted him to continue to look at her until Grayson grabbed him. "I don't believe you've ever done anything clever in your life. You're too stupid." She could tell he was losing control. She could see it in his eyes.

Logan lunged for her and grabbed

her around the neck, choking her. Grayson moved like lightning and tore him off her.

"What the hell, Olivia," he shouted as he slammed Logan against the wall. "Why didn't you move away from him?"

She coughed the words, "I should have." She rubbed her neck and said, "I wanted him to keep talking."

She looked at Jane, who appeared to be so stunned she couldn't move. Olivia took her hand and pulled her to her feet. She put her arm around her friend's shoulders and said, "Come on. You're going to the hospital."

THIRTY-ONE

It was almost nine before Olivia arrived home from the hospital. Grayson had followed her in his car and waited until they were inside her apartment to give her hell again.

"If he had a knife . . ."

"He didn't."

"If he . . ."

She went into the kitchen to get something to drink. "You had your gun on him. What could he do?" Too late, she realized it was a dumb question.

"How about use you as a shield? He

could have snapped your neck. He could have—"

"But he didn't."

Ronan arrived, interrupting the lecture Olivia knew Grayson was about to launch into.

Olivia told him to help himself to whatever he wanted to eat or drink. He grabbed a Coke and sat facing her.

Grayson wanted to pace. "Should have checked sooner," he told Ronan. "When Olivia mentioned that Logan was an addict, I should have checked to make sure he was still clean . . . do my damned job. I wasn't paying attention. She could have been killed."

"Jane's going to be okay," Olivia reassured.

Ronan smiled. "He was talking about *you*."

"Oh."

"Nothing more impulsive than a devout cokehead," Ronan remarked. "Where is Logan now?"

"He was taken to the hospital to have his stomach pumped and then to jail," Grayson answered. He shook his head. "Everything that came out of that bastard's mouth was a lie. He didn't live in a halfway house, and he only worked for the car rental agency a couple of months." He came around the sofa as he said, "And he sure as hell didn't go to any meetings. I'll bet he was getting high every night."

Olivia turned to Grayson. "Did you know he was poisoning Jane?"

"Once I found out everything out of his mouth was a lie, I called Dr. Pardieu and told him my suspicions. He confirmed that it all added up. I told him we'd bring Jane in. I wanted to make sure you were safe, and I'd stopped to warn you when I got your call."

"We went to Logan's apartment," Ronan said. "It was a real dump. We found the arsenic there."

"The poison only stays in the blood a couple of days," Grayson said. "Logan timed it so that when she went back into the hospital, it wouldn't show up. He was giving her small doses, just enough to weaken her. I think he was hoping it would make her cancer come back."

The doorbell rang, and he went to answer it. A lovely blond, blue-eyed young woman with a bewitching smile was standing there, waiting for him to let her in.

"Collins," he said.

Her smile widened. "Grayson."

Introductions over, she rushed past him. She was yelling before she reached Olivia. "I told you Logan was a sleaze-bag. Didn't I tell you?"

"You might have mentioned—"

"If I had a gun . . ."

"Don't finish that," Olivia blurted. "There are two FBI agents here."

Collins whirled around. "Two?"

Ronan was standing right behind her. They stared at each other for several seconds, neither saying a word. Olivia watched, fascinated. She could almost see the electricity flowing between them.

Grayson introduced them. Collins smiled up at Ronan, then turned around and continued her rant.

"I called Sam and told her. She didn't believe Logan had changed either." Hands on hips, she faced Grayson. "How did you finally figure it out?"

Olivia groaned. Collins had inadvertently gotten him worked up again. He went through the process, and by the time he was finished, he was furious once more.

"Don't ask any more questions, Collins," she pleaded.

"Just one," she countered. "How did you find his apartment?"

"He put his address on the application at the rental agency."

Ronan was having trouble paying attention to the conversation. He couldn't seem to make himself stop staring at Collins.

"I'm getting a Popsicle. Want one?" she asked Olivia.

"Sure. Grape."

Five minutes later, Grayson and Ronan stood side by side watching the two women.

"Why do you like Popsicles?" Ronan asked.

"We got hooked on them when we were going through chemo," Collins answered matter-of-factly. "The cold soothed the blisters in our mouths."

Both women put the Popsicles in their mouths at the same time. Grayson moaned, "Ah, come on."

Olivia knew what he was thinking. Her tongue swirled around the tip of the Popsicle, her gaze locked on his. "Want some?" she innocently asked.

"Jeez," Ronan muttered.

"I've got to get out of here," Grayson said, glaring at Olivia.

Ronan gave him an understanding slap on the back. "I'm right behind you."

THIRTY-TWO

Ray Martin was sitting in jail, charged with the attempted murder of Olivia MacKenzie. Grayson and Ronan still weren't convinced they had the right man. They needed to be sure.

They brought Carl Simmons's alibi in for another interrogation. Her name was Vicky Hyde Clark, and she was a paid escort. Simmons was one of her best clients. He always overpaid her for her services, and he didn't mind being seen in public with her. She considered him a good friend.

Vicky was tall, thin, and wore a dress

that was a little too tight. She wasn't pretty, by any means, and there was a hardness about her and a look that suggested she'd been through a couple of wars.

She sat at a table across from Ronan, who had a file open in front of him. Grayson leaned against the wall behind the agent and stared at Vicky. He had yet to say a word to her.

He was an expert at intimidation, and he knew he was scaring her, all without moving a muscle or uttering a sound.

"I've told you everything I know," Vicky whined. "Carl's one of my dearest friends . . . he used to be, anyway, but now that he's going to prison for all that fraud business, I don't see how I can help you. I understand . . . Carl's innocent until proven guilty in a court of law, but we all know . . ." She took a breath and said, "I told you the truth. Carl was with me that night you asked about . . . you know, when that girl got shot. Carl was in my bed all night."

She kept nervously glancing at Grayson, then back to Ronan. "I don't know what you want from me," she cried. "I haven't done anything wrong."

"Just a couple of questions, Vicky, then it will be over and we'll take you to lockup," Ronan said smoothly.

"What's this?" she gasped. "Lockup? Why?"

Grayson finally spoke. "You lied to us."

"No, I . . ." She couldn't hold his stare.

"Like I said, Vicky, just a few questions and we'll be done," Ronan repeated. "Where did the ten thousand dollars come from? You made a five-thousand-dollar deposit in your savings account and a five-thousand-dollar deposit in your checking account. You made those deposits on the same day, exactly one week after Olivia MacKenzie was shot."

She was so rattled she had to think about the question a minute before blurting, "It was money I saved."

"That's another lie," Ronan said. He tried to sound disappointed.

"I don't know what you're talking about. I really don't."

Ronan's voice hardened. "We traced

it, Vicky. The money came from Carl Simmons's account."

"No, no, it didn't. I saved all that money."

"Carl withdrew that precise amount," he said. He didn't have proof that Carl had done any such thing, but he was going to see if Vicky would take the bait. "And you deposited that amount. There's only one conclusion we can draw. Carl gave you the money. So now I have to ask, why? Could it be for the alibi you gave him?"

She hadn't asked for an attorney, so Ronan kept at her, question after question, trying to wear her down.

Grayson spoke again. "You're going to prison for a long time if you lie to us. You're as much responsible for shooting Olivia MacKenzie as Carl is."

"No. Why would you think—"

"You're lying for him to give him an alibi, so you're in it with him," Ronan said. He slapped his hand down on the table, and the sound reverberated around the small room. Vicky jumped.

"Tell her about the proof we have that

she's lying," Grayson told Ronan. "The other proof."

What the hell? Ronan had no idea what Grayson was talking about, but he nodded and said, "I will. I'm getting to it."

"There's more proof?" Vicky was scared and unsure now.

"I don't understand," Ronan said, shaking his head. "Carl's going to go to prison for his other crimes. Why are you protecting him? You certainly don't have to worry about giving the money back to him."

Grayson knew they were going to have to let her go. Aside from the fact that Vicky had deposited ten thousand dollars, everything they claimed to know about her was fabricated. He wasn't through messing with Ronan, though. "Go ahead, Agent Conrad. Tell her about the other proof."

Ronan was going to have to come up with something, and Grayson couldn't wait to hear what he would say. He knew his friend's mind was scrambling.

Vicky panicked. "I want a deal."

"You what?" Ronan asked. He'd also

been thinking they were going to have to cut her loose.

Grayson stepped forward and leaned on the table. "What kind of deal?"

"I'll tell you what really happened, and you don't put me in lockup. You let me go for good. No charges . . . ever."

They nodded, but before they spoke their agreement or disagreement, she blurted, "Yes, I lied. He made me. He was with me that night, but only for a little while. He left early. He seemed to be in a real hurry."

"Did you see what he was driving?" Grayson asked.

"I did. I'd never seen it before, so I asked him about it. It was a brand-new SUV. One of those big fancy ones. He said it belonged to the fleet that they used whenever lawyers from other branches were in town."

"What color?" Ronan asked.

"Black. Real shiny black."

Grayson walked out into the hall. Ronan followed him. "A black SUV doesn't prove anything."

"Unless we can show where it's been," Grayson said and then added, "GPS."

Ronan smiled. "Of course. Simmons spends most of his time in New York. He can't be that familiar with D.C. He might have needed directions to Olivia's apartment."

"Or maybe even Martin's house to plant a gun. If he programmed an address into the GPS, there would be a record."

"It's worth a shot."

"Let's go find that SUV."

Carl Simmons's misery started and ended with Olivia MacKenzie. She had set out to destroy her father and him, and she had succeeded. He tried, but he hadn't been able to shut her up or stop her relentless quest.

Carl had estimated he had at least another good year to draw more and more rich investors into the Trinity Fund. He'd tucked away a little bit in foreign banks, but he simply hadn't had enough time to hide what he'd need to live on. It was too late now. He had to figure out a way to get out of the country.

He'd made sure there weren't any papers to prove he was a silent partner in the fund. Nothing in writing to damn him. That was only slowing the Feds down, though. Eventually they'd have enough to fry him.

Yes, it started and ended with her. He'd tried to stop the woman by threatening her, but she didn't scare that easily, so he took it to the next step and went to her employers to discredit her. That didn't work either. Killing her seemed the most logical solution.

Kline needed money and agreed to do it, but he backed out at the last minute. Simmons decided that he would have to pull the trigger himself. Three bullets and he still couldn't get rid of her.

He felt confident he'd covered his tracks pretty well, but then finding out about Ray Martin was a lucky break. His arrest was covered in all the papers, so Carl took advantage of his good fortune and decided to hide his gun at Martin's house. Simple as could be. Martin would go down, and maybe Olivia would be so shaken she'd worry about the shooting and back off her persistent prying. He actually thought it was a possibility . . . that is, until she started messing with Robert's deal with Jeff Wilcox. She brought in the lawyer, Mitchell Kaplan, and Carl knew that pit bull wouldn't stop until their whole operation was exposed.

All they'd needed was a little time, a few days for them to clean out their accounts and hide what was left of the money before they took off and disappeared, but when he learned about her visit to Jeff Wilcox, he could almost hear the clock ticking down the minutes before he and Robert MacKenzie were destroyed. Carl should have killed Olivia then, but he had to act quickly, so he'd tried to use the mental illness ploy to get her hauled away to an institution for a few days. He never should have trusted those idiots, Kline and Vogel. They screwed up everything, and if he'd just been a little quicker, he would have gotten away before the Feds showed up.

Carl refused to be defeated. They may have arrested him, but he was smart enough to convince the judge to release him on bail. Obviously they'd underestimated him. He had a plan. He was going to leave in the middle of the night, drive one of the fleet cars that wouldn't be recognized, and hightail it to Miami. He had connections there, people who could get him out of the United States.

Everything was in place. He was all set to leave that night, but then he got the phone call that changed everything. An inside source, an attorney who had a contentious relationship with the FBI and who owed Simmons a favor, called to let him know his bail was going to be revoked. The Feds were on their way to his house to take him in. He was being charged with attempted murder. The source told him about the evidence. The GPS had damned him, and Carl knew there wasn't any way out of this now. Even if he tried, he couldn't get away.

When he'd been arrested for his white-collar crimes, he hadn't panicked. Even if he didn't make it out of the country, at the very worst, he'd be sent to a minimum-security prison, or as the media liked to call these facilities, a country club. Now that he was going down for attempted murder, minimum security was off the table. The judge would put

him in a hard-core federal prison, and
Carl knew he couldn't handle that. Just
thinking about it terrified him.

He'd rather die.

The more he thought about it, the
more sense it made. He would die. It
would be quick and over. No long years
of terror in prison. He'd go out on his
own terms. And he wouldn't go alone.
Yes, he'd take her with him. It was fitting, wasn't it? She'd caused all this pain
in his life. She had been his ruination.
Now he would be hers.

He already had the fleet car waiting, a
dark blue Honda. It was parked on a
street a couple of blocks away. He'd removed the license plate and swapped it
with one he found on another Honda in
a parking lot.

He had to act fast. Once the Feds
discovered he wasn't at his small D.C.
apartment, they'd put out a search for
him. He knew he couldn't evade them
long. He took the gun he kept in his safe
and hurried down the street to the waiting car. He drove to Olivia's apartment
building, pulled into the garage across
the street, and waited. Darkness was

descending. It was Saturday, and he hoped she'd go out. He'd follow her and ambush her. It wasn't much of a plan, but he hadn't had time to figure out something more elaborate.

There were other cars parked on the street across from the entrance to her building. People were sitting inside them. Newspeople, he knew, waiting for a chance to talk to her about her father. He might just get lucky and shoot a couple of them, as well. They certainly hadn't been kind to him. Why should he care about them?

Carl decided he'd have a better vantage if he joined the other vans and cars. An Acura left, and he pulled into its slot behind a white van. It was a great spot. A red SUV honked at him because he'd gotten to the space first. Like the other vans and SUVs and sedans, he kept his motor running. Slinking down in his seat, he waited. Condensation quickly covered the windshield and windows, making it difficult for anyone walking by to see inside.

Carl had brought a flask of whiskey with him. He took a long swallow and

felt the liquid burn his insides. The whiskey gave him courage. Before he killed
himself, he hoped he could watch Olivia
die. He smiled thinking about it and took
another swig. It would all be over soon.

Grayson paced in Olivia's apartment
while he waited to hear that Simmons
had been picked up. Agents were on
their way to Simmons's apartment now,
and it shouldn't be much longer before
Grayson got the call that the bastard
was in handcuffs. Only when Simmons
was in lockup would Grayson stop worrying.

Olivia was getting ready to go out.
Grayson was taking her to a dinner party
honoring Dr. Pardieu.

She had taken the news about Carl
Simmons well and admitted she was
actually more relieved than surprised.

"The GPS was his big mistake. He left
a clear record that he'd driven to Martin's house to plant the gun," Grayson
told her. "Are you happy now that you
know it was indeed Simmons who tried
to kill you?" he asked.

She laughed. "Happy? This will put him away forever, so yes, I guess I am."

Grayson had told her that as soon as Simmons was picked up they could leave.

The bedroom door opened, and there she stood. She wore a black dress with a V-neck that showed just enough cleavage to make Grayson nuts.

"You look beautiful," he told her as he pulled her into his arms and kissed the side of her neck. "Every time I get near you, I want to take you to bed."

She felt the same way. She kissed him on his cheek and pulled away. "We're going to be late if we don't leave now. It's a thirty-minute drive to the restaurant."

"I haven't heard about Simmons yet. We're going to wait—"

"Couldn't we get in the car and start driving?"

"Olivia . . ."

The warning in his voice didn't deter her. "If we get to the restaurant and Simmons still hasn't been taken into custody, we'll turn around and come back. I don't want to wait here, then drive like

crazy to get there before it's over. It's
Dr. Pardieu," she said. "I can't miss it.
He's like a father to me."

He relented. "Okay, we'll leave now,
but you have to promise you'll stay in
the car and not balk if we have to turn
around."

She smiled. "I'm not sure about the
balking, Grayson. I'll stay in the car, but
I feel I'm entitled to a little balking."

He helped her with her coat, kissed
her neck again, and buttoned his suit
jacket. "Ready to walk the gauntlet?"

"How many reporters did you see?"

"Three vans, a couple of SUVs. They'll
try to swarm as soon as you step outside. Keep your head down," he told her.
"I'll get you out of here as fast as I can."

"You should park in the garage from
now on," she suggested.

"They're down there, too," he replied.
"More than are on the street. When we
get back, I'll talk to the doorman about
sweeping the garage."

He pulled up her collar as the elevator
door opened in the lobby. "Ready?"

She nodded. Grayson took her hand
and strode past John. She waved to him

as she was being pulled through the door.

A door opened on every car that was parked across the street, and cameramen and reporters came running. Grayson noticed a blue Honda opposite the apartment entrance. It hadn't been there when he'd arrived. The sedan was squeezed in between two vans. As Grayson hurried Olivia around his car to get to the passenger side, out of the corner of his eye he saw the door of the Honda open and Carl Simmons step out into the street.

Olivia was blinded by camera lights. She put her hand up to shield her eyes, unaware of the danger.

Simmons swung his right arm up, and Grayson saw the glint of steel. He moved so quickly, Olivia didn't have time to brace herself or react. He threw her behind him, and she fell to her knees before he flattened her with his body. In one fluid motion, he covered her and trained his gun on Simmons.

He shouted to the reporters, "Get down, get down . . ."

"What—" was all that Olivia could utter. Grayson had knocked the wind out of her. Gunshots stopped her from asking questions. She squeezed her eyes shut and prayed Grayson wouldn't get hit. Protecting her, he'd made himself a target.

Camera lights illuminated the scene that was unfolding. Simmons ran toward them, shooting again and again, trying desperately to get Olivia. Grayson fired only one shot. That was all he needed. The bullet sliced into Simmons's black heart. His arms flailed, his legs buckled, and he crashed spread-eagle to the ground, face-first.

The noise was ear-piercing. People were screaming and running every which way. Olivia's heart pounded in her chest, and she couldn't catch her breath. Grayson lifted her, checking to make certain she hadn't been hit by one of Simmons's bullets. Her dress was ripped all the way up to the top of her thigh, her elbow was scraped, and she was shaking from head to toe.

Grayson's eyes showed fear mixed with his rage. "Are you all right? Did he—"

"I'm okay," she whispered, surprised by how weak her voice sounded. "What happened?"

"Carl Simmons."

Stunned, she asked, "He's here?"

"He's dead. Can you walk? I want you to get inside. Tell John to lock the door. Don't talk to anyone. Just sit and wait for me. I need to get to Simmons's gun—"

"Go," she said.

John held the door for her, blocking two eager reporters from entering. He bolted the door behind her and led her to the security room behind the desk. "No one will bother you here, and you can watch the street, see what Agent Kincaid is doing."

Grayson ran across the street. Pushing reporters out of his way, he knelt beside Carl to check for a pulse while he called it in.

Others had called 911 already. Within bare minutes, police and agents filled the street. Olivia waited patiently, but her chest was getting tight, and she knew she was going to be in trouble if she didn't use her inhaler. She then realized she didn't have her purse. She must have dropped it when Grayson pushed her. John found it under the car and brought it to her, and once she'd used her inhaler, she felt immediate relief. She put her head back, closed her eyes, and tried to calm her racing heartbeat.

She thought about Grayson and how calm he'd been while that maniac was shooting at them. He was completely in control, until it was over. Then his composure turned into fury that Simmons had tried to hurt her. He had put his life on the line to save hers, she realized, and her eyes filled with tears at the thought of what could have happened to him.

Knowing it would be some time before Grayson was finished, she went back upstairs. She stripped out of her clothes, washed her hands, and cleaned the cut on her elbow. She slipped into her silk robe and curled up on the sofa to wait for him.

He arrived a half hour later and found her standing at the kitchen window, looking down at the street.

"Is he really dead?" she asked.

"Yes."

"What was he thinking to come here? With all the reporters . . . He couldn't have thought he'd get away with it."

"He wanted to die, but he wanted to kill you first."

"He really hated me, didn't he?"

"Yes, he did. You stopped him from destroying more innocent people's lives. The world's a better place without him." Grayson tossed his tie on the table. "You took your clothes off," he commented.

"Yes."

He took a step toward her and stopped. "It's not too late. We could catch the end of the party I guess."

She took a step toward him. "I don't want to go out. I could fix dinner . . . microwave something. Are you hungry?"

He slowly looked her up and down, smiled, and said, "Yeah, I'm hungry."

Lifting her into his arms, he walked into the bedroom and kicked the door shut behind him.

THIRTY-THREE

Grayson wouldn't leave Olivia alone. He was determined to marry her, and nothing she could do or say would change his mind. He had listened to her protests for two months, but he was persistent.

"If I were to get sick again, you'd have to suffer with me," she argued. "Are you ready for that?"

"How about I toss you out if you get so much as a cold?"

"I'm serious."

"What happens if I get sick?" he countered.

The question gave her pause. "I'd take care of you."

"Marry me." He was backing her into her bedroom while he made his demand. "I'm not asking. I'm telling you. You're going to marry me."

She promised to think about it. He knew what that meant. She'd be thinking about it six months from now.

"When you wake up, you'll have a ring on your finger. I'm done waiting." He pulled her to him and began to undress her.

"You think I'll sleep through you putting a ring on my finger? I'm a very light sleeper, Grayson."

"When I'm finished with you, you're going to be so exhausted, you'll sleep through anything I do to you."

He wasn't exaggerating. He began to make love to her with gentle caresses and slow, wet kisses. He soon became more demanding, and he brought her to the brink again and again, but each time he pulled back and made her wait. When she finally screamed for release, he gave in. The last thing she remembered was

Grayson leaning over her and whispering that he loved her.

He stayed over that night and slept with her wrapped in his arms. When Olivia woke up, he was in the kitchen. She could smell bacon, and she could hear him whistling. She rolled onto her back and stretched her arms toward the ceiling. She saw the ring then, a gorgeous emerald-cut diamond.

Grayson heard the rich, joyful sound of laughter coming from the bedroom. It was music to his ears.

He had his answer.

THIRTY-FOUR

Their wedding was to be a small affair in her aunt Emma's living room. Olivia couldn't make up her mind if she wanted to invite her mother and her sister, but Natalie made the decision for her. She called late one evening, and her voice was absolutely frigid.

"Still blaming me, Natalie?" Olivia asked.

"You are to blame," her sister said resentfully. "I don't think Mother or I will ever be able to forgive you."

"Have I asked for forgiveness?"

"I have a message."

"Oh?"

"The message is from our father. He has such a kind heart."

"Right."

"He said he's ready to forgive you, but you have to face him when you apologize."

There was dead silence on the phone for at least twenty seconds. Then Olivia began to laugh. Some things—and some men—never change. Logan Weston was one example; Robert MacKenzie, another.

It was such a beautiful spring day, Emma decided to have the wedding outside in her garden. By the time she finished with the caterer and the florist, the yard looked like a wonderland.

Dr. Andre Pardieu walked Olivia down the aisle. Her maids of honor were Collins, Jane, and Samantha. Olivia had told Grayson that Samantha had to be at the ceremony, and if she couldn't get leave, then everyone would go to Iceland, and they'd get married there.

Grayson in his tux set her heart on

fire. This beautiful man loved her. As she walked toward him, she felt as though she were floating. All her worries had vanished. She was no longer afraid of what might come. With Grayson at her side, she could face anything. He was her lover, her friend, her strength. It would be all right to lean on him every now and then.

There was much to celebrate. Collins had finally received word that she could begin training to become an FBI agent, and she was thrilled. Ronan kept his distance, but Olivia noticed he hadn't taken his eyes off Collins. She couldn't wait to see what might come of the attraction.

Agent Huntsman was late for the ceremony, but he had the most wonderful excuse. He pulled Olivia and Grayson aside to share his news. "I've got a wedding present for you," he began. "We finally caught up with that bitch, Gretta Keene. She was in New Mexico under an assumed name. She's behind bars now. And guess who else?"

Olivia gasped. "Eric Jorguson?"

"That's right. We nabbed him, too."

Huntsman couldn't stop smiling. "We've got everything we need to prove Jorguson was laundering money, and now it looks like we'll also be able to go after some of his other clients. It's a mighty fine day, isn't it?"

Olivia thought it was a fine day, indeed. Every one of Grayson's buddies was drooling over Olivia's three best friends. And the girls certainly knew how to flirt, even Jane, now that she was looking so radiant. She'd started dating again and was truly happy.

Ralph and his father were invited— Henry had put them on the list. Mary and Harriet were busy protecting the cake and keeping the boys out of mischief.

Ralph Sr. fell under Samantha's spell. He hung on her every word. She was launching into "the story" when her friends joined her.

"There I was . . ."

Collins, Jane, and Olivia finished the sentence for her. ". . . in seat twenty-eight A on flight twenty-seven forty-three. . . ." Laughter followed, drawing smiles from the guests.

The photographer wanted a picture of the bride with her maids of honor. Olivia gathered them on the terrace. They stood together smiling into the camera. Sam whispered something the others found hilarious, and they had a good laugh.

Contentment washed over Olivia. The Pips were together again. They had come through the storm, and the sun was shining.

EPILOGUE

A year had passed since the wedding, and Olivia had settled comfortably into married life. Patrick continued to keep the household running smoothly, and she helped with carpools and home-work.

Grayson hadn't committed yet, but he was giving serious thought to accepting a promotion at the agency. As an incen-tive, they had agreed to his demands: He could take on individual cases from time to time and not be tied to a desk, and Ronan would continue to be his partner for those investigations. The new position would mean that his work schedule would be predictable and he could spend more time with his family.

Olivia and Henry had become very close. Their busy lives kept them occupied during the week, so Olivia made it a point to reserve the weekends for family activities. One Saturday in late June, Olivia and Henry were at a local farmers' market that was set up on the edge of a city park. She wanted to pick up some fresh vegetables for their dinner, and she'd promised Henry they would see the latest Transformer movie when she was finished. Grayson and Ronan were tying up a case, and Ronan was going to drop Grayson off at the park to meet them and spend the rest of the day with them.

Henry had one of his handheld game players and was trying to destroy aliens while Olivia and he strolled among the crowded stalls. She kept her hand on Henry's shoulder, guiding him. They stopped in front of a stall containing fresh tomatoes. As she was sorting through them, she glanced across the market to the parking lot beyond. Grayson was walking toward her. Her heart-beat quickened, and her breath caught in her throat. Oh, he was such a hand-some man. In all this time together, she still hadn't gotten used to him. When-ever he walked through the door at night, she reacted the same way. Always with excitement and wonder. She thought it a miracle that he loved her.

He reached her and leaned down to kiss her. Henry was so intent on his game, he didn't realize his uncle had joined them.

"Sorry I'm late. After all this time, Eric Jorguson wants to make a deal," he ex-plained. "It's not gonna happen. He can't give us anything we don't already have."

"I can't despise the man," she whis-pered so Henry wouldn't overhear. "If he hadn't attacked me, I never would have met you."

"Not true," Grayson said. And though he wasn't usually poetic, he added, "We were meant to be together. I would have found you."